D1430159

WHITE STAG
TO
QUEEN'S PAWN

MARTIN MACDOWALL

Copyright © 2008 Martin MacDowall
All rights reserved.

ISBN: 1-4196-9352-2
ISBN-13: 9781419693526

Visit www.booksurge.com to order additional copies.

IN MEMORY OF
DAVID TELLING

TABLE OF CONTENTS

Glen Torridon — January 8th 1959 9

Drumochter Pass — January 9th 1959 23

Glen Cannich — Saturday July 9th 1955 27

Glen Cannich — Saturday August 27th 1955 35

Auld John – Glen Torridon May 1956 57

Dr. Ken Urquhart — October 1958 73

The Rescue — January 9th 1959 85

Los Angeles — October 15th 1958 103

Ross MacDonald — December 12th 1958 137

The Shunt — December 15th 1958 153

The Crises — December 20th 1958 171

The Return — January 8th 1959 183

Inverness — January 16th 1959 203

Beinn Eighe Summit — January 17th 1959 221

Los Angeles — January 1959 229

The Return to Torridon — April 1959 235

Mhairi — May 1959 245

Douglas Hamilton — October 1969 259

"Sir's Week" Glen Torridon — October 1969 283

Christmas at Moulin — December 1969 291

Lance Ericsson — Christmas 1968 305

Strahearn — Spring 1970 321

Colin Macalister MD FRCS — September 1970 341

Yorkhill Hospital, Glasgow — September 1970 361

Glen Torridon — November 1970 389

Return to Strahearn — January 1971 401

University of Houston — May 1979 419

Marischal College — July 1979 427

The Graduation Ball — July 1979 449

Innerleithen — July 1979 465

Drew Findlay, Houston, Texas — September 1993 483

Scotland — November 1993 495

Inverness — November 1993 519

Morgan City, Louisiana — November 1993 525

London — November 1993 535

Glen Cannich — December 1993 551

South Beach Miami — December 1993 575

Station Hotel, Inverness — December 1993 591

Torridon Lodge — Christmas 1993 595

London Gatwick — January 16th 1994 617

Bill Whyte, Inverness — January 18th 1994 633

Dalcross, Inverness — January 19th 1994 643

Beinn Eighe — January 25th 1994 659

Glossary 663

Acknowledgments 669

Additional Author's Notes 671

FORWARD

The title of Stalker in Scotland is regarded as a prestigious and highly regarded professional occupation.

The culling of deer is monitored and controlled by the Deer Commission for Scotland founded in 1996 as a replacement for the Red Deer Commission. The objectives of the Commission are: Furthering the conservation, control and sustainable management of all species of wild deer in Scotland, and keeping under review all matters, including welfare, relating to wild deer. More information is available online at http://www.dcs.gov.uk/

The culling of Stags (Bucks) commences on August 20th each year and ends on October 20th. Hunting Stags is an important part of any Estates income and hunters can pay large sums for privilege of going on the hill with the Stalker and shooting a Stag with a suitable rifle. The Stalker is in charge of all activities related to stalking and must be obeyed. A typical stalk starts in the early morning with the Stalker locating herds of deer on his March (Territory). He then makes a decision which Stag he is going to stalk and kill. His choice can be based on many factors including identifying an old Stag in declining health that may not survive the winter, or a Stag with poor antler growth, a switch, which has antlers without branches, or a Stag with too large a herd of Hinds to successfully cover over the period of the rut.

Having identified the Stag to be culled the Stalker makes his way up the hill with the hunting party usually consisting on no more that 3 or 4 people which would normally include a Ghillie (Gaelic for a hill laborer) who would help in bringing the dead Stag down the hill. The stalk can take some time and the distance covered can often be between 7 to 10 miles which makes for quite strenuous walking through heather, bracken and peat hags (bogs).

Once the Stalker is in position he puts the hunter with a rifle into a firing position and may advise the hunter when and how to make the shot. Once the Stag is dead the Stalker or the Ghillie gralloch (field dress or disembowel) the beast and drag the beast down the hill to an point that can be accessed by an ArgoCat, a small all terrain vehicle which can seat up to four people or two people and a couple of deer.

The Hinds (Does) are culled from October 21st to February 20th in any year. This cull is usually carried out by the Stalker with a Ghillie sometimes helping.

The deer meat is butchered by the Stalker and hung in the Estate Larder to await collection by a town or city butcher purveying venison.

Despite the driving snow the victim loomed large in the telescopic sight.

"Just a little closer," breathed the stalker.

The prey turned slightly as if some imagined sound or presence had alerted her.

Bam! The Mannlicher .270 barked, the target swayed slightly as the bullet struck, her legs buckled and she fell motionless. A vermilion stain spread outwards from the body as the pristine snow blossomed red.

Eilid Stuart rose, brushed the spindrift from her Barbour jacket and slowly walked the 150 odd yards up to the body tucking her flowing blond hair back under her deerstalker cap which the wind threatened to whip off her head at any minute. A glazed, lifeless brown eye stared back at her; quickly she opened her hunting knife and pressed the sharp point to the corner of the eye. Not a flicker. The hind was quite dead. Eilid had accomplished her second cull of the day in appalling weather conditions.

As the stalker on Sir David Vickers's estate it was her responsibility for the culling of hinds between the end of October and the middle of February of the following year. The cull was an essential part of Estate management throughout the Scottish Highlands. Deer were overpopulating the hills and glens and an annual cull was the only way the deer population was kept in check as the damage to crops and newly planted trees became excessive.

For an Estate the size of Sir David Vickers there was a specified annual number of Stags and Hinds she was permitted to take off the hill. Stags were hunted during the rut which stretched from August 20th through to October 20th in any given year; Hinds from October 21st through to February 20th. She was behind with the cull and it was for that reason she had decided to go on the hill despite the bad weather. She had shot only 22 so far counting the two that lay close by; normally she would have taken out at least half of the 60 hinds she took off the hill each year.

The two hill ponies whinnied noisily as the north wind's strength increased and the falling snow became almost horizontal in the open corrie. Eilid decided that enough was enough for that day. She was frozen and the weather was deteriorating rapidly. She had rolled the hind over to gralloch the animal when the heavens were illuminated by a blinding flash, followed by a thunderous explosion which seemed to come from the summit of Beinn Eighe. Despite the bitter wind for a moment she felt a searing heat from the blast.

Quickly she pulled her binoculars out of her Barbour and scanned the area below the triple buttressed towers, the feature that makes Corrie Mhic Fhearchair (say Corry Veechker*a*char) on the north-face of Beinn Eighe so unique.

She was at the lower west end of the corrie and, as she looked up and over to her right, cascading debris briefly filled the lenses of what she later discovered were parts of an aircraft, the driving snow then obliterated her view. She had no idea of what could have happened. Slinging the Mannlicher over her shoulder she made her way up the corrie traversing from west to east.

There were fires raging in different parts of the snow-covered mountainside. Great sections of painted aluminum covered the ground clanking and wailing in the wind, which whipped up from the lochan below.

It took her twenty minutes of hard climbing to get to the level where the first of the wreckage could be seen and a fire raged. Eilid was completely stunned. Her mouth she discovered was as wide open as her eyes as she tried to take in the enormity of the scene in front of her. The first obvious thing that told her it had been an aircraft of some sort was part of a wing tip, standing wedged vertically in the snow.

Suddenly the wind dropped and the snow came down more gently hissing and fizzing as it met the flames of the still burning sections of the aircraft. It was that lull that allowed Eilid to take stock. She looked all around her. It was an unbelievable sight. One she would take with her to her grave. The detritus of death littered the corrie. For a brief moment she could see broken bodies, bloodstains on virgin snow and personal belongings scattered from suitcases that had lost their contents in the crash. Perhaps, she thought, there just might be one or two survivors. She knew nothing about aircraft or the forces associated with them; all she hoped was that she could help someone get out of this hell alive. It seemed, at first glance, to be a futile wish.

There was hardly a body in one piece, some clothed in tatters, some unrecognizably scorched black, others almost as naked as they day they were born but all with dreadful injuries and with limbs, and in some cases heads, missing. Eilid was used to blood and guts, but that was with animals. Old John's death came back to haunt her as she reached one body after another to see that they had that deathly gray pallor which indicates only one thing. She turned from the fragmented wreckage and started to make her way down from where she had come. The authorities had to be informed and it would be many hours from now, as she would have to get to off the hill to reach a telephone and raise the alarm.

It was then that she heard what sounded like the bleat of a sheep. She stopped frozen in her tracks, every fiber of her being strained for other sounds. There was nothing. Just the howl of the wind freshening again as renewed flurries of snow swirled in the corrie.

Then she heard the sound again. It was more like a wail, a cat's, no...a baby's cry. She stopped again. Maybe her imagination was playing tricks on her. Maybe it was just the wind milling through the wreckage of the doomed aircraft. She moved on down a few steps and then she heard it loud and clear. It *was* a baby's cry. She turned immediately and made her way to where she thought the sound had come from. The wind howled, the snow started coming down thicker than ever. If I don't get out of here soon, thought Eilid, even I might not make it, let alone anyone else. But she could hear a more repetitive sound now coming from below her as the wind blew up the corrie. She started down to where there was no wreckage to be seen. This can't be right she thought, it must be connected with the 'plane and there are no parts of the 'plane to be seen, I must be mistaken. Then she heard the cry louder, more agitated this time and it was right below her feet. Panic stricken she looked everywhere.

Snow, there was nothing but pristine snow. Then it came again. It was right in front of her! My God, she thought, whatever it is, it's under the snow. Again in front of her she heard the baby's cry, and then she saw it. It was just a gray corner of some kind of fabric standing out against the snow's white purity. But something it was. Eilid dug frantically at the snow around her and uncovered the gray carrycot that might well have been Jens Ericsson's tomb. The carrycot miraculously had been shot from the tail of the plane, fallen 700 feet, tobogganed another 500 feet and ended up, almost completely covered in snow at the bottom part of the corrie. Eilid couldn't believe her luck and the baby's good fortune. Now she had to get it off the mountain and keep it alive. She touched the baby's skin. God, it was frozen. She had to get it to some heat, and that was easier said than done. The wind had picked up again and virtual blizzard conditions existed. There were blankets and sheets in the carrycot but now these were wet and cold and she discovered the baby had been strapped in. Quickly she undid the straps and picked the covers up with the infant and started off down the hill just as fast as she could go. Her mind was working frantically. How was she going to get the child off Beinn Eighe without it dying? She had done a quick triage on the baby and nothing seemed to be broken. At least it was pink and yelling lustily. Eilid reached the hind she had left before the events of the day had diverted her to greater things. An idea was quickly forming in her mind; she could only hope it would work.

Leaving the baby to one side she took off her Barbour jacket and put it on top of the infant as some means of protection against the wind and the snow. Quickly, she gralloched the hind she had just shot. The hind's innards were still warm, as she had hoped. She continued with the disemboweling at record speed. Now came the difficult part. With her hunting knife she made slits through the skin of the hind's belly, which now lay in folds as a result of the field dressing. The baby had stopped bawling by now, she didn't know whether this was from the cold or from being reunited with what it thought was its mother. It was that thought that stopped her in her tracks. The mother and the father had to have been on that 'plane. This child was an orphan. Her skin crawled and the hair at the back of her neck stood on end as those terrible thoughts hit her. She had to save this poor little mite at all costs; it was the sole survivor and she its only hope.

She grabbed the child and the blankets and her Barbour jacket and placed the infant inside the warm belly of the hind. Next she took the skein of rope she always took on the hill and threaded the rope as you would as if lacing a shoe, until the stomach of the hind was closed and the baby cocooned in the hind's warm belly. She then fetched the Shetland ponies that had been standing now for several hours seemingly impervious to the gale and the snow. Fortunately she had put deer saddles on both. More rope came into play. She cut lengths for attachment to the deer saddle on one of the ponies and tied them to the hind's hind legs. Then, when she was sure everything was in order, she moved the ponies out of the corrie, one with a hind slung across its back on the deer saddle and the other pulling the hind converted into a sledge complete with child. The journey back was a nightmare. The snow was getting heavier all the time. Eilid was frozen by this time. No amount of beating her arms round her body could coax any feeling into her hands and arms. Her thick Fairisle sweater was covered in snow, somehow the heavy wool seemed to attract the flakes and they stuck like a freezing white overcoat.

The only thing in her favor was that the wind was now at her back and that she was going downhill as fast as she could muster the ponies. As she made her way thoughts swirled in her mind about the catastrophe she had just witnessed. She would have to tell the authorities, which would be the police at Loch Carron. God knows when she would get there, she thought. So she trudged on, looking for the easiest path down as the snow had obliterated the well-worn path that wound itself up the mountainside. Then she thought about Auld John, what he would have done. He would probably not have had a clue in how to tend for an infant. She wondered if it was a little boy or a girl that she had saved. Then she thought ruefully, I haven't saved it yet, we all could end up like frozen statues. She had been going for over two hours now and it was getting dark, only the reflection of the snow helped her to see the path to follow. The hind had been dragged belly up but had tipped over to either one side or the other on occasion, so Eilid had been going backwards and forwards righting the "sledge" and running back to take the pony's bridle and lead on. Even the ponies were finding the going difficult as the snow built up and they plowed into drifts that they couldn't see or were too tired to go around. It was time to take a look at the baby.

"Whoa there Shelagh, whoa there." The ponies stopped. The wind wasn't quite so bad here as they got some shelter from an outcrop of rock directly behind them. Anxiously she brushed the snow off the hind's body. Gently she prized open the stitched up hide so that she could see inside. The body was now getting cold but there was still some relative warmth when she stuck her fingers in a little bit deeper. All she could make out was a bundle. Nothing was moving. She put her hand in farther and she felt something move, either a hand or a leg. She hadn't too far to go now.

As she left the relative shelter of the outcrop the wind whipped up again and spindrift almost blinded her completely. Quickly she got the ponies going forward again and she flailed her arms for the umpteenth time in an attempt to get some warmth in her and to remove the snow from her sweater. Now she was crossing the big burn that cut across the path before the hillside flattened out some and became moor. Then she would be only a mile from the road and two miles from home. This was when she wished she had a ghillie and not waited until the spring, as Sir David had suggested, to think about hiring one. She hoped the peat fire she had left smoldering that morning was still on and offering some heat. The ponies whinnied as they recognized familiar territory.

The ponies and child-loaded hind reached Eilid's cottage in the pitch black at just after six o'clock. It had taken Eilid over three and a half hours to do what she normally did in under two, but her progress was remarkable given the circumstances. Quickly she took the hind off one pony and put it in the deer larder. She cut the ropes from the other pony and tried to unfasten the rope she had used to lace up the hinds belly. This proved impossible as the rope had become frozen and stiff so she carefully used her knife to slice away the fastenings. The hind's belly was stone cold by this time but she lifted out the Barbour wrapped package and went into the house. The pleasant warmth and smell of the peat fire wrapped itself around her as she bundled the baby inside the cottage. Going into her bedroom she placed the infant, still in its carrycot blankets onto her bed. Gingerly she peeled off the layers one by one. The blankets were soaked in the deer's blood but they weren't frozen, cold maybe, but not frozen, that was the important thing. There was the baby's little face, its eyes all screwed tight shut, covered in blood, which had dried hard. For goodness sake, thought Eilid the wee soul's covered. She dashed into the bathroom and ran the hot water. Soon almost scalding water poured into the washand basin. She poured in cold until the temperature was lukewarm. Moistening her softest facecloth she then proceeded to gently wash the baby's face. Suddenly its legs kicked and it began to cry. It was a miracle; it was literally alive and kicking. She smiled to herself at her homemade joke. She would give it a bath that would warm it up. It was wearing a little blue romper, which made her guess the baby was a boy. She'd soon find out. The baby began to cry more lustily and his lips were moving obviously searching for something. The bairn's hungry, that's what wrong, he's starving, she told herself. Now came Eilid's quandary, she knew nothing about babies except they needed lots of looking after. When she lived in Glen Cannich she had often seen her mother's friends reach for a dummy or pacifier to stick in the child's mouth to shut it up. Surely this baby would have had such a thing. Back she went to the blankets she had just bundled up. She opened them up one by one this time and, sure enough, stuck with blood to the corner of one was a dummy teat. There was something else in the blanket, something lumpy. She peeled off the sticky cover and there was a little teddy bear in a soldier's uniform. He even had a little tin hat with 'Tommy' written across the front. It was a wounded soldier too; he had a bandage that was wrapped around the left side of his body. It had been badly stained by the hind's blood. Eilid decided she would clean it up later. Food for the baby was now high on the priority list.

She cleaned the pacifier and tried it in the little boy's mouth. It worked, but only for a moment. Detecting no milk the baby opened up again at a higher pitch. My God, thought Eilid, I can't stand too much of this. The ponies whinnied from outside. Dear God, the poor horses, I've forgotten the ponies. Leaving the baby screaming on the bed she got back to the ponies and removed their tack, led them into the stable and put them in their dry stalls. Grabbing some straw she rubbed them down until they were almost dry and she left them with a huge helping of oats and as much hay as they would need for a while. Back she dashed into the cottage. The baby was still wailing. What was she going to do? She asked herself. She needed milk and fast. Her only option was to go to the store in Torridon village. It would be closed but she could rouse Mistress McBride to get her some milk. She dashed out to the Land Rover having put on a fresh sweater and her Barbour jacket and left the baby lodged between two pillows on her bed. He would be safe, she thought 'til she got back.

The Land Rover proved difficult to start as the glow plug didn't heat the system fast enough due to the cold. Finally the engine fired in a great puff of diesel and she shot out of the barn towards the village. She was thankful for the Land Rover's four-wheel drive; it took to the snow like a duck to water. She drove right through substantial drifts until she reached the road. Everything was white in the glare of the headlights and if it hadn't been for the poles that marked the passing places on the single-track road she'd have been in a ditch in no time. She was driving much too fast but her adrenalin was flowing and she knew she didn't have a lot of time. The baby she had rescued had been through an unimaginable experience. Hopefully it wouldn't remember much about it but there had to be scars, especially when it was reunited with people who didn't really want the child, some relatives who lived who knew where. It was then, her mind racing as she careened down the road to the store that an outrageous idea began to form in her mind. She would adopt this child! Her experiences with men had convinced her she would never marry; this was a fantastic opportunity for them both, child and want-to-be mother. If she kept him, who would know? She asked herself again and again until she reached the store. Eilid leaped from the Land Rover and threw herself at the door of the house that adjoined the store and battered on it frantically. Light came through the fanlight as a door was opened from inside.

"Mercy, mercy, what in the name of the wee man is going on? Who is it at this time of the night, and what might you be wanting?"

"Mistress McBride, it's Eilid, Eilid Stuart," as if there were Eilids all up and down the Glen.

"Wait a minute now, patience, patience, lassie." The door opened just a crack. "What is it you'll be wanting then; I was nearly away to my bed."

"I'm terribly sorry Mistress McBride but I've got a sheep that's lambed prematurely. The ewe died but the lamb's still alive and I've no means of feeding her. Could you let me have some milk from the store? Please."

"My now there's a strange thing lambing in nearly the middle of January. Well we're here to help, that's what I always tell the folks, we're here to help. Come away in."

Eilid stepped into the house and followed Eliza McBride into the store. Mrs. McBride went to a shelf and produced a large tin of National Dried Milk. There you are my dear, now you know how to make this up do you?"

"No, not really, but I suppose I'll find out from the label."

"Aye, aye right you are. You just mix it with water, and let it cool, make sure it's not too hot."

"How much do I owe you?"

"It's two shillings and sixpence."

"Mistress McBride I've come away without any money can you put it on the slate for me?"

"Not a problem, not a problem anything for one of Sir David's best employees." She leered at Eilid as if to say, I know what's going on between you two.

"Thank you, I'll be off then."

"Aye now, so you will, and just how do ye think this wee lamb's going to get its milk?"

"Oh, oh right, I never thought about that."

"There ye go now, all you young girls have no idea of how to raise or look after a family."

Oh God, thought Eilid, I can't wait for the lecture that was sure to follow.

"You're so right Mistress McBride, what do I need? Do you have a baby's bottle?"

"Indeed I have. One of the finest, with a choice of teats mind you. It's only just come from Inverness but it's expensive, ye know?"

Eilid was sure it would be. "Right then Mistress McBride put that on the slate too, I've got to be off and thank you so much again."

Eilid got back to the cottage in record time, snow not withstanding. The baby was on the bed still bawling loudly. Quickly she put on the kettle and made up some formula. She took the bottle from the package and selected a suitable teat. The formula was far too hot. How do I cool it quickly, she asked herself? I must be daft, she thought, with all this snow about. Outside went the bottle and in two to three minutes the little boy was sucking down the dried milk mixture like there was no tomorrow. Eilid was in a tremendous state of elation at her achievements. The baby would be fine, she would keep him and not say a word to anyone; there would be talk, but so what? This was a chance in a lifetime, the baby needed a mother and, possibly a father, she was reluctant to concede, but she was confident she could do fill both roles.

Then all the events of the day hit her like a ton of bricks, the little boy was quiet now but lying on the bed with his eyes wide open taking everything in around him. She realized she was hungry, and most of all, utterly exhausted. Picking him up again she carried him into the parlor and sat him on her big chair. She went into the kitchen and got some venison stew of doubtful age and freshness, out of the cool larder, but what the hell! She was starving.

The stew smelled wonderful to her as she put it on the hot plate of the Aga cooker. Back she went to see her new arrival. He was fast asleep, breathing contentedly. She felt his Romper it was wet at the back, she had forgotten, how stupid, the baby would have a nappy and after all he'd been through I bet it needs changing, she thought. She began to think that her lack of knowledge with babies was going to be a problem. She decided not to waken him as he was sleeping so soundly. Eilid brought her meal into the parlor and sat picking at the stew with a lack of enthusiasm. Suddenly she wasn't hungry any more her 'wee prince', as she had provisionally named him, needed all her attention. As a new mother she wasn't really doing very well, in fact, she said to herself, "I'm a miserable failure."

Pouring herself a Macallan, the one luxury she allowed herself, she sat and thought about her decision to keep the baby. The malt whisky relaxed her to the point where she fell asleep in an almost upright chair. She wakened, catching herself falling forward, before she hit the floor. The little boy was stirring slightly as if having a disturbed sleep. Suddenly he awakened with a jolt and looked around without a sound. Then he whimpered very softly. It was time, thought Eilid, he hasn't been out of those clothes for probably 24 hours. Off came the blue romper, then a little vest. He was squirming now arms and legs going in every direction. There was a brilliant flash of light, then it was gone. Eilid thought she had imagined it but as the baby tossed and turned it happened again. She leaned forward and looked more closely. Then she saw the yellow ribbon round Jens's neck.

"Well, well now, what's this my wee man?"

She gently lifted the ribbon from round his neck. There on the end was fastened a ring with a huge blue stone, she didn't know what the blue stone was but she supposed the white surrounding stones were diamonds. She had only once been close to diamonds and that was when her Grandmother had come from Stornoway on her last visit to see her mother at Cannich. Granny had a large diamond ring, which she claimed Eilid's Grandfather had won in a game of cards from a Russian seaman. Eilid didn't know if the story was true or not but it was a good yarn.

My heavens, she said to herself, this is beautiful. She took it from the ribbon and placed it on her wedding finger. It was a perfect fit. She held it out in front of her turning her hand from side to side and watched the brilliants flash; the deep rich glow from the blue stone was hard to describe. Well fancy that, she thought, I have an engagement ring and a baby.

Off came the baby's vest. His little chest was heaving up and down and his legs pumped the air. It was as if he had been given freedom to move about at last. Next came the nappy. It had a large pin securing it near the top.

She could see that his little buttocks were raw as she removed the nappy. I'm not really ready for this. I'm only twenty-one; maybe, just maybe, I'm making a mistake. She cleaned up the infant's posterior and dredged it with talcum powder. What on earth was she going to use as a replacement? A towel that would have to do, the idea popped into her head. She had plenty spare towels in the bathroom as she had augmented her supply when her mother had come to stay. She searched for the right size and came across a hand towel, that would have to do until she could get proper diapers.

It was then that she stopped and stared at the infant. How could she have missed that? Covering the left side of his chest was a white bandage or surgical dressing which went under his little left arm all neatly stuck in place with tape. What was this all about she wondered? It didn't seem to prevent him moving his arm about as he flailed away obviously relieved to be free of clothing, especially the damp stuff. Eilid was in a quandary; clearly this little fellow had been 'in the wars'. Then she remembered the beat up and stained Tommy Teddy. Someone had made that to copy what had happened to the child. How very clever, she thought. She resolved to try and remember to clean the muck and blood off Tommy. But what was she to do with this dressing? If only she had a telephone, she could have talked to her Uncle Ken, the doctor, in Pitlochry. But there was only one phone box in the glen and that was miles away. Her wee prince started to cry again. *Now* what could be wrong, she wondered. He lay on his back girning away making motions with his lips again. He couldn't possibly be hungry again? Could he? He was. As the newly prepared bottle of formula came close he stopped crying and sucked lustily. Eilid was in heaven. She felt all maternal, protective and tired, she was so tired. Once or twice earlier that evening she had caught herself nodding off, but she had managed to stay awake on account of the baby.

She was still concerned about the dressing. Clearly this indicated an accident or maybe an operation of some sort, she couldn't be sure. The dressing was so professionally applied; she could tell that much just by looking, it had to have been put on by a doctor or a nurse. She would let things be for the evening and decided to look at what was under the dressing in the morning when the light would be better. Next she had to make up her mind on where the baby was going to sleep. She possessed nothing like a cradle or a cot to keep him secure. She leaned back in her chair, eyes closed, thinking about what she was going to do, not just for that evening, but also for the rest of her life. Eilid's strong will and determination drove her to carry most challenges to a conclusion satisfactory to her, even although her decisions might often fly in the face of common sense. She was nearly dropping off to sleep again when she had another brain wave. The bottom drawer of the chest of drawers was huge; the baby would fit in that perfectly.

Then she could use the sleeping bag that she had had for years and used in the summer when she stayed out on the hill in the shieling on some nights watching her father's livestock. Quickly she got up, pulled out the drawer and started on the makeshift cot. By the time she was finished with it she was quite proud of herself. The folded sleeping bag made it soft and comfy and the sides of the drawer were still deep enough to keep the baby from moving too much. There hadn't been much movement from him at all that evening except when she had changed his nappy. She wondered just how old he was. She was useless at judging the age of babies of this size. He could be six months or three months, Eilid didn't know one way or the other. So Eilid's little prince spent his first night in Scotland in a dressing table drawer sleeping right through until seven o'clock the next morning.

At that time of the year in the far north the dawn didn't break until just before nine o'clock. By that time Eilid had cleaned her 'wee prince' using a facecloth and warm soapy water. She had considered a bath but that would have to wait until she looked at what was under the dressing. She had changed his makeshift nappy back to the real thing that she had washed and dried in front of the Aga. After the ablutions were complete she decided to take a look under the bandages. Being as careful as she could she peeled back the surgical tape. It was like none she had ever seen being paper-thin but not leaving any residue when she lifted it back. Her little prince came through the whole exercise with flying colors. His little face screwed up with a burst of tears now and then when she hurt him, but there wasn't any sustained crying. Eilid left the top piece of tape on and lifted the white pad very gently. Slowly she hinged it upwards. Then she could see the red weal of a scar that started almost at his back and came forward towards his chest about an inch below his armpit. She could see the stitch marks clearly. The wound looked red and was oozing in one or two places. Gently she touched a yellow area. The little boy jumped as if stung and immediately burst into tears. Eilid was at a loss, she didn't really know how to cope with this situation. This child was recovering from surgery; there was no doubt about that. From what she could see he would need medical attention soon. There was nothing for it, Uncle Kenny had to be brought into the picture. Her mind was working at breakneck speed as she considered her options. The estate was deserted over the winter months, Sir David didn't come near the place until May and that, if what she had in mind was going to work, would be fine. She had no way of contacting Sir David. He could be anywhere in Britain or Europe for that matter. That was it, she would take the boy to Pitlochry and stay, if her Uncle Kenny would let her, until April that was about ten or eleven weeks away. No one would miss her. She decided it was worth the risk.

For the next two hours she loaded up the Land Rover with what food she had in cans, and some venison she had been keeping in the outside larder as good as any deep freeze in the wintertime. In went the drawer for her little prince complete with sleeping bag and Tommy Teddy. Some cans of Paraffin were added as she decided to take a Primus stove. Goodness only knows what the weather might be like on the way south to Pitlochry; she didn't even consider that the roads might be impassable even to the Land Rover. Eilid was locked in and focused on target. Finally she piled all her big sweaters on the passenger seat along with an extra pair of boots. Then she went to the stables where the ponies were, "enjoy your holiday", she said to them as she patted them and they nuzzled her. Opening the stable door wide she picked up a huge boulder and placed against the open door. No matter how hard the wind blew it would stay open and give the ponies their freedom to come and go as they pleased. Then she opened the door to where the hay was stored. That done she was certain they would be able to look after themselves until she got back. They wouldn't go hungry, she told herself. At last, she was ready to go. In went the baby, who had been as good as gold all this time. She looked down at him and smiled; suddenly he smiled a lovely little smile back that made her glow all over.

"My God" she shouted out to herself, "the bottle and the milk, I nearly forgot the whole damned lot."

Back she went into the cottage and packed the formula and Mistress McBride's expensive feeding bottle. Doubts began to form in her mind again as she drove down the snow-covered track to the road turning to the right up the Glen.

DRUMOCHTER PASS —
January 9th 1959

The weather was cold and cloudy with milky gray clouds scudding across the sky promising more snow. She had no idea how long the drive would take her, she had only done it once before and that was to attend Auld John Robertson's funeral and then drive the few miles from Struan to look up her mother's brother, a doctor in Pitlochry. She figured it was at least 150 miles but she wasn't sure. The ten miles or so to Kinlochewe went without incident although she had some anxious moments when the Land Rover slipped to the sides of the narrow one track road. She couldn't afford to go into a ditch on this isolated section of her journey; there would be no one to help her. Finally, having got to Kinlochewe she filled the Land Rover to the top with diesel. Few filling stations kept diesel so she had decided that if and when she saw one she'd top up, just to be on the safe side.

She was just out of Kinlochewe when a thunderous roar filled the air and two RAF bright yellow Bristol Sycamore helicopters passed low overhead and banked towards Torridon. Suddenly her conscience pricked her. They must be looking for the crashed plane but after all the snow they'll never see it, she thought. I should have told them where it was. But to do that was sure to scupper any plans she had for the acquisition of her wee prince. These thoughts ran riot through her mind but she ruthlessly put those feelings behind her. And so she drove on. The A 832 was still single track for another nine miles until the junction of the A 890 at Achnasheen when the road became wider and better.

It was now about eleven-thirty in the morning and so far she felt she was making good time. Inverness seemed to appear out of nowhere and she drove through what was a virtually deserted town for a Friday. Her troubles began as she climbed the long hill out of Inverness to Slochd summit getting closer to the Grampian Mountains by the minute. The snow was very deep in places where the wind had created drifts across parts of the road. While the earlier road had evidence of some traffic, tire tracks began to disappear as the snow got deeper. To make matters worse it started to snow again. Eilid was getting concerned. Her wee prince hadn't made a noise for some time and he seemed to be content lying in his big wooden drawer. As she got nearer to Aviemore the snow became heavier. The wind had also increased and it was becoming more difficult to see. The single electric windshield wiper growled noisily as it tried to shift the increasing weight of snow. Then the snow stopped. Elated, Eilid increased speed and drove the next few miles in relative comfort.

The heater in the Land Rover was doing a good job keeping her warm but she had begun to notice that the inside of the roof behind her was frosting up. By the time she got to Kingussie the wind had increased and the snow had started again with a vengeance. She pressed on with the speed of the Land Rover decreasing rapidly as the snow deepened and the visibility became poorer and poorer. Eilid's biggest challenge was coming. She had to get over the summit of the Drumochter Pass, which, at over 1,500 feet above sea level, hosts some of the wildest weather in Scotland. In forty-five minutes she had made it through Dalwhinnie. It had taken her that time just to drive the seventeen miles from Kingussie. The Land Rover was getting colder and slower. She was now on the long climb through the pass. The snow swirled and the wind howled relentlessly. The baby began to whimper. Eilid tried to get the Land Rover past twenty miles an hour, but it was no good, the snow was getting thicker and falling heavier by the minute. Still she kept going. It was getting darker and darker as the mountains on either side of the pass closed in. Only the snow poles on either side that told her where the road was; otherwise she could have driven anywhere, there was just a great white plain stretching out before her. Without any reference point she could only reckon that she must be near the top of the pass. She was crawling now and trying to fight the panic that was beginning to grow within her. Then the Land Rover's engine petered out. She had no idea of what had gone wrong or what to do. She tried the starter. It whirred again and again but the engine simply would not fire. She was stuck in a wilderness with a baby she had just rescued from a similar situation not twenty-four hours earlier. She began to cry. Not for her own plight, but out of frustration and for the baby. There was nothing else for it she would have to try and wait it out until some kind of help came. The snow was drifting at an alarming rate. She clambered into the back and pulled out the Primus stove. In no time she had the stove going and had made a bottle up for her wee prince, followed by a can of Heinz tomato soup for her. The baby had gone ominously quiet again. At least the soup was warming and the Primus cast a blue glow inside the vehicle as it roared away. Drips of condensation from the roof started to land on the baby. She grabbed a towel and wiped away the melting patch on the green metal roof directly above the stove. She looked at her watch. Twenty past three. Already it was getting dark. She felt the infant just to make sure he was warm. The sleeping bag was doing the trick and he was warm as toast. She wondered about the stove burning in a confined space. While it gave warmth she was beginning to feel drowsy, the air inside the Land Rover beginning to feel heavy with Paraffin fumes. She turned the stove off almost gasping for air. Back to the front she went and tried to slide open one of the windows. It opened only a crack to reveal a wall of snow. The Land Rover was buried. They were entombed on the Drumochter Pass.

Eilid sat motionless stunned by the outcome of what should have been a simple journey, which had placed herself in this circumstance. There was nothing to be done. She sat in the driver's seat watching the uninsulated dark green roof of the Land Rover ice up.

So it has come to this, she thought, conceived in a raging blizzard as the bastard daughter of the Laird's son Alasdair, she was going to die in one; the irony was lost on her as her mind went back to the circumstances that had destroyed her stable family life in Glen Cannich. It had started with the gift of a Mannlicher rifle on her eighteenth birthday from her Grandfather, albeit illegitimate Grandfather, Sir Andrew Ballantyne. Her mind drifted as she recalled happier times..........

GLEN CANNICH —
Saturday July 9th 1955

The day for celebrating her coming-of-age had dawned wet, dreary and dismal. A "gey dreich day", Kathleen Urquhart had pronounced, succinctly using an old Scot's expression to sum up the miserable weather in a word, as she helped Catriona her daughter, Eilid's mother, make preparations for her Grand-daughter's eighteenth birthday.

"Well, it might be cold and gray outside, mother, but for the birthday girl the sun's shining," Catriona had observed. "Just hand me over the pastry 'til I put the top on this steak pie. I think five of these should do. Mind you, knowing the appetite of some of the young men in the village, it might be as well to have one in reserve."

Eilid's birthday had actually been on Monday July 4th and she had wanted to have the party earlier on Saturday the 2nd, but her grandmother would not hear of it.

"That's tempting fate that is," she had declared, "having a birthday party before the day will bring bad luck on you."

Catriona had agreed, which was just as well. There had been so much to do at the farm she was way behind in her preparations for the 'grand party' as Angus, Eilid's father had called it, which was to be held in the Village Hall.

Her birthday party had been planned for some months. While twenty-one was still the age of majority in Scotland, eighteen was regarded as a milestone, a sort of coming-of-age. All the Stuart's friends in the village had got together to organize what was really to be a 'Grand Party'. It wasn't just for Eilid, it was for everyone who had watched her grow up to become one of the most attractive and well-liked young ladies the village had ever known. Old Hamish MacDowell had promised some "punch" for the party, and to all the men attending he donated the first dram — 'to get the evening off the ground' — as Hamish put it.

Angus had managed to get a local Scottish dance band to come from Inverness. One of the stalker's sons on the neighboring estate played the piano accordion in the band so, with a bit of judicious pressure, the band had offered to play "just for the beer". The evening was set in the village hall which Catriona and Kathleen had decorated with as much bunting and ribbon as they could lay their hands on. It was to be a sit down dinner for about 40 people with Catriona feeling nervous that the five huge steak and kidney pies she had baked wouldn't be enough to feed everyone.

By five o'clock the weather had started to brighten. The rain eventually stopped and by six a watery sun had filtered through the clouds to brighten Eilid's day. Catriona and her mother had made Eilid's party dress from a pattern they had found in one of the latest teenage fashion magazines. It was the latest 50's style and Eilid had thought she looked fabulous. The dress was blue with a boat neck, a hooped layered net petticoat that caused the calf length dress to resemble a ball gown. A broad white elastic belt completed the picture with low-heeled shoes to match.

Eilid's grandmother, Kathleen Urquhart, had got terribly emotional when she saw her granddaughter looking so beautiful and mature.

"There's just one wee finishing touch it needs," she had smiled at Eilid.

Off she went up to her bedroom to come back minutes later with a gold cross on a fine gold chain. She faced Eilid.

"Turn round."

Eilid had done as she was told.

"Mercy me," her Grandmother had said, "you look really lovely in a dress, you should wear one more often, and you're so tall, you'll need to dip a bit to help me."

Eilid bent her knees. Slowly Kathleen fastened the chain round Eilid's slender neck.

"There now, let's see you."

She had turned around again to face her mother, grandmother and her father, who had just come into the room.

"My, my but you just look so fine, that's my special birthday present to you. It was your great-grandmother's cross, Eilid, and she gave it to me when I got married and I've had it ever since. I don't wear it very often for the chain was getting so fine I was frightened it would break and I'd lose it, but your Dad got a new chain just the other day, so I want you to have this to keep you safe with the Lord's blessing." Kathleen stepped back to admire her granddaughter again.

She remembered being quite overcome. Without a word she had stepped forward, hugged her grandmother and had given her a big kiss.

"Thank you, thank you, Granny, it's the first jewelry I've ever had. I'll always wear it to remind me of this happy, happy day," she had said.

With that Granny and granddaughter had given one another tearful hugs. Angus had produced one of his mammoth red handkerchiefs from a jacket pocket.

"My, my, we've got a fair bit o' moppin' up tae do here." He gently dabbed his mother-in-law's cheeks. Since Angus had returned a hero from the war Angus had gone up in Kathleen Urquhart's estimation, she had even invited him to refer to her by her first name.

"That wis awfy kind of ye, Kathy, ah jist don't know how tae thank ye enough. Ma lass looks splendid doesn't she mither," he had turned to look at Catriona who was standing smiling wistfully with a mind full of mixed emotions. My God, Catriona had said to herself, if he only knew...... Now was certainly not the time for negative thoughts, she told herself. She had a party to organize and a hundred other things to do before the evening was over. Catriona had but one regret. She had asked Sir Andrew to attend but he had sent a very nice note apologizing for not being able to be there. In fact the tone of the note had rather upset Catriona. There was not one mention of wishing Eilid a happy birthday or anything. Catriona had been bitterly disappointed and had thought Sir Andrew's response very strange. It wasn't like him to miss a chance to see his only living relative.

The sit down meal had been a roaring success. There was just enough steak pie to go around complete with suede turnip, mashed potatoes and carrots washed down with jugs of ale that old Hamish had provided along with the "Fruit" Punch as his present to Eilid for the evening, however the Punch remained untouched. Even the younger attendees didn't seem to like it.

The Beauly Dance Band was in great form. Anyone with a wooden leg would have got up to dance, so infectious was their rhythm and beat. They never seemed to tire, nor did the villagers. Dance followed dance in profusion. All the old favorites were catered for, the Gay Gordons, Strip the Willow, the Highland Barn Dance, Dashing White Sergeant, the Military Two-step, the Pride of Erin Waltz, and the St. Bernard's Waltz and, of course, to finish the dancing off, the Eightsome Reel.

Every boy or young man in the village had danced Eilid off her feet. By ten-thirty everyone including Eilid was exhausted. Angus, Catriona and Kathleen were delighted the party had gone so well. Everyone had been well behaved even although a lot of beer had been consumed. Angus had kept a close watch on the younger lads as he saw the odd half-bottle of whisky coming out of an inside pocket and tipped into the beer. There wasn't a young man there who hadn't tried to make an impression on Eilid. But none had any success. There was an aristocratic look about her that evening, her mother thought that seemed to place an invisible barrier between her and the young village would-be blades without seeming to offend. It was like an aura emanating from her daughter that Catriona had never noticed before. Her little girl had grown up.

At eleven o'clock the lights had been dimmed and Angus wheeled in a huge birthday cake that had taken three of Catriona's best friends about two weeks to bake and decorate. Covered in frosty white icing with a huge pink ribbon round the middle, the cake sported 18 blue candles sitting on top of a charming Highland scene of a Hind and her fawns grazing in a clearing of pine trees. It truly was a work of art. There were oohs and aahs from the revelers as the cake, mounted on a trolley, was slowly pushed to the center of the room.

Angus had turned to each corner of the room in turn, "Charge your glasses," he commanded. "Happy Birthday Eilid," he shouted for all to hear, and, following Angus's lead the assembly burst into song, first with 'Happy Birthday to you', followed by, 'For she's a jolly good fellow'.

With great poise and presence she had blown out all the candles with surprising ease. All her friends had crowded up to the cake and had helped her make the first cut through the icing and into the rich dark fruitcake beneath. The cake had been distributed with relish. It was no secret that Mary McLennan, regarded as the best baker in the village, had used at least two bottles of whisky in its making. As midnight approached everyone got prepared to leave. Sunday was the Sabbath and all revelry stopped by tradition just before Sunday came in. The farewells to the Stuart family had just begun when a hush fell over the assembly. The double doors had opened quietly to reveal the Laird, Sir Andrew Ballantyne silhouetted in the entrance.

"Sir Andrew," everyone gasped. There stood the Laird dressed in his kilt and highland finery looking every inch a Knight of the Realm. From his Highland bonnet, set on his head at a rakish angle, to the Prince Charlie jacket then on down to the kilt in Ancient Stuart of Bute tartan to the silver buckled shoes he became quite the most elegant man at the party. The sgian dubh protruding from the top of his right stocking completed the picture.

Angus and Catriona had rushed forward in greeting.

"Mercy me Sir Andrew, you look just like a Highland Lord," Angus had quipped.

Catriona had hugged Sir Andrew affectionately and had given him a huge kiss on the cheek. "I knew you wouldn't miss Eilid's eighteenth," she had whispered in his ear.

Eilid to had crossed the floor and gone over to Sir Andrew. The Laird had never seen her more beautiful. She too gave Sir Andrew a kiss and a hug, like she had always done since she was a little girl.

"My, my, what brings you here, Sir Andrew," she smiled, teasing him.

"Well," Sir Andrew had said, "Would you believe I was just passing and I thought there was a bit of a party going on and I just stopped by to see what all the noise and fuss was about, and there you all were. Is it somebody's birthday?" he had smiled back at Eilid continuing the little play-acting.

"Highland Lord's don't go around unarmed, you know, so Angus if you'll go into my car out there there's a case lying along the back seat. Bring it in, would you."

While Angus had gone off to do as he was bid all the partygoers had surrounded the Laird shaking hands with him, and wishing him well. The villagers were well aware that the pain and sadness from losing first his wife to a heart attack, which then had been followed by Alasdair's death in the Battle of Britain, still dwelled within him. Since the latter event he had always seemed to be a rather sad and very lonely man. But not tonight, the Laird was in fine fettle. He soon caught the eye of Hamish MacDowall and demanded a large Macallan.

Old Hamish had been astounded. "Well now Sir Andrew, I don't know if I'll be having any of that. The war's over, but there are still shortages everywhere."

"Havers man," Sir Andrew had said, "call yourself a publican with no decent malt, we'll have to make some changes around here."

That had done it.

"Well now I don't sell it in the pub, you know, but I might just have some in my personal stock, if you wouldn't mind having a wee dram of that?" Hamish had inwardly groaned as he could see Sir Andrew ordering drinks all round from his precious hoarded supply of Macallan.

"That'll be fine Hamish, I'll be right here." Sir Andrew had winked at the locals, knowing well that Hamish kept all the good malts for himself and his cronies.

Angus had come back from the Laird's car carrying a large rifle case.

"Ah, well done Angus, you're a good man."

Hamish had slowly emerged from the gloom with a bottle of Macallan and one glass.

"What's all this then," the Laird had asked, am I the only one drinking?"

Hamish had dreaded this. His worse nightmare was about to come true.

"Well sir Andrew, you were the only one who asked for the malt. It's just been beer for the men and punch for the ladies, eh, all at my expense you know." Hamish had tried to make his point.

But Sir Andrew had been in a great mood for devilry that night. He had driven up from Glasgow that day through the appalling weather to get to the Lodge just in time to have a quick change into his Highland Dress and get to the party. He knew it had to close down before the Sabbath and well he knew that his timing was calculated to cause problems.

"Who'll join me in a quick drink to toast the birthday girl," Sir Andrew filled his glass, held onto the bottle and went round the circle of men that had gathered round him. Whisky glasses had appeared as if by magic as the Macallan was judiciously poured into every glass the Laird could see, until, in front of an almost fainting Hamish, the bottle was empty.

"Slainte," the Laird had cried, raising his glass.

"Slainte mhath," 'Good health to you' had come back the cry.

And Hamish's best malt had disappeared as if by magic.

"To the Laird," a villager had cried and another loyal toast was drunk.

It was time to go. The Laird's arrival had been the metaphorical icing on the cake for Eilid and her mother. As the people filed out of the door each shook the Laird's hand as if it were Sunday at Church shaking hands with the priest after the service.

"Sir Andrew, whit dae ye want me to do wi' this case?" Angus had stood holding the rifle case in the now near empty hall.

"Just bring it over to the table," Sir Andrew had beckoned so Catriona and she had followed. Sir Andrew, dipping into his sporran, had produced a tiny silver key. He had turned to face Eilid,

"Here Eilid, this is yours".

He had then picked the case up and laid it on the table. Sir Andrew went on to explain,

"I wanted Eilid to have this in private, just with her family."

Catriona's heart had leapt at his words, my God, if Angus even suspected. She had closed down her mind as Sir Andrew went on,

"Eilid, this is from me to you, you have all the talent, so your father tells me, to become a great stalker. You could be the first lady stalker, as far as I know, in Scotland. You need the right equipment, though, to help you achieve that. I hope this gift makes you realize your ambitions. Please do not be too proud to accept it. It comes with all my best wishes and I hope you use it with same skill as your father."

Catriona's palpitations had started with a vengeance. Had Sir Andrew really mean Angus, for Angus was a great shot, or was there a deeper, deadlier meaning to be construed.

Eilid had opened the case. There lay the most beautiful rifle she had ever seen. The wooden stalk was of the finest deep-grained wood and it seemed to continue up the barrel of the rifle, encasing it both top and bottom. Only at the very end of the wood encasement did the snub gunmetal gray barrel protrude. She had carefully picked it from its resting place and had looked at it as if mesmerized. There were even two triggers. She had never seen anything like it.

"My God," exclaimed Angus, "a Mannlicher .270 what a beautiful rifle."

Her mother had been almost in tears.

"Oh, Sir Andrew, this must have cost a fortune," Catriona had given him a hug with all her might as the Laird patted her on the back enjoying every moment of contact with the wonderful young lady he almost regarded as his daughter-in-law.

Eilid too had kissed Sir Andrew. There was something quite special about the Laird, she didn't quite know what, but she had known him now since she was a babe-in-arms and he had become someone who had always shown a great interest in her and valued her opinions on all things. She loved him for that. There were other times when she would catch him looking at her with a sort of wistful, knowing look. But she thought that was just her imagination. She supposed it was just because his life was empty. No family, no wife, just a lonely, but very loveable old man.

Eilid had placed the rifle back in its case. "Sir Andrew, I'm not too proud to accept this. But I do know I'll make you proud...I'll be the best, truly I will. Thank you, thank you, with all my heart."

"My dear I know you will." Sir Andrew had kissed her gently. "Many, many Happy Returns."

Eilid had applied for, and was granted, her Firearms Certificate. She adored Sir Andrew's gift as if possessed magical powers. It was forever being talked to as she stripped it down, cleaned and oiled it incessantly, although she had still not used it. Angus had taken it to the Lodge and had sighted the rifle. He thought it the best firearm he had ever handled. Beautifully balanced, with a standard and hair trigger, the gun was almost too good for his daughter. Angus was a crack shot himself and Sir Andrew's rifle made target shooting even more enjoyable. The cardboard box complete with a bull's-eye blackened out in the middle would be placed in the safety of the old quarry. The magazine held five shots and Angus would let fly at the target as fast as he could work the smooth bolt action of the gun. It was incredible. He could get a two-inch grouping from 150 yards.

It had been late in the month when Angus had decided it was about time to see if his daughter could use Sir Andrew's gift. On a bright Saturday morning father and daughter had taken the Estate Land Rover up the single-track road towards the head of the Dam and the disused quarry. The rifle was in its case and Angus had brought plenty of ammunition, the first lesson, he had thought, might be a slow and difficult one.

A new cardboard box had been duly marked up with a bigger than normal bull's-eye, a dry spot was selected where they could spread-eagle themselves and the box had been placed about 100 yards away, Eilid's Barbour jacket was spread on the ground, while Angus rolled his up tightly for something to rest the rifle on. Out came his telescope to augment the binoculars hanging round his neck.

"Right now," he addressed his daughter, "jist look doon the telescopic site and tell me whit ye see?"

"Nothing," Eilid had said, "it's all black."

"Aye, right, it will be tae. Ye've got yer eye too close tae the scope; draw back a wee bitty and now take a look."

"Oh, oh, that's miles better," Eilid had exclaimed as the rocks in the quarry seemed to leap towards her.

"Right," Angus had continued, "jist find the box, an' then tell me whit ye see?"

The rifle waived around for a minute and then became still as Eilid sighted in on the box and the bull.

"I've got it, Dad, it looks so close, you couldn't possibly miss."

"Aye, that'll be right. We'll see aboot that. Now pit yer left hand along the barrel, where the wood is rough, yer right jist rests here on the stock so ye can place yer finger on the trigger. Get yer right cheek well intae the gun and grip the rifle firmly yer right hand twisting wan way and yer left the ither, as if ye were tryin' tae wring oot wet clothes."

"It feels awful uncomfortable, Dad".

"Ah ken, ah ken, but ye'll get used tae it. Now jist pretend yer aboot tae pull the trigger, take a deep breath and slowly let it out. When ye think the rifle's steady and the cross hairs are on the bull, squeeze the trigger, dinae pull it now, it's very light, jist squeeze it gently."

Eilid tried the routine with the unloaded rifle until Angus thought she had the basics right.

"Okay, right, let's have a go wi' some live ammunition now." Angus crouched over his daughter and slid back the rifle bolt and placed 4 rounds in the magazine and one "up the spout". Quietly he had slid the bolt into position and put on the safety catch.

"Right, away we go, get intae position, when yer comfortable push aff the safety, like this," Angus had shown her, "then take aim and fire. That's aw' there is tae it."

She had done as she was bid. There was the loudest crack from the rifle as the first shot went off. The bang reverberated round the quarry as if three or four rifles had been discharged. Eilid couldn't believe the noise. It was as if she had suddenly gone deaf.

Angus had scanned the box with the binoculars.

"Well it's either missed or it's through the bull," he declared. Up came the telescope. "Aye it's missed the box completely. Try again, and this time squeeze that trigger."

Boom! The second shot went out. This time Angus had it tracked. "Too high, yer awa' too high."

The other three shots had shared the same fate, left, right, over under, no matter how Eilid had adjusted herself, the whole thing felt uncomfortable and just not right. Angus, not known for being long on patience, had begun to get upset. Christ, he had thought, I've a daughter who so far has been as good as any man on the hill and she cannae hit a barn door from inside the bloody barn!

However he had stilled himself with a deal of effort. He had sensed too, that Eilid was getting frustrated.

"All right love, let's gie it a try again."

Five more shots and the cardboard box had remained unmarked.

Angus had begun to fray at the edges.

"Christ Eilid, yer no' listenin' tac whit Ah'm telling ye. Aim the bloody thing, yer a' owr the place. Try tae relax."

Relaxation was the last thing Eilid had had on her mind. She was had gradually become more and more frustrated, the harder she tried the worse it seemed to get. Worse, her father had expected her to become a crack shot after two lessons. It just wasn't fair.

"Look Dad, it's no use. I'm trying the best I know how, truly I'm really trying but everything feels upside down, if you know what I mean."

"Upside down, upside down, whit the Hell does that mean?" Angus had glared at her.

"Dad, let's go home. You're getting upset and so am I. By upside down I mean holding the rifle this way doesn't seem right. Something's wrong with me. I don't feel comfortable".

"Stop right there," Angus had cried. The light bulb in his head had just gone on. Quickly he gave her the master eye test.

"Eilid extend yer right arm and point yer fore finger at the bull on the box up there."

Eilid had done as she was told. "Now close yer left eye an' tell me if your fingertip is still pointin' at the bull."

"No it's not," said Eilid, "it's moved away to the right."

"Right, noo close yer right eye, an tell me whit happens."

"Nothing it's great it's still pointing right on the bull."

"There we go then, that's it, yer left eye is your master eye." Angus had suddenly remembered that Eilid wrote with her left hand when she went to school at first. That was it! The Scottish educational system had no time for left-handers; Angus remembered. For when a lefty tried to write with a metal nib pen and black ink, they smudged everything they wrote as they pulled their hands across the page. That *was* it! Eilid had been actively encouraged to use her right hand with a rap on the knuckles with a ruler every time her left hand came into play. No wonder she couldn't shoot straight.

"Ah'm sorry ma' wee lass. Let's try this. Pit the rifle on yer left shoulder. Now pit yer right haun' on the barrel, use yer left haun' tae squeeze the trigger, try that."

The minute Eilid had reversed her holding of the rifle Angus knew she was home. Without a moments hesitation she went through the same routine he had taught her.

Bang! The cardboard box rocked. Angus let out a yelp!

"Right through the bull, right through the bloody bull!" he roared.

Four more shots had found the enlarged bull; all were in the black. Angus couldn't believe it. By God his daughter could shoot and this was her first day with Sir Andrew's rifle.

"Try five more Eilid."

With a smooth action he couldn't begin to imagine someone of 18 could possess, he had watched as Eilid fired off another 5 rounds into the bull in record time. The cardboard box was now peppered with ten shots, all still in the black.

"Five more an' we're done for the day."

Once again the left-handed Eilid was right on target. The cardboard box finally disintegrated as the last two shots had knocked the center of the box to bits.

Angus had never been so proud. He had a crack shot for a daughter. He couldn't wait to get home to tell Catriona.

He had driven at high speed down the Glen, back to the farm. Catriona had heard them coming into the yard as she finished putting dinner in the oven. It was a dinner that was never to be eaten.

Father and daughter had come into the farmhouse arm-in-arm.

"Well, well," Catriona had said, "some cat's got the cream! Tell me all about it..."

Angus and Eilid one after the other had told of the morning's events.

"I told Dad something wasn't right when I held the rifle right handed, I just couldn't explain it, but then it all worked out."

"An' she's a cracking shot mither, time after time she was in the bull. Look at this Ah brought the box back, look at it shot tae ribbons all in the middle." Angus had been unable to contain himself.

"Ah've never seen anyone dae something like that so easily, no left haunded anyway, except, except, young Alasdair Ballantyne, my God that man could shoot, an' he was left haunded jist like Eilid here."

Catriona's heart had been somewhere around her front teeth as Angus stopped wittering on. The silence that had ensued could have been cut with a knife.

Angus had turned on his heel to face Catriona, his face like death.

"You, upstairs." Catriona had known it was all over.

Both her parents had gone up to the bedroom and closed the door. Catriona knew what was coming. For 18 years she had hoped her secret would die with her.

"She's the Laird's bastard, isn't she?" Angus yelled.

"Of course not Angus, Sir Andrew's a gentleman, he wouldn't lay a finger on me," Catriona had tried to put a slightly haughty but brave face on it.

"Don't play wi' words. Damn fine ye know who Ah'm talking aboot. Alasdair, the brave Alasdair, it's his wean down there isn't it? She's no' mine, an' niver wis. Jist tell me the truth. It wis Alasdair that bairned ye, wisn't it?"

"Angus, listen to me, she's your daughter, she loves you and she loves me. Don't carry on with this it'll destroy everything. Please, Angus please, let's just talk about it."

"Talk aboot it, aye talk aboot it, let's have a wee fireside chat an' it'll a' go away." Angus then had done something he had never done before. He had grabbed Catriona by the throat and hissed,

"She's no' mine, is she, tell me the truth, tell me the bloody truth."

"Let me go. No, Angus she's not yours. I wish she was but you can't have children, surely you know that. Even the medical in the army must have told you there was a problem after that injury at the Shinty match."

"Why wid the Army tell me that? Ah mean we jist had to fight them, no' fuck them!" Angus had exploded with unconscious humor as he pushed Catriona away from him.

"It was all an accident. One night that was all, we…" Catriona had tailed off as Angus cut in.

"Some bloody accident". Angus interrupted. He was in full flood now. The veins stood out on his head, which had gone almost purple with rage.

"An' ah suppose the Laird knows a' about this, eh?"

"I don't know, I don't think so," Catriona had lied.

"Well ye can get oot o' ma house, yer no better than a common whore."

"Angus please, don't do this."

"Ah havnae even started yet. An' take that bastard daughter wi' ye".

"Angus please, calm down, just think, no one else knows, not even Eilid, but they will if you do what you're going to do. It'll tear our family apart."

"Family, whit bloody family. You've got the family no' me."

"Please Angus you're using the language of the gutter, what if Eilid hears all this?"

"Ah'm past carin'. My God what a mug I've been. All these bloody years and Ah've supported Andrew Ballantyne's bastard granddaughter, well nae maer. Out youse both go, the night. Ah tell ye whit, Ah'm aff tae the pub when Ah get back neither of ye had better be here, Ah'm warnin' ye, git while the goin's good."

Catriona had been in tears. "Angus, Angus please don't do this. Eilid doesn't know. She thinks that you're her Dad, what am I going to tell her."

"You should have thought aboot that eighteen years ago." And with that Angus had clattered down the stairs, strode by a terrified Eilid who had never in her life seen her father in a mood like this, flung open the door and had disappeared down the road to the village.

Silence.

Eilid had sat in the one of the living room chairs, too frightened to move. Catriona had sat on the bed upstairs holding herself tightly, swaying to and fro, sobbing silently, her mind in turmoil. She had never seen Angus become violent but she knew enough to take his warning seriously. There had been no doubt in her mind that he'd come back from the pub drunker than drunk. Then the trouble would really start for when Angus had a good drink in him he was prepared to take on the Russian Army. She was in shock, particularly on how she was going to break the news to Eilid. Well, it had to be done. Into the bathroom she went and washed away her tears. Slowly she had gone down the stairs to find Eilid sitting like she had seen a ghost.

Eilid well remembered the conversation.

"Eilid"

"Mother"

"Your Dad's taken leave of his senses. Well a bit anyway. I need to sit down and talk to you about what's happened. Dad wants us to leave this house tonight. He's gone to the pub in a rage and when he gets back he wants us out of here. I'm frightened that'll he come back drunk and there will be trouble. The only thing I can think of us doing is to go to the Lodge for the night, let your Dad sleep it off and see if he's changed his mind in the morning."

"Mother, what's gone wrong. We had a great day out there, Dad was so proud of the way I could shoot with my rifle and suddenly it's all gone wrong. Is it something I've done?"

"No, no, of course not my love, it's nothing to do with you; and yet I suppose in a way it is. If you hadn't shot so well maybe your father would never have started to think the way he did. You see you shoot just like your father."

"Mother, you're not making sense. I might be even better than Dad, is that's what's bothering him. I just shoot with the rifle the other way round, I use my left eye."

"You could say that's what's bothering him, that's the way your father did shoot."

"Mother what are you trying to tell me?"

"Angus Stuart's not your father."

Eilid had been shaken to her very foundation.

"My God, who then is my father?"

"Alasdair Ballantyne, the Laird's son. He never lived to see you. He was killed, shot down, in the Battle of Britain. That's where you get your blonde hair and your ability to shoot so well."

Eilid had been stunned into silence. She had sat and stared at the floor with her head in her hands for what had seemed like ages. She had no idea of what to say or where to begin.

Continual sobbing had racked her mother and she remembered her crumpled face as she had looked at her daughter for some sort of comfort.

"Mother, who else knows?" Eilid had asked.

"Until fifteen minutes ago only me and Sir Andrew."

"So, *that's* why Sir Andrew has always treated me as someone special." Suddenly it had become clear to Eilid that the special attention Sir Andrew had heaped on her for years was for a reason.

"Does that mean Sir Andrew is my Grandfather?" She had looked her mother in the eye.

"You could say that," her mother had sobbed, "you're his only living relative, illegitimate of course, but you are his son's daughter."

'My God, mother, what a mess, how did all this happen?" Eilid had wanted to know everything, despite still being in shock.

"It's a long story," her mother had began, "away back when I was twenty-five we had a freak snowstorm here in the glen. I had to prepare the Lodge for Sir Andrew and his guests as they always came to the last week of the cull. I had taken old Meg and the trap, we relied on ponies then, up the road to the Lodge. The snow had just started but in no time the weather turned to blizzard conditions and the snow had started to drift and make the road almost impassable in places, but I soldiered on. By the time I arrived the snow was so bad I had to unharness Meg and put her in the hill ponies stable. Well, I was in the middle of lighting the range when I heard a noise from upstairs, I nearly died of fright, so much so that I was about to leave when Alasdair Ballantyne appeared at the head of the stairs. He was such a handsome man, tall, blond, he just fair took my breath away.

We had met many times when he visited the estate and there was this attraction between us, never more, for your father was a gentleman and he always stayed polite but I could tell there was something just under the surface that told me he thought me attractive. But you never dwell on these thoughts, they'll just haunt you, after all he was the Laird's son and I was the Stalker's wife, the class distinctions were more severe then."

"How long had you been married to my Dad?" Eilid had asked.

"Oh about three years, I had been a nurse in Raigmore hospital when they dragged your Dad in for treatment, he had been injured in a Shinty match, and without going into a lot of detail I'm sure that was the reason we couldn't have children. Not that your father would ever admit to that. Anyway we grew friendly and when he was released he came back the following week and asked me to marry him."

"Alright," Eilid had said, "back to Mr. Ballantyne."

"Aye, aye, of course back to Alasdair. Well he helped me make the beds and with some of the other chores and when it was time for me to leave the blizzard had closed the road and you couldn't see your hand in front of your face. There was nothing for it but to stay the night. I found an end of ham in the deep pantry and some eggs so we sat in front of the fire ate the ham and eggs and talked to one another for ages. He was such an interesting man. He had traveled all over Europe and was aware of the events taking place in Germany that eventually led to the War.

I had remembered that Angus kept a bottle of Glenmorangie some-where as an emergency, if you like, and finally I found it tucked away in the top corner kitchen cupboard, I nearly fell off the stool fetching it and Alasdair had to rescue me. When he put his arms around me like that it felt so wonderful. He was so warm and gentle with me so we went back to the flickering fire and drank the malt; it was like a dream, he was so romantic. We spent the night sleeping together. I hate to say this but your father, I mean Angus, never showed me the love and ten-derness that I had on that one night with Alasdair.

All good things have to come to an end, so they say, the next morn-ing the snow had stopped but the road was still blocked so I had to jump on Meg bareback and ride back to the farm. I met your father half way back on his way to the Lodge to find out what happened to me. I told him Alasdair Ballantyne had just arrived that morning and that he had been hill walking by Kintail, had sheltered in the shieling by the loch overnight and set out early for the Lodge that morning.

It was December when I discovered I was pregnant."

Her mother had ended her story on that poignant note.

"So my father never suspected?"

"No, no, I told Angus on Hogmanay that we were going to be par-ents and he went daft. We had been trying for three years to have chil-dren, so he was over the moon."

"Until today." Eilid had said. "Mother, I've never known any other father. He's been a great Dad. He's taught me all I know and I love him for that. Remember when Miss Bain at the village school wanted me to go to some fancy academy in Inverness? Well my Dad wouldn't have it and while I might have ended up better educated I would have missed the years on the hill and the wonderful times I've had with Dad. Let me go down to the pub, it'll be alright, you'll see. I'll bring Dad back at it'll be alright, I promise you."

Eilid had been convinced she could placate her father and keep the family together, but she hadn't realized the depth of injured pride in her father.

Oh God, Catriona had thought, out of the mouths of babes and sucklings…. she has no idea what's just happened or what's at stake.

Maybe, just maybe, it could work. It depended on how much whisky Angus had consumed before she got to the village. Logic had never been Angus's strong point even Eilid knew that. It was still light, but the nights were starting to draw in. It would be dark by about ten o'clock.

"All right, on you go. But just be careful; think of your Dad as a loaded gun about to go off. And if he's the worse for wear, just leave, you can't talk sense to him when he's drunk."

"Mother, you can't talk sense to him at all, drunk or sober. It's all emotion I know that. Leave it to me if I'm not back by dark then you'll need to be concerned." Eilid had sounded confident, convinced that she put things back together again.

Catriona had marveled at her daughter's common sense and her intuitive knowledge of Angus. She was so right. It's always emotion with Angus. Shoot first and ask questions later that was Angus's style. And Eilid was only eighteen.

"Do you not want some dinner first, there's a steak pie in the oven, well it's venison actually, you must be starving?" Catriona asked.

"Mother, how can you think of food at this time?"

"All right, all right, I only asked."

Eilid had put on her hill boots, grabbed her Barbour jacket and had gone off down the road to the village. It was normally a good twenty-minute walk to the pub but Eilid did it in ten. It was a Saturday night and the pub had been packed. She jostled her way forward.

"Hi there Eilid, yer Dad tells me yer a dab hand wi' the gun eh?" Allan Fraser had shouted over the din.

"Aye, it's only one day, though Allan."

"There's the thing, yer right, there's the thing."

She had searched everywhere but she hadn't been able to see Angus anywhere. Finally she had made it to the bar.

"Jeannie, have you seen my Dad?"

The barmaid looked surprised. "He was here a wee minute ago, look in the ither room hen, he's maybe in wi' auld Hamish."

Eilid had gone through to what was referred to as the 'Lounge Bar'. It was shrouded in cigarette smoke. What a place. The smell of the beer pervaded everywhere with the odd whiff of a cheap cigar and even cheaper whisky. There, through the gloom she had seen him, hunched over a pint of heavy and a large whisky. He hadn't seen her. He had been sitting by himself, looking stunned and very unhappy. Eilid had approached.

"Dad, what's the matter?" I heard you and Mother having a set to. I've come down to take you home."

"Fuck off!"

Eilid had never, ever heard her father speak to her like that.

"Dad, it's going to be all right, come back home with me, my Mother and me want to talk to you. This is not the place."

"Fuck off!"

"Dad, this is not the way. Until just now I didn't know you were not my real father, but that doesn't matter to me. It's you I want as my father, you've always been my true Dad."

That did it. Angus had lashed out at some unseen monster. The pint of beer and the whisky went flying across the room.

"Are you bloody deaf? Whit part of fuck-off do ye no' understaun?"

Patrick the bouncer had come into view.

"Is there a problem Mr. Stuart?"

"No, no problem Pat, jist get ma daughter oot o' here and get her home where she needs to be."

"Nae problem, Mr. Stuart." Then he had turned to Eilid, "Come on hen, you come wi' me. This is not a place for young lassies." He had grasped Eilid by the elbow and went to march her out of the room. But it wasn't going to be so easy. Eilid sensing what Patrick was about, side stepped as he had grabbed her arm and had used his forward motion against him with the slightest of shoves. Patrick, who had also had few drams too many, went staggering across the floor, to the hilarity of the occupants of the lounge bar.

"Way ye go Patrick, ye couldnae bounce a rubber ba'" shouted one old worthy.

Patrick had not been amused. "Oh so we've got a right smart arse here hiv we? Come on lady, oot."

But Eilid was not to be moved. She had sat beside Angus and had grabbed his arm.

"Dad, please, don't be like this. I need to talk to you."

Patrick had loomed.

Angus relented. "Patrick two pints and two haufs, if she's old enough to come in here, she's old enough tae drink."

"Right ye are Mr. Stuart, Ah'll get Jamie tae bring them ower."

Angus had looked at his daughter through rheumy eyes. She looked wonderful, gorgeous, even in jeans, a sweater and a Barbour jacket. And she wasn't his. Eilid took off her Barbour. Her long blond hair cascaded down over her shoulders; her electric blue eyes pierced the cigarette's fog. There wasn't a man in the room that didn't turn and stare. And she wasn't his. How could he have been so blind all these years? Cover the bottom part of Eilid's face and she was Alasdair Ballantyne to a tee. Reverse that, and she had Catriona's soft lips and pretty nose. She was really a true combination of them both. The bitter bile rose in his throat as he thought about the years he had loved his child. His child. Now someone had taken that away from him. That someone would pay. By Christ they would pay.

Jamie had finally arrived with the drinks.

"Dad, you know I don't like beer and I've never touched whisky."

"Drink"

Eilid had taken a tentative sip of the beer. It tasted awful; bitter and sour. She had turned to the whisky and took a quick sip. Fiery, but better. She had then reached for the water jug on the table and added a splash. Another sip. That had tasted much better. She had thought she could get to like this. She had felt the whisky's warmth course through her. She sat back and had looked at Angus. Her father was focusing on some piece of wall about fifteen feet over her left shoulder. Neither spoke. About five minutes went by.

"Whit did yer mither say tae ye?"

Eilid had related what her mother had told her minutes before. She had thought her words hadn't sunk in, but they had made their mark. Downhill was downhill. It was time to start climbing.

"Jesus Christ whit a story. That auld bastard Sir Andrew knew all along jist whit he wis doin'. On ye go hame tae yer mither. Tell her tae stay where she is. Ah'll no' be hame the night."

"Dad, where will ye go?"

"Auld Hamish will look after me. On ye go. Finish yer drink and go back tae yer mither."

And with that Angus drained what was left of Eilid's pint as well as his own.

"Can I sit with you for a while?" Eilid hadn't wanted to leave right away, especially with her father in a foul mood.

"Aye, well alright. Just as long as it takes ye tae finish yer whisky."

So Eilid had stayed sipping away quietly at her whisky. She really had hated the place. It was thick with cigarette smoke, which had made her eyes nip. She had thought about her mother, more than likely packing to get out and go to the Lodge. On reflection she shouldn't have let her alone, but it had all happened so fast and all that she had wanted to do was to keep her mother and father together. There was nothing to be gained by revealing all to the general populace of the village. A bit of scandal about the Stuarts was just meat and drink to the gossipmongers, of which there were plenty. She had thrown back the last off her whisky like a drinking professional that had caught the attention of quite a few in the bar.

"Jist wan o' the lads, is that lass of your Angus. Is this yer first time here hen?" Roderick MacLeod, one of the regulars, had asked the question.

Eilid had said it was.

"Well don't be stranger, ye fair lighten the place up, yer a bonnie, bonnie lass. Ah didnae think an ugly soul like yer faither there could have such a bonnie bairn!"

Oh God, Eilid had thought, this is neither the time nor the place.

But Angus had taken it in his stride. "Whit wid you know about bonnie bairns Roddy, eh?"

It was well known that Roderick's two daughters were without doubt the ugliest two spinsters in the village. That had got a laugh from the crowd and Roddy mercifully shut up.

Eilid had said goodbye to her father and had given him a big hug and an even bigger kiss, whispering, "I love you Dad, don't ever forget that."

She had hurried out of the Lounge and through the Public Bar to the exit. It was getting dark now; she had been in the pub longer than she anticipated. As she had walked quickly up the road she thought she had heard footsteps behind her but she had paid no heed. She had walked this road at night many times. As she turned up the hill towards the farm road she had heard a noise again, this time it wasn't behind her but to her left where trees lined the road as it branched off uphill. She had wondered what it could be. It could have been a young stag or hind moving through the trees, or a stag getting the velvet off his antlers as the rut was getting closer.

Then she had heard it again. It wasn't footsteps, it was someone panting, breathing heavily. There was a crash as the thick tree branches were parted ahead of her by a wild-eyed Patrick McKeown, the bouncer from the pub.

"Ah, ha! There we are now," fat Patrick was drunk and out of breath. "Jist no' so fast young lady of the smart arse, I've got something tae say to you."

Eilid had had no time for this. "Make it quick Patrick; I'm on my way home."

"Well, no sae fast now. I've got a wee bone tae pick with you. That wis jist too smart a move ye put on me there in the pub, an' aw' the people laughing at me, an' me the bouncer."

"Patrick, you didn't need to try to strong arm me out the door, if you had asked politely I'd have left."

"Bollocks! Ye hung on tae yer Da fur dear life, you were no' fur goin' out wi' oot a struggle, Ah might be daft, but Ah'm no' stupit."

Eilid had thought of a very bright answer, but she canned it. It would only rile Patrick the more and she wanted to get to her mother before it was pitch black. So she had said,

"I'm sure you're right, Patrick."

But it wasn't going to stop there.

"Too bloody true I'm right, an' you know it. Anyway here's the deal gie's a wee kiss tae make up an' it's aw' forgotten."

Eilid could see what was coming. "No, not right now Patrick, look my mother's ill in bed and I promised I'd be back before dark, some other time."

"Bollocks!" Patrick exploded again. "That'll be right. Yer Ma's ill in bed so you go doon tae the pub fur a drink, pull the ither wan it's got bells on it."

Eilid had had to concede that while he might be drunk, his logic was pretty much on the mark.

"Seriously, Patrick"

"Aw go tae Hell."

And with that he had put his arms around Eilid and tried to get his lips to meet hers. The sour smell of beer overlaid with whisky had been all-pervasive. Eilid had recoiled as best she could from the encircling arms. But Patrick was strong. He wasn't the local bouncer for nothing. She was held in a vice like grip. His lips had met hers, no matter how hard she squirmed. Then he had forced his tongue in her mouth. It was disgustingly indescribable. She had never been kissed by a boy before, not in any romantic way, and this was awful. She brought her teeth down and had chomped on his tongue.

Patrick had recoiled "Jesus Christ! Are ye mad woman? Whit in God's name dae ye think yer doin' Ye've bit ma tongue, Christ it's blee-din'. You wee bitch. You've done it this time, let's se whit yer really made of wi' yer blond hair and yer goody-two-shoes attitude. Try Pat-rick on for size."

The next thing Eilid had known was that she was on her back. Pat-rick had put his left leg behind hers and pushed. The frantic Patrick was on top of her, his knees straddling her. His hands moved under her sweater grabbed her bra and pulled hard. The catch at the back gave way and his right hand had moved onto her left breast before she could even move.

"Patrick, Patrick stop. I'm sorry, I'll give you your kiss, just let me go."

"Too bloody late for that now lady. Let's see whit kind o' fancy drawers ye wear."

"Patrick, for God's sake, this is not right. Stop now before you get into real trouble."

But Patrick had been deaf to any pleading. The zip to her jeans had been undone as his right hand moved from under her sweater. His left elbow had pinned her in the middle of her chest. His breathing was heavy and labored as he fumbled with his own trousers. Eilid had been petrified. She was going to be raped. She knew it, she could hardly breathe let alone move as Patrick's full weight was upon her. Then his right hand moved back inside her jeans clumsily fumbling as he tried to get into her pants. The weight suddenly lessened as he had sat up. Her legs were still trapped though. Patrick reached into his trousers and as she had elbowed herself up his huge erection sprang from his pants. His face had got close to hers and she had smelled his hot, fetid breath again. His left elbow had been on the ground now as was his right. As he had gone forward on his knees all the weight was suddenly lifted for a second.

It had to be now or never. Eilid had jerked her right knee up with all her might and made contact with Patrick's crotch. It was the strength in her legs that did the trick. Patrick had gone flying almost over her head. But she had been just too quick to get up. As she had lifted her head his right boot had caught her in the mouth and had split her lip. But she hadn't cared; she felt no pain as she scrambled to her feet as a roaring Patrick had tried to get to his. But he had been no match for Eilid's speed and agility. Still face down he had got to his knees when Eilid grabbed the waist of his pants and pulled hard. Right below his knees had come his trousers, underpants and all. His great white hairy backside had loomed into view. Patrick, only half way up, couldn't move his legs and he was just about to struggle out of his entrapment when Eilid's boot had caught him in the same place where she had kneed him. Patrick had collapsed writhing in agony clutching his bruised gonads.

"You bastard Patrick, you bastard. Don't ever come near me again or you'll get worse than this." She had yelled at him.

Eilid had been shaking violently as she pulled down her sweater, yanked up her jeans and took off into the night and had left Patrick gasping and writhing on the ground.

She had got home at about a quarter to eleven to find her mother in the bedroom packing a suitcase.

"Mother, Mum, stay where you are. I spoke to Dad you've to stay here tonight at least, he's not coming home so you'll be safe with me."

The words had come pouring out falling over one another in her haste to tell her mother that the dire threats made by her father wouldn't be carried out.

She had, of course, forgotten about her own looks.

Her mother had thrown a fit.

"My God Eilid, what's happened to you darling? Your face is all covered in blood, your sweaters torn and your right eye's all bruised. Was this your father? For if it is I'll kill him."

"No mother, no, no, Dad wouldn't do this to me. Big Patrick McKeown attacked me." She had blurted out

"Attacked you, sweet Jesus what ever for?"

"Mum, I think he was trying to rape me."

Then, in a rush, it all had come home to her, the attack, the struggle and Patrick's bestiality. The whole horrifying incident came back in a rush and had shocked her. Eilid had burst into tears and had collapsed onto the bed shaking uncontrollably. My God, Catriona had thought, what a day, never in all my years have we had a day like this. Catriona sat beside her and had hugged her daughter for all she was worth, rocking her gently to and fro. Catriona bit her lip as she tried to hold back the tears. Here she was almost forty and her husband was going to throw her out of the house, her daughter, her and Alasdair's beautiful daughter had just been attacked by one of the locals, what was happening to the world?

Softly she had got up from the bed and went into the bathroom. She had filled a hand basin with warm water, had added a little Dettol and had gone back with balls of cotton wool to bathe her poor baby's face. Carefully she removed Eilid's sweater and what was left of her brassiere. She had helped her into a soft wooly dressing gown and then removed her boots and the rest of her clothing. Carefully she had looked her daughter over. Eilid's left breast was scratched in a couple of places. Her lip was split slightly and she'd have a shiner of a right eye. There were one or two other bruises but otherwise she was intact, thank God, she had breathed.

She had been half way through cleaning up her daughter when Angus had burst into the house.

"My God, Eilid that's your father, I thought you said he was staying at Hamish MacDowall's for the night." Her mother for the first time Eilid could remember had sounded in a panic.

"That's what he said mother." Eilid had looked wild-eyed at her mother as she heard her father approaching up the stair. The door had opened softly to reveal an agitated Angus. He had looked nearly as disheveled as Eilid.

"Ma wee lamb, tell me it's no' true." He had taken in the anguished look on his daughter's face and had feared the worst. Eilid, in fact, had now calmed down quite well. She was more concerned now with her father's return and her mother's safety. She couldn't take any more, not in one evening anyway.

"Dad, Dad, I'm fine. Why did you come home? Is it alright for Mother to stay.... you told me it was."

"Aye, aye, that's no' ma concern the noo. It's whit happened tae you Ah'm mair concerned wi'." Her father had scrutinized her closely.

"How did you know Angus?" Catriona spoke her first words.

Angus hadn't looked at his wife. He had just put his head in his hands and had said,

"It's an awfy business, an awfy business. It wis big Patrick wasn't it ma wee lamb?"

Eilid had just nodded her head.

"Ah thought as much. Ah knew he didnae like bein' made a fool o' in the bar an' Ah got tipped aff that he was goin' tae sort ye oot. Well more fool that bugger, he got sorted oot by baith members o' the family."

"But how did you know Dad?"

"Well Patrick cannae haud his tongue, can he. He boasted tae some o' his friends whit he wis aboot tae do. Well, of course nuthin' gets by auld Hamish. The only thing wis Ah let ye down. I didn't think he'd be sae daft tae dae something when Ah wis in the bar. The fella must be mad. Well anyway back he comes a' beat up like an' the boys piss themselves laughing. So Hamish widnae tell me whit had gone on, so Ah asked wan o' the ither folk whit a' the laughin' wis aboot. So they tell me it's some lass Patrick fancied an' he'd been sent packin'. Ah knew then whit the score wis."

"Dad, what did you do? Please tell me."

"He needs tae go tae the Hospital."

"My God, Angus, as if we don't have enough trouble." Catriona had blurted out.

Angus had turned on her. "An' who wis the cause o' a' the trouble, eh? Can Ah ask ye that?"

"Dad, what did you do to him?"

"Broke his bloody jaw! He's lucky he's still alive. He'll no' be back in this village again, no' if Ah've got onything tae dae wi' it."

Eilid had been delighted. At least her father hadn't killed him. And the fact that everyone knew what had happened pleased her. She knew she was lucky to escape relatively unscathed but she was also glad her wits, strength and speed had pulled her through. She had got up from the bed, had thrown her arms round her Dad and had said,

"Thank you Dad, I knew you would always protect me. I just wish you had followed me up the road and then none of this have happened. But it's not your fault. Thank God I got away. That Patrick's horrible. I never want to see him again."

"Eilid, do you want to go to the police?" Catriona asked, "that would be the right thing to do."

Before Eilid could answer, Angus had cut in.

"Dinae be so daft, woman. Mair guid's been done the night than the police would ever do. The word's got round. Don't mess wi' Angus an' his family. Ah'm proud of ye lass. If that man had harmed as much as a hair on yer heid he'd be deid by now, stone cold deid."

Both mother and daughter had believed him. It had been a terrifying, shocking, unpleasant and exhausting day for everyone. Angus had brought out three glasses and poured them all a large Malt Whisky. Not a word had been raised in objection. Silently they had sat sipping the smooth golden liquid. Each had been wrapped up in their own thoughts as the whisky slowly took effect. Catriona and Eilid had gone upstairs together arm-in-arm. Angus hadn't moved. Morning had found him still fast asleep in his chair.

Patrick McKeown never returned to the village. It was rumored that he went to live with a relative near Glasgow and was never seen in Cannich again.

She relived the events engraved in her mind as she tried to keep warm in the entombed Land Rover. It was now pitch dark, finally she fell into a fitful sleep only to dream of John Robertson whose tragic death had precipitated her elevation to Stalker at Sir David Vickers Glen Torridon Estate and of her Uncle Ken, the doctor to whom she was heading.

AULD JOHN –
Glen Torridon May 1956

It was in the spring of 1956 when Eilid came to Torridon at the tender age of 19 to work or labor under the tutelage of John Robertson, an experienced stalker of 58 but who looked more like 78. John had been with Sir David Vickers for many years on the Torridon Estate and Auld John, as he was known locally, was extremely diffident about having any female work with him on the estate.

'It's no right," he confided to Sir David, "this isnae the place for women, this is man's work, she'll niver dae whit a guid ghillie could dae."

And that, as far as Auld John was concerned, was that. David Vickers knew better than to try and placate his stalker. All he said to Auld John was that his very good friend Sir Andrew Ballantyne had asked him for a favor and that he was prepared to accommodate him. Let's see, he had said, how Eilid works out, if she can't do the work she would have to go and that he, Sir David, would take care of that eventuality. After six weeks at the Torridon Lodge, Auld John wasn't saying too much. For the first month he had to run the gauntlet of scorn from his colleagues and friends. None of that daunted Auld John, he readily accepted the fact that Eilid was outstandingly good looking, his "pin up" as he came to call her. But while he didn't criticize, neither did he praise. To all the questions his pals fired at him in the pub, Auld John would take it all in his stride and say she was doing "nae bad" for a woman. Inwardly he was just amazed at Eilid's stamina on the hill, and when it came to using the rifle Auld John had to admit he had never seen anything like it. She was a natural, a crack shot; she could do things with her Mannlicher that he could never equal.

It was one day on the hill they had to deal with a runner that remained fixed in his mind. It was the second stalk of the year and Sir David's guest would have been lucky to hit a stag if it was at the end of the rifle. Auld John, knowing this, had got as close to the stag as he could. It was about an eighty-yard shot, broadside on and the bullet went wide of the mark hitting the stag somewhere mid-body. Frothy pink blood appeared indicating the shot went through a lung as the stag took off up the hill at breakneck speed.

"Aw shit," Auld John had cried, taking off after the wounded beast. But when he looked up the hill to see how far he had to go Eilid was about two hundred yards in front of him carrying her own rifle. As Eilid got to the top of the hill she stopped in dismay. The stag had gone over the estate's March and was miles away. She stopped till Auld John caught up.

"What do you think, John?"

"Well, first of all that stupit bugger shouldnae be oot on the hill, and secondly that beast is just over our March. Let's take it oot if we can. Ah' cannae abide hivin' wounded animals come from my land on tae someone else's. The problem is there's nae cover. He's stopped now but he's in wide open territory."

"John, you stay here with our guest and leave it to me,"

"Dae ye think ye can get close enough for a shot?"

"I don't know, but I'm going to try."

"Well now, jist one thing, if the beast moves farther on tae the neighbor's side, ye'll have tae let it go. Ah cannae hiv ye winding that hill."

Eilid nodded her assent and took off back down the hill to keep the horizon clear from her to the stag. That would only last for so long for the wounded stag was now grazing on a wide-open piece of the hill with virtually no cover between it and the watershed summit.

Auld John had just got back to his guest when he heard the crack of the Mannlicher. He couldn't believe it. Eilid couldn't possibly have got as close to loose off a shot in the time since he had left her. Telling the guest to stay where he was he raced back up the hill and looked down to where the stag had been. Pulling out his binoculars he could see the stag on its side, stone dead. Then he tried to find Eilid. Eventually he picked her out wending her way towards the beast. He couldn't believe it. The shot must have been taken all of four hundred yards from the target.

In about two hours they had gralloched and dragged the stag onto their territory again to where the pony could pick it up. Never had they seen such a relieved guest who firmly believed his shot had killed the stag, or mortally wounded it, as he said. Eilid had just looked at Auld John and John at Eilid summing it up with a slight shake of his head. Later on, back at the estate larder, John was butchering the stag and found that Eilid's shot had taken the bottom corner of the stag's heart right off. It was fantastic accuracy from such a distance.

It was in the spring of the following year that Catriona came to visit her daughter. Almost two years had passed since she had seen Eilid. They had kept in touch by letter and Catriona was happy that her daughter was making her own way in life, albeit in a menial way. There was an old bothy on the estate that had been a shepherd's cottage of sorts but it had fallen into disrepair. Auld John had told Sir David to get rid of it because it was a haven for hill walkers and mountaineers who came to Torridon to scale the triple buttresses at the back of Beinn Eighe. However Sir David had had a better idea and asked Eilid if she would like to live there if he, Sir David, put it in decent shape. Eilid was delighted with the idea. She never liked staying in the Lodge, especially when guests were there. She had a tiny room with an even tinier window and nowhere to keep any personal possessions. Those had to be kept in the lockers Sir David provided for the stalkers and it was always a nuisance to go from her room and pass through the main body of the lodge especially in the evenings when all the guests would be lounging about after dinner having the odd dram or two, or three. She could never get past without at least one or two of the guests attempting to engage her in conversation or make a pass at her. She hated that. It was as if she were part of the estate property for the use of the guests. She was always polite but very firm. No, she wouldn't join them for a drink, thank you very much. No she didn't have a boy friend and yes, she confirmed, she kept herself to herself.

By the time Catriona visited the old bothy had been transformed into a comfortable cottage. Sir David had made sure all the essentials were installed and even went as far as to let her have an old coal fired Aga cooker that he moved out of the lodge to replace it with an oil fired one. The cottage had four fair sized rooms two up and two down with a proper bathroom and a big kitchen which was formed by making a lean-to at the back which ran the full breadth of the cottage. At the front of the cottage about 100 feet from the front door was a small Loch or Lochan with copses of tall pines dotted here and there. When the weather was fine the whole setting was almost idyllic. When it was foul the wind and driving rain shook the cottage to its very foundations as the wind funneled between Beinn Eighe and Liathach plucking at the roof as if to send it sailing into the surrounding peat hags.

It was an emotional meeting between mother and daughter. They stood at the side of the road and hugged one another to death, oblivious of the stares from the dozen or so passengers who were traveling on to Gairloch. As the bus took off in a puff of diesel smoke Eilid stood back and looked at her mother. She had changed little. Maybe a few more crow's feet round the eyes, but apart from that she looked well. Her hair was longer, fuller and it suited her, framing her face and making it more attractive. Down the glen they bounced in the Land Rover chattering away like school children going on a picnic. Catriona had heard by letter from a friend that Janet McVey had moved in with Angus and as far as she was concerned that was just fine. She told Eilid that she had got a good job as a cook in one of the local hotels and was 'seeing' a trawler captain. "Nothing serious," she assured Eilid, "we're just good friends". Eilid told her mother all about Auld John and how well they got on together despite John's original misgivings about having a woman working for him. Auld John had taught her so much more about stalking than Angus ever had and on some of the days when John's arthritis was giving him pain she had actually done a successful stalk. Also he had let her keep the traditional bottle of whisky that is given to the stalker for the first stag shot by a guest.

"What about boy friends?" Catriona had inquired. "There must be some nice men hereabouts that would suit you?"

"None that I've found or seen so far. I'm fed up with advances or offers from Sir David's guests; they're always having a go at me. Let me fly you down to London in my private plane and so forth, and the laugh is", she continued, "they're all married and they think I don't know. But before they get up here Sir David has given us the names of the next of kin just in case there's an accident or an unexpected illness."

"Aye, you're quite right, Eilid; have nothing to do with them. I'm sure if you stepped out of line Sir David would have you out of here in an instant."

"I'm quite sure he would, mother, and I've no reason to go chasing men. I'm only twenty and I still vividly remember that awful night with Patrick McKeown." Eilid shuddered involuntarily as she recalled the encounter.

"At least that was one thing Angus did right. He made sure Patrick would never come back to the village again." Catriona looked left and right as they approached Eilid's bothy.

"My goodness Eilid this is beautiful, what a grand place and you've your own wee loch too," her mother enthused as they arrived at the cottage.

"Wait 'til you see inside. The beds are a bit basic but they're comfortable enough. I'm going to drop you off, so take a look around. I've got to take the Land Rover back to John. It's the only transport we have around here except for the bike and I use that to go up and down to the village and go to the Lodge to attend to the ponies. I'll be back in about fifteen minutes."

True to her word Eilid was back in less than fifteen minutes accompanied by Auld John who's nose, he admitted, was bothering him so much so that he wanted to meet Catriona.

"Hello, hello now, there you are. My, my, I can see now why you've got a beautiful daughter." John looked Catriona up and down.

"Thank you very much, you're too kind," said Catriona shaking hands.

"So what are you going to be doing now that you're here?" asked Auld John.

"That's a good question," answered Catriona. "This place is truly beautiful but it really is in the middle of nowhere."

"Aye. Aye, that it is. But there's the village and it has a fine wee shop. It'll take you about an hour to walk to it from here and then if you go on a bit further there's Diabeg right there on the sea. Now that's worth a visit. You'll meet the local fishermen and if you're around when they come in they'll give you some nice fresh haddock or maybe even sole."

"Well I'm sure I'll find something to do, Eilid and I have got a lot of catching up to do and I'd love to get to the top of Beinn Eighe, it looks such a dramatic mountain."

"Aye indeed, that it is. That's all part of Sir David's estate and going round the back of the Beinn is even more interesting into Corrie Mhic

Fhearchair. That's more dramatic. Three great columns of rock tower skywards and there's a fine lochan at the entrance to the corrie."

John's descriptiveness made Catriona sense John's keen appreciation of the countryside and the pride with which he controlled Sir David's Estate.

The week passed all too quickly. Catriona had a fine time just being with her daughter. As a bonus the spring weather held up with sunshine almost everyday. She enjoyed her quiet walks on the surrounding hills and she enjoyed cooking some wonderful meals for Eilid and John. There was no shortage of a variety of food. They ate grouse, pheasant and venison that Auld John had put "intae some contraption Sir David calls a deep freeze." There was fresh salmon from the local rivers but the best of all was the Sea Trout, which John Robertson managed to acquire from the Gamekeeper at Loch Maree. To Eilid and Catriona no fish had ever tasted so good. The Sea Trout was lighter than Salmon in color, texture and flavor. Catriona fried the pink-fleshed fish in a pan in the same way she had taught Eilid, with lots of butter, a dressing of oatmeal and a generous sprinkling of lemon juice; no other fish came close to tasting so good and so fresh.

As for Auld John, he had never eaten so well. His wife had died some years earlier and most of the time he couldn't be bothered cooking, so he lived on cold beef or cold venison sandwiches, or sometimes cooked up the odd bacon and egg for dinner instead of breakfast. As the week ended Eilid promised her mother that she would come to Stornoway at the first available opportunity. The only real problem was that Sir David now relied on her to help John with the lambing and the calving, then followed the stalking, so it meant it would be the end of October before she could possibly get free. Going to Stornoway during the winter months was certainly not an attractive proposition. But she promised to write and send some photographs. There was even a rumor that a phone was to be installed in the Lodge but so far it was only a rumor. At least her mother had seen that her daughter was happy having made the transition from Angus and Cannich. Sir David seemed to be a kind if rather quiet man who very much left John and Eilid to their own devices. As long as the Estate ran at a small profit Sir David was happy. Coming from London to Torridon was a change of venue Sir David was happy to make. Like

Sir Andrew Ballantyne, he provided hunting, shooting and fishing for all his associates and contacts in the City at reasonable rates, and without charge to his special friends. Auld John loved it when his Sir David's friends came. Because they were charged nothing for the stalking, the whisky was distributed more liberally and the tips were doubled or even tripled.

Eilid's technique as a stalker improved immeasurably by the time her first season came to a close. She had become something of a legend in the Highlands as story after story was told in local bothies, pubs, and homes, about the blond ghillie on the Vickers' Estate. Embellishments about her good looks and prowess with a rifle grew. Rumor had it that she was Sir David's mistress but this piece of conjecture could never be verified as neither of them had ever been seen together. If any of the stories bothered Eilid she never showed the slightest emotion when one of the locals asked her to confirm a rumor or not. She would smile sweetly, tilt her head and engage them with her piercing blue eyes and watch them wither under her stare. She became adept at answering all questions about her person with a question.

"Do you think it's true then, Mistress McBride?" She would reply to owner of the general store in Torridon, who would make the most out-rageous forays into Eilid's past. Eliza McBride was her most formidable interrogator who possessed a carapace-like imperviousness when it came to asking the most rude and impertinent questions. She had no qualms asking any question of anyone no matter how personal and this inquisi-tiveness gave her the reputation of being the most knowledgeable person in the glen when it came to local gossip or scandal. By God, Eliza had told herself, she was going to get to the bottom of Eilid Stuart and her myste-rious arrival at the Torridon Estate no matter how long it took.

But she hadn't reckoned on Eilid's wiles nor Auld John's phlegmatic and taciturn nature. Eilid made sure she went to the store when there was certain to be at least one other person there. Then she would hand Mrs. McBride a neatly written note of what she required and tell her she'd pick it up the very next day. Eliza's wish to engage Eilid in a long conversation was thus thwarted to her ongoing frustration.

A year and six months went by. It was now early August 1957. Eilid had celebrated her first Hogmanay in Torridon and then her twentieth birthday, both in Auld John's company. They were a strange team but they had come to fit together well. Secretly John Robertson would have done anything for the tall lithesome blonde who looked after him when he was feeling under the weather. She was just too easy to look at. Her hand-eye co-ordination was so good that any task she performed was akin to poetry in motion. When he knew Eilid wasn't looking his way he would watch her with an unbridled fascination. Like Mrs. McBride he couldn't even begin to understand why someone so attractive and accomplished didn't find a decent job, which would have paid three or four times more than the tiny stipend Sir David paid her for being his ghillie.

In fact Sir David had joked that he had seriously thought of taking her down to London with him to see if she would make a good secretary. But it was said in jest when Sir David and John had been celebrating a fine stalk and a successful day on the hill. Auld John had laughed at the suggestion. It had been a hollow laugh, though, for the thought had just struck him of what he would do, or how he would manage without her. The more he thought about it, the more Sir David's suggestion preyed on his mind. Eilid had said nothing. He was sure she would have said something if Sir David had asked her, even in jest. However, it became an obsession. He would wake and sit bolt upright in the middle of the night as the ghouls and ghosts of uncertainty invaded his mind. After another restless night he resolved the very next day to ask Eilid about London. He picked Eilid up in the Land Rover the following morning.

"Is there something the matter John?"

John shook his head vigorously. "Why dae ye ask?"

"Well you look like the cat's got your tongue."

"Whit the hell does that mean?"

"It means you're not giving me a proper answer."

Silence. They drove down the road about two miles heading for the village.

"Have ye ever been tae London?"

"London? I've never been out of Scotland."

"But wid ye like tae go tae London?"

"My God John, what is all this about?"

John blushed. He didn't embarrass easily but he was making a complete mess of the whole thing. He was on edge so much all the subtle questioning he had planned and rehearsed was blown. He just wanted to get it over with.

"Did Sir David Vickers talk to you about going to London with him?"

"No, he didn't. Why would he ask me a daft thing like that?"

Suddenly a huge weight was lifted from Auld John's shoulders. He turned and beamed at Eilid.

"Aye, ye're right, why wid he ask ye a daft thing like that?"

Eilid kept looking at the stupid smile on John's face. John kept his eyes firmly fixed on the road about ten feet in front of them. John could feel Eilid's eyes boring through him.

"John?"

"Whit?"

"John I'm not daft, what's going on?"

He turned and looked at her stupidly with his silly grin still lighting up his face. Eilid had seldom seen John smile. Occasionally on the hill he'd permit a smirk or a quiet grin when one of the guests did something stupid, but smile...never.

"John out with it, come on, out with it."

"Aye, well, all right. Ah suppose Ah owe ye an explanation. Sir David told me he had thought of inviting you to London to see if he could make a secretary oot o'ye."

"And you thought I wouldn't say anything to you, if he had?"

"Aye, well, no, Ah jist wondered," Auld John floundered for words.

"Well, no, not a word was said about London. I've never been there and having heard about it I'm glad he didn't ask for I would have said no. Even for a visit. I could never be cooped up in an office, whether in London or anywhere, what did Sir David actually say?"

John repeated almost verbatim what Sir David had said. He left out the bit about her being better looking that any of Sir David's present staff, that didn't need to be said.

"Well, John, thanks for telling me. Were you worried?"

"Well, no, no, Ah mean if ye had wanted to go, that wid have been fine wi' me..." he tailed off.

"John?" Eilid put the eyes back on him, full beam this time.

John stopped the Land Rover and looked over at Eilid.

"Ah wis worried sick."

"Thank you, John, you've made my day. I love it here. I would always discuss something like this with you. It would be very wrong of Sir David to go behind your back on a subject like this."

With that Eilid smiled at John, leaned across the gearshift between them so that her blonde hair cascaded over half her face, reached out with her hand for John's face and gave him a big kiss on the cheek.

Auld John thought he was about to die. A long extinguished fire suddenly flared in the old man as the combination of Eilid's smell, her hair and her soft supple lips on his cheek brought back buried memories from his youth. Clearing his throat loudly, he crashed the Land Rover back into gear and took off down the single-track road.

Little did either of them suspect that they would be separated within six weeks.

It was mid-September and already there had been a touch of frost almost at sea level. Both Liathach and Bein Eighe had a powdering of snow around their summits. The colors were beginning to change earlier this year than last. There was a full complement of guests coming to the Lodge so John and Eilid would be fully occupied for the stalking season save when the weather was too bad to go on the hill.

August had so far proved uneventful. The rut hadn't started until the first week in September and now the deer had started to form into herds as the stags fought for control of the hinds. The colder weather had brought them down off the tops to lower ground. Conditions were perfect.

There were six in the party as John at the head of the line and Eilid bringing up the rear silently marched in single file in the corrie between Liathach and Bein Eighe. Auld John then wheeled left to go behind the big buttresses of Liathach. He then spied a large herd of deer to his right. He stopped the party while he got out his trusty telescope and scanned the beasts in front of him. He quietly closed the scope and came back to Eilid.

"What do you see?"

"Well, there's a big stag up there at the greenish patch, behind the hinds, looks like an eleven pointer."

"Aye, I've got him. Is that all?"

"No, there's another stag behind that big rock way up there on the left."

"Ah didnae see anything up there."

"Look at the big rock just before you get to the sky line, all you can see are the tips of his antlers."

John moved the telescope and braced it against his stick as he scanned towards the rock Eilid had pointed out.

"Michty me, ye're right. All ye can see are the points for he's lyin' doon. He looks like a fair sized beast though."

"I think he's going to ambush the old fellow up there on the right."

"Aye, well ye might be right. But Ah'm going tae go for the old beast there. He's not in good shape and if yon big stag is young Ah wid rather hiv the herd go tae him. Anyway it's no' an easy stalk an' Ah think Ah've got a rookie on the rifle. Still he wis no bad wi' the box, Ah mean at least he hit the bloody thing."

They smiled together. It was forever an unknown quantity bringing untried and untested people to stalk for the first time.

"Eilid, you wait here wi' the others. Ah'll take oor mannie here up and see if I can get him close enough for a shot."

An hour and a half went by during which time the rest of the party became cold and impatient.

"Come on, Eilid, what's going on," cried George Jenkins, a City Stockbroker. "We're bloody frozen."

"Nothing's going on except they're getting fairly close now. It's a difficult stalk. There's not much cover and the hinds are all arrayed in front of the stag. But if anyone can do it Auld John can."

"Well I vote we get out of here, we're all freezing." Miles Ashley spoke up echoing the feelings of the others.

Eilid jumped on the insurrection quickly. "You'll all just stay put. To move now would most certainly spoil the stalk. You all know the rules, you move only when John gives us a signal and I'll be the judge of when that might be. I'll keep you posted as the stalk continues."

The three guests all sat down again with a look of disgust directed at Eilid. Eilid appeared not to notice. She had plenty of experience with the English wimps, as she called them, coming up to the Highlands for the first time and thinking they would stroll out of the lodge and kill a twelve pointer. This group epitomized her broad perception of those who worked in the City of London. They wouldn't know what hard work is she surmised, all talk and no action.

She raised herself up on her elbows and took another look through her binoculars. John had done a magnificent job. He had actually got right up to where the first hinds were and the big stag was standing still at the back of the herd looking up the hill. Eilid followed the stag's line of sight. The stag from behind the rock had got up, it hadn't moved, but now the old stag could see very clearly what was bound to be his adversary. The old stag let out a roar and for a reason unknown the hinds barked in unison and scattered, running swiftly up hill and left, away from the possible confrontation. Eilid watched fascinated. Auld John got up from what must have been their final position, clearly he had been preparing Steve Fillmore for the shot.

What happened next was like a slow motion horror movie. As Auld John stood up he waved his handkerchief at the party beckoning them up while at the same time Steve Fillmore got up from his horizontal position, swiveled left to look at John, and as he turned the rifle moved with him. There was tremendous crack from the .270. John must have been carried ten or twelve feet by the shot to collapse on the heather.

"My God!" cried Eilid, "John's just been shot!" And she took off at breakneck speed up the hill to where John lay, not caring or looking if the others were following. The others not having seen anything but on hearing Eilid's cry took off hard on her heels. Eilid got to the spot well ahead of the remaining three. The Steve man was just standing completely dazed, not knowing what to do. Eilid took in the whole scene at a glance although she was terrified at what she might see. Auld John was sprawled out on the heather, slightly propped up by a hummock he had fallen against, looking as if he was just resting. One eye looked as if there was a dark patch close to its corner but he looked quite peaceful. The other three guests arrived puffing and panting. Eilid told them to stand back as she relieved Steve of the rifle. Quickly she slid open the bolt to remove the casing in the chamber, and removed the magazine. The rifle was safe.

"Hold that," she handed the rifle to Miles.

Steve was blubbering away, "He told me to put on the safety, I'm sure I did, I really don't know what happened, he'll be all right won't he?"

Eilid stayed silent. She walked forward to John's body almost frightened to touch it. There was something just beyond his head lying in the grass and she couldn't quite make out what it was, then as she got closer she started back in horror. It was John's brains, lying almost intact completely blown out of his scull. Her stomach churned wildly as nausea almost overwhelmed her. She turned away and took a deep breath. She stepped back to the group who were still staring at the body of the stalker.

"He is going to all right though, isn't he," Steve blubbered on some more.

Eilid approached him and grasped him by both shoulders and looked straight into his eyes. "Steven, John's dead, you've blown his brains out, so for God's sake be quiet and let's deal with this disaster as best we can."

"Miles, take the keys to the Land Rover and off you go down the hill as fast as you can and go to the 'phone box just before the Lodge, dial 999 and ask for the police at Loch Carron. Tell them what's happened and they'll know what to do…we'll need an ambulance as well…." she tailed off. Her mind was whirling now as different ideas and options flooded her mind. She had to get word to Sir David; he had to be informed as soon as possible. He was in London and all she had was his office number, by the time they got off the hill it would be dark. She didn't have a clue as to what to do next. If the police were to get involved then she really should leave the body where it lay, on the other hand rigor mortis would set in as well as leaving Auld John to become a victim of any preying animal that might be attracted towards the corpse. They would have to somehow get the body off the hill, but it would have to be carried some distance to where it would be accessible for the pony.

"Steven, Nigel, George," she addressed the other three as Miles left helter-skelter down through the corrie with the Land Rover keys. "Were going to try and carry John a-ways. Here's what were going to do, take our hill sticks and cross them over between the two of us, we'll sit John on them. Steven, you'll have to take his arms and throw an arm over each of our shoulders so that he's sitting slumped forward. His arms will fall off but I've got my skein of rope so we can tie his hands together keeping his arms in place. Have you got all that now?"

Steve, by this time was sitting doubled up rocking himself as silent tears flooded his face. He just couldn't cope with the enormity of what had happened.

"I don't think I can help you, I've never touched a dead body before, Jesus Christ this is awful."

"Jesus Christ, so it is. What do you mean you think you can't help us? Listen you, you caused the problem! I really don't give a shit whether you've handled dead bodies before, neither have I, there's a first time for everything, so let's get on with it, we've got a long way to go."

George and Nigel nodded their assent as George picked up Auld John's fallen stick and stood silent and ready.

"George, give me a hand to move the body; I want to leave the place as we found it, I'm sure the police will want to see where the accident happened. Let's move John over here a bit on the down slope and we'll surround the perimeter of the area with stones. I'm not sure what the police will want, but in the circumstances that's all they're going to get."

Eilid went behind the body and put her hands under John's armpits. She was surprised at how little blood there had been, but as she tried to move John his head lolled forward exposing a huge exit hole at the back of his head. The nausea began again. George had the legs but they barely moved the body a foot.

"Christ," said George, "he's a dead weight. Sorry I didn't really mean to say that." And he laughed inanely.

But joking apart he was right. John was a dead weight. They had to persuade Steve to get a grip on himself and take a shoulder before they could achieve a clear lift out of the accident area.

The stones were quickly put in place and the task of trying out Eilid's theory of crossed sticks and arms over shoulders began. It took 30 minutes of maneuvering to get the body sitting between Nigel and George, Stephen stood behind just in case the corpse fell backwards. They slowly made their way downhill, stumbling over stones, dragging their feet in the heather and stopping at any rock against which they could prop the body to prevent the loading process starting all over again. They had come about three miles that had taken them four hours with rest stops and taking turns at carrying John's body. At last Eilid could see the Glen Torridon road in the distance. It couldn't have been more than a mile and a half away. Not surprisingly there was no sign of the police or an ambulance.

"Okay," said Eilid, "here's where we leave John. I'll run on down, you three stay with him and I'll fetch the pony. It'll take me a while longer for I've not got the Land Rover but I'll be as quick as I can and I'm sure to get here before dark." It was already five-thirty but it didn't really get dark until about seven-thirty, so Eilid figured on getting the pony to the party in an hour or less.

She was harnessing Shelagh, one of the ponies, when the shock of what had happened hit her. She started to sob, quite uncontrollably, then the sobs turned to tears coursing down her face. Old John Robertson was dead. The picture of him in her mind, as it always is, was that last picture as he lay dead on the heather, the grayish pallor of death seeping through his weather beaten face. It was as well the pony knew the route they were taking by heart for Eilid couldn't see a thing. Her body heaved as she shook with attack after attack of convulsive sobbing until she crossed the road and got on the route between Liathach and Beinn Eighe. Finally she gathered the pony, and astride the deer saddle trotted on, wiping away her tears lest the guests would see her grief in the open. As she got higher into the corrie she saw headlights coming down the road in the gathering twilight. The last thing she wanted now was to talk to the police, if it was them. So she kicked Shelagh on towards the waiting party and old John's body.

The funeral was a somber affair albeit held in a charming little church almost two hundred miles south of Torridon near the tiny village of Struan, in Perthshire. There in the churchyard, at the confluence of the river Garry and Errochty water, they laid John Robertson to rest. Eilid had traveled down on her own in the Land Rover and met Sir David and Sir Andrew Ballantyne close to the village. It was just under a year since she had seen her grandfather; she called him Granddad when they were in private and he adored her attention. Eilid saw a change in Sir Andrew: he looked more drawn and rather gray, but he professed to being fit and had been looking forward to his visit to Torridon in October. The terrible accident, on which the coroner's court returned an open verdict of death by misadventure, clouded the whole season. Sir David had canceled all further stalking and had given clear instructions to his Factor to closely vet any applications for stalking the following year. If the people coming to The Estate had no experience of using a rifle they were not be allowed on the hill. Sir David's Factor told him that asking for such detailed information might just drive guests away. Sir David had said he didn't care, he was not going to lose anyone, guest, stalker or ghillie on the hill, due to inexperience with a firearm, and that was that.

As she left Struan, Eilid remembered her mother telling her that she had an uncle, her mother's brother, Dr. Ken Urquhart, who lived in Pitlochry about 15 miles south of Struan. Sir David had given her as much time off as she needed and had not yet broached the subject of who was to take Auld John's place. Sir Andrew, meantime, had said to Eilid he could see no good reason why Sir David wouldn't offer her the job of stalker. Eilid felt badly about that, it was she had said to Sir Andrew, as if she was filling dead men's shoes. Sir Andrew had characteristically hit the nail on the head when he said to her, "Well, it wasn't you who shot Auld John now, was it?"

They parted company with Eilid saying that if the job was offered, she 'would think about it' which as far as Eilid was concerned was as good a commitment as her Granddad was likely to get.

Pitlochry turned out to be a fine town with many fancy hotels and fancier shops. Loch Faskally had been created about ten years earlier by the damming of the River Tummel to produce Hydro electricity. The Falls of Tummel were no more; the dam had ended all that. A few vapid eddies and swirls were all that remained of the famous falls, sacrificed in the name of progress. The surrounding countryside, however, was, Eilid thought, just picture perfect. Being early autumn the trees sported their farewell tones of red, brown and gold. Where deciduous intermingled with evergreen, spruce, and pine, the contrast was more dramatic. Eilid found the little suspension bridge that spans the Tummel just below the dam and from there gazed out over Loch Faskally. Then as she walked up the hill on the west side of the Loch she could see the mountain of Beinn Vrackie with its sharp, almost razor-edged peak, standing like a huge sentinel over the town. In a way it reminded her of Beinn Eighe but her Beinn was more perfect, more conical. Thoughts of home brought back memories of Auld John and a feeling of terrible emptiness swamped her and wouldn't go away. He had been a true friend and mentor to her and she never had a real opportunity to express her gratitude to him. Who would have thought that on that one day in Torridon a stupid, fateful mistake would cost John his life? My God, she thought, I'm getting really maudlin. So she shook off her mood of depression by stepping out, heading back to the Land Rover resolving to find her Uncle Kenneth.

Eilid soon found her doctor uncle, in one of the local pubs. She had found his house by looking up his address in a telephone directory and had driven up the hill to the little village of Moulin where he lived. She had knocked on his door several times when a next-door neighbor appeared asking who she was and who might she be looking for. The neighbor, as well as just about everyone in the village, it turned out, knew Ken Urquhart's routine almost better than Ken himself.

"Och aye, it's past six, Kenny will be in the pub," pronounced the chatty neighbor, "your box will be fine here," he smiled in the direction of the Land Rover. "Just go down the road a wee bitie, he'll be at the bar in the Moulin Hotel."

And so it proved to be. Eilid recognized him from photographs her mother had let her see. Ken had been a fine strapping man with a mop of unruly reddish hair and a warm disarming smile. But it was a morose and overweight Ken that sat at a table near the bar drinking a large scotch with a pint chaser. Eilid asked the barman, nodding in his direction, if he was indeed Dr. Ken. The barman had nodded 'yes' back. Eilid went up and introduced herself. Clearly Kenny, as he was referred to, had had more than just one drink.

"It's Catriona's daughter, I don't believe it. Look at you, my God you look wonderful. Look, everybody, this is my niece Eilid down from Inverness to see me!" his unhappy demeanor changing to a warm, welcoming smile.

He twisted in his seat pointing out Eilid to the small assembly. People nodded approval and some smiled warmly in her direction.

"I'm not really from Inverness, Uncle," she whispered.

"Ach don't bother your head about that, they'll no' care anyway. Here, Johnnie," waving at the barman, "this calls for drinks all round!"

And so the party started. News of Kenny's philanthropy spread like wildfire. In no time the pub was crowded with Johnnie, the happy barman, pouring whiskies and pulling pints as fast as he could. Kenny was delighted that Eilid enjoyed a whisky. Johnnie, who had now recognized that Eilid was quite the most attractive girl he'd ever seen in his bar, ported over Macallan after Macallan to the table. The young men had also taken note of her slender figure and long blonde hair that spilled over her shoulders now that she had taken off her Barbour jacket. They were like moths round a candle, all talking animatedly to Kenny but not taking their eyes off Eilid.

Eilid was mightily relieved when at closing time, Kenny offered her a bed for the night at his house. She certainly couldn't have driven anywhere and she was contemplating asking for a room at the hotel. Another whisky appeared at the table. Eilid looked up at Johnnie.

"It's on the hoose, Eilid, well, it's from me really," said Johnnie giving her a knowing wink.

"Thank you very much, you're too generous and I don't really think I can drink this down as it's closing time."

"Nae bother, lass, take yer time. I've got you in as a hotel guest. You can drink all night now if you like. Room number 12, just in case anybody asks. But the polis won't be in here tonight." He grinned again as he referred to the local constabulary who were happy to stretch the licensing laws just as long as the odd dram came their way.

All the young blades, deeply disappointed at being ejected at closing time, mooned around the entrance to the bar in the hope of catching sight of Eilid again. But Eilid and her uncle were catching up on family history.

Ken was a successful general practitioner and well liked in the town. Ten years earlier, he had told Eilid, his wife Phyllis had run off with an Irish laborer who had worked on the building of the Tummel dam. He had never recovered from the insult.

"A bloody Paddy, and a navvy to boot. I don't know which attribute was worse," he had said to Eilid. They had had no children and after 5 years their divorce became final. Kenny was still bitter about it, Eilid could see that. Apparently he had started drinking after his wife's elopement, not too much at first, just a bit at night to help him sleep and to get rid of bitter memories. At eleven-thirty they gave up. Eilid had never drunk so much in her life. The room was rocking quietly as she stood up and helped her uncle to his feet.

"Steady the Buffs," shouted Kenny as he staggered from his seat. Eilid put on her Barbour with more than a little difficulty and then put her arm round Kenny to give him some support. Together they staggered wildly to the right.

"Christ, it's the blind leading the blind," Johnnie remarked dryly as niece and uncle virtually fell out of the door he was holding open for them.

Dr. Kenny's house belied the owner's looks. It was clean and neat to the point of almost being antiseptic. Kenny didn't smoke, Eilid was grateful of that; she hated cigarette smoke more than anything. It somehow reminded her of the awful night in the Cannich Inn and the aftermath with Patrick McKeown. She hadn't really got over the shock of that night and she wondered if it was that experience that made her wary of men; every glance, every comment, was suspect no matter how innocently made.

Kenny showed her to her room and where the bathroom was. Her room was small but well decorated with lined curtains and a soft plush carpet that moved up and down when she trod on it. Very plush, she thought. What a difference from her minimalistic furnished cottage in Torridon with only cheap mats thrown here and there to combat the cold and the bareness of the stone flagged floor. She had picked her rucksack out of the Land Rover and brought it into the house. Eventually, for her eyes weren't focusing too well, she retrieved her flannelette nightdress and pulled it on, went to brush her teeth and say 'goodnight' to Kenny but she didn't have to bother. Loud snores coming from behind Kenny's bedroom door told their own story.

The smell of bacon frying and the aroma of coffee wafting through the house wakened her. She had a splitting headache and she realized she was starving. Slowly she eased herself out of the bed and slowly crept towards the kitchen. Kenny was just coming in the front door having picked up the daily newspaper. He looked marvelous. Hair all neatly combed, shaved, a clean crisp white open necked shirt, dark slacks and black casuals made him look a dashing figure. It was as if he had never had a drink in his life. Eilid couldn't believe her eyes. Kenny looked at her carefully.

"Uh huh, a wee bit peekie this morning, are we?" Eilid could only nod. Even that hurt.

"Aye we'll fix that in a minute, we've got all the tools, all the tools." Kenny was too damn cheerful for words.

"I'm really sorry, pet, I should have known you never had drank so much, it was too much for me as well, and I've still got the bloody bill to pay, that's the worst part. I hope Johnnie goes easy on me. Still, here we go, have a cup of coffee and I'll get something to help your headache; you have got a headache?"

Eilid placed her hand on her forehead and groaned and sat down at the kitchen table. Uncle Kenny looked her up and down again. Even when she was ill she looked fabulous. She could get a job as a model, or a beautician, anything really unrelated to what she did. Her flannelette nightdress didn't exactly flatter; it was probably just as well he thought, he still had a keen and appreciative eye for the female form. Eilid sipped her coffee as if it was hemlock.

It's not that bad now, is it? Freshly ground this morning you know."

"Uncle Kenny, it's fine. I'll be okay in a minute."

"Right now here's the cure, just down it in a one. Don't even smell it."

Eilid took the proffered glass. It looked like whisky; it smelt like whisky, it *was* whisky!

"No really, Uncle Kenny, really I couldn't." The smell was killing her.

"Come on now, hold your nose if you like and down the hatch, doctor's orders." He sounded quite stern.

Eilid did what she was told. Over the liquor went in one, burning her throat on the way down. She grabbed the coffee and took a deep swallow.

"There you go now, good girl. It's what's called 'the hair of the dog'. You'll be fine in fifteen minutes." And, by Jove, Kenny was right.

In another ten minutes she was woofing down Kenny's big fry up of bacon, egg, sausage, potato scone, black pudding; the full Monty. Another two cups of coffee washed the whole breakfast down and Eilid felt as right as rain.

"Uncle Ken, that was wonderful, you're a great cook."

"Aye needs must. When that cow Phyllis left me I had to learn quick. I've got some great recipes. Once I get to know the chefs in the local hotels I go along there with my card and I ask them what they consider their best dish is, and off they go. In fact only once have I not been invited along for a complimentary tasting. Then after a few drams they'll not only give me the ingredients, I get the details on how to cook it. So you can see I'm not suffering by the weight I've put on. Of course this is the first time we've met but I'm sure you've seen photographs of me at your mother's wedding."

"Yes, I did, Uncle Ken. You were in your kilt and you looked fabulous. You have put on a bit of weight, but I suppose that's more the drink than the food." Eilid was being her brutally honest self.

"Aye, right you are there, again. You're just like your mother aye telling me what's bad for me. Oh, and another thing, just call me Kenny, everyone else does. And drop the uncle bit, it makes me feel so damn old."

"I'm sorry Uncle...... Kenny," Eilid caught herself, "I wasn't trying to preach; I'm just worried if you go on like this, the Medical Board or whatever it is might just take away your license."

"Your quite right, lass, quite right. They're out to get me.

"I'm sure you can handle them. You certainly seem to be well liked in the village."

"Don't be fooled by that, Eilid, that's the friendship you get when you buy friendship. These villages in the Highlands don't change much. Although I've been here for over twenty years, I'm still an outsider. Even though I'm more of a Highlander than they are. My first language was Gaelic, I had to learn to speak English, and so did your mother. But that doesn't count for anything; you're still an outsider. But the number of people who regard me as such is going down as the village grows. Tourism is getting stronger. It always was good, but it's growing. You know they're talking about having a theater right here in the town, for the summer months of course, and they'll have plays staged locally, the Theater in the Hills, is what it's going to be called."

So the conversation continued and Eilid told him what had happened to her mother and Angus leaving out the real reason for their parting. What had happened after that, she diplomatically left out the bit about Patrick McKeown, and how her mother's life and hers had gone downhill from there. She told him about Sir Andrew and how he had helped her leave home to go to Torridon to work on Sir David Vickers's Estate. She filled in the gaps about John Robertson and the hellishness of his death and how it all happened so suddenly.

Kenny had interrupted at that juncture as he could see Eilid was getting very upset and close to tears. He asked her if she thought she had sufficient experience to become Sir David's stalker. That had brought her back quickly.

"Of course", she said. "You know I haven't been offered the job yet, but I'll take it if Sir David offers it to me. I think he knows I'm competent enough."

Kenny didn't doubt it for a minute. He didn't say it, but he thought that if Eilid became stalker Sir David could name his own price for guests to come to Torridon. Who wouldn't turn down a chance to go stalking with the beautiful Eilid? They'd have to be nuts not to want that.

"Good for you. Maybe when you get the job, and I mean it's not a question of will you get it, but when, and we can have a wee get together, you, your mother, and me eh? That would be grand now, wouldn't it?"

Eilid agreed. And those comments made her wish she were back in Glen Torridon again. Back to her small but comfortable cottage with its spectacular views of the Loch and the surrounding mountains.

"Kenny, I'll have to go. Thanks so much for giving me a place to stay and giving me some valuable lessons. I'm only twenty-one but I've done so much in the last couple of years I feel older. I don't want to take advantage of Sir David's generosity so I'll get back to the Estate. I really don't know when I'll see you again, but I hope it's soon. You're a wonderful Uncle, and I'm sure a great Doctor, just make certain it stays that way."

And with that she planted a moist kiss on Kenny's lips that made him think how glad he was to be a relative, and not consider the consequences of reciprocation. The girl didn't have a clue of how she came across to men. She was like a time bomb, waiting to go off. He just hoped it would be with the right man. So they hugged and kissed again, uncle and niece. Kenny waved until the Land Rover was out of sight, as she turned right down the hill from Moulin to Pitlochry. Neither of them knowing how soon they would meet again and in quite the most bizarre circumstances.

It was the Tuesday evening after Eilid's return from Perthshire when she saw the headlights of a vehicle approaching her cottage. She put on the outside light by her vestibule as a welcome. She was sure it would be Sir David. As it turned out she was right, but instead of one, she had two knights of the realm step out of the car. Sir Andrew Ballantyne, her grandfather and patron, had come along too. Eilid couldn't have been more delighted.

"Sir Andrew!" she called out and rushed forward to give him a kiss.

"Where's my 'Granddad ' tag then?" he chided.

Eilid moved her eyes in Sir David's general direction.

"It's all right, my pet, Sir David knows all about us," he spoke loudly,

"Isn't that right David?"

David Vickers nodded his assent as the threesome entered Eilid's cottage. From his inside Barbour jacket pocket, Sir Andrew produced a bottle of 18-year-old Macallan with what could only be called a flourish. Eilid's eyes rolled in her head. Memories of the Moulin Hotel bar flashed in front of her as she looked at the bottle of malt.

"Well, don't just stand there lassie, you must have some glasses?" Sir Andrew proceeded to uncork the bottle and throw the cork away. Eilid's worst fears had been realized.

"Granddad, of course I've got glasses, Edinburgh crystal no less, a set of six whisky glasses from a very satisfied client. He very kindly sent them to me when we had a dram to celebrate him getting a Royal and we only had tumblers. He sent six to me and six to John, wasn't that nice?"

"Well you've got a dozen now," chimed in Sir David. "Auld John left you all his possessions. It's not really a Will, it's more a letter of administration, he had no relatives left you know, but it's as good as a Will in Scotland.."

Eilid felt all her emotions well up in her again. She had known Auld John liked her, but to leave all his meager possessions to her was just too much.

"Oh, God, oh, my God'" was all she could say as she bit her lip to prevent the tears that were ever welling up in her eyes when she considered John's untimely demise.

"There, there," Sir Andrew hugged her close. "You mustn't grieve, lass, this is not what Auld John would want now, is it?'

And, of course, Sir Andrew was right. John never felt sorry for himself, only for others who didn't, couldn't or wouldn't see the wonders that John saw every day in his beloved Torridon.

The 18-year-old Macallan helped calm her. The smooth malt whisky was as fine as she had ever tasted as they sat round the flickering fire.

"Eilid, I'm sure you know why we're here." Sir David started off the conversation. "I've asked Andrew along because I thought you might have some reservations about taking on John's job and responsibilities. I hope you don't. It's my pleasure to offer you the job if you're prepared to take it." Sir David stopped and looked closely at her.

Silence.

Sir Andrew cleared his throat noisily.

"What do you think then, Eilid? Do you want some time to think it over?"

"Can I stay in my cottage Sir David or do I have to move to the Lodge to the rooms that John had?"

"My dear, you can do whatever you want."

"Then, I'll accept Sir David, and I hope you'll never regret making me stalker. I'm proud and honored."

"Well said," Sir David raised his glass.

"Hear, hear," called out Sir Andrew. "I give you a toast, Eilid Stuart, Keeper and Stalker of the Glen Torridon Estate."

The appointment was duly sealed with another large dram.

Sir Andrew was ecstatic. "I'm pleased for you and for David. I think you'll make a fine team. The only thing now is to find a decent ghillie that'll work for you. That might be hard. There's not too many men willing to work under the instruction of a woman, no matter how talented."

Sir David pooh-poohed Sir Andrew. "Nonsense man, there's a bunch of lads who'd like to work with Eilid, mark my words."

"Aye, David, but for all the wrong reasons. With Eilid's looks, they'll be knocking on the door all right, but we're not looking for suitors, it's workers we want, not bloody romancers."

And so the discussion went on with Eilid taking hardly any part. She politely declined the third Macallan and left it to Sir David and her Granddad to polish off the bottle.

It was almost midnight when the two estate owners made their way home in an ebullient state. They enjoyed one another's company, and, while Sir David was fifteen years Sir Andrew's junior, there was little difference in their political or commercial opinions. The next day Eilid wrote a long letter to her mother telling her about John Robertson's untimely death, the funeral, meeting her Uncle Ken for the first time, and being appointed as Stalker on the Vickers Estate. It was now mid-

November and Eilid explained that because of the circumstances she would be unable to come to Stornoway for Christmas or New Year but that she hoped that her mother and Kenny could meet sometime in the spring before the lambing started. Eilid had the Hinds to cull from October the twenty-first through to February the twentieth. Sir David had made the decision not to take on a ghillie as the stalking season was over. The winter cull took about sixty hinds off the estate each year and Eilid figured she would have her work cut out to meet her target over the next two or three months. It depended very much on the weather.

December that year turned out to be cold and very wet with snow on high ground at times. The low cloud persisted almost up to the New Year and Eilid was about half way through the cull with only about seven weeks left. And so it was that she came to be on the hill on a miserable day early in January 1959, trudging through a fresh fall of snow with two ponies, heading round the foot of Beinn Eighe, in deteriorating weather, when events took place that would change her life for ever, including the lives of others she had never met.

THE RESCUE —
January 9th 1959

Eilid wakened to a burning bright light. She almost felt it before she saw it. She opened one eye to be blinded. We're dead, we must have died and we're on our way to Heaven. Then she heard voices; far from heavenly ones.

"Here, Tammy, here, it's a car near buried. We're bloody lucky we didnae drive right over the thing. See, here, gie me that shovel."

The bright light moved to the side as the huge snow plough turned to the left. Eilid could now begin to see a man frantically shoveling away the snow that had piled up on the side.

"Christ Tammy, it's a Land Rover, an' there's somebody in it."

A second man appeared and he started moving the drifts with his gloved hands. Soon they were in open vision as the snow was wiped off the windshield and the side windows. Eilid opened the door and fell out, her legs giving way under her.

"Here now hen, get up, the last thing ye want is to be sittin' in the snow, eh now?"

Her long blond hair blew in the wind as the snow plough driver helped her up.

"Thank, thank you very much," was all she could manage to say.

"Christ hen, yer lucky. We weren't supposed tae dae this section 'til the mornin' but it wis Bob who said let's see if we can get tae Kingussie and pick up they wiper blades. One of ours broke, early on," Tammy explained.

"There's my baby in the back."

"Whit?"

"My baby's in the back, I hope he's okay."

"Merciful Christ! Bob, there's a bairn in the back can ye see him? How old is he miss?"

Turning to Eilid.

"Four months." She nearly said 'I think', but she stopped herself short.

"Is he in some kind o' box miss?"

"Aye, he is. It's an old drawer from a chest of drawers. His carry cot got wet and ruined."

That was true certainly.

"Dear God, ye've had an awful time, where are ye going?"

"I was trying to get to Pitlochry, to my Uncle, he's a doctor. The baby's sick."

"He seems to be aw' right," Bob shouted as he opened the back door from the freed Land Rover and peered in the makeshift cot. "He's well wrapped up, but I Ah think we should take the wee soul intae the warm o' the cabin 'til we get ye goin' again."

'Was it the snow that jist stopped ye then?' Tammy asked.

"No, no it wasn't. That's what bothered me it just sort of stopped."

"Ye mean the engine, like."

"Yes, the engine just stopped."

Tammy was familiar with women and vehicles. In his opinion the female race shouldn't have been allowed out on the road as not one of them had a clue about what happened under the bonnet.

"Aye, well it'll be the diesel."

"Oh no there's plenty of fuel, I topped it up at Kinlochewe."

"For heaven's sake lassie, where did ye come from?"

"Glen Torridon." Damn, the words were out before she knew it. She hadn't thought quickly enough. It's a small world in the Highlands of Scotland. She was relieved to hear when the snow plough driver told her it was a part of the world with which he wasn't familiar. But he had been to Loch Maree, which was past Kinlochewe, on the same road.

"No, it's no' the quantity of fuel that's the problem, hen. It's the diesel. It freezes up when it's really cauld. The top o' this pass is as cauld as it's goin' tae get, on a road, anyway."

"You mean the fuels frozen solid."

"Well no' exactly. It co-agu-lates," Tammy pronounced the word slowly as if he wasn't quite sure if he had said it properly. "It gets thick, waxy like, an' when it gets thick, it disnae flow, an' so the engine stops."

"Can it be fixed?"

"Och aye, we'll see what we can do."

Bob had come back from the snow plough, having put the baby in the warm cabin. "My word, he's a great wee chap that, no' a peep out of him. An' he's wee face is froze, so it is."

"Thank you Bob, that's really kind of you. My name's Eilid, by the way."

"Eilid, my that's an unusual name, but nice eh? Pleased for tae meet you miss, it could have been in better circumstances, so it could."

"Bob, get yer arse over here an' stop chattin' up the lassie."

"Ah'm jist introducin' myself, so I am. I'm mair polite than you, so I am."

Eilid was getting the jist of Bob's way of speaking waiting for the add-on at the end of every sentence. Tammy was getting the remaining snow cleared away from the Land Rover. The snow had long stopped and the wind had quieted down so there was little drifting.

Eilid went over to see if she could help. "Do you need anything?" she asked Tammy.

"Well we'll need something to burn under the tank here, a wee fire, like. Ideally if we had a wee drop o' paraffin that wid be great, because we could pit it in the tank an' thin doon the diesel."

"I've got paraffin, I brought it for the Primus stove."

"Away wi' ye then, that's bloody marvelous. We'll have ye on the road in no time."

So Eilid got the bottle of paraffin out of the back and Tammy did the rest. Back he went to the snow plough and got some old newspapers, poured a little paraffin on them and then, placing them under the fuel tank and the line that led to the engine compartment, he set the paper alight.

"Will it not explode?" Eilid said, getting alarmed.

"No, no hen, this is diesel, no' petrol, it'll be fine."

The fire eventually went out and Tammy seemed satisfied.

"Right, quick, in ye go and turn the starter. Hold it over mind 'til the glow-plug gets goin'."

"Thank you, I *do* know about that." On the second crank the engine fired. Huge plumes of white smoke shot out of the exhaust as Eilid revved the engine.

"Right now, just keep it goin'. Bob bring the wean."

In a couple of minutes the baby was installed in the back that was slowly beginning to thaw out.

"I don't know how to thank you both, you've been so kind. You saved our lives."

"Ah don't know about that, but it could have got right nasty during the night. It wis our pleasure miss, wasn't it Bob."

"Oh aye, it was, so it was."

They both waved as Eilid slid the Land Rover into gear and started off up the pass again. Soon she got to the summit at just over 1,500 feet and the road started to go down hill. The Land Rover stopped laboring and the road began to wind more as she headed towards Pitlochry. It was now almost nine o'clock at night. Outside the snow reflected off her headlights as she drove carefully round some treacherous bends. Soon she was passing Struan, and she could just make out the outline of the church where Auld John Robertson was buried. She had about twenty miles to go. As she passed through Blair Athol an almost full moon lit up the countryside all cloaked in white. The sky had cleared and she could see the stars twinkling. The snow began to get crispier as the clearing sky brought a sharp frost. She wended her way slowly through Killiekrankie taking care on some sharp bends and accelerated hard up the hill.... she was almost there, she told herself.

The Pitlochry street lights cast a welcome glow on the road, as she turned left up the hill to Moulin and Uncle Kenny's house. It was just about ten o'clock. She was tired and famished and she was sure the baby was as well. At last she pulled into Kenny's drive. Thank goodness there was a light on. She could see her Uncle getting up from his chair as he saw her headlights coming up the short drive.

She opened the door of the Land Rover and nearly fell, the ground was like a skating rink.

"Sweet Jesus it *is* Eilid. You know I thought it was your Land Rover but the white roof put me off."

Kenny laughed. He was in a good mood seeing his attractive niece again and sooner than he had dared hope. He liked Eilid's company, she didn't act particularly feminine, he told himself but she certainly she looked feminine. Kenny supposed it was all the years on the hill acting as a ghillie and then as a stalker that made her think and act like a man.

"Well come away in. What brings you here in such hellish weather?"

"It's a bit of a long story Uncle Kenny….I sort of need your advice. First of all I have a passenger I need to bring in and introduce you to."

"My goodness, I feel so rude, I didn't see anyone else in the Rover with you. They must think I'm terrible."

"It's not quite like that Uncle Kenny, it's a baby."

"Jesus Christ, does your mother know?' Is it *your* baby?"

"Well not exactly."

"Not exactly," Kenny shouted the words. What the hell does that mean?"

"Just what I said, not exactly."

"Eilid, I love you dearly, but you're losing me. Bring the child or baby in, whatever, let's look after the him or her…."

"It's a him."

"Right let's look after the him then and get you something to eat, you look famished, and then we'll have a wee dram and you can tell me all about it. How does that sound?"

"Marvelous."

And so Eilid's 'wee prince' was brought into the house and Eilid went to work changing his nappy, feeding him from the bottle and marveling that after the nightmare journey he showed no adverse signs. She purposely didn't go near the surgical dressing, that was for later. She really hadn't made up her mind what she was going to tell her Uncle at this stage and she thought she would wait for the questions that were bound to be asked.

By the time she finished and she had placed the baby in his special 'cot' for the night, Kenny had made a casserole of Pheasant. He was an expert at preparing a quick and delicious meal. Mashed potatoes and French beans completed the simple meal that seemed like a feast; everything tasted superb. Eilid ate every morsel. Then came the Macallan. For another evening she was exhausted, her eyes started to sag as the smooth malt whisky hit her.

"You look beat, Eilid, and I'm sure there's a long story attached to this. Do you want to wait until the morning and tell me about it over breakfast?"

"No. No, I don't. What's happened is important to me. It's been non-stop for the past couple of days, and while I'm tired I've got to tell you what's going on."

"I can see, and I'm pretty sure that you've not been pregnant then."

"No, no nothing like that. Not after my experiences with men."

"All right, let's make this easy, whose baby is it?"

"I don't know. But I want to keep it."

"Whoa, whoa, not so fast lassie. It's not so simple as that. Did you find it by the side of the road then?"

"Well sort of."

Kenny was about to lose it for the second time. "For Christ's sake Eilid, how about…how about just telling me," and he reached forward and held both of her hands and looked her straight in the eye, "the truth."

Eilid faltered. She had thought Kenny would want to be supportive and go along with her wishes. The conversation and the plan she had mapped out in her mind crumbled. She had never seen her Uncle as serious as this. The hard drinking devil-may-care attitude she had experienced earlier on her first visit had gone. He was very professional and all doctor.

"Let me bring the baby to you. You need to see something." Eilid was close to tears.

"All right, let's start there."

Eilid brought her little prince into the room. She took off the little romper he had been wearing when she found him, removed his vest and showed Kenny the surgical bandage.

"This child's had an operation, of that there's no doubt. Let's take a look. Carefully he uncovered the wound. It looked redder than it had in the morning.

"This has gone septic, you were right to bring him to me. It's not bad and I can clear it up in a couple of days. I'll do a bit of work on it now, replace the dressing and we'll see what he's like in the morning."

Eilid's Uncle then proceeded to show her just what a good doctor he was. Very gently he cleaned the parts of the wound that were showing signs of going septic. He was very gentle but firm. The baby cried, but more out of tiredness than pain.

"How old is this bairn? I mean you do know its age?" Kenny looked up at his niece.

"I'm guessing three to four months, but I don't know Uncle Kenny, I really don't know."

"All right. I can do no more this evening. I'll probably give him a shot of penicillin tomorrow. I'll go to the surgery in the morning, it's Saturday and somebody else is doing locum for me. Let's sit back when you've got him down and then we'll talk."

Kenny poured a second Macallan. He sat back in his chair, propped his glasses on his forehead and said, "Shoot".

By this time Eilid had decided to tell him the truth, the whole story. Kenny listened spellbound, not saying a word until Eilid had finished.

"Jesus, you've had the experience of a lifetime in just two days. Let's tackle the points one at a time. First of all you've saved the child's life. Secondly, you've abducted it for want of a better word, thirdly, you want to illegally adopt it, fourthly you have not informed the authorities on the whereabouts of the crash, and fifth, and last, it is your assumption that everyone on the aircraft, including the child's mother and father, perished. Does that about sum it up?"

Eilid said nothing and just nodded glumly. Put like that she sounded like a criminal. Uncle Kenny hadn't missed a point and his assumption, that Eilid wanted to keep the baby, was correct.

"Tell me Eilid, why would you not hand the child over to the proper authorities? There could be family still alive, even it's Grandparents, for example, who would look after the infant. By all accounts, he has had some very major surgery. He's either had a lung operated on or a heart operation, even more serious. This child might never be well. How will you look after him? You have your job and your responsibility to Sir David, it's a hard physical job and you have the unique position of being the Laird's Stalker, a girl, well a woman, sorry, at the age of twenty-two.".

"I won't be twenty-two until July."

"All right, twenty-one then. It's as if you haven't thought this thing through, and I'm sure it's not like you. You've made a spur of the moment decision and assumed, rightly or wrongly, that I would help you in all of this."

"I thought my mother would be able to look after the baby for a while. She's lonely back in Stornoway and Sir David's been wanting me to move into the Lodge. There's room enough for both of us and my mum would like that."

"Shit, deeper and deeper. Your mother's going to know about all this then is she? She'll not wear it, I can tell you that now. She'll think you've gone completely daft and, if she knows I got involved, I'll get it in the neck as well. I think you'd better think this whole thing through."

Eilid began to cry. She sat, silent, tears coursing down her face staring at an invisible point somewhere in the room.

Kenny went on. "You've never even had a boy friend, have you? And a good looking girl like you should have someone. So if we say the child is yours, how did you get pregnant? Who was the last person to see you in Torridon?"

"Mistress McBride in the General Store there," Eilid sobbed.

"Well she'd know you weren't pregnant when you left, and then you turn up with this bairn ...." Kenny tailed off.

"I wear big sloppy clothes all the time, like an Anorak or a Barbour, I could be ready to drop the thing and she wouldn't know." She sniffed, wiping her eyes with the back of her hand. Kenny had to admit that she could be right, but that was only answered one problem.

"Is there a real reason why you want this baby so much. You're young, you've got your whole life before you, there'll be a man some-day and you'll get married and have your own children."

"Twice men have been near me, one tried to rape me the night my father discovered I was Alasdair Ballantyne's bastard daughter. I can't begin to tell you the shock to the whole family. It destroyed my father, I can see and understand that now, and my mother was left to pick up the pieces. I learned to hate all men. I just hate men coming near me. I know men find me attractive, that's why I wear sloppy sweaters and hide my figure. Don't you think I can't see them leering at me and thinking dirty thoughts? They are, you know. I had a happy life until that night, now I've lost my mother; my father doesn't want to know me although I still regard him as my Dad. He brought me up, taught me all I know, apart from what I learned from Auld John and now he's dead. All I've got left is my Grandfather, Sir Andrew Ballantyne a gentleman in every sense of the word, but now that I'm at Torridon I've only seen him twice in eighteen months. So you see anything I've ever had to hang on to, to call my own has gone. That's why I want this child."

Kenny sat back astonished. All of this Alasdair Ballantyne stuff was new to him. So Catriona, his sister, did have dark secrets after all. Then there was Eilid, who because of her two past experiences had serious problems about the male sex. He listened as she poured out all the injustices she felt had been heaped upon her over the last two years. In a way Kenny's heart went out to her. What the hell, he began to think, maybe there is a way. He would be fifty later that year and his career was over, he would never be more than a General Practitioner. The threat of being struck off the register had abated a bit, but he didn't really care. He knew he was the best doctor in the district and all the locals knew it. His outrageous behavior and his drinking bouts were all just part of the Kenny legend.

"All right, here's what I'm prepared to do. It's conditional. Sooner or later they're going to find the aircraft, maybe, just maybe, there will be survivors. If it turns out there are no survivors, then, and only then I'll consider helping you keep this child."

Eilid knew instinctively no one could have survived that crash, she didn't want to go into any description with her Uncle, the horror of it all was still fresh in her mind. The blood stained snow, body parts, personal effects scattered everywhere and the fires burning in impossible conditions. It was a picture seared into her mind that she would never forget.

"What are you going to tell my mother?"

"The truth."

"But I thought you said you couldn't or wouldn't do that."

"I'm going to tell her you've taken delivery of a child. There's no lie in that. If I know Catriona she'll be delighted. My wee sister won't be asking any questions. The only thing is she's looking after our mother and doing a fine job."

"How old is granny now?" Eilid asked.

"She's sixty-nine and she's keeping well at the moment but she has these bouts of arthritis when she finds it impossible to move around, and that's when your mother moves in to help. Now let's see if there's been anything on the news about that 'plane crashing."

Kenny switched on the radio. It was close to eleven o'clock and the news program came on at eleven. They listened intently but there was no mention of an aircraft having crashed or even having gone missing.

Saturday dawned crisp and clear with a hard frost. The sun rose, a big red ball on the horizon. Pine trees sparkled as if they were Christmas trees in the blinding light. For a moment she paused to appreciate the breathtaking scenery. Eilid had risen early at seven. Something in her subconscious had told her to check on the baby, but he was fast asleep in his drawer looking quite at peace. It was when she went through to the kitchen she discovered Kenny had already had his traditional tea and toast and was gone. She made herself a cup of tea and turned on the radio. Half way through the broadcast she heard the item about a Transoceanic Stratocruiser being reported missing. The RAF Air and Sea Rescue unit based at Lossiemouth, on the Scottish East Coast, had received a "Mayday" distress signal but no further facts were available. All that was known was that the flight's final destination was Los Angeles in the United States and that there was a flight crew of eleven and thirty-four passengers on board. A helicopter search was continuing for the missing plane. Eilid's heart raced as she thought about her involvement and her lack of responsibility at reporting the wreck. But she had made her choices, there was no turning back and it looked now as if her Uncle Kenny might just help her.

Kenny returned from his surgery at eight thirty armed with dressings and other medications. By nine o'clock the baby had been given a shot of penicillin, his dressing changed, fed and cleaned up. He was a brave little soul, quite happily burbling away and didn't even flinch when Kenny gave him the penicillin shot. Eilid had remarked on that.

"It's because I'm the best," Kenny told her, "it's the velvet touch. Anyway I put so much ether on his bum it would be numb."

"Oh then," laughed Eilid, "he had the numb bum."

"Precisely," answered Kenny, pleased to see his niece smiling for the first time since she had arrived. "Anything on the 'plane?" he asked.

Eilid told him about the news report indicating that it hadn't been found but that it had been reported missing.

"Well we'll have to wait then, won't we," said Kenny. "Oh, I nearly forgot." And at that he turned on his heel and went back out to his car. Eilid watched as he carried what looked like sections of something into the house. Into the spare bedroom he went where Eilid slept and assembled a cot in next to no time.

"Where did that come from Uncle?"

"You know we've had that in the surgery for years, just in case we had to keep a baby overnight for observation. I think it's been used once, it's ancient I'm sure but the child can't go on sleeping in a bloody drawer, he'll grow up with a complex or something. By the way does this child have a name? You keep referring to him as your 'bonnie wee prince', so have you given it any thought?"

"I thought of something Highland really, like Hamish or Rory or something romantic, what do you think, Uncle?"

"Well if I were you I'd think about your surname."

"What do you mean?"

"Well, it's Stuart, isn't it? He went on as Eilid nodded. "And this wee fellow is your bonnie wee prince. Now you *must* have heard of Bonnie Prince Charlie."

"Of course, of course, I see what you're saying, he could be Charles Stuart, what a great idea, and what a grand romantic and historical name, a name that's been famous and might well be again."

And from that moment Jens Ericsson was reborn as Charles Edward Stuart, the name of the Young Pretender, Bonnie Prince Charlie, and as Kenny pointed out, Charlie actually came from the Gaelic *Tearlich* meaning Charlie.

Niece and Uncle went shopping in the town of Pitlochry with Charlie now named if not yet christened. Kenny had thought hard and long about what he was about to do and he had made his decision, unless something occurred to alter that, Eilid would be the lawful mother of this child. Of one thing he was certain, she would make a wonderful, caring mother. Kenny was spending money like it was going out of fashion. A carry cot, a pram, not a huge one but one that converted into a carry cot, perfect for stowing in the back of the Land Rover and finally he went into the jewelers with Eilid to buy a wedding band. It was only then that he noticed that she was wearing the huge sapphire and diamond ring on her wedding finger. He grabbed her by the sleeve and without a word turned her around and marched her straight out of the shop to the wide mouthed astonishment of the staff.

"Jesus, where did you get that?"

"It's just a ring."

"I know what it is, where did you get it?" Kenny was riled up and it showed.

"It was on a ribbon round the baby's neck."

"My arse in parsley, that *will* be right, every baby has a bloody sapphire ring round its neck, where did you get it?" Kenny was getting louder now and red in the face.

Before Eilid could answer, he took hold of her and shook her hard.

"Now just where did you get that ring?" he hissed at her through clenched teeth.

Eilid was terrified. Kenny was in a blind rage.

"Uncle believe me, it was round the baby's neck, I just tried it on and it was a perfect fit. Why are you so upset?"

"You promise me, on your mother's life that's the truth."

Eilid began to cry. "Uncle Kenny, I promise with all my heart that was how it was, when I got him to my cottage and took off his wet romper suit, there it was on a yellow ribbon, hanging round his neck I promise you, please where else did you think it came from?"

"From one of the poor bastards who got killed on the plane, you just helped yourself to it and removed it from someone's finger."

That awful thought had never occurred to Eilid. She quickly came to underststood Kenny's mind set, but she was shocked and cut to the quick to think her Uncle considered her so low as to do any such vile act. She stood silent for a minute as she took in the enormity of his suggestion. She turned to him, her deep sharp blue eyes blazing.

"I might be a lot of things, but a grave robber is not one of them. You might well be my Uncle, and I love you dearly, but I resent that accusation. What would I possibly want with a fancy ring? I wouldn't even know if it was real. I'm a stalker, I'm a simple person and you've hurt me deeply. Let me take the child and go, I'll get out of your life for people you think are the likes of me should not be in it."

Kenny realized she was right, of course. He had acted hastily and the thought of how she might have acquired the ring made him over-react.

"Eilid, I'm truly sorry. I should never have said what I said. I believe you. Please forgive me, I'm just a bit blinded by what you're doing with your life...and mine," he added, "and I thought you might have come by the ring in different circumstances."

Eilid bit her lip, near to tears again. Her life was back on a roller coaster of emotion. Ever since that fateful day in the Glen Cannich quarry when her father discovered she was a natural shot holding the rifle left handed the stability of the life had gone completely to hell.

How she wished she could have turned the clock back and erase those terrible weeks and months that followed.

The silence between Eilid and Kenny continued as both considered their positions. Eilid weighed up the pros and the cons. There was infinitely more good than bad in her Uncle, the positives far offset the negatives. She understood very well while why he had doubts about the origin of the ring. She decided to accept his apology. Turning to him, she brushed back her long blond hair and kissed him softly full on the mouth.

"Thank you Eilid, thank you," was all that an emotional Uncle could say. And after he cleared his throat, and surreptitiously wiped a film from both eyes, he said, "Come on we'll go to another jewelers and make an honest woman of you."

Fifteen minutes later a wedding band was added below the great sapphire and diamond stone. To the perfunctory world Miss Stuart was now a married lady. Despite the apparent settlement between them there was still some unease. In truth they were really just getting to know one another but the upset had caused niece and uncle to stand back and examine one another in a more measured way. Outwardly they chatted away amiably as they wheeled Charles up the hill to Moulin in his brand new pram enjoying the crisp, cold January air, but there was a reservation in the way they held their conversation that had never existed previously. It was Kenny who was more ill at ease, and it was a strange feeling. It was as if he needed to justify himself to Eilid on his concern about the ring. Here he was, he told himself, a fine GP, somewhat avant-garde in medical terms, almost thirty years older than his niece, feeling some debt of obligation towards her. He was also prepared to lie to help her in her obsessive, hair-brained scheme, to possess this child. The whole thing was lopsided. Was it his love for his sister that made him think this way? Or was it just Eilid who was so attractive, so beautiful that made him want to do a favor for his kith and kin, which could be to his cost. He was deep in these thoughts as they continued up the hill towards his house.

As they passed by the Moulin Hotel Kenny suggested they go in for a drink, as it was almost five o'clock, opening time. They marched into the bar to meet Johnnie the barman from Eilid's previous visit.

"My Gawd, look who's here, could ye no' stay away? Nice tae see ye miss," as Johnnie came forward and gave her a kiss. Then he saw the carrycot with the baby. "Jesus, we've been busy since I saw ye last, no, no, it cannae be yer bairn eh? I mean ye weren't pregnant in September, well I didnae think ye were"…and Johnnie tailed off as Kenny gave him a hard look. Johnnie got the message.

"Right then, what'll it be?" becoming the professional bar tender again.

"Just the usual Johnnie, but no beer for my niece."

"Righty-oh then, two large Macallans and a pint o' heavy coming up."

The drinks appeared and Johnnie, forever nosey, peeked into the carrycot to look at Charlie.

"Ah take it it's a boy, eh?"

"Aye it's a boy," Kenny answered.

"Fancy that." said Johnnie. "Is the faither here?"

"No, he can't leave Torridon."

"Oh aye right, right, I understand, talking aboot Torridon did ye hear the news?"

"No," Eilid and Kenny chorused together.

"Well, there wis some big 'plane crash, right up near ye, miss. An American plane they said crashed intae Beinn Eighe. They've jist found the wreckage, nae survivors, a' deid." Johnnie finished matter-of-factly.

Kenny and Eilid looked a knowing look at one another.

Kenny and Eilid returned to the house in the dark. It was getting markedly colder as they walked the short distance from the hotel to their warm home. Charles was then fed, bathed and put into his new bed with fresh diapers and a new dressing. Already there were signs that the infected wound was healing and Charlie gurgled away happily as Eilid and then Kenny tended to him.

"I wonder who you really are little fellow and what's your real name, we might never find out eh? Well it doesn't matter now, you'll be in good hands wi' young Eilid, I'm sure of that." Kenny chatted away to the baby.

Uncle Ken was as good as his word. On Monday he registered the birth of Eilid's new son and declared the father to be a certain Callum Stuart of Birnam who Kenny knew was an old recluse of about eighty-five living alone in that village. He hoped, just for the record, that he was still alive as the Registrar filled out the Birth Certificate. There was no requirement for age. In a matter of five minutes Jens Ericsson an American Citizen, became a British Citizen bearing the name Charles Edward Stuart. Next Kenny got on the phone to Stornoway and spoke to his sister Catriona who was overjoyed to hear that her daughter had given birth and was well. On the subject of the father Kenny did a great job of fluffing it out, telling Catriona that not even he knew and with the trauma Eilid had gone through she was better not to know and never ask. Catriona remembering the upset when Patrick McKeown had tried to rape her daughter didn't probe. Kenny told her that Eilid was due to return to Torridon sometime in April and that she, and her mother's presence, would be welcome. Having dispensed with legal formalities and sorted out Eilid's mother Kenny reverted to being a doctor and dealt with the increasing line of patients in his waiting room.

That night he went home to find that Eilid had cooked a wonderful dinner consisting of Scotch broth, roast chicken with stuffing, roast potatoes and green beans all ready and waiting for him. Charlie was in good fettle and grinned away toothlessly through the bars of his cot. Kenny then told Eilid what he had done and gave her the Birth Certificate telling her to keep it in a safe place and not to lose it. It was a legal document that would be required from time to time and he said that it would stand up to any scrutiny.

"Who is Callum Stuart, Kenny? His name is also Stuart does that not sound a bit odd?"

"Havers lassie, the place is riddled with Stuarts and this one is in Birnam. I treated him for a broken leg when I was doing locum there about ten years ago, he's a filthy old devil, a recluse, and he keeps himself to himself so there's no danger of him ever getting any communication of any kind on this subject and if he did, he wouldn't open the letter anyway. He was a fine fisherman though," Kenny ruminated, "showed me one of the best salmon beats on the Tay.

So there you are, he's all proper and legal now and he's yours and your mother won't be asking you any questions either but she's looking forward to seeing you at Torridon. I told her to bring our mother, it'll be a break for her as well and she'll want to help. I just still wonder if we've done the right thing and I can't help wondering what Charlie's real name is."

"Please Uncle Kenny, let's not go down that road. What's done is done and I'll never discuss it with anyone and I know you won't, will you?"

"Jesus, for what I've just done I can't. I really would be in the soup. We can find out you know, I'm sure they'll publish a passenger list in the newspaper."

"No, please Uncle Kenny, it would only confuse things and upset me."

Kenny concluded she was right so he kept quiet and ate his dinner in silence.

By Tuesday all the papers carried the story on the front page. "Doomed Airliner crashes in mountains" screamed the Daily Express. "All die in Strat disaster," read the Daily Record. The photographs showing the crash site were of poor quality. The snow had covered up most of the wreckage and it would probably be spring before parts of the aircraft could be recovered. The story told of how the Inverness airport had picked up the Stratocruiser's last distress signal reporting two engine failures and that they were attempting to get to Dalcross to make an emergency landing. Of the passengers and crew there was no mention except to confirm that they had all perished and that their names were being withheld until the next of kin had been informed.

Eilid went to bed at eleven that night having talked to her Uncle about all the hopes and dreams she had for her Bonnie Prince.

"Aye he's Bonnie Prince Charlie now, remember. I just hope he doesn't create the havoc like the original. Scotland, or at least the Highlands, never recovered." Kenny said with finality.

Wednesday, October fourteenth, 1958 was Red Ericsson's day. The cigar couldn't have been bigger nor the grin on his face wider as he drove to Cedars-Sinai hospital in Los Angeles. Twin boys, they had said, and your wife is doing just fine. It was a warm day for mid-October and the sun beat down on Red's new 1958 white convertible as he drove quickly through the traffic. The radio schmoozed out the Everly Brothers latest hit, "All I Have to Do is Dream", but Red didn't hear any of the close harmony, his mind was firmly focused on other things. Twin boys! His love and respect for his wife grew by the minute as he contemplated the years ahead and the fun he would have with his sons. Karen had had a rough pregnancy; she could hardly keep a meal down for the first four months. She had also suffered from swollen ankles and high blood pressure to the point where her obstetrician had ordered her to bed for a month. Red had found a marvelous old nurse-come-midwife to come in and look after Karen, just to make sure she followed doctor's orders. He knew only too well that his wife would hate the confinement of the house, let alone the bedroom. At twenty-seven, Karen was a keen sportswoman and loved to play tennis and swim at the local Country Club.

As he made his way through light traffic his mind drifted back on how they had first met. She had come to Texas to visit an old college friend. He was in Texas to start a new job with an oilfield contractor as Special Projects manager. It was on a Friday in April 1956 and Houston was jumping. Elvis Presley had taken over the Pop Charts with songs like Hound Dog, Don't be Cruel, and Love me Tender. He and his new-found buddies had gone to one of the better restaurants in town to celebrate, and Red was holding sway at the bar when in walked two of the best looking chicks imaginable. Red stared as he watched the Maitre D' usher Karen and Michelle over to a nearby corner table in the restaurant and ply them with menus and a wine list. Red's story died on his lips as he beckoned Tony over.

"Jeez, Tony, where did those two come from?"

"Don't know Mr. Ericsson, sir. I think one's local but the other, the small dark haired lady, is from Los Angeles I think I heard her say," the Maitre d' replied obsequiously. Red had already established himself as a big tipper for the right sort of service or information.

"Okay Tony, here's what we're gonna do. Take over a bottle of Cristal on ice with my compliments and see where we go from there"

"Certainly sir,"

The Cristal Champagne was duly proffered to the two young women with as much flair and pizzazz as Tony could muster, which was considerable. Not that it was too difficult to present a one hundred dollar plus bottle of Champagne, which Red, with all the experience of his twenty—eight years, considered to be superior to Dom Perignon. Red strained to hear their reaction above the racket at the bar. He heard the Oohs and Aahs as the gift was accepted and the cork popped expansively. Tony filled the flutes to two thirds and replaced the clear Champagne bottle back in the cooler.

The ladies turned to look at their beneficiary in the general direction of the bar and raised their glasses in a toast.

Tony reappeared smiling broadly. "The young ladies would like to thank you in person Mr. Ericsson".

"Well done, Tony," he slipped the Maitre d' a twenty.

"Hang on guys, I've got a little business to attend to," he announced to the gang. Red eased himself off the bar stool and stood up, his six foot two frame towering above the others. He ambled over in the direction of the two women.

"Ladies, welcome to Texas!" Red spread his hands expansively as if he owned the State. "My name's Red Ericsson and it's my pleasure to see y'all here". He gently shook hands with each of the girls in turn. Red had huge hands that had often been likened to a bunch of bananas. The girls smiled in turn as they introduced themselves.

"What brings y'all to Houston, as they say in this City?"

Karen's smile lit up the room. She had perfect dazzling white teeth and a wide mouth with generous vermilion lips. The darkest of brown eyes beckoned like deep whirlpools. She had jet black page-boy length hair which framed her finely boned face to perfection She was extremely slim with accentuated breasts in proportion to her slender frame. "I'm Karen", she arched her hand gracefully towards Red. Bending forward Red gallantly planted a kiss as he stared into her deep brown eyes. His heart looped the loop.

"And I'm Michelle." Red acknowledged Michelle without even taking his eyes off Karen. "I'm the one who lives in Houston, in fact I'm one of the few Houstonians born and bred in the city. My Dad's a surgeon who works at the Medical Center. Won't you join us for a glass of your excellent Champagne?"

"Well, just a glass, as you can see I'm with some colleagues over there at the bar. Where do you live in Los Angeles, Karen?'

"Beverly Hills, my Dad's a film producer."

"Really", Red's eyebrows arched in feigned surprise. "So your family must be pretty well off, I guess?"

"Stinking rich," said Karen with a giggle. Red threw back his head and laughed. Here was someone who didn't mess around. Was she joking, though? He didn't think so. The big brown eyes seemed too honest.

"So how about you, Michelle?"

"In poverty, that's why I hang on to Karen as a friend."

The Champagne was clearly taking effect. These girls were obviously out for fun.

"Let me settle up some unfinished business with those guys over there. You ladies are quite delightful and I just hope you wouldn't be too proud to allow me to buy y'all dinner?

"You mean you wouldn't let one of your buddies join us and make up a foursome?" Michelle clearly saw the way things were going, and not her way.

Red immediately recognized his faux pas.

"I do apologize, that is so rude. I sure didn't think to get one of those fellas over here and do some introductions, I just can't imagine I could be so discourteous." Red launched the lifeboat.

"Well, now, Red, there's about ten guys over there and we just need one, why don't you let Michelle pick one out and you can tell us all about him." Karen certainly wasn't backward in coming forward. Red warmed to her even more, if that was possible. He was already madly in love with her, but that wasn't the question.

"Of course, you can. Who do you fancy?" Red eyeballed Michelle.

"What about that guy in the dark blue suit and the wax top. He looks real muscular, he could be a marine".

"Oh right, well he wasn't in the Marine Corps but he's a kinda fitness freak. Works out all the time, that's Dan Walters, we call him 'Danny Boy'.

"Why Danny Boy?" Michelle asked.

"Watch this," Red shouted over to the group. "Hi Danny!"

On Red's shout Danny slid off the high bar stool. He stood about five foot off the ground.

"My God," Michelle exploded, "he's a dwarf". Michelle who was about five foot ten and equally as slim as Karen with long brunette hair and an hourglass figure couldn't possibly see herself having a good time with 'Danny Boy'.

"Okay Dan, order another round for the boys and put it on my tab." Red extracted himself from the situation without anyone getting his or her feelings bruised. Karen thought, hmm.... neat move.

Eventually Michelle picked a very elegant looking man who was dressed conservatively, also in a dark blue suit, complimented by a white shirt with blue pinstripes, and who, in contrast to everyone else, was wearing a tie. John Hollingsworth, who turned out to be English and who was an accountant in the same company as Red, was eventually declared the most boring fart on the planet by both Michelle and Karen as they animatedly talked over the evening's events during the cab ride back to Michelle's parent's home in River Oaks.

"Come on then, what did you think of Red? He's nuts about you." Michelle was all excited.

"Wellll," Karen drew out the word, "he certainly knows his way around women, but he is attractive. Never have I ever seen such green eyes and the reddish hair. I don't like red hair as a rule, but this is a soft-ish red, sort of…"

"Strawberry blond!" Michelle butted in.

"Well, not quite, but close. That's a girl's hair color. I can't see Red agreeing to that description. He wants to meet me on Saturday night, by the way, if that's okay with you. I thought you could invite Jim Jarvis to join us, I certainly don't want to be on my own."

"My, we've got it all worked out then," Michelle sat back arms crossed looking aloof and staring into her friend's eyes. "Gee, I like Jim, but we're not exactly dating. Rumor has it he's just busted up with Jane Grayson and he's become all bitter and twisted."

"All the more reason to ask him out. Anyway I didn't mean it quite like that, it was just a sort of suggestion."

Michelle had been wonderful and Karen didn't want to cause prob-lems. There was no doubt that Red had a keen interest in Karen. For her part she was certainly quite taken with Red.

Out of nowhere she said to Michelle, "I wonder what his real name is? Red's a nickname because of his hair, it's probably something awful. Let's sleep on it. I have his phone number so I'll call tomorrow and see if he still wants to go out".

They paid the cab driver and climbed the front stairs together arm-in-arm.

Saturday was a day of action. Red had confirmed beyond 'any possi-ble shadow of doubt', were his words, that he would be deeply offended if Karen and Michelle didn't join him for dinner and dancing, in that order. He laughingly asked if he should invite John Hollingsworth back for one more try and Karen had joined in the fun and said that Red was bringing him along, right reason or none. The shrieks from Michelle would have been heard Downtown. Karen, with Red still on the phone, had to convince her that they were only joking and that the dreaded Hollingsworth would not be there. Karen filled Red in on Jim Jarvis, who worked in the oil business as well, and Red had said bring who you like. Off the girls went to manicure, pedicure, hair and eyes were done and legs waxed for the big event.

"All right," said Michelle, "where's the Big Man taking us?"

"Not a clue," said Karen

"Come on Karen, he must have said where we're to meet him."

"No, he didn't, truly. But we're not meeting him anyway, he's coming here in a limo to pick us up."

"Oh, my God, what'll my father say?" Michelle was suddenly all concerned.

"What would your father say, indeed? I mean he knows we're being picked up."

"How come".

"Because I told him, you silly goose. I wouldn't give your address to Red without asking your father's permission. He seemed quite pleased, no kidding."

"Well, if that doesn't beat all, I suppose I'd better get Jim to come round and he can go with us?"

"Done," laughed Karen. "Michelle, I'm having a great time and I want you to have a fabulous time as well. I talked to your mom about Jim and she told me how you feel about him, so I wanted it to be one big happy party. I hope I haven't done anything wrong, have I?"

Michelle said nothing and gave Karen a big hug. Her smile told Karen everything.

Jim duly arrived at six forty-five and Dr. Turner opened a bottle of Champagne some grateful patient had donated to the Turner wine cellar. At seven o'clock on the dot the stretched Limo arrived. The liveried driver rang the doorbell and waited while the girls completed their finishing touches and sashayed out in their ball gowns to the waiting auto. As the chauffeur opened the door there was Red sprawled back in one of the opulent seats like some Eastern Potentate clutching a glass of Champagne and smoking a large cigar. Michelle introduced Jim. Red motioned to Karen to sit beside him. He reached over and gave her the politest kiss on the cheek. God, thought Karen, he's so masculine, and that cigar smells so good!

The Limo took off at a crawl to allow Red to pour more Champagne into the waiting glasses.

"I have to tell you ladies you look absolutely fabulous, don't they Jim." Jim, still scarred by the Jane Grayson rejection, could only mumble "yeah great". He really thought that Michelle looked particularly stunning in her midnight blue gown accentuated with silver accessories, handbag, belt and shoes. Karen by comparison looked radiant. She had chosen a bright red gown that combined superbly with her dark hair and sun tanned complexion. The lipstick matched the dress perfectly. Stiletto heels hoisted her tiny frame up another three inches but she still looked tiny beside Red.

"Okay, Red, where are you taking us?"

"The Petroleum Club".

Jim's jaw dropped way open. "You mean *the* Petroleum Club?"

"Sure do, unless there's any other in town."

"You mean you're a member at the Petroleum Club?"

"Yes sir, I am."

Jim sat stunned. He knew how prestigious and fabulous the Petroleum Club was. He could only dream of becoming a member some day.

Michelle knew just how impressive the club was. She had been there once when the President of some oil company, who was a patient of her father's, had invited the whole Turner family for dinner. Situated in the Rice Hotel it was beautifully appointed and had some of the most famous Texas oilmen as its members. The quality of the food was legendary, the wine list exemplary. On Fridays and Saturdays it had the best quartet to dance to in the city.

Clearly the Champagne from all quarters had helped relax everyone; the night was typically Texan, clear skies with myriads of stars sparkling just as if they had been placed there to illuminate the evening. Even Jim loosened up and danced with Michelle again and yet again until they ended up locked in an embrace in the middle of the dance floor impervious to any onlookers who applauded politely when they finally kissed.

While Michelle and Jim danced, Karen tried to find out more about Red. He surprised her by telling her he was Canadian. His father had been a farmer and a rancher who had emigrated from Norway and moved out west just before the depression. Red was born in 1928 so he was just two years older than Karen. Red was the third of four children, born to Jens and Else Ericsson, two girls and two boys. They all lived in a three-room house with no running water and no electricity. Karen listened, fascinated. Red's mother cooked on a wood-burning stove that also heated the house. They used kerosene lamps for light and a bit of extra heat during the long cold Canadian Winters. Bath night was on a Saturday night, Red explained. They all washed in a great big tub on the kitchen floor, his sisters got in first, then the boys. The toilet consisted of a two holer, outdoors. Karen wanted to ask all about that, but Red was on a subject close to his heart, so she kept her questions 'til later. His father, Jens, farmed with six draft horses and he raised cattle, pigs, chickens and turkeys. He also planted and grew some grain and cut acres of grass for hay. The family had twelve cows that had to be milked every morning and night. That became Red's chore when he was old enough and he would milk the cows by hand every morning in the log barn before going to school. It was freezing cold in the winter and always dark even with the kerosene lamps turned up. The Ericsson's sold milk and cream to a local dairy and Red's mother made butter and cheese for home consumption.

Red went to a one-room schoolhouse. He enjoyed school immensely and was a good student. He was always interested in what the other students were doing who were two to three years ahead of him. At the end of his first year in school he was promoted from the First to the Third grade. Red was always top of his class and he participated and enjoyed all sports especially hockey. He started skating on a frozen lake when he was six years old.

The waiter poured some more wine and broke the spell of Red's childhood memories. He looked over at Karen who was leaning forward enthralled by his story.

"Karen, I'm terribly sorry, I'm going on and on and I must be boring the pants off you. Michelle and Jim seem to be having a wonderful time, come on, let's dance."

"Red, Red, you're not boring me at all. It's a fascinating story and I want to hear all of it, but, okay, if you want to dance, let's join the others."

Even with her stiletto heels Karen had to stretch to get her arm round Red. For a big man he was like gossamer on his feet. This was their first dance and it was as if they had been partners forever. They billowed round the floor becoming more and more aware of each other's presence. As the music stopped they returned, flushed with their new-found fascination for one another, to join Michelle and Jim at the table. Karen was dying to learn more about Red, but he out of politeness kept the conversation going with Jim and Michelle.

"Red, what's your real name, I mean your given name?" the wine had helped Karen pluck up sufficient courage to ask.

"Oh, you're better not to know that, really."

"Is it really that bad?"

"Well I'm happier with Red, even my family called me Red from when I was about five. My hair was redder then."

"So you're not going to tell me?"

"Only if you insist."

"I insist!" Karen was not about to let go now.

"Well, it's Adolph."

Karen could have sworn Red even blushed slightly.

"My God…I see what you mean. You would be going to school when the real Adolph was doing his stuff."

"You've got it in one. My mother always called me by my proper name. It was a joke, well, for the other kids anyway."

"Adolph Ericsson, I think it goes quite well. In fact I think it's a lovely name. I'll call you Adolph from now on." Karen's jaw took on its firm, determined set.

"Then I can't see you again."

"Really."

"Yep, really"

The first battle of wills loomed, ready to spoil the evening.

"Well, if you give me a kiss, you might just persuade me to change my mind." Karen capitulated with grace.

"I might just have to think about that," Red smiled his best laconic smile. "How do I know I can trust you?"

"Trust me, trust me, you great Norwegian oaf, how dare you to suggest a lady's word can't be trusted." Karen's eyes were alive with fire as she rounded on Red. "I wouldn't kiss you if you were the last............"

Her words died as Red picked her up like a tiny doll off the floor and kissed her full on the lips. Any tenseness left Karen's body as the kiss continued. Dancers stopped to stare at the couple, as Karen, her feet now completely off the floor, dangled attached to Red it seemed by lips only. The band stopped in mid tune, silence took over as the kiss went on and on and on. Karen and Red held one another in a fierce embrace oblivious to their surroundings. Fortunately the band's drummer had a sense of good timing and he began a quiet drum roll which got louder and louder until at the moment Karen and Red parted there was a crash on the cymbals to the delight of the crowd who clapped, whistled and yelled their good wishes on the young couple.

"All right, it's Red," Karen said breathless and blushing. The band, right on cue, struck up the Great Pretender one of the hits of the year as the crowd continued to applaud and smile warmly at them.

"It's as if we've just gotten engaged," remarked Red. "So how about it Karen, will you marry me?"

Karen was in a daze. Was Red for real? She knew then that she loved him. She was twenty-six, had many boy friends but none like this. It was as if there was some form of animal magnetism that attracted them. But it was too soon to judge. She couldn't be such a fool. And what would her parents think?

She smiled sweetly at Red and said, "I might just have to think about that."

Red smiled. "Well it wasn't "no". There's a good start". And with that he put his arm round Karen and led her to the dance floor.

The next three months seemed to fly by. Red traveled to Los Angeles at every available opportunity and Karen, for her part, took a flight to Denver, where Red was still living, when she could get time off from her job as a Personal Assistant to some Hollywood mogul.

She learned more about Red as the weeks went by. Red's new boss had a ranch near Steamboat Springs and they both enjoyed riding. Whenever they met in Colorado they would go to the Lazy Y Ranch tack up two ponies and head off into the mountains. It was during those long treks that Red told her more about his childhood. How at the age of twelve a neighbor, trying to help with the milking, kicked over one of the kerosene lamps and set the barn on fire. As the nearby pond was frozen all they could do was stand and watch in horror as the barn burned down with the cows still in it. After that his father sold the farm, and took a job with a grain company. The family moved to a town of about three thousand people. The electric light switches and the wonder of running water and indoor plumbing fascinated him and his brothers and sisters. They had no telephone but they had a car. The town too had its own fascinations with a movie theater, and various stores. Red loved his new school as each class had its own room.

He was still top of his class and a keen hockey player, but because of the age differential it was difficult for him to compete with the older bigger boys. Red became very aggressive in sports, kept his top grades, but he admitted that his teachers had serious problems with his delinquent behavior.

At sixteen he had graduated from High School and was awarded a scholarship to McGill University and enrolled in engineering. It was about this time that he discovered the joys of alcohol and women, though as he politely explained to Karen, not necessarily in that order. During the summer months he worked on oil drilling rigs for a buck thirty-five an hour. Red was in hog heaven. He loved the nomadic, almost gypsy style, life. He would move to a different town every two to three weeks where he would discover new bars, new women and new guys to fight. He graduated from University when he was just twenty and, while he had many offers for positions as a chemical engineer, he chose to work in the oil fields where the pay was much better.

And the rest Karen knew. He was in Houston to take over as a drilling engineer manager on special projects for another Scandinavian called Mats Frosteman, a Swede, who had a small, but very profitable oil drilling company. Mats had, and did all the things Red admired. Mats was tough minded, worked like hell, flew his own airplane and owned a ski lodge in the mountains, the ranch they had just left and, just like Red, loved women and good Scotch.

Despite Karen's parent's objecting strongly to their only daughter taking the plunge with someone they regarded as a roustabout.......
they were convinced Red stood for 'Red Neck'.......they grudgingly gave their blessing. With Karen's strong will and personality they never really had any choice. Three months later Red and Karen were married, with all due pomp and circumstance, in the Cathedral Chapel of St. Vibiana in Beverly Hills. Red, a staunch Protestant, realized he was not going to get his own way in everything so he put a brave face on it and took the necessary tuition to follow the Roman Catholic service. He found it all very fascinating, if not a bit over the top, but for Karen, he would have sacrificed much more.

Red's wanderings down memory lane ended as the entrance to the hospital appeared. He swung the car through the wrought iron gates and gunned the accelerator. The huge bunch of flowers slid across the back seat as he took the first corner, sidewalls squealing. He bit hard on the cigar, looked for a parking spot, ignored the fact that it was reserved for a doctor, and screeched to a halt.

He leaped out of the convertible, grabbed the flowers and sprinted to the Hospital entrance. An orderly gave him a suspicious look as he crashed through the door, not having any clue as to where he was going.

"Maternity'" he yelled at the orderly.

"Other way, down here, and it's on your right," the instructions were hardly given and Red was off in the general direction indicated.

As he strode down the corridor he had the misfortune to meet Staff Nurse Anderson. Agnes Anderson was Scots, a spinster of fifty-two, efficient to the point of agony and who did not suffer fools gladly. She represented the epitome of British nursing. Florence Nightingale would have been proud of her. Her crisp starched apron was in complete keeping with her character.

Red's six-foot-two frame came to an abrupt halt as the diminutive Agnes Anderson barred his way.

"Now where do you think you might be going?" The Scottish burr was evident in the emphasized 'where'. The delivery was less than friendly.

Before Red could offer any explanation he caught another salvo.

"And what, pray, is that filthy thing clenched in your teeth?"

Red had truly forgotten about the cigar. He removed the offending object, gave her his best smile, and said, "It's a cigar".

"I can well see that. Fortunately it's not lit or we'd be out the door. This is a Hospital, sir. Cigars are smoked in bars and other loose places of enjoyment."

"Well I was kinda celebrating, my wife's just had twins." He waved the bunch of flowers in Anderson's face by way of explanation.

"You men, you're all the same. No idea of what your wife has gone through, especially with twins. Come on then, follow me, but *get rid of that thing!*"

"Yes Maam!" Red emphatically agreed, pitched the twenty-dollar cigar in the nearest trashcan and followed Anderson to the Maternity Ward. The Staff Nurse stopped at the door.

"Up there on your left, on you go".

The strong hospital smells were now getting to Red. The combined antiseptic and ether aroma were beginning to bother him. I can't wait to see Karen and I can't wait to get out of this place, he thought. He crept forward frightened at what he might find. He need not have bothered. Karen was sitting up, in bed like the goose that had laid the golden egg. She looked fantastic, radiant even. Red threw the flowers on the bed, grabbed her, and kissed her passionately.

"No, Red, we can't, not here, it's a public ward!" She laughed as she teased him. He laughed as well. His tension subsided.

"How are you darling? You've had a tough time, but believe me I'll make it up to you. When did you know you were having twins?"

"About thirty minutes after you dropped me off. They did some kind of new fangled scan and there were two heartbeats, not one, now we've got two darling boys."

Karen had been right about her parents being stinking rich. Brett Stahlman was a very successful Hollywood producer and director and was completely totalitarian. He was not used to being argued with on any subject. But Red was just as determined that he wasn't going to bend any farther. He had already agreed to make Hollywood, or to be more precise, Beverly Hills, their place of residence until Karen delivered the baby. He was sure Brett and Karen's mother, Rosemary, had it firmly in their minds that once the move was made their home would become permanently near to them. As it was, the house Red had leased was stretching him financially and the commuting at the weekends was beginning to try the patience of Mats, his boss. So far, however, as far as Frosteman was concerned Red was doing a fine job, but all this traveling, Mats knew, must be getting Red down. To be fair to Mats, Red worked right over some weekends and never went home to Karen, but it was the long term that bothered Mats, despite the fact that he did have Red's assurance that once the baby was born, Red and Karen would head back permanently to Texas.

"Right then, where are the boys?"

"Well they're very small, one's over five pounds, but the other is slightly under, they think. He was so small they didn't weigh him. They're both in incubators, which is normal for children at this birth weight. I think we can go to the nursery and see them once the nurse comes round. They're very strict about me getting in and out of bed, you know."

"I can imagine, I just ran into Staff Nurse Anderson as I came in, she sure is feisty, isn't she?"

"She certainly is," Karen agreed, "she's just as tough on the Nurses as well. Everything has to be 'just so' otherwise there's hell to pay. She told me she was trained in the old school of British nursing at Glasgow Infirmary. She's handled all sorts. She also told me that every Saturday night in casualty was like World War II all over again. Glasgow seems to be a rough place."

"Well I wouldn't know," said Red, "but Saturday night can be rough in any city, if you're in the wrong part of town." His mind flashed back to some of the rabble rousing he had taken part in over the years. He was sure Nurse Anderson would have strongly disapproved of him if she had an inkling of what Red was like in his roustabout days.

One of the nurses came down the ward and stopped at Karen's bed.

"So this is the lucky man then?" She smiled at Red, taking in his tall frame and sandy colored hair. "I'm Jane Colby, I'm assigned to Mrs. Ericsson during the day. I suppose you'd both like to see the boys?" Mrs. Ericsson do you feel up to walking down to the nursery?"

"Of course. I'm never felt better."

"Well you think you do, but you were in labor for eight hours, did you know that Mr. Ericsson?"

"No I didn't. I have to tell you that your people are not the most communicative. All I was told was that Mrs. Ericsson is in labor and is progressing satisfactorily. I didn't even know she was having twins. Now I don't want to complain, but I think y'all need to brush up your act."

"I can understand you being upset, but I think everything's fine now. Let's go and see the boys." Jane Colby smiled sweetly.

With that Jane ushered Red away from the bed, drew the curtains around Karen to give her privacy as she got her feet on the floor and put her dressing gown on. As Karen emerged Jane led the way to the nursery.

The nursery must have had about twenty cribs with babies of different size, color and weight safely kept behind a huge glass screen. Three nurses could be seen in attendance. Jane opened the Nursery door and beckoned them in.

"The incubators are in a separate room," she explained. Quietly she opened one of the double doors to where the incubated babies were. There were about six incubators occupied. Two Red could immediately see had the name in large print 'Ericsson' at the foot of the contraption. Jane Colby was right. His sons were tiny. The larger of the two seemed to be more active and he seemed pinker than his brother.

"What's wrong with the little one Jane? He seems sort of blue."

"Oh I don't think there's anything to bother about Mr. Ericsson. He's more than likely got a touch of cyanosis. It's due to a temporary shortage of oxygen when he was being born. That's why he's on oxygen now. We expect that to clear up within twenty-four hours."

Jane's confident and positive manner put Red at ease. He put his arm round his wife as they stared at their future heirs. It made Red more determined as he stood there watching over the little mites that he would work harder and build a better future for them than he had as a boy.

"When do they get fed?"

"Every three hours or so," Karen blushed.

"You mean you're feeding them?"

"Red darling, that's what these are for," and she cupped her hands under her breasts, which were already enlarged by a seemingly endless milk supply.

"I didn't mean it like that, but my mother couldn't breast feed for some reason, we were all raised on a bottle.........well I think we were."

"You would hardly remember now, would you Mr. Ericsson?" Jane laughed.

"Come on then darling, there's not much more to see, so let's go back to the ward."

As they walked back Jane had said the boys would probably be in their incubators for about seven days, and if she wanted Karen could go home without them that would be fine. She would come in just at feeding time. Karen was in two minds about this. It seemed to be so callous to be leaving them so soon after they had come into the world. Red didn't like it one little bit. He thought Karen should be with the children, although he had to agree that the accommodation left something to be desired. They decided on a compromise. Karen would stay an extra three days and then come home for the anticipated four days before the boys would be released from Cedars of Sinai.

Red got home at about seven o'clock. He had already called the in-laws who were agog with the news of twins. Red assured them Karen was fine and he thought her parents would be allowed to visit the next day, once the boys had settled down.

He ate mechanically at a local restaurant. If he had been asked ten minutes afterwards what he had eaten, Red wouldn't have had a clue. Parenthood had somehow overwhelmed him. Mats, his boss, had told him it would be like this but Red never expected or experienced such a metamorphosis in such a short time. Suddenly he was a father, and he liked the feeling. He just couldn't wait to have the boys and Karen home.

He was into his second Scotch when it hit him like a ton of bricks. The nursery! The nursery was supposed to be all ready. The drapes were new, the paint fresh, there were Bambi like animals stenciled tastefully on blue gray walls, but there was only one crib! Shit, how could he be so dumb, two babies are coming home. In his euphoric state that important detail had gone right over his head. It wasn't just the adding of another crib, the room had been laid out for one child, now there were two.

Rosemary! That was the answer. Quickly he dialed the Stahlman's number. The maid answered the phone.

"Who eez pleez?"

"Luz, it's Red, just tell Mrs. Stahlman it's Red"

"Si, Signor, I geet right away."

Rosemary came on the phone in ten seconds flat.

"Red, is it Karen?" What's wrong?" Red could nearly feel let alone hear the panic.

"Rosemary, relax. Everything's fine. I just have a problem with the nursery. It's organized for single occupancy. Now we've got two. I thought you might be able to help."

Rosemary gushed. "Oh Red, how nice of you to think of me. I'd be delighted. Now I know this interior designer Mary Linton, she's English, of course, but she's just the person to do a wonderful.........."

"Rosemary, Rosemary. No".

"Well I just thought."

"I know, but it's your touch I want, not some English broad."

"Well she's hardly a 'broad' to use your coarse expression..." his mother-in-law's voice became disapproving.

"Rosemary, look if you don't want to do this…"

"But I do, Red I really do."

"Well then, let's say tomorrow night round about seven. I'll be back from the hospital and we can discuss what needs to be done then."

"Thank you Red, thank you, I'll be there, you can count on me." It was all gush again.

Just what I was afraid of, thought Red. But his strategy had paid off. At least one of the Outlaws, as he called them, might just be on his side. Rosemary was an older carbon copy of Karen, except she didn't have the drive and backbone. She was decidedly high maintenance. Before she married Brett her indulgent life style had been one of mansions, maids, chauffeurs, limousines. Her father had owned a chain of supermarkets in California, which he had sold to an even bigger chain, reputedly for millions. He never worked again and neither, it seemed, did anyone else in the family. Her brothers were reputed to be complete wasters who spent their time drinking, gambling and whoring in the tinsel town environment of Las Vegas.

It was five o'clock the next afternoon when Red turned up at the hospital. Now that he knew where he was going he strode on down through the long corridor to the maternity wing, almost into the waiting arms of Staff Nurse Anderson who had clearly been lying in wait for him.

"Jesus Christ, what have I done this time?" Red exploded.

"Don't you use your blasphemy on me young man, I'll thank you to come with me a minute."

"What's this all about? I'm here to see Karen and my boys."

"This will only take a couple of minutes, there's some paper work that needs filling out."

"Shit, you people are so tied up in bureaucracy."

"Mr. Ericsson, *please*. Just follow me."

For a quiet life Red did as he was bid. Nurse Anderson showed him to an office down one of the many side corridors that led to his destination. The occupant of the office got up as Red went in. He extended his hand.

"How do you do? I'm Doctor Levine, Mr. Ericsson, I work with Dr. Crawford Head of Cardiology and he asked me to have a word with you. This will only take a few moments of your time."

Red sensed right away that something was not quite right. Dr. Levine's demeanor was somewhat superior and off-hand and he took an instant dislike to this very young intern who was now lounging back in his swivel chair, his feet propped up, not quite on the desk, but on a top drawer he had opened. His tie was loose around his collar that had been unbuttoned at the top. This was the first display of unprofessionalism Red had seen at the hospital. The fact that Nurse Anderson had effectively ambushed him had put him right on edge. Red said nothing and sat down. The doctor adjusted his glasses and opened a manila folder, which was already in his hand. Red looked at this young doctor with the spotty face, big nose and the slicked back hair. The horn-rimmed glasses Red supposed were an attempt to make himself look more mature, but Red reckoned if he was twenty-four, he'd be lucky.

"Have you given your boys names yet?"

"No. We're discussing it." That wasn't quite true; they had chosen Lance for a boy and Ingrid for a girl, after Red's mother. Since the twins arrived the business of choosing names had been forgotten.

"Why?"

"Might I suggest you do more than discuss it?"

"Well it's not that simple. We had chosen a name for a boy, we didn't expect two." Red felt he was justifying himself and his dislike of the doctor grew. "Why?" Red finally asked.

"I would have thought that would have been obvious, even to you. It would give us a way of identifying them, wouldn't it, and that would help us".

Red bit his tongue. It made sense, though, thought Red. "For the moment let's call them small and smaller". He made an attempt at humor.

"Very good. Very witty". Levine oozed sarcasm. "Okay, that'll do. It concerns 'smaller' then." Dr. Levine stretched back even farther in the swivel chair, steepled his fingers and peered down through his horn rims.

"At first we weren't quite sure but now we're concerned about 'smaller's' color. Sometimes this can be caused by a lack of oxygen at birth, I think Jane Colby, sorry, Nurse Colby briefly explained that condition."

"She did."

"Well…I'm afraid it's not quite as simple as that. Your son is what is sometimes referred to as a 'blue baby', and that's not good; it's a heart condition. The medical term is Tetrology of Fallow. Basically it means that your 'smaller' son has a hole in his heart, that's why he's so blue."

Red froze.

"What can be done about that," his desiccated voice came out as a hoarse croak.

"Well, that's what I wanted to talk to you about."

"Does Karen know?"

"No. Not yet. But we're, or rather you're going to have to tell her at some stage. But I think we need to discuss our options."

Red's recent euphoria and his idyllic life were melting away right in front of him. The hospital smell was getting to him again, and the doctor's supercilious attitude didn't help. He breathed deeply to try and stop his own racing heart.

"Okay, give me the bottom line. Will 'smaller' live or die?"

"I take it you mean in the immediate future, Mr. Ericsson, everyone dies, sooner or later." Levine stopped and smiled smugly.

That did it for Red. His huge banana hands swung into action. He shot forward over the desk, grabbed the doctor by the lapels hoisting him forward out of the swivel chair. Levine's face ended up about three inches from Red's.

"Don't you fuck with me, you son-of-a-bitch! Damn fine you know what I mean, you supercilious bastard. Now I'm going to put you down, and we're going to discuss this in terms I can understand with no smart assed quips, is that clear?"

Levine's face, in direct contrast to Red's now matched the color of his hospital coat. He was so taken aback he was literally at a loss for words. Red shook him like a rag doll.

"Do we understand one another?"

"Yes", gasped Levine, "for God's sake put me down. This is an assault you know."

"Assault my ass, mister, you'll know when you've been assaulted. Now talk."

"Well, you need to meet with the Senior Cardiologist, Doctor Crawford, I'm supposed to be taking you there, but I'm very upset at your attitude. I didn't mean you to take me seriously when I made that comment." Levine nervously smoothed away at his white coat trying to remove the creases put there by Red.

"That's my problem", agreed Red, "I can't find any humor in the situation at all, and so let's just let it go at that. Is Dr. Crawford coming here or do we go to him?"

"He's supposed to be here shortly, they've been doing x-rays on 'smaller' and I expect he'll give us his findings. You know there is a surgical procedure that may cure his problem. It's a highly specialized procedure done only by a handful of pediatric surgeons, so it wouldn't be done here in Cedars of Sinai."

Just as Dr. Levine finished the door opened and Dr. Crawford entered. He made straight for Red and shook hands warmly. A tall gangly man with a slight stoop and graying hair, Crawford was the perfect TV Doctor. He took the dangling stethoscope from around his neck and stuffed it into his white coat pocket, saying, "We won't be needing that," as he sat down beside Red rather than opposite him. Red took to Dr. Crawford immediately.

"Ah, Mr. Ericsson we have a problem with one of your sons…"

"Call me Red, everyone else does."

"Ah yes, quite, quite. As I was saying we have a slight problem with the smaller of your twin boys."

"We've christened him 'smaller' actually," Red butted in again.

"Ah, quite, quite, very good, I'll start again. As I was saying we have a slight problem with your smaller son, shall we say? He has a heart condition that requires attention, maybe not immediate attention but certainly within the next two or three months if he's going to survive.

Now the chances of his survival are, and I'm putting my best estimate forward, about 60-40. The operation is tricky and it really depends on the expertise of the surgeon who's going to do the job. Now there's someone in the Baltimore area, who has quite a bit of expertise in this procedure. He is quite difficult to get hold of, though, as there's quite a demand for his skills. Whether you can get him within the time frame we require could be debatable. There is, however, another option. Now I hesitate to suggest this, but this surgeon is quite the best man in this field with the highest success rate. He is someone I have talked to on a professional basis now and again. He is without doubt the original expert in this type of operation and he developed this technique. I can only say that if it were my son I would try to get this gentleman to save my boy. Now, his name is Mr. Ross MacDonald, a Scotsman of great talent who has his practice in Harley Street.

"Where's Harley Street?" Asked Red, immediately associating the name with motorcycles.

Levine gave Red a withering glance, which fortunately Red either ignored or didn't see. Dr. Crawford by contrast didn't miss a beat.

"In London," he continued. "England," he added as an afterthought remembering that Red was Canadian.

"What's your best advice Doctor?"

"Well right now that's rather difficult to say. It's all about your son's ability to stay relatively healthy so that he can undergo the surgery. If we have an emergency situation then there would be no question of him going abroad. I'm not quite sure how you'd get from here to there, but it would entail a long, probably exhausting flight, not just for your son, but for whoever accompanies him. I'm assuming that would be Mrs. Ericsson."

"Dead right, it would, but I'd try and get someone to go with her. That would be her mother without doubt, wild horses couldn't keep her away."

Red was beginning to balk at the thought. Karen and Rosemary together in a crisis would be like another crises about to happen.

"Well, now, you see, I wouldn't go for the obvious, unless Mrs. Ericsson's mother is a professional nurse. I think you'd really want someone who can care for the child before and after surgery and is not as emotionally attached as the mother or grandmother. I think you want to give that some consideration. Now it's still early, you have time to consider the issues and make a decision. There's going to be the initial strain on your wife, Karen, isn't there?"

Red nodded.

"So," Dr. Crawford went on, "let's see how 'smaller' gets on in the next few days and we can make a considered judgment of to whom and where we can go. Meanwhile with your permission I'll make a Transatlantic call to Ross MacDonald, and if he's at all available I'll let you know. The next thing will be to send over your son's x-rays and his Medical Records for Macdonald to examine. I'll leave you now with Dr. Levine, you'll be in good hands and I'll be in touch. And by the way if you or your wife need to talk to me further about this, here's my private number. My secretary can always reach me if I'm not immediately available. Good luck, Red." He grasped Red's huge hand, shook it warmly, tripped over a manual of some sort lying on the floor and exited stage left.

Red left without saying anything to Michael Levine and made his way to Karen's ward. Just as he got to the entrance Staff Nurse Anderson just happened to be there. She grasped his arm by the elbow and ushered him into the Nurse's office.

"Mr. Ericsson, I'm fair heartbroken about the wee one's condition. Are you going to tell your wife now?"

"No I'm not, well not right at the moment. Dr. Crawford thinks we should, or rather I should wait 'til we see how 'smaller', as we've called him gets on. I'm scared to death, but I'll put a brave face on it. There's no point in two of us worrying ourselves to death until we have more facts."

"Aye, your quite right there," her Scottish brogue becoming more pronounced. "I mean this now, if there's anything I can do, or help with, you must ask me. She's such a lovely lass, she can do well without all this, especially when she's got one healthy boy to look after, the strain is sure to tell."

"That's very kind of you Nurse Anderson." Red could see now that underneath the bluff and bluster she had a kind and caring heart. He warmed to her. "I'll let you know when I'm going to tell Karen and we can work out a plan of what to say, and, more importantly, how to say it. I'll need to get going, though. She'll be beginning to wonder what's kept me, I'm half an hour late as it is…the traffic's been terrible," and at that Red winked at the Nurse and opened the office door.

Karen was sitting in a chair by the side of the bed still looking radiant. She smiled widely at Red as he strode down the ward, looking neither to left or right.

"I thought you'd got lost,"

"The traffic was terrible," lied Red, "and then my favorite Nurse grabbed me at the door".

"Who might that be? Not Nurse Anderson?"

"Yup."

"What did she want?"

"She's after my body, but her Scottish Presbyterianism won't let her tell me straight out."

"I can just see you and Agnes Anderson having a romantic affair… she's got to be fifty something."

"Well…the older the fiddle…"

"Red, I'm familiar with that expression, I know the follow-on, but I do not wish to hear it, thank you very much."

"So how are the boys?" he changed the subject smoothly so that Karen quite forgot what Nurse Anderson really wanted him for.

"Well they're fine. I think the little one doesn't look quite so blue, but they've got him on oxygen all the time now and I don't know whether that's a good thing or not. There's a Dr. Crawford been looking at him and I thought he might say something to you or me, but so far he hasn't reappeared. The big boy is just fine. He eats like a horse, he takes all the milk I can give him and as the small one has a problem with breast feeding, they've got him with a tube down his throat and they're feeding him formula."

So they chatted on and then they both walked down to the nursery to see the boys. It was as if there was telepathy when Red just blurted out at the point when Karen was going to say something about names.

"What are we going to call those two?"

Karen had already thought about it.

"Well we were going to call a boy Lance, after my grandfather".

"I don't know if it had anything to do with your grandfather, I just liked the name." Red interrupted.

"Okay, but let's stick to Lance. What was your father's name?"

"Well it wasn't Adolph, thank God, it was Jens."

"That's a nice name, and it carries on the Norwegian connection, why don't we call the bigger one Lance and the small one Jens."

"That's fine." Red agreed. "Lance and Jens," he rolled the names around. That's pretty neat. You can't shorten them anyway. I hate names you can do that with, like Patrick becomes Pat or William becomes Bill or worse still Willie."

"Alright so that's all set. I'll get my parents to tell the Priest so that he can organize the christening."

"Well let's not rush into this, darling. I think we might just be being a tad premature."

"Oh Red, we're not into this religion thing again are we? I thought you had agreed the boy, or boys were to brought up in the Roman Catholic faith."

That wasn't what Red was concerned about at all and he could have bitten his tongue when he said what he just had said. Karen had thrown him another safety line, so he grabbed it.

"Well, I said that would be okay to educate them at a Parochial school, you didn't turn out too bad, but do we really have to go through all this baloney, I mean the wedding was bad enough."

"Oh it was, was it?"

Red had shot himself comprehensively in the foot.

"I didn't mean it like that. The attendees were wonderful, just the service did go on a bit," Red's vocal shoveling tried to fill up the hole.

"I thought it was a beautiful service, you know I did, and all right, suppose we did have Mass, I think it was the right thing to do."

"Quite right, darling," he gave her a hug and a kiss as they got back to the ward.

God, Karen thought, he can be so condescending. However she said nothing and went back to her bed.

Rosemary turned up promptly at seven o'clock to help with the rearranging of the nursery. The additional crib had already been purchased, and was decorated, wouldn't you know it, Red thought, to exactly resemble the first. Red could well have done without Rosemary that evening, but mother-in-laws are tough to discourage and Rosemary Stahlman was no exception. He was still shaking from the revelation on Jens, as 'smaller' was known at present. Brett, Red was certain, would throw money at the problem, but that wasn't the answer. Some specialist out there had to have the answer and Red was determined to get it even if he meant going overseas..

He told Rosemary that Karen would be coming home in two days time and that she, and Brett, would be more than welcome. The boys would stay a few more days in the hospital in the incubators until they gained some more weight. He did not elaborate in any way about Jens's condition. That would really trigger an unnecessary situation that he could well do without at the moment.

Rosemary left an exhausted Red at about ten-thirty with the nursery now looking like something out of a film set. Red poured himself a large Scotch, switched on the TV sat back and promptly fell asleep. He was wakened by the shrill ring of the 'phone at what seemed like the middle of the night. He screwed up his eyes to read the hands on his Rolex. Christ, it was the middle of the night or at least almost four o'clock in the morning.

"Hello".

"Red, how are you? What the hell's going on?"

Red instantly recognized the voice of Mats Frosteman.

"Hi Mats, what's the problem? It's four in the morning, for Christ's sake."

"What's the problem? Shit you're not here, that's the problem! And it's six where I am!"

Mats had obviously got some problem out in the field, and he, Red wasn't there to fix it.

"Mats, I'll be back in two to three days at the most. There's been a kinda complication."

"You bet your life there's been a fuckin' complication…I need you here, *now*!"

Clearly Mats was in no mood to listen to any excuses. He had the bit between his teeth. This was the old Mats tough and ruthless. Flexibility didn't exist in Mats' dictionary.

"Mats, listen to me, I can't get there right away, I've got a sick child. Anyway what's the matter?"

"I'm sorry you've got a sick kid." The words carried as much concern and conviction of an actor in a soap opera. "The crew on the Comanche Peak rig has gone on strike."

"Fire their asses. I'll get you another team. Better than them, and we'll finish ahead of schedule, I promise. Mats, when have I ever let you down?"

There was a long silence. "Okay, okay, but you get here tomorrow, right?"

"Right." Red slammed down the phone. Jesus, this was all he needed. God knows when the hospital would release Karen but it was sure to be some time in the afternoon. He would need to try and get a flight out of LAX by late afternoon, if there was one. He went to the wet bar, poured out the ice diluted Scotch and fixed himself a stronger one. Sleep was out of the question now. He would wait until eight and then call the hospital. Once he had a picture in his mind he could deal with it. He'd probably have to rely on Rosemary…there was a thought. But she'd do well; Red was sure of that; it was Karen he bothered about more than anything. Mother and daughter went together like oil and water. After the third Scotch and a large cigar he nodded off at about five-thirty. He couldn't have been asleep for more than thirty minutes when the damn phone rang again. Slightly bemused this time he picked up the phone.

"Hello".

"This is Brett Stahlman here." Oh God, he knew immediately by the strident tone there was a problem, or if there wasn't, Karen's father was about to make one.

"This is Red, isn't it?"

"Yes sir."

"What the hell is goin' on with my li'l darlin'? I demand to know."

"Mr. Stahl...I mean Brett what's the problem?" Jesus did those words sound familiar.

"Did I waken you?"

"Well, I had just dropped off........."

"Dropped of, dropped off! I have no idea how you can sleep with the problems you and Karen have. Not to mention that you haven't discussed the problem with Rosemary and me, and Rosemary bein' just out of yor house not a few hours ago."

"Brett, if you could tell me what all this is about it would help." Red was playing for time and trying to find out just what was going on. He was sure Karen hadn't spoken to her Dad about Jen's condition but there was no way of telling the way Brett beat around the bush.

"Why it's the smallest twin, as if you didn't know, he's apt to die at any minute and yor there sittin' on yor ass not tellin' anybody anything."

"Well it's not quite like that Brett........."

"Oh really, you tell me what it's not quite like. I have my only child in the hospital, she's had a tough time with those boys, she's a plucky little girl, an' as far as I can tell she's been brain washed by you sir, not to tell me or Rosemary a damn thing, an' we're her parents. I feel I've just lost my little girl who would tell her Daddy everything."

Red had the receiver about twelve inches from his ear by this time as the tirade reached a crescendo.

"If it hadn't been for Michael Levine's daddy speakin' to me I wouldn't have known a thing."

"Michael Levine, Michael Levine.....who the hell is Michael Levine?"

"You damn well know Red, don't pull that one on me, the young kid was just trying to help you and you nearly killed him."

Jesus, thought Red what *is* going on.

"Right, *that* Michael Levine." Red thought it better to 'fess up' rather than have a further prolonged harangue from Mr. Brett Stahlman, producer and director.

"Yeah, *that* Michael Levine. Well let me tell you that Danny, his father, a close friend and colleague of mine for many years, who happens to be the studio physician assigned to look after the health and well being of all the stars and cast members while they're on set, came up to me, puts his arm on my shoulder and says, "Brett, you have my prayers and sympathy. And I think it's a joke. So I give him the bit about sympathy being a word in the dictionary between shit and syphilis, and he looks at me and says, 'You don't know, do you, you don't know?' And I say what are you trying to tell me? So then he backs off and says 'I shouldn't be telling you anything but if I were you I'd have a word with Karen.' So I did."

"Great". Red was reeling now wondering what was going to come next. He felt that if Karen had said anything that might cause fireworks he would have heard from her.

"What did she tell you?"

"That's why I'm phoning you, she said there was a problem with the smaller twin and that I should speak to you. That's what I mean when I say I've lost my girl."

"But she didn't say he's dying?"

"Not in so many words, but I can tell when she's upset, I'm her daddy, you know?"

Will I ever be allowed to forget it? Red thought.

"Well I'm sorry you feel that way, and it's not her fault, it's mine. I didn't want to worry you and Rosemary about something that is really still being checked out. But I will tell you what I know as you're going to have to know sooner or later. Jens, the smaller of the two has got a heart problem."

For once there was silence on the other end of the line.

Red continued. "It's like this, Dr. Crawford the cardiologist says he's got a hole in his heart. That's why he's had difficulty breathing and he looks blue all the time. Right now he's being well looked after and they're trying to help him with oxygen and feeding him by a tube down his throat."

"Jesus Red, I wish you had told me sooner."

"Brett, I only found out the facts today and I was hoping to have an answer before Karen came home so that we could all face the problem as a family." A nice touch that, thought Red.

"You're right son, you're so right." It worked. Red listened as Brett was drawn into the family circle. "I want the very best for my grandson, whatever it takes. When will we get a prognosis?"

"I'm waiting to hear from Dr. Crawford some time this morning. He's been making enquiries for me."

"What kind of enquiries?"

"It looks as though the poor little mite will have to have an operation as soon as he's fit enough to stand the strain. Not too many people do this kind of thing, the medical term is Tetrology of something...I can't quite remember the second part. Crawford says there's someone in Baltimore, he thinks might be available but he also knows of a Ross Macdonald a Scotsman practicing in London who pioneered the technique in the United Kingdom."

"My God, getting to London, that's a hell of a long way." Red really could hear the concern in Brett's voice now.

"Look Brett it's nearly seven o'clock and we've been talking for nearly half an hour, let me get showered and shaved. I've also got problems in Houston; I had Mats my boss on the phone at four this morning blowing down my ear. He wants me back in Houston tomorrow...I don't know what to tell him."

"Tell him you can't do it, tell him this is your life and you have an emergency."

"Well I've tried to do that but when Mats' blood's up he's not inclined to listen."

"Fuck Mats then. We've got ways with dealing with people like that. You're under enough pressure as it is without that horse's ass pushing you around." Red could hardly believe his ears. Here was Brett the protective father-in-law performing a 180-degree turn in fifteen minutes.

"You have to remember that Mats has been real good giving me time off and going along with me living in Los Angeles and still keeping my job in Texas."

"Now I understand that son." Brett's condescension was getting to be too much for Red. For the second time in the last ten minutes Brett had referred to him as son. Brett went on "But this is what I think. Karen is going to need you, there's this problem that's got to be resolved and you need to be here to see it through. That's the bottom line as I see it. You have to tell Mats that."

"I'll try, but it won't be easy. His crew has quit on him and I can fix it, I think, in about five days. Nothing is going to happen right away unless Jens takes a turn for the worse and that can happen whether I'm here or not. This is what I'm going to do Brett, it's not so much I need the job but I do have a loyalty to Mats. I'm going to go to Houston tomorrow sometime. You can look out for Karen while I'm gone. I'll leave it to you to tell Rosemary what you feel is right but I'll let you know what's going on with Dr. Crawford. So let me hang up and I'll get back to you just as soon as I get any information."

The father-in-law was silent for a moment. He was actually beginning to warm to Red. At first when they met Red had seemed to be a shallow red-necked gigolo who was out to steal his beloved daughter. He was just too smooth for Brett who, as a director, watched false emotions ebb and flow daily on a Hollywood set. But he was beginning to realize there was a hard core to Red that wasn't all bad. That Red loved his daughter he had no doubt, well, as certain as any one could be in the rock n' roll days of 1958.

"Okay. I'll do what's necessary. But make sure you phone Karen everyday and I'll keep you updated on what the situation is with Jens. If it looks like things are getting worse then I want your word that you'll come home right away. Okay? Deal?"

"Deal," responded Red and hung up the phone.

By eight o'clock that morning Red had made arrangements to fly to Houston that late afternoon out of Los Angeles to Houston's Hobby airport.

He was just about to jump into the shower when the phone rang for the third time that morning. For God's sake, he thought, can't anybody leave me alone? It was beginning to fit to a pattern, four, six and eight o'clock.

"Hello".

"Mr. Ericsson?"

"This is he."

"Jack Crawford."

"Oh, hi there, good morning doctor." Red's heart skipped a few beats…something was up!

"I thought you'd like to know that I just had a long distance call, trunk call they say in Britain, from Ross MacDonald. It's about four o'clock there, I mean in the afternoon, so the day's nearly over for them but I thought you might like to hear what he said."

"Sure thing, fire away."

"Well the first good news is he's interested in your or rather Jens's case. I have to send the x-rays and medical report to him airmail. He'll then review what I send him and what's to be done. Like me he feels time is not on our side. Now I've explained that so far Jens is showing a slow but steady improvement. He's eating or rather taking his milk better. We've taken the tube out, much to your wife's relief and he manages a bottle quite well, all things considered. I've said that if he continues on this path that he might be in a position to get out of here and go wherever at the end of November or early December, that would make him just five or six weeks old."

"Will he be well enough to make the trip? We are talking going to England aren't we?"

"Yes we are. Now let's just see though, if I can get hold of the surgeon I know about in Baltimore, he may just be available. That would save an enormous amount of traveling and be much easier on your son, your wife and your whole family. Don't you agree?"

"But I thought you said Ross Macdonald is the man for the job?'

"Indeed I did. But there are other factors that come into the equation. If the journey to England is too arduous on Jens then he may not arrive in a fit condition to be operated upon. That's just one of my concerns. The other is having got there, he's got to get back. Same rules apply. Will he be fit to travel after what is going to be a pretty hazardous bit of surgery? And remember all the time there will be the other twin…"

"Lance".

"Yes quite, Lance will be without his mother. I cannot imagine she would even consider taking two tots, no matter how healthy, on such an expedition."

"Jeez, Doctor you make it sound like he's going to Africa. How long a journey is it?"

"Well the last time I went to England was out of Idlewild in New York. That was three years ago on a Pan Am clipper. That seemed long enough. We stopped to refuel at Gander in Newfoundland and then went on to Prestwick in Scotland and then to London. It seemed like forever with all the stops. I think it took about sixteen or eighteen hours. Mind you they look after you very well, but that's from New York, which is roughly three thousand five hundred miles. You've got to get to New York, that's another two and a half thousand miles if I'm not mistaken."

Red was silent as the Doctor's words sank in. It was going to be some undertaking.

"Right Doctor, I see what you mean. Why don't you do what Ross Macdonald asks, send him all he needs right away and at the same time put a feeler out for the man in Baltimore".

"All right Mr. Ericsson…"

"Please, Red."

"Ahem, yes, quite so, Red, I'll do that right away and I'll keep in touch. You should be able to pick up Karen and Lance today, probably just after noon. Call Nurse Anderson if you would and she'll confirm the time"

"Thanks Doctor, Karen and I really appreciate all you're doing. These are our first kids as you know and we're a bit green at the game."

"I understand. But think of it this way, you can only be green for a year. Bye." And with that the good Doctor was gone.

It was a blustery day in early December at Los Angeles International Airport. The Ericsson and Stahlman families were gathered at the airport along with an anxious Agnes Anderson. The whole arrangement could have been described as an adventure to save Jens Ericsson's life, however the assembled party appeared anything but enthusiastic. Only two would be going on the aircraft with the baby. Agnes Anderson, co-opted and coerced by Red and mother-in-law Rosemary, had eventually agreed to go to London with Karen and Jens. Red had come to regard Agnes as one of the most honest and direct people he had ever met. She met problems head on with a refreshing sense of nursing professionalism and plain common sense. She had little or no time for people who were sorry for themselves and who looked to the system to make them whole without as much as making a reasonable effort. Nor did she hold the medical staff in awe either.

"Just remember," she had said to Red on one of the evenings when they talked about the trip to London to have Ross MacDonald operate on Jens, you can fix your mistakes with a few nuts and bolts, doctors bury theirs."

Everyone stood and gawked at the Transoceanic Airways Boeing Stratocruiser as it sat on the tarmac. The double-decked fuselage and the greenhouse type cockpit were regarded as state of the art. The aircraft looked huge. The four Pratt and Whitney 3,500 horse power Wasp Major engines looked barely adequate to pull the plane into the sky. Agnes and Karen looked at one another nervously. Red put an arm round each.

"Don't be having second thoughts now, these planes are as safe as houses, they've been making this trip for 10 years now…so plenty of people have made this journey before you. And in any case from what I hear the food on board is real gourmet. This plane has a galley and the stewardesses prepare hot meals for you, so whadya think of that?"

Agnes Anderson was not to be so easily convinced. She had never flown before in her life and had made her way to California via the Queen Mary to New York and thence by train to Los Angeles. The whole trip had taken about two weeks. She found it hard to believe that some 30 hours later she, Karen and Jens would all find themselves in London.

She had asked Dr. Crawford about Ross Macdonald as a person. He had been fairly non-committal.

"I've only talked to him on medical matters over the phone, Agnes. He's not one for long conversations. I don't know whether he doesn't like to talk much or the cost of the phone call is too rich for his Scottish blood."

He flashed Agnes a lopsided grin. Agnes was not in the least amused.

"Let me tell you Doctor Crawford........."

Jack Crawford cut her off throwing up his hands in mock surrender...

"All right Agnes, all right, I was only joking."

He received another withering glance from his favorite nurse before she strode off to attend to her many duties.

Red had talked to Mats about the Boeing Stratocruiser, which Mats said had been nicknamed the Statuscruiser because of its opulent interior. Depending on how the interior of the aircraft was configured, it could provide pretty spacious accommodation for up to eighty passengers, Mats told Red,

For long haul flights the 377 could be converted to a sleeper with twenty-eight upper and lower bunk units. This was the model Mats had traveled on with Scandinavian Airlines System or SAS, as it was known. Red had also gone into all of the details of how to get to London. Brett Stahlman had helped as Red shuttled from Houston to Los Angeles keeping Mats, his boss, appreciative of his dedication to the company and his job, and at the same time keeping his father-in-law's volatility at bay. The Transoceanic scheduled crossing was the only flight that fitted all their needs. Flying at over 25,000 feet the Boeing 377 had a range of just over 2,500 miles and a cruising speed of 300 miles per hour.

This particular Transoceanic flight had the 28 sleeper configuration and special arrangements had been made to fit baby Jens' incubator into a section of the lower berth compartment. The flight left at six o'clock that afternoon. Although it wasn't yet dark the low gray scudding clouds made for an eerie light that served to accentuate the huge airplane as the ground crews fueled and victualed the airliner for the first leg of the flight which would be to Chicago, O'Hare, then to New York Idlewild, refueling there, on to Gander in Newfoundland, from there to Prestwick, Scotland and finally to Heathrow, London all in all a flight lasting some 28 hours and 6,027 miles.

For once there was unanimity in the Ericsson/Stahlman household. Brett was surprisingly quiet as he looked over the huge aircraft. Rosemary Stahlman had been keeping close to her little Jens and her daughter all day. At first Red was taken up with all the arrangements as he talked to the flight attendants who couldn't have been nicer as they explained the route of the flight and the arrangements they had made just in case there were any problems with Jens. Oxygen was on hand if it was needed and the area where the incubator was to sit had substantial restraints to prevent any turbulence dislodging Jens in his little Cocoon. Red marveled at the sumptuous interior of the airplane, the attractiveness of the stewardesses and rather wished he was going on the trip.

It was just after five and it was almost dark with the weather still looking gray and ominous. General boarding would start in about 10 minutes and it was time for Karen, Jens and Agnes Anderson to pre-board and get settled before the other passengers took their seats.

On went Agnes and Jens first as the ground staff helped with the incubator. Red had even given Agnes a big hug and a peck on the cheek that nearly had the stalwart Scot misting up, but Agnes bit her lip and cast her thoughts to her duties, turning away without looking back. The remaining good-byes were tearful; Karen hugged her mother and then her father in turn. Even Brett Stahlman had to wipe away the odd tear as he bade farewell to his only child. Red walked to the foot of the steps with Karen.

"Darling," there was a huskiness in Red's voice. This would be the first time they would be apart for more than a few weeks. "Darling, take care, I know you're both going to be fine."

"I know, I know but I'll miss you so…" Karen's words tailed off as her emotions took hold.

Red didn't say any more. Their hopes and dreams were all in front of them. Taking Karen in his arms he gave his beloved wife the longest parting kiss. Red turned quickly and walked back to the terminal building. Staring through the heavy plate glass the family watched the huge Stratocruiser start its four engines, one at a time, taxi to the end of the runway and take off in a great roar of raw power as the engines at full throttle lifted their loved ones into the low scudding clouds, disappearing from sight in a few short moments. Red shook Brett's hand and thanked him again for all his financial help, he kissed Rosemary and they parted company. Red was going straight back to Los Angeles and then on to Houston once he had settled in the Nanny who was to look after Lance while Karen was in London. Brett and Rosemary had decided to drive north to stay with friends in the movie industry who had just moved into a house in Carmel on the Pacific coast. They had agreed to keep an eye on the Nanny who had come with the best possible references from an English company specializing in providing domestic staff of the highest caliber.

As soon as Red got home he tried to call Mats and tell him would be in Houston in two days time. As it turned out Mats wasn't in and Red left a message with Kristin, Mats' stunning looking secretary to pass on the message. Kristin had told him they were all thinking about him and Jens, and that he shouldn't hurry back, things were fine and that Mats was in a good mood. They had just landed the large drilling contract they had been bidding for in West Texas so things were 'cool'.

Jens fell fast asleep just after take off. This gave Karen and Agnes a chance to look over the Stratocruiser. The seats were wide and spacious and 'couchettes' pulled down from the overhead space providing snug but comfortable sleeping for those passengers who got bored with the constant drone of the engines as the plane headed north-east on course to Chicago, their first stop.

Karen was amazed at the comfort and amenities Transoceanic offered their passengers. There was smoked salmon, Champagne, pâté of the finest quality, followed by a selection of fine wines to accompany a menu that would have done a five star restaurant proud. Agnes, having never been on any kind of aircraft before was truly amazed by the experience. If this was flying, give me more of it, she thought as she dug into her filet mignon and sipped on a glass of wine. Many of the passengers came downstairs to the bar, which was set up on the lower deck. They stood around smoking, chatting and drinking 'highballs'. Invariably they asked about baby Jens until there wasn't one person on board who didn't know about Jens and his problem.

Agnes eventually tried to sleep having climbed up the little stair-ladder the Stewardess brought her to access her couchette. She drew the curtains tight shut, but try as she might sleep wouldn't come. The noise of the engines and the overall excitement of the trip proved too much for her; she didn't want to miss one moment. While Karen had said she would keep an eye on Jens, Agnes still felt responsible. After tossing and turning for a couple of hours she got up, went to the toilet, brushed her teeth, splashed some water on her face and went to have a look at Jens. The baby was still sound asleep and was so still that even Agnes began to wonder if he was all right. Then she remembered Dr. Crawford had given Jens a "small sedative" just before take off. Clearly it was doing its work. Little Jens was out to the world. Karen had fallen asleep in her seat and rather than wake her and tell her to lie down, Agnes sat in one of the empty seats at the back so that she could keep an eye on the baby and the incubator.

She must have dozed off because someone was shaking her and she wakened with a start. There was no one there, but it was the plane that was shaking. Agnes was terrified. The plane bounced up and down and shook all over like a wet dog trying to dry itself. The cabin lights had been dimmed and she couldn't see if there were any of the stewardesses to ask what was wrong. Just as she was about to panic the Captain's voice came over the intercom advising everyone that there was some turbulence ahead and to make sure they had their seat belts fastened. More like a parachute we need, Agnes thought dryly, convinced the plane was going to end up in the ocean or whichever part of land they were over.

Karen too had wakened up with the Captain's announcement and couldn't for a moment see Agnes who had sat so far down in her seat praying to the almighty to save them that Karen could only just see the top of her head. Karen got up and walked back as the Stratocruiser bucked and swayed.

"Agnes, are you okay? Don't worry, this is quite normal and I'm sure it'll be over soon. We always get this when we fly to Houston, it's quite normal really".

Agnes rolled the whites of her eyes and gave Karen her best stare, which said, 'I don't believe a word you're telling me', to the point where Karen burst out laughing at Agnes's white face.

"It's all very well for you young lady, you've done this before. When will it stop?"

Their short conversation was brought abruptly to an end as one of the stewardesses seeing Karen on her feet called to her to please sit back down and fasten her seat belt. The rocking and rolling went on for about another ten minutes and then it was mercifully calm again. Nurse Anderson breathed a great sigh of relief and decided she needed a wee whisky, 'for medicinal purposes only you understand' as she breezed past Karen to get to the bar before any other passenger beat her to it.

"Agnes, I didn't know you liked Scotch? Karen had never ever associated Agnes with drinking.

"Oh I don't as a rule Miss Karen, but this is just to settle my nerves if ye don't mind."

"Mind, of course I don't mind you dear lady, you've given up your regular life style to come with me on this trip and I can't thank you enough. Go have a belter. Jens is fine and if he wakes up soon I'll feed him".

"Thank you Miss Karen, but I wouldn't describe it as a belter, more of a wee libation."

"Fine," said Karen and on your way back maybe you could bring me a glass of water I seem to be awful thirsty."

Agnes moved off down the aisle to the bar nodding her head at Karen's request. In no time the glass of water appeared on a silver salver held by one of the stewardesses.

"Mrs. Ericsson,"

"Thank you"

"Now you don't have to send your Nurse for anything, just press this call button here and either Shirley or I will be here to get you whatever you want."

"Thank you, I realize that but Agnes just wanted to make herself useful, she's not used to all this sitting about, I think she's getting bored."

"I understand. It's a long flight. Try to get some sleep while you can. Young Jens is showing you all the way........he's been as good as gold"

"So far", answered Karen crossing her fingers, "he was given a mild sedative by our doctor just before he came on board. I'm not quite sure how long it will last."

"If you don't mind me asking Mrs. Ericsson, just what is wrong with your baby?"

So Karen told Carol her story about how she had given birth to twin boys, how one was fine but the other, by some freak of nature had a defective heart and how there was a wonderful surgeon in London who was going make Jens all better. And as the Stratocruiser droned on through the night Karen poured her heart out to the sympathetic Carol while Agnes slept fitfully in her upper level bunk, the Scotch having done the trick. Because of a strong tail wind they reached Chicago in five and a half hours to find it was early next morning as they had just lost two hours with the change in time zones. More food kept coming as the stewardesses kept producing fresh wonders from a well-designed and well-provisioned galley.

The weather was much colder in Chicago and they were allowed to stay on the aircraft, as the refueling did not take long. The next leg to Idlewild was mere 740 miles where there would be a crew change for the even longer flight over the Atlantic.

Jens had become more fractious during the last eight hours of the flight, the sedative had clearly worn off. Agnes proved more than her worth tending the sick baby as if he were her own and giving an exhausted Karen a welcome break from feeding and diaper changing. Finally they arrived at London's Heathrow Airport and passed through immigration without any problems.

The hotel Bentley was there to meet the weary travelers and the chauffeur could not have been nicer as he packed the bags and manhandled the incubator into the back seat. Traffic seemed light for a Wednesday so their driver had said and they arrived at Claridges Hotel in London's Mayfair in less than an hour.

Checking in at Claridges was an experience. They were taken straight to their rooms and a hotel representative came to them and took all the relevant information from them. He confirmed that indeed Madam had a suite with a sitting room and two bedrooms on the second floor with slightly limited views but very well appointed. It was now mid afternoon and both Agnes and Karen helped clean up Jens and put him down to sleep and crashed out for about four hours.

It was pitch dark when Karen wakened to Jens crying. She went to him and calmed him down feeding him a little made-up formula.. Once he was calm she left him and jumped in the shower, luxuriating in the hot water and wonderful shower gel the hotel had provided. She grabbed one of the soft toweling robes, threw that on and went to see what was wrong with Jens, who by this time was screaming blue murder and was looking bluer as the seconds went by. Again Karen gently rocked him and fed him again. Soon he was quiet and relaxed gently falling asleep in his mother's arms as she sat in one of the hotel bedroom's luxurious armchairs. She began to feel almost human again and her mind wind milled with impatience and what the future might hold for her son as she contemplated her visit with the famous Ross Macdonald.

Just after lunch on the following day the hotel car took Karen and Agnes with Jens to London's famous Harley Street where every medical specialist who was anybody had their clinic. They were ushered into a waiting room by a severe looking nurse who said that Mr. Macdonald was expecting them and that they would not be kept waiting very long.

They had only just sat down when another door in the waiting room opened and a middle-aged gentleman with a ruddy complexion accentuated by gray hair greeted them. Almost six feet tall he peered at them through a pair of half-moon glasses perched on the end of his nose. He wore a slightly shabby Harris Tweed suit that looked like it had never been cleaned or pressed.

He smiled a thin smile as he came forward to greet them.

"How do you do, I'm Ross Macdonald."

They all shook hands and made their introductions. Professor Macdonald invited them into his surgery. The room was pale green and on the walls there hung a number of diplomas in gilt frames. There were one or two highland scenes depicting lochs and mountains, but apart from those, and a large Mahogany desk, the room was sparsely furnished.

"Please sit down." He motioned to the only two other chairs in the room and Agnes Anderson put the bassinette holding Jens on the professor's desk.

Macdonald reached in and gently picked Jens up.

"There now wee fellow, let's have a look at you."

Jens' grimaced as unknown hands picked him up and an unknown face stared into his. The professor quickly put him on a nearby table at which point Jens began to cry and his face turned blue. Karen immediately jumped up to go to his side.

"Just sit over there please, Mrs. Ericsson, he'll be quite all right with me."

Karen abruptly sat down feeling very much put in her place.

"Right now wee man let's see what's going on with you". The cold stethoscope touched Jens' little chest and increased his wailing to ear splitting proportions.

Karen looked frantically at Agnes who signaled with her eyes to stay put and say nothing. Jens' wailing continued.

Ross Macdonald peered over the half-moons and looked at Agnes Anderson. The look was enough. Agnes rose from her chair and went over to the baby.

"There now, there now Jens, this man's going to help you get well, there, there wee chap just calm down."

Macdonald recognizing a Scot's accent said,

"Which part of Scotland are you from then?"

"Glasgow," replied Agnes.

"Ah, really. Well that can't be helped. Not a city I'm familiar with really. I come from Mallaig originally. My great-great-great Grandfather was with Bonnie Prince Charlie when he raised his standard at Glenfinnan in 1745."

"Fancy that." Was all Agnes could think of saying.

Jens' wailing abated as the Professor continued his examination.

His soft hands moved deftly over the infant's body as he pressed his stomach and turned him over face down and looked at the diaper clad child on the table.

The examination went on for another two minutes by which Karen was becoming more and more agitated. She hadn't said two words since she had met Ross Macdonald and she had so many questions she wanted to ask. She had come all this way and she felt she deserved more attention than she was getting. Her lips pursed as she tried to keep her patience under control. She felt she had been living on her nerves for more than three days now and it was beginning to show. The flying time lag had also taken its toll and she was just about at the end of her tether.

The Professor finished with Jens and indicated to Agnes to put the baby's clothes back on again. His stethoscope went into the pocket of his white coat, sat down at his desk and looked over some notes.

He then went over to the wall where there was viewing box and flicked a switch. The screen illuminated to a dazzling white. All this time his back was to Karen and it was as if she didn't exist. He clipped an x-ray onto the screen and closely examined the picture. He repeated the process with another x-ray.

"What do you think doctor?" asked Karen unable to stay quiet any longer.

"Well, he's definitely blue." Macdonald then started to write totally unaware that his remarks had inflamed Karen.

"Well," she bit her tongue, "what can you do for him?"

There was a long silence. Agnes Anderson died quietly in the corner wishing she were somewhere else. The dour Scottish Professor was not used to long conversations and she had quickly realized that Macdonald was a man of few words.

"Well", the Professor nodded his head, "let's do it."

"Do what?" Karen leaned forward in her chair to catch any more words of wisdom that might fall from the Professor's lips.

"We'll do a shunt"

"What's that?"

Macdonald permitted himself a rare thin smile. He looked over his glasses straight into Karen's eyes and said,

"That's what you came all this way for, isn't it, to repair the hole in your son's heart?

Karen's face lit up at the sound of those words, she had just found a savior for her child.

"You're at Claridges aren't you? I'll call you and tell you when I can do it next week, oh and by the way, my fee will be 500 guineas."

The car ride back to Claridges took only ten minutes. Karen was silent as she tried to work out in her mind if she liked or disliked Ross Macdonald. Finally she turned to Agnes, who seemed to be deep in her own thoughts and said,

"Agnes, what's a guinea?"

"One pound and one shilling, it's an old unit of sterling."

"So that's five hundred pounds and five hundred shillings"

"Correct, that's five hundred and twenty-five pounds."

"Right, I wonder what that is in dollars? It doesn't seem much does it? Not for making Jens well."

"That's about $2,000 dollars Karen"

"What do you think of him, Agnes?" Karen's mind was clearly not on money.

"Typical doctor or Professor, if you like. Can't deal with people at all. He's probably a very shy man. He comes from Mallaig originally, which is a remote village on the northwest coast of Scotland. If he was serious child, and I think he most certainly was he wouldn't have many friends growing up. I think you've come to the right man. You may not like him but he seems totally professional and I'm sure he'll be dedicated to any patient in his care."

"I didn't say I didn't like him Agnes, he was just a bit abrupt, I guess. And how did he know we were staying at Claridges?"

"Well that's just like a doctor, no bedside manner worth a damn, and you have to admit people don't normally speak to you that way Miss Karen, so your not used to it. As for where we're staying he'd have found that out from Dr. Crawford."

"Just what do you mean by 'people don't usually speak to me in that way'? And as for your theory on Jack Crawford he didn't know where we were going to be staying in London? It was a friend of daddy's who suggested Claridges at the last minute, he said it was much better and quieter than the other hotels we considered."

"You're used to getting attention, that's all. I suppose he must have found out some way. Didn't you tell his receptionist how to get in touch with us?"

"I don't know if I like that, makes me sound kinda spoiled, and I don't think I am." Karen retorted pouting.

Agnes was on the point of saying 'if the cap fits, wear it' but she thought the better of it. Karen did not brook criticism in any way and Ross Macdonald had treated her matter-of –factly and she wasn't used to that.

"Miss Karen relax. Jens is going to be fine. Let's get over the time dif-ference. I'm fair weary and then when I go to bed I can't get to sleep."

Agnes neatly turned the conversation away from a possible confron-tation. She kept trying to remember that people in the United States were not used to her somewhat blunt Scottish approach.

James the doorman resplendent in an ornate top hat, a gold liveried footman's coat, black polished leather boots and gauntlet style gloves greeted them as they arrived back at the hotel.

"Madame Ericsson, Miss Anderson, Master Jens. I trust you have all had a good day."

James wagged his gloved finger at Jens' peaked face, which was just visible under the swaddling blankets that covered him up in the little carrycot. Karen marveled at the quality of service. They had only been two, or was it three, days in the hotel but already the doorman knew them by their respective names. Not only that but it applied to the Concierge and whoever was on reception. Pick up the phone for ser-vice and you were addressed by your name. No wonder Claridges was famous.

"James, thank you. We've had a most encouraging day with Profes-sor Macdonald. I think he can do something for my little boy and I'm very pleased."

"I am too for all of you Madam," James smiled warmly as he opened the door to allow them to pass into the Hotel's snug interior.

A huge beautifully decorated and lighted Christmas tree had suddenly appeared in the hotel lobby. Karen had forgotten it was so near to Christmas. Suddenly she began to feel homesick and she had only just arrived. This just wouldn't do. Getting a grip on her emotions she took Jens from Agnes's arms and was about to go to the elevator when the Concierge saw her out of the corner of his eye. Excusing himself from another guest he hurried over to Karen.

"Mrs. Ericsson," he spoke in a low voice, "there was a trunk call from the United States not two hours ago. I believe it was your husband phoning from Texas somewhere. The number is on a note I had placed on your bedside cabinet. Just pick up the phone and one of our operators will do the rest. It might take a while to get through, at this time of the year you have to book transatlantic calls."

"Thank you George, you're real swell."

"My pleasure, Mrs. Ericsson."

Karen and Agnes went up to their room on the third floor. A smartly dressed bellhop manned the elevator. The sitting room was filled with three vases of beautifully arranged flowers. Where the hotel got such wonderful flowers in the Wintertime Karen couldn't imagine. She took the cards from their respective envelopes. "Much love, mommy and daddy" read one. "I'll always love you." She didn't need to see from whom that card came. Her eyes misted up. Then she remembered the phone call. She looked at the note in her bedroom as Agnes put Jens down for the night. The little boy was exhausted from all his recent experiences and he was looking bluer than ever, so much so that even Agnes was becoming alarmed.

Karen placed the call to Houston via the hotel operator who promised she would get a response within the hour. Karen went through to Jens's cot, which was close to Agnes's bed.

"What do you think Agnes, will he be all right? He's gone real blue this afternoon."

"Aye, you're right there ma'am. Let's put him down and see if he improves in half-an-hour, if he doesn't and his breathing is still as labored, then I think we need to get some medical help."

149

"Agnes, are you hungry? I'm starving; let's get Room Service to send up something."

"Great idea," agreed Agnes.

In 30 minutes Jens' breathing had improved and the blueness had abated. They could relax, for a bit anyway, so ten minutes later they sat down at an exquisitely laid table to a meal of Scotch Broth, ordered by Agnes, melon and Proscuitto, followed by some excellent poached salmon with a hollandaise sauce that was, as Karen put it, to die for. The waiter had suggested a bottle of Sancerre, which complimented the meal perfectly, or so Karen thought. Agnes, on the other hand, not being a wine drinker thought the wine dry and sour, "gie wersh" was what she had actually said and explained it was a commonly used Scot's expression when something made your mouth pucker akin to sucking a lemon. Karen decided there was much more to Agnes than met the eye.

The meal over they decided to watch some British Television. A dark walnut console that housed the black and white Phillips fourteen-inch TV stood in the corner of the room. They had just switched on when the telephone rang. It was the hotel operator. She apologized for taking so long to get a connection but Mr. Ericsson was on the line from Houston in Texas.

"Red, Red, is that you," Karen shouted down the line.

"It's me honey, are you okay?" Red's voice didn't seem at all like him; the distance and the under-ocean cable playing tricks with his voice.

"Oh Red, I'm fine and so is Agnes. It was a long flight but we made it safely and tell daddy the hotel is wonderful. It must be costing an awful lot but tell him everyone is so nice and helpful I can't believe it."

"What about Jens?"

In the excitement Karen had quite forgotten about her little boy.

"What about Lance?" she countered not to be outdone.

"Why Lance is fine, so Bendy Wendy tells me."

"Who the hell is Bendy Wendy?"

"It's just my nickname for Wendy the Nanny, she's such a shy person I can hardly get two words out of her."

"Well Jens is okay. He did well on the airplane thanks to Doctor Crawford and more especially to Agnes, she's been wonderful Red, I don't know what I'd have done without her."

"What did the doctor say?"

"It's Professor actually, Ross Macdonald is a Professor, Red. He says he can fix Jens so that he'll be fine. He's going to do the operation next week sometime. He's going to call me, I suppose on Monday and tell me when."

"Shit, he's taking his time. He knew you were coming, so what's the hold up?"

"Red, darling I don't know. He doesn't say much, and I think if I ask too much I'll upset him. His fee is going to be five hundred guineas"

"What the hell is a guinea?"

"I had to ask Agnes the same thing, its one pound and one shilling, altogether about two thousand dollars.

"Just you tell him who's paying the bill, that'll bring him into line."

"Red, believe me he's not like that. I really don't think he cares about the money."

"Bull Shit, everybody cares about the money. Do you want me to phone him and set him straight?"

"Darling that's the worst thing you could do. Please leave it with me. It'll be all right. And, as he's Scots, Agnes has got a few tricks up her sleeve."

Karen had no idea of what, if any, tricks Agnes had. She just had to get Red off the subject of brow beating Ross Macdonald. She had seen quite enough of the Professor to know that the bullying tactics used by Red on his roustabouts would just kill any possible association with the Professor.

"That's the girl, I knew Agnes would be able to handle him. Darling I miss you so much and it's only been a few days. Come home soon."

"Darling I will and it will be with a Jens who's fit and well and can play with his brother, I promise. How are mommy and daddy?"

"Oh they're fine. They enjoy being in charge. Your Dad's between films so he's at the house every day, bird-doggin' Bendy Wendy.

"Darling I'll have to go, it's bed time and we're all tired. I'll call you or Daddy when I have some positive news from Ross Macdonald."

"Okay, I'm going to 'phone your folks tonight and tell them y'all are fine. Love ya, honey."

"Love you too, Red, take care."

And with that Karen put down the 'phone feeling much better, went to bed and instantly fell fast asleep.

True to his word Ross Macdonald called the very next day.

"Ross Macdonald here, Mrs. Ericsson."

"Please, call me Karen."

"Mrs. Ericsson will be just fine, thank you."

Oops! Thought Karen I've upset him already.

"Bring Jens to Brompton Hospital on Monday at six o'clock in the evening. Register him with the Staff Nurse on duty and we'll get him set up for the operation on Tuesday morning. The hotel will tell you how to find us, or I suppose they'll bring you there."

"Oh I'm sure they will Professor, they've been wonderful to us already."

"Aye, I've heard they're not bad from some of my previous patients. I've never had the occasion to stay there, of course, and from what I hear I doubt if I could afford it. Well I'll bid you good day for the time being."

It took three hours on Sunday to get a transatlantic call to Red. He was still in Houston but he told Karen he was going back to Los Angeles either on Tuesday or Wednesday. "Call your Mom and Dad," he had said, "because when I get to LA I want to know how the operation has gone." Karen agreed. She'd call on Tuesday and tell them all what had transpired. Monday dragged for both mother and nurse. Jens' health seemed to be deteriorating. His breathing was becoming more labored and his color was now distinctively blue. The operation couldn't come fast enough they concurred. A walk in Hyde Park had been planned but the British weather didn't co-operate. Monday turned out to be a dark, wet, dismal day. It was still dark at nine o'clock that morning as the wind whipped low clouds heavy with rain across London's West End and the City. Heavy showers lashed on and off intermittently making going out impossible.

By four o'clock that afternoon Karen and Agnes had consumed enough tea and biscuits to last them a lifetime. It was beginning to get dark again and the street lamps cast an eerie glow over the saturated streets. Agnes had prepared Jens for the journey. He looked all the world like a tiny Eskimo papoose with only his little face peeking out from all the clothes and blankets Agnes had wrapped around him. At five the hotel Bentley was at the Hotel entrance ready to take them to the hospital. The Concierge had told them, even in heavy traffic the hospital was only ten to fifteen minutes away but Karen decided she would rather be early than late and in any case the two ladies had decided that the safest place for Jens was in a hospital.

Peter the Concierge was right. Ten minutes later the Bentley smoothed up to Brompton Hospital. Both Karen and Agnes looked out at the dingy gray brownstone building with alarm.

"Are you sure this is the right place Colin?" Karen addressed the chauffeur.

"This is it ma'am. T'ain't so bad when you're inside like, but I 'ave to say it don't look too invitin' ma'am on an 'orrible day like this."

Colin jumped out and held the door open. Karen was out first and Agnes passed Jens to her. He hadn't cried or made a sound for the last two hours and that seemed ominous. Jens didn't like to be lifted and laid too often and he usually made himself heard. The silence worried Karen as she went in through the entrance to the reception area, which was manned by a nurse in crisp, antiseptically white, uniform. The familiar hospital smells came back to Karen as she gave her details to the nurse.

"We're expecting you Mrs. Ericsson, Professor Macdonald has told us to make you as comfortable as we can. Let me first of all get a Porter to take Jens to his ward, check him in with Staff and then I'll take you to see him. How's that?"

"We're in your hands," said Karen without a vestige of humor.

The Porter duly arrived and took Jens from Karen's arms. Jens was still quiet and breathing shallowly.

"Poor li'l buggar," said the Porter looking down at the baby's bluish face, ol' Macdonald will put that right, I'm willin' to bet." And off he went pushing the gurney at what seemed like breakneck speed.

Karen was exhausted, emotionally drained. She didn't know whether to be relieved or sad at Jens going off. She felt relieved in a way, but then she felt guilty at feeling of relief. She just prayed everything was going to be all right. She reached over, took Agnes's hand and held it tight.

"There, there now Karen don't you fret. When we see him tomorrow he'll be fresher than a daisy, all pink and shining, I promise you," said Agnes.

"Oh how I wish that could be true," Karen's voice wavered, close to tears.

"Don't you worry, my dear, your wee lad couldn't be in better hands, isn't that so nurse?" Agnes looked over at the nurse on reception for support.

"Mrs. Ericsson, Agnes is quite right. Since I've come to this hospital I've seen miracles performed, miracles I tell you. That Professor Macdonald is so special, he's the best there is, I promise you." That was the third time that day Karen had the 'promise' word thrown at her. She nodded and tried to smile back at the nurse's reassuring words.

The rapid clicking of busy feet echoed off the bare concrete corridor floor. A stout, blue uniformed nurse appeared clutching a clipboard. She took stock of Karen and Agnes immediately.

"Mrs. Ericsson, your son is in his little cot. He's fine, or, if you like, he's looking better now as we put him in an oxygen tent. His breathing is very much improved and I think he'll be better equipped to face the morning if he has a good night's rest, don't you think so, Nurse Anderson?"

It was a rhetorical question and the Staff nurse did not expect a reply. Agnes nodded without saying a word.

"Oh by the way I'm Joyce Potter, Staff Nurse here at Brompton. Any problems bring them to me. There's not much I can't fix if I know about it."

I bet, thought Agnes. What an officious lady, thought Karen, realizing in her second thoughts that she was probably extremely efficient and good at her job.

"If you want to come up and see Jens you can, but he's comfortable and he's fast asleep, so it's up to you." The suggestion was that a visit would not be welcome. Agnes looked at Karen.

"When can we come in tomorrow, Staff?" Agnes posed the question.

"Well now, that I'll have to find out, but I think, and don't hold me to this, about noon would be fine. The operation is scheduled for nine o'clock tomorrow morning and the Professor should be finished in under an hour. There's the closing and then transferring so I would think, unless there were to be complications, about noon would be okay. If you leave me your number though I'll phone to confirm." Joyce Potter smiled warmly.

"Fine, then I think we'll just leave Jens in your capable hands, don't you think so miss Karen?" Agnes took the initiative.

Karen nodded. "Yes that'll be fine Staff. Here's our number. If we're not in the room the hotel will get a message to us. Thank you for your time. I'll see you tomorrow." And with that Karen and Agnes returned to the waiting car.

"What you need now Miss Karen is a good drink. It's out of your hands now and he's in the best possible care. Let's go downstairs to the bar and, as you say in the States, let's have a highball."

Karen thought Agnes's idea was a great one. She had been on edge since they left Los Angeles. The long flight, Jens's diminishing health, being away from Red and from home had made her appreciate her husband and home all the more. It had been impossible to relax and it had all added to the stress she was now feeling. Karen bathed and put on her prettiest dress. Her figure wasn't quite back in shape, but eyeing herself in the long bedroom mirror, she thought she didn't look too bad. The vermilion lipstick had been applied with a touch of panache and it complimented her dark hair, eyebrows and eyes magnificently. For the first time in more than eight months she felt like a woman again.

Agnes, not to be outdone, made the best of what she had. Her gray hair had been neatly coiffed, her makeup subdued, a little rouge on the cheeks, and a touch of eyeliner helped to accentuate her vivid blue eyes. She had put on a very ornate white blouse complete with jabot which, together with her Anderson tartan-plaid hostess skirt made her look very sophisticated indeed.

Karen couldn't believe the transformation. Agnes looked about ten years younger and somehow taller and elegant, it was the high-heeled shoes had done that so Karen concluded. She had never seen her in anything other than her flat nurses shoes and uniform. Karen told her she looked beautiful and she meant it. Again, she said to herself, Agnes Anderson has hidden depths probably never to be completely revealed. So they hit the cocktail bar arm in arm and virtually stopped all conversation. First it was Karen's stunning good looks and quiet elegance that drew attention followed immediately by Nurse Anderson transformed into aristocratic elegance by her formal Highland wear. A small table was immediately made available for them as they moved their way into the opulent bar area. A waiter sat them and came over with a Carte des Vins.

"What is Madame's pleasure this evening?" the waiter bowed deeply.

"I would like something with a little bit of fizz but not too dry, what can you suggest?"

"Champagne, of course Madame, but if you would like something a little out of the ordinary may I suggest a Kir Royale?"

"What's that?" Karen and Agnes asked in unison.

"Well Madame it is a touch of Crème de Cassis topped up with Champagne. Most refreshing and very popular."

"Sounds interesting, good enough for me," Karen ordered the drink. "Agnes do you want the same?"

"Not I miss, I'm much too plebian. Glenlivet and a touch of water please." Agnes beamed at the waiter who was quite taken aback, but remained totally composed.

"Certainly Madame."

The drinks were duly served in great style and little canapés found their way to the table. Karen and Agnes sat in their newfound euphoria taking in everything around them.

"Here's to Christmas at home," toasted Karen.

"Amen to that." Agnes toasted back

"Do you think it's possible Agnes? Seriously?"

"Well it depends; I think it's pushing things a bit. It's a big operation and to get to Los Angeles in time for Christmas means flying out of London no later than December 23rd, that's just seven days after the operation, I don't honestly think it's possible. But we could be home for New Year, now that would be the thing to go for."

"Agnes is New Year more important than Christmas to the Scots?"

"Aye, it is that Miss Karen. We're a heathen lot. We all wait for Hogmanay and Ne'erday and the general population gets close to alcoholic. Well that's in Glasgow anyway."

"What's Hogmanay? And Ne'erday?"

"Oh, New Year's Eve and New Year's day to you Sassenachs."

"My God Agnes, stop drinking. You're talking a whole new language, what's a Sassen…whatever?"

"It's just a name we give to the English."

"Really? Well I'm not English."

"No your not. You're quite right but we sometimes tend to use it in a more general manner for those who aren't Scots It comes from the Gaelic word for Saxon, therefore English."

"Well let's talk about New Year then and try to get back in time for that."

At that Agnes's face lit up as she contemplated New Year with her sister who was married and lived in Vancouver, Canada.

"Okay then Agnes let's finish our drinks and get off to bed. I sure hope I sleep, tomorrow's going to be the big day."

"You will Miss Karen, you will, and tomorrow will be a great day, honest."

Ross Macdonald arrived promptly at eight o'clock on Tuesday morning. The rain had stopped and a keen north wind blew out of a steely blue sky. He wore a heavy overcoat, leather gloves and a black Homburg hat. He swept past the nurse on reception mumbling 'good morning' as he hurried off in the direction of the pediatric ward. The Staff Nurse was there to greet him as he came in.

"How's the wee chappie then?" Ross asked using the classic Highland double diminutive.

"He's fine Professor. He had not a bad night once we put him on oxygen. His breathing is a lot better now and I think he'll be up to the operation." Joyce proffered her opinion.

"Aye, well I'll be the judge of that. What's his blood pressure like? Temperature?"

Macdonald listened placing his stethoscope over the baby's chest and back.

Finally he straightened up.

"No time like the present. We'd better get on with it. All right Staff give him a wee dose of Chloral Hydrate and we'll have him in the OR in an hour's time, all right?"

"Fine Professor," Joyce Potter went off to do the Professor's bidding.

Macdonald made for the operating theater and the scrub room. He bade his two surgical assistants 'good morning' and once in his scrubs went into a deep conversation with the anesthetist. The operating theater was the best that money could buy despite the restrictions of the National Health system, which the Labour Government, under Clement Atlee, had introduced in 1948. The lighting was state of the art as was all the back up equipment. As the surgical team entered, one of the theater nurses took the Professor's instruments out of the sterilizer and placed them in position to commence the operation. Joyce Potter wheeled the little boy in to what must have looked like a scary movie set. All the surgeons were dressed in green scrubs and had face masks and close fitting surgical caps on. Little Jens couldn't have cared less. He was very drowsy now and quite relaxed. The Staff Nurse lifted the baby off the gurney and placed him on the operating table under the big bright lights.

There was a quiet humming from the equipment but other than that silence prevailed. A wool blanket covered Jens's body, save for the top of his chest. The anesthetist reached over with a mask and covered Jens's mouth. Nitrous Oxide, otherwise known as 'laughing gas,' was gently applied and had him quickly sedated. Very carefully the anesthetist pushed a tube down the little patient's tiny windpipe and fiddled with the knobs on the various cylinders by his side. Carefully they all watched the child's vital signs displayed on the monitors. Heart rate was stable and blood pressure acceptable for a child with Jens's condition. The anesthetist nodded at Macdonald,

"He's yours Ross."

Macdonald turned the baby on his right side so that his left side was exposed and with his scalpel and made a lateral incision about three-quarters of an inch below the armpit. Working quickly with scissors and forceps he enlarged the opening.

"Retractor" The theater nurse handed him a small retractor to allow the surgeon to move the left lung out of the way. His assistants moved in and helped hold the lungs away from the area around the heart. Deftly Macdonald reached into the tiny cavity and found the subclavian artery and proceeded to place a ligature on one side of the artery similarly tying off the other associated arteries. He then occluded the pulmonary artery on either side where he proposed to make the connection with the subclavian artery. Then clamping the subclavian farther back from its junction he made an incision in the subclavian artery and pulled it down towards the pulmonary artery. Placing the two arteries side by side he then made an incision in the pulmonary artery. Macdonald was working quickly and his colleagues watched the true genius of the man as he handled tiny arteries without the aid of any magnification.

"How's he doing David?" he asked the anesthetist never taking his eyes off the open chest cavity. The nurses handed him swabs and forceps at the right moments without having to be asked.

"He's fine, Ross, doing fine."

Next, with one of his assistants help in holding the fine silk, he sutured the two arteries together effectively diverting blood that normally would go to the arm to now go to the lungs. This was the tricky part. Sewing such small arteries together required the utmost skill and technique. An incorrect stitch now could cause severe hemorrhaging. So far the whole operation had taken twenty minutes. The sewing now over Macdonald removed the clamps and ligatures and checked for bleeding. There was none. He then removed the eight or so swabs that had been used.

"All right Colin, you can close now."

Colin Macalister, Ross Macdonald's protégé took a chest tube and with more silk and with the help of his colleague closed up Jens's chest. The physical change in Jens's color was immediate. All the blueness had disappeared and he was now a healthy glowing pink! The miracle Karen had hoped for had happened.

David Brown the anesthetist looked at Colin. "Fantastic eh? It never fails to amaze me, and he makes it look all so easy. Look at this wee lad, now his mother won't know him. Colin, I'm going to keep him on the ventilator, we'll put him in an oxygen tent where we can make sure his breathing is okay. Later we'll see if we can get him off it and let him breathe on his own"

"Fine, David. I'll come in later tonight and just make sure all's well. What's the situation with the mother?"

"Ross has gone down to see her; she's in the waiting room." David said.

"She's from the States, isn't she?" Colin had heard she was film star material.

"She is and she's a bit of a looker. From California I think. Joyce who knows all things tells me her father's a film producer."

"You're kidding?" Colin's eyebrows arched.

"No, I'm not and he's a pretty famous one at that. She's staying at Claridges with her nurse."

"Jesus Christ! That costs a fortune. Ross will be on to that one. Wait 'til she gets the bill." Colin laughed.

"You know, I don't know if Ross is like that, I think it's more the prestige or power, I don't think it's money. He lives quite modestly, you know."

David knew Ross Macdonald was a modest man at heart.

"Do you think we'll meet the mother?" Colin was fishing now. Being single he could always appreciate a fine figure without getting into trouble.

"Well if you hang around you probably will. Go and ask Choice Joyce if she's heard from the mother. If she has she'll have an idea of when she'll be here."

"Great idea." At that Colin Macalister beetled off to find the Staff Nurse.

Joyce Potter headed for the Waiting Room where Karen and Agnes had been sitting for some hours now. Ross Macdonald's visit was a welcome break in the monotony and he assured Karen that the operation was successful. She just had to wait and see her son around noon, so the Professor had said.

"Agnes, Mrs. Ericsson, come in, come with me"

"How is he, was the operation really a success?" Karen couldn't wait to blurt out as they walked smartly along the long corridor.

"Come and see for yourself," Joyce beckoned to them to come to the main elevator.

They got off at the third floor and smelled the ether and antiseptic that seemed to prevail in every hospital. Joyce strode forward leading them to the Intensive Care ward. She slowed as she approached the door and signaled to them to be quiet, holding her index finger up to her lips. The door opened slowly. There were only three people in a ward that could have held twenty or more. Quickly Karen took in the old lady, painfully white and clearly in pain, then a young man who lay on a hospital bed with IV drips and wires protruding from different parts of his body.

"Car accident," Joyce whispered as they made their way to the tiny cot at the end of the ward.

At last Karen looked down at her little boy. He was still out for the count and the ventilator was still in place. An IV drip was attached by surgical tape to his right wrist. But the change, the change was miraculous. Her little boy was pink and well. The alteration in his color was even more dramatic to Karen than it had been to the hospital staff. Jens had never looked as good as this. The long journey, the nights filled only with agonizing worry, the concern as to whether Jens would live or die. It was over. He looked like a reborn infant; in fact he *was* a reborn infant. He'd be a normal child and be able to play with his brother Lance.

"The tube will come out later today once he's come round from the anesthetic," Joyce told them. Doctor Macalister is in charge of Jens at the moment, he's our senior registrar, if you'd like to see him?"

Joyce proposed the meeting that Colin Macalister had asked her to surreptitiously organize.

"That would be wonderful, thank you." Karen gushed happily.

Agnes was still watching Jens breathing steadily. She too was amazed at the change for the better in his condition. It was indeed as if a miracle had happened. Colin Macalister came sweeping in to the ward just as Agnes got off her knees.

"Ah," Macalister joked, "praying are we?"

"Aye, well, it would hardly be out of place, now, would it?" Agnes stared at the Doctor.

"Only joking," said Macalister, "so you're from Scotland then by the sound of the accent."

"That I am," Agnes drew herself up to her full five foot five.

"And this must be the very beautiful Karen Ericsson?" Colin Macalister held out his hand and shook Karen's warmly.

"What do you think of Jens now?"

"Doctor, it is incredible, you have all been so kind. I did see Professor Macdonald just after he had finished the operation and I'd like to fix a time when I can visit with him again."

"Right, his secretary will most probably make the call. He'll want to review the case with you and give you some instruction on cleaning and dressing the wound until you get back to the United States and get him under medical supervision."

"Will he need intensive care?" Karen suddenly became concerned.

"No, no nothing like that. But we just want to make sure the wound stays clean and heals properly and that his general health continues to improve. Do you star in your father's films?" Colin changed the subject in midstream. She was so good looking, he couldn't take his eyes off her and to make matters worse it was obvious to everyone, including Karen.

Karen poured on the charm. "I'd love to be in one of my Daddy's movies but I'm just not good looking enough. She flickered her eyelashes at the Doctor and smiled warmly. Colin Macalister's heart flipped.

"Oh, oh, never that's just not true", he countered. "I think you're one of the most beautiful women I've ever met.........truly." He added as if any emphasis was necessary.

Karen had him over a barrel. She linked her arm through Colin's, which was thrust deep in his white doctor's coat pocket and said,

"Come over here closer to Jens and tell me all about the operation and everything."

She moved gently towards Jens's bed flirting outrageously with the 'captured' Doctor, pulling him along with her. Colin's face had gone bright red. Normally Agnes would have been horrified at the way Karen seemed to throwing herself at Colin. But even Agnes's Presbyterian attitude was beginning to melt with the exposure to some of the better things in life which she had never thought she would have the where-withal to enjoy, but was now enjoying immensely.

Karen had had a tough time, she told herself, and the relief of Jens's successful operation had brought back the little girl in her again, which had been missing for the past three or four months. Agnes saw Joyce smiling and she and Joyce exchanged glances and tried not to laugh out loud. It was too funny. Colin Macalister had become instantly besotted with Karen, and Karen was making the most of it. Karen sat Colin down on the edge of the bed, faced him square on and opened her deep brown eyes to full beam, smiled charmingly and said,

"You can begin now."

"Well..." Colin was back to spluttering again, "it's sort of difficult to explain in layman's terms, but I'll do the best I can and stop me if you don't understand anything." And so he launched off into the story of what Ross Macdonald had done in about an hour and a half to make her son well and lead a normal life. Karen stopped him when he mentioned a 'normal' life.

"Will it truly be normal, doctor?" she gazed into Colin's eyes.

Colin averted his eyes to somewhere over her left shoulder and explained that it was Ross Macdonald's job to assess how successful the operation might be after he had carried out a number of tests.

"So what you're saying is that he might not be normal?"

"No, I didn't quite say that, but there's a number of factors to be taken into consideration, I mean he might not be able to run a four-minute mile." Colin referred to Roger Bannister's feat four years earlier as the first person in recorded history to run a mile in just under four minutes.

"Well I didn't think he'd be able to do that but that's an extreme, I think you're evading the question Doctor Macalister, that's what I think. I suppose we'll have to talk about it later," she pouted her lips in feigned disapproval and got up from the bed indicating the conversation was over. A bit of Colin Macalister quietly died as he considered a lonely evening ahead without Karen.

"Well, you know, you could wait and talk to the Professor. I am sure he'll call you tonight after he's been in to see Jens. If you want to stay awhile I'll make sure you won't be bored. I can show you the OR where it all took place."

"The OR?" asked Karen.

"Operating theatre, dear", Joyce and Agnes chorused together.

"Of course, how silly of me. No. It's a very kind offer but I have to get back to the hotel and phone my husband in Texas to tell him how Jens is."

Another bit of Doctor Macalister quietly died at the mention of Karen's husband. He jolted back to reality.

"Of course, of course, I should have realized. He must be terribly anxious."

"Yes he is. But it's not so bad for him. He's working real hard all day, so it takes his mind off things. But when he gets a moment I know he'll try to call. It takes so long to get through now, I suppose it's because we're so close to Christmas all the transatlantic 'phone lines are busy."

The small talk continued for a few more moments about Jens and when Ross Macdonald might call when Karen had a great idea.

"Doctor Macalister," she grasped his arm,

"Colin, please, just call me Colin, eh…but you might just want to call me Doctor when the Professor's around."

"Of course, that'll be just fine Colin," Karen squeezed his arm for emphasis. Colin's temperature shot up two points.

"Well, what I was thinking Colin was I heard you say you had never been to Claridges. The food is really very good, and," she snuggled up to him, "as it's getting close to Christmas how would you and Professor Macdonald like to join us, that's Agnes and me, for dinner on Saturday night? That's the twentieth I think. You do get an evening off don't you?"

"Yes we do. But it all depends on what's going on surgery-wise. As the Professor specializes I think he tries to keep Christmas and New Year fairly free, so that just leaves emergencies. I'd love to spend an evening with you but I can't speak for the Professor, the invitation would have to come from you miss."

"Karen, Colin, it's Karen."

"Yes, yes, of course." Colin stammered, went beetroot red again and closely examined a spot on the polished linoleum floor.

"Well of course I'll ask him, just leave it all to me. I'm sure he'd like an evening out. I bet he never gets asked out. I'll phone him first thing in the morning, leave it to me, Colin."

That's just what I'm bothered about, thought Colin, smiling back at Karen. He was quickly having second thoughts. He wished he hadn't been quite so precipitate in accepting Karen's invitation. He had never socialized in any way with Ross Macdonald short of having a quick snack with him in the Hospital's Cafeteria, that was the closest he had come to being with him in a non-professional capacity. Would Ross Macdonald accept? Suppose Karen didn't tell him that he, Colin was invited as well. God, it would be all over. There existed a distinct protocol in the medical profession and Karen Ericsson was blowing a hole right through it. She should have asked Ross Macdonald first, and then ran it past the Professor to find out if his assistant could join them. The decision at that point would be the Professor's.

All these thoughts flashed through his mind as he escorted Karen and Agnes to the hotel limousine, which was waiting for them at the main entrance. He almost said something to Karen as they parted, but he was so keen to see her again he rationalized that Ross wouldn't accept and he would have Karen all to himself that Saturday, well Agnes would be there but he was sure that she would get the picture and excuse herself at an appropriate moment. He waved them away from the entry in animated style as the chauffeured car pulled away. He had never felt like this in his life before. He was, he realized, head over heels in love with someone else's wife and he didn't give a damn! He danced through the reception area past the astonished nurse on reception and to a very disapproving look from Staff Nurse Potter, Choice Joyce to the doctors.

Agnes could see what was happening. Karen was just being a downright flirt. Agnes could imagine that the poor young doctor, who had probably studied and worked all sorts of hours just to get to where he was, and who also probably had never had a serious relationship with a woman, was now totally captivated by Karen. She mulled over Colin's question as to why Karen hadn't become a film star. After all her father was a big producer in Hollywood and could pull all the necessary strings to get her a part in a movie. She had all the moves and the looks Agnes had certainly seen that. It was Oscar winning stuff. So on the short drive back to the hotel she asked.

"Karen, why was it that you never went into films or rather movies as you call them?"

"Why do you ask?"

"Well you've put on a great performance with Colin Macalister, now I know you love Red and that you can't wait to talk to him, but that poor doctor doesn't know whether he's coming or going....he's fallen in love with you, you know."

"That's Bull, Agnes. He might be a little bit infatuated with me, he'll get over that."

"You haven't answered my question. I thought all young girls would love to be screen stars, why not you?"

"Not good looking enough." Karen answered abruptly.

"Fiddlesticks," said Agnes. "Try again."

"I didn't pass the screen test."

"Oh, so you did try. What made you fail the screen test?"

"Producer didn't like what he saw."

"Really, who was the producer?"

"Brett Stahlman."

"You mean your father?"

"Yup, the one and only."

"Well for goodness sake....I can hardly believe that..........."

Agnes's words tailed off as the car arrived back at the hotel.

Karen was relieved. She didn't want to discuss the subject and it was so irrelevant now in any case. Once again James the doorman gave them the royal welcome.

"How are you Madame, has everything gone satisfactorily?"

"Thank you James. Jens's operation was real successful. I'm just rushing in to 'phone Jens's father, it takes so long to get a call to the US at the moment."

"I understand Madame and at the sake of appearing presumptuous I booked a call through the Concierge to the United States for you, I would think that it will come through shortly Madame. Peter the Concierge assumed it would be the Houston number."

"Oh James," Karen looked at Agnes in astonishment, "how wonderful you are, thanks a bunch, you're real sweet." And with that she reached on her tiptoes and planted a big kiss on James's cheek. For a brief moment James was completely taken off-guard. He didn't quite know how to respond.

"Thank you Madame, you are too kind," James bowed and taking Karen's tiny manicured hand he gently kissed it trying his level best not show his discomfort at this very unusual situation. Karen rushed on into the hotel followed closely by an equally astonished Agnes who was beginning to wonder what Karen would get up to next.

Karen got a connection to Red in about fifteen minutes thanks to the foresight of the hotel staff. She positively bubbled down the 'phone. Red has never heard her so ebullient in months, she was back to being the vivacious, petite charmer he had married.

"Yes darling the operation was a complete success. Jens looks wonderful, he's as pink as a carnation, honest. He was sleeping when I left

him. The staff are all just wonderful and I think we made the right decision to come to Ross Macdonald. I haven't got all the answers just yet.
I think I'm meeting with the Professor tomorrow and he'll tell me how
good Jens recovery will be. There's also a very nice Doctor Macalister,
Ross Macdonald's assistant. He's a real cool guy and I'm sure very talented. He's the sort of man who would do well in California; they don't
get paid very well in England you know. They have this National Health
Service plan which gives free medicine to everyone. I have no idea how
they can get free health care, but keeping the doctors poor seems to
be one way. Anyway darling," and she dropped her voice to her special
little girl pout, "we're not going to get home for Christmas darling,
New Year is on, but not Christmas. I was sure we'd be a complete family
for Christmas. I sure miss Lance darling, how is he anyway?"

"Growing like a weed and eating like a horse," Red's distorted voice
ebbed and flowed over the transatlantic connection.

"Oh, that's marvelous."

"Gee, honey I'm so sad you aren't going to be home for Christmas
and that goes for your Mom and Pop too. Still New Year is better than
nothing and we'll all be able to celebrate 1959. It promises to be a big
year."

"Darling, I can't wait. London's fine and the people are so nice but
the weather is wet and cold all the time. We don't go out in it, but it's so
gloomy, I guess that's the word, it makes everyone kind of sad looking."

"Well the weather's real grand here in Houston. And I understand
from your Mom that it's fine in Los Angeles as well. I think it's maybe a
little warmer here. It's like seventy-five during the day and down to the
high fifties at night. By the way Mats sends his best."

"Thank him for me darling, I'll call you tomorrow once I've had a
word with Ross."

"Leave it for a day honey; I'm going to be in Dallas tomorrow. Tell
you what, call me on Friday, I'm sure to be back in town by then."

"All right. Love you darling."

Red blew kisses down the receiver making a sound like whales vent-
ing at the other end of the line.

Ross Macdonald's secretary called at ten o'clock the next morning to say that the Professor would like to see Mrs. Ericsson in an hour's time at his Harley Street office if that would be convenient. Karen, having agreed, reserved the hotel car for the trip to Harley Street but asked that it return without waiting. The weather had improved to the point where sunshine flitted between the scattered wintry clouds and she figured she would walk along Oxford Street on her way back to the hotel. Karen was ushered into the waiting room at about eleven fifteen. Ross Macdonald greeted her warmly.

"Well, so you've seen your wee boy, what do you think?"

"Oh Doctor…sorry, Professor, it's a miracle!"

"Aye, doctor's just fine by the way. He looks grand though. He's got a-ways to go yet but the operation was a technical success, we've got to wait now and see if he'll get over all the trauma of his ordeal, it's quite a big thing, you know."

"I can imagine."

"Well he was a bit below weight when we got him, but I think he'll pick up now. Joyce Potter is very competent and you'll have met Colin Macalister, my assistant, I suppose."

"Oh yes, he's a real cutie, in fact I wanted…"

Ross Macdonald abruptly cut of her conversation with a wave of his hand.

"Cutie, eh, cutie… that's not quite the word I'd use for young Colin. He peered down his half-moon spectacles looking perplexed.

"Let me tell you about Jens. What I've done is a temporary measure. At some stage when he's older, and I mean by that ten or eleven or so, he's going to require more major surgery. We're not there yet. There are some great strides going on in the heart surgery department, in fact I'll be left behind. It's chaps like young Colin who will be the new breed of surgeon in the next ten or so years. So you might want to keep in with Doctor Colin."

Macdonald looked up at Karen knowingly. Karen's face was a mask.

"Jens will probably have a semi-normal life."

"What just do you mean semi-normal?" Karen cut in.

"Well, he'll be able to do most reasonable things but high levels of exertion will be a problem for him. Basically he's got a damaged heart, the shunt is, at best, a means of bypassing the immediate problem of getting oxygen to the lungs, hence the improvement in his color. But you never know. With the right sort of activities he may go farther than any of us would dare imagine. So my message to you is this, as he grows keep him active within a range of activity that doesn't distress him. Any sign of stress or distress should be avoided and to any outsider he should not be a weakly child. Imagine, if you will, a badly asthmatic child, that child would probably have more impairment than Jens. So, look on the bright side my dear, and I'm sure you'll have a wonderful time with your son in the years ahead."

The Professor finished his lecture, sat back and steepled his fingers peering at Karen through the half-moons again.

"Any questions?"

"Yes Professor, when do you think it will be safe for him to travel?"

"You're flying back, I take it?"

"Yes we're taking the same route as we took to get here. All in all it's about 26 hours and it may be longer depending on the weather. We had hoped to be home for Christmas."

"Well, I'm afraid that's not going to be possible. It means you'd have to fly out of London on the twenty-third at least which is just six days from today and eight days from the operation. That's too soon. But if all goes well you could be home for New Year, now there's a thought."

"Yes, I think Agnes sets more store in getting home for New Year than for Christmas."

"Aye, well she's Scots of course." The Professor did not elaborate. As a Scot he considered his statement required no further explanation.

"Professor Macdonald," Karen leaned forward in her chair, "would you do me the pleasure of dining with us at Claridges on Saturday evening?" Karen tried to make the invitation as English as she could and stared back into the Professor's eyes.

"Well that's most kind, most kind. Do you know I've never eaten there, and I hear it's very good. My wife has gone to her sister's over the weekend and unless there are any emergencies which young Colin can't handle, I may well take you up on that."

"Well that would be just great. You know Agnes Anderson will be there too, she's traveled all the way with me to look after Jens and another thing I did, rather on the spur of the moment invite young Colin, as you call him, to join me as well. So you may want to reconsider. I really should have asked you first..." Karen tripped over her words as she tried to explain but the Professor cut her off with his hand.

"My dear lady, think nothing of it. I'll be interested to see young Macalister in action. And Agnes is the lady from Glasgow of course. An interesting combination as Colin Macalister comes from Edinburgh." He smiled his typical thin smile. "Now, if there is indeed an emergency you do know he'll have to excuse himself, but we'll keep our fingers crossed and we'll look forward to a wonderful evening."

Karen couldn't believe it. Ross Macdonald was as nice as ninepence, to use a recent English term she had picked up. The Professor cleared his throat slightly. "Mrs. Ericsson, there is just one other small matter."

"Oh sure, fire away."

"My account."

"Oh heavens yes, golly gee, I'm sorry I kind of forgot about all that."

"There's no rush, no rush at all. Mrs. Sanderson will let you have it on your way out, I just wanted to let you know there are no additional charges and I've billed you my standard fee for an operation of this sort which, as I told you at our first meeting, would be five hundred guineas."

"Doctor, that's real kind of you. Red and I sure appreciate that." Karen shook the Professor's hand warmly and exited the office via the efficient Mrs. Sanderson who presented her with a heavy parchment style envelope with 'Mrs. Red Ericsson' written in beautiful copper-plate script.

Agnes couldn't believe the news that the Professor was really going to join them for dinner. Just to be in Ross Macdonald's presence was an honor, never mind spending a whole evening with him.

"Do you think my tartan hostess skirt will be acceptable? I mean I've worn it before, the night you and I went to the bar."

"Your hostess skirt will be just great. I'm going to wear what I wore that night as well; we're buying them dinner, not putting on a fashion show. What I will do though, is talk to Bruno the Maitre d' and ask his advice on wines. I know nothing about French wines and I might also ask him about his recommendations for dinner."

The dinner, organized by Bruno, turned out to be a great success. Ross Macdonald and Colin Macalister shared a cab and arrived promptly at seven thirty for cocktails. They were both dressed in Dinner Suits with Ross Macdonald sporting a bright red carnation in his lapel. The professor permitted himself a small Glenlivet and was accompanied by Agnes. Karen, having fallen in love with Kir Royale, ordered one and was about to persuade Colin Macalister to have the same when he said he wasn't drinking. Technically, he said, he was on duty. He would allow himself a little wine with dinner, but that would be all. Agnes could see that Colin was very much in check watching his P's and Q's in Ross Macdonald's presence.

It started out as a simple meal. The first course was the finest Scottish Smoked Salmon with thinly sliced brown bread. Karen had found out from Colin that one of the Professor's favorites was smoked salmon. This was followed by a small bowl of cock-a-leekie soup. Karen had never heard of such a soup. But again it was a Scottish dish recommended highly by Agnes and Bruno. And at that point Karen had drawn the line. There may well be three Scots attending this dinner, she had said to Agnes, but I'm going to choose the main course. The white burgundy, a 1954 Mersault was replenished as the Lobster Thermidor arrived. The presentation of the dish was totally dramatic as Bruno entered the dining room with a platter of four large lobsters flaring spectacularly on a huge silver salver. Side salads of crispy lettuce, thinly sliced tomato with French dressing were all that complimented the crustaceans. None of Karen's other guests had ever heard of Lobster Thermidor. It was voted an outstanding success. The sauce, Ross Macdonald commented, was quite the finest he had ever tasted, the pieces of Lobster tender and the gratinéed topping on the sauce perfection itself. There was a lull in the eating and more wine followed little goblets of lemon sorbet, which had the effect of cleansing the palette. A selection of French soft cheeses was then offered followed by individual ramekins of crème brulée.

The party was just finishing off desert when Bruno, the Maitre d', approached Ross Macdonald and whispered urgently in his ear. Macdonald excused himself and headed for a telephone in the lobby. Colin Macalister looked nervous.

"I hope it's not an emergency. That would spoil a wonderful evening Karen. You and Agnes have been perfect hostesses. I think even the Professor had a good time."

"Well he certainly didn't leave any food," Agnes remarked enthusiastically. She had enjoyed a wonderful evening. Once she had got to know Ross, she realized what a shy and self-effacing man he was. He was really terribly self–conscious in a social setting. In the hospital, which was his domain, it didn't show at all but elsewhere he was like a fish out of water. Ross Macdonald came striding back to the table.

"Ladies, we have to excuse ourselves, we have an emergency and we must leave for the hospital immediately. Colin?"

Colin Macalister was on his feet in an instant. Karen and Agnes showed their concern.

"I hope it's nothing too serious," Karen commented.

"We won't know 'til we get there," the Professor commented dryly.

"Anybody we know?" asked Colin.

Macdonald looked at Colin directly keeping his eyes fixed on him.

"It's Jens…he's had a set back."

"Oh no, oh my God!" Karen screamed.

Ross turned to Agnes.

"Agnes, please look after her, this might be serious and it may not. I have to go, but as soon as I know what's wrong you'll be the first to know."

"Right, I'll do what I can, please call me as soon as you know anything. Do you think we should come to the hospital?"

"No, no that's not necessary right now. As I said I'll be in touch once we have all the facts and we have examined Jens." He turned to Karen.

"Karen," this was the first time he had ever referred to her by her Christian name, "Karen, be brave, he's in the best place and in the best hands." With that he gave Karen an awkward hug and disappeared with Colin on his heels.

Karen thought she was going to throw up. She suddenly felt nauseous. My God, she thought, how can this be? Jens was doing so well. She sat, stunned, unable to move from the table. Other guests, clearly aware that something was awry, whispered animatedly amongst themselves. It was no secret that the famous Professor Macdonald had been dining with them and for him to leave in such a precipitate way affected everyone in the dining room. All eyes surreptitiously crept over towards Karen and Agnes. Bruno finally approached.

"Madame, is there anything at all I can do?"

"Thank you Bruno, Jens has had a setback,.....perhaps a prayer?"

"My deepest thoughts are with you Madame, and a candle will be lit for your son, he will be fine, I know this." And with that Bruno backed away to attend to the other diners.

It was eleven-thirty when Colin Macalister phoned the hotel and got put through to Karen who was sitting staring at a blank wall with Agnes equally as anxious sitting on the edge of a settee.

"Karen, it's Colin."

"How is he?"

"Not well. He's gone very blue again and his breathing is bad. His temperature is high and he's running a fever."

"My God Colin, you mean the operation hasn't worked?"

"No it's too early to say yet. The Professor is with him now. We've taken x-rays so we'll know very shortly what's wrong."

"Colin, can I, or can we, please come to the hospital. They'll be no sleep for anyone here tonight."

"I don't know if Ross would want that."

"Well to hell with Ross for a moment. This is *my* child, *my* baby. We'll be over."

Before an open mouthed Colin Macalister could say anything Karen slammed down the phone.

The hotel car once again made the journey but in half the usual time. Karen and Agnes decanted without the usual ceremony of having the doors held open for them. The night receptionist greeted them.

"Mrs. Ericsson, Mrs. Anderson, Doctor Macalister said to expect you. Will you please go to Ward Ten? It's on the second floor, Professor Macdonald will be there."

"Thank you." Karen took off almost running to the worn out elevator at the end of the corridor. Agnes, still in her tartan plaid, couldn't move so quickly but she needn't have rushed. Pressing the button on the antediluvian elevator elicited only a long hydraulic sigh as the machinery started to turn. The second floor corridor was empty when they arrived after an interminable wait for the lift. Karen made her way to Ward Ten, Agnes again bringing up the rear.

The Professor was in the middle of an empty ward. Karen wide eyed and in tears now feared the worst. She collapsed into the Professor's arms.

"There, there, lassie, he's going to be fine, he's going to be fine." Ross patted Karen's back as if she was some favorite sheepdog.

"Truly."

"Yes, truly. He's got a case of pneumonia, not that that's a good thing, but we can clear that up. He's in an oxygen tent right now. That's why we've moved him out of this ward back into intensive care. Come on, let me take you to him."

With that the Professor took Karen's arm and walked her the length of the institutional corridor to the section marked Intensive Care in bold blue letters. Karen and Agnes immediately saw Colin Macalister standing by a crib. There was an oxygen tent draped over the crib and an IV drip connected to Jen's little arm.

Karen couldn't help but rush up and hug Colin. Agnes stayed in the background watching.

"Colin, what's happened to my boy, look at him he's gone all blue again. Does this mean the operation hasn't worked?"

"Karen, you've not to worry, that's normal in a case like this."

"Colin, so far since I've come here nothing's been normal. This is a slice of life that I'm not used to handling...now if Red were here...."

Her words and the mention of Red stung Colin into retaliation.

"Look Karen, I know to you nothing's been normal, but we deal with this day and daily. You came over here looking for some miracle to make your son whole, and we've done our best. You have, believe me, the best man in the world at doing this sort of thing, and now you're inferring what we've done doesn't work, well frankly I resent that. Your son has an infection. It's affecting his pulmonary system, his lungs. He can't breathe properly and that's just the same as being a 'blue' baby".

"So what are you and the famous Professor going to do about it?"

"If you'd give me a moment to explain, I'll tell you. We've started Jens on a course of Penicillin, that should clear up the infection but it may take some days. The worst thing that could happen is that you won't be getting home anytime soon, not for New Year anyway."

"I don't really care when I get home, as long as it's with a healthy child. So there!"

The super pout came into maximum effect. God, Colin thought, she looks so beautiful when she does that, eyes blazing, ready to take the world on.

"Go home, go back to the hotel, there's nothing you can do here." Colin turned to Ross Macdonald, "Professor that's right isn't it."

"Absolutely. Mrs. Ericsson, thank you again for dinner I'm so sorry it should have ended in such unfortunate circumstances, but alas that's life. Jens will be fine. His condition is normal where there has been major surgery particularly in his run down state. Please, please, do not concern yourself. We shall meet tomorrow. I'll phone you myself, even Mrs. Sanderson gets a day off."

Agnes, still in the background nodded at the Professor's words. She moved forward and took Karen's arm and started walking towards the exit. Karen stopped.

"There's just one thing Agnes," with that she went towards the crib, lifted the tent and kissed her little son on the forehead.

"Goodbye my little angel, Mommy will see you in the morning." She turned abruptly biting her lip and joined Agnes who was by this time half way to the exit.

It had been a long sleepless night for both of them. The euphoria of having dinner with Ross Macdonald had completely evaporated in the wake of Jens's set back. Agnes had tried to reassure Karen that all would be well, but she could well understand the nagging doubt in Karen's mind that perhaps the operation had not been a success despite all the assurances from both doctors. Karen had finally got through to Red who was in Los Angeles for the weekend. Like Karen, he too was taken aback by Jens's condition. He could tell by Karen's metallic like voice she was just about at the end of her rope. Her spirits kept fluctuating between happiness and disaster. No amount of cajoling on Red's part could convince her that the pneumonia could be cured and that Jens would be fit and well again. She was in a dogged state of depression refusing all assurances of future improvement. Red had to eventually hang up the phone with Karen still in a subdued state. He was going over to Brett and Rosemary's for Sunday dinner, taking Lance with him and he was due there at six o'clock sharp. It was now two in the morning London time.

Karen decided to go to church, as it was Sunday. Peter the Concierge had suggested St. Paul's Cathedral, as it was quite the most prestigious Roman Catholic Church in England. Karen asked Agnes if she would like to join her and it was then that she discovered Agnes came from strong Presbyterian roots and regarded anything Papist as an anathema to society.

"I shall pray for Jens in my own way," she announced staunchly.

Karen backed off very quickly. She respected other religions. After all she had married Red, he was Protestant and it had never been an issue. Another of Agnes's hidden depths had come to the surface.

The service in St. Paul's was moving and spectacular and was held mainly in Latin that brought an almost overwhelming degree of pomp and circumstance to the proceedings. Karen made a generous donation to the church and asked one of the priests to pray for her son. As the day was bright and clear she decided to walk all the way back from Ludgate Hill to Claridges.

Her walk took the best part of three hours. She felt tired but at the same time invigorated by the walk. The fresh air had done her some good. James the regular doorman was not on duty but the relief doorman addressed her by her name as she entered the hotel.

"Good afternoon Mrs. Ericsson, did you enjoy your walk Madame?"

"Yes I did thank you. You said good afternoon, what time is it?"

"It's just past one thirty Madame. There's been a Mistress Anderson looking for you Madame and if I may say so she seemed rather agitated."

Good God thought Karen, its Jens, something else has gone wrong.

"Oh thank you eh…"

"Charles, Madame, at your service."

"Thank you Charles, I'll get hold of Mrs. Anderson right away."

Karen didn't wait to go to her room. She phoned Agnes from the hotel lobby.

"My God Karen, where have you been? We've been looking all over for you."

"I walked back from church, I'm sorry it took me much longer than I expected. What's wrong Agnes, Charles the doorman said you were looking for me."

"It's quite good news for a change. The hospital phoned. It was Joyce Potter. They've got Jens's temperature down, he's got some way to go yet, but he's on the mend. I wanted to tell you as soon as possible."

At that moment Karen believed in the power of prayer. Her attendance at Mass had been worthwhile. Thank you God, thank you God, was all she could think of saying to herself, over and over.

"What was that Karen?"

"I was just thinking aloud Agnes, I'm sorry. That's great news. Can we go to the hospital then?"

"Joyce didn't say you couldn't, but I think you'd be better to stay away. It only upsets you to see him lying there. Why don't we go tomorrow morning and give him another night to improve?"

"Yup. Let's do that Agnes. That darn hospital sure gets me upset."

The days came and went and the activity in the hotel became more frenzied as Christmas Day crept closer. By Christmas Eve Jens was almost back to normal. Karen's spirits rose like an emotional barometer buoyed by the recovery in her son. Telephone calls across the Atlantic took on the frequency of local calls. Karen didn't even contemplate the cost; she had to convey the good news to Red and to hear Red's voice assuring her that all was going to be well and that her homecoming was going to be so special he could almost taste it. Karen and Agnes had now been in the hotel for almost a fortnight and were on almost good friend terms with most of the staff. What Karen didn't divulge to the friendly staff Agnes did, because the kindly Londoners were so interested in Jens's well being she felt she it was akin to telling good news to good friends.

They had just returned from Brompton Hospital where Colin Macalister had said that if Jens's progress continued they could all go home early in the New Year, but not in time to celebrate New Year. Jens would probably not be released until the end of the first week in January. Agnes was upset and while she tried hard not to show her disappointment it became evident to Karen that she was saddened in not being able to honor her commitment to her sister in Vancouver that they would be together to bring in 1959. They were discussing this over dinner served in their suite when the phone rang and Peter the Concierge announced they had a visitor.

"A visitor? Who can that possibly be?" Karen could only think of Colin Macalister or Ross Macdonald bringing evil tidings on Christmas Eve.

"What does he look like Peter?"

"Very much like Father Christmas, Madame"

"You're kidding."

"Would I jest with you Madame?"

"Where's he from?" Agnes asked, thinking that it might well be another ruse by Rupert Bentley-Jones to gain access to Karen.

"Madame, he says your husband sends him to you. He has given me his business card and I can assure you his motive for being here is quite proper. I think it would be appropriate to say he is the bearer of gifts and good tidings."

My heavens, thought Karen, would the English ever stop their flamboyant way of speaking? "Peter that's wonderful, send the gentleman up, and what's his name?"

"Chris Cringle, Madame, it is not a name with which I'm familiar."

It was Red's doing all right. No one in England had heard of Chris Cringle.

"Okay Peter, lets cut the cackle; send the guy up."

"Right away Madame."

Two minutes later there was a soft tapping on the door.

"Come in." Karen called. Then she remembered that she would have to open the door from her side to let anyone in. She strode forward and yanked the door open. Sure enough there stood Father Christmas.

"Yo-Ho-Ho" cried the bearded messenger. "Merry Christmas to one and all!"

Karen and Agnes collapsed in gales of laughter they were sure to the man's embarrassment.

"Do please come in," Karen did her best to suppress her laughter.

"I bring you greetings from a far off land with a present for you, fair lady and for you dear lady."

Agnes noted the demotion from fair to dear but she nevertheless gladly accepted the beautifully wrapped package from Santa.

"Dear Ladies, may you have a wonderful Christmas and a Happy and Prosperous New Year," Santa continued to gush. "Oh, and there's one other thing I almost forgot, it's larger but it's for your little boy." A larger parcel appeared from under his tunic and Karen took it smiling.

"Please stay and have a drink with us, after all your working on Christmas Eve."

"Dear Ladies nothing would give me greater pleasure, but I have a family of my own who await my presence." And with a cheery wave he opened the door and was gone.

"Goodness me, I wonder what all this is about?" Agnes was itching to open her present. "Now when I was a little girl I wasn't allowed to open my presents until Christmas Day but I don't know what the American custom is. As far as I'm concerned to Hell with Glasgow protocol let's see what we've got."

Karen had been standing all this time as though mesmerized. She knew it was all Red's work. She gingerly picked up the small parcel and read the card. 'Aspreys, Bond Street,' on one side. 'To my Karen, Happy Christmas to my dearest darling' on the other. Tears came into her eyes. She had almost forgotten the spirit of Christmas with the concern over Jens's health and being so far away from her loved ones. What a wonderful surprise. She kept staring at the box, not wanting to do anything but hold something that came from Red.

Agnes broke the spell.

"Well, to open or not to open, that is the question?"

"The Hell with Scottish protocol. You open yours first Agnes."

"Right-oh'. Agnes tore at the paper to reveal an elegant slim dark blue box. There was a card inside. "To Agnes, for all you've done for the Ericsson family, wear these with pride.' Agnes gingerly prized open the box.

"Oh, my God Miss Karen, you're man's gone daft," lapsing into her Scottish brogue with all the excitement. Agnes held aloft a beautiful two strand pearl necklace.

"Oh, Agnes it's beautiful, so beautiful, it'll suit you perfectly. Now let's see what I've got."

Karen gently undid the ribbon around the small box and then carefully took apart the ornate wrapping paper to reveal a dark blue jewelry box. She pressed the little catch to open the lid and there, before her was the most exquisite sapphire surrounded by diamonds.

Agnes peered over Karen's shoulder, "My goodness miss, it must have cost a fortune!" she exclaimed. "Quick, try it on."

Karen removed the ring from the box and tried to put it on the fourth finger of her right hand. But try as she might the band-size was too small so she had to put it on her pinkie where it moved around being too slack. It looked totally out of place on her little finger. Nevertheless the ring was beautiful and Red must have guessed her ring size. Probably before she had the twins, she thought, it would have fitted perfectly.

"Oh, let's not worry Agnes, it's so beautiful and it's so kind of Red to think of us being here alone for Christmas. Let me try and call him right away and we both can thank him."

"What about the other parcel? What's in that?"

"Oh right, I'd forgotten all about that. Let's open that one." She looked at the card and it read, 'To Jens, our brave little soldier'. Out of the wrappings came a small teddy bear, but different from any other Karen had seen. It was dressed in a khaki British Army uniform; he had a British soldier's little tin hat with the name 'Tommy' written across the front. Around his midriff there was a bandage stained red on the left hand side and there was a white patch over one eye.

"Mercy me, isn't that the cutest thing you've ever seen," Agnes gasped. "What a wonderful wee teddy, wounded just like Jens, doesn't that just take the biscuit. That man of yours is really resourceful, how on earth do you think he got all these presents to us from about six thousand miles away. He must have had the teddy made especially for Jens and probably the ring for you and maybe even the pearls for me. We'll never be able to thank him enough."

Karen's eyes had completely misted up with Agnes words. She tried hard not to cry but it was all too much: the wonderful presents that had just made their Christmas special and the teddy for Jens that was so appropriate. She just let go and bawled. Tears streamed down her face as she let go all the pent up emotions inside her. Agnes went to the bar and poured them both a drink. So they sat down, Agnes smiling, sporting her new pearl necklace and Karen mopping up her tears, looking lovingly at her ring as they toasted one another the happiest of Christmas's. Eventually the Champagne and the malt Whisky proved too much for either and they both fell asleep on the large settee in the sitting room. The phone rang at just past two o'clock in the morning wakening them both. It was Red calling from Los Angeles. It had taken him ages to get through as everyone was phoning a loved one or ones on the other side of the Atlantic. The call went on forever. First Karen, then Agnes, effusive in her thanks, and then back to Karen to give Red more kisses for her wonderful ring. She said it looked wonderful and the size was perfect and what a wonderful man he was for remembering. She told Red how Jens was improving and how they hoped to be back early in the New Year. After forty-five minutes they finally hung up and staggered off to bed exhausted. It was already well into Christmas Day.

They left the hotel around mid-morning to go to the hospital and give Jens his special Christmas teddy. Karen could see the improvement in Jens every day now, clearly the crises was over and it was just a matter of time when he would be allowed out. Colin Macalister had said it would be best to have him at the hotel for a few days before subjecting him to the long flight home and he felt that if Jens's improvement continued he would get out on New Year's Day or just before. Karen decided that it was time for Agnes to return.

"Agnes, why don't you fly back for New Year and go to your sister's, please. I'm sure I can manage with Jens, he's going to be fine and the stewardesses are so nice on the plane they'll help me if I need any. Remember Jen's won't need all of the bits and pieces we came out with, he'll be in good health."

"Miss Karen, I couldn't think of leaving you here to cope. Think, if there's another set back, what about that? I'd be fair sick leaving you to cope on your own. I know Dorothy would like to see me, and I'd like to show off my pearls, but they'll be plenty of New Years in the future."

"Seriously Agnes, you should go. You've been real generous with your time. How about agreeing to this, that if Ross Macdonald or Colin Macalister says Jens is sure to get out on or before New Year, you'll go back. You would have to leave on the twenty-eight but that would get you to Vancouver just in time for the celebrations, what do you think?"

The idea was attractive to Agnes. Karen had never mentioned it but she was sure that for her to stay in the hotel was costing her a small fortune and she really would have liked to see her elder sister who hadn't been in good health recently. She weighed up all the factors and decided to take Karen's offer.

Boxing Day came and went and Karen discovered that it had nothing to do with anyone fighting in a ring but a British Victorian or Edwardian era tradition of sending the domestic staff home with boxes of presents on the day after Christmas as a reward to them for having been on duty on Christmas Day.

Two days later Karen hugged Agnes on a blustery, cold winter's day at Heathrow Airport as she prepared to take the return flight to Los Angeles. She bade her final farewell waving to someone who had become a firm friend. She had this sudden feeling of emptiness now that Agnes was gone.

On December the thirty-first, Hogmanay to Agnes, she picked up Jens from Brompton Road hospital and brought him to the hotel. He looked wonderful. His little green eyes shone as she carried him into the hotel lobby with the staff lined up on either side of the foyer to form a phalanx to welcome the little boy. Both Ross Macdonald and Colin Macalister had said their farewells at the hospital however Colin had said he might look round in the next two or three days just to see that Jens had adjusted from his long stay in hospital and to show Karen how to change the dressing that covered his wound. Joyce Potter had already spent some time with Karen going over the procedure and Karen hadn't said a word to Colin as she had secretly hoped he might visit her before she returned home.

New Year 1959, the last year of the decade, came in with a bang. Karen could hear the noise from the revelers as they went from street to street carousing and singing until well after midnight. Jens was feeding well enough from the bottle now and she had just put him down to sleep in the small hours of the morning when the phone rang. She assumed it was Red but she had an even better surprise when she found it was Agnes on the other end.

"It's not New Year here yet, she shouted down the phone, we've still got six hours to go but I took the chance that you wouldn't be in bed, it's so lovely to talk to you." Agnes shouted down the phone. "I tried at Midnight, your time to get through but all the lines were busy. How's my wee boy?"

"Oh, Agnes, it's so lovely to hear from you too. Jens is just fine. He's put on quite a bit of weight and he's got such rosy cheeks, you'd be proud of him. How's your sister and how's Vancouver?"

"Well my sister is fine. She's so pleased to see me and I must thank you again for letting me come back for New Year. Vancouver's fine too except it's been raining a bit today but it's not too cold. We're going to have a grand old time this evening."

"Well that's great Agnes. I'll talk to you when I get back, I expect it's going to be in about ten days time. The doctors want to make sure Jens is strong enough to make the trip."

"Quite right Miss Karen you don't want to take any chances. All the best and Happy New Year, Cheerio then!" And Agnes was gone off to celebrate her Hogmanay.

Karen had to laugh at the 'Cheerio' bit. Agnes didn't use it very often but it was amusing when she did. Karen guessed correctly that it was a strange Scottish way of saying good-bye. The 'phone call made her homesick, but only for a moment, soon she would be heading for home a week from today Karen calculated. She couldn't wait.

Colin Macalister called on Sunday late morning to say he had some free time in the afternoon if he could call. Karen was delighted. Life in the hotel had become so boring without Agnes. Jens tied her down more than she had thought. She was no longer free to roam around London and she began to wish she hadn't insisted so strongly that Agnes go home. That was being uncharitable she told herself, Agnes had been a loyal companion and given her the most wonderful support when she needed it most. She decided that she would dress up for Colin. She chose a pinafore dress in deep blue corduroy and she wore it over a polo necked sweater which she thought accentuated her breasts to the full. Her hair was longer than when she arrived in London. Just over pageboy length it sat alluringly on her shoulders. Her deep brown eyes, a little mascara, the bright vermilion slash of lipstick accentuated her good looks to the full. The sheerest nylons complimented her slim legs and the dark blue shoes completed the outfit. I look absolutely ravishing, she told herself.

It was 3 o'clock when Colin arrived. When Karen opened the door Colin Macalister melted almost completely. He had never seen any-one quite so stunning. He had seen Karen in all sorts of situations. The stressed out mother, the hostess at dinner in December, the flirtatious American at the hospital, as Joyce had called her. But this was different;

she was looking like a film star. It was the only expression he could think of that fitted the woman standing before him.

"My God," he said, "you look…you look stunning." He stammered. He was not at all prepared for this. He had had erotic dreams about Karen and he had decided that he would be very professional and stay aloof from whatever little innuendos Karen might throw in his way. He knew she was flirting with him, and he knew she was unattainable, but this was different. This was open warfare on a new front.

"Colin, it's so good of you to come". She was getting used to English mannerisms and style. She grasped his hand and led him into the sitting room of the suite.

"I've ordered afternoon tea, it'll be here real…sorry, shortly."

"Oh, oh, that'll be fine."

"Or would you like anything stronger."

"Oh Lord no. I'm still on duty until midnight tonight."

"For Heaven's sake Colin, when did you come on duty?"

"Well it's been one of those weekends, Saturday at seven o'clock."

"You mean in the evening?"

"No, the morning."

"My God, you must be exhausted. Sit down, let me take your jacket." Karen removed Colin's jacket and then set about loosening his tie. God, she smells wonderful, Colin thought as Karen's heady perfume floated over him like an inviting mist.

The knock on the door broke Colin's reverie. The waiter entered with a trolley full of scones, crumpets, tea breads of all varieties and French Cakes covered in white fondant, beautifully decorated with piped chocolate and marzipan.

"Cream sir?" The waiter was pouring.

"No thank you, just as it is will be fine."

"This is Doctor Macalister Tim," Karen addressed the waiter. "He's come to check up on Jens."

"Quite so Madame, quite so, Madame." Karen was sure Tim didn't believe one word of it. He had already drawn his own conclusions from

Karen's dress and Colin's glazed eyes. "Is that to your liking Doctor", as he placed the black sugarless tea on the table at Colin's side.

"Fine, thank you."

"Will that be all Madame?"

"Thank you, Tim."

The waiter bowed and exited.

"Well, let's start with who I really came to see. How is he?"

"Wait a minute Colin, what do you mean by 'who you really came to see'. You mean you didn't come to see me. Gee what an insult! I'm hurt, very hurt."

"No I didn't mean it like that, I meant in a professional capacity."

"Oh really?"

"Well I mean you're not the one who's sick, are you?"

"How do you know?"

"Well look at you, you're the picture of health and beauty." Colin frantically tried to retrieve the situation, but Karen had other plans.

"How do you not know that I need your medical help desperately?"

Oh, Christ, thought Colin here we go. "I don't of course. I would do anything for you and you know that." He couldn't believe the words as they poured out of his mouth.

"Colin, really, you are the greatest guy, truly. You know, I think more about you than you realize?"

"No, no I didn't know that…in fact I don't think I want to know that."

"Why not? You're talented, *very* attractive and single." Karen kneeled by his chair.

"But you're a married woman."

"Well I know, but I'm here all alone in a strange land. Who knows when we might meet again?

"I was going to talk to you about that." Suddenly Colin was all business. "Do you think there arc openings for people like me in the United States?"

Crap, thought Karen, that's what this is all about, getting to the States. But then she remembered Ross Macdonald's words. 'If I were you I'd keep in with him, Jens will need surgery at some time in the future.'

"Well sure, sure; they'd welcome a man of your caliber there in a heartbeat. Jeeps, there's a pun in there somewhere. Would you like me to do something for you? I know a lot of people who would be glad to talk to you and my father knows even more."

Colin nodded his head as if to accentuate Karen's every word. He was now on his third crumpet following the demolition of four scones, the poor man was starved. Karen got up from her kneeling position and refilled his empty teacup.

"That would be great," he said with his mouth half full. "Aren't you going to eat anything, Karen, these crumpets are really good."

"No I'm not. I'm going to have a glass of Champagne and I hope you'll join me."

"No, no. I can't do that. Remember I'm still on duty".

"Until when?"

"Midnight."

"Well pick up the 'phone and call the hospital and find out what's going on. It's now four o'clock, so that's eight hours to go. You haven't slept, I can see that, and you probably could do with a hot shower."

A hot shower and a nap did it for Colin. He was dead on his feet. The hotel rooms were so luxurious compared to his bed-sit in Kensington he didn't dare dwell too long on the subject.

Karen just smiled her most fetching smile. "Come on then, finish that last French Cake and here's where you go."

"Wait 'til I call the hospital."

Colin handled the situation well. He explained that he was with Mrs. Ericsson and Jens and that he would be delayed as there was a slight problem with the little boy's dressing. Any emergencies were to be passed to him at this number. He was assured by the hospital that all was quiet and that he would be called if needed.

The bathroom was large and opulent. Karen had even laid out a hotel toweling robe for him when he got out of the shower. He showered and shampooed and in fifteen minutes he felt like a new man. He was just about to get out of the bathroom when there was a gentle knock on the door. He opened it gently to have a flute of Champagne pressed into his hand.

"Thank you, Karen." Was all he could manage to say. The Champagne was ice cold and delicious. I could get used to this sort of life, he told himself. He finished combing his hair and went back into the sitting room of the suite. Karen was stretched out on the couch with a glass too. The pinafore dress had been replaced by a diaphanous silver negligee that had been carefully draped over her body to provide maximum allure with minimum exposure with the exception of one leg, which was exposed up to the thigh.

"Ah, there you are!" Colin stammered again stating the obvious. "I think I'll just get out of this robe, which is very nice, by the way, but I think it might be more appropriate if I was dressed."

"Colin, shut up and come over here," Karen beckoned him towards her with her index finger. "Sit down." She swung her legs round and put her feet on the carpet to make room for him. Colin did as he was bid. He could hear his heart pounding so hard he was sure Karen could hear it too.

"Colin, I thought you might just give me a hug or even a cuddle before I go back to Los Angeles. I would like something more than just your professionalism and good looks to remind me of you."

"I don't suppose there's any harm in giving you just a hug," his words sounded less than convincing, his voice thick with lust, almost breathless. He put down the almost empty glass of Champagne on one of the side tables. Karen got up very slowly, made for the bottle in the ice bucket, and came back to give him a refill. She had said nothing. She stood with the bottle still in her hand.

"Doctor Macalister, please stand up." Colin obeyed. Karen took his now full glass and put it back on the table. She gently put her hands on his wrists and pulled him to her. It was too much for Colin; he could feel himself being aroused immediately. He freed both his hands and wrapped his arms round Karen. The silk silver negligee accentuated her firm body. He could feel her breasts rising and falling as he bent over and kissed her full on the lips. What happened after that was almost a blur. Karen's tongue searched for his as they kissed again and again. All the pent up emotions they had for one anther were released in an unstoppable flow. The negligee fell open and he put his hands inside 'til he felt the small of her back. Nothing had ever felt so good to Colin in his life. Her skin was so smooth and the natural perfume of her femininity overpowering. Gently she lifted his right hand and placed on her left breast. Colin was having a problem containing himself. As he caressed her gently any self-restraint left him and his tumescent phallus sprang through the toweling robe. Karen felt his moist erection on her leg. She stood back from him slightly, looked down demurely and said,

"We'll have to do something about that, won't we?"

She led him to the bedroom and as she moved across the floor her negligee fell from her leaving her totally naked. Picking it up she threw it casually over the bedside lamp dimming it to a glow. Colin dropped the dressing gown in a frantic rush but Karen slowed him down. She sat on the edge of the bed and stopped him so that he stood in front of her. "Take me like this, Colin, it's much more thrilling."

Thirty minutes later they made love again. This time slower and more conventionally until Karen had her complete satisfaction.

"Thank you darling that was marvelous," she kissed him again.

"What time is it?" Colin asked.

"About seven-thirty, darling"

"My God, that late, I've got to get back to the hospital, I've got things to do before I hand over to John Cochrane who takes over from me. Will you be okay?"

Karen thought, my God typical male, wham, bam, thank you ma'am and off. But she smiled sweetly and said,

"Of course, I'll miss you, Colin, but I'll be fine. Please come and see me one more time before I leave. Then with any luck we'll meet again in California."

"When do you leave?"

"Thursday, four days from today. I want to get your résumé to take back to Los Angeles with me.

"Oh, right, you mean my CV?"

"No, I mean your résumé"

"It's the same thing. We call it a CV in Britain."

"What does it stand for?"

"Curriculum Vitae. It's Latin."

"What does it mean?"

"Résumé" Colin laughed.

"No seriously, what does it mean?"

"It means an outline of a person's educational and professional history."

"That's a résumé!"

"All right, Miss America, you win, but I've got to go. I'll bring my paperwork to you on Tuesday and I'll have some medication you can give Jens to keep him quiet for at least some of the trip, oh and I'll personally change his dressing. ......and Karen, darling, thank you for everything."

Colin left the hotel feeling exhilarated and ashamed all at the same time. He had just committed the most egregious breach of professionalism and he wondered what the ultimate consequences might be if anyone were to find out.

The weather had turned bitterly cold in the first week of the New Year. A biting north wind blew out of a crystal blue sky as the hotel car took Jens and Karen to Heathrow airport for the trip back to Los Angeles. The farewells at the hotel had been long and emotional. Karen had kissed Colin goodbye when he had called in with Jens's medication for the long flight to the United States. Still shy and embarrassed about his lack of self-control on the previous Sunday, he was distant and cool. Their conversation was stilted and it was obvious to Karen that Colin couldn't wait to leave.

The Transoceanic Boeing 377 Stratocruiser had come into Heathrow two days previously and, having given the Captain some concern with performance, had to have maintenance carried out to the Hamilton Standard propellers on engines three and four. All pilots flying Stratocruisers recognized that both the 377's engines and propellers were, at the very least, temperamental and had caused the loss of several aircraft due to the problems associated with one or the other. In fact Pilots referred to the Stratocruiser as the best three-engine plane to cross the Atlantic. The main problems related to the four water-injected Pratt and Whitney cylinder radial R-4360 engines, which could overheat sometimes without warning and the Hamilton Standard propellers that suffered from unpredictable material failure. Both the engines and propellers were at the height of piston airliner technology.

Hank Kelly, a laconic forty-six year old six-foot-six Texan, who was the Captain of Transoceanic flight 27 back across the Atlantic, arrived from his Heathrow hotel at seven-thirty in the morning. He wanted to make sure that the maintenance items he had ordered had been carried out. His schedule was to leave Heathrow and refuel for the Trans-Atlantic trip at Prestwick in Scotland, then fly to Gander, then on to Idlewild, thence to Chicago and finally to Los Angeles. New York was as far as he went and he was looking forward to taking in a Broadway show while in New York. He had a crew of eleven with only twenty-seven passengers, one of them an infant. The configuration of this Stratocruiser was for 50 seats with a rear fuselage Stateroom on the lower deck which could sleep three adults and which had been reserved for a Mr. and Mrs. Ericsson. This particular airliner had sleeping berths for all of the passengers. The interior of the plane was tastefully decorated and boasted both a lady's and a gentleman's dressing room.

Hank checked the work on the engines and props as best he could. The crew chief took him round the engines and showed him the work that had been done, it all looked okay to Hank. Take-off was scheduled for nine-thirty that morning so he went to the Pilot's Mess to meet with the rest of his crew. His crew consisted of his co-pilot, flight engineer, radio operator and navigator. He had flown with all of the crewmembers many times but the navigator John Brock was new to him. The remaining crewmembers were all stewardesses who had been flying for Transoceanic for nearly over six years. Hank was a well-respected Captain with over 13,000 hours on Stratocruisers.

By nine o'clock all the passengers had cleared immigration and were on board the aircraft. Hank had already warmed up the engines so that the cabin interior was warm. It was still bitterly cold outside. Snow, which was already falling in parts of Scotland, was forecast for London later in the day. Karen and Jens, now looking the picture of health, were ensconced in the rear lower deck stateroom that boasted its own lavatory and a fine view.

At just after nine-thirty Transoceanic 27 took off, the four engines at full-throttle lifting the 142,000-pound airliner into the bright January sky. Karen felt a rush of elation. She was on her way home...at last. On her final day at the hotel Ross Macdonald came to see her and Jens, and, for the last time, changed Jens dressing, patted the baby politely on the head and gallantly kissed her hand wishing her Bon Voyage.

"Tell Doctor Crawford to call me at any time if there are any problems with Jens and also if he has any patients as fine as you." He allowed himself one of his characteristic thin wintry smiles. Karen beamed back, flashing her perfect white teeth.

She settled down with Jens who was in his carrycot gurgling away happily as the stewardess brought a full English breakfast with lashings of good hot coffee. It was so nice to have American coffee again, even Claridges didn't know how to make decent coffee and anything else she had tried in England had been a milky mixture that tasted of chicory.

The bright sunshine at takeoff was soon replaced by thin gray cloud and the flight to Prestwick took just over two hours because of a strong headwind. There was thicker low cloud with flurries of snow as they reached the west coast of Scotland. Hank eased the Stratocruiser into the Prestwick approach stack at 5,000 feet and Ground Control Approach began talking him down for an instrument landing on Runway 31. Hank was talked down to about 500 yards of the runway's threshold until he had visual contact.

"Landing flaps. Full flap. Landing lights on," he called out to the co-pilot as he tried to steady the plane, which was being buffeted by the strong northeasterly wind.

The Stratocruiser touched down safely, the propellers thrust into reverse, and the brakes applied. The passengers were invited to stay on the aircraft for re-fueling, which they were told would not take long. The Stratocruiser was the first commercial airliner to have an under-wing manifold-type fueling system. 7,500 US gallons of fuel could be pumped in fifteen minutes or less.

Seven more passengers joined the aircraft at Prestwick chatting away amiably to the London passengers as they came on board, thankful to be out of the cold. Forty minutes later Transoceanic flight 27 took off again at fifteen minutes past noon heading northwest up Scotland on the way to Gander in Newfoundland. The great airplane was buffeted badly after take off and Karen, in the tail section, was tossed around as the tail yawed from side to side in the gale. Hank leveled the plane off at 23,000 feet. He would climb to 28,000 to cross the Atlantic once he had burned off fuel and the aircraft was lighter. Now they were almost straight into the wind and above the worst of the clouds. The constant buffeting stopped as the Stratocruiser's cruising speed was reduced from the normal 300 miles per hour to about 270. The next section of the flight would be boring and Hank handed over to his first officer and headed for the galley and some coffee. After talking to some of the stewardesses he decided to go and introduce himself to the passengers. His walk-about was hugely popular. Hank was film star material and he molded himself on John Wayne, who was a becoming a very popular actor in the movie industry. Having covered the upper deck he thought he would take a look at what he thought would be the honeymoon cou-ple in the stateroom. He tipped his cap to the passengers who were now lounging in the lower cabin where the bar was installed as they smoked and drank to while away the eight hours it would take them to reach Gander. When he reached the stateroom Kathy, the stewardess respon-sible for that section, warned him to be quiet and not waken the baby.

"Baby," said Hank, "whose the baby?" really thinking Kathy was mak-ing a joke about the occupants.

"No really Captain, it's Mrs. Ericsson and her young son, he's only three months old and he's had major heart surgery by a top English surgeon." Ross Macdonald would have turned white at being referred to as English.

"No kiddin'" Hank was fascinated. He gently tapped on the state-room door. Karen opened the door gently and looked into the tall Tex-an's face.

"You must be the Captain, it's Hank, Hank Kelly, isn't it?"

"Muh pleasure ma'am," Hank was even more fascinated.

"You seem to know more about this flight than me, I guess"

"No, not really, you know Mats Frosteman I think?"

"'Deed Ah do ma'am, Mats and me go back a long, long ways. Now how in tarnation would you know Mats?"

"My husband works for Mats."

"Well Ah'll be doggone. Ericsson, that sure don't ring any bells for me, what's your man's first name?"

"Red."

"Jesus…pardon me ma'am, Ah mean, bless muh soul. You mean you're the li'l lady Red's bin talking about. Ah jes cain't believe that. Ah know Red real well. Many-a-night we've tied one on…well ah mean we've had a few refreshments like ma'am. Ah never knew his last name was Ericsson"

"Hank, first of all I know my husband, he can well and truly 'tie one on' secondly can you quit this ma'am nonsense and call me Karen?"

"Well now, you are his li'l ole' lady an' no mistake. Muh pleasure Karen." Hank stuck out his hand. Karen shook it politely.

"Ah've got to be gettin' back to the flight deck right now, but why don't we meet later an' have a li'l ole chat about Red and Mats an' yor li'l baby here. He's doin' fine, so Ah hear."

"He's much better Hank, and he'll be much better when we get back to Los Angeles."

"Amen to that ma'am…Ah mean….Karen. Muh pleasure."

And at that precise moment the plane began to have severe buffeting and strong vibrations running through the airframe.

"Told yah", yelled Hank as he sped off up the spiral stair to the upper deck.

Hank got to the flight deck in a matter of seconds, it was as if all bedlam had let loose. The second officer was yelling at the flight engineer as he fought to control the aircraft, and the radio operator was shouting at the First Officer. The only person who was quiet was John, the navigator, who was pouring over his route map.

"What's goin' on Bill," Hank yelled at the co-pilot.

"Number one engine's oversped." Bill Phillips replied, "That's what's causing the vibration."

"Feather the son-of-a-bitch then," said Hank as he climbed into his seat. "I have control," he called to the First Officer as he placed his hands on the control column.

"She won't feather, that's the problem, and she's not responding to the throttle at all."

"Okay, got ya'" Hank thought quickly.

"Chris," he called over his right shoulder to the flight engineer, whose seat was at right angles to the pilots' seats, "starve number one of oil, and let's shut her down."

"Okay Captain, will do."

The action Chris took did stop the engine, but the rogue propeller continued to refuse to feather and was now windmilling slowing their airspeed from 270 miles per hour to about 175 mph. The 'plane was descending at more than 1,000 feet per minute from 21,000 feet.

"Where's the nearest airport, son?" Hank called out to the young navigator.

"The closest to us is Dalcross, Inverness, on the east coast, sir."

"How far?"

"I'm just trying to work that out sir, I'm not exactly sure of where we are."

"Shit," said Hank under his breath. "Get a back bearing from Prestwick and don't take too long son, 'cause that's where we've got to head."

Hank continued to fight with the Stratocruiser for the next five minutes by which time the altimeter told him he was now below 10,000 feet.

"I need that fix, son," he called out to the navigator.

"Frank, send out a Mayday," Hank instructed the radio operator.

"Heading zero nine fiver Skipper," John Brock called out.

"Thank you son, will do. Now where the hell are we?"

"Take over Bill, while I have a look-see." Hank scrambled out of the captain's seat and staggered over to John Brock's station.

"Show me, son, where you think we are."

"About here", John stabbed the map in front of him with his index finger.

"Show me Dalcross."

"Over here. It's about sixty miles, sir."

"And you've got us here." Hank's finger pointed to a place on the north-west Coast of Scotland with an unpronounceable name.

"Yes, sir near Shiel...., something sir." John tried to figure out how to say Shieldaig.

"Okay, the heading you gave me will take us almost due east." And with that Hank went back and took control again.

"Chris, let's see if we can get some more power out of these engines as we're losing too much altitude. John tells me we're less than sixty miles away from Inverness, that's Dalcross Airport and we'll have to dump most of our fuel before we land. So we're gonna be busy."

At that Hank gently eased open the throttles on number two and number four engines. At that point things went from awful to terrible. Number four engine backfired and stopped making power. Chris quickly shut the engine down and successfully feathered the propeller. Transoceanic's Enterprise of the Skies was reduced to a two engine aircraft. Things on the flight deck were now desperate. The weather was appalling and the aircraft was being buffeted severely. The plane was now heading almost due east in an attempt to reach the Moray Firth, Dalcross's location.

In the main cabin people were terrified. Because of the darkness and the foul weather they could just make out that only two of the engines were working and that the plane was descending rapidly. The stewardesses worked hard at trying to quiet the passengers and for the most part they did a good job, telling them how many hours Captain Hank Kelley had flown and what a great pilot he was. Karen sat in her stateroom looking out at the snow that was now visible, as the Captain had put on the landing lights. Jens was fast asleep in his little carrycot with Red's sapphire ring strung on a piece of ribbon round his neck. Karen had devised this as a safe place to keep the ring as she thought it would act as a good luck charm until she got it sized to fit her back home.

What happened next was almost entirely due to the inexperience of John Brock the young navigator. The extra time he had taken to establish the aircraft's position had put them on a course traveling almost due east up Glen Torridon. Hank had just said to Bill, his second in command,

"Jeez, Ah sure hope we make this, ain't there mountains in this part of Scotland?"

Those were to be his last words as the wallowing Stratocruiser hit the very summit of Beinn Eighe. The crash tore the bottom section of the plane off as the two remaining engines pulled the aircraft left and forward. The port wing split from the fuselage rupturing the fuel tanks and the whole of the front section of the plane exploded in a huge fireball as it catapulted the remaining 1,500 feet into the corrie below. The passengers never had any chance of survival, for those whose necks were not broken immediately upon impact the remainder were blown to smithereens in the subsequent explosion. Death came so suddenly, not one passenger had even uttered a scream as their lives suddenly ended. The clock on the destroyed flight deck stopped at 14:18 hrs.

Back in Los Angeles a devastated Red Ericsson could barely bring himself to telephone Brett and Rosemary Stahlman. The news had been vague at first, Transoceanic had called and said that the plane was over-due but that there had been some severe weather in the area and that in all probability the plane had made an emergency landing somewhere. That had been Saturday evening. Red had been expecting Karen and Jens to arrive the following evening at Los Angeles airport. By Sunday late morning a representative from the airline had visited Red with the grim news that the aircraft was indeed missing but that there was no news of where it might be. So Red was slightly more prepared for the truth when it finally hit, he would never see Karen and Jens again. He just *had* to call and at least warn them that there might be bad news.

It was Luz, the Mexican maid that answered the phone. "Mees Rose-mary no heer sir, you wanna speak meester Stahlman?"

"Yes, that would be fine Luz, thank you."

"Red how are ya' son," Brett's bluff voice bellowed down the 'phone.

Red told him everything as quickly as he could. There was a long silence.

"Jesus Christ," Brett's voice was barely a whisper, "But there could still be hope, Red couldn't there?"

"A slim chance, it's all we've got to hang on to….I mean what do they mean by 'missing'" Red's voice was cracking as he thought about the worst. Brett said nothing for a while and then said, "I'm coming over".

Father and son-in-law sat in stunned silence, each holding a drink, which remained, untouched as they watched the television news. The second item to come up was a report on the missing Stratocruiser, pic-tures of the Stratocruiser were flashed on the screen as they repeated the Transoceanic message of "missing" somewhere in the North of Scot-land. A report on the weather at the time was also given but there was no further news available. Red went through to the nursery and looked down at the sleeping Lance, looking all nice and warm in his little cot. The room was decked in yellow ribbons and cuddly toys for Jens's homecoming. Red's eyes filled at the very thought of what might never be for both his beloved wife and infant son. He went back through to the Den to sit with Brett. They sat into the wee small hours talking inconsequential rubbish hoping against hope that there might be good news. Eventually, exhausted by worry, Red fell asleep and Brett went home. He would tell Rosemary in the morning when she came back from a trip to Sacramento.

Red wakened early on Monday morning with a bitter sinking feeling in the pit of his stomach and a blinding headache. Going into the bathroom he popped a couple of Alka-Seltzer into a glass and could hardly wait for the fizzing to stop before he drank. What the hell, I can't go on like this, he thought, I'll phone the airline.

He was put through to the nicest of ladies at a special department set up by Transoceanic to handle calls from the next of kin.

"Mr. Ericsson, Red Ericsson is that correct sir?" Beverly Schwartz was a sympathetic and well-trained psychologist employed by the airline for eventualities just like this.

"Yes that's me," Red confirmed.

"Mr. Ericsson, there is someone scheduled to come over to speak with you later today, will you be in?"

"Well sure I will, I just wondered if you had an update on the status of Karen's flight?"

"Well yes we have Mr. Ericsson, but I'm not authorized to give those details over the 'phone."

"Jesus Christ woman, why not? That's got to mean it's bad news, eh?"

"It's not very encouraging Mr. Ericsson, I have to say that."

"Can I come over and talk to you? I mean I would like to know right now whether my wife and son are alive or dead, can you do that for me?"

Beverly gave her location at Los Angeles airport to the emotionally drained Red and he said he'd be with her in half an hour. Red found the office faster than he had reckoned and he was sitting in front of Beverly in less than twenty minutes from leaving home.

"I'm Beverly Schwartz, Mr. Ericsson, please call me Beverly." In any other set of circumstances Red would have warmed to Beverly, she was a very attractive lady. At thirty-seven she had a slim build with short bobbed blond hair, blue eyes and a retroussé nose. People sometimes mistook her for Doris Day, the film actress. She thought she actually looked better than Doris Day but she kept those thoughts to herself. She sported a ring on her engagement finger but no wedding band.

"Call me Red as well, it saves time."

"All right Red, as you surmised it's not good news. The wreckage was located today in a remote part of Scotland. The RAF has sent helicopters to the crash scene and right now I have to tell you there are no signs of survivors. However," Beverly rushed on, "it was late in the day when they found the aircraft and it gets dark at about three-thirty in the afternoon it's so far north so they haven't had a chance to do a full reconnoiter of the crash site. The weather's been a factor as well but it's improved and it should be clear tomorrow."

"Do you mind if I smoke?" Red was reeling from the news.

"No, not at all, feel free." Beverly pushed an ashtray towards him.

"Mr. Ericsson...Red, I'm real sorry, I don't know what to say."

"There's nothing you can say Beverly, I don't envy your job, have you had a lot of this?"

"No this is the first bad accident Transoceanic has ever had. Something real serious must have happened as Hank Kelley, the pilot, was one of our most experienced."

"You mean Hank Kelly from Houston, Texas was flying that plane?"

"Do you know Mr. Kelly?"

"I most certainly do, he was a close buddy of my boss Mats Frosteman and he and I had many a good night on the town. That's just awful, I can't tell you what a nice guy he was the girls just all loved Hank."

"Yes indeed they did, Red."

"So you knew him as well?"

"This is Hank's ring", Beverly held up her left hand to show off the baguette diamond, "we were engaged to be married."

"Jesus, I'm so sorry, now I feel terrible and you've got this job to do."

"Yup". Beverly was trying to keep control but her bottom lip was quivering.

Red stood up, reached out, and held her hand tight not saying a word.

"It's hard you know." A tear quietly ran down her cheek. Red produced a clean handkerchief and gently mopped it up.

"Yup," said Red and they sat back down together.

"Okay, I'm all right now. Here's what's going to happen. By tomorrow morning, which will be about four o'clock in the afternoon in Scotland we will be preparing a 'plane, to fly all the relatives who want to go, to Scotland. I assume you would want to be on that?"

"Dead right."

"Anyone else in your family?"

"Oh yes, I don't know whether Karen's mother will go, but I could bet Brett Stahlman Karen's father will most certainly want to go."

"Is that Stahlman the movie producer?"

"Yes it is. And Karen was his only child."

"Don't 'was' just yet Red, we can't give up hope."

"Beverly, I hear you, but even if someone managed to survive in that weather they'd surely die of exposure? Don't you think?"

"Yes I suppose your right and without details we just don't know anything. If part of the fuselage remained intact it could provide shelter, you never know."

With that one remaining hope in his heart, more than in his mind, Red took off to the Stahlman residence. It was now about nine-thirty in the morning. It was going to be a long day. Red found Rosemary Stahlman in a state of utter grief. She lay in her bed weeping uncontrollably. Brett had already sent for his pal, the studio doctor, to give her a sedative before she did something stupid. There was nothing Red could do by staying but he told Brett of his meeting with Beverly Schwartz and the offer by Transoceanic to fly all the relatives to Scotland. He would have more news in the morning. Brett said he would go with the provision that Rosemary had stabilized to the point where he felt he could leave her. Red had never seen Brett in a grimmer mood. But at least he was keeping his emotions under control.

Red got home just before twelve. He checked on the Nanny and then peeked in to see Lance who was already trying to move around at just at three months. His little legs kicked the air and he continually clenched and unclenched his hands. He was a big drooler too. Time and time again 'Bendy Wendy' as Red had christened her wiped his mouth in a vain attempt at keeping it dry. But he still developed a little rash round his lips by the end of the day. He told Wendy the news about the 'plane. Although she had only met Karen once when she was interviewed for the job, Wendy immediately burst into tears and fled from the room. My God, thought Red, that's all I need.

Going into his study he 'phoned Mats and told him the story of Hank and Karen and Jens. Mats was stunned as well. He could hardly talk.

"Red," his voice shaking I can't believe your lovely wife might be gone along with Jens, after the successful operation, what a waste, what a Goddamn waste and then Hank, my God what a day. We've all lost loved ones. Hank Kelley was probably my best buddy. He was engaged you know to a very pretty girl, well lady she was about six or seven years his junior, I've seen photographs of her. She's an absolute peach. She works for Transoceanic too, but they kept their engagement a secret as the airline doesn't like to see its employees getting together, if you know what I mean."

"You mean Beverly Schwartz?" Red dropped the bomb.

"Yeah, yeah exactly, do you know her?"

Red told him the story. Mats told Red to take any leave of absence he might want to get everything taken care of. Red thanked him profusely and said he'd make up the lost time when he got back to Houston. He just didn't know though when that might be. Then Mats said a strange thing to him.

"You know, you might be better off in Houston with Lance, I can't imagine you living in L.A. with the in-laws, you might want to think about that."

That was Mats all right. Don't beat around the bush. It was almost like telepathy, for Red in his waking hours, and there had been many, had considered what he would do with his life now that Karen was not coming back and living in Los Angeles was not one of them.

He had just put the phone down from speaking with Mats when the 'phone rang.

"Red Ericsson." He picked it up.

"Mr. Ericsson, Red is that you."

Right away he knew the voice by the Scottish burr.

"Agnes, Agnes Anderson, how are you?"

"Red, I'm fine. But I just heard where a Transoceanic flight, like the one I was on with Karen has gone missing over Scotland. I just hope and pray that's not the one wee Jens and his mother were on, is it?"

"Agnes, I don't know how to tell you this, but it is that plane. I think we've lost them."

Hang on fella, he said to himself, as he felt his voice choke up again.

There was no reply from the other end.

"Agnes, Agnes, are you there?"

"I'll have to call you back," was all Agnes could manage to say in a voice choking with tears and emotion. The phone went dead.

Red pulled out his big handkerchief and wiped his misting eyes for the umpteenth time. Agnes must be blaming herself for coming home to celebrate New Year that was the type of person she was. She would have been on that flight with Karen and she would have perished as well, but she wouldn't think of it that way, it would be more to Agnes like a desertion in the face of danger, which was all complete nonsense, but he was right, those were Agnes's feelings precisely.

It was almost an hour later after he had placated Wendy the tall gangly Nanny from Lancashire, when Agnes called back. She had taken a grip on her emotions and she asked all about the possibilities that the airline had got things wrong. Red told her of his visit to the airport that day leaving out certain details. Was there anything she could do? Agnes had asked. Red said he wished there were. Then he had an idea.

"Agnes, I'm going to go to Scotland with Mr. Stahlman to fetch Miss Karen and Jens home and if you could maybe just look in to see if Wendy is okay with Lance, that would be great."

"It'll be my pleasure Red, and if I think I need to stay with Wendy then I shall, Lance will get the best of care."

"Thanks Agnes. I'll leave a spare set of keys with Wendy so you can come and go at any time. The rates will be just the same as I paid you before, if that's okay."

"Indeed it's not okay. You'll not pay me a penny; this family's been so generous with me I can't think of any way to repay you. All I can do is offer my services, and I just so hoped it would be to Miss Karen and Jens." At which point Agnes lost her composure, burst into tears, and hung up the phone.

Red spent the rest of the day packing and making arrangements for a funeral should one be required in Los Angeles. He called Beverly Schwartz later in the day to find out if there had been more information. Beverly was terse as she mechanically told Red that the crash site had been reached and that there were no survivors. The plane had burst into flames on impact and with all the fuel on board there were hardly any recognizable bodies. The airline was asking for dental records to try and establish some individuals' identity. Red's last hope was gone. Manfully he went to Karen's dentist and asked him for whatever x-rays he had of her teeth. The dentist was only too glad to help and was shocked to know that Karen was a crash victim. Then he phoned Brett. Brett said he couldn't go, Rosemary was too emotionally stressed out to be left alone. Brett told Red to do what he thought was necessary and to bring home whatever there was of his daughter and grandson for a family funeral. Red said he'd keep Brett up-to-date on events not knowing what he'd find when he got to Inverness, which was where the bodies had been taken.

After an almost sleepless night Red spent the rest of the day phoning all Karen's friends and their mutual friends to tell them of the disaster.

He was met with a stunned silence from virtually everyone. All of the contacts had heard of the airliner going down but no one had suspected Karen and Jens were on it. They all fervently wished Red a safe trip and some even asked if it was wise, for if something happened to Red, Lance would be orphaned. The thought had never occurred to Red and he blew it off, saying he couldn't *not* go and that was that. But the thought stayed with him as he made his way to the airport that afternoon.

The lounge that had been set aside for the victims families was crowded with everyone talking in hushed whispers. The room had a deep air of depression as people searched for a friendly face or for someone to talk to. Beverly Schwartz entered after Red had got there and they shook hands and chatted about how long the flight might take. They were going to follow the same route as Karen and Agnes had taken with stops in Chicago, New York, Gander and finally Prestwick where they would transfer to a smaller aircraft to take them up to Dalcross Airport at Inverness. It would be a long haul and many of the passengers, not surprisingly, looked fearful of flying. The weather at Los Angeles that day didn't help. There was a strong cold wind blowing in from the Pacific with low gray clouds, just like the day when Karen left, Red thought. Was it only just over four weeks ago he said goodbye to his gorgeous vivacious wife? He couldn't get the events of the last four weeks out of his mind and the changes had been wrought in his life since then. The euphoria of Jens's successful operation, then the setback preventing Karen and Jens returning from London in time for Christmas or New Year, then the black finality as news of the missing aircraft turned into a reality of misery for relatives and loved ones. And here he was today making the sad trip to identify his wife and son, if he could, and bring them back home. All of this in just over a month, he couldn't get the time span out of his mind. Christ in Heaven he thought today's the thirteenth; it was like a black omen descending on him. Red was so deep in his thoughts he didn't notice Beverly approaching with some details on the flight. He started as she touched his elbow.

"Sorry Red, you were deep in thought, did I startle you?"

"I'm fine, I'm okay Beverly, I had just realized today's January the thirteenth."

"Yes, I know, but who's superstitious?"

"Not me I suppose, but my life's been turned inside out as has yours in the past few weeks."

"Yeah, tell me about it," said Beverly bitterly. "We were looking forward to having a real nice time Hank and I. You know he had a little itty-bitty ranch left to him by an Uncle in the hill country near Austin, Texas. He was going to quit flying big 'planes and try and start his own little commuter airline. We talked about what we were going to do and have. Horses, a few head of cattle, a couple of big dogs, it all sounded kinda idyllic, away from the city, our own little spread..."Beverly tailed off at the bitter sweet memories which was all she had left of her fiancé. "See that little lady over there," she pointed to a small but refined lady of, Red guessed, mid sixties. "That's Hanks mother, she's 78 and she's going over to bring her son back. She had four boys; she lost two in the war, and now Hank. Let me tell you something, she's still clear minded and not maudlin in any way and she can still laugh and have a good time, she's a remarkable lady."

"Yep, Beverly, those kind of people are an inspiration to us all, when you look round at a time like this you can always find someone who is worse off, or suffered more than you. I would have put her at early to mid sixties she's fantastic."

Beverly called Mrs. Kelly over and introduced her to Red. She had a firm handshake and a dry eye, as she looked Red over.

"My, my you remind me of Hank when he was your age, you must be still in your twenties or early thirties."

"Right on the money ma'am I'm thirty." Red smiled back at her.

"Beverly tells me you know Hank, is that true?"

"Yes, I did....or I do." Shit, Red thought what an awful mistake to make. "I'm sorry ma'am."

"Well don't be, it's an easy mistake to make and we are all under the same cloud, so let's make the best of it, if you knew Hank he wouldn't be grieving for you, he'd be out with the boys having a drink and saying what a great guy you were."

What a lady, thought Red, she certainly had the measure of her son and there must be some deep, deep sadness there, but you would never know it.

"Ma'am you're right. Hank and I tied a few on now and again with Mats my boss, he was quite a guy."

"Just like his father, he was, when it came to drink, he never knew when to stop. The fighting Irish you know, a few glasses of John Jamieson and they'd take on the Russian army." She laughed.

Beverly sensing it was time to go, put her arm round Jean Kelly and made for the exit. Red followed and they were soon seated in the opulent interior of the Stratocruiser. Red wanted to be close to Beverly but she had her seat next to Mrs. Kelly on the upper deck. For whatever reason Red had been assigned to an aisle seat in the lower deck. But it didn't really matter, apart for the sleeping arrangements there was plenty space to move about. Take off was the most spectacular part of the flight as the Strat surged forward down the runway and eased itself into the bumpy air. Once they had got to 23,000 feet the turbulence ceased and the passengers all relaxed. The flight crew worked their tails off bringing drinks and all sorts of delicacies to the passengers. God knows what this is costing Transoceanic thought Red, but underneath he didn't give a damn, whether it was their fault or a generic fault in the aircraft didn't matter one iota. He had lost his Karen and little Jens and there was nothing anyone could do to bring them back.

Prestwick was dark and cold although it was almost ten o'clock in the morning. It was as if the dark gray clouds had followed them all the way from Los Angeles. The passengers piled out of the plane glad to be at their destination, tired but certainly not hungry, Transoceanic's flight attendants had seen to that. By eleven o'clock the clouds miraculously parted and a watery sun shone out of a vivid blue sky. Red joined up with Mrs. Kelley and Beverly as he had done at every stop. The refueling at Gander, Newfoundland had been the worst. The place was literally freezing and the local facilities failed to keep the travelers warm, it had been, after all, the middle of the night.

A BEA Vickers Viscount turbo-prop aircraft had been commissioned to take the thirty-two passengers to Dalcross, Inverness. The Scottish crew were cheerful, sympathetic and looked after their passengers as if they were royalty. It was just after mid-day when the Viscount touched down at Inverness. The good weather had held and the views of the Grampian Mountains from the aircraft were spectacular. They were close to Ben Nevis, the highest mountain in Britain, when the pilot came on the intercom and said he was going to bank the 'plane to allow them a better view of what he called the soaring serenity of the mountain. He hoped, he said, that despite their grim journey his passengers would be able to take a little of that serenity with them. Sure enough Ben Nevis stood out like a huge white sentinel looking down over the town of Fort William and Loch Linnie.

Once the passengers had collected their luggage they were taken by bus to the Station Hotel in the center of the town. There, various medical and airline officials, who would organize the viewing and identification of the bodies, met them. This was the part they had all dreaded most. The passengers whose next of kin were not recognizable gave over what dental records and other information they had to assist in the gruesome process. Others, whose relatives had not been burnt or charred beyond recognition were taken to a room and briefed on what they might expect. Beverly, Mrs. Kelly and Red fell into the latter category, which made Red even more uneasy. He wanted to remember his vivacious wife the way she looked when she had left him four weeks earlier. His concern, and it was a real one, was that the last picture that you see of anyone after death is the one that you tend to remember. That final picture returns to haunt you time after time.

So it was with trepidation that he talked to the medical orderly that had been assigned to him at the local hospital. Jock MacNab was a crusty old hospital porter of about sixty. He had a full head of crinkly iron gray hair, bushy eyebrows and a craggy face with a bulbous-like nose that looked like it was cracked by the little red veins that populated it. He was about two inches short of six feet and he wore dark trousers and a heavy dark green woolen sweater. He had a slow and soft way of talking which made people strain to catch every word. He was a master at getting everyone's attention without so much as raising his voice.

He flipped through a clipboard with what looked like a tabulated list of names.

"Ericsson, is that right Mr. Ericsson, if I can ask you, what does the "A" stand for?"

He must have my name from my passport Red figured; no one has used my real name for years. He was not about to get into an explanation with Jock as everything else he possessed had his name as Red.

"It must be a mistake; my first name begins with "R".

"Oh really, now there's a thing, a mistake already and we've a-ways to go to make sure the identification process is accurate. You were the husband of Karen Ericsson, were you not?"

"Yes, you've got that right," Red retorted impatiently.

"Aye well now sir, don't be getting upset. I'm just trying to do my job as quickly and as accurately as possible. I've got an "A" here as your first initial and I need to see some proof that it is an "R". What does the "R" stand for by-the-way?'

"Red".

"Mercy now, you mean your parents christened you Red."

"Not quite."

"What do you mean by not quite, sir?" Would it not be better if you just let me see your passport sir?"

"Jesus Christ, I've flown six thousand miles to be here and now I'm faced with Scottish bureaucracy, this is Bull Shit!" Red exploded. He was tired, hungry, needed a shower or a bath and probably a good night's sleep.

"Well I'm not sure on the variety of shit sir, and I can see you're tired. I am only trying to make certain that it is the next of kin that makes an identification of the deceased, I'm sure you understand."

"Okay, here's my passport." Red handed the passport over as if it was glued to his hand.

Jock flipped it open. "There we are now, Adolph Christian Ericsson, that wasn't all that difficult, now was it sir...they should have called you Ace sir, that would have been more appropriate." Jock smiled benignly.

There was something familiar about all this Red felt, here he was saying goodbye to his wife and, on the first occasion they met, she had insisted on having his proper name. It was unreal Red concluded as if Karen was trying to reach out to him in some way. It's the eight-hour time difference that's catching up on me he figured as he shook his head.

"Right now sir, if you'll follow me I'll take you to the morgue." Red followed Jock to the elevator and they descended to the bowels of the hospital. The familiar odors reached Red again as they wended they're way along seemingly endless corridors.

Jock stopped at a set of double doors and opened them carefully. There was a gurney in the room with a body draped in a sheet. Jock carefully examined the toe tag.

"Aye here we are sir, Karen Ericsson, is that right."

"Yep." Red choked on the word.

"Let me warn you sir, there's multiple lacerations and contusions to the head area. They've cleaned your wife up the best they can. Her right arm has been severed at just below the elbow and both legs were broken. She's a bit of a mess sir."

Jock stood at the top of the gurney and folded back the sheet to reveal Karen's face. The sight was indescribable. Red's first reaction was to say it wasn't her. Her face was swollen and puffy, black and blue and he could see where there had been a huge open wound to her head that someone had clumsily sewn up. Suddenly he felt nauseous and faint.

"Yes, that's her; I just need to sit down for a bit."

Jock quickly pushed a chair towards him and he slumped into it leaning forward, head between his knees. God, this was worse than he ever imagined. Brett and Rosemary could *never* see their daughter like this. He sat quiet for about five minutes. Jock came up to him.

"All right are we now sir?" I'm so sorry this is an awfy business. At least, and I don't want this to sound daft in any way sir, but at least you've got somebody to identify. There's this too sir," Jock handed over a brown envelope.

Red slit the package open and peered inside. There was Karen's wedding band, engagement ring, gold Rolex watch she had been given by her father on her twenty-first birthday, a single strand string of pearls, one or two bobby pins and that was it. He sat and contemplated the contents; this was the final moment he had come to dread. The contents in this miserable brown envelope were all that was left of his wife.

"All right," Red said to Jock after a long silence, "let's get the rest over with."

"How's that sir?"

"My son, Jens, he was with his mother on the 'plane."

"He's not on my chart, sir but that doesn't mean to say he doesn't exist. What I can tell you is that he's not here anyway. Let's go back up to administration and see if they can tell us something."

Red followed Jock until they arrived where they had started.

"Wait here, sir, I'll be right back."

Jock wasn't right back as he promised. Fifteen minutes went by, then twenty. Fatigue was getting to him. He was just nodding off when a tearful Beverly and a stalwart Mrs. Kelly came along the corridor. Red got up, didn't say a word, and embraced the two women as best he could.

"That was awful," sobbed Beverly.

"Yeah, same for me. How are you Mrs. Kelly?"

"I'll not get over it," she said matter of factly. "That's my third son, I've never really got over the other two, but this is very difficult." She looked Red straight in the eye, never flinching, not a tear in evidence. It would probably hit her later, thought Red. He was busy supplying a handkerchief to Beverly when Jock reappeared.

"Mr. Ericsson, sir, could we have a quick word?"

"Certainly Jock." Red moved away from the ladies to the privacy of a corner.

"We have no record of a child's body being found, sir. Our head of Psychiatry will be out shortly to talk to you sir."

"You mean they haven't found my son?"

"That's what it looks like sir, I'm awfy sorry, I thought you knew."

"Christ Jock, how was I supposed to know, you're the first person I've spoken to who knows anything about this."

"You were supposed to be informed at the Hotel, sir. It seems there's been a mix up."

"All right Jock, it's not your fault. Thanks for all you've done."

And then suddenly Red remembered. The sapphire and diamond ring, where had that gone.

"Jock, just before you go, there's one thing I forgot. I bought my wife a sapphire ring for Christmas from an English jeweler. I've never seen it but it should be a big ring, blue in color with diamonds around it, you haven't seen it have you?"

"No sir, I haven't. But I wasn't the one who dealt with the personal effects. That was a combination of the Rescue boys from the RAF and the pathologist who did the autopsy. Which finger would she have been wearing it on sir?"

"Fourth finger, right hand I suppose."

"She did lose her right arm, if you remember, sir."

"Oh, shit, yes, you're right. That's what must have happened. They didn't find…"Red tailed off.

"To my knowledge sir, no they didn't find the arm, or at least they didn't identify the arm. There were quite a few limbs sir."

"Right, yeah right Jock. Thanks. I'll wait for your shrink."

"Doctor Evans sir, he's Welsh." The way Jock said it if Welsh was a disease, Doctor Evans had it.

Eventually Red was shown into an office just after Mrs. Kelley and Beverly had left for the hotel. They all agreed to have dinner together that evening if they could stay awake.

Doctor Evans was a small man with sandy hair, brushed forward to cover up the receding portions. He had twinkling blue eyes, neat little hands and feet and freckles, which covered the upper part of his face. He talked very rapidly and was clearly hyper, a strange characteristic thought Red for a psychiatrist. He was very straight forward with Red whom he quickly assessed was not to be fooled with. They shook hands and the doctor sat down.

"I know how you're feeling, or at least I think I do. You've said your farewells to your wife and now you have to do the same to your son. Well it's not going to be easy. There are the two scenarios. Jens, it is Jens isn't it?"

Red nodded.

"Right Jens was what, three months old?" A tot, for want of a better word"

Red nodded again.

"Well the plane did go up in flames, so many people were burned beyond recognition, all that fuel and everything, and if that happened to Jens, there would be no trace, I'm afraid, his poor little body would be consumed. The other possibility is that he was catapulted from the plane and became buried in the thick snow somewhere on the mountain. Lost, shall we say until the snow melts which I'm told could be next week or next month. The weather is so changeable you know. But I'm also told the snow is much deeper in the corrie, so months might be nearer the mark. Either way, and I can see you're a realist, your son is dead. We just don't have a body. No one could have survived that crash and then the inferno."

Evans paused and looked at Red. There was nothing the good doctor had said that Red would have disagreed with.

"Just where is this mountain."

"Beinn Eighe?"

"Whatever."

"You'd probably get better information from Jock, he's a local. But basically it's on the west side of the country, a beautiful part of the country, called Torridon. By road it's about fifty miles from here. Some of the roads are single track, it's pretty barren and there's very few people."

"Single track. What's single track?"

"Well the name fits the description. It is a one-vehicle width road with passing places. Can get quite exciting if you meet one of the locals coming quickly the other way. The passing places are marked, you can see them when the road is straight, but it seldom is."

"Could I go there?"

"You want to see the crash site?"

"Well, I've come all this way, Karen is an only child and I'll be asked questions."

"I understand."

"Can I rent a car?"

"Certainly. But if you really want to get into the corrie you would need climbing or hill walking gear. It's rough and wild up there. Tell you what. The RAF are still cleaning up, I think I can persuade them to give you a lift on one of their choppers up there and you'd be up and back in a couple of hours."

"You're kiddin'?"

"No. Do you want me to try?"

"Sure thing, I'd be real grateful doctor."

"You're at the Station Hotel aren't you?"

"Yes."

"Okay let me call you tonight and see what I can set up. Oh, and just one other thing. Only you can go, don't tell anyone about this otherwise I'll really be in the shit."

"Understood."

At that they shook hands and parted.

Trevor Evans, as good as his word, called Red early the next morning.

"Red, it's all set up. Take a taxi to Dalcross a Bristol Sycamore helicopter will pick you up at ten hundred hours, that's ten a.m. to you. They'll fly you to the corrie and bring you back. The only caveat is that you have to stay as long as they need to be there. That could be ten minutes or ten hours, understood?"

"Doctor, thanks a bunch."

"Trevor will do. Let me know how you get on when you get back"

"You've gotta deal Trevor."

The bright yellow RAF Air Sea Rescue helicopter from Squadron 275 touched down from Lossiemouth at zero nine fifty-five hours exactly. Red had mustered all the warm clothing he had, which wasn't much, plus a loaned anorak from the hotel porter who used it only at weekends when he too went into the hills.

The RAF crew saluted politely when Red climbed on board and he was shown to a seat and given a headset to wear. He was also offered a bright orange jump suit that he gratefully put on. He was frozen. The trip took all of twenty minutes but it was breathtaking. The pilot virtually followed the road up to Kinlochewe at an altitude of about five thousand feet. There in front of them was Loch Maree and to their right the great hump of Slioch, looking much grander than it's three thousand three hundred feet, due to the coating of snow. Then the pilot banked left down Glen Torridon and gained altitude slightly as they approached the pinnacle peak of Beinn Eighe. To the left Red could see the huge mass of Liathach approaching. Then as they descended over the rim of the mountain into the corrie Red could clearly see what was left of the Stratocruiser. The tail plane was still visible jutting up like a huge aluminum shark's fin firmly stuck in the snow. The pilot pointed to the summit of the Bein. Red strained forward to get a better glimpse. You could see the scars and pieces of airframe where the giant airliner had struck. Then the Sycamore banked sharply and headed down, down, down into the corrie.

Touch down was in a tremendous flurry of snow as the downdraft from the helicopter's rotors created a huge white cloud. The engines were switched off and they sat still until the rotors had stopped turning. One of the crewmen slid the door open and pulled out a short aluminum ladder that stopped just short of the ground. The winchman stood at the foot of the ladder and beckoned to Red to come out.

The glare from the snow-filled corrie was incredible. Even with his dark sunglasses on Red was blinded by the reflected light from a cold morning sun, which stood low on the horizon. There was now total stillness in the corrie, the only noise came from the waterfall spilling out of the small loch at the foot of the corrie. Red stood surveying the wreckage, or what was left of it. Some parts had been removed; others were too deeply embedded in the snow to be removed. It would be spring before the clean up would be complete. This was it. This was where Karen and Jens had died, and Hank Kelley, for that matter. There was a lump in his throat that was almost choking him. He was glad he had on dark glasses for tears were welling up within him. He coughed and sniffed. He had to get back in control. The winchman was walking up a well worn track that lead to one of the larger parts of the aircraft which turned out to be part of a wing.

As he looked more carefully he could see the blackening under the new snow. The blackening caused by the exploding aircraft as it bounced off the top of the mountain and catapulted, past the three soaring rock towers into the corrie below.

Red turned to the RAF crewman who had stopped to light up a cigarette.

"They wouldn't have much of a chance?"

"None, it was pretty brutal."

"Were the passengers found all together or were they..." Red tailed off.

"All over the place. When the plane struck the top up there the bottom section of the airframe must have split open and many of the people were catapulted out of the plane down the mountain, those towers are about fifteen hundred feet you know, to end up in this corrie. Those were the lucky ones. They most likely died right away from the fall if their necks weren't already broken when the aircraft hit the top."

My God, thought Red, does he have to go into the gory details.

But the crewman was on a roll now and he warmed to his imaginary picture of the disaster.

"The ones that were trapped in the main fuselage were worse off. They were blown all over the place when the aircraft exploded and then the ignited fuel would cover them. A petrochemical fire reaches incredible temperatures in next to no time, like 1,800 degrees Fahrenheit. That's why it's been difficult identifying the bodies. Burned to a crisp they all were."

"Thanks, thanks for that," Red said sarcastically. But it went right over the crewman's head Red reckoned.

"Don't mention it, sir."

"I won't. Is it okay if I go up here a bit?"

"Yes, sure, go anywhere you like, sir, just don't touch anything if you don't mind. Not that it matters really, but the experts want to come back and check out a few things."

"Thanks," said Red and got going on up the corrie traversing from west to east and climbing as he went. Apart from the scars made by the Stratocruiser crash this was a beautiful place he told himself. The more he thought of it the more convinced he became that he should leave Karen here with her son. They died together; their remains should be together. And so as he climbed, puffing and panting in the cold morning air, he put together a plan. He would come back and scatter Karen's ashes in the corrie to be with her son's remains. He knew he would meet with tremendous resistance from the Stahlman's. Being Catholic, cremation was not an option, they would want coffins and a burial service. He was lost in those thoughts when the pilot of the helicopter gave him a yell and a wave that indicated they would be heading back shortly. Red started back down resolved to carry out his plan.

Back in Inverness he went to find old Jock MacNab at the hospital. Old Jock had just come on duty at noon so he came to talk to Red when he heard he was looking for him.

"Jock, what's the deal, when can I get my wife's body released to me?"

"It's up to you sir. Now identification's complete you have some papers to sign and we'll turn it over to the undertaker of your choice."

"Who do you recommend?"

"The best in town is McLaren's sir. They've been here in the city father and son now for as long as anyone can remember. Will I give them a call?"

"That would be just great Jock, oh and Jock thanks very much for looking after her," he slipped Jock a five pound note.

"Thank you, you're too generous sir, dinae you worry sir I'll take care of everything and she'll be with McLaren's tomorrow. They'll prepare her for the journey home."

"Jock, thanks a bunch." Red strode out of the hospital and made off to the hotel to find out where the nearest Catholic Church was.

The hotel porter directed him to St. Brides. There he met with one of the Fathers who looked not too senior and fairly fit. He would have to be for what Red had in mind.

"You want to what?" the astonished priest could hardly believe what Red had just said.

"But these are special circumstances."

"That may be, but no priest in his right mind would do what you're asking. It's against our very principles. I take it you're not Catholic?"

"Correct," said Red. "I'll pay well, I know it's asking a lot but I just want her funeral to be private but correct."

"Well I've never heard of one on top of a 3,000 feet plus mountain in terrible weather."

"How do you know the weather's going to be terrible?"

"At this time of year it usually is."

"But you don't know that." Red could see he wasn't getting anywhere.

"The answers 'no'. I've never heard of such a thing, you're from the United States, then?"

"Yes I am."

"Ah well," the priest shook his head as if that explained everything.

Red headed for the door and didn't look back.

He was going to discuss his dilemma with Beverly and Mrs. Kelley over dinner, but he thought the better of that as Mrs. Kelley was sure to be a staunch Catholic and he was certain his idea and his view would be an anathema to the old lady who already had suffered quite enough. As for Brett and Rosemary Stahlman, he'd deal with them when he got home. Back home, that was where he wanted to be. Back home with Lance to try and get closure on the tragedy.

He had finished dinner and was in the bar trying out a malt whisky old Jock had recommended when he saw one of the RAF personnel come in. That triggered another thought. Surely the Air Force would have an interdenominational chaplain who would be able to help him out. He had the number of the Leuchars Squadron so he decided to call in the morning. Who knows, he thought, I might just hitch a lift again and that would make things a lot easier.

True to his word old Jock had McLaren the undertakers pick up Karen's body first thing in the morning. By the time Red found the McLaren office a member of staff was waiting for his arrival. Red introduced himself to a tall skinny lady called Lizzie, Mr. McLaren's assistant she assured him. Did Mr. Ericsson want the body prepared for the long flight home? Red explained he wanted to organize a cremation at the earliest opportunity. Lizzie coughed a bit and asked if it was his late wife's wishes to be cremated. Red said no, but in the circumstances it was what he wanted. Lizzie then reminded Red that the paperwork she had received on Mrs. Ericsson indicated that she was Catholic and did he, Mr. Ericsson, know that it was not the policy of Catholics to be cremated. Red had then proceeded to frighten the life out of Lizzie by telling her she had quite enough to do living her own life and not meddle in others, particularly those who were past caring. All of this was conveyed in a tone and style that Lizzie would remember for a very long time. Especially the green eyes, the electric and haunted deep green eyes.

Red was alone, apart from the RAF Chaplain, who attended Karen's cremation. The ashes were handed to him after the ceremony in a nondescript box. The next day Red met the Sycamore helicopter at the same time and place and flew to Beinn Eighe. Through the intercom the chopper pilot said,

"So you want on the summit Mr. Ericsson?"

"Only if it's feasible, I don't want to put anyone's life at risk."

"Piece of cake, sir. Will the Chaplain be getting out too, sir?"

"Yes, he will. We won't be more that five minutes."

"Righty-oh sir, we'll just keep her turning over."

The pilot flew straight to the summit this time however the wind was so strong that it was impossible to land.

"I'm afraid we're going to have to land in the corrie sir," the pilot said via the intercom system. Again the bright yellow Sycamore circled down to where Red had been before. The Chaplain and Red stared up at the summit it seemed a long way away.

"You'd best get a move on sir, you've got two hours then we've got to get out of here. We're told there's a bit of bad weather coming in from the west."

The crewman looked at his watch to emphasize the sense of urgency. Red and the Chaplain looked at one another and started off for the summit. It was a hard climb, and Red, despite having bought a pair of what he was told were climbing boots, kept sliding about on the snow. Finally the reached the top of the snow covered scree and moved onto patches of rock, which being steeper, had little or no snow. But it was hard going. The Chaplain, who it turned out, was a keen rock climber, and being fitter and having the right equipment, was away out in front of Red scouting for the easiest route to the top. Higher and higher they climbed until the helicopter was just a spot in the distance.

Forty-five minutes had passed and they had reached the arête, which ran up to the summit. There was some quite difficult rock climbing involved and without the Chaplain's help Red was sure he would never have made it. Finally the wind whipped around them as the came out of the protection of the ridge and they made their way to Beinn Eighe 's peak. There were still quite large chunks of aircraft lying around and

Red could clearly see where the rock had been scored and soil uprooted by the huge body of the Stratocruiser. Together they stood on the summit, breathless with their exertions. The view was quite unbelievable. There below them stretched Loch Maree with the great hump of Slioch overlooking the loch. To their left they could see the black snow capped Cuillins of Skye. Directly below them was the Corrie Mhic Fhearchair, which the Chaplain explained was a Gaelic name pronounced 'corry veechker*a*char' which meant corrie of the son of Farquhar. The Chaplain didn't know who that was historically.

The service, if it could be called that, was short and to the point. The Chaplain did his ashes to ashes bit and Red cast Karen's remains into the wind to be carried onto the resting place of her son below. Red had a sense of peace within himself. He had done what he felt was right and proper. Her life had ended in tragic circumstances but the surroundings were so beautiful he felt it fitting that here she should stay with Jens. It was over. He could get back to the US with the others and pick up the pieces of a shattered life.

He turned to the Chaplain and said, "Thank you, you've been most kind in helping me fulfill my wish. That's one thing I won't have to do again." Red couldn't have been more wrong.

It seemed even longer getting back to Los Angeles and it was. Head winds buffeted the aircraft as it flew the reverse route against the jet stream. Stiff, tired and bored beyond words Red and his two flying companions disembarked at Los Angeles. It was there that a most fortuitous piece of good luck helped Red. Apparently twenty-seven makeshift coffins had been loaded and only twenty-six had been claimed. All of the passengers were asked if they were sure they had not forgotten to pick up a relative or loved one. That was when Red confessed to having forgotten his charge. He was just so relieved to get home, he told the sympathetic ground crew member; it had all gone right out of his head. He signed the delivery ticket for someone called Bain claiming that it was his and quickly destroyed any evidence that might link him and the Bain body. What had obviously happened was that one Scottish passenger who perished had been inadvertently loaded on the return aircraft instead of staying in Scotland. Well, Red thought ruefully, you'll get a better send off than you'd ever get in Scotland. He had returned to his in-laws with a body in a box.

His welcome from the Stahlmans was as emotional as it was tearful. Of course Rosemary insisted on seeing the body. Red had been prepared for this. He had pulled Brett aside and explained to him the nature of Karen's injuries and advising him never to let anyone open the makeshift coffin. He finished up by whispering to Brett that not all the parts of the body were there. While he was not telling a lie, the manner in which he confided to Brett inferred that perhaps the head was missing. Brett blanched at the thought. Red had never seen him so white, so quiet and introverted. He could only imagine how they felt, as he would never forget his memories of Scotland and what had happened there.

The Stahlman funeral was a grand affair. The casket was of the finest quality and the priest who knew the family gave a magnificent eulogy, there was not a dry eye in the packed church. Brett and Rosemary had laid out a magnificent buffet for the close family friends who were invited back to their huge house in Beverly Hills. Red was exhausted.

Never had he talked to so many people he didn't know and, indeed, didn't care to know. Agnes Anderson had been the best person ever. She organized Red, took care of Lance and helped Wendy, the Nanny, without any fuss.

Agnes's first meeting with Red had been worse than anything he could have imagined. She was absolutely distraught with grief and cried openly about the demise of Karen and little Jens. She felt guilty, she said, for being in the United States when her place was with Miss Karen. Red finally stepped in and stopped her from all her self-recrimination. What the hell good would it have done, he said, if Agnes had gone down with the plane? At least he had her and all that she stood for. Loyal, honest, efficient and strong willed. He couldn't imagine a better person to help Lance face the difficulties of growing up without a mother. Without reservation he wanted her to be Lance's Godmother, tutor and mentor. Would she accept?

Agnes was overwhelmed. Yes, she had said, she would like to do that but there were one or two questions and one or two things she would like to make clear before she accepted. They agreed to meet as soon as possible after Karen's funeral. It was five o'clock or just after when Red got home. Wendy had fielded calls from Mats Frosteman and Beverly Schwartz. He called Mats and told him he would be back in Houston a week on Monday and that he had decided to move to Houston permanently. It would take a bit of time finding a house and so forth, but he was prepared to make the move a permanent one. Mats expressed delight at Red's decision.

Next he called Beverly who was in Austin, Texas. She told him the funeral had gone well, if funerals are supposed to go well. Mrs. Kelly had been very brave up until the moment when they lowered the coffin into the grave. That had proved too much for the stoic mother and she collapsed. She was staying with Beverly overnight at her hotel. Red said that when he came to Houston he'd make a point of visiting with Mrs. Kelley. Beverly was preparing to return to Los Angeles and pick up the pieces of her life again. There were so many shattered dreams, she said. Red agreed.

He had considered meeting Agnes Anderson that evening but he was too tired. So he called Agnes, put her off until the morning, poured himself a Scotch, sat back to watch TV and fell fast asleep.

Suddenly there was a soft touch on his shoulder, he slowly drifted back. It's Karen he thought she's trying to waken me up and then reality hit as he became more conscious. It couldn't be Karen. Slowly he opened his eyes to see the Nanny, Wendy looking down at him.

"Mister Ericsson sir, it's 'alf past eleven, would you not be more comfortable in your bed?"

"Yeah, I would Wendy, thanks," his gruff voice didn't convey thanks at all but that was nothing to do with Wendy.

"You mean it's eleven thirty Wendy?"

"That's right Mr. Ericsson."

"For Christ's sake speak English."

"But I *am* English Mr. Ericsson."

"So you are Wendy, so you are."

"Mr. Ericsson, we 'aven't really 'ad a chance to speak. Can I say 'ow sorry I am about Mrs. Ericsson and poor little Jens. I was so looking forward to 'aving them back sir, it's such a tragedy and I'm so, so sorry."

"Thanks, Wendy. And I should be thanking you for the great way you've looked after Lance while I've been gone, I mean it when I say you've done a real fine job."

He reached forward and gave the gangly Wendy a brief hug and a kiss on the cheek. Wendy stood back, curtsied as if he was royalty, turned bright red and ran out of the room.

Red picked up what was left of the Scotch and headed for bed.

Agnes Anderson turned up promptly at eight o'clock the next morning looking as elegant as Red had ever seen her. For an elderly lady, Red thought, she looked quite attractive. They sat in the kitchen and Red poured them both a coffee.

"Okay Agnes, shoot, what's on your mind?"

"I've got two things...well maybe three things I need to say. First is where are you going to live? Your work is in Houston and there are only memories here for you now. Second is if I take the job and you get married again where does that leave me? And lastly if I do take this job will I have the final say in your son's education? I'm only talking about the formative years, up to ten let's say, those are the most important. That wee lamb is never going to know his mother and she was a princess. I can't be that, I'll give him all my love, you know that too, but I can't give him a mother's love and that's what he'll never have."

"Jesus Christ Agnes, had you thought about this before I mentioned it? Or did you go and speak to your attorney?"

"First of all Red I wish you wouldn't blaspheme, if you do it now you'll do it in front of the child, and no, I haven't spoken to my lawyer, but this is my position. I'm no spring chicken but I've worked hard all my life, Miss Karen, thanks to your or her father's generosity showed me a different style of life, I liked that, thank you. I don't want to accept and in ten months or a couple of years I'm out of a job because you fall in love with someone else, or you start another family and then I'd be in the way, I just want to make sure it's what you want long term, not what you need in a crisis."

"Well, there's one thing for sure, the Scots don't miss you and hit the wall." Red sat back and considered all that Agnes had said.

"Here's what I'm prepared to do. I can't read the future any more than you can but you *know* how much I loved Karen and she loved me, and in time, yes, I might find someone to replace her. Right now I doubt it. One thing I can tell you is that I'm getting out of here and moving to Houston. I'm in oil and Houston is oil. On the education front I don't have a problem with your request although I think I should be consulted about where and by whom my son gets taught. So I'll get a legal contract drawn up which we'll both sign, if that makes you happy and that will be that."

"Red you'll do no such thing. I'll be happy to do what you ask, I'm prepared to live in Houston, don't know much about it except it's in Texas and I'll take your word on the education, you'll be consulted but all I want is your agreement that I'll have at least ten years with you and Lance, your word as a gentleman is enough for me. If I have to leave before then you'll pay me whatever money is due for twelve months, plus, and I'll leave this to you, a payment to compensate me for the living accommodation I'll have to find together with related expenses."

Red held out his hand. "It's a deal."

Agnes and Red shook hands and the next week Agnes moved in to the Ericsson household to take charge. Wendy went back to Britain with a handsome bonus and glowing reference to look for a new job.

At what was referred to as the Sunday family dinner Red broke the news to Brett and Rosemary that he was moving to Houston on a permanent basis. Rosemary burst into tears. Brett went bananas.

"You son-of a-bitch, I jest noo you'd do this to us. Take our only livin' memory of Karen away. We want to see young Lance there jest as much as you do. I forbid you to do this. Yor gonna get yor ass sued, that's what I'm gonna do if you move out of here, ain't that right Rosemary baby?"

It was a rhetorical question but that didn't stop Rosemary putting in her two cents.

"I've never thought I'd see the day when we'd be treated like this, you're an evil monster, that's what you are Red Ericsson."

"Christ you two, you would think Houston is in Russia. It's five hours flying, tops. When the new jets come in it'll be even quicker, you can visit as often and for as long as you like. Agnes Anderson has accepted the position of housekeeper and she's the best person I can think of to look after your grandson. If I stay here it's more than likely Mats will get someone to replace me. I'm good at what I do and I hope to have my own company someday, but I can't do that staying here. You'll be welcome anytime, I promise you."

"Well I'm jest pissed off at you Red. You make this decision without as much as a word to my good lady wife, as if we've not been through enough these past months."

"It's hardly been a picnic for me." Red butted in.

"It's our only child we're talking about and you don't seem to be able to understand jest how we feel, ain't that right Rosemary, honey?"

Red knew all along what had been in his in-laws minds. They, not Red, would have had a controlling interest in Lance's destiny and Red wanted no part of that. He had been left one precious gift from the woman he loved and he was going to see that Lance would get the very best of everything. In that there lay an inherent danger but at that point in time Red was oblivious to the danger of spoiling his only child.

Red was getting sick of the conversation. It was going nowhere.

"Look, I came to tell you of my intentions, I didn't come for an argument, all we're doing is destroying the memories we had of Karen. No amount of yelling or threatening can bring her back, so save your breath and just thank God you have a Grandson left that you can visit at any time. I want you both to think carefully about what I've said because I'm going now, I want no part of this 'family' meal."

With that Red folded his napkin, pushed back his chair and strode out of the room to the screams and yells of both Rosemary and Brett.

He arrived home to a chicken potpie that Agnes had in the oven.

"Did you not make that for tomorrow's dinner, Agnes?"

"Hardly, you're off to Houston tomorrow, or have you forgotten?"

"No, I haven't but you knew I was having dinner at the Stahlmans, didn't you?"

"Aye that I did. And have you eaten anything?" she stood looking at him arms akimbo in her best nurse routine.

Red broke into a broad grin. "Shit, you know I haven't, Agnes."

"Well then, sit down and I'll dish it up."

"But how did you know?"

"I jaloused there would be a battle, they want Lance, don't they."

"I figure, but what's this 'jaloused' word?"

"Oh never mind I go back to old Scottish words when I'm upset, it means I guessed or figured out…and I know, I know, speak English Agnes before you say it."

Red laughed again. "Right you are Agnes you jaloused that correctly."

They both laughed and sat down to Agnes's delicious chicken potpie.

THE RETURN TO TORRIDON —
April 1959

It was early April and the trees were still bare although there were signs that spring was just around the corner. It was time to return to Torridon. Young Charles, now just over six months old was a bouncing healthy baby. Eilid's Uncle Ken had treated them as if they were his family. He allowed Eilid and the baby to come and go as they pleased while he kept a watchful eye on the little boys health, but there had been no crises. Charles grew stronger and more vociferous as the days went by and Kenny's only stipulation was that Eilid have dinner ready for him when he came home in the evening.

As the days grew longer and the weather warmer Eilid and Charles had become familiar sights as Eilid pushed her little pram up and down the Moulin Brae to and from Pitlochry. At first local talk had the child as Kenny's but they soon discovered that Eilid was in fact his niece, so tongues started wagging again, and no end of gossip was manufactured as Eilid maintained her silence over her child or where she was from. Johnnie the barman at the Moulin Inn knew, but when asked, he pointed his finger to the north and say, "she's from up there somewhere, Inverness I think."

For the gossipmongers she became then Dr. Ken Urquhart's niece who had a child out of wedlock. She had come to her Uncle's to have the child because her family had thrown her out, the scandal being more than they could bear. But on one thing they were all agreed. She was the most attractive young lady they had ever seen. Her tall lithesome body moved with a special grace, her long blond hair tied back in a ponytail bobbed jauntily as if to match her good spirits. She was cheerful, polite, and superbly evasive if asked a direct question. If she had a good figure to go with her charm and pleasant look it was seldom revealed, as she wore big sweaters and ballooning anoraks which hid her hourglass figure. That she was fit, there was no doubt, and her electric blue eyes seemed to sparkle brighter as the days slid by and her homecoming came closer.

The one indelible mark she made on her stay was at the local gun and rifle association. Kenny had taken her along one evening to meet his friends in the club or so he had said. In fact he had been prompted by the young membership to bring 'that good looking lassie of yours along'. Kenny obliged. For once she wore tight jeans and a thin turtle-neck lambs wool sweater that had been her mothers. It was a deep shade of blue and followed the curves of her body in the most revealing fashion. Her hair hung down to her shoulders, the ponytail gone.

Jesus, thought Kenny as they left the house with young Charles safely in the hands of Barbara the receptionist from his practice, this is going to be some evening. And how right he was. If Eilid was the flame every man became a moth, almost to the point where Kenny had to exercise crowd control.

The rifle association had a range out at the back all properly set out and buttressed with sandbags. Stances for practice were set at about eight feet from one another and it could accommodate six people at any given time. Range etiquette was controlled by one of the members so that a cease fire was an orderly affair with rifle breaches open on each of the stances as members went forward to retrieve their target.

Invariably shooting came into the conversation as the young blades plied Eilid with question after question. 'How long was she going to be around?' 'Was she married?' 'Where was the baby?' And on and on until she was becoming pretty fed up with the way the evening was going. Eilid decided to ask about the range. Each member took a turn at explaining how it worked and the safety routines they followed, making her wistful as she remembered Auld John's tragic death caused by care-lessness with a rifle on the hill.

One asked," Have you ever used a rifle?"

"Oh, yes"

"Really?"

"Do you use it often?"

"A bit here and there."

They all grinned at one another.

"Would you like to have a bit of target practice while you're here?"

"I'd love to." And Eilid wasn't joking. She had been away from the hill too long and she had begun to doubt if her accuracy might be affected through lack of practice.

So Eilid was taken to a stance, and given a rifle with five bullets in the magazine.

"Ah," she said when handed the rifle, "a Sako .270 eh? I think I've used one of these once before"

The would-be Pitlochry suitors all looked at one another again. This was supposed to be a bit of fun, a bit of baiting, but she certainly looked as if she knew how to handle a firearm.

"Ready," cried the range orderly.

"Yes, fine thank you." She raised the rifle to her left eye. The Sako had just iron sights and Eilid actually preferred these on occasion. There were times, she considered, when a telescopic sight tends to give the user a false sense of security.

"Fire at will," said the orderly.

Bam, bam, bam, bam, bam. Eilid ripped off the five shots in short order.

Kenny watched in awe, his mouth wide open.

The members also watched mesmerized as the tall blond moved the bolt using her left hand with polished lightening speed, the empty cartridge casings cascading to the ground. They were amazed.

"Did ye see that Hughie?" said one.

"Just. It was so damn fast I nearly missed it. The thing is though did they hit the target?"

They turned to the orderly. "What's the score?"

"I'm not sure. I really can't tell in artificial light. It's either a complete miss or else..." Jim didn't finish his sentence. Eilid had laid down the rifle breach open and Jim was off to the butts to fetch the paper target.

Back he came to the astonished group of members his forefinger poking through the center of the target.

"Look at this. I've never seen shooting like it. She blew the bloody bull away. Five shots right through the middle and she's never fired this rifle before. That's not amazing, that's miraculous. It's a half-inch grouping at 100 yards"

Eilid sidled over to her Uncle.

"I think it's time to go, don't you?"

Kenny caught the drift. Quietly he said to her, "Aye, we'll away then. I think you've made your point."

"Gentlemen thank you. I've got to go back to the baby, feeding time"

"Where did you learn to shoot like that?" Jimmy the astonished orderly asked.

"My father was a good shot and he taught me. Nice to see you all, 'bye." Eilid exited with Kenny arm in arm.

That was an interesting answer thought Kenny. From what Eilid had told him Alasdair Ballantyne had been a crack shot and it was Angus Stuart that had taught her. How neat. One answer, two fathers, nary a lie.

The consternation among the astonished members of the rifle association was incredible. It was as fine a display of marksmanship has they had ever seen.

The group all said their farewells and agreed that Eilid was quite the best looking and most talented female they had ever seen at the club.

As Eilid drove down the last stretch of single-track road towards the turn-off to her cottage she scanned the moor looking for the ponies. She was so focused on what she was doing she didn't see the Royal Mail van coming towards her. It was only at the last moment when the driver blew his horn that she got her eyes fully back on the road and saw she was about to have a head-on collision. She swerved hard left onto the heather and stopped just short of the Mail van that had also braked to a stop. The carrycot had shot forward with the violent braking. Eilid piled out of the Land Rover to see if Charles was all right and at the same time apologize to Eric the 'postie'.

"Eric, I'm so sorry, it's my fault. I wasn't looking at the road."

"Aye, Mistress Eilid, well I could see that. What was on yer mind?"

"Nothing really, Eric; I've been away for a few months and I was looking for the ponies, I had to turn them loose."

"Well now there are two ponies down the road a bit towards your cottage, they're lookin' gey scruffy, but otherwise they seem to be fine."

All the while Eric was talking Eilid had opened the back door of the Land Rover and checked inside to see if Charles was fine. He was just starting to come to from a deep sleep and he began to bawl lustily. Eilid clambered into the back to pick him up.

"My, my, that's a bonnie bairn ye have there Miss Eilid. It's no' yours is it?"

Eilid knew this had to come in one form or another and from anyone who knew her.

"It is that Eric, he's just wakened up so he's a wee bit upset."

"Well now aren't you quite the one, rushing off and having a wean and no one here knows. I see your man isn't with you, he'll be coming later no doubt?"

Well, she thought, I might as well start the way I aim to finish.

"No there's no man in my life Eric. It's just me and Charles."

"Aye, quite, quite, yer sometimes better without all the complications eh?"

"Aye you're right Eric, well forgive me again for giving you a fright, I'll need to be off, Charles needs fed."

"Aye right you are Miss Eilid and welcome home. I'll be right behind you though, there's something I forgot to pick up from Mistress McBride, so on you go."

Eric smiled what he thought was a knowing smile. If you really knew the truth, thought Eilid you probably wouldn't believe it. But the story had started. Before the day was out everyone who was anyone in Torridon, Shieldaig or Kinlochewe would know that Eilid Stuart had given birth and that there was no father.

At last she passed the lochan and drew up at the side of her cottage. It was a wonderful feeling. She was home, and home with a baby.

239

She knew there would be a spate of questions from mother and grand-mother but she had prepared herself for that, and as Uncle Kenny had said, 'it'll be a seven day wonder, lass. Just let it all go over your head.'

The house was damp and cold. The cold didn't bother her as much as the damp. It was all pervasive eating into her bones with a chill that was hard to shake off. Quickly she built and lit the fire leaving Charles in the Land Rover with the back door ajar. He was better off there instead of fighting off the ill humors of the cottage. For a change the weather co-operated. The skies cleared in the afternoon, and a balmy south-westerly blew gently up the Glen. All of a sudden spring was in the air. Eilid opened all the doors and windows to let the sunshine warm the cottage and chase away the gloom and the damp. By about six o'clock that evening the cottage was clean, dry and warm. The ponies had also returned seeing the familiar dark green Land Rover parked at the door. Charles had now been placed in Uncle Kenny's cot, as it was called and was trying to imitate a crawl. There was a distinct change in the baby's attitude; he too seemed more relaxed and content. It was as if he had realized this was home and he had come to stay.

Despite the thrill of coming back to her cottage she had a miserable evening. The unpalatable can of stew became more unpalatable and being alone didn't help. With no one to talk to she decided to go to bed early but she tossed and turned for hours until exhaustion finally made her go into a deep sleep which was full of ghoulish dreams of bodies in the cor-rie lit by the flames from the Stratocruiser inferno.

She wakened to Charles crying; feeding time again. She looked at her big watch, six-twenty. It was light by then. Sunrise was at about five-thirty and already the days were lengthening, the vernal equinox having passed two weeks prior to Eilid returning to Torridon.

She picked the baby up, removed the soiled diaper, washed his little bottom, powdered him and had a clean toweling nappy on in less than ten minutes. She had become an expert. Her mother would be proud of her. Catriona and her Granny Kathleen were supposed to be arriving on the following week. She had a lot to do. The Lodge had been empty without any fires burning since October the previous year. The beds would need airing and the house cleaning but as long as the spring like weather held up she would manage alone. Her only dread was meeting

Eliza McBride, which she most certainly would have to do if she needed provisions of any kind. Eliza was the only store in the village unless she drove the odd ten miles to Kinlochewe. Suddenly the ten miles became an attractive proposition for she was sure she would get nothing but poison from Eliza McBride.

By midday the weather was warm enough for Charles to sit out in his pram in sight of the Lodge front door, so Eilid could keep an eye on him while she cleaned. She was in the middle of lifting some heavy blankets to take them downstairs when a voice called out.

"Hello, hello, anyone there?"

She dropped the blankets and made her way down the stairs. Outside was a tall tousled red-headed boy of about seventeen, Eilid guessed. He had a profusion of freckles all over his face and ears that stuck out like Dumbo. He was skinny with what appeared to be enormous feet, or maybe it was the huge boots he was wearing, sticking out from a pair of blue dungarees that were far too big for him. He wore a thick dark sweater under the dungarees and he had a small rucksack on his back. His pale blue watery eyes seemed to be troubled by the bright sunlight for he squinted up at Eilid from the baby's pram.

"Hello, I'm Eilid Stuart, can I help you?"

"Oh, you're the Eilid girl, I mean the Stalker, is that right?"

"That's me."

"I was told by my father that there might be a job going here?"

"What sort of job?"

"I heard Sir David was looking for a ghillie."

"Well he is, but are you not a bit young to work on the hill? It's hard work you know, especially during the rut when we've the stalking parties."

"You are Sir David's Stalker though, is that right?"

"Yes, I told you I'm the Stalker; do you have a problem with that?"

"No, no I don't miss, your just awful young and too good-looking as well." he grinned impishly displaying a crooked set of front teeth. It was an infectious sort of smile though, Eilid thought.

"Do you have a name?"

"Oh, aye, sorry miss, Hamish Ferguson, at your service" and he spread his arms palms up as if giving a presentation together with the cheeky grin.

"How did you get here?"

"I walked miss; is this your bairn?"

"You walked here, from where?"

"I got a lift to Kinlochewe miss."

"You walked about ten miles not knowing if they'd be anyone here?"

"No, I heard from someone you were back in the Glen and I thought you would be far away."

Eilid looked him up and down again. At least the kid showed pluck and ghillies were hard to come by. No one wanted a laboring job that offered no security and very little future. For Eilid it had been different but that was all due to Auld John's sudden demise.

"Well, come away in, and yes that's my baby, Charles that is, he's my son. I've just put on the kettle and I'll make a cup of tea. You must be famished. Have you had anything to eat?"

"Not since this morning miss."

"All right I've got some good cheese sandwiches and I've got a couple of apples so that should see us through."

So they sat and ate Eilid's sandwiches over a mug of steaming hot tea and talked about the estate and what Hamish's duties would be. The pay was low but the accommodation was all found, the cottage went with the job. Hamish had seen the cottage on his way to the Lodge and he hardly dared to hope that it might just be his. Eilid decided to take the bull by the horns.

"Hamish, how would you like to start today? I think you're a good lad. You can help me clear up in here and you can stay in the Lodge tonight. You can help move me in tomorrow and we'll swap then. You can have the job for a three-month probationary period, if we get along then you stay and we'll increase your pay a bit. If you don't work out

I'll probably know in a month and we'll part, okay, how does that suit you?"

"That's great miss; fantastic miss."

"And another thing, call me Eilid."

"Right away miss, I mean Eilid."

"There's just one more thing, you'll have to go home and tell your parents or at least call them. Let me drive you up the road to Kinlochewe and you can either get a lift from there to get you home or stay the night, depending what your parents say.

"Thank you Eilid. You don't have to take me up the road to phone. There's just my father, my mother died two years ago and he's not expecting me home."

"I'm sorry about your mother, that's too bad, but will your Dad not be concerned about you."

"Not really."

"Are you sure?"

"Positive. He told me not to come back until I had a job."

So that was it. Poor Hamish he'd been thrown out the house.

"Do you have any brothers or sisters?"

"Aye there are seven of us. I'm the eldest. There would be eight but my ma died trying to have the last bairn."

"That's awful. What does your father do?"

"He's a painter at the local distillery. He's a randy old bastard and never sober."

She had touched a raw nerve. Hamish's lips had drawn into a tight line and his eyes went dark as he thought about his father.

Eilid put her arm round Hamish's shoulders.

"And I suppose all you have is in that wee rucksack?"

"You're right. I was never going back, not back to him anyway. I'm just sorry to leave my sisters; my brothers can look after themselves."

"How many sisters do you have?"

"Just the two miss, sorry, Eilid."

"How old are they?"

"One's fifteen and the other is eight."

"Do you all live in the same house?"

"No, two of my brothers stay with my Gran and they help out. That works out fine. I just wish Mhairi was at my Gran's."

"Why?"

"Well it's difficult. It's difficult to tell you miss."

"Well let's leave it for now." Eilid decided not to pry. She could tell it would bother Hamish if she pushed, but he had given her a very good idea of what was going on in the Ferguson household and her thoughts of what might just be going on made her skin crawl.

"Right, we've talked enough. Come upstairs and give me a hand with these blankets."

Sir David's estate now had a new ghillie and new child.

Catriona and Kathleen finally arrived from Stornoway on a Monday having taken all weekend to sail from the Hebridean city to the mainland and thence by train and bus to get to the end of the road leading to Torridon. Eilid had waited for over two hours for the bus to come as there had been delay after delay which Catriona hadn't been able to communicate to her daughter. It was nevertheless a joyful reunion. Eilid hadn't seen her mother since the previous spring and it had been three years since she had seen her Grandmother. Eilid noticed changes in her. She was more stooped, looked grayer and moved much more slowly. But she could still smile and laugh and that, she told herself, was a good thing. Three generations stood and hugged one another for ages and then helped Granny into the Land Rover and took off down the road. No mention of the baby had been made and they chatted away animatedly as Granny took in the wonderful views of Beinn Eighe and the surrounding countryside as they made their way to the Lodge.

Thanks to Hamish's invaluable help the Lodge was looking wonderful. There were two of best rooms set aside for Grandmother and mother and Hamish had proved to be very useful with a paintbrush. He had started out to be an apprentice painter and follow his father but it had been clear from the outset that an indoor job was not for Hamish. It also turned out he was allergic to certain paint solvents and his skin would react violently from time to time. He was pleased to quit, so he had said to Eilid.

Soon Eilid had her guests comfortably ensconced in the Lodge. Suitcases were unpacked and tea served. It was now about four o'clock in the afternoon. Catriona sat back, looked at her daughter, smiled and said,

"If I didn't know better I would never know you had a baby. You've lost all the weight you must have put on and I think you're slimmer than ever. So are we not going to see Prince Charlie then?"

"Of course, he's full of vim and vigor, because I put him in his cot when I left to pick you up. Hamish told me he fell asleep so he's all raring to go."

"Is Hamish the father?"

"No he's not; he's the new ghillie and a great asset he is to me. He's only seventeen but he's a great worker."

"Who is the father, Eilid? I mean he's got a responsibility," Catriona said looking straight at her daughter.

"Mother, let's not discuss this, please. It's no one you know and even if you did know it wouldn't help. He's got no money and he's not interested in helping."

"How did this all happen?"

Eilid thought this is not the way it's supposed to go. Kenny told me he had taken care of this and she's going on and on.

"Mum, I'd rather not say."

"Eilid, I am your mother and you *are* my only child, I think I've a right to know."

"Mother, it happened in circumstances I'm not proud of, but I decided to have Charles and that's that. Can't you just accept the fact that he's my son and I appreciate your offer of assistance in helping me in bringing him up."

"My God, Eilid, you're a stubborn child. You're just like your father."

"Which one?"

Those words stung Catriona in a way that caused her almost physical pain. She looked at Eilid, and it was then she realized it was an Eilid she had never seen before and did not know.

"Your true father, Alasdair, of course. If he hadn't been so stubborn and convinced that signing up with the RAF was the right thing to do he'd probably be with us today instead of being dead for the last twenty years."

It was saying the word twenty that brought the reality home to Catriona. It *was* twenty or almost twenty years, wasn't it and not a day had gone past that she hadn't thought of him in one way or another. Her emotions took over and tears started to fall, softly at first, but then more rapidly. Embarrassed she dabbed furiously at her eyes and turned away from her daughter. It was this sight that changed everything for Eilid. She threw her arms round her mother, realizing just how much she had gone through over the years. Terrified that Angus Stuart would find out that Eilid was not his and then horrified when he did. This entire burden she had carried for years with no one to support her. Katherine, Catriona's mother never knew that Eilid was not Angus's and the truth, Catriona supposed, would have brought her to an early grave.

"Mother, mother I'm sorry. Let's sit down when Granny's gone to bed and I'll tell you all about this. There are conditions, though, and you'll have to abide by them before I tell you the whole truth."

And so it was later that night that Eilid told her mother the whole story about Charles and the airplane crash from which he was the sole survivor. The only thing she asked her mother to promise her was that she would never speak of what she knew, not even to her brother Kenny who had put his whole career in jeopardy by aiding and abetting Eilid in the illegal adoption.

Surprisingly Catriona did not share any of her brother's misgivings. Instead she was amazed that Eilid had saved the baby against almost impossible odds. Convinced that both the child's parents were dead helped her rationalize her view that Charles would have a better home and a better upbringing than he would as a foster child somewhere. Not for one minute did she consider there might be other siblings in the family nor indeed that one parent or grandparent might be alive and longing for the child they now considered had perished. Those were side issues not worth considering. Her daughter was radiant with happiness at having a child and there had been a dearth of happiness over the past three years. Catriona would play her part. Her lips were sealed even to the existence of a fake Birth Certificate that Eilid had let her see. The Stuart conspiracy was safe with her and she would help Eilid to ensure that Charles would be brought up in the best possible way.

The next few weeks were idyllic. Clear sunny spring weather had settled into the Glen and mother, daughter and grandmother enjoyed the company and attending to both Charles and Hamish. Hamish had almost become one of the family. He was willing and quick to do any tasks assigned to him. Eilid could see his gaunt figure filling out as he enjoyed the cooking of all three ladies who took a pride in trying to fill him with the best food available. For his part Hamish thought he had died and gone to Heaven. He just loved his little cottage and he spent hours cleaning and improving or fixing anything that he thought needed attention. He never talked about his family and Eilid had asked her mother not to ask too many questions of Hamish.

Lambing had now started in earnest and the days were filled with rounding up the newly born and the ewes to dip them and color them for identification purposes. It was hard work. Sheep grazed on about eight thousand acres, about half the estate. It was late one evening, just as April was about to give way to May, when Eilid and Hamish sat late round the big fire in the Lodge, exhausted after a hard day rounding up sheep on the hill, when Hamish turned to her and said,

"Eilid I met Eric the postie when I was coming here this morning. He had heard something about my father, and while I tried to get him to say more he wouldnae. So I'm a wee bit concerned."

Eilid looked at him and she could see he was troubled.

"Hamish why don't you go home this weekend? I'll take you to Kinlochewe and you can get the bus from there."

"Are ye sure Eilid? I don't want tae leave you with all these sheep still to do. Leave it 'til next week and we'll be done, then I can go."

"Hamish, if you're worried then I'm concerned. You've never really told me much about your family life and I haven't pried, but if you think you might be needed back there go now, to hell with the sheep. I can finish the rest, unless you want me to come with you?"

"No, no that'll no' be necessary. I can look after myself.

"Take three days and get back on Sunday. I'll take you to Kinlochewe and when you get back I'll be waiting to pick you up."

"But how will you know when I'm going to be there?"

"There's only one bus that comes up from Garve on a Sunday, be on it."

"I'll do that. Mind you I could hitch a lift…"

"Enough. I'll see you Sunday."

"Yes Ma'am." And Hamish saluted as he fled out of the Lodge before Eilid's boot could meet his hindquarters.

Sunday. Eilid sat at the end of the road to Torridon. The MacBrayne's bus from Garve had long gone and there was no sign of Hamish. She sat fuming until six and with no Hamish she drove back to the Lodge for Sunday dinner.

"Where's Hamish?" Her mother asked as Eilid stormed in.

"I have no idea."

"Well something must have happened Eilid, it's not like Hamish. If he could have got in touch with you he'd let you know I'm sure."

"Don't rub it in mother. The phone was supposed to be connected to the Lodge a year ago, but it hasn't happened yet."

"Well darling, I'm not the government, I'm sure they must be a reason for them not getting more phone lines down the glen."

"Yes, there is, it's money. They don't care. How many people live in the Glen, ten, twenty sometimes forty at a push? They don't care we're not significant. And anyway the government is in London. If they had property up here you bet your life there would be a proper phone system installed but you're talking about the Post Office and this is Scotland. We're nothing. We don't matter."

Catriona was astonished at her daughter's outburst. She had never suspected that Eilid even knew or cared about the plight of the Scots in the Highlands. There was no doubt the people in the Highlands appeared to be second class or maybe even third class citizens in the eyes of the MP's in Parliament. But those thoughts she had kept to herself for many a long year.

Monday. Eilid was up at first light. She couldn't sleep for thinking about what might have happened to Hamish. He had become such an invaluable part of Sir David's Estate she couldn't afford to lose him. Charles hadn't even wakened. Softly she crept out of the Lodge and got in the Land Rover. She was about to drive the ten odd miles to Kinlochewe when something made her turn up the track to her old cottage. I've just got a gut feeling, she told herself. She approached the cottage slowly. The Land Rover slid silently to a halt. It appeared the cottage was empty. There were no lights on and the storm door was shut tight. She walked up to the door apprehensively. Nothing. Nothing to indicate someone was at home. She knocked on the door. Silence. She shrugged her shoulders, she must have been wrong. She turned to leave when she heard a faint noise from inside. Hamish had come back, but God knows when. She was going to go back and leave Hamish in peace but she thought the better of it and so she knocked harder on the door. At last she heard Hamish.

"All right, all right, I'm coming. For God's sake, it's the middle of the night."

The door was pulled open and a disheveled Hamish peered into the morning light.

"Hamish, what the hell happened to you?"

"Sorry Eilid, it's a long story. I'll come over as soon as I get drawn together. I couldn't get word to you and we didn't get here until three o'clock or thereabouts this morning."

"Was it your father who held you back?"

"No, I wish it was. It was Mhairi."

"You mean she came all this way with you?"

"Aye she did. We got a lift from a truck coming out of Garve and he dropped us of at the end of the road at Kinlochewe. But it was that late there weren't any cars coming down the Glen, so we walked."

"Mercy me; you both must be tired."

"And famished." Hamish added.

"All right; take your time. Come up to the Lodge and my mother will give you and Mhairi some breakfast."

It was about ten o'clock when Mhairi and Hamish appeared looking weary. Mhairi was like Hamish. She was tall for her age, with straight red hair, pale skin and freckles. She had the same wishy-washy insipid blue eyes as Hamish but with a pert little nose and ears that were petit. She did not speak at all and was clearly painfully shy and very diffident about being at the Lodge at all. She wore the same blue dungarees that Hamish had worn when he first met Eilid.

Catriona took over.

"Mhairi, come over here and give me a hand with breakfast."

Mhairi nodded and went forward to the Range where there was a big frying pan filled with sausages and bacon sizzling away furiously.

"Just turn that bacon in a couple of minutes will you. I'm off to tend to my grandson. Will you be all right now?"

Mhairi nodded yes, and concentrated at the job she had been given. Meanwhile Hamish and Eilid had gone back outside. She could tell that Hamish was dying to speak to her.

"Okay Hamish, tell me what's going on."

"I couldn't leave her there, at the house. She's in a terrible state. My father came in last night drunk as usual but this time he was worse than ever before, the old bastard. He used to get Mhairi to do things for him, you know?"

"No I don't know you're going to have to tell me."

"Well when I say things I mean dirty things, miss." Hamish was back speaking as if to his schoolteacher again. His eyes never left the ground and Eilid could see he was coloring bright red with embarrassment.

"Let me help you out. You mean he got your sister to touch him in a sexual way?"

Hamish nodded too ashamed to look at Eilid.

"Has he touched Mhairi or worse?"

Hamish studied the ground more closely. "I don't know. She won't speak about it," he whispered, "but last night was terrible. I had come back from Rab Kennedy's, a friend of mine and there she was, sitting in the living room, in floods of tears her arms wrapped round her, looking terrified. So I just said to her she was coming with me and she didn't put up a fight. We grabbed what clothes she has and put them in the rucksack and we hitched a lift..."

"Don't be sorry, you've both been through a lot. Does your father know that Mhairi is here with you?"

"I don't know. He'll have guessed Mhairi's gone with me but he doesn't know where I am. We hardly spoke when I first arrived. I just told him I had a job, it was permanent and I was leaving home. He said about high time too. And that was end of conversation. See if he's done anything bad to Mhairi, I'll kill him, I really will, I'll kill him."

Eilid could see Hamish was on the point of breaking up emotionally. She came up to him and put her arm round his narrow shoulders and gave him a big hug. He fought back the tears with the aid of a big red handkerchief he pulled out of his trouser pocket.

"Come away in and get some breakfast. How do you like your eggs?" Eilid decided it was time to change the subject; they would talk more on this later.

In about half an hour all the food was gone, devoured by the Fergusons, as if they hadn't seen food in days. Catriona poured more tea and tried to strike up a conversation with Mhairi, but to no avail. The little girl was clearly in a shocked state and to her these people were strangers. Monday was virtually a wasted day. By the time evening came Hamish could hardly stand and his eyes were closing from fatigue.

Mhairi had taken to the baby like a duck to water. With so many brothers and sisters both Kathleen and Catriona reckoned she had been quite the little mother since her own mother's death. The rest of the week seemed to fly in and by Saturday all the sheep and lambs had been marked, dipped and sent back out to roam on the hills. The new assembled family seemed to find a routine that suited each and every one of them. Mhairi looked after Charles during the day and then she went back to the cottage with Hamish. Eilid and Hamish worked the hill, fixing broken fences and repairing some of the old dry stone dykes that crisscrossed the land. Eilid often wondered at the amount of back braking toil that had gone into the building of miles and miles of dykes. Just gathering the stone was work enough and then the building of the dyke, an art in itself, where no mortar was ever used, only the skill of the artisan to lay the stones and set them in such a fashion that a dyke would last for a hundred years or more.

Catriona and Kathleen, daughter and mother, spent their time cooking and cleaning and heaping masses of loving care on little Charles who was now getting quite plump with all the food the family foisted on him. He seemed to have a healthy appetite and crawled about the floor of the lodge at an alarming rate keeping grandmother and great grandmother on their toes as he scooted from room to room.

It was the third Saturday in May when Sir David Vickers and Sir Andrew Ballantyne came to visit. Sir Andrew had not seen Eilid for more than six months and he had missed his granddaughter terribly. He wished Eilid would write more often and reply to his letters that told of his loneliness and pain. His health had deteriorated during the year and he had his gall bladder removed which left him weak and feeling rather sorry for himself. So when David Vickers phoned and said would he like to join him to do a tour of the Cannich and Torridon Estates Sir Andrew accepted with alacrity.

The two Lairds could not have been more astonished to find what had taken place in the short seven months since they had congratulated Eilid as Stalker to the Torridon Estate. Sir Andrew in particular did not know whether to be overjoyed or dismayed at the discovery of Charles Edward Stuart. Sir David, by contrast, was not so much astonished by the child, as the fact that Eilid had obviously had an affair of some sort. She had never struck Sir David as being a promiscuous person, and, to his knowledge, when he left the Glen there was no one she was close to, let alone any sign of a man in her life. However they accepted the situation in what could just be described as good grace and, as they had arrived just in time for the evening meal, joining the assembled family of Stuarts and Fergusons for dinner. Catriona's Cullen Skink, a fish soup from the Orkney Islands, started the meal followed by spring lamb with roast potatoes, carrots and cauliflower.

Mhairi had made a contribution with a jam roly-poly, which was so light, and delicious the whole table treated her to a round of applause. Sir Andrew declared it took him back to his days at Boarding School where the only food worth eating had been the steamed puddings. Mhairi blushed to the very roots of her hair and became even more embarrassed when Sir David announced that she would be 'cookie' for the guests who would start to arrive in late August for the stalking. Eilid had quietly told both the Lairds about the circumstances of Mhairi's arrival and they were both shocked by what they heard and told Eilid she must go to the police. However when they learned there was no mother and that all the children were now under the grandmother's care they felt it was right to let sleeping dogs lie as an arrest would only stop Hughie Ferguson earning. Eilid had established, after many attempts at broaching the subject, that Mhairi had been touched quite inappropriately by her father, but fortunately never more than that. She was certain, of course, that had Mhairi stayed with her father, the outcome would have been unspeakable.

Sir Andrew and Eilid spent many hours together. They would go down the road to Diabeg and look out to sea over a bay that was once, Sir Andrew told her, the crater of some long extinct volcano. At other times they would walk on the surrounding hills and it was on one of these days that Sir Andrew talked about the Stratocruiser crash and how he had known some people associated with the disaster. Eilid covered by saying she had been at her Uncle's at the time and had missed all the action. She had never been back to the spot since that fateful day in January, as her memories remained very vivid on the grim event. Sir Andrew told her how he felt his Estate at Glen Cannich was going down hill because Angus, her surrogate father, had lost interest in himself and in the Estate. He didn't know how to handle the situation. He had known Angus all of his working life, apart from the war years, and now at forty-seven, his days out on the hill in all weathers and his addiction to whisky were taking their toll.

Sir Andrew said he hoped to live long enough to see his great grandson grow up and he indicated his determination to give the boy the best possible education. At sixty-five he felt he might not have many years left but he would make suitable arrangements to pay for Charles's future education.

It turned out to be the best possible week for both men. They ate and drank heartily, walked and talked a lot, went to Loch Maree and dapped for Sea Trout bringing home two beautiful eight pound fish that Catriona cooked to perfection. Mhairi continued to work wonders with pastry and general baking to the astonishment of all. Catriona had asked her how she had learned to bake so well, but Mhairi would blush and say nothing

Granny Kathleen got closest when she watched her baking short-bread one day. What she produced was a miracle that melted on the tongue and Kathleen saw that she referred to no recipe book or manual. She instinctively knew what to use and how to put the ingredients together. Kathleen had asked her,

"How do you know what to use, Mhairi?"

"I just know miss."

"Forgive me wee lass, but how do you know to use rice flour in shortbread, someone had to teach you that."

"No miss, I just watched my mammy, she was a great baker."

And it was then that they all learned Mhairi could hardly read, but to compensate she had developed a near photographic memory. Show her how to do something just one time and her mind encapsulated it.

"Ah tell ye all what," granny declared, "wi' a talent like that she could make a fortune in any hotel or pub, mark my words." Sir David and Sir Andrew readily agreed.

The next day was to be the last for Sir Andrew at Torridon. He and Eilid had a long walk over the Estate looking at the sheep and the ponies grazing contentedly. The weather had been kind to them and there had not been any rain during the week. Now as they walked through the bracken and peat hags on their way up to Liathach they could see clouds gathering which meant that the weather might break during the next day or so. Sir Andrew talked about Cannich and Eilid's father and he asked if Catriona had ever spoken to Angus or written to him. Eilid said that as far as she knew not one word, written or spoken had passed between them since her mother's departure almost four years earlier.

They climbed as high as Sir Andrew wanted and looked back eastwards down the Glen. The day too was drawing in and they walked back in silence in the beauty of the gloaming. Suddenly a herd of deer plunged across the gully in front of them quickly making themselves scarce by racing up the next steep escarpment as if none existed.

"There we are now, did you see that big Stag Sir Andrew? He was a Royal last year, twelve points no less and I think he might have more this year. It's difficult to tell because he's still in velvet but I don't want to lose that one. He'll improve the breed around here and that's what I want to do for Sir David."

"I'm impressed my dear. You're going the right way about it. How does Sir David treat you?"

"He gives me every freedom. I just couldn't have had Charles without the flexibility he allows me. I told him I had to borrow the Land

Rover to go to see my Uncle in Pitlochry and he never batted an eye, 'that's what it's there for', was all he said. Who else would be so generous to allow my mother and my grandmother to stay in the Lodge with me? I don't think there are too many estate owners that would let me have that sort of freedom and flexibility. Of course it'll all change by August, in time for the stalking; Mhairi and I and Hamish will be the only ones here. We seem to have found a cook in Mhairi I think we'll have some well pleased guests."

"Eilid, I'm very proud of you. You know Sir David talks about you all the time; how attractive you look and how intelligent you are. He wonders sometimes if you wouldn't like to quit this life style and take a job elsewhere; in the City maybe."

"Granddad, we've had that sort of conversation and I think he asked Auld John to ask me if I would like to go to London. I can't think of anything worse. I'm happy here in the country, I know I don't have many refinements but that's the way I am. And I'm very independent, you know."

Sir Andrew laughed. "Just like a Ballantyne, just like a Ballantyne. I'm glad we've had this conversation for there are two things on my mind. One is Charles and his education, now that's a-way-off yet but you can't plan too soon for important things like that. Then there's Cannich Estate, I've no living family except you, so you've helped me with your honest answers."

"What do you mean Granddad?"

"Oh nothing much, it was just a silly notion I had in my head." And farther on the subject Sir Andrew refused to be drawn. "Oh, aye, and there's another thing, I've got something important to give you, I very nearly forgot. Remind me at dinnertime, would you otherwise I shall forget. It's really something you must have."

That evening, after everyone had gone off to bed, Eilid and her Granddad sat totally relaxed in front of the log fire, each with a whisky, watching the flames flickering and dancing up the chimney, immersed in their own thoughts.

It was Eilid who broke the silence.

"Granddad, you told me to remind you of something you had for me, if it's convenient, now........"

"Oh, aye, there I go again, nearly forgot. Eilid go into my bedroom and on the dresser there's a big brown envelope. Bring it to me please, dear."

Eilid fetched the envelope and Sir Andrew slowly took out his penknife and slit it open. He carefully emptied the contents of the package onto the low table in front of the fire. Eilid couldn't see anything in detail the lighting was so subdued. There were a couple of photographs, some metal objects, what looked like envelopes containing letters and a slim bar of ribbon or something.

"Eilid, it's about time you had these. This is all that's left of my son Alasdair, your father. As you know he died in the war, one of the heroes of the Battle of Britain. These are his letters to me, given to me by my lawyer, the letters from your mother, and photographs of him in his uniform and standing in front of his Spitfire, the day before"...Sir Andrew stopped and swallowed hard, "the day before he was shot down." These are his medals. This one is the DFC, the Distinguished Flying Cross one of the greatest honors the country could bestow on the brave pilots whose actions thwarted the Luftwaffe. I want you to have these, they're yours by right."

Eilid was close to tears. She could see her Granddad was too. She went forward to him and gave him a hug resting her face on his shoulder. "I wish I could have met him. I think about him often and my mother has never let me see a photograph or anything."

She picked up one of the photographs and looked at it. It was an old black and white shot of a tall blond airman dressed in a flying suit and mufti leaning against the wing of a fighter plane. It had been a cloudy day and it was difficult to see much detail. She picked up another. And there smiling warmly was her father. No wonder, she thought, my mother wanted him, he looked so handsome and attractive. He was in RAF uniform with his cap held in his hand so that his blond hair was quite visible. Eilid stared at the picture for a long time. How she wished she could have known this man. That was where the blond hair came from, no doubt about that at all. She picked up the medals one by one each with their different colored ribbons and placed them on the table again. The letters she would read later.

She turned to her Granddad again. Talking his face in her hands she gently kissed him murmuring, "Thank you, thank you," as tears slowly coursed down her face to be joined by Sir Andrew's as the emotion of the moment overcame both of them. Eilid had no idea of how long they stood there just leaning on one another as the fire burned lower reflecting on their faces, granddaughter and grandfather in a warm embrace.

Gently, Eilid put all of her father's memorabilia back in the envelope, and, taking her grandfather's arm, made their way slowly upstairs.

It was a few days after Sir Andrew had left the Glen that Eilid showed the contents of the envelope to her mother. Catriona was both astonished and hurt that Sir Andrew hadn't seen fit to let her see the letters and all of Alasdair's possessions but she knew there was a closer bond between Sir Andrew and Eilid, better than she could have hoped, but it didn't remove the bitterness she felt all summer long.

It was the autumn of 1968 and Charles's tenth birthday approached. Not knowing the exact date of Charles birthday Eilid had made it November Thirtieth, St. Andrew's Day. She considered the date somewhat apposite as St. Andrew, being the Patron Saint of Scotland went well with Sir Andrew Ballantyne who was basically Charles own patron saint if the truth be told.

Not a year had gone by without some financial assistance from Sir Andrew who was as proud as only a great-grandfather can be without prying into hows and wherefores of Charles mysterious appearance in Eilid's world.

Charles had not developed like a normal child. He was thin and pale for a boy his age and as he got older he tired easily. He did not readily join school games and the other boys bullied and taunted him at times when he didn't participate. His inabilities took on a 'don't' attitude rather than a 'can't' attitude and he became tacit and withdrawn unless he was home with Mhairi or Hamish. Nevertheless Charles had struggled on manfully determined to do his best and not let his mother down.

The growing-up process which began as a wonderful experience for Eilid now became a cause for her concern. But she remembered the intervening years and how happy they had been for both surrogate mother and child. Charles's first steps, then his first words, his first day at the local school, all became milestones in Eilid's memory.

Charles was eight when Eilid took him on the hill with her for the first time. That day had troubled her. He seemed to have little energy and he also seemed to have trouble getting his breath on some of the steeper passages of the climb. Eilid could only hope that his health would improve but she had begun to accept that there was something fundamentally wrong with her son, but she didn't know what.

Over the years Charles had asked about his father and what had happened to him. Other boys all had daddies why not he? Eilid told him that his father had died in a terrible accident and steered away from the subject as quickly as possible.

His lack of physical strength and endurance was made up for in no small measure by his intelligence. Charles was clever. By the time he was five he was the best reader in the small village school and at eight he had mastered arithmetic and was finding simple algebra easy.

He and Hamish Ferguson had become firm friends and Charles looked up to Hamish like a big brother and, on occasion, like the father he had never known. Hamish proved to be an expert at woodcarving. Just as his sister Mhairi had shown her expertise at cooking and baking so Hamish could take a piece of wood and fashion it into something wonderful.

Charles became fascinated with woodcarving and he and Hamish would spend the long summer nights together using simple tools to carve all sorts of wonderful shapes out of driftwood they had found by the shores of a Loch.

Charles also became spellbound with the History of Scotland. He was an avid reader of books on the early Scottish monarchs and the stirring deeds of William Wallace and Robert the Bruce. Later on he would read of the demise of Mary Queen of Scots beheaded by her cousin Queen Elizabeth the First of England. Then, after Elizabeth and Oliver Cromwell, how there came about the Union of the Crowns in 1606 which made James VI of Scotland, Mary Queen of Scots son, King James 1st of England. Finally he read about Bonnie Prince Charlie, the Prince whose name he bore, and the 1745 rebellion that ended at Culloden field where many Highlanders were massacred by the English and Scottish lowlanders, supporters of King George I.

And so it was that history and wood carving gave Charles his early interests rather than football or shinty that occupied the time and focus of his other young school friends.

Eilid was now thirty-two and had taken on a maturity that made her look even more attractive. Stalking at Torridon was at a premium. Sir David Vickers may not have known it but he was the toast of the Glen. People flooded into Torridon in the hope of just catching a glimpse of Eilid, the tall, stunningly beautiful stalker striding up the hill in search of stags. Money flowed into pubs and shops like never before and the local tourist industry took off in a way no one could possibly Fhave envisaged. Sir David, always a salesman, had told his colleagues in London about his 'model of the glen' as he put it. One look at Eilid's photograph was enough to make them want to book the whole of the stalking season for themselves. However Sir David judiciously metered the would-be stalkers week by week. The prices for a week's stalking in the Glen went higher and higher, but there were never any refusals.

Not only did the stalking reach a level of finesse never before experienced by regulars but with Mhairi as cook a week at Torridon Lodge took on a gourmet-type pilgrimage as tales of Mhairi's remarkable culinary art grew.

Many of the visitors would embellish their week's adventure with stories of their conquest of Eilid to the scorn of others who had tried. To all her guests she remained professional, polite and evocatively alluring. It was that year that someone did turn her head and it happened in the most unusual way.

It was almost at the end of the stalking season and Eilid was driving the Land Rover up Glen Torridon on a dull Sunday afternoon when there was an almighty bang and a front tire went flat. It was Murphy's Law that as she got out to survey the damage, rain, which had threatened all day, became a reality and arrived in horizontal sheets soaking her, and everything else, in minutes. It was in the midst of this when she saw headlights of a car coming toward her. The car stopped and the driver, who was alone, got out and walked round the Land Rover. He was wearing a lightweight kagul that covered his body and legs and although the wind made it flap wildly around him he didn't seem to mind the rain. His hair was plastered to his head by this time. The driver identified himself as Douglas Hamilton and told Eilid to get into his car and he would take care of the rest.

"Do you know anything about Land Rovers," she had asked and he just nodded and held the car door open for her. In five minutes he had changed the wheel in the most appalling conditions. He opened the door for her and she rushed back into the Land Rover and continued on her way. Her hero, who looked very much in control of everything, had said only two or three words, accepted her profuse thanks with a nod and a wave and continued on down the road.

When Eilid returned to the Lodge later that night she discovered Douglas Hamilton was one of four guests who were staying for the week. Two of the men she knew and had been at Torridon before but she soon discovered that the Hamilton brothers were guests of Sir David. This usually meant Sir David would be up later in the week to find out how the 'newcomers' had done. If he was lucky he would be with them on the hill when they bagged their first stag and watch them get bloodied which was the main attraction of bringing novices on the hill. Eilid knew instinctively that these men were experienced, maybe not at stag hunting, but both Douglas and Peter Hamilton looked very calm and confident. She had warned Sir David about bringing complete novices to the Glen after the dreadful demise of Auld John, all due to the inexperience of a fool of a person with a firearm who should never have been allowed to go stalking in the first place.

The men all smiled warmly as Eilid came into the dining room. John Rogers, a paying guest who had never missed a year in eight, introduced the Hamiltons.

"So we meet again." Douglas smiled again and shook her hand. Peter, his brother, deciding to be more chivalrous, gallantly kissed Eilid's hand overwhelmed it seemed either with her beauty or her position as stalker on Sir David's Estate.

"Mr. Hamilton," Eilid turned to Douglas, "I can't thank you enough for changing that wheel for me. It would have taken me all of half an hour and I would have been completely soaked. How did you manage to change that wheel so quickly?"

"First of all call me Douglas. This is my younger brother Peter, he has always been a problem to the family," he grinned and waved his hand in Peter's general direction. "Now John and Mark," he motioned in the direction of the regulars, "don't need your help, but we most certainly do. Please join us for a drink after you have had your dinner and we'll discuss the tactics for tomorrow." He smiled warmly again in Eilid's direction.

"Do you not mean strategy?" countered Eilid.

"No, no, we know the strategy is to kill the seven stags we've been allotted, it's the tactics we've got to discuss."

The next morning confirmed what Eilid had thought about the Hamiltons. They certainly knew how to use a rifle. Peter was good for a four inch grouping round the bull, but Douglas was remarkable, every bullet found the bull at 100 yards, about an inch grouping. Eilid was impressed but she didn't say anything. First on the rifle that day was to be Douglas. They walked up the hill in the usual single file format stopping now and again while Eilid used her binoculars and her telescope to scan the hill for deer.

"What do you see Eilid," Douglas Hamilton asked at their third stop.

"Well there are two stags up there in the corrie. The big older one is just above that greenish patch right of the boulder, about one o'clock. The other is coming across the corrie, at about nine o'clock. He's about five years old and he's got a fine head on him. I won't be shooting him"

"What about the one who's lying down in the heather, above the big fellow but to the right at about three o'clock?" Douglas whispered in her ear.

Quickly Eilid scanned the part of the hill Douglas had indicated with her binoculars. She couldn't see a thing. Out came the trusty telescope that had been left to her by Auld John. Sure enough there was something there. She adjusted the focus slightly. It was a stag, lying down in a peat hag. There was not a sign of movement.

"I think that beast is dead, Douglas, its eyes are closed and if you look carefully he's sort of over to one side."

"You can see that?"

"I can with the telescope, let me try your field glasses. My goodness, these are wonderful binoculars, where did you get them?"

"Government issue," Douglas smiled an enigmatic smile.

"You work for the Government?"

"Well not exactly; in a roundabout sort of way."

"Really?"

"Yes, really."

Eilid decided to check out the stag lying in the bog. Fortunately there were small gullies and many blind spots in the terrain between the party and the big stag with the herd of hinds so that they reached 'Douglas's' stag without detection. Eilid had been right, the stag was dead. She turned the body over looking for something that might have caused his death. It was Douglas who spotted the holes first.

"Eilid, look here at his hindquarters."

Eilid examined the bullet holes that riddled the poor beast through the lungs and the bowel area. The stag had been shot many times, but not through the heart, it had bled to a long, slow death as a result of its wounds.

"My God, who or what could have done this?"

"Well we might not know who, but what killed him is an old fashioned Tommy gun or Sten gun. This stag has been killed by automatic fire."

"How do you know?" Eilid looked at Douglas, perplexed.

"Oh trust me, I know."

"It must be the poachers working their way up the country. I had heard of similar incidents around Inverness but I never thought it would get this far north." Eilid looked perplexed.

"Aye, but remember it's free meat to these people, and they don't give a toss how many they wound or maim, there's a market for venison and that's what this is all about."

"Well there's nothing we can do about it now, but these are wonderful binoculars you have, they're better even than mine. I'm glad you spotted this beast. Let's continue with the stalk. I'll get Hamish to take this one down after we've got that big stag up there with all the hinds."

So began a mutual admiration pact between the two or so it seemed to Hamish as a casual observer; he had never seen Eilid quite so animated when carrying on a conversation as she did with Douglas. Carefully she stalked the stag with a herd of about seventy hinds. It was a fairly long and difficult shot of at least 150 yards. There would be no possibility of getting any closer as there were hinds all fanned around the stag and to attempt to get closer would alert them. One bark from a hind and the herd would take off. Eilid crawled over to a suitable hummock of coarse grass and took another look through her telescope.

"It's not an easy shot," she whispered to Douglas, who had stayed back behind her as she spied on the herd. "See what you think, come up here," she beckoned with her right hand and indicated where the stag was. Douglas moved up slowly almost like a professional and carefully peeked over the small ridge that was hiding them from the deer. The stag was so far back that all Douglas could see was the beast's head with a magnificent set of antlers. Quickly he counted eleven points, but what a wide set of antlers. The stag must have weighed at least 250 pounds. He turned to Eilid and she slid him the rifle.

"It's ready, just slowly put off the safety; do you think you can make it? I won't be put out if you feel you can't."

Douglas gave her a slow smile. "I think I can ," he mouthed back at her. The rifle was just at his shoulder when a hind came over on top of them and barked just once.

"Quickly!" She hardly had time to finish the word as Douglas pulled the trigger. The herd erupted in flight running upward and spreading all over the corrie. Eilid stood up. There was no sign of the stag. She looked down at Douglas who hadn't moved apart from rapidly reloading the rifle.

"Got him!" was all he said and smiled broadly. Eilid turned the binoculars up to where the stag had been. Sure enough he was there, stone dead lying in the heather. Douglas got up slowly, opened the breach, depressed the next round and slipped the bolt back in place with the trigger depressed. Just the same safety drill as Eilid observed. Slinging the rifle over his shoulder he started up the hill without a word. They both got to the stag at about the same time. The beast's glassy eyed stare told them he was quite dead, but still Eilid opened her hunting knife and pressed the point in the corner of the stag's eye. Not a flicker. She grabbed one of the antlers to move the body over for the gralloch and it swung about madly.

"My God, I don't believe it right through the top of his head and you've taken away the top of his skull, you'll have to glue the antlers together look it's shake, rattle and roll." Eilid laughed.

"Jesus, so it is, so much for that. But that's all I could see was the top of his head." Douglas explained as Eilid bled the stag from the chest cavity. "I must say I'm parched, must have been all that wine last night."

"Douglas, there's a wee burn down there if you want to get a drink."

"Good idea", said Douglas and off he went the few paces down the hill to drink from the burn. Little did he know that Eilid was waiting for his return with hands cupped with blood from the chest wall. As Douglas stepped forward she came from behind and plastered his face with blood.

"You bugger," wailed Douglas, "I forgot about that." He stood looking like some Pictish Chief who had just returned from a bloody battle. He dug in his pocket for a handkerchief to wipe off the offensive matter sticking to his face, but there was a loud shout from the assembly.

"No, no you can't do that. This is your first stag, that's the tradition.

The gore's got to stay on for the day."

Douglas grudgingly accepted his fate but vowed revenge on Eilid, who had never laughed so hard in such a long time. There was something attractive about Douglas, Eilid thought. Was it because he respected her professionalism on the hill or was it because, unlike other men she had known, he made no comment on her looks, spoke to her as an equal, and sometimes even ignored her presence? Eilid wasn't sure that she liked the indifference he sometimes showed, but from Douglas's point of view that was his trump card. He knew if he showed respect to women he liked, they would come 'round sooner or later. It was a waiting game. And if it didn't happen....well...there was the whole world out there, or was there? He had to admit to himself he had never quite admired and respected any woman as he did Eilid.

It turned out to be a quite perfect day. The wind stayed coming from the south-west and by the time the sun was sinking over Liathach two more stags, not counting the dead beast they found, were culled. The stalking party had walked about twelve miles, dragged the stags for the best part of five or six, to where the ponies could fetch them. They all voted that a serious après stalk was called for.

Mhairi filled the bill with her usual flair. The menu consisted of smoked haddock mousse, wild duck soup, steak and kidney pudding followed by a heart stopping jam roly-poly with lashings of custard and fresh cream. The wine flowed as did the malt whisky afterwards and the tales of valor and expertise grew more and more elaborate as the evening progressed. Eilid had been invited to dinner that night on Douglas's insistence. Normally the stalker was invited to share diner with their guests on one night only but Douglas would not hear of it. As was the custom he presented Eilid with a bottle of whisky for his first stag. It was a bottle of 18 year-old Macallan, which Eilid had not tasted since the night Sir David and Sir Andrew had come to her cottage to tell her she had the job as Stalker on the Torridon Estate.

Eilid had slipped outside to get some fresh air. The dining room had become stifling; Mhairi had gone back to the cottage with Hamish as she just wanted some peace and quiet before she too went to bed. She had checked on Charles who was sleeping soundly. Without Mhairi's help with Charles she didn't know how she would have managed during the stalking season. So deep in thought was she that she didn't hear Douglas come up behind her.

"Penny for them," was all he said as he sat down beside her. "Tired?"

"Just a bit, I think it's the wine. I'm not used to drinking so much. Are you not tired?"

"Fresh as a daisy, actually, I thought we might just take a wee wander, as you might say, down the Glen."

"You mean walking?"

"Hardly, I thought we might just wander down in the Land Rover to see if the poachers might return tonight." Douglas turned to face her.

Eilid put down her glass. "You know I forgot all about that. I doubt if they'll come tonight, they must have gone down to Inverness to unload their kill. I can't imagine they'll be back so soon."

"Eilid, you're not thinking. The weather's perfect; there's almost a full moon; it's cold enough for the deer to come down the hill, almost to the roadside at night, they might never get a better opportunity."

Eilid knew he was right. There was something strange about Douglas that attracted her and scared her slightly at the same time.

"Douglas, can I ask you something? Were you in the Army?"

"No, I can answer that honestly, I was not in the Army. Why?"

"Well there's something about you that speaks of the military, I think. My Dad was in the Gordon Highlanders you know?"

"I didn't, was that during the war?"

"Yes."

"Tough times," added Douglas.

"I suppose, but for him they ended up tougher in peace time," said Eilid

"How do you mean?"

"It's a long story; it doesn't matter." Eilid decided this was not the time and place to reveal her thoughts to Douglas, no matter how nice he might appear.

A long silence followed as each sipped at their drinks contemplatively, neither wanting to make the next move.

"About tonight," Eilid broke the silence. "Do you really think they'll come back?"

"I would if I were them. They've gone undetected by now, they must be feeling confident."

"Do you think we should go down the Glen, or rather up the Glen and see if we can find out what's going on?"

"I think it would be a good idea. Even if we don't catch them red-handed at least they'll see there's a presence and it would be a very bold poacher who would try and take out some stags when the Stalker or Game Keeper is about."

There certainly was some sense to what Douglas suggested. It was now after midnight and Charles was sound asleep. It would be unusual for him to waken before Eilid and Douglas returned. In any event the other three guests were there and Eilid knew them well enough, two of them anyway, to know that Charles would be in good hands if he happened to waken unexpectedly.

Douglas and Eilid had just got into the Land Rover and started it up when Douglas asked,

"You have the rifle with you, don't you?"

"No. I didn't think we'd need it."

"Well I'd think again." He chided her gently. "Suppose we meet these characters with a Sten gun, for example, we might have to defend ourselves, I would certainly take the rifle, and ammunition of course."

"Douglas, I might be daft but I'm not stupid," Eilid came back on him, "of course there will be ammunition." And with that she leapt out of the Land Rover and came back in a couple of minutes with the Mannlicher.

The skies had cleared sufficiently for some fitful moonlight to filter through, half lighting the hills in a softish glow. Eilid doused the headlights as they reached the main Torridon road. There was sufficient light to see where they were going without forewarning anyone of their approach. But they spied no one and nothing seemed to be moving as they finally arrived at Kinlochewe. It was now after one in the morning. Eilid turned the Land Rover around and they made their way slowly back down the glen. They were almost at the road that turned off to Hamish's cottage when they heard the short staccato bark of an automatic weapon, then silence.

"It came from over here," said Douglas pointing at the foot of Liathach. Slowly they pulled into a passing place and turned off the sidelights. The Land Rover was now practically invisible. Slowly they both eased themselves out of the Land Rover and closed the doors as quietly as possible. There was another burst of gunfire and this time they could see the flashes from the very base of the hill, not at all far off the road.

Douglas bent down into the drainage ditch at the roadside and picked up some dark peat moss and rubbed it over his face. Then he turned to Eilid.

"Permit me," he said, and proceeded to plaster the dank peat all over her face.

"Is this your way of getting me back for the blooding today," she hissed.

"No it's not. Nothing stands out in the moonlight like a white face and you have one." Douglas's teeth flashed in a quick smile. "Let's go."

He moved off down the road quickly but quietly, his Vibram soled boots making hardly noise on the asphalt. Suddenly there was more gun fire, but closer this time. As they approached a small quarry, which had been gouged out of the hillside for road metal many years before, they saw a big dark van parked in a far corner. The glow of a cigarette told them that someone was standing by the van. Quietly, Douglas moved up the hill at the side of the quarry so that he and Eilid would be looking down into the quarry in good cover if, and when, anything happened. They didn't have to wait long. There were noises above and to the right of them as two men dragged a dead deer down a steep slope to the entrance of the corrie.

"Haw Jim. Gie's a hand fur Christ sake 'till we get this big bruiser intae the van." The cigarette went out as the smoker moved to give the other two a hand with their trophy. The van doors swung open and with a mighty heave the carcass was loaded onto the tailgate and then dragged forward out of sight. The two disappeared again and about five or six minutes passed when the second carcass was dragged down the hill and the same exercise repeated.

Eilid looked at Douglas. "What are we going to do?"

"Just watch for the time being. They must have another one to fetch."

And Douglas was right. What looked like one headless stag and two hinds were loaded in less than 40 minutes.

"Jesus, Hughie, let's take a break. Gie's a fag and then we'll get oot o' here. No' a bad night mind ye. Three beasts in less than two hours, by Christ the Sten's the thing; nae messing aboot. Dae ye think we hit that ither wan that ran away?"

The question was addressed to his partner who had the Sten gun slung over his shoulder. Douglas was looking at it through his binoculars. "Sten Mark 2" he said to no one in particular, "with a silencer."

"Aye I think Ah winged it but it's off and gone the now. Maybe we'll find it the morra when we come back."

The conversation made Eilid's blood run cold. Shooting indiscriminately into a herd like that gave the poachers no idea of how many they hit or maimed. The ones that dropped they picked up and left the others to their fate, which was what had happened to the stag they had found dead that day.

"I think we'll get rid of these hoodlums, don't you think Eilid?"

"What are you going to do?"

"Give them a surprise and some of their own medicine. Give me the rifle, please."

"Not before I know what you're going to do, please Douglas you can't just shoot them in cold blood!"

"Well I could actually, these are bastards, but I promise you I'll only shoot at them if they return fire, okay?"

"I suppose you know what you're doing." Eilid reluctantly handed over the rifle.

"Listen Eilid, I know what I'm doing. I'm going to give these bastards the fright of their lives, get rid of them, and save you taking any responsibility on the subject of discharging a firearm in a public place, okay?"

"Right." She responded.

Douglas had clearly taken command. The three poachers were starting to move to the van when the first shot took out the vehicle's windshield.

"Fuck me," cried Jim the driver. "Did that Sten of yours go aff Sanny?"

"No, no way, we're bein' shot at. Tak cover."

The owner of the Sten gun dropped behind a rock and didn't move. There was complete silence. Sanny was just starting to crawl on his belly to the van when Douglas's second shot blew out a tire. Sanny now had an idea of the general direction of the gunfire. Douglas watched as he loaded a magazine into the breach and, crouching, let go a burst in Douglas's general direction.

The next shot went right through Sanny's shoulder and the Sten went spinning into the depths and darkness of the quarry.

"Jesus Christ, we've got tae get oot o' here," Hughie yelped frantically as he ran to the van, opened the door, and clambered in. Douglas held his fire. Jim had now got to Sanny's side and was helping him back to the van too.

The van engine sprang to life as Jim turned the ignition key and drove out of the quarry with the flat tire flapping loudly and then, to Eilid's complete surprise, turned right down the road towards Torridon village and Diabeg.

"We've got them now!" Yelled Douglas, as he made off down the side of the quarry carrying the rifle at the trail, let's go to Loch Carron and tell the police what's going on."

An exhausted Eilid and a tired but elated Douglas arrived back at the Lodge just as dawn broke. They had contacted the police and an Inspector from Portree in Skye had asked them to wait at the Loch Carron station where he would interview them about the events of the night. It had taken over two hours for the Inspector to make his way to Loch Carron. By that time Eilid and Douglas were nodding off, not from tiredness, but with the sheer boredom of waiting for the local constabulary. Hardly a word had passed between them, but Douglas knew instinctively that Eilid had approved of what he had done. The wounded man would live, and live to tell the tale. That was exactly what Douglas wanted. Sir David's Estate would be free from poachers for some considerable time.

The Inspector turned out to be a tall, thin, gray, elderly and serious man with an almost Sherlock Holmes nose who quite properly regarded 'Glen Warfare,' as he called it, totally unacceptable. He started by asking what shots had been fired by whom and Douglas used a degree of journalistic license to say the first shots had come from the poachers. He didn't say at whom, but it was the Inspector's slightly misplaced assumption that the poachers had opened fire on Eilid and Douglas first. The going had been tough at first as firing a weapon at anyone is considered quite outwith the law in Britain, even in the most extreme circumstances. The Inspector was becoming very difficult when Douglas asked if he might have a private word with him. Whatever Douglas said or did resolved any difficulties. Eilid and Douglas left the Police Station at about five-thirty in the morning; it was now pitch black as the earlier moon had disappeared.

"What did you do to make the Inspector back off like that, Douglas?"

"Oh, I used my natural charm. What else sweet maid?"

"Douglas you really are so full of. . . . . . well I won't say it, it's not lady like."

"Ladies, I don't see any ladies!"

Tired as she was that comment called for retaliation; Eilid wasn't quite sure if he was half joking or whole earnest but she was about to find out.

"You great shit!" She screamed and drove her elbow into Douglas's side with a force that knocked the wind out of Douglas and very nearly put the Land Rover in the ditch.

"Jesus Christ, Eilid, you'll have us over." Douglas clutched his side in pain. Then he reached over, grabbed the steering wheel, almost sat on top of Eilid, stamped on the brakes and brought the Land Rover to a screeching halt in the middle of the road. It was sill dark. He moved back to his side of the vehicle, put his arm round her neck, brought her face to his and kissed her. Softly at first, then as Eilid almost unconsciously responded he kissed her deeper and deeper until her lips parted and his tongue found hers in combined passion. Eilid could feel something happening to her that she had never ever felt before. It was frightening and exhilarating all at the same time. Suddenly she found herself wanting Douglas, in a way that was embarrassing to her. Slowly she pushed Douglas away and he acceded.

"Whew," she said breathing outwards her voice taking on a huskiness she couldn't control. "Douglas, that was wonderful, seriously, but I've never had anyone like you before."

"What about Charles's father? He must have been kind of, shall we say, persuasive, eh?"

"That's not a subject I discuss, but he was certainly not like you."

"Come *on* Eilid, you must have had plenty lovers. You can't look like you and not get attention from men."

"It's not that kind of attention I want, truly, I could tell you some terrible stories but I'd rather not dredge them up. All it does is to remind me of things and events I'd rather not remember."

"All right, let's say no more." And at that Douglas leaned over and kissed her lightly on the lips again. He was backing away when Eilid pulled him to her and kissed him with ferocity that astonished even the worldly-wise Douglas. If I didn't know better, he thought to himself, this woman's never made love. He just didn't know how close he was to the truth when he broke their embrace and said,

"Later, darling, we've got to get back."

Eilid's spirits soared like one of the great Golden Eagles in the glen. 'Darling', 'darling,' no one had ever called her darling before, except maybe her mother and she couldn't remember when last that was. Eilid drove down the glen with a jauntiness that was reflected in her driving. Eilid had someone she loved and she thought loved her. It was a moment to savor.

Mhairi was just up when they returned to the Lodge. Charles was still fast asleep and there was no sign as yet of the other guests as it was just past six o'clock. The smell of the bacon frying and the coffee being brewed lifted their spirits. They told Mhairi briefly what had happened and she was amazed that they had been up all night and wanted to know more about the poachers and why they hadn't rounded them up. Douglas explained that that was a job for the police and they had left it like that. Eilid and Douglas were just finishing their breakfast when a police car drew up outside the Lodge.

The Inspector they had seen earlier got out of the car and walked to the door. Eilid, on seeing him coming beckoned him in.

"Would you not like a cup of tea or coffee Inspector, and Mhairi will let you have some bacon on a roll, does that sound good?"

"Indeed it does," Inspector Robertson agreed. "Can I have a cup too for my driver?"

"We'll do better than that. Mhairi away and invite the poor soul in, it's a gey dreich morning to be sitting out there."

Eilid looked at the Inspector and he nodded his approval. Mhairi moved off to do as she was bid. The young policemen came in, thankful to see a warm fire and smell the bacon frying in the pan. The first cup of coffee didn't touch the sides and Mhairi rushed to give him a refill.

"Don't you be spoiling him now miss," The Inspector chided more cheerful now than he had been previously.

"My name's Mhairi, Mhairi Ferguson, sir."

Your not one of the Fergusons from near Garve are you?"

"Aye, that I am sir."

"So you'll be old Hughie's daughter then?"

"Right again, sir."

"You must like it here?"

"Oh *yes* sir. I wouldn't leave for the world."

"Better than being at home I suppose?"

Goodness thought Mhairi, no wonder he was a policeman, question followed question. But there was a purpose in the Inspector's questions, which soon became clear.

"That it is sir."

"Does your dad still drink a lot?"

"I don't know sir. Haven't seen my Dad for"...she stopped and screwed up her freckled face, thinking hard..."well on ten years it must be. You'd be best to ask Hamish when he comes up from the cottage. He sees him now and again."

"You've a sister, haven't you Mhairi?"

"Aye I have, Allison, sir."

"And she'll be about how old?"

Mhairi thought hard again. "I think she'll be about 18, sir. There's seven years between us."

"Why did you leave home, Mhairi?"

Eilid watched as Mhairi became agitated. Silence.

"Was it because of your father?"

Eilid watched as Mhairi went bright red to the roots of her red hair and she started to retreat to find refuge in the kitchen. Eilid jumped up and put her arms around her.

"Do we need to have this Inspector?"

"No, no, forgive me; it was not my intention to interrogate the lass. That's just the policeman in me. I'm very sorry." He went towards Mhairi to give her a hug, but she backed off out of Eilid's arms and made a rush for the sitting room, dabbing furiously at her eyes.

While she was out of the room Eilid told the Inspector what she knew about Mhairi and her father and how the little waif of fifteen had forgotten all about her father and never wanted to go back and see him again.

"There's a purpose to all this though, isn't there, Inspector?"

"Indeed I'm afraid there is. You see we've heard reports that old Hughie is, shall we say, for want of a better word, hitting on Allison, Mhairi's sister who is now eighteen. No one in the family will do anything, otherwise we'd have the old devil behind bars before you could say knife. But we are powerless unless either the daughter speaks out or one of her brothers reports the old man. That was the reason behind my questions and I'm truly sorry I've dragged up the whole mess."

Eilid and the Inspector joined Douglas and the young policeman from the corner of the kitchen where they had gone to have their conversation.

"Where did Mhairi go?" the young officer asked.

"I don't know, I think she got some bacon fat in her eye, away and see if she's all right John."

The Inspector pointed to the living room into which Mhairi had bolted.

Mhairi eventually emerged on the arm of the constable looking much more composed and smiling slightly at the young man, who, it seemed, had also taken an interest in her. The Inspector pushed aside his plate having eaten well. Not content to give the police just a roll and bacon Mhairi had provided a full cooked breakfast.

It was Douglas who asked the obvious.

"Inspector, I'm sure this is not a social visit. What happened last night?"

Inspector Robertson smiled his thin smile. "I wondered when any of you were going to ask."

He pushed back his chair and was just about to speak when Peter Hamilton and the two regular guests appeared for breakfast.

"Well now, what's been going on, you lot? Bust up the town last night did you, is that why the police are here?"

Douglas looked at his younger brother in a way that probably only siblings understand. The look said 'shut up and buzz off.'

"Right then chaps, Peter blundered on, let's have breakfast, you have left some for us Inspector, haven't you?" he said looking at the empty plates.

Peter got no response as the Inspector, Eilid and Douglas got up and moved to the living room.

"Goodness!" said a far too jovial Peter, was it something we said?" as the party took their leave.

Eilid and Douglas sat on one of the big sofas, the Inspector commandeered a big armchair and the young policeman sat on the arm of another lounge chair.

"Sorry about that," Douglas apologized for his brother. "Please go on."

"Right, as I was going to say, and this will interest you, I think we've caught a band of very well organized poachers. One of our cars picked up a trail of blood on the road, obviously dripping from a shot beast, and followed it all the way to Diabeg."

"You can't be serious," Eilid looked at the Inspector amazed.

"Aye, indeed I am. They had a boat moored in the bay there; Diabeg is a pretty deserted place at this time of the year, which suits their purpose. They were about to unload the slaughtered deer when our boys were on them. Now another thing, the boat wasn't wasting its time either. The bloody thing, pardon me ma'am," he looked at Eilid who just smiled back, "was full of salmon and lobster to boot. These people had netted salmon, poached lobster creels belonging to local fishermen, and loaded up venison. It was a gourmet's dream on the high seas. Now, how far down the coast they would have sailed we don't know yet, but I bet it wouldn't be too far and then they would re-load another van and drive the goods to London where they'd get top price. Aye, the Special Branch did well last night." Inspector Robertson smiled encouragingly at Douglas.

Douglas gave a quick shake of his head, looked very serious for a moment and then turned away from the Inspector.

Eilid said nothing but clearly there was a lot more to Mr. Douglas Hamilton than met the eye. She was about to ask Douglas something, thought the better of it and went through to see how Mhairi was doing. All the guests had been taken care of and John, the young policeman was giving a helping hand with the dishes. It was at this point young Charles came into the dining room looking very much the young Laird. His auburn hair had become slightly more reddish as the years progressed. He was tall for his age but his pallor was that of someone who did not enjoy good health. He wore a heavy green shirt of twill, open at the neck, a kilt of Urquhart White Line tartan. He wore dark green stockings with matching tartan flashes. A sgian dubh was tucked into the top of his right stocking. A brown leather sporran sat on the apron of his kilt.

"Good morning Charles," the guests and Mhairi all chorused.

"Good morning," he softly responded.

He smiled at all the guests. "Where's Mr. Douglas?"

"He's through there with your mother talking to Nosey Parker," said Mhairi.

Charles laughed at the name. "Who is Nosey Parker?"

"This man's boss," and she pulled young John towards her playfully.

"God," whispered John under his breath, "don't let him hear you calling him that, they'll be no living with him, it's bad enough as it is."

John fell immediately silent as Inspector Robertson came into the room with Douglas and Eilid trailing.

"Hello young man!" The Inspector tried his charm at Charles who looked curiously at the police uniform.

"Have you come to take mummy to jail?"

"No I wouldn't do a thing like that, why would I?"

God, he's off again, thought Eilid and Mhairi simultaneously.

"Well she shoots things you know," Charles looked straight into the policeman's face with his huge green eyes.

"Does she really, well I think she probably has the right to shoot things, don't you think so?"

"Well I don't know. She's going to shoot Mrs. McBride down at the local store, you know. She's a nasty lady and I heard mummy telling grandma she could kill her."

Eilid couldn't believe her ears. She put up her hand to protest, but The Inspector stopped her with a look.

"How long ago was this?"

"Oh last year when grandma visited, I wish she would come back, I like grandma, and she likes me." Charles averred, assuring the Inspector that it was a mutual admiration society.

"Well thank you for all that information and I'll keep in touch with you now and again if I may."

"Oh, any time. I'm here most of the time; this is school break for the tattie howking." Charles made a face at the thought of digging up the local farmers' potato crop.

Eilid waited 'til the Inspector and young John headed for the door and got beside the Inspector.

"I only just said…"

But the Inspector cut her off with a wave of his hand. "We all wished we had killed Eliza McBride, at some time or another" he smiled a genuine smile for the first time at Eilid, and went on, "however, when I need to know all the family secrets, I'll know who to talk to first."

He laughed as he exited the Lodge with young John rushing to open the police car door for him. Eilid's exhaustion came back with a rush. The night's activity combined with the complete lack of sleep was catching up on her. There wasn't any way she could take the guests stalking that day. She made a decision, which she hoped would not back fire on her. She made her way into the dining room where everyone was leaning back in their chair having polished off another of Mhairi's heart stopping breakfasts when Mhairi came in with the sandwiches made up for each of them to take on the hill.

"Have you seen Hamish?" she looked over to Mhairi.

"Aye, miss, he's just outside spying the hill. You can't see him for the Land Rover.

"Oh right, okay Mhairi I just wondered where he was."

Eilid went outside and talked to Hamish.

"Hamish, can you be stalker today? How do you feel about it?"

"Great Eilid, just great." This was the opportunity Hamish had longed for, to show *his* skills on the stalk. But now he felt strangely nervous. The guests were not strangers and they knew some of Eilid's techniques. They'd be watching him closely.

"All right now?" Eilid saw the flash of failure in his eyes. "You can do it, I know you can, you're better than many who call themselves Stalker up and down the glens," she gave him a fierce hug.

"What about the ponies?"

"I'll get Charles to watch for you firing the heather, it'll be well on by that time and I'll have slept, I'll bring the ponies up to you."

"That'll be just fine."

Hamish put away his telescope and went into the Lodge to get the hill party together.

Eilid saw nothing of Douglas until just past one o'clock. The weather had held up quite nicely for stalking with gray skies, a light Southwesterly wind, and no rain. Charles had done a wonderful job scanning the hills with his own personal mini-binoculars, one of the many gifts from Sir Andrew. So far he reported no firing of the heather and so Eilid went to find Douglas. She found him perched on a rock with a small poachers' rod quietly fly-fishing the Lochan hard-by what used to be her cottage. He heard her coming despite the fact that she tried to sneak up on him and give him a surprise.

He reeled in as she approached. "Any luck," Eilid asked.

"One bite and I lost it; I think it was foul hooked. Big fish though, would have done you and me fine for lunch. By the way, how's Hamish doing?"

"No smoke yet, unless Charles has missed it."

"No he hasn't missed anything. I've been keeping an eye out and there's been nothing. At least with the wind the way it is the smoke will drift our way."

"Douglas, what do you do for a living?"

"I'm own a garage and I'm the Land Rover concessionaire for the North of Scotland; that's from Perth up."

"No wonder you changed the wheel so quickly."

"Well, not really. All those linkage rods and things are truly a pain in the arse, I cheated. I've got a small hydraulic jack in the back of the Rover. Gets the vehicle up in seconds and there you are…easy as pie."

"But there's more to you than that, isn't there?"

"I suppose so."

"Do I get to know, or are you going to be the mysterious stranger in my life for ever?"

"Not for ever."

"What does that mean?"

"It means not for ever, some day, I'll tell you about me."

"Douglas I like you, I like you more than anyone I've ever met." Her voice slowed now, all kinds of emotions were swirling within her. There was a huskiness when she spoke again.

"No man has ever kissed me like you did last night, correction…this morning. I want to know where I stand in your emotions."

Eilid's naivety touched his heart. Douglas knew instinctively by her ingenuousness she was not used to romance or having a man in her life. There had been none. He could see that now. How Charles had come into the world was literally and metaphorically a misconception of the first order. He would have to handle this very carefully. He liked her, he knew, did he love her? Maybe. He hadn't really asked himself the question. There had been so many fine women in his life; this was not the time to commit.

"Eilid, I love you dearly. You're beautiful, talented, and quite out of my league. I could never measure up to your style and quality of life. I live for the most part in London, far from here. I have managers who look after my business affairs in Scotland and I'm seldom in Scotland. I visit Perth, for example, about four times a year."

"But you'll come back and visit won't you?" Her voice was pitched now, almost shrill.

"Of course, I couldn't think of a nicer place to be with a woman who likes me. And I like her. I promise I'll be back and I'll write, but only if you promise to write me back."

"Oh I will, I will," Eilid eagerly agreed.

Romance for two had come into the Glen. First to Eilid, who was prepared to pine for almost a year for Douglas's return, and secondly to Mhairi who had captured the heart of John Chisholm, the young policeman who drove Inspector Robertson's car. It would be some time before Eilid and Douglas consummated their love for one another in critical circumstances which brought them together again. Mhairi and John had not taken long to have their night together, although there were necessarily long intervals between their love making, as John had to initiate many and varied ploys with the police force to get down the glen to meet his loved one.

'Sirs' week, as it was called in the glen, drew near. It had become tradition that Sir David, as Laird and owner of the Estate, invited other peers to stalk in the last week of the stag cull. Sir Andrew had always been his first choice and the two of them still shared a mutual admiration and a strong liking for one another. Sir Andrew was now seventy-five and while he took the odd stroll on the hill his stalking days were over. David Vickers still included him in the party but invited one or two other younger peers with whom he was friendly to join him.

Mhairi excelled herself in preparing for the visitors. Her love for John Chisholm had apparently given her wings and she gaily flew through the days before the guests arrived on the Sunday, making the most wonderful pasties and bridies for them to take on the hill with equally light-as-a-feather vol-au-vent canapés as appetizers before dinner.

Eilid was equally prepared to enjoy the week. There was a backlog of stags to be culled and the three peers who would be stalking had thirteen stags to get in the six days before the cull ended. There was actually one day left for culling as the 20th fell on a Monday of the following week that year; however she reckoned that only Sir David would stay if there were any stags left. All of the guests were excellent shots so she looked forward to a week of good sport.

It was Sir Andrew who was first to arrive early on the Sunday morning and take everyone by surprise. He looked remarkably fit dressed in his tweed jacket and breeches as if he was ready for the hill. Eilid thought his face looked a little thinner but his eyes sparkled as brightly as ever and his mind was just as incisive.

"For goodness sake Granddad, can you not let us have a wee bit time to ourselves?" Eilid chided. "We've just got rid of a party who ate us out of house and home, there's hardly any food left, no shops are open, so it's all home fare."

They embraced for a long time, holding one another close. Eilid and Sir Andrew had a very special relationship that had developed quietly over the years. Sir Andrew could now see in Eilid those qualities, which he had admired so much in his son. Age seemed to have made him much more aware of the fragility of life and he was becoming more emotional as the years progressed.

"Eilid, you look beautiful, but, as they say in the United States, what else is new? He stood back and smiled up at her. "Well now, there's a new twinkle there I haven't seen before, what's that all about?"

Eilid didn't know quite what to say. There had been an emotional goodbye with Douglas Hamilton the previous day, and while she was sad to see him go, her heart followed him all the way home. She was in love and she had finally realized it. It was a wonderful feeling. Surely none of that showed?

"What me? What do you mean?" she colored as she tried to answer Sir Andrew in an off-hand way.

Sir Andrew reached out and took both of her hands in his and, looking her in the eye, said "Eilid, how well do you know me? Have I ever been wrong about you?"

"Granddad, all right. I think I'm in love."

"That's wonderful. Would I know who this lucky man might be? It's not Charles' father is it?'

"Lord no Granddad. We've had this conversation. No, it's Douglas Hamilton."

"A ah! I thought he might appeal to you."

"You mean you know him?"

"Of course, the man's a legend."

"A legend? What does that mean?"

"Douglas Hamilton was in the SAS, one of the top men in the SAS."

"What's the SAS?"

"You must have heard of the SAS?"

"No I haven't."

"You mean you've slept with this man and he didn't tell you he was in the SAS?"

"I did not sleep with Mr. Hamilton, whether he was in the bloody SAS or not."

Andrew Ballantyne smiled inwardly. At least he had got the information he most wanted to hear. He was almost certain there had never been a man in Eilid's life but after the arrival of Charles he wasn't so sure. His granddaughter could have had any man on whom she set her sights. There was little doubt in his mind on that issue. He just wanted to check her resolve and he felt almost ashamed that he had doubted her integrity.

"Let me tell you a bit about the SAS. The SAS stands for Special Air Service and is one of the best known and respected elite forces in the world. The SAS consists of small raiding units of four to five men and was the brainchild of a Captain David Stirling. The SAS are used for special missions and can infiltrate behind enemy lines. I suppose they could best be described as small Commando units. They have seen action all over the world. They are a very secretive bunch and not too many people know about their existence."

"So Douglas was really in the army."

"Well yes, you could say that. I think anyone would take it as an insult if you suggested they were 'in the army'. As I said they are very elite part of the army. Very few qualify for the Winged Dagger badge, which is the emblem of the SAS. Only about 10% of those who seek entry in the SAS succeed. Douglas was in the Air Troop, which is one of the most hazardous units to be in. The objective of 22 SAS is to parachute out of aircraft at a great height, 25,000 feet for example and land deep behind enemy lines. These very brave individuals were nicknamed the Ice Cream Boys because they always wore sunglasses and had a great sun tan; they remind me a bit about Alasdair really."

"He's not still in the SAS, is he?"

"No he's probably a bit past it, he's getting on you know."

"He can't be thirty-five yet, at least I don't think so."

"Nearer forty my dear, nearer forty."

"Doesn't look it, though does he?"

"No I have to give you that, but then you don't look thirty-two, do you?" Sir Andrew smiled.

"Well I don't think I have any gray hairs, if that's what you mean."

"Away with you lassie. Anyway I'm glad you've found someone and I'm sure Douglas must think a lot of you. Good luck to you both."

"Granddad, the night we chased the poachers away Douglas was being questioned by Inspector Robertson about all the shooting that had been going on and the Inspector, who, let me tell you, is like a dog with a bone, wouldn't let up on the use of firearms that night. He was getting very difficult with Douglas when Douglas took him out of the interview room and either said something to him or showed him something, because after that the Inspector backed off and couldn't have been nicer."

"I think Douglas is in some way still connected with, shall we say, Special Forces, and he probably identified himself to the Inspector. That would help explain what happened."

"You're probably right, you usually are."

"And where's my great-grandson then?" Sir Andrew quickly changed the topic.

"He went down to visit Hamish at the cottage at eight o'clock; they were going to take the ponies up the hill. You know Charles loves to get out on the hills but he has to take a pony. His breathing is getting more and more labored as he gets older. I think I'm going to take him to see my Uncle Ken in Pitlochry some time soon, just to give him a check up."

"Aye that would be a grand idea for what I'm going to talk to you about now will have an impact on his ability to play games and so forth."

"What do you mean Granddad?"

"I'm talking about your son's education, Eilid. It's no secret that he's very, very, bright but he's not going to get the education hereabouts that will stand him in any good stead. I would like to see him go to University, and that requires that he acquires the necessary qualifications to gain entry. I think he needs to go to Public School and I've already made the arrangements, but he's your son and I need to talk to you about this and get your approval."

It was as if the clock had been turned back twenty years. Eilid had had the same conversation with her mother and father about the merits of going to a school away from home. Miss Bain, her old school mistress had wanted her to go to Inverness Academy, which was a sort of Grammar school but neither Eilid nor Angus had wanted any part of Miss Bain's suggestion, despite Catriona trying to change their minds.

"Granddad, this is very kind of you, but I'm not sure if it's right for Charles. He's got all his friends here, all he needs is here, and I'm not sure if his health will stand the strain."

"For God sake, Eilid, broaden your horizons. There's a whole new different world out there. Charles is either going to be a part of it or he's going to end up some type of recluse whose never gone farther south than Inverness. At least give him the opportunity, the bloody child is stifled living here, he needs to go out and stand on his own two feet."

Eilid had never heard her Granddad speak like this. He was the Sir Andrew Ballantyne of old, planning the future of someone he knew he would not be able to help in the years ahead. Eilid was amazed at how strong; even strident his voice was at his age as he almost pleaded with her to set her son free. The situation was not altogether lost on Eilid. Charles association with Hamish and Mhairi was all very well, but he needed broader experiences than she could provide.

"Granddad, I know there's a lot of truth in what you say. What arrangements have you made?"

Sir Andrew leaned back, took off his glasses and polished them assiduously, replaced them, steepled his fingers and started to talk.

"When Charles arrived, I was surprised, as we all were, at the suddenness of events. Nevertheless he is your child, and I have a duty as a grandfather, and probably as a Godfather, which I regard as the role, that I should adopt with Charles, to provide assistance with his education and well being."

Eilid sat back. This was going to be a long speech. It was as if he had taken up his seat in the House of Lords.

"When he was two years old," Sir Andrew continued, "I put his name down for Strahearn, it's where Alasdair went and it has a long tradition of academic excellence and of equipping young boys for the future. They are strong on sports and on leadership. I think Charles would benefit greatly by attending Strahearn and I have formed a trust so that the school fees will never be a burden to you, and indeed the way I've set up the trust, according to Clive Pritchard, my lawyer it should ensure that there will be sufficient funds left over to see him through University. Now Charles will start, subject to your agreement, of course, next September, just before his twelfth birthday. So what do you think of that?"

Eilid just sat back and stared into space. It was virtually a fait accompli. It was the first time she felt she had lost control of her son's future. She knew Sir Andrew meant well but the suddenness of what had just been proposed and the persuasiveness and robustness of Sir Andrew's proposal had virtually left her breathless.

"Granddad, what you have done is most kind, can I have a few days to talk it over with Charles, he's quite adult you know, and I'll let you know how he feels."

"Quite, quite m'dear; I'm sure to you this is all a bit sudden. I just worry that I shan't see my great grandson established in a good Scottish school. I'm sorry if you feel I'm rushing you into making a judgment or decision, and perhaps I should have discussed it with you earlier, but it's still almost a year away. Nearer the time we'll all go and visit the school and we'll meet the masters and the pupils, what do you say to that?"

"Fine Granddad. But let me first broach the subject with Charles and see what he says."

"Splendid, splendid, I knew everything would be fine,"

It took two or three days for Eilid to mention school to Charles and that he would be leaving home for up to three months at a time. To her astonishment Charles was all for the idea. One of the many books he had read was Tom Brown's Schooldays by Thomas Hughes and the thought of all the excitement and intrigue at a boarding school fired his imagination. He simply couldn't wait to go.

Sir Andrew was, of course, delighted but sensing Eilid's dismay at the alacrity of Charles's acceptance, effectively cutting the umbilicus, played down his satisfaction at what he considered to be a job well done.

Saturday night at the Lodge was one of grand celebration. The thirteenth stag, the last in Eilid's quota was shot by Sir Andrew, quite a feat at seventy-five. It was David Vickers who put them both up to it, encouraging Sir Andrew and getting Eilid to really cull a stag she had not intended to shoot. But it happened to be well down the hill, almost tethered, as Sir David had put it, and after a short walk and a quick stalk an Imperial was bagged by Sir Andrew. The coincidence of the stag having thirteen points on its antlers and he being the thirteenth beast to be shot was not lost on the old man. He was as pleased as punch.

Mhairi threw herself into the Saturday night celebrations with unsurpassed verve and culinary skill. Eilid had earlier shot a young Stag for skinning when Douglas Hamilton had been there and she had kept a haunch to feed the final guests of the season.

The menu consisted of a small lobster salad followed by Scotch Broth, then came the haunch of venison marinated for three days by Mhairi in a mixture of red wine, herbs, vegetables and spices, the true contents of which Mhairi refused to reveal to anyone. The venison was so tender Sir David vowed that he could have carved it with the blunt side of the carving knife; the vegetables were kept simple. Roast potatoes, a pastry boat with fresh redcurrants, al dente French beans, and small carrots. At least an hour passed before the replete guests and Eilid were served with Edinburgh fog; a creation of meringues floating on a thin crème Anglaise, with whipped cream as a topping.

The wines brought by the guests matched each course to perfection with a rich full-bodied Chateuneuf du Pape complementing the venison superbly. Sir Andrew ate and drank to the full; he doubted if he would be able to make the trip again. His own estate at Cannich took up most of his time and he was, he had to admit slowing down. So somewhat in his cups, he rattled his wine glass, stood up and proposed a toast to Eilid.

"Here is to my dearest granddaughter, my only surviving relative, who has given me a great-grandson with the name of Charles Edward Stuart, a name famed or held in infamy depending on your political leaning; to Eilid and her son I wish long life and happiness to enjoy it."

The other knights were flabbergasted. Never for one minute did they expect that Eilid could be related to Sir Andrew. They looked askance at David Vickers as if to imply the old man had lost his mind. But if they expected some lack of recognition from David it was certainly not forthcoming. He was first on his feet; raised his glass and turning to the seated Eilid, drank deeply. The others immediately followed suit, a flurry of 'hear, hears,' followed.

Eilid was overcome with embarrassment. Not for a second did she think that Sir Andrew would admit that she, Catriona Stuart's bastard child, was his close relation. She felt somehow she had to respond. Slowly she got to her feet.

"Speech, speech, speech," yelled the guests in unison.

Eilid just as slowly raised her glass. "This is my favorite week in the year. I think you know that, for you come time and time again, and that is the true measure of enjoyment. Sir David was kind enough to see that I had a talent and commitment to this Estate, and I hope I haven't let him down. I cannot do all of this," she spread her hands palms up over the dinner table, "on my own. I owe a debt of gratitude to the Fergusons, Hamish as ghillie and Mhairi, his sister as cook or rather grand chef, for the enjoyment we all share on the hill and afterwards at this fine lodge." Eilid still with her glass in hand walked back to the kitchen and beckoned for Mhairi and Hamish to come out and join her. Slowly they joined Eilid to thunderous applause and cheers from the well-oiled crew at the table.

"Bravo, well done, well said young lady"

Then to a man they stood with charged glasses, looked at each in turn and drank the toast to Eilid, Hamish and Mhairi.

"I'm not finished though, gentlemen." Eilid words rang out clear. She couldn't believe she was doing this and nor could Hamish and his sister.

"I rose to propose a toast to the guests, without you, and your support, we would not survive. We wish you to know this and please accept our appreciation. The toast is 'the loyal guests'."

Hamish and Mhairi were hurriedly furnished glasses filled almost to the brim. They followed Eilid as she rose her glass to each guest in turn with a particular long look at her Granddad, which said I love you. Then she sipped the wine and sat down. It was the first time she had ever attempted a response and she was glad she had. She too realized that Sir Andrew's days at Torridon might well be at an end. What she did that night pleased Sir Andrew to the very roots of his being. Not only was Eilid a beauty, she had intelligence and a positive attitude. It was difficult not to be in love with her all of the time.

CHRISTMAS AT MOULIN —
December 1969

Eilid decided to take Charles to see Uncle Ken and stay for Christmas. She was certain that for Ken it was a lonely time of year and, as he hadn't seen Charles for the past ten years, it would be an occasion to introduce Charles to his great uncle and get a medical report at the same time. Eilid was becoming increasingly concerned about her son's health. While he excelled academically he certainly did not in any sporting activity. It was painful to see him try to run just to keep up with the other school children. He would rapidly get breathless and take quite some time to recover. She had telephoned Ken to say they planned a visit. Ken was ecstatic. He could only imagine what Eilid looked like at age thirty-two. His friends at the rifle association still talked in amazement about the tall blond girl who came and gave them all a lesson on target shooting, the like of which they hadn't seen before or since.

It was December twenty-second 1968, a Sunday, when a new Land Rover arrived at Kenny's cottage. Charles had eagerly been craning his neck to see the sights as they drove up the hill from Pitlochry. Kenny came out to greet them as the Eilid pulled up at the door. It was a raw chilly evening, and Kenny had lit the big fire in the living room. In addition he had bought a Christmas tree, the first time for years he had acknowledged there was such a thing as Christmas. Charles eyes were all aglow as he came into the comfortable bungalow and looked around.

Kenny could see why Eilid was concerned. The boy was thin and pasty colored, his slightly reddish auburn hair looked wispy and thin. Only his eyes, sharp green eyes, had life. He was breathing heavily already and that was just moving from the vehicle to the house. Kenny reckoned he was tall for his age which made him look even more gaunt as he wandered around from room to room.

"Oh, this is really nice mother, it's so...." Charles searched for the right word....... "cozy!"

"You've been here before you know," Kenny looked down at him smiling. It was only then that Eilid saw the crinkly lines around his eyes, other than that he hadn't seemed to age at all.

"Oh Uncle Ken, don't confuse the lad."

"I'm only telling him the truth, that when you were just born, here's where you stayed with your mother,"....he turned to smile at Charles again, "when you were a wee bairn."

Eilid turned to Kenny, "And don't you be going giving him all this Scot's dialect stuff, Kenny Urquhart, all you'll do is confuse him."

"I'll consider myself severely told off then, Miss Eilid. And do I not get anything after ten long years? Or have you forgotten your manners?" He stood back arms akimbo looking at his niece.

"Oh sorry Kenny, with all the excitement…" she reached forward, took both his hands in hers, pulled him to her and kissed him as she always did, full on the lips. Somewhere in Kenny's soul a small fire rekindled. He almost had a problem letting go, her lips were so soft and inviting. You're a dirty old man he told himself, finally pulling away.

"Well now, that's a better deal than I remember, you must have been getting some practice with the boys then?"

Eilid went bright red. Kenny always knew how to get her going. It was her Achilles Heel and she rose to the bait every time. God, but she was so good looking, he just couldn't take his eyes off her.

"I'll have you know that only recently I met a gentleman and we are"…she stumbled slightly, "we are seeing one another, so there."

"Christ, wonders will never cease. You've been to bed with him I hope?"

Eilid went even redder, if at all possible.

"Can I ask you not to take the Lord's name in vain in front of Charles and I have *not* been to bed with this gentleman. That's why he is a gentleman; he would not ask that of me." She tossed her long hair haughtily, glaring at Kenny.

Jeepers, thought Kenny, I've really lit the fire.

"I only asked."

"And if I had, do you think I would tell you?"

"Well, I am your Uncle, Doctor and gynecologist, if push comes to shove. I've a right to know. So what you're telling me is lies Eilid Stuart."

"You damn well know I'm not, and you're just....just...." she searched for a suitable insult... "an old fart!"

Kenny threw his head back and laughed out loud at Eilid's embarrassment and frustration. Putting his arm around her he said, "Come on, let's get you moved in, dinner's cooking, and I've got a new Malt I want you to try. What does Charles like to eat? I've been branching out in the cooking a bit; it's Spaghetti Bolognaise for dinner, made the sauce myself."

"That sounds great. How about some wine? Sir David and Sir Andrew bring some excellent wines to the Torridon Lodge and I'm getting used to some pleasant red wine now and again."

"You know Eilid, I drank the last bottle of red about a week ago. While I finish off here, I've just got to boil the spaghetti, why don't you nip down to the Moulin bar, Johnnie's still there still asking after you. He'll get you the best bottle of red he's got and tell him to put it on my bill, but don't be too long now, I'm sure Charles will be alright with me?"

"He'll be fine, I'll away down and talk to Johnnie." At that she walked out grabbing her anorak as she went.

Being a Sunday the Moulin Bar was closed but the hotel restaurant was open. Johnnie came dashing out into the hotel foyer when he saw Eilid through the restaurant's glass doors. It was almost as if he'd seen a ghost.

"My God, if it isn't Miss Eilid, how are ye? It's awfy good tae see ye back at Kenny's again. Did ye bring the bairn?"

"Indeed I did Johnnie. He's getting to be big, a wee bit pale, but he's going to be tall, just like his father," she added as a piece of validation that there was a father, somewhere.

"Yer no so short yersel' Miss Eilid, ye've got these big lang legs of yours. Is the bairn like ye?"

"My goodness Johnnie all these questions."

"Aye but Miss, I wis feart ye'd no come back again. We all fair miss ye, an' see for them yins in the Rifle Association, did you show them a thing or two, eh! Bloody marvelous ah' call it. Knocked the wind right oot their sails so ye did; bloody marvelous," he repeated. "Whit can Ah dae for you?"

"Johnnie, you're so kind, it's great to see you looking so good after ten years. Kenny wants to know if you've got a decent bottle of red wine he can have, he's made spaghetti for Charles and me."

"Miss Eilid, since ye were here last let me tell you that the new owner has got a great wine list, let me see whit they have." Johnnie darted off on his mission, two minutes later he was back clutching a bottle.

"Here ye are miss, an' its wi' the manager's compliments, miss. In fact he's going to come in tae say hello." Johnnie proffered the bottle to Eilid. Amarone was emblazoned on the label. Eilid had never heard of the wine. Anything at the Lodge was French and this seemed to be of Italian origin. She looked at the bottle quizzically.

"It's awfy good, so the manager said miss. He said that if ye're eating Italian ye might as well drink Italian. He'll be here in a minute, ye can ask him yersel."

The words weren't out of Johnnie's mouth when the door between the hotel and the bar flew open. Eilid looked up and there in the threshold was Douglas Hamilton with a grin as wide as the river Tummel.

"Merry Christmas, darling!"

Eilid had never been so close to fainting in her life. Thoughts of Douglas and where he was and what he was doing had been with her every day since he had left the glen. She stood rooted to the spot as Douglas put his arms around her and kissed her passionately. Her knees went weak, and she could hardly breathe. Finally she gasped, "Oh Douglas, is it really you?"

"The very man," said Douglas breaking the embrace. Johnnie was leering down at them like the village idiot.

"But how did you get here, you're not the manager of the hotel are you?"

"Of course not. But I just heard that you might be at Kenny's for Christmas and I thought why not? I wasn't doing anything special, so I thought I'd do something special and come to see you. Eilid, I've missed you so much."

"Me too, Douglas; look come and meet my Uncle Kenny and have dinner with us, I'm sure there will be plenty food."

"No, no I couldn't do that, I'd be encroaching."

"Well you'll just have to encroach, for dinner's going to be ready."

In three minutes they were back at Kenny's house. Eilid rang the doorbell, not wanting to walk in with a stranger.

"It's open," Kenny yelled from the kitchen. So Eilid went in with Douglas now carrying the bottle of wine.

"Uncle Kenny. Not only did I find some wine but I ran into this 'gentleman' I was telling you about when I arrived."

Kenny looked up from the kitchen range and saw Douglas.

"How do you do? I'm Doctor Urquhart" And the next thing Eilid knew they were laughing and slapping each other on the back.

"Hello Mr. Hamilton, nice to see you again." Charles came forward, smiling.

"Why thank you Charles, it was more than you're mother could say."

Eilid took in the whole scene her blue eyes getting narrower and sharper by the second. Something was up. There was a conspiracy, she was sure.

"You bugger, Uncle Kenny." She turned on Douglas. "And that goes for you too, you great ape."

Kenny turned his most professional look on Eilid. "Can I please ask you not to use a profanity when young Charles is within earshot?"

"Oh, oh, you two, you *are* absolute buggers! I don't know how you've done this but I propose to find out." Eilid carried on pretending to be enraged by what had been a plot to get her to meet Douglas again.

"Well, before you start your Highland Inquisition I suggest we eat this spaghetti or it will all be sticking to the wall. Douglas, you pour the wine, maybe it'll sweeten this old maid here."

That did it for Eilid. She thrust herself forward, took a great swipe at Kenny, who dodged the fist, stuck out his foot at his charging niece, which Eilid promptly tripped on, regained her balance only to ricochet into Douglas, who fortunately had put down the bottle of wine. She struggled against Douglas's enveloping arms, but he was too powerful. All she could do was squirm and yell at them both which added to the hilarity of the whole situation. Both men were laughing so heartily that even Charles, not really realizing why, joined in the laughter.

"Surrender?" Douglas asked.

"No surrender… truce though?" Eilid asked.

"Let's eat dinner with the enemy then," Douglas laughed and released Eilid as Kenny dished the spaghetti into great bowls covering each helping with a rich meaty sauce. It smelled delicious and it turned out to be delicious. They discovered too that the Amarone was superb. Soft, rich and round was the way Douglas described it. Young Charles got stuck into the spaghetti even although it proved a challenge to get it to stay on his fork. Kenny showed him how to use a spoon in conjunction with a fork and gave him his first lesson in eating long spaghetti.

"Okay," said Eilid half way through the meal, "the jokes on me and I appreciate this is a great conspiracy, but how did it all come about. I, apart from Kenny, was the only person who knew I was coming to Pitlochry on the twenty-second, so how did you find out," looking hard a Douglas, "unless you two know one another from somewhere." She swiveled in her chair to look at Kenny at the other end of the table.

"Pretty good eh?" Douglas smiled at Kenny.

"Aye, not bad, she's not so slow on the uptake as you might think." Kenny grinned back.

"All right," said Douglas taking another sip of the wine, "shall we tell her Kenny?"

"I see no reason to, do you?"

"No, you're probably quite right, but I'm trying to make peace."

"Oh, aye, of course, you've got a sort of vested interest there, haven't you?" And he grinned an evil grin at Eilid just to tease her some more.

Eilid started to rise slowly from the table, heading in Kenny's direction. Ken could smell trouble, she was a strong lass, one belt from Eilid and he'd be sure to remember it. He held up his hands in mock surrender.

"Okay, okay, just sit down, we get the message." He looked at Douglas. Douglas nodded imperceptibly. Kenny motioned with his hand in Douglas's direction.

"You want me to start, is that the way of it? Right, Sir Andrew told me you were coming to Pitlochry to stay with your Uncle Kenneth, as he put it, over Christmas. So I asked him Kenneth's last name and he said Urquhart. And I said I used to know an Urquhart many years ago, is he by any chance a doctor and he said he was, and added quite the finest in the area. Well when I was in the Commandos we used to hold maneuvers on the moor and hills around Spean Bridge and when any of us got into a scrape there was this doctor who would fix us up, his name was Kenneth Urquhart. So I phoned Kenny, he remembered me and I said I was his niece's lover, so here we are!"

"I hope you didn't believe that last bit, Uncle Ken." Eilid was back of the defensive again.

"Why not? Douglas has always been honest for as long as I can remember."

"Well it's just not true and he's making fun of me and I wish he wouldn't."

"I know, I know how you are, I'm only joking and you're rising to the bait every time. I wish that big salmon in the Garry I've got my eye on would take the fly as quickly as you, we'd be having a feast."

"So you were in the Commandos then, Douglas?"

"Yes I started off with them, and later joined or qualified for the SAS. And before you ask any more, I know Sir Andrew's filled you in on some of the details surrounding the SAS so we can skip that bit of conversation."

"What age were you then?"

"A raw recruit, twenty–two I think I was. Ready to fight the North Korean army, or something like that."

"Were you sent to Korea?"

"No, it was just about over then, or so we thought. It took another year, July 1953 really to get the truce declared."

"So when did you join the SAS?"

"Eilid, does it matter? I'm out of it now. I have a sort of civilian status connected to the police force, but that's it."

"Just curious, that's all."

"Aye, just so. Curiosity killed the cat…didn't it Charlie?"

Charles looked up.

"Kenny don't call him Charlie, it's so common."

"Well you used to call him your wee Prince Charlie when you brought him here, well, I mean, when you had him here," Kenny quickly corrected his mistake hoping that Douglas would pass it over which he seemed to do.

"I know, I used to call him Charlie, but my mother put a stop to that," said Eilid

"I knew it, I knew it, that sister of mine Catriona, she *is* a bloody snob. She's always had delusions of grandeur."

"That's not true Kenny, why would she ever have married Angus?"

"I'm not going to debate the point. Anyway how is my wee sister?"

"She's really well. I mean looks really well. She's fifty three now and looks forty three."

"That's Catriona for you. Always was a beauty, and she's passed it on to you. Except your taller, blond and got the Ballantyne blue eyes and you shoot left handed. Douglas, have you ever seen her shoot?"

"Oh yes, she gave me a lesson the first time I went on the hill."

Charles was put to bed, Kenny added logs to the fire, and the three-some sat down to enjoy Kenny's latest malt. There was a long silence as they sipped the whisky, each, it seemed, lost in their own thoughts. It was Kenny who broke the silence.

"Tell me about Charles. I can see right off he doesn't look well, but tell me what the problems are."

"He can't exert himself in any way," Eilid's voice was strained. "He can't run and can't play with any of the others at school. When he's really bad his lips go blue and he looks as if he's going to faint. Look how skinny he is. True he doesn't eat a lot, but it's a challenge for him to gain weight. There's something not right, Kenny, that's why I want you to examine him for me. You know Andrew is hell-bent on sending him to Strahearn next year, the way he is now I don't think he'll be able to make it."

"Aye well," Kenny was about to mention the signs of the operation when Eilid brought him first to Pitlochry, but Eilid's sharp look cautioned him. If only Douglas wasn't here, he thought, we could discuss what the problem might be. "He's young enough, that if it's anything serious we should be able to take care of it."

As if on cue to Kenny's thoughts Douglas announced his departure. "Folks I'm tired. It's been a long but wonderful day. I'm going to turn in before the hotel shuts me out."

Douglas said his farewells to Kenny and Eilid walked with him to the door. They kissed in the little porch that Kenny had added since Eilid had been there last. Eilid felt the blood rushing to all sorts of places in her body. There was no doubt in her mind; there never had been anyone like Douglas. Eventually he broke from her embrace and set off down the road. Eilid returned to the warm fire and her Uncle.

"You know he could have stayed here if you wanted." Kenny looked at his niece over his spectacles that he had put on to read the newspaper.

"I know Kenny. I know you wouldn't mind. I love him with all my heart. I suppose I want to make love to him, the problem is, I never have."

The following morning was a repeat of dreich Sunday. Dreich Monday rolled in, probably colder than the previous day as the wind had veered to the north. Charles went quite happily with his Great Uncle to the surgery. Eilid had elected to have breakfast with Douglas at the hotel and then plan their day. Over porridge, Loch Fyne kippers, lashings of wheat toast and Dundee marmalade the two yet-to-be lovers talked animatedly about the upcoming Christmas. Uncle Kenny's tree still had to be decorated and Kenny had left it undecorated deliberately as he knew Charles would want to be involved. Off the two went arm in arm striding down the hill to Pitlochry to see what was left in the shops by way of Christmas tree decorations.

Meanwhile Kenny was carrying out a full examination on young Charles. He didn't like what he found and made an appointment for Charles at the local hospital to have some x-rays taken on the following day.

That evening Kenny and Eilid sat down after dinner to discuss Charles's health. Douglas conveniently went down the road to the pub.

"It's obvious Charles is in need of medical attention, I'm sure it's all to do with the operation he had, I'm presuming in London, but I still don't know what it's about. If we knew his original name it might help, but it would also raise more questions than answers. So basically we're in the dark. I'm going to put him on some medication that might increase his flow of blood and try to get rid of the blueness he gets from any exertion. I have to warn you though that this may only be a palliative and I'm concerned that when he goes to Strahearn he'll be automatically subjected to the rough and tumble of any boarding school."

"Do you think we should take him to a specialist before he goes to Strahearn?"

"That's a good question. The problem with that is that if he needs some sort of major surgery it may affect his entrance to the school. You've told me that Sir Andrew has already pulled a few rabbits out-of-the-hat to get him in before the acceptance age, and I don't think he'd want to do something like that again, particularly if it concerns the boy's health. The last thing Strahearn will want is the liability of having an invalid or a potential invalid at the school."

"Remember it is nine months away. If we were to do something now he might be fit and well by the beginning of September when the autumn term begins." Eilid suggested.

"That's certainly true but you've got to think this one through. If you take him, or even I take him to a specialist, like me they're going to recognize something pretty major has been done to this child. So who's the first person they're going to ask for details?"

There was a long silence. Kenny's point was well made. Eilid wouldn't have a clue what to say to any specialist and if she did say something about an operation that would most certainly open up Pandora's Box as to when, where and by whom. A myriad of questions would most certainly follow. The prospects for a proper examination faded in her mind but at the same time made her even more apprehensive about her son's health. So eventually she decided to let the matter be and enjoy Christmas with Charles, Kenny and Douglas.

Christmas dinner at the Moulin Hotel turned out to be a fine meal. Kenney had vowed he was damned if he was going to cook on Christmas Day and so they all enjoyed each other's company, even Johnnie the barman turned up to toast the family a happy Christmas. The next few days were almost idyllic. The weather was cold and clear and Douglas, Eilid and Charles spent their time making visits to historical items of interest in the area.

Douglas then suggested they climb Beinn Vrackie. Kenney fortunately intervened and said he'd look after Charles giving Douglas and Eilid the day to themselves. The view from the summit of Ben Vrackie was marvelous, below them to the south stretched the town of Pitlochry while to the north they could see some of the Grampian peaks as well as the Falls of Bruar they had visited the previous day appearing as a white ribbon of water in the near distance. All of this reminded Eilid of Struan and the quiet little Church with the graveyard where John Robertson was buried.

Eilid turned to Douglas as the wind splayed her long blond hair behind her. Her cheeks were rosy red from the cold and the exertion and Douglas thought she had never looked lovelier.

"Douglas, could you take me to Struan tomorrow? There's something I need to do."

"Sure, you know it's my last day, I promised my mother I'd be home for New Year so I need to leave tomorrow, so if we go in the morning would that be okay?"

"That'll be fine, thank you."

"What's with this Struan place anyway?"

So Eilid told Douglas the whole tragic story about Auld John's demise and how she ended up by default as the youngest Stalker in Scotland, as well as being female to boot.

"My God, why didn't you tell me all this before, I would love to see the place, including the falls on the river Gary."

So the next day they set out, after one of Kenney's super breakfasts to the little Church that nestles at the conflux of Errochty water and the river Gary. Douglas couldn't imagine a more tranquil and apposite setting for a church. They found John Robertson's grave with the rose bush Eilid had planted seemingly braving and surviving the winter. Then they browsed through the graveyard examining the old gravestones, some flat on the ground, some clearly centuries old with the names eroded by wind and rain.

It was at the south entrance to the Church where Douglas found the most moving monument. Here a father had buried seven of his children as they died one after the other, some weeks apart, some months apart caused by a plague of diphtheria that had swept the glen in the 1860's. There was no embellishment of any kind, which made the memorial all the more poignant. The complete lack of sentiment or emotion only helped to accentuate the agony that this desperate father surely must have endured as he watched his children die one-by-one, helpless, as the dreadful affliction took his children from him. It was the first time Eilid had seen Douglas so visibly moved emotionally. His SAS training, she thought, had probably taught him to suppress his emotions at most levels, just in the same way a doctor does when he or she has to remain emotionally detached when conveying the prognosis to a terminally ill patient. It was then and there that Eilid knew she truly loved Douglas Hamilton and she vowed that if he asked her to marry him, she would say 'yes'.

It was on Tuesday, the day before Hogmanay that Kenney's guests bade their farewell and went off in their separate ways. The drive back to Torridon was quick and easy. There had been no snow and any early morning frost on the roads melted quickly in the vapid warmth of a winter sun.

Eilid arrived back at the Lodge by late afternoon and found everything to be shipshape. She was pleased to see Hamish and Mhairi had kept the Lodge tidy.

"Sir David would be proud to see the Lodge in such fine shape for this time of the year," she told them. "Mind you we haven't had any bad weather yet, so tomorrow Hamish you and I are off to cull the Hinds before we have a repeat of what happened to me about ten years ago."

Eilid's mind raced back to the events of that day.

"Was that when the American plane crashed into the corrie?" Hamish asked.

"Yes it was. The weather was so bad the rescue teams didn't get there for two days. But there were no survivors, all those poor people; there was nothing that could be done."

"So you were the one to report it then?" Hamish was curious.

"No, no, I was at Pitlochry having Charles." Eilid brushed the matter aside. She wished she hadn't made mention of the weather or the plane crash all those years ago. Her secret was still safe. Only her mother and her Uncle Ken knew and they would never tell.

The evening ended with the Eilid's memories haunting her. She bade Hamish and Mhairi goodnight and went to bed to get ready for 1970; the next decade was almost with them.

For Lance Ericsson Christmas was a time for getting his every wish fulfilled. Agnes Anderson, still a bright sixty-one year old had tried to prevail on Red not to spoil his son quite so much, but that was like talking to the wall. Red doted on Lance and Lance knew it. He was big for his age, and was a complete contrast to his twin. He excelled at all sports, he was impatient when being taught anything, and basically wanted to arrive without having traveled. He was also becoming, Agnes had to admit it, more than she could handle. His demands became more flamboyant and unreasonable and if she dared deny the child anything it became an issue that he brought to Red's attention. Red was not blind to Lance's little games but he seemed to go along with them just the same, which made Agnes get so mad it tried her patience and composure to the very limit.

Many changes had taken place in the ten years since Karen's death. Red had now his own drilling company and was getting into the Petro-chemical business with some influential and wealthy backers, all 'old money' from Dallas and Houston. Red's decision to move back to Houston with Lance and Agnes had not only angered the Stahlmans, it had alienated them in a way Red was at a loss to understand. For the short time he and Karen had been together he had done everything to keep the Stahlmans happy, commuting from Houston to Los Angeles every two or three weeks. The traveling had been slow and tedious but Red had never complained, as they wanted, indeed demanded, to have their only child close to them. With the new jet aircraft Houston was a short 3 to 4 hours away, but as far as Lance was concerned he had no Grandparents. The Stahlmans never visited or phoned. It was as if Lance and Red had died with their daughter.

Red's closest friend and protégé, Mats Frosteman had died five years earlier in a tragic Scuba diving accident off the Cayman Islands. No one really knew what happened. Mats had gone diving without a 'buddy', which was something no Scuba diver should ever do. He had rented a Condominium right on the beach and his wife and family were to join him the following week when the school semester ended. He apparently had gone out one night, wadded into the sea in his Scuba gear and was found floating in the Caribbean next morning, not far off the beach with his BC fully inflated. Whether Mats took a heart attack first or his death was due to equipment failure could never be properly ascertained. His wife, son and daughter were devastated by his death, as was Red. There had been a long legal battle with the Life Insurance Company, for while Mats had a Life Insurance Policy in excess of two million dollars he had never divulged to the Insurers that he Scuba dived or flew his own plane. Red did his best to keep the family together during the months after Mats' death. It turned out that Mats, while seemingly very wealthy, had amassed a great deal of debt. There was only one thing that Red could do and that was to sell off Mats' assets to help get the family clear of the creditors who had started to hound them. Meanwhile the legal battle raged with the insurers who were adamant that they had no liability to pay due to the lack of disclosures on Mat's part. The legal costs and complexities kept escalating with a solution never in sight. Red eventually sold the company, the ranch, and the ski lodge, which went under the auctioneer's hammer for about $300,000 dollars less than Mats had paid for it. When the dust had settled the family had just under a million dollars to sustain themselves for the remainder of their lives. Finally the Insurers did pay up half of the Policy value, so the outlook for the Frosteman family improved by another million dollars.

From the wreckage of Mats' empire Red took the best men he could afford, leased some equipment, and became a workaholic. For the next five years Lance saw his father only on rare occasions and when he did Red showered him with gifts and money not realizing that his son was becoming the most obnoxious child to attend the exclusive Memorial Jesuit School.

Women seldom figured in Red's life. It had taken Karen's death to bring home to him what he had probably realized all along that she was the only woman he had really, truly, loved. These feelings were now accentuated with the bitter poignancy of her absence. No one, he had decided, could even come close to taking her place. He reverted to the habits of his younger days, getting roaring drunk with the roustabouts in the field and sleeping with whoever took his fancy for what was strictly a one-night-stand.

As the years slipped by Agnes saw the changes that the loss of a wife and mother were wreaking on the lives of Red and Lance. There was seldom any laughter; there was the increasingly constant harping from a spoiled brat who wanted for nothing. Red became more serious and introverted as he built his empire to the god of fame and fortune. Agnes did her best to balance her job of housekeeper and surrogate mother but with her advancing years it became more difficult to accept a style of life that was becoming virtually unpleasant. In 1968 Red bought a huge house in the prestigious River Oaks area of Houston and Lance and Agnes moved in, with Red absent in Libya somewhere doing another oil deal.

Red made certain that he would be home for Lance's tenth birthday on October the fourteenth 1968. The party was held in the garden of Red's new home that covered about three acres. A huge tent was erected in the garden just in case there might be rain. However the Houston weather obliged with clear sunny skies and low humidity with the temperature in the low eighties, perfect fall weather for outdoors.

The party was organized and catered by a company specializing in this sort of event for young children. There were magicians, clowns, jugglers and even a mini-petting zoo where children could see and touch tame animals, conditioned to deal with high-spirited youngsters. Every member of Lance's class was invited, along with certain other children of his age in the neighborhood. There was a super barbeque run by a black chef with the tallest chef's hat they had ever seen. He took delight in serving jumbo hot dogs, hamburgers, cheese burgers, all the junk food kids love, telling them over and over there was plenty more where that came from. On another table there were lashings of birthday cake and every possible type of soda all floating in ice filled buckets. In fact Red had wanted to set up a proper Soda Fountain with ice cream floats but Agnes had fortunately prevailed and said there was enough food ordered to have the children sick for a week and that irate parents would probably sue Red.

As it turned out everyone voted the party an outstanding success. The Birthday presents for Lance stood in a heap in the huge entry hall. It would take him at least all of one day to open them, Agnes reckoned, and then he had the chore of writing letters to each and every person who had given him a present. Lance hated doing this but Agnes's

Scottish moral rectitude would not tolerate discourtesy or bad manners and on this she never wavered. She was thankful that Red gave the application of these disciplines his full support.

Red watched all the activity without getting involved. He had been thinking of Karen and the day on which Lance and Jens had been born. It had all gone so quickly in one way, but there were moments when the picture went into slow motion as Red's memories of Karen would come alive, usually when it seemed obvious that Lance lacked a mother's love and care. As the party revelers started to leave just before dark Red decided it was time for his special present to his son. Quietly he went to the back of the huge mansion where he had someone make a small addition to the garage, so small it passed without being noticed. Red opened the little door and a golden retriever pup bounded out, his little tail wagging furiously and licking anything and everything in sight. Red attached a small leash to the tiny collar and made his way to the front garden.

"Lance, Lance son, come over here, I've got something to show you."

Lance came over at the trot, and Red let the puppy go. The little pup bounded straight to Lance legs and body all over the place as if he had India rubber for a body. Lance knelt down to the onrushing pup and was rewarded with a canine face wash as he was licked all over. Lance had never had a pet and this simple present made him happier than any of the gifts he had received so far.

"Oh Dad, is he really mine? Can I keep him?"

"Of course he's yours, but you can only keep him if you look after him and train him to be a good dog. You'll have to walk him at least twice a day and remember never to let him off the leash if you take him out of the garden. Providing the gates stay closed he'll be in no danger from passing traffic. Is that a deal?"

"Deal," said Lance and they shook hands. Off they went hand in hand with the puppy going helter-skelter between and round them.

An exhausted Agnes watched them go off thinking this was the first time she had ever seen Lance truly happy. Here was something that was finally his, he had a responsibility to look after it, and the retriever in turn would be a loyal friend and companion. It was a stroke of genius on Red's part, or so Agnes thought. She turned to go into the house pulling her cardigan around her as there was a slight chill in the air when she saw a large car pull up to the electrically activated entrance gates. There was a telephone communicating to the house to allow the gates to be opened. As there was no one in the house she decided she'd wander down and see whose parents had been sent back by what child to pick up something they had forgotten. She shielded her eyes against the glare of the headlights as she made her way down the long driveway. The lights were turned off as the driver could see Agnes straining to verify who was there. She could now see that it was a huge white Cadillac with a driver and a passenger. Something else looked strange and then it came to her, the car had out-of-state plates. It was probably some friends of Red's that he had forgotten to tell her were coming. As she got to the gates the driver's door opened and the burly driver got out of the car. There was something about the face that she sort of recognized. The driver spoke.

"Agnes, is that you?"

"My God, Mr. Stahlman, I don't believe it. Is that Mrs. Stahlman who's with you?"

"It sure is Agnes. We drove all the way from LA to be with our grandson on his tenth birthday and by the looks of things there's been a grand party."

"Oh yes, it's been wonderful, wonderful. Goodness what am I doing talking to you through the bars like this. Let me open the gate and let you in."

Agnes pressed the concealed button that opened the gates from the house side of the drive. Brett eased the Cadillac through and stopped. Rosemary Stahlman got out her side of the car and gave Agnes the warmest of embraces.

"Oh Agnes it's so good to see you, it's been all these years and you haven't changed a bit."

"Thank you. It's so nice to see you too." She couldn't return the compliment. Rosemary Stahlman looked a wreck. Agnes knew she was a few years younger than she but the woman before her looked more like seventy-five rather than sixty-five. Rosemary opened an elegant cigarette case, took out a cigarette and lit it in one smooth movement. She excused herself and offered one to Agnes.

"No thanks, Mrs. Stahlman, I don't smoke. Never have."

"Land sakes Agnes call me Rosemary, we've known one another for such a long time, let's be pals."

"Let me get in the car then Rosemary and get you up to the house. Red's out in the garden with Lance and the new pup, he gave him a golden retriever for his birthday and they've gone off round the garden with the puppy."

All this pals' stuff was getting to Agnes. She smelled the reek of Bourbon as she got in the car. No wonder Rosemary was so friendly; she was as high as a kite. Somehow she had to get to Red before he walked into the most unwanted surprise of the decade.

"Sure is some pad Red's got here, eh, honcy?"

Brett turned to look back at Agnes. "Jeez Agnes how big is this thing?"

"I think it's about eleven thousand square feet. But there are parts of it I haven't visited yet." Agnes gave a dry laugh. Comedy right now was not on the agenda. "Just pull over here Mr. Stahlman, you'll not have far to go to the front door."

"For Christ's sake Agnes call me Brett, you're not at Cedars-Sinai now. We're friends from way back."

Here we go again thought Agnes.

"Brett it is then. Come away in." Agnes was sounding more Scots by the minute, which she did when she got nervous. "I'll get hold of Red and Lance and tell them you're here."

"Hell no, Agnes, you'll do no such thing. Think of the surprise Red will get when he sees us. You just lead us to the bar, I'm sure this pad has one an' we'll jes be fine and dandy."

"It's got two actually. One in the family room here," she ushered them in, "and one in the pool room; it's more of a pub-like bar."

"This one will be jes fine. Mother, what'll it be?"

"The usual for me, Hon."

"Okay, let's see what Red's got by way of Bourbon. Well whadya know Hon, Old Charter, right up your street. Agnes, you'll join us, I'm sure, in a toast. What'll it be?"

"Well, I'd rather wait until Red gets here but you can pour me a wee Glenmorangie, no ice now mind, and I'll help myself to water."

"Boy the lady knows what she wants, you got it. I'll have a Manhattan. I figure I can mix one of these up in this swell place, he's got all the fixin's, I always said Red didn't do things by half."

Just then the phone rang. Great, thought Agnes. "I'll take this in the kitchen," she shouted over her shoulder as she scuttled out of the family room leaving Brett looking for Maraschino Cherries. She quickly got rid of the caller who was a parent thanking Red for the wonderful birthday party. Hanging up the phone she got to a set of French doors at the rear of the house and opened them up gingerly less the Stahlmans would hear her. Just to the right of her were Red and Lance heading back with the pup.

"Red, Red, you've got to come here right away."

"What's up Agnes, you look as if you've seen a ghost."

"Just about. Brett and Rosemary Stahlman have just arrived."

"Jesus Christ. You've got to be Goddamn joking? Sorry Agnes let me rephrase that. You've got to be joking."

"I wish I was. They've driven all the way from Los Angeles to celebrate Lance's tenth birthday. They arrived in this huge Cadillac about fifteen minutes ago. Rosemary is drunk, and looks like hell and Brett has put on so much weight I hardly recognized him."

"Jesus, they'll expect to stay the night?" It was a rhetorical question for Agnes knew the answer to that. "Thanks for the warning Agnes, I appreciate that. Where are they now?"

"Depleting your bar; they insisted I have a drink, they've poured me a wee Glenmorangie."

"Well that's probably about the first useful thing they've done since they got here. Let me get Lance to put the pup in his kennel and then we'll be through."

Agnes hurried back to the family room where Brett and Rosemary had ensconced themselves, each in a deep leather armchair. Rosemary had just lit what had to be her third cigarette. The smoke curled up to the high timber beamed ceiling and disappeared in the gloom. Agnes realized they were sitting almost in the dark; only the lights from behind the bar were on so she busied herself going round putting on a table light here and a standard lamp there until the room looked more cheerful.

"Well Agnes, you're lookin' great. Red must be takin' real good care of you. I've jest turned sixty-eight myself so I'm slowin' down a bit. An' Rosemary had a bad touch of flu in the spring and that set her back a bit but we're both fine now an' we're lookin forward to seeing our little grandson."

"Let me tell you he's not so little for ten, he's probably the tallest in his class, not the smartest mind you, but the tallest."

There was a flurry at the entrance of the family room as Red and Lance came in. Red had just told Lance that his grandparents were here to see him and the boy was totally at odds with the situation.

"But Dad, you told me I had no grandparents, just last year you told me that."

"Well, yes, I think I did say something along those lines, so I have got to tell you I'm sorry. I hadn't heard from them since your Mom died, I don't know why that is, but maybe, now that they're here, they'll explain it all to you." Red was sure they'd be no explanation but he continued to hope he might receive some sort of backhanded apology.

Rosemary staggered to her feet as Lance entered the room. Brett was still holding sway behind the bar.

"Well, well, well, look who's here. Lance, it's your grandma and grandpa all the way from California. They came by covered wagon I figure because it's taken them ten years." Red couldn't resist the sarcasm.

"All right Red we know we owe you an explanation but don't let's start out on the wrong note, jes button yor lip for a minute and we'll explain."

"I can't wait." Red stared at Brett. If looks could kill Brett would be under the Saltillo tiled floor of the bar. "Rosemary, how are you?" Red walked over to his inebriated mother-in-law and gave her a perfunctory kiss on the cheek.

"Red it's so nice to see you an Agnes once again, we just couldn't wait."

"Tell me about it." Red's sarcasm was biting but Rosemary was in no state to recognize snide remarks, however cutting.

"And this is Lance." She turned to her grandson and held him out at arm's length. "My word Brett he's just the spittin' image of Karen, isn't he honey?"

Agnes was on the point of throwing up. Never had she heard such maudlin claptrap in all her life. There was not one part of Lance that even resembled Karen Stahlman. He was his father's double, down to the auburn slightly reddish hair and the intense green eyes and if he kept on growing he would be taller than Red's six foot-two.

Brett never said a word. He just stared into his drink for a minute and then lumbered over to Lance.

He bent over, proffered his hand and said, "Howdy buddy."

"Howdy," said Lance in reply.

"Are you truly my mother's father?"

"Yup, sure am".

"She was a beautiful lady my mom, wasn't she?"

"The most beautiful, son."

"Do I really look like her?"

"Nope, not from the outside, but from the inside. I can see your mom smiling out of you. She was a feisty young lady, and I've only just set eyes on you, but I recognize that you have her nature, that spark. It's the spark she had and it comes from within, an' that means you're somethin' special, so there."

Red had to hand it to Brett. He carried his first encounter with Lance superbly, and indeed there was an element of truth to what he had just said, Lance did have that unruly, devil may care attitude, it was that spark that had made him love Karen like no other.

"Agnes let's see what we've got for dinner, or better still, with all you've had to do today let's go out to eat. We've got some really good restaurants here. Manuela, one of our maids will look after Lance, for he's beat and she can prepare the bedroom for you and Rosemary upstairs."

Brett held up his hands. "Easy on now Red we didn't jes want to impose like that; we did this kinda on the spur of the moment. We had decided to take a trip to San Anton and by the time we got there, why Rosemary remembered it was Lance's tenth birthday and there we were not 200 miles away, so we jes took off like, found your address from a friendly mailman. But before Lance says goodnight we have this special present for him, and for you too, I figure. Hold on 'til I go to the car."

Rosemary lit another cigarette and Red replenished her drink, about her third by this time, as Brett went off to the Cadillac. Agnes left to get hold of Manuela and tell her which bedroom to prepare, having established that two Queen size beds were preferable to a King. Lance sat at Rosemary's feet as she tousled his hair with her drinking hand, the cigarette burning away in the other. Red poured himself a Scotch and looked Rosemary over. Even in subdued lighting, she looked a wreck, he thought. The cigarettes and the booze had taken their toll on what had been an attractive woman. Now she was just a poor lush, living out her time with nothing to do, Red figured, and not many friends to do it with. There was a tremendous banging and thumping coming from the hallway. Red put down his glass and went through to see what was going on. Brett Stahlman had the front door ajar and was trying to maneuver a huge object that must have weighed a ton through the door. Whatever he was wrestling with was all wrapped up in crisp brown paper and was about five feet tall by about three and a half feet wide.

"Hold on Brett, let me help. You'll give yourself a heart attack."

"Red I'm fine, it's jest a bit awkward, even though you have a big door."

"Well it needs someone just to hold it open for you, that's all."

The large double front doors were on rising hinges, which made them close automatically. Red held one of the doors wide open and Brett struggled through puffing and blowing.

"Here let me give you a hand." Red got to one end of the package and lifted. Jesus, it is heavy, he thought. Brett had done some kind of job getting it out of the car thus far. The two men now carried the parcel into the family room and laid it to rest against one of the sofas.

"Thanks Red, it was heavier than I thought. I'm getting too old for this sh".... stopping in mid word when he remembered Lance was there. "Let me open this up for you." Brett pulled out a pocketknife and cut the heavy brown string that had held the brown paper. The paper fell away to reveal a quilted matt protecting the contents. Red could now see it was a gilt picture frame as one of the ends of the quilt had opened slightly. Brett reached up and gently removed the quilting to reveal a painting.

"Let's get it over to the wall here and set it up right. It goes vertically, like this," and he and Red hoisted it upright and placed it against the wall. At this point Red was too close to the painting to identify what or who it was; it was Agnes returning from the bedrooms that let out a scream,

"Oh my God, it's Miss Karen." And indeed it was. Red stood back and looked at the painting. Whoever the artist was had done a fabulous job. It must have been from a photograph for there was Karen looking her most beautiful wearing a red dress, the red dress she had worn to go to the Petroleum Club on her first date with Red.

Red couldn't speak. He had a lump in his throat the size of a fist. It was Karen as he remembered her, not like the last picture in his mind from the morgue in the hospital at Inverness.

"Come over here Lance". Lance moved from Rosemary's chair so he could see the painting. Agnes Anderson stood frozen in time as the painting brought back so many memories for her.

"Lance this is a painting of your mother, your mom, and it's very, very like her."

"She was beautiful, wasn't she?"

Everyone in the room just nodded so awestruck by the painting to say anything. The emotion was almost palpable as the occupants stared at the portrait. It was Brett who broke the silence in a voice cracking with pent up feelings.

"Lance son, this is the mother you knew only as a baby and we thought you should have something, and that we could bring her back into the family."

It was all too much for Brett, who, like a good film director, had rehearsed his lines again and again, but when it came to the bit with Karen there, looking down on him, he just fell apart. Tears coursed down his worn face and Rosemary joined in by sobbing, quietly glued to her chair. It took all of Red's and Agnes' self control not to join them. Red was sure Agnes wouldn't break down and, as long as she held up, he would be fine.

Breakfast was a somber affair. Agnes scrambled eggs, broiled bacon and served up hashed browns to everyone including Lance and Manuela, neither of whom could figure out what all the heavy silence was about. The proposed dinner at a local restaurant from the previous evening had died on the vine with Red ordering Chinese food to-go. Red had already called one of his contractor friends and by eight o'clock that morning Karen's portrait took pride of place at the top of the staircase. Red was ambivalent about the portrait. On the one hand it was a marvelous likeness of Karen, on the other a constant reminder of his loss. He was sure Brett Stahlman had meant well and it was fitting and proper that Lance's mother was recognized in some way in the family home, but Red couldn't help having reservations. Nevertheless he accepted the gift on his and Lance's behalf with good grace. The Stahlmans left by ten o'clock that morning and Red figured it would be another ten years before they communicated. He hoped not, for it would be nice if Lance could go to Los Angeles when he was in his teens and Brett would love to show him around Hollywood. Red would have to play the wait-and-see game.

It was two weeks before things got back to normal in the Ericsson household. Agnes could see the emotional strain that had been put on Red with the impromptu Stahlman visit and the gift of Karen's portrait. Old wounds that she thought had healed opened up again. Red took to burying himself deeper into his work, sometimes not coming home at all, falling asleep in the office after drinking too much. Agnes could only imagine his pain but at the end of two weeks after the in-laws visit she collared Red one evening.

"Red Ericsson, look at yourself, you're a bloody disgrace. Your shirt isn't even clean, you haven't shaved in two days and you need to close your eyes to stop the bleeding! You look closer to fifty than forty."

"Agnes for Christ's sake…"

"Don't you for Christ's sake me. Don't you think that portrait of Karen beckons to me every moment of every day? I should have been with her on that plane. That was my duty and I was guilty of dereliction. I know the Stahlmans opened up old wounds, mine as well, but you don't see me sitting round feeling sorry for myself pouring myself a malt whisky at any time of the day or night. I think what Brett and Rosemary did was a kind act. All right, they could have called us and told us they were coming, the San Antonio visit was, as you would say, a piece of Bull Shit. They carted that painting all the way from Los Angeles as a surprise. Don't forget Brett is or was a film producer, don't you think he liked the wee touch of the drama?

So here's what we're going to do, you'll be home tomorrow evening at six o'clock prompt, you'll play with Lance and MacDuff, you and I will have a drink and then I'll serve my chicken potpie and you'll be in bed at a decent hour, and no excuses!"

Red was used to Agnes laying down the law from time to time but he had never seen her so mad. Her blood was boiling and she meant what she said. Red knew that to deviate from Agnes's plan could have dire consequences. He hung his head meekly in compliance. Anyway, he loved her chicken potpie. It reminded him of his younger days in Canada and his mother's cooking. It was comfort food and it was just what he needed.

"Okay Agnes, see you at six, I promise. I'm going to jump in the shower now and I've *got* to go back out to dinner. I have some wealthy Arab clients in town. I'll try not to be late."

Agnes threw him a "that'll be right" glance and went off to find out what Lance was up to.

The following evening Red was home just before six. He played with Lance and MacDuff, the name given to the dog by Agnes. There was some obscure reason for her choice of name, the pup had been born by Caesarian section, and she muttered something about Shakespeare's

Macbeth and said the name was apposite. All of this was lost on Red but he and Lance liked the name, so MacDuff it was.

Agnes and Red sat down to dinner at about eight. The potpie was wonderful. Agnes made such good pastry that just melted in the mouth Red reckoned she could market the product. Knowing she liked slightly sweeter wines than Chardonnays he had opened a bottle of Piesporter that Agnes quietly sipped.

It was towards the end of the meal they began to talk about Lance and how the puppy had changed him quite a bit. The responsibility of looking after the dog had made him less aware of his needs and he was not so much of a spoiled brat, although he still did more or less what he wanted despite objections from Agnes.

"Red, it's just over ten years now and I can't be around for ever. And look at this house, what the hell are we doing in something that's a mini hotel? There's you, me, Lance, Manuela and Rosa, who comes in part-time if we have a lot of people staying, but really, just to walk from one end to the other wears me out. I'll be sixty-two next year and my sister is still in Vancouver, a widow now as you know, and she wants me to join her some time soon. Now it's not going to be right away, but I just need to tell you what's in my mind."

"Well you always have Agnes, thanks for that and I have been think-ing about it. The big house is because my business. It can be a risky busi-ness and if anything happened to financially wipe me out I would still have the house and most of the contents. Under the Texas homestead laws that can't be touched. So it's more of a safeguard than anything else. You're quite right it is too big for us but you can't get all this land with a wee house, as you would say."

Agnes smiled. Red always pulled her leg about her Scot's accent at least once a week.

"There's the security issue as well. Lance is my only child. We have all this land where he can play safely with MacDuff, have his friends over to the Tree house, swing on ropes and not be a bother to you or the neighbors, for that matter."

Agnes could see there was a lot of sense in what Red said and she wanted to ask a personal question, she just wasn't sure how Red would react. "Red, do you not think you'll ever marry again? Is there not one girl in town that takes your fancy? You're probably the most eligible bachelor in town. You're wealthy, you're handsome, this house needs a wife and Lance needs a mother."

"Agnes you're right. I just haven't met anyone who has remotely attracted me the way Karen did. I have my fling when I'm out of town with the boys and up to now that's been fine. Love 'em and leave 'em. No complications, no commitment."

"That's not the way to live your life. You're a family man at heart. You come from a big family although I have to say I've never heard you speak of your brothers and sisters. I thought you might like to invite them down some time for a visit."

"That wouldn't work. It's a bit like the Stahlmans. I haven't talked to them in years. They know where I am if they want me. The phone line works two ways you know."

Agnes just nodded. This was not the first occasion she had raised the subject and once again Red gave her a standard two-line answer.

"Well I just hope you find someone. You're too young to be a widower. You could have more children you know, this house needs filling."

Red was silent. 'You know Agnes, I think if Jens had lived and only Karen had died or been killed, it would have been different. Starting over again with Lance at ten would be a mistake. I've got my son and heir and together we'll build an Empire. The timing is right. I waken up at about 5 o'clock every morning with the blood surging through my veins just with the excitement of what the day ahead has in store for me. I love this business and I just hope Lance loves it as well. I know I spoil him, and I can't help it. It's bad for him, but he'll find his own level, you'll see."

"Would you not consider sending him off to a private school somewhere, like a boarding school where there's strict rules and disciplines to be followed. It would help him stand on his own two feet and teach him some values."

"No damn way! Why would I want to do that? Okay I bought this Mansion for the reasons I've given you, so why would I send my boy away when I want to be with him as often as possible? It doesn't make sense Agnes."

But Agnes knew that it did. A good boarding school was what Lance needed, probably in a year's time, but she could see that Red was dead against the idea.

And so the Ericsson household progressed into 1969 joining with millions of others staring at the TV as Neil Armstrong and Buzz Aldrin walked on the moon after the Lunar Module Eagle made a safe landing in the Sea of Tranquility on July the twentieth of that year.

Richard Nixon occupied the White House, Spiro Agnew was Vice President and a gallon of gas cost 36 cents. Another event, not quite so awe inspiring as the moon landing, took place fourth months earlier with the first flight of the world's only supersonic aircraft, Concorde 001, flown by Frenchman André Turcat.

MacDuff grew from a pup into a gentle and loyal companion to Lance. Red's travels increased and his company, Petrotex, grew to become one of the major players in Oil and Gas industry in Texas, and Agnes Anderson soldiered on with no mention of a replacement being considered.

STRAHEARN —
Spring 1970

Eilid and Charles had been invited to Sir Andrew's house just outside Peebles, a pleasant market town in the Scottish Borders. The purpose of the trip was to visit Strahearn boarding school, just outside the
city of Perth.

The drive to Peebles was most picturesque and took on a dramatic
quality when they crossed the River Forth by way of the relatively new
Forth Road Bridge, which had been opened by the Queen in September
of 1964. Charles was awe struck at the huge suspension cables and towers that supported four lanes of divided road across the river. To his left
he had a full view of what had been up until then the only Forth Bridge
built in 1890 with its famous three cantilevered sections carrying the
railway to all points north.

Eilid decided to divert through Edinburgh as they were not expected
at Sir Andrew's until late afternoon and she and Charles wanted to take
this unique opportunity to see Edinburgh Castle and Princes Street,
famous for its beautiful gardens. They were not disappointed. The great
castle soared above them as they drove down Princes Street, which
looked so beautiful Eilid just had to park the Land Rover and take
Charles for a walk through the gardens. There was a profusion of color
everywhere and then, as an added surprise, they came upon the Floral Clock whose hands were planted with bright yellow marigolds and
watched with all the other curious tourists as the hands jerked round
every minute as if defying gardening and engineering logic. It was the
first time Eilid had ever been any further south than Pitlochry and the
volume and speed of the traffic made her nervous at first. But as her
confidence in heavy traffic grew she noticed that if she drove a little bit
aggressively other drivers backed off due to the substantiality and size
of the dark green Land Rover. Soon they were back on the road finding
their way west and south through Penicuik, thence to Peebles and "The
Neuk" which was the name Sir Andrew had given his house located on
the outskirts of Innerleithen.

It had been a long journey but worthwhile, letting Charles see there was more to life than the Highlands of West Scotland and the delights, if they could be called that, of Inverness. They drove up the long driveway to what was really a Mansion. Sir Andrew had referred to it as his house and made it seem modest, as if it were a little bungalow nestling in a local village. Eilid should have known better. Sir Andrew was always guilty of understatement. "The Neuk" had a huge manicured lawn surrounded by a variety of shrubs and bushes. Further back from the lawn still were large rhododendron bushes, which, Eilid imagined, would be a riot of color in early spring.

Rose beds bordered the lawn with five or six varieties of roses in various stages of bloom. As they drove up close to the front door, with the Land Rover making a loud crunching noise on the gravel drive, they saw Sir Andrew. There he was in the garden wearing an old tweed jacket and a pair of threadbare cavalry twills, a huge straw hat covered his head and he was clutching some sort of spray that had a cylinder at the far end and a long tube with a protruding handle. As they watched, fascinated, Granddad pumped furiously as a fine spray of insecticide shot out the other end landing on the roses.

Sir Andrew stopped pumping as he heard the Land Rover approach, put the spray gadget down and made his way towards them. Eilid thought he looked better and fitter since she had seen him last at the Lodge in Torridon.

"My, my, you're a sight for my poor old sore eyes. Let me clean up before I give you all a kiss and a hug. These bloody greenfly are eating up my roses. I try to get some ladybirds from the locals to fight them off, but it's no use, they're everywhere. So I had to declare war. Trouble with that is I kill the ladybirds as well, but what can one do?

Come on in. I'll get Fitz to get your bags and show you to your rooms. You must be exhausted driving that piece of junk all the way from Torridon."

"Don't say that Granddad, it's only a year old and it runs really well. Being diesel it's a bit noisy but we get used to it don't we Charles?"

"Yes we do. It's a bit bumpy though, it's as if the tires are too hard. We bounce along all over the place. How are you Great Granddad?"

"Thank you for asking young man. Tell me how do I look?'

"I think you look fine, for an old man."

"Well I asked for that didn't I?"

"Charles that was very rude, even though your Great Granddad is an old man." Eilid laughed and Sir Andrew laughed with them.

"Aye, I tell you, I miss the direct honesty of the Highlands sometimes, even if it does dent my ego. Did you stop in and say hello to your Uncle on the way down?"

"No we didn't have time for that. Uncle Ken had some business in Perth that afternoon but it was before we got there and he had to head back home as he had a surgery that evening in Pitlochry. But we're going to drop in on the way back."

"Good, good." And quietly to Eilid in an aside, "the wee fellow needs looking at, don't you think, he's awfully pale."

Eilid said nothing and nodded.

Sir Andrew ushered them into the huge hallway which had stags' heads mounted in every possible place. The walls were in rich oak linenfold paneling and serpentine marble tiles covered the floor interspersed by a tiger's eye marble inset in a diamond pattern. The effect was quite Baronial. While Sir Andrew went to clean up, Fitz, Sir Andrew's butler took care of the bags from the Land Rover and showed them to two of the eight bedrooms, complete with ensuite bathrooms.

After Eilid and Charles had unpacked they were directed to the Drawing Room where Fitz without asking poured a substantial Macallan for Eilid.

"The water is over here Madame, if you wish some"

"Fitz, please call me Eilid. I'm virtually in the same business as you, so let's be friends, especially as Sir Andrew is my Granddad."

"Sir Andrew told me you'd say that miss, and that's fine. I take it the Macallan is in order?"

"I suppose he told you about that as well."

"Correct Eilid, and a great deal more."

"I can imagine"

Fitz just smiled. "Eilid can I ask you something, if you don't mind?"

"Depends what it is, ask away."

"Eilid, now that's a name I'm not familiar with, where does it come from?"

"Oh that's easy. It was my grandmother who came up with that shortly after I was born. My father, Angus Stuart, was Sir Andrew's stalker, and Eilid is Gaelic for a hind or female deer. My parents thought it appropriate."

"Thank you for explaining that. I think it's a charming name, and most apposite. Your beauty matches that of the finest hind on any hill. It's a pleasure to know you."

Eilid was taken aback at the Butler's eloquence to the point where she didn't know how to respond except to say 'thank you' and blush slightly. Then she thought about Fitz's name.

"Can I ask you the same question, where did Fitz come from?"

"Ah, that's easy. My name is Liam Fitzgerald, but ever since I was a youngster at school in London everybody called me Fitz. So here I am almost forty-five and anybody who's ever known me calls me Fitz."

"Well I think it's a grand name. Do you have any ginger beer? Charles has taken a liking to ginger beer. I think it's the name more than anything else. He thinks the 'beer' tag sounds very grown up."

"Yes we have that on hand, I'll just get Sir Andrew's G and T before he comes down. He likes it 'just there' when he comes into the room."

Sure enough Sir Andrew arrived all spruced up right on time for Fitz to hand him his regular Gin and Tonic as he collapsed into a large wing backed chair.

"Ah, there we go now, that's much better. I think I rather overdid it in the garden today, but I've had a hot bath and once I have this," he waved the drink in Eilid's direction, "I'll be just fine. Fitz, have we got young Charles something to suit his palate?"

"Yes sir, your granddaughter tells me he likes ginger beer and here it is. I've taken the liberty of putting in just a touch of limejuice, makes it all the more refreshing. There you are young sir, tell me what you think of that?"

Charles took a gulp. "Smashing!" Was his reaction.

"Well now Fitz, what do we have for dinner?" Sir Andrew asked turning to Fitz.

"Well you told me to keep it simple Sir, and simple it is. We have some Cock a' Leekie soup followed by Steak and Kidney pie, with potatoes and cauliflower from the kitchen garden and then I have some rhubarb tart with ice cream."

"That sounds just grand. What do you think Eilid?"

"Fantastic, Granddad, eh Charles?"

Charles still immersed in his huge glass of ginger beer just smiled and nodded. Eilid knew he loved Steak and Kidney pie. They sat back each with a drink as Sir Andrew explained what they were going to be doing the following day.

"Here's what I've done. I sent the results from Charles' last test to the Bursar at Strahearn, as you know he's a good friend of mine, normally there's a somewhat perfunctory entrance examination but with Charles' results he immediately waived that. The question of sports came up and I said that Charles was more of an academic. By this time the Headmaster had joined us and as he is very keen on sports, particularly rugby he asked me some more rather difficult questions. I said that in the part of the Highlands where Charles came from there was not much call for rugger and that once he saw boys playing the game and he got an understanding of it he would probably want to join in. So I really avoided the issue we know about."

Sir Andrew picked his words carefully. He wanted to have Charles to be a part of the conversation but he didn't want to dwell on his health issues. There would be time enough for that.

"So tomorrow morning we're going to leave here after breakfast at around ten o'clock, I'm not much of an early riser these days, then we'll get going to Strahearn. It shouldn't take us more than two hours, with Fitz driving, probably less. We'll meet the Headmaster and the Bursar and, as the school summer break doesn't happen until the end of July, we'll be able to see and talk to some of the masters and the boys. Now the thing is Charles, this is your decision. If you don't like the feel of the place you don't go. Now I mean that. Your going to be there for probably five years, I've made that provision, and there are always other schools, so speak up if there is anything that you think would not be in your favor by you going there. Is that fair enough?"

"Yes Granddad, that's fine." Charles spoke firmly and with conviction.

He and Sir Andrew seemed to get along together.

"Right let's go through to the dining room, Fitz will be ready for us."

As they crossed the hallway between the Drawing Room and the Dining room Eilid saw a large painting on the hall wall. It was of a young man in uniform with his officer's cap set at a jaunty angle exposing a mop of blond hair. She could see the medal ribbons just above the left breast pocket of his tunic. Sir Andrew saw her staring at the painting,

"Yes, that's Alasdair, your father. You have your mother's lips and nose and your father's eyes and hair. I had this painted from one of the last photographs taken of him. I took the liberty of adding the medals he was awarded a bar to his DFC and the DSO, both , posthumously." Sir Andrew smiled grimly.

Sir Andrew was right about the eyes and the hair. The artist must have known Alasdair for the eyes were a piercing blue and Eilid doubted if their intensity could have been preserved in a photograph which was probably black and white anyway.

Charles stood beside his mother looking at the painting as well.

"Is this my true Grandfather?" He asked.

"Yes, that's the Grandfather who never lived to see you or your mother, for that matter. He died a hero as one of the 'few' in the Battle of Britain." Eilid explained.

"Oh, I've read all about that in my history books. It's an amazing story of how a few fighter pilots saved Britain from destruction from the German bombers. I bet you're proud your Dad was one of them?"

"I've never thought about it that way, Charles. I heard such a lot about him from my mother and Granddad here; I just wished he could have shared all the fine things we have today. It seems such a waste of life. But that was the war. So many people ended up without a husband or a father. Come on then let's eat." Eilid changed the subject rapidly.

And with that she gently pushed Charles through the door to the dining room. Twelve to fourteen people could have sat at the huge mahogany table, Eilid guessed. It looked slightly incongruous with only three place settings at one end with a huge silver candelabra placed just beyond the china. The candlelight cast a warm glow over the table. There were all sorts of silver coasters and vessels on an equally large mahogany sideboard. Although it was still daylight the candles were needed in the room that was darkened by rich deep green flock wallpaper.

"Is Fitz not joining us for dinner, Granddad?"

"No, no. He likes to do his own thing in the kitchen and I leave him alone. He prefers it that way."

"What a pity, he seems a highly intelligent and most cultured man."

"You're right he is. He is well educated and he knows all about the finer things in life, which makes him the perfect butler. His family was originally very wealthy but they lost all their money in some dreadful investment which ended up making the family broke. The shock killed his father, who suffered a heart attack, and his mother ended up in a mental institution. Fitz sold their house, he got quite a lot of money for that, but he likes what he does. He has food and board free in a fine house, he gets to drive my Rolls-Royce…"

"You mean you have a Rolls-Royce, Granddad!" Charles interrupted.

"Of course," Sir Andrew looked down his glasses at Charles as if there would never be any possibility that he would not own a Rolls.

"Can I see it, please? I've never seen one before, I've seen pictures…"

"Charles, stop interrupting your Granddad," Eilid admonished him, but she had rarely seen Charles so excited.

"It's quite all right my dear, quite all right. Of course you can see it, in fact you'll be riding in it when we go to Strahearn tomorrow."

"Gosh really, that's fab," squeaked Charles with so much excitement he nearly choked on his Steak Pie.

"Well as I was saying," Sir Andrew picked up the thread of his conversation again, "Fitz gets to drive the Rolls and with the money he got from the sale of his house he manages to pay for the hospital his mother is now in and for anything else by way of a luxury he might want. I don't make great demands on him but he has a job. I don't pay him much, mind you, but he likes things just the way they are."

"Has he ever been married?" Eilid asked.

"Do you know, I don't know the answer to that. I've never asked and he's never told me. I know he sees some lady friend, for want of a better word, but it seems to be a platonic friendship. He loves to play Bridge and so does she. I think that's the only attraction. Other than that he reads a lot and he likes to fish on the Tweed; on my beat of course."

When dinner was over, Charles went straight to bed leaving Eilid and her Granddad the Drawing room to themselves. First on the agenda was Charles's health. Sir Andrew thought that he looked paler than ever and that his breathing seemed labored and erratic. Eilid agreed and said how concerned she was, especially when he was keen to go to Boarding School. If he hadn't been so keen it would have been easier to keep him at home, but to Charles this was the beginning of a great adventure and he wasn't going to miss it.

"What is it that's really wrong Eilid? Does Kenny not have any ideas?"

"He's pretty certain there's something wrong with Charles's heart."

"Goodness me," Sir Andrew was instantly alarmed. "That could be terribly serious, you know it was a heart attack that killed my wife."

"No I didn't, I'm very sorry."

"Oh I've got over that a long time ago. Alasdair was just a teenager. It was apparently some congenital heart defect that no one knew about. She was only thirty-nine. We only had the one child. It was Alasdair's loss that affected me deeply. Never really got over that one." He stared into his glass. There was a long silence broken only by the ticking of a Grandfather clock in the far corner of the room.

"Well, the thing is Eilid," Sir Andrew eventually continued, "this problem has got to be faced. I can pull the strings to get Charles in, and his academic qualifications are not in question, but a boys' only Boarding School is a rough and tumble place. I just hope he can hold his own."

"I hope he can too. If it doesn't work, we'll just have to pull him out of there, and you'll save a lot of money."

"I'm not interested in the money. In any case I set this trust up ten years ago when Charles was born and it has done very well. I've got plenty to last me the rest of my life. It's the loneliness I can't stand. So I take myself off abroad and I meet and talk to all these people and become friendly with them. These are people, let me tell you, with whom I normally wouldn't pass the time of day. I do it to be sociable and all that happens is I return home more frustrated than ever, having met American widows or divorcees who have more money than sense and are invariably loud mouthed and over made-up. It's just so…what's the word…vexatious, I suppose."

He stared into the empty gin glass for the second time. It was then that Eilid began to feel sorry for her Granddad. He was trying hard not to be sorry for himself but the façade was breaking down.

"Well, here's hoping Charles succeeds, Granddad and you can visit him and take him out on the Leave Out weekends. It's too far for me to come and you know he likes seeing you, especially if you come in the Rolls. I didn't know you had a Rolls either. You always come to the Highlands in that Volvo Estate car."

"I like the Volvo. It's not very fast, but it's rugged and dependable and it's got plenty of space. I wouldn't dream of taking the Rolls on these narrow single track roads you have up there."

"Well, like Charles, I'm looking forward to sitting in a Rolls-Royce."

"I just thought I'd put on a bit of the dog for the School. Tell me Eilid when did you last see or visit Angus?"

"I haven't seen him nor been in touch with him since I left Cannich. There's no point really. He knows I'm not his daughter and that's that. He's more than likely brought that woman from the village, what's her name, to live in with him."

"You mean Janet McVey?"

Eilid marveled at Sir Andrew's memory. As usual It was flawless.

"You're right. Janet McVey. Is he still seeing her?"

"Seeing her? She's moved in with him. Therein lies my problem. Your Dad has taken to the drink and to Janet. She can tell him how to spend his money before he gets it. I don't think the farm is making him any money at all now. The place is going to rack and ruin. I'm seriously thinking of telling him to get himself another job."

"Granddad he'll be fifty-seven this year. Where would he get another position? You know it's difficult in the Highlands right now."

"Well, I probably won't do anything but I thought you might just have a word with him."

So that was it. Sir Andrew wanted Eilid to be the go-between and give Angus the 'gypsy's warning'.

"Granddad if I thought for one minute it would do any good I'd go and talk to Janet McVey. But for me to roll up there, especially with Charles and tell him the place is a shambles and he'd better pull his socks up would be like a red rag to a bull. Criticism

coming from anyone is bad enough, but coming from *me,* I daren't think about his reaction."

"Aye, aye, you're probably quite right. It was just a thought, just a thought. Not a very good one. I'll drop the subject and pray that Angus does something to save himself. Right, it's time for bed and I'll see you in the morning".

Sir Andrew gave her a warm hug and a kiss and off he went. Eilid sat for a bit contemplating everything that Sir Andrew had said about Angus. She had learned that Sir Andrew didn't have much time for idle chatter, when he said something, no matter how innocent; there was an ulterior motive or a purpose behind it.

The next day the party set off in grand style for Strahearn Public School. Situated in a village near Perth the school was in a rural setting. At one time it had been a stately home belonging to some Baron or Earl but now it was a famous school where learning, sports and other activities were mixed in what were considered to be in suitable proportion to build bright, self reliant, leaders in society. The drive took just under two hours and was something that Eilid and Charles had never experienced. The Rolls Royce swept along in complete silence in distinct contrast to the Land Rover in which, at times, it became difficult to hold even a reasonable conversation. Fitz handled the car superbly and the passengers were treated to another view of the Forth road and rail bridges as they made their way to Perth skirting Edinburgh to the west and heading due north to just before Perth where they turned off the main road onto a country road to reach Strahearn.

They reached the imposing gates of the school in good time for their meeting with the Headmaster and the Bursar. Fitz drove the Rolls through the gates and proceeded down the long drive lined with tall lime trees. Members of the school, who happened to be walking on the drive, turned to face in towards the car, removed their caps and saluted politely as the Rolls slid by.

Eilid was immediately impressed by the grounds, which were in immaculate order. The driveway narrowed as they passed what seemed to be a deep tree filled gully on their left. A few yards further on the drive led to large pebbled open area in front of what was the original mansion. Three or four much smaller cars were parked there so Fitz drove up as close as he could to the imposing ornate oak doors, complete with wrought iron brackets and studs.

Charles was in awe. The entrance to the school reminded him of castles he had visited near Inverness. Fitz dutifully opened the car doors and the party decanted to be met by a smiling bursar who had just seen them arrive.

"Andrew, welcome to Strahearn once again. A pleasure to see you, a pleasure," the Bursar gushed suitably at one of the school's main benefactors. "And this will be Charles?" He stooped down to shake Charles's hand and then he turned to Eilid. He really couldn't quite believe what he was looking at. Before him stood this tall, blond and elegant lady, she could be a film star, the Bursar thought. He was quite overcrawed.

He proffered his hand to Eilid and quickly realized his mouth was agape. Suddenly aware of his lack of manners in staring at her he burst into what was almost a eulogy.

"My dear lady, you must be Mrs. Stuart. I am honored to meet you, welcome to what we call the Big House. May I say how attractive you are and how you lighten up even a day filled with sunshine. I can assure you that Charles, if he joins us, will be in the best possible schooling environment in Scotland. I shall personally see to it that he gets every attention. Andrew told me he had an attractive Granddaughter but, as always, he is too self-effacing. You are truly the crème de la crème as Miss Jean Brodie might say. If there is anything you need while you are here you have but only to ask."

The Bursar finally stopped groveling and let go Eilid's hand, taking note of the large sapphire and diamond ring Eilid had chosen to wear on her wedding finger.

Sir Andrew was astonished. Never in his life had he seen his old friend Henry Blake act this way. True, like himself Henry was getting on in years, and he probably had very few occasions when he could meet someone as attractive as Eilid. He had to agree with the Bursar's comments when she wore a skirt or a dress she looked fabulous. Eilid had chosen to wear a Heather Tweed suit with an open jacket, a straight skirt just above the knees, a sheer white shirt-type blouse, closed at the neck with a beautiful Cameo brooch which had been her grandmother's. The whole ensemble was set off by neat shoes with a matching handbag. She was quite the picture of elegance. Sir Andrew hoped she would walk with smaller steps. He had to admit to himself that her apparent grace evaporated slightly when Eilid took off with what could only be referred to as an agricultural gait leaving most others behind. Eilid did not let him down, however. Her walk was extremely stylish, her steps almost mincing. What Sir Andrew had failed to realize was that the straight tweed skirt Eilid restricted her to such an extent that only small lady-like steps were possible.

Eilid took Henry Blake's compliments in her stride smiling demurely while placing her hand on Charles's shoulder. The Bursar continued to smile inanely while Sir Andrew stood behind him winking furiously at Eilid and son.

"Come along now, we have an appointment with the Headmaster and I'm sure he's just dying to meet you. If you have no objection, I'll lead the way."

Going through the solid oak doors was like entering into another century. Dark Oak paneled walls were made darker still by the Cardinal

Red ceramic floor tiles which had been polished for years until they almost gleamed in the murky gloom of the entrance hall. A white ceiling with oak beams and a white narrow frieze did little to add light. Two small leaded glass windows at either side of the entrance doors gave the only view to the outside world.

"Come this way then," and the Bursar scuttled forward down a long and equally dark passageway to yet another oak door with fielded panels. The sign on the door read Headmaster in gold leaf. The party stopped at the door and waited while the Bursar knocked and a voice cried, "Enter".

The Headmasters office, or study, as he preferred to call it, was in direct contrast to the gloom of the adjacent surrounding corridors and entrance hall. The walls were paneled in oak but the wood had been bleached and 'limed' which gave it a wonderful light and almost translucent effect and accentuated the figuring in the oak superbly. Behind the Headmaster's desk there was a huge bay window which looked out onto an equally huge lawn with surrounding grounds. A cricket pitch had been set up almost in the middle of the green sward. Where the immaculate grass lawn ended there were rhododendron bushes on a steep slope backed by a mixture of mature deciduous and evergreen trees.

"John Forsyth," the Headmaster rose from behind his desk to introduce himself to Eilid and Charles. He was impressed with Eilid's strong handshake as well as her good looks. John was an aficionado of all good-looking women and Eilid Stuart scored an instant ten on his one to ten scale. He looked at Charles and wondered how such a fine woman could have such a wimpy looking child but he shook Charles by the hand and was pleasantly surprised at the firmness of that handshake as well.

He then welcomed Sir Andrew, who he knew well and for whom he had great regard.

"Please, sit you all down." He beckoned to the sofa and the armchairs around his desk.

"So Alasdair Ballantyne was your father?" The headmaster smiled warmly at Eilid.

"Yes he was. Did you know him?"

"No, he was well before my time; I'm not *that* old you know." John turned on his Pepsodent smile.

"Sorry, I just wasn't thinking. Yes, and like Charles I never knew him but my mother re-married an Angus Stuart from Beauly and he was a good father to me."

"Well, that's quite a story. We do have photographs of Alasdair here at the school. You can tell he has blond hair, just like yours, that's something you've inherited from him. I think it looks better on you than on him." John Forsyth oozed charm.

"Thank you, you're very nice." Eilid too poured on the charm in an attempt to soothe the ruffled Headmaster's feathers. "I think Charles was concerned that you might put more emphasis on sports than learning, he had heard something to that effect. As you can see he is small for his age and he has this bronchitic condition which my Uncle, who is a very well known GP in Pitlochry, tells me will improve." Eilid lied convincingly.

"Ah, now then Mrs. Stuart, I was coming to that. Has Charles played in any sports while at his local school?"

"No he has not. I hope you won't discriminate because of that. He has had a few difficulties breathing of late, but he is now on a prescription drug, again prescribed by my Uncle Dr. Urquhart in Pitlochry, which has helped tremendously."

Sir Andrew stood by as Eilid told the most convincing lies to John Forsyth. He did not like the smell of this. Mendacity of this magnitude had a habit of coming back to haunt you, and he was right to be concerned. But John Forsyth, forever the ladies man, swallowed it hook, line and sinker from the striking blond before him.

Forsyth realized he was walking some form of tightrope. Just how wide the tightrope was caused him concern. Clearly Sir Andrew's Great Grandson was not a well boy. He was not happy with the child's pallor, but on the other hand the mother sounded very convincing. Strahearn had very limited medical facilities for dealing with a true medical emergency, and therein lay his concern. He wanted to oblige Sir Andrew as much as possible as he had been a great benefactor to the school donating money for new rugger pitches and new squash courts. He decided he'd talk in private to Sir Andrew on the subject later on.

"Well, I'm sure you want to see the rest of the school and I'll be happy to escort you through the Big House, as we call it and then we can go across the valley to the classrooms. Henry I'm sure you have plenty to do so if you don't wish to join us I'm sure Mrs. Stuart and Sir Andrew will quite understand."

"Oh not at all, I've set aside the afternoon, nothing would give me greater pleasure." Henry was not about to be diverted from this tour if he could help it. Just to be seen with Eilid Stuart was, he was sure, complimentary to him.

John Forsyth tried to hide his annoyance with little success and asked them to accompany him into the Masters' Dining room for a light lunch. The room was nearly empty with just a few masters rising from their seats to welcome the party.

"Not too many of your staff eating eh, John?" Sir Andrew spoke for the first time in almost twenty minutes.

"Not really. It's lunchtime for the boys as well, so there is always a master at every table. Just to ensure good manners are observed."

"Ah, right, understood." Sir Andrew nodded.

After lunch the headmaster, with Henry Blake still in tow, showed Charles the Common Rooms where Prep was done for the next day's classes. There was an 'Activity Hour' before Prep and boys could chose almost any activity that they fancied from practicing or playing any kind of sport, to woodworking, or taking part in Scouting activities or just plain reading, which they had to do in silence, if that was their choice.

The dormitories were austere. The windows were curtainless, the floors bare hardwood, the beds iron framed and all sagging in the middle with bright red woolen blankets as top covers. Dressing gowns of all shapes and colors hung on hooks on one of the walls. The particular dormitory Charles saw slept about twenty boys with not much space between the beds.

The school library was a much finer room. Charles concluded that it had always been a library as the bookcases were beautifully carved and were hung with glass doors to protect the books. Four large tables inlaid with leather complete with matching chairs took up the floor space.

The walk across the so-called valley to the school was by way of an iron bridge, which they had seen from the Rolls on the way to the Big House. Teaching areas were therefore completely separate from the living quarters the Headmaster explained. The school buildings were more modern and built in brick with dark slate roofs. The classrooms were arranged around a quadrangle consisting of a large area of grass to break the monotony of asphalt paths that led to the various classrooms. At the north end of the quad there were Tennis courts laid out together with the four very new squash courts donated by Sir Andrew. A plaque to this effect modestly called the area Ballantyne Court with no other detail of the benefactor.

Back the party went to the Big House and admired another drive lined with Beechnut trees to what had been the family private Chapel. The masters and prefects could access this from within the Big House; others had to use the drive no matter the weather. Charles saw a rugger game in progress and asked if he could go and watch. The Bursar expressed his delight in taking Mrs. Stuart and her son down to the playing field to watch play at close quarters. This gave John Forsyth the opportunity he had been waiting for to ask Sir Andrew about his great-grandson's health.

"Well John, I really have to take Eilid's word for all of this. Urquhart is really the man to talk to if you have any concerns. I see Charles once or maybe twice a year and I have to confess he's not getting any better. He does look pale and he certainly doesn't look robust enough to play rugger." Sir Andrew was as candid as he could be without destroying the opportunity he had bequeathed his great-grandson.

"Well, I'm concerned. What his mother is telling me I'm inclined to believe. She is astonishingly attractive by the way; I can't imagine why some virile young blade hasn't snatched her up. She is a single parent, is she not?"

"Aye, that she is. It's one of Eilid's mysteries, she's never said who the father is and I don't believe anyone knows except Kenneth Urquhart. She apparently went to him in the January of 1959 to have the child. I assume there must be a Birth Certificate somewhere but to be truthful it has never been a concern of mine. She reminds me so much of Alasdair it's like my son has been reincarnated in female form.

You should see her shoot by-the- way; blow the balls off a stag at three hundred yards!"

"Seriously?" John Forsyth chuckled.

"Seriously. She is a crack shot, so be careful John especially if you and she end up anywhere near a rifle"

"Well I'll remember that. Look Andrew, here's what I'm prepared to do. Let's have Charles come for a year, no strings; he can leave at any time if it isn't working out. I think the boy is bright, very bright actually. Let's see how he gets on and if it goes well, I mean academically then we will all be happy. I understand sporting activities will be curtailed for the time being, and if we take those out of the picture then there shouldn't be a problem. How does that sound?"

"I think that's a very acceptable compromise and one which I'm sure Eilid will accept. You know she is not keen on him boarding at all, and it's me really who started this whole boarding school business. I think a good Scottish education cannot be beaten, just look at the inventors, engineers and philanthropists this tiny country has created. So it was Charles who wanted, nay, begged to come to boarding school and I think it would be terrible if he were denied the opportunity. I thank you for your offer. Now I've been thinking as we've been talking, National Health in this country is a bloody disaster. Why don't I take out some very substantial form of private Health Insurance for Charles and if he needs anything major done to him, why the insurance will kick in, we'll get the best people and the school would be relieved of all liability. How does that appeal to you?"

"Marvelous Andrew; we've got a deal then. Just sell it to Eilid. I would just love to see her come down to visit Charles at the Leave Out weekends."

"Now John, I know you only too well and I can see that sparkle in your eye."

"Andrew it's more than a sparkle, if that goes I might as well roll over. But don't concern yourself, your granddaughter's safe with me." He smiled broadly.

"You know John that's a statement that truly bothers me."

The two men laughed heartily together as Charles, Eilid and the Bursar approached.

"Well you two seem to be having a rare old time together." Eilid smiled her blond hair cascading forward as she bent down to put on her shoes that she had been carrying. The rugger field and the surrounding area had been so muddy the Bursar had found an old pair of rugby boots, which turned out to be a good fit. Eilid did not have tiny feet.

"Well yes, we've been talking about old times. How did you like the rugby Charles?" Sir Andrew turned to face him.

"Granddad, it was super, just like Tom Brown's Schooldays. I just wish I could play, that's all I wish."

The eleven year-old's wish was so fervent, it seemed to touch everybody's heart. There was a long silence. The John Forsyth hunkered down and looked at him squarely,

"You will young man, you will, once we get you here."

Charles literally jumped for joy.

"You mean you'll have me, you'll accept me?"

"Yes indeed, if your mother agrees of course."

Eilid just nodded affirmatively, and smiled first at Sir Andrew, then at John Forsyth, turned round, picked Charles up effortlessly and gave him a big kiss.

"There, there, isn't that wonderful Charles. And you will play rugby and squash, we'll work towards that."

She had absolutely no idea of what she was promising but it seemed to be the right thing to endorse the Headmaster's comments. She also had every faith in Uncle Ken. Her next stop after returning to Innerleithen was to her Uncle's house in Pitlochry.

It was time to go. All the words of thanks had been said. Fitz had returned with the Rolls Royce having spent most of his day in Perth shopping. Everyone gathered round the Rolls as they said their farewells. Eilid shook hands with Henry Blake the Bursar and as John Forsyth proffered his hand Eilid took it, pulled John to her, and gave him a soft and warm kiss on the cheek.

"Thank you so much, "she murmured in his ear.

The effect on John Forsyth was electrifying. He clutched Eilid's other hand by the wrist and held her close to him, their bodies just apart.

"No thank *you* so much. You have my word that I shall do everything to make Charles welcome and to progress his education. It has been my pleasure."

Reluctantly he released Eilid and stepped back as Sir Andrew, Charles and finally Eilid got into the car. Fitz put the Rolls in gear and gently crunched his way over the gravel to the asphalt driveway that led back to the school gates.

Sir Andrew was tired. For a man of seventy-five it had been a long day. As he closed his eyes his mind was still turning. Was Eilid just an innocent abroad, or did she really know what she was doing with men. For a long time he had doubted that there was any guile in what she did, she always seemed so innocent and ingenuous but now he wasn't quite so sure. There was a skillful fox-like quality in what she did, did he imagine this or was he putting too much into his granddaughter's actions. They seemed so spontaneous, was it an act or.........and at that point he dozed off to dream of fly-fishing for salmon on the Tweed.

Two weeks later a letter arrived at the Torridon Lodge addressed to Charles Edward Stuart Esquire. The letter advised Charles of his acceptance at Strahearn and was signed by John Forsyth the Headmaster. The letter contained all sorts of information on school uniform and where to get it. There was one item Charles did not need to buy and that was a kilt. Kilts were regulation wear on a Sunday complete with a stiff collared white shirt with studs and French cuffs, a Tweed waistcoat and matching jacket completed the Sunday ensemble. Charles did have a kilt, but not the other articles. His enthusiasm was intense. His first term started on September seventh which was for new entrants. The following Sunday the other pupils would arrive which gave the new arrivals time to become acquainted with the school system, organization and disciplines.

COLIN MACALISTER MD FRCS —
September 1970

There are moments in life when luck or good fortune, whatever the name, plays a key part. September of 1970 was to provide one such occasion that saved Eilid's credibility and Charles's life.

Colin Macalister MD FRCS was now Senior Registrar at Great Ormond Street Hospital for Sick Children in London, an important position for a cardiovascular surgeon of only 39. His mentor Ross Macdonald now only did consultancy work and had virtually retired. Colin had married a very attractive English girl named Jennifer Simpson, two years after he heard the news of Karen Ericsson's tragic death and that of her son Jens, the child he and Ross Macdonald had operated on only weeks before.

The news of the Stratocruiser's crash in the Scottish Highlands affected him badly when he learned there had been no survivors. All his future hopes and dreams of having a medical practice in the United States instantly evaporated with the news of the tragedy.

TV, Radio and the newspapers all sensationalized the crash at the time but because of the remoteness of the location and the lack of contact with the crash site for almost two days, there were few pictures or photographs. Reporters contented themselves with what little news they could glean from relatives who were accessible to them. There was virtually no news of American passengers save for file photographs of a Boeing 377 and quite a bit about Hank Kelley, the Stratocruiser's pilot, who was something of a Second World War hero having flown and survived twenty-two bombing missions into Germany. Colin had hoped against hope that it wasn't Karen's flight. It brought back the unforgettable memory of his night with Karen and how she had seduced him in her hotel suite. He freely conceded to himself that he had been a willing victim. The real tragedy was the death of the baby. Ross Macdonald had carried out a wonderful operation to make the child survive and have a normal life for at least a number of years by which time, they hoped, correctly as it transpired, that a more permanent solution to Jens' problem would be found.

Jennifer, Colin's wife was a talented athlete as well as an accomplished cook. She was five years Colin's junior, still played hockey for the former pupils' team of her Grammar School and was keen on equestrian sports, as well as squash and tennis. To these activities she added hill walking. She had thought of mountaineering and had gone to Scotland once with her father just to explore the possibilities. Her father had been a keen mountaineer or rock climber in his younger days and spent many weekends in the English Lake District doing some of the harder climbs combined with nights of serious drinking flitting between the famous or infamous Old and New Dungeon Gill pubs in Great Langdale. To her father's mixed emotions of regret and relief Jennifer found that she couldn't stand heights, and while she didn't quite suffer from vertigo, sheer rock walls were not for her, but she did take to hill walking as an enjoyable pastime.

One evening when she was visiting her parents in Maidenhead, Surrey, she met Sir David Vickers who was on the board of the same Merchant Bank as her father. Sir David was extolling the virtues of Eilid his stalker and Mhairi, his legendary chef. Jennifer asked all sorts of questions about the location of his estate in the Highlands, and in particular about stalking which she had heard him speak of.

Sir David, who regarded Jennifer almost as a niece, and who he considered could give Eilid a run for her money in stamina if not in looks, gave a fine dissertation on a week's stalking in Torridon. Jennifer asked if it would be possible to hill walk while Colin did some hunting. She wasn't sure if she was up to seeing any animal being killed let alone killing anything herself for she had no experience of handling firearms. But, she said to Sir David, Colin might just love a break and the introduction to stalking. Sir David explained that she could not hill walk while the annual cull was in progress but that she could accompany the hunting party on the hill, adding that at times the stalking party covered ten to twelve miles in a day. Jennifer was enthralled by the idea. Colin would love the complete break away from work, he would be back in his homeland for a week or more, and they would be on the hills together. That combined with the camaraderie in the evenings generated by Mhairi's now legendary cooking gave it all the ingredients of a holiday made in heaven for them.

Sir David promised to phone her with available dates, if there were any, for stalking that autumn. To that end he called Eilid later in the same week that she had received the news of Charles being admitted to Strahearn.

"Do you know, there's nothing, nothing at all. I've even got some party in the first week of the rut in August, which I wouldn't put your friends on anyway because it's a waste of time." Eilid scanned through her bookings while on the phone with Sir David.

"The only possibility is that I get a cancellation, and that hasn't happened for a while. David, how important is it to you that this couple comes to Torridon?"

"Eilid my love, it's just a favor for a good friend of mine. It's his daughter actually, pretty young filly, loves to hill walk. Her husband is an up and coming star in medical circles so I'm told. He is Scots but I don't think he's ever been stalking before. He just works so hard that Jennifer, that's her name, felt that a week at Torridon would be a complete break, but if we can't do it, we can't do it."

"Is he a specialist, this doctor fellow?"

"Oh yes, he's a heart surgeon, quite famous in London circles so I hear, but it's of no consequence, I know you don't like people on the hill with no experience at all, especially after Auld John's demise."

"You're right there, but let's just see what happens. I have one or two still to confirm and I don't have the money from them yet, so let me call you in a fortnight and I may have something." Eilid hung up thinking about Charles and his probable heart condition.

She had visited Ken Urquhart on her way back from Sir Andrew's house in June but all that Ken could tell her was more or less what he had surmised before, that as a baby Charles had some heart surgery and that his health was deteriorating more rapidly as he got older. Kenny was very concerned about Charles going to Strahearn and said so.

The first two weeks of the stalking season were almost over and there had been no change in the bookings until on the last day of that fortnight a regular client called to say his wife had suddenly taken ill and that he would have to cancel. He would quite understand if his deposit was forfeit but there was nothing he could do but cancel this year's trip.

Eilid was warm and sympathetic. His deposit would be returned by the next post and she wished his ailing wife well before saying goodbye. Next she called Sir David.

"Your Doctor chap's on, Sir David. Monday 14th to Saturday 19th of September, I'll expect them to arrive as usual on the Sunday evening in time for dinner."

"What happened, someone cancel?"

"Yes, their wife took ill."

"Eilid you're wonderful, Jennifer and Colin will be so grateful. I'll get them to send you a cheque right away."

"Well if they're friends of yours there's no need. I'll leave it to you."

"No, I'll get the cash. They'll think I done them a big favor after telling them there was not a hope in hell of getting on the hill this year."

"You're probably right. Fortunately that's the Sunday after Charles goes to Strahearn so I'll be here to welcome them. I don't mind if I'm not around for some of the regulars, they know to expect me on the Monday morning, but when it's new people I like to be present to welcome them."

The end of the first week in September was frantic. All Charles school clothes were laid out and counted. Four gray shirts, two school ties, four pairs of gray socks, two pairs of kilt socks, two dozen handkerchiefs, four vests, four pairs of 'bum fugs' as Eilid liked to call underpants and on and on. Mhairi had been elicited to sew name tag labels on everything and Charles had insisted on his full name being on the tag which made it huge when combined with his school number, which oddly enough was forty-five, the significance of which was lost on most, but not on his mother. When Mhairi, Hamish and Eilid had checked and double-checked everything it was packed in a huge trunk with Charles's name boldly written on it together with the address of the school. This would be sent by train a few days prior to Charles leaving the Glen and would be waiting for him when he got to Strahearn. The farewells were tearful as Charles got into the Land Rover with his mother for the drive to the school. Mhairi hugged and kissed him over and over again and Hamish, forever the gentleman shook his hand warmly and wished him every success at the school with an admonition to not forget to write often. It was at that point that Hamish held up his hands in horror.

"Stop, stop for goodness sake. I've forgotten something," and off he raced into the Lodge. Seconds later he came out with a present, wrapped in brown paper.

"Charles, this is from Mhairi and me. Open it when you get to school."

And with that he gave Charles a huge hug. Mhairi and he waved until the Land Rover disappeared from view and then went back into the Lodge now strangely silent and empty. It wouldn't be for long however, a six man contingent was supposed to arrive from somewhere near Bristol later that day, prepared for Mhairi's fine cooking and the promise of good stalking on the following day. Eilid arrived back at the Lodge late that evening having seen Charles safely ensconced in his dormitory that had a pleasant view over the rugger fields. Beyond the rugger fields there was a fruit farm and then a wide, fast flowing river.

She was physically and emotionally drained. For the first time she had left her son in the care of others who were not related to her in any way; there was a trace of irony in that thought she mused, but she put those thoughts behind her. Charles, in contrast to other boys his age or just a little older, looked taller than most but skinny by contrast and pale and wan.

Eilid was glad to be home. When she left the school Charles had already made friends with some of the new arrivals who were missing their mothers already. Charles didn't seem to bat an eye and took everything in his stride. It was as if his body had found some new inner strength to drive him on. Mhairi had left a cold plate out for her with a carafe of wine and she ate alone by the living room fire's dying embers. The weather was cloudy and mild with a moderate wind coming out of the south-west. She would see what kind of people she had for the upcoming week early next morning at breakfast. As it happened the weeks' stalking turned out to be very strenuous.

The mild weather kept the stags near the mountain tops and the rut had only just begun with most of the stags still running together.

The visitors from the south were fortunately all fit and in good spirits and they had organized themselves so that only four went on the hill at any one time. Eilid appreciated their consideration, as a party of eight, Hamish joining them as Ghillie, was a difficult number to handle on the hill. She remembered from the previous year that most of the party were fairly good shots, there had been only one complete miss and at the end of the week the visitors had culled five stags with only eight shots being fired, a good outcome as far as Eilid was concerned. On other days the two not going on the hill went off fishing, some to Loch Maree and others to local rivers in search of salmon. The weather remained kind with a few heavy showers towards the end of the week.

The guests were most generous and left Eilid with a whole case of Glenmorangie 10-year-old malt whisky. They tipped Hamish and Mhairi generously and vowed to return the following year. For the departing guests Sunday was a dreadful day with rain lashing the glen and not a hill in sight. But the group of six left in such good spirits not even the foul weather could dampen their good humor as they headed home south to Bristol.

Dr. Colin Macalister and his wife Jennifer had left London before first light in dry but cloudy conditions and had headed up the AI. They had hoped to try out the M1; Britain's first section of Motorway that would cover the seventy six miles from St. Albans to Birmingham, but as this had been subject to delay after delay it wasn't going to open until later in November of that year, so Colin had read.

Colin had no option, therefore, but to use the A1 that ran up the east side of the country from London to Edinburgh, the best route available in 1969.

Hamish had been putting more logs on the fire in the large living room when he shouted to Mhairi that he could see lights coming down the glen. Mhairi guessed that it had to be her guests so she began to prepare the meal. The table was all set in starched white clean napery and the wine glasses gleamed in the light from the table lamps around the room. For good friends of Sir David's Eilid had, as usual, opened and decanted a bottle of one of Sir David's better clarets, a 1951 bottle of Chateau Phelan Segur. She remembered too that Colin Macalister was a heart surgeon of great reputation. So she reckoned that with just the right amount attention she might get a little free advice on what could be done to improve her son's health.

Jennifer and Colin literally staggered into the welcoming light and warmth of Sir David Vickers's Lodge. Hamish was first to greet them, followed by Mhairi. Quickly she led the two exhausted travelers to the big settee in front of the fire, told them not to move and poured two large Macallans porting them on a silver salver with a small crystal jug of water. Colin didn't hesitate for a moment. He took the proffered glass, and looked at Jennifer.

"Colin, you know I don't like whisky, never have, never will. Marie do you think I could have a gin and tonic, please?"

"Certainly ma'am. My name is actually pronounced Varie, it's Gaelic, it looks like Marie but an 'Mh' in Gaelic has a 'V' sound."

"Jennifer, for God's sake this isn't St John's Wood. Try the bloody whisky. It's like nothing you've ever had." Colin was on his feet now. "I mean darling when in Rome........."

"Well I'll have just a sip then. Let me add a little water." She carefully took the jug and added about half as much water again to the glass of malt. She sipped tentatively as if it might contain arsenic.

Mhairi hovered in the background.

"My God darling you're right. This is sooo smooth. I can't believe it; I've never tasted anything like it. It's almost like the finest Cognac. Mhairi forget the G & T. this is going to be fabulous."

The Macallan was doing its job, mellowing the travelers as they heated themselves by the now roaring fire. It was at this point they heard footsteps coming towards them. Eilid had come to greet her guests. Colin looked up at the approaching figure. Quickly he took in all the ladies attributes. Tall, long blond hair spilling over her shoulders, electric blue eyes, an aquiline nose, slim, very athletic looking, she could be competition for Jennifer, Colin reckoned.

"Good evening, I'm Eilid Stuart. Sir David has told me a lot about you. Welcome to Torridon. You must be exhausted. It's such a long drive."

"Have you ever done it?" Jennifer asked pointedly.

"No I never have. I've never ever been to England, let alone London, but I can imagine it's a long way."

"You've no idea, have you?" Jennifer was like a cat that had just been attacked. Was it the way Colin had looked at Eilid or was it just raw feminine instinct, the threat of competition.

"I'm not sure what you mean, but I do know London is about 650 miles from here on not very good roads, anyway I'm sure you must be starving, Mhairi's set up the dining room for you and dinner will be served shortly. It's simple fare tonight, but I think you'll enjoy Sir David's claret."

"It seems everything around here is pretty simple." Jennifer's tongue was on the point of scalding, but if Eilid was supposed to react there was not a blink, not a flicker, to denote she was being attacked.

"You're right Mrs. Macalister, we lead a simple life, there are few complications, and if there are, we try to iron them out. Now Mhairi will leave after she's served the steak and kidney pudding, there's cloutie dumpling and custard afterwards which Hamish will help you to and we'll see you at nine thirty for breakfast. Is there anything else we can do for you?"

"Well if we don't know what breakfast consists of, how do we know we'll like it?" Colin's honest opinion was that Jennifer was rapidly becoming a pain-in-the-arse, but if Eilid thought likewise it certainly didn't show.

Eilid smiled sweetly. "There's traditional Scottish porridge, followed by bacon, eggs, potato scone, black pudding, sausage and if you like, baked beans. Nothing is compulsory and if you prefer a Continental Breakfast we can do toast and coffee. It is a long day on the hill, and if you can eat a hearty breakfast then I recommend it to you. Hamish will also ask you what you would like on your sandwiches for the hill. Mhairi has most meats, ham, roast beef, rare of course, chicken, pheasant, and fruit if you wish. I think we might be out of bananas but that'll be fixed by tomorrow evening. See you in the morning." And with that she was gone.

"My God cloutie dumpling *and* custard, I haven't had that in years."

"Colin just what is 'cloutie dumpling'?" Jennifer looked confused.

"Well a clout, is old Scots for a cloth and the dumpling is just a mixture of dried fruits like currents, raisins, grated apple, sugar, bread crumbs, suet, mixed spices, cinnamon, ginger, treacle, self raising flour, and milk all mixed together in a big bowl. Then the cloth is scalded with boiling water and then sprinkled with flour, the mixture wrapped up in the cloth and put in a big pan full of water, on a plate, to simmer for about two or three hours. This is going to be a great trip darling, thanks so much for organizing it for me."

"You're welcome. I didn't know we were going to have a bimbo who masquerades as a stalker."

"For God's sake Jennifer, act your age. Eilid Stuart is a married, or rather widowed woman with a son. She has been at the Lodge for more than ten years. She would not come highly recommended by Sir David if she was some kind of floozy."

"Well all I know that the minute she walked into the room she had eyes only for you, come on Colin you must have seen that?"

"Bollocks! You've gone mad. It's been a long day. Let's eat, sleep and see what tomorrow looks like through refreshed eyes."

Colin was in no mood to discuss the Eilid versus Jennifer match any longer. Mhairi's meal was delicious but they ate in silence. Not even a few glasses of the Phelan Segur could break the ice and they collapsed into their bed before ten o'clock.

Monday morning dawned cold and clear. There was a stiff breeze blowing out of the north-east that would have, as Mhairi remarked, "cut you in two," as she served breakfast. Jennifer ate heartily, she had slept well and she appeared to be in better humor although Eilid hadn't yet appeared. At about ten minutes to nine, Eilid came through the door to the sitting room with Barbour trousers, jacket and green scarf. Her hair was tied back in a ponytail and she had a green beret in her hand.

"Good morning, how are you all this morning? I hope you slept well, and if you're still drowsy there's a wind out there that'll blow the cobwebs away. Mrs. Macalister are you coming out on the hill today?"

"Absolutely, if that's all right?" Jennifer looked over at Colin for confirmation.

"Well it's Eilid's call as to who goes on the hill." Colin looked over deferring to Eilid. He had been well warned by Horace, Jennifer's Uncle that the stalker was in charge of all things relating to the stalking including any trophies that the guest might like to take home in the form of antlers and so forth. Technically, Horace had said, anything that was culled on the hill was the stalker's, to do with as he or she liked. In most cases if a client wanted to keep the antlers the stalker gladly allowed that for a customary five-pound tip.

Eilid smiled and said, "That's fine with me, I'll be outside setting up the box for you to try the rifle. Will you be shooting Mrs. Macalister?"

"Heavens no! I've never seen a gun let alone handled one."

"We can soon fix that, but it's your decision. You've got two full days to yourselves before your father and your uncle arrive and we've got eight stags to get this week if we can." Eilid turned towards the door and the Land Rover parked outside.

Colin turned to Jennifer. "Come on darling, why don't you have a go?"

"Colin, I'm not about to make myself a fool in front of that woman, and that's that."

"Well if you don't try, you don't do. So what's the point of coming up on the hill?"

"I just want to stretch my legs. It was a long day yesterday all cramped up in the car. Colin was sure there was another reason but he kept quiet and said, "I'm just concerned it could be an equally long day and it is bloody cold out there."

Jennifer insisted she would be quite fine, thank you very much, so she went up to their bedroom and dressed for the hill. She had a ski jacket, which was very warm in a bright pink so when she came out to see what was going on Mhairi and Hamish went into fits of laughter as they could imagine the Eilid's reaction to the color scheme. The dark blue salopettes weren't too bad, but the shocking pink jacket, wow!

Eilid was busy setting Colin up with the rifle and the cardboard box with a target pasted to it down by the burn. She had him on the ground behind a convenient rock with his Barbour spread out to keep him dry. Then she told him to zero in with the scope on the target and squeeze the trigger when he thought he was aimed at the bull. There was no ammunition in the rifle but she wanted Colin to get an idea of the pressure that was needed when he squeezed off a shot. When Colin felt comfortable and he had the feel of the rifle Eilid loaded five rounds in the magazine and pushed the first round home with the bolt, putting on the safety catch as she handed the rifle back to Colin.

"Right, it's ready to go. Just flick off the safety with your thumb and then take a deep breath, take aim and as you exhale slowly and when you think you're on target, squeeze the trigger." Eilid stood behind Colin with the binoculars trained on the cardboard box. Boom! The rifle barked. Colin lay there astonished at the noise.

"Reload, reload. Don't just lie there!" There was urgency in Eilid's voice.

Colin worked the bolt frantically. The empty casing flew from the rifle and another round shot into the chamber.

"Am I allowed to know how I did?"

"Well....not bad, not bad at all." Coming from Eilid that was praise indeed. "Your about two inches to the right, about two o'clock above the bull."

"Okay. I'm pleased."

"That's just one shot though; carry on with the other four."

Eilid went back to her binoculars and just caught a glimpse of an apparition in deep fuchsia somewhere to her left. The rifle boomed again and again until the final shot. Colin got up and left the rifle lying with the breach open.

"Come on then, let's see how you've done." Eilid was striding ahead covering the hundred yards between the rock and the target in rapid steps. Colin had to run at first to catch up. Also coming behind was Jennifer at a good clip. One thing she could do was run and so she caught up with the pair about twenty-five yards from the box.

"Having fun?" was all she said, looking at her husband with that expectant look in her eye that all men are supposed to recognize and understand but never do.

"I think I've done quite well, for a first time." Colin qualified his remark.

He turned to Eilid.

"My, my, that's a bright cozy jacket you have there Mrs. Macalister."

"Yes it is. It's part of my ski wear which I brought because I just thought it might get cold at this time of year."

"Aye, well that was a good thought. Your man's done very well. I mean the doctor," as Colin looked doubtful. "You've a four inch grouping to the upper right of the bull, for a first timer I'd say that's first class. Any of those shots would be a kill. So I've no fear in taking you on the hill today or any other day."

"Could Jennifer have a go, Eilid?"

"You mean with the rifle?"

"Well I thought she might want to become involved in the stalking, it was just a thought mind you, Jennifer's not too keen, although she'd like to come along just for the walk."

"What do you want to do Mrs. Macalister?"

"In truth I don't think I could kill a Stag, but I'd like to come with you on the hill if I may."

"You may indeed. But we'll have to get you something to cover that Belisha Beacon you've got on."

"I beg your pardon, this is a Giovanni Bergamo."

"Mrs. Macalister, I don't really care who made it. It's more who's wearing it. I'd be delighted for you to join us on the hill, but that outfit just won't do. Deer are not color blind and every beast in the Glen will be able to see you coming for miles around."

"Well I'm certainly not going to take it off. I'll freeze up there."

"Mrs. Macalister," Eilid's patience was becoming stretched by the second, "no one said you have to take it off, we just have to find something more suitable to the surrounding colors to put over it."

"Well I certainly didn't bring anything in camouflage. No one told me there was a color ban on certain clothes. I don't see why I . . . ."

"Jennifer, please. Just be quiet. Eilid will help you out with something." Colin Macalister was also getting quite annoyed by his wife's performance. It was as if she had a burning jealousy of Eilid, and Eilid had not done one thing to warrant Jennifer's demeanor.

Eilid said nothing, turned on her heel and walked all the way back to the Lodge. Hamish was just emerging having had breakfast with his sister and saw Eilid approaching fast.

"I have it here." Was all that Hamish said. He held up a musty dark green kagul that way back in time someone had left behind in the Lodge. Both Hamish and Mhairi were squirrels and threw away nothing. It was at times like these that Eilid just loved Hamish. It was as if he had the gift of second sight. He had seen Jennifer Macalister with the fluorescent ski jacket and knew what the outcome would be.

"Thanks Hamish," was all Eilid said as she grabbed the Kagul.

"Mrs. Macalister if you put this over your ski jacket we can proceed to the hill."

"What, put that musty old thing over my Giovanni Bergamo, I don't think so."

Eilid looked at Colin and shrugged. Colin could almost feel the fire in her electric blue eyes so intense was her look.

"Just a minute Eilid, please." Colin got hold of his wife by the elbow and moved her barely out of earshot.

"Jennifer, if we're going to have a good time here put on that fucking Kagul, and that's my last word on it, otherwise we're back home, understand?"

Jennifer stared at Colin. She had never quite seen him so mad. She put the Kagul over her fuchsia jacket and moved back towards Eilid. Eilid said not a word, turned on her heel and went to the Land Rover. In a few seconds they were heading down the track towards an awe-inspiring view Liathach, as Eilid explained to them that the name translated into the Gray One from the Gaelic. Its huge mass got larger as they approached it from the Glen Torridon road.

The day went quite well. Jennifer uttered not a word and Eilid put Colin into his first beast almost at the place where Auld John had met his untimely end. It was a clean miss and the Hinds and the Stag fled the corrie when the rifle went off. Colin was very upset.

"I had that damned thing in my sights, no question."

"I agree," said Eilid, "but why did you close your eyes when you pulled the trigger?"

"I didn't, well I wasn't aware that I did," Colin was perplexed.

"Well Doctor Macalister, you did. If you can imagine it's like following through at golf. Keep your eye on the target at all times and see the bullet strike. Now don't concern yourself. This is your first stalk. It's one thing shooting at a cardboard box, quite another when you have a big stag at the end of your rifle."

"Your right; there's a lot in what you say. Oh and by the way, would you just call me Colin, I'd truly prefer that."

"Will Mrs. Macalister mind?"

"Probably. She's not been in a very good mood since we arrived, and this is her treat to me. I can't understand it."

"Well it's maybe the first time she's been on the hill stalking, and it's not the first time I've had a problem by being the boss on the hill so to speak. Maybe she resents that."

"More like your good looks and blond hair," muttered Colin. But if Eilid heard she gave no sign as they went back down the hill to Jennifer who had been behind a rock for what had seemed like ages as Eilid had stalked the stag. It had only been thirty minutes but already Jennifer was frozen. However she said nothing and walked on, the last in file, as they traversed the hill looking for another herd that Eilid had spied from the road.

Below at the Lodge, Hamish heard the shot, waited for the smoke from the fired heather but as none appeared he assumed, quite rightly, that there had been no kill. He just hoped they didn't have a runner, a wounded stag, for that put Eilid in the foulest of moods as she had to spend all sorts of time to find out where the stag had gone and whether or not it was mortally wounded. He went back into the Lodge and joined his sister in another cup of coffee.

The hill party stopped at just after noon to shelter behind a large rock in a gully to have their sandwiches in an attempt to take shelter from the biting Nor-Easter that had been blowing all day. Jennifer had hardly spoken, but there hadn't been much conversation anyway. Colin was still embarrassed by his miss despite Eilid's assurances that the next time he would know what to do. They ate in silence as the wind whipped around them. In twenty minutes they were back on the exposed mountainside going after the other herd. Colin was astonished at the Stalker's eyesight. She could see animals that he couldn't even see when they were pointed out to him. Colin began to think he had faulty eyesight or inferior binoculars or both but his inability to spot a stag or a herd of deer was confirmed by Jennifer who had excellent eyesight but to whom the herds of deer remained invisible.

It was two o'clock when Eilid asked Jennifer to stay put behind a rock as she moved forward in a crouch to the next herd that was just over the horizon. In no time at all Eilid and Colin were crawling on their hands and knees trying to keep out of sight from the herd. Eilid motioned Colin to stop as she gently moved forward and took a look over a mound of heather covered peat just in front of her. She was back in a moment. She put her mouth to Colin's ear and whispered,

"The stag's just about eighty yards away at the back of the herd. He's standing straight on but I want you to wait until he turns and then take your shot. Okay?"

"Okay," confirmed Colin. My God he thought I can hear my heart pounding, I have to calm down. But try as he might his heart rate increased to where he thought the hinds would be able to hear his approach, so great was the thumping in his chest. They reached the heather covered tuffet and Eilid took off her Barbour jacket and rolled it into a sort of ball. She left it on top of the mound and slid Colin the rifle.

"Safety's on."

"Okay," Colin croaked moving forward an inch at a time. Ever so slowly he peeked over the mound. He could see the hinds. My God they were close he thought. But where was the stag? Suddenly he saw it standing perfectly still head on to him. It was only because the stag moved his head slightly that Colin was able to see him, so well was he camouflaged. The stag's natural color blended into the earthy browns of the peat hag he was standing in as well as being camouflaged by the surrounding brown bracken. Quietly he slid the rifle forward and took aim. The stag was still head on.

"Hold on," Eilid whispered. "Wait till he turns."

They lay their freezing for what seemed like an eternity until a hind barked. The stag started to turn.

"Now, now," hissed Eilid

Boom! Eilid's old Mannlicher barked. The noise was deafening as Colin quickly reloaded.

"It's all right he's gone, he's gone."

Colin couldn't bear to look. He was sure he had got the stag. He was sure he had even seen the bullet hit and the shock wave that rippled up the stag's body. He forced himself to look. The stag was still there swaying imperceptibly, and then it crumpled in a heap without a sound.

"Well done, well done!" Eilid rose to walk forward as the hinds fled from the immediate vicinity.

Jennifer was disgusted with the graloching or field dressing of the beast. She was even more affronted when Eilid did the traditional bloodying of Colin. It was absolutely heathen she thought.

"Come on then darling, where's the camera?"

"If you think I'm going to take a photograph of you looking like that Colin Macalister you can think again."

"Come on Jennifer, it's what we came all this way for."

"I will not."

Eilid stepped in. "I'll take the pictures if you give me the camera."

"But you hands are covered in blood and God knows what else," protested Jennifer.

Eilid could see that Colin was getting upset again. Jennifer was really too much.

"Give me the bloody camera!" Colin exploded.

Jennifer, eyes wide open with astonishment at the second cursing of the day, she stood silent and tight lipped, as she handed Colin the camera.

"Thank you."

Eilid washed her hands in a nearby burn where she had dumped the stag's innards and took photographs of Colin, the stag, the stag and Colin. Jennifer refused point blank to appear in any of the photographs, no matter how Colin tried to cajole her. Eilid had gone off to the nearby summit, which looked down on the Glen and gathered as much dried material as she could find and then lit the heather with a little help from a bottle of lighter fluid she secretly kept in her Barbour. The welcome smoke was seen by Hamish at the Lodge and he set off with two ponies, just in case there was a second kill that day.

That night at the Lodge Colin was in great humor. Mhairi's food was as wonderful as ever, particularly following a few drams with Eilid in the larder as they both drank while she prepared the stag for the butcher's truck which would come to pick up the carcasses later on in the week. Jennifer's demeanor had improved slightly but the staff at the Lodge remained wary of the "spiky wifie" as Mhairi had described her. The wind was due to continue out of the east for a few more days so Eilid decided to stalk round the back of Beinn Eighe the following day. Jennifer decided that Inverness was a much better venue than the hill and declared just a bit too forcibly that she had no intention of going out in the cold weather to freeze her backside stuck on some hillside for God knows how long.

By nine o'clock the next morning Eilid and Colin Macalister set out from the Lodge. Hamish had been told to give them a three-hour head start before he set off with the ponies. The day was clear and bright and although the north-east wind had abated slightly it was still bitterly cold. Stalker and client moved quickly over the track between the bases of Liathach and Beinn Eighe. In the cold northern light the Ben looked spectacular, its sharp summit standing out like peak in the Swiss Alps. By eleven o'clock the couple had reached the waterfall that flowed out of the Lochan at the foot of the Corrie Mhic Fhearchair. They stopped to eat some of the sandwiches Mhairi had prepared for them before climbing into the corrie. Eilid was constantly looking through her binoculars at two particular spots.

"Do you see anything?" Colin asked.

"Uh, huh. There are a couple of herds up there. One's got a really big stag and right now he's chasing off a couple of nobbers, so that's keeping him occupied. I think we'll go for him."

Eilid put her binoculars into the pocket of her Barbour and stood up. Colin followed her lead and grasping his stick fell in behind her. As they made their way up the scree towards the Triple Buttresses something flashed in the bright sunlight. Colin tried to see what it was but he couldn't with his naked eye. Pulling out his binoculars he took another look. It was silver or actually aluminum and the wind was pulling at a piece of the metal making it flap so that now and again it caught the sunlight.

"Eilid, what's that I see in the corrie?" He pointed with his stick in the general direction of the object.

"Oh that, it's just part of the undercarriage of an airplane which crashed about 10 years ago. The RAF took most of it out but for some reason they left the bigger bits."

She looked at Colin who had suddenly gone silent and was staring at the piece of wreckage.

"My God, I can't believe it, I just can't believe it." Memories of Karen Ericsson flooded his mind.

"Doctor, are you all right?" Eilid looked at him, concerned.

"Yes and no, actually. I have to ask you, was this an American plane, a Stratocruiser, by any chance?"

"Yes, I think that's what they called it, everybody on board was killed." Eilid's own memories of the incident flooded back.

"Why do you ask?"

"Well I was one of the surgeons who treated this very sick baby. After all our work he and his mother were on this 'plane taking them back to Los Angeles when it crashed and, as you say, there were no survivors."

Eilid's heart was pounding. Her mind raced as she took in all Colin Macalister had just said. She tried to sound as nonchalant as she could. She had stopped walking now and they faced one another on the steep incline.

"What sort of operation was it?"

"It was to fix a hole in the baby's heart. We did what's called a shunt."

"And that made the baby well again?"

"Well the operation was a success, if that's what you mean. He was all blue when we got him but he was returning home, literally in the pink, when this tragedy occurred."

"Would that have been a permanent fix?"

"What makes you ask that?"

"Just interested really. I have a friend in Inverness whose baby had something similar done five years ago." Eilid lied convincingly.

"Oh, right, I see. Well what we did then was the best technology had to offer, now they have heart bypass surgery which would have let us do a permanent repair, you know, fix the faulty valve."

"So what you did wasn't permanent?"

"Not really. It's all academic but if little Jens had lived, round about now young Jens would need proper heart surgery to fix him up."

"Oh his name was Jens, that's a Scandinavian name isn't it?"

"Yes it is. But this baby was from the United States, however his last name was, if I can remember, was something like Magnusson or Christiansen or something."

Colin reached back in time. Karen, Karen what the hell was her last name? How could he possibly forget? Then it came to him.

"Ericsson," he said out loud. That was it Ericsson."

Eilid had heard enough. Now she knew what was wrong with Charles, she even knew his original name, Jens Ericsson. There was one last fact she had to have.

"Colin was the father killed as well?"

"No he stayed back in Los Angeles I think, or somewhere in Texas, I'm really not sure. Jens was a twin, so that's why the father stayed at home."

That was just what she had not wanted to hear. Colin Macalister's words stung her with a ferocity she could hardly bear. The child she rescued was *not* an orphan after all. Her mind went into a tailspin. Uncle Kenny was right, she had, eleven long years ago, deprived a father of his child and a child of his brother.

The rest of the day was a blur. She successfully stalked and Colin shot the big stag, Hamish came up with the ponies and they left the hill early. Colin didn't mention a second stalk neither did she. Only Hamish made a passing comment on the other stag he had seen on the way up but Eilid said she was finished for the day and so the party all went back down the hill together. Both Colin and Hamish noted that there was a strangeness about Eilid. She spoke even less than usual, her conversation becoming even more sparse as they made their way back to the lodge.

George and Horace Simpson arrived on the Wednesday by which time Eilid seemed to have returned to normal. By the end of the week there were eight stags in the larder, three very pleased clients and a slightly thawed out Jennifer who had been lectured to by her father and told in no uncertain terms to get her 'head out of her arse'. She was almost friendly to Eilid by the time Saturday came around. Mhairi excelled herself at the traditional Saturday night dinner and was voted "Chefesse of the Year" by a well-oiled Horace Simpson. There would be a few sore heads on Sunday morning before the long drive back to London began.

Eilid stayed longer in bed on Sunday morning than she had for many a year. She wasn't asleep, but she lay in the luxury of her bed, all nice and cozy thinking about Colin Macalister and what he had said. Discovering the fact that Charles's, née Jens, father was possibly alive and well in the USA and that there was a brother preyed on her mind. She had been so certain those eleven years ago that the child was an orphan. Or was it just her desire, her obsession that made her think that way? It was she who told Kenny at the time not to examine the list of crash site victims in detail. The responsibilities were hers and hers alone. She loved Charles as only a mother could and the thought of losing him, either to failing health or some other means was an anathema to her. She decided she was playing mind games too much so she rose at eight-thirty and went down to the kitchen in the Lodge to find Hamish pouring himself a mug of coffee.

"Good week then Eilid?"

"Yes, I liked Doctor Macalister. I have to say I found Jennifer heavy going, but there we go, there's not much I could do about that."

"Aye, she had a bad attitude. She was as Mhairi said a spiky lady and for no reason."

"You're right Hamish. But let's not talk about it right now. We've got a full house tonight with six arriving from Yorkshire somewhere. Tell Mhairi just to make a regular steak and kidney pie this time, I expect they'll arrive in time for dinner. They know the ropes and they'll expect some good claret, so I'll leave it to you to get the wine from the cellar and chambré it before they get here."

"Nae problem." Hamish was becoming quite a wine connoisseur with all the experience he had gleaned from the guests at Torridon Lodge.

"Hamish, do you fancy a roll and bacon?"

"Magic. That would jist hit the spot."

"Right off you go and get the bacon and I'll see if we have any rolls left."

It was just as she was going to the larder that the phone rang.

"Hamish can you get that?"

"Aye, no problem."

Eilid found the rolls and was making her way back to the kitchen when she heard Hamish.

"Aye, right I'll get her right away sir, right away."

"Who is it?"

"Do you know a John Forsyth? He says he's a headmaster or something, he's kind of rambling on…"

"Give me the phone Hamish."

Hamish handed Eilid the phone. Immediately Eilid had a sinking feeling in the pit of her stomach that all was not well.

"Mr. Forsyth, Eilid Stuart."

"Ah, right Mrs. Stuart sorry to bother you but we have a problem with Charles."

"Really, what sort of problem?"

"Well he is the San right now…sorry Sanatorium and he is not terribly well I'm afraid."

"Just tell me what the problem is." Eilid cut right to the chase.

"Well, I mean he's not breathing very well and he's gone awfully blue. We're rather concerned and I thought I should phone you." John Forsyth's voice sounded strained at the other end of the line.

"Quite right, thank you. What happened?"

"Well it was just a schoolboy prank, you know, these things happen…" John Forsyth tailed off as Eilid cut in.

"Just tell me what happened Mr. Forsyth."

"Well yes, I mean the boys were horsing around in the Dorm, sort of running the gauntlet for the newcomers and it's harmless really, just a line of boys with pillows standing in line whacking the newcomers with pillows, and I'm afraid Charles collapsed. I mean he's alright for now, well I mean he's in bed and being looked after by Matron."

"I'll be with you sometime this morning, meantime I suggest you get Charles on oxygen to help his breathing."

"Mrs. Stuart I knew you'd be distraught. Please don't concern yourself he's in very capable hands. Can I ask you if you've ever had anything like this happen before?"

"No, not like this. Charles suffers from shortness of breath on occasions after exertion but he's never been confined to bed."

There was a long silence at the other end.

"I'll see you when you get here Mrs. Stuart, and I'm sure all will be well." John Forsyth didn't sound the least convincing. Clearly he was a worried man and so he should be, thought Eilid. Thank God for Colin Macalister. At least she knew or thought she knew what was wrong.

"Hamish!" Eilid screamed.

Hamish came running.

"It's Charles, isn't it?"

"Aye it's Charles and he's taken ill. I have to leave for Strahearn right away It'll take me a good four hours to get there. Can you and Mhairi look after the guests?"

"Of course, if we can't do that by this time, we're bloody useless."

"No, understand that's not just for tonight, but I mean for the week, I may not be here at all, depending on circumstances."

"You mean take them on the hill as the stalker?"

"Precisely. This is your big chance, Hamish. Get one of the lads from Kinlochewe to ghillie for you, there's plenty will be glad of the opportunity and treat these people to some good stalking. I've taught you all I know; now you have the chance to put it into practice."

"God, Eilid, I've prayed for this moment, but hearing you say it fair gives me the shits. I think I can do it.........

Eilid cut him off abruptly placing a hand on each shoulder and facing him head on.

"Hamish I know you can do it. I'll call this evening and let you know what's happening." Hamish could hear the tension in her voice as she spoke. He said nothing, nodded in all the right places and gave her the thumbs up. Before he knew it Eilid was upstairs packing a bag. In fifteen minutes she was downstairs.

"Hamish, I'm taking the Land Rover, I never thought, what are you and Mhairi going to do for transport?"

"Not a problem. We've got Inverness police department at our disposal.

"How do you mean?"

"Young John Gilchrist, the police driver, he's still got the hots for Mhairi."

"I know what you mean, but must you use such a disgusting expression?"

Hamish just grinned. There were times when Eilid's propriety left him wondering. It was as if she was modern and old fashioned all at the same time.

"All right so you're fine with transport. I've got to go. Hamish," she turned to give him the full power of her laser-like blue eyes, "you're in charge, don't screw up!" And with a toss of her long blond mane, she was gone.

Eilid drove the single-track road from Torridon to Kinlochewe like a woman possessed. The only picture in her mind was that of Charles lying in the Strahearn Sanatorium close to death. Fortunately an early Sunday morning in mid-September attracted no traffic and she sailed round blind corners without encountering any other vehicles. She pressed on through Garve towards Inverness with her foot hard on the accelerator. Sunday traffic in Inverness was light and she was soon on familiar territory some two hours into the journey as she went over the Drumochter Pass heading for Pitlochry. Her mind was racing. Uncle Ken was sure to be at home. She stopped at Calvine and made a phone call. Kenny answered. Quickly she explained Charles's condition and Kenny said he'd meet her at the foot of the Moulin Brae as she came into town.

Kenny took over the driving and as they sped towards Perth. Eilid told him all about Colin Macalister, her week with him at the Lodge and what she had found out. Kenny listened intently and when she told him of the shunt operation her Uncle almost leaped out of the Land Rover. "Tetrology of Fallot" he exclaimed. "I should have guessed it all along. But why would an American child come over to England for that operation? That's the fascinating part. I suppose we were ahead of the US in that field then," he continued to mutter away to himself as they took the bends in the road at top speed.

They reached the gates at Strahearn by twelve-thirty, they had averaged about fifty miles an hour Kenny said, not bad for the turns and twists the road took following the river Tummel towards Perth. They drove immediately to the main house and a Prefect had been posted to look out for Eilid's arrival.

"Mrs. Stuart, Mr. Stuart, welcome to Strahearn." He shook hands politely with them both.

"I'm Doctor Urquhart actually," said Ken. "I'm Mrs. Stuart's Uncle."

"Oh, I'm sorry, I just thought..."The Prefects words tailed off. "I've to take you to the Headmaster's study right away."

Eilid and Kenny followed the polite young man closely. There must have been some telepathic communication, for as they approached the Headmaster's office John Forsyth stood framed in the doorway.

"Ah, Mrs. Stuart and?" he turned to shake hands with Ken.

"Doctor Urquhart, I'm Eilid's Uncle," Ken introduced himself.

"Very pleased you're here," John Forsyth could not have been more sincere. "I'm not going to comment on Charles's condition except to say that he's more stable, so please come with me."

They were both ushered into the Headmaster's car and driven across to the School Room area where the Sanatorium was situated. Quickly, they followed the Headmaster into the San, as it was called. A small, slim, middle-aged figure in a dark blue uniform with a starched white apron and a nurse's cap came out to greet them.

"How do you do, I'm Nurse Johnson." She smiled warmly at them. "Please come with me."

Off she went down a corridor adjacent to the office and opened the door into a light, airy ward that held about a dozen beds. Only one was occupied. There in the middle of the ward was the pale, wan face of Charles Stuart partially covered by an oxygen mask. His eyes opened at the sound of the party coming through the door. He tried to prop himself up on one elbow but the effort seemed too great and he sank back onto the bed. Eilid rushed forward seeing his efforts to raise himself, while Nurse Johnson clucked away disapprovingly.

"Charles, what did I tell you, you've not to do that."

Charles rolled his eyes at his mother in some form of response. Eilid put her hand on his forehead. It was frighteningly cold and clammy. Kenny was already taking his pulse, it was very weak. He took his stethoscope out of his pocket and placed it over Charles's heart. There was no mistaking the irregular beat. Even with oxygen on supply Charles was short of breath. Kenny looked at his fingernails, his nails were clubbed, rounded and very prominent, his lips were blue, all the signs were there. Charles was very ill indeed.

Ken Urquhart stood back from the bed. There was no doubt in his mind that Charles required evaluation for heart surgery and quick. He turned to the nurse.

"Nurse Johnson, do you know of a good cardiologist in Perth?"

"There are two I know of. Both are excellent."

"Would you give me their phone numbers and I'll try and speak to them. We have an emergency situation."

"Right. I'll get on to it." Nurse Johnson clattered away on her heels to get the cardiologists' telephone numbers.

Eilid was sitting on the bed beside Charles stroking his forehead. Kenny beckoned to her with his head that he wanted a private word. John Forsyth diplomatically moved off towards the office.

"Uncle Ken, what's wrong?"

"It's the shunt. It needs to be undone and a permanent solution found to fix his heart."

"Can that be done?"

"Now it can. It's not quite common practice. As you know heart transplants are being carried out with a modicum of success, who would have thought that ten or eleven years ago."

"Where will he have to go?"

"Well, I'm going to recommend Yorkhill in Glasgow. I know one of the surgeons there and I'd trust him with my life. So as soon as possible we'll move him down to Glasgow. I'm just waiting for the cardiologist to come and confirm my findings then we'll be off."

It was now only one-thirty. By two-thirty the cardiologist Ken had spoken to had confirmed Ken's opinion. Ken had then 'phoned Yorkhill hospital to get Charles admitted as an emergency. The ambulance was already waiting and by five o'clock that afternoon Charles was in the Intensive Care unit at Yorkhill hospital in Glasgow.

The resident cardiologist took over and talked with Ken Urquhart. George Eliot, the surgeon who would do the operation was not expected in until the following day meanwhile Peter Fleming, the cardiologist, said Charles would need a catheterization and once that was done they would review the findings with Eilid and Kenny. The operation would probably be in a couple of days as Charles needed to not only go through some tests but get 'tuned up', as the cardiologist put it, for what was a very serious operation.

Meanwhile Eilid paced the hospital waiting room like a caged tiger with Ken and Peter Fleming in deep conversation. Fed up with the waiting she found a phone and tried calling The Lodge at Torridon. She had put at least four shillings in the phone box and got through on the second attempt. It was Mhairi who answered the call.

"How is he? Is he going to be all right?" Mhairi blurted out when she heard Eilid's voice.

"Mhairi, call me back on this number, the money will run out. And yes, I think Charles is going to be fine, I hope so anyway."

In a couple of minutes the phone rang in the hospital hallway. It was Hamish on the other end.

"How is he, Eilid?"

"He's very ill. I've never seen him quite this bad. He's gone that peeked way again, but worse than you or I ever saw. I've got some very good doctors working on him right now. He's going to have to go through some very tricky heart surgery. Uncle Ken's here with me thank God, without him I don't know what I would have done. He's told me about the operation and he's been blunt and honest with me. He's says there's about an 75 percent success rate, give or take, so I'm really scared in case things don't work out and I lose my wee boy."

"My God, what are they going to do?"

"Properly repair the hole in his heart that he's had since he was born."

"Michty me. I didn't know he had a heart problem, you never said."

"Well there was no point in talking about it. It was always there. I just didn't know that the operation he had when he was born wasn't going to last for the rest of his life. That's just my ignorance. I think he's going to be fine, though."

"I take it then that you're not coming home, I mean not for this week anyway?"

"Right you are. It's too early to say when I'll be home. If all goes according to plan Charles will be in hospital for about three to four weeks. He can't go straight back to school, so he'll come home with me until he feels well enough to go back to Strahearn. But I plan to be back next Thursday if he's all right, it's just too early to say yet."

"You mean you're going to leave him in the hospital on his own, after an operation like that?" Hamish couldn't believe what he was hearing.

"That I do." Eilid sounded adamant.

"Eilid, don't be so bloody daft. We can manage just fine, really we can. We broke the news to the guests tonight, no problems. They just send their best wishes for Charles's speedy recovery and it goes without saying that comes from Mhairi and me as well."

"It's not that I don't think you can manage Hamish," Eilid said, "but I can't stand being in this place. The smell of the ether is bad enough without the general claustrophobia."

"Have you told Sir Andrew?"

"Good God, you know I haven't. He'll think I'm terrible. I'll have to phone him right away.......he'll kill me."

"Eilid, look, why don't I phone Sir Andrew? I'll explain what happened and I'll give him this number we have for you. He can try to get hold of you later."

"Aye that's a good idea, but I might not always be around. This is just a public phone in the hallway."

"Oh right. He'll just have to take his chances then, for I'm not going to go into a long explanation of what's happened to Charles."

"No. That's understood. Hamish why don't you phone him now, he'll more than likely be having his pre-dinner gin & tonic and tell him to phone this number right away. I'll hang around for ten minutes or so."

"Right, I'll do that now. And Eilid, all the best." There was a break in Hamish's voice as he said that and hung up the receiver. Eilid walked to the end of the hallway and met Kenny coming the other way.

"What's happening now?" She asked.

"Well they'll be doing some more tests and there will be more tomorrow when George Eliot the surgeon gets here. There's nothing much we can do at the moment. Why don't we go to the cafeteria and get something to eat. It'll maybe cheer us up."

They were walking back to the exit when the phone in the hallway rang again. Eilid picked it up.

"Granddad, it's Eilid." She recognized Sir Andrew's voice full of concern at the other end of the phone. Quickly she explained all that had happened without mentioning the 'shunt' operation, what was about to happen and tried to calm the old man down.

"Granddad as soon as we know anything I'll call you, promise."

"We, who's we?"

"I picked up Uncle Ken on the way down and he came with me. Being a doctor he took charge of everything so after the operation Charles might just be able to live a normal life. Wouldn't that be the best of news?"

"It would be the best possible news, my dear. I just hope these chaps know what they're doing."

"Uncle Ken knows one of the surgeons and he says he'd be happy to have him operate on him, so that's good news too, isn't it."

"Wonderful, wonderful. Get back to me when you can. Charles will be in my prayers tonight I assure you."

"Thank you Granddad." Eilid hung up.

Ken and Eilid sat in the hospital cafeteria picking away at greasy fish and chips which was the only thing they had found at least half appealing on the limited menu. Eilid wanted to go back to be with Charles as soon as possible.

"Ken, do you think the hospital would let me stay close to Charles, at least for tonight?"

"I doubt it, but you can always ask. I need to get someone to cover my practice while I'm here with you so I've got to stay somewhere as well. You know we should find ourselves a place for the night. It's coming up to ten o'clock, you must be exhausted. I don't know that there's anywhere nearby where we could stay. We'll probably have to go into town and find a hotel."

Eilid posed the question of staying in the hospital with the on-duty Staff Nurse but she was gently told that the hospital had no such arrangements. She was good enough to suggest a couple of Bed and Breakfast places almost within walking distance of the hospital. George Eliot, the surgeon would meet with both Ken and Eilid early the following morning.

The Bed and Breakfast lodging proved to have clean, airy but slightly cramped bedrooms. Mrs. Robson, the widow who owned the house, was a short stout lady with a ruddy complexion and graying hair. She was friendly and helpful and asked when uncle and niece would want breakfast and how many days would they be staying.

Eilid told her the circumstances of her visit and said the she would probably be staying for at least one week until she was satisfied that Charles was well and truly on the mend. Kenny said would wait until the operation was over then return to his practice in Pitlochry by train. Mrs. Robson said she welcomed the business and that they could stay as long as they liked.

The next morning Eilid and Ken had breakfasted by eight-thirty and were at the hospital just before nine. The on-duty Staff Nurse said that Charles had had a comfortable night and that George Eliot had already made his rounds and would be talking to them later that morning. They were allowed to visit Charles who was propped up in bed still looking anything but well. His face was gray and his lips distinctly bluish.

Eilid spent about thirty minutes with him while Ken, being acquainted with the surgeon, went off to find George Eliot. He found George still wearing his suit and white doctor's coat coming along one of the many corridors his stethoscope round his neck. He recognized Ken immediately.

"Ken Urquhart!" he exclaimed, "how many years has it been?"

"Don't ask George, too damn many," as they pumped each other's hand.

"Well it's great to see you, you've put on a bit of weight since I saw you last, are you still in that country practice near Perth somewhere?"

"Pitlochry, I'm still in Pitlochry."

"Ah that's right, I remember now. You'll know I've seen your niece's wee boy, he's in a pretty bad way, but I think we can do something for him. I've seen Peter Fleming the cardiologist and he's done the catheterization and so forth." Another fifteen minutes passed as spoke to one another on a doctor to doctor basis. Suddenly George stopped speaking. "Some of what I'm going over I should be saying to your niece. How about fetching her and bringing her to my office, that's the last door on the right down there," he waved his hand in the general direction of where he had been heading.

"Champion," said Kenny, "she's with Charles now, let me get her."

"By the way Ken, what's her name?"

"Eilid, Eilid Stuart."

"That's a new one on me, never heard that before."

"It's Gaelic," said Ken without elaborating as he strode off in the direction of Charles's ward. Fifteen minutes later Eilid and Ken were sitting listening to George Eliot describe what he was proposing to do.

Dr. Eliot explained the total correction procedure of Tetrology of Fallot to her. It sounded very complicated but the surgeon kept it in layman's terms. Basically Charles would be put on a heart bypass machine, the shunt previously performed would be undone and a Dacron patch would be stitched over the hole in his heart and the obstruction in the heart chamber removed. The whole procedure would take about six hours, then the heart bypass would be disconnected, his heart re-started and Charles would be taken to recovery in the Intensive Care ward. Recovery time would be about three to four weeks; in sixteen to eighteen weeks he might just be a new man if the operation was a success.

"It sounds painful," said Eilid. "I don't think Charles has ever suffered from as much as a headache, apart from the constant shortness of breath, he's been pretty healthy."

"That's a good thing," the surgeon continued, "he'll be sedated for a few days; the pain can be quite severe. We're going to slice him right up his breastbone."

"You're joking?"

"I'm afraid not. I have to saw through the sternum to get into the chest cavity, use a spreader to push aside the rib cage and then the real work starts."

"My God the poor wee soul, I never thought for a minute he'd have to go through something like that. You're right, I'll have to stay here certainly until the end of the week or longer."

"I would certainly advise you to stay until he's out of the woods. There's plenty of things to see and do in Glasgow. Today I'm going to get some blood organized. Are you the same blood type Mrs. Stuart?"

"No she's not," cut in Ken. He had been waiting for that. Checking Eilid's blood type could only serve to prove one thing and that was that Eilid was not Charles's mother.

"Not a problem, not a problem," George Eliot went on, "we'll take care of that for you. If everything goes according to plan I'll operate tomorrow morning around seven-thirty, so maybe if you talk to Staff she'll let you know if you can come around mid-afternoon and take a wee peek at him. Now he'll be on a ventilator probably for up to three days then we'll see how he does on his own, all right." George Eliot got up, the conversation was clearly over.

Eilid and Kenny rose to leave and as they were going out the door George Eliot called to Ken.

"Ken, a quick word."

Ken indicated to Eilid that she should carry on and he went back into George Eliot's office closing the door.

"Shoot," Ken said.

"You didn't tell me she was a looker, you old bugger."

Kenny laughed. "I thought I'd let you find out for yourself."

"Goodness me, she is quite the most attractive lady I think I've met. The husband must be a lucky man. Where is he, by-the-way?"

"He isn't," said Kenny, "there's never been a husband. It's a long story and I'll catch up with you later."

"Aye, quite, quite. I was just curious though. What does she do for a living?"

"She's a stalker, a good one too so I hear, and she's a crack shot with a rifle."

"Bless my soul, I thought you were going to tell me she was some kind of model."

"She could be, couldn't she?" Kenny winked, smiled broadly and exited George Eliot's office.

Kenny caught up with Eilid and they left the hospital together. It was a fine autumn day with hazy sunshine.

"I need to go for a walk," said Eilid, "get this hospital smell out of my lungs and blow the cobwebs away."

"Let's go to Kelvingrove Park," Kenny suggested, "it's not far. We just need to cross Sauchiehall street and we're there."

The park was quiet as they talked about Charles's upcoming operation as they walked slowly along the banks of the river Kelvin.

"Do you think Charles will ever be able to go back to Strahearn? Eilid asked.

"Well depends again on how the operation goes. Eliot's a good man, one of the best but what he's got to do is truly a tricky procedure."

"No. I didn't mean that Ken. I'm hoping for the best that my wee boy will come through this with flying colors. What I meant was we've frightened the life out of John Forsyth, the headmaster. We really didn't level with him when we talked about Charles going to Strahearn. It wasn't only me. I was ably aided and abetted by my Granddad who truly misled the headmaster about Charles's condition."

"Oh, now I see where you're coming from. Yes, you're right. I think Sir Andrew might have to do a bit of damage control there, if you know what I mean?"

"Well I'd rather have my Granddad tackle the problem, he knows John Forsyth and the Bursar really well. We did take out a special health insurance for Charles just in case something like this did happen, but I'm concerned that Forsyth might think something like this could reoccur."

"Well, it's highly unlikely and I can give him some assurances on that subject. Let's go back and wander up Byers Road and get something to eat.

"And drink," said Eilid.

"Amen to that," said Ken and off they went to find the Curlers pub.

The next day dragged with agonizing sluggishness. While their little Bed and Breakfast place was fine they had to be out of Mrs. Robson's house by nine-thirty at the latest and allowed back in after five in the evening. Ken phoned the hospital a couple of times to be told that the operation on Charles was in the words of the Staff Nurse, "progressing satisfactorily."

Finally three o'clock came round and they were told they could see Charles in intensive care for a few moments only. They reached the hospital and were ushered into a waiting room. Fifteen minutes passed and George Eliot came in wearing his green scrubs.

"George, we didn't hear you coming. How is he?" Asked Kenny, bouncing out of his chair.

"It's gone very well. The hole's repaired and the obstruction removed.. We've moved him to Intensive Care. With a bit of luck he'll be on the mend in no time. Youth is on his side, he's only eleven isn't he Mrs. Stuart?"

"Yes he's eleven but he'll be twelve at the end of November."

"Well as I say, he's got youth on his side. You can hopefully expect to see a quite different Charles. No more shortness of breath, no more blueness.

Eilid stared at the surgeon. All at once she became emotional.

"Dr. Eliot I don't know how to ever thank you. You've changed Charles's life and my life with your skill and dedication, thank you from both of us."

"It's my pleasure. Now I'm being cautiously optimistic when I say this but I reckon if we take good care of him he'll be walking around in ten days." George Eliot ran his fingers through his hair.

"Really!" Eilid and Kenny chorused.

"That's what I hope for anyway. Come along." And he walked off in the direction of the Intensive Care wards.

The ward was in semi-darkness and they followed the surgeon closely as they made their way to Charles's bed. In the gloom all Eilid could make out was a little bump in the bed surrounded by wires and tubes. Monitors hummed in the artificial twilight with lines and squiggles traversing the screens in continuous motion. It was like some space odyssey, Eilid had never seen anything like it. The twentieth century had come home to her with a bang.

Charles looked awful. His pallor was gray and he looked very ill indeed. His breathing, through some tube down his throat, seemed labored and uneven. Eilid began to sob. Immediately Kenny was at her side.

"This is why I didn't want you to see him right now. No one's a pretty sight after six hours of surgery. Just leave the nurses to do what they do best, isn't that right George?"

"Absolutely," George Eliot concurred. He turned to Eilid, "I promise you he'll be looking much better in the morning."

"Thank you again," Eilid said to the surgeon. Then turning to her uncle, "Uncle Ken, I'm so glad you came with me. I don't know if I could have got through this without you."

Ken wrapped his arms round his niece and gave her a big hug.

"That's what I'm here for lass. What did I tell you last Christmas, I'm your Uncle, doctor and gynecologist."

"Uncle Ken, I love you." And then she gave him that most disconcerting kiss of hers, full on the lips.

George Eliot turned away politely and headed for the door. Kenny and Eilid took their cue from George and headed out but not before Eilid had planted another kiss on Charles's forehead.

They made their way out arm in arm. As they walked a tall, well-built man came towards them. For some reason Eilid thought the person looked familiar. Then he stopped. Immediately Eilid saw it was Douglas Hamilton. She couldn't believe it.

"Ken, it's Douglas."

"Douglas, how do you mean Douglas?"

"Douglas Hamilton, my Douglas, oh my God I don't believe it!"

She rushed forward to be picked up and held high in the air by the only man she cared about.

"Douglas, Douglas, it's you. How on earth did you get here?"

"Pretty easy actually, just drove down from Perth."

"But how did you know?"

"Well Sir Andrew phoned the garage, you know, the Land Rover franchise I have in Perth, passed on the message about Charles, and here I am."

"But how did you know I'd be here?"

"It was a pretty safe bet. Andrew phoned the school and the Headmaster told him which hospital you'd gone to, if I didn't find you right away I knew that Charles would be here, and that you wouldn't be far away."

"I don't believe it. Great to see you again so soon." Ken Urquhart pumped Douglas's hand. "We were just off to our Bed and Breakfast place which is all very well but we really need a hotel where Eilid can stay, so you can help us if you like.

"That's another reason why I came. I've an old army pal who has a flat in Kew Terrace, just off Great Western Road; that means you're only a couple of miles from the hospital. It's ideal really. He's in London right now so we have the run of that for about a week or maybe more. I've to pick up the keys from a neighbor and we're good to go."

Eilid had to sit down on one of the nearby benches. Meeting Douglas was so wonderful, and at such a time of crises. She was deliriously happy and emotionally drained. It had been a long, testing, three days.

The Land Rover was left at the hospital and Douglas first drove them to Mrs. Robson's B & B where they settled their bill, picked up their bags, and then proceeded on to the flat in Kew Terrace. Eilid was given the ground floor bedroom that was huge and airy with large windows looking out onto the back of the property which had mature deciduous trees just beginning to turn as autumn approached.

Douglas and Ken went downstairs where there were two other bedrooms sharing a bathroom. Eilid had thrown some of her underwear and a couple of shirts into a washing machine she found in the large and gloomy kitchen.

They assembled in the Lounge which was on the same level as Eilid's bedroom but even larger. It was pleasantly decorated with a white ceiling, an ornate center flower and cornice complimented by pale Adam green walls. Douglas poured them all a drink and finally sat down beside Eilid.

"How is he then? Holding up?"

"You wouldn't think so to see him lying in that ward, but Ken and Doctor Eliot say he'll look better in the morning," Eilid turned to look at Ken for some reassurance.

Ken just nodded. "He'll be fine. You wouldn't look to bright having been knocked out for six hours."

"That's a helluva long time, isn't it. Just what were they doing?"

Ken went through the operation procedure once again as Douglas's eyes continued to get wider and wider.

"My God, this is serious shit then, isn't it?"

"Aye, it certainly is. But he'll be certain to look better in the morning. I don't know about you two, but I'm famished. Let's go out and eat and then it's early to bed for me."

September sunlight streaming in the window wakened Eilid with a start. At first she didn't know where she was, she had slept so deeply, but then with a rush all the events of the previous day came flooding into her mind. She glanced at the alarm clock on the bedside table it read nine fifteen. Damn she thought, the others will be up and dressed. She opened the bedroom door and listened. There wasn't a sound from downstairs so maybe she was the first to waken after all. By nine forty-five she had bathed and dressed. Before doing anything else she picked up the phone and dialed the number of Yorkhill hospital given to her by George Eliot. It rang at the nurses' station in Charles's ward. A Staff Nurse answered and Eilid introduced herself.

"Mercy me, Mrs. Stuart. We thought you all had gone back to Inverness, so we did."

"Why did you think that?"

"From whit I was told you all jist disappeared, no address, no 'phone number, nuthin', out the door and away."

Eilid was stunned.

"My God, you're so right. We never even considered giving someone contact information, I'm so sorry. How's Charles's?"

"The wee lamb is just fine, he had a good night and he's lookin' much better."

With the use of the 'wee lamb' expression memories of her father using that phrase when she was a child came flooding back. For a second she wondered how and where he was. She assumed he was still at Cannich. She had heard nothing from him nor he from her for almost twelve years now. She amputated the memories almost as soon as they began.

"That's marvelous news. Is he awake?"

"Well, he's come round once or twice, but he's very drowsy. It'll be a wee while before he's fully awake. He was under that anesthetic for over six hours you know?"

"Yes, I do know. I'm very sorry I didn't phone earlier. We were all so tired; yesterday was a long day for everyone. When can I come in and see him?"

"Just when you're ready miss, just when you're ready. We'll be here."

Noises were coming from the downstairs bedrooms as Eilid hung up the phone. Ken and Douglas were up and about. The welcome smell of coffee came wafting up from the kitchen.

"Are you men decent, I'm coming down." Eilid called out as she made her way down the stairs.

She laughed when she saw Ken still in his striped pajamas; hair all tousled hovering over the coffee percolator that was bubbling away on the stovetop.

"Do you know anything about these bloody things? I'm not really sure how it works." Ken looked perplexed as the water gave another surge up to the glass top. "By the way, how's Charles, I'm sure you've phoned?"

"Aye I did. I got a right telling-off from the Staff Nurse."

"Why so?"

"Well we all went out of there last night and didn't leave an address or a phone number where we could be contacted. She was quite sarcastic."

"My God, but she's right. I can't believe we did that. It's with Douglas coming and everything. I'll apologize to her myself, I take it he's fine then?"

"Still drowsy, but fine."

"Great. We'll get some breakfast and then we'll go and see him."

The words weren't out of Ken's mouth when Douglas appeared all showered and shaved his dark hair slicked back.

"What's for breakfast then?"

"Typical man, marches in and expects to be served right away," Eilid smiled.

Douglas bent over and kissed her in front of Ken.

"Good morning to you too, how's our boy?"

"The nurse says he's coming round and we can visit at any time."

"Ah here we are, bacon, eggs, sausages," Douglas was crouched down in front of the open fridge, "somebody must have known we were coming."

"Okay," said Ken, I'll handle breakfast; you two have some catching up to do. Take your coffee upstairs to the lounge and I'll call you when it's all ready."

Despite the protests from Eilid and Douglas who wanted to help, Ken would have none of it and chased the two of them upstairs to do as they were told.

As they sipped their coffee Eilid and Douglas exchanged stories. Eilid told him about Colin Macalister's visit and how he was now a famous heart surgeon omitting to tell him the whole story about Charles's origin. Douglas agreed that having Colin as a guest had been fortuitous. Douglas had been abroad, the Middle East, he told Eilid, but was suitably vague about exactly where he had been and mentioned Land Rover exports a number of times. He had only been in Perth for a couple of days when he received Sir Andrew's call telling him about Charles. The rest was easy. He had packed an overnight bag, called his friend who owned the flat, whom he knew was in London, and had driven quickly to Glasgow. They were in the middle of a discussion trying to determine when Charles would get out of hospital and where he would recuperate when Ken called up from the kitchen to say the food was on the table. They shared a quick kiss and went down to breakfast.

They continued their discussion over breakfast and brought Ken into the conversation. Ken agreed that Charles certainly couldn't go back to school until he had healed up properly. He said he would ask George Eliot what sort of time frame the surgeon had in mind for a complete recovery.

By ten thirty they had set out for the hospital in Douglas's car. Eilid couldn't wait to see how Charles was, and Ken could see the strain of her recent experience was beginning to show. Her face had lines of worry and she looked tired despite the long sleep she had had the previous night.

A different Staff Nurse ushered them into the ward. Charles was still lying flat on his back with a ventilator doing his breathing for him. There were a couple of IV drips attached. His eyes were closed but there was a tremendous change in his color. Gone was the blueness and the grayness. His complexion was like that of a normal boy of ten.

"He does look better, thank God," said Eilid. "When will he get off the machine?" she turned to the Staff Nurse.

"Two more days probably. Dr. Eliot will be the one to decide that. Anyway you can see he's on the mend. Before we all forget let me have your phone number."

"Sure," said Douglas. "I'm sorry about last night, it's my fault really I had just come down from Perth and in all the commotion we walked out of here without thinking." He opened his diary and read off the number to the nurse who wrote it down on the starched cuff of her uniform.

"Thank you for that. If anything happens you can be assured we'll call you. If you don't hear from us then you can take it all is well. There are set visiting hours but Dr. Eliot told me to forget those, it seems he knows your uncle, Dr. Urquhart, pretty well." The Staff Nurse smiled.

Eilid and Ken thanked her and all three left the hospital to go back to the flat.

By Friday Charles was off the ventilator. Ken Urquhart had headed back to Pitlochry in the Land Rover the previous day leaving Douglas to look after Eilid or "vice versa" as Kenny had said, grinning hugely.

Eilid and Douglas arrived mid-morning to find Charles now propped up in bed and looking even better than on their previous visits. He opened his eyes as his mother and Douglas approached. Charles smiled wanly. Eilid knelt by the bed, close to tears, and held his hand.

"There now my wee Prince, you're going to be all better now. No school for you for a few months. Once you're out of the hospital we're going to go home and Mhairi and Hamish will look after you. You'll miss the rest of this term but the doctor thinks you should be able to back to Strahearn after the Christmas holidays."

Douglas also knelt by the bed to talk to Charles.

"How's my brave soldier? Have you any pain?"

Charles nodded his head feebly, woozy from the pain killers.

"That's too bad. Be brave the pain will soon go away. You've just got to rest now and the nurses will see that you get well as quickly as possible."

Charles opened his mouth to speak but nothing came out. His lips formed the word 'water'. Eilid picked up the glass of water on the bedside chest and propping Charles forward let him sip from the glass.

"The wee soul must have been parched," Eilid turned to Douglas, as Charles kept on drinking for what seemed like an age.

"Seems that way," said Douglas. While Eilid held the glass for Charles, Douglas went back to stand at the foot of the bed and gave Charles a smile. When he had stopped drinking Charles managed a smile back.

"What happened?" Charles gasped.

Eilid and Douglas stared at one another. *They* knew what had transpired but they had completely forgotten that poor Charles hadn't a clue as to what had happened to him.

"I'm going to let Douglas tell you what you've been through. You took a little turn at the school and we had to bring you here, you're in a hospital in Glasgow."

Eilid got up and let Douglas pull up a chair. As simply as he could Douglas explained what had happened, why Charles had been so ill, and what the doctors had done about it.

"The good news," Douglas finished off, "is that you'll be like the other boys now and you'll be able to join in sports and many of the games."

"Rugger, will I be able to play rugger?"

"We'll have to see, but I don't see why not."

"Goody", was all Charles said.

Douglas had asked Ken about that possibility for they remembered how keen Charles had been to play rugger. Ken had said that it was pretty unlikely that George Eliot would like Charles to engage in any contact sports after such an operation. Douglas thought about Ken's comments but he felt now wasn't the time to dampen the child's hopes. Eilid and Douglas stayed around the bed for about an hour and were asked politely to leave as Charles was tiring. They promised to visit the next day.

That night Douglas took Eilid to the Rogano Oyster Bar and Restaurant just off Glasgow's Exchange Square. This was a popular spot for many Glaswegians and the bar on the ground floor was famous for its Art Deco designs in plastic paint that covered the walls. Douglas plowed into a dozen oysters while Eilid tried the Parma ham and melon. A full Dover sole meunière on the bone followed for each of them with shoestring fries. The whole meal was delicious. A bottle of Sancerre was demolished as Eilid relaxed for the first time in almost a week. They got back to the flat in Kew Terrace just after eleven o'clock. Douglas lit the big log fire in the front lounge and they sat there in its reflected glow sipping coffee and malt whisky in that order. Douglas an Eilid were alone at last!

They sat in silence for what must have been half an hour, leaning against one another, their backs against the big sofa sitting on the floor staring into the fire.

"Ready for bed?" It was Douglas who broke the silence, the huskiness in his voice betraying his emotions.

"Yes, I think I am, but not without you."

Douglas's heart leaped. "Are you sure you know what you're saying?"

"Yes I do. Just be gentle with me I've never done anything like this before."

Douglas was about to say, 'where did Charles come from then', but it wasn't the time or the place. Eilid stood up her blond hair spilling over her shoulders and they kissed. Softly at first but then with increasing fervor as the wine and the spirits drove away any inhibitions.

"Come on, come into the bedroom," Eilid whispered. Eilid was already barefoot as they gently opened the bedroom door. The heavy curtains were drawn and the room was dark as night. Quickly Douglas took off his pants and shirt. Eilid was doing the same with her blouse, her back to Douglas. Douglas reached out to find out exactly where she was to find her bare back. He slid his hands up and round to her front.

The blouse had come off and there wasn't any bra to struggle with. He cupped his hands round her firm breasts and he felt her nipples harden as he gently moved his hands over them. She giggled like a little girl, as if embarrassed by what was happening. Her pleasure heightened as Douglas skillfully massaged her until her breasts were enlarged and more voluptuous. He could hear her panting slightly.

Eilid had never felt like this before. Douglas's touch was like velvet she wanted him so badly she was afraid the moment would suddenly be snatched from her. Quickly she turned to face him.

"Oh Douglas, Douglas," she gasped.

He kissed her again all over her neck and then his mouth found her breast and the ecstasy started anew. Quietly he moved his hands over her hips and her panties gently slipped over her hips to the floor. Her body yielded to his touch and he gently caressed the lips within lips as he felt the fire within her.

"My God Eilid, you are ready for me," he croaked huskily. By this time he was tumescent. They collapsed on the bed. She arched her back and their lovemaking began.

Douglas rolled onto his back, exhausted. Eilid lay there not really knowing what had happened, save for the fact that she had been made love to for the first time in her life. She wasn't sure that it was all that wonderful, the lead up to the act she liked, but it was all over so quickly. She lay staring blindly at the ceiling not knowing what to say.

Douglas broke the ice. "Jesus Eilid, that was magnificent."

"I'm glad you thought it was good, I'm not a very good judge you know."

"How could you not be good, you're the best ever."

Oh well she thought, at least I stand up to comparison. She considered the back-handed compliment as she drifted off to sleep. It must have been in the early hours of the morning that she wakened to the same feeling of ecstasy. Douglas had wakened and was caressing her breasts again. She became more and more aroused and she reached out to him. This time their lovemaking was not nearly as frantic and it lasted longer until Eilid began to feel something happening deep inside her that she had never experienced before. They climaxed together in an explosive passion that she wished would never end. Now she *was* sure. Making love *was* marvelous. This time she didn't want to let Douglas go and she kissed his exhausted body all over until they both fell asleep in one another's arms.

Morning dawned fresh and clear with just a hint of frost in the air. Douglas had gone downstairs to shower and dress. By ten they were back at the hospital to see a marked improvement in Charles. This routine continued for another ten days as their initial lust turned to love and respect and their being together became so natural that Eilid thought this must be what it's like to be married. Their time alternated between visiting Charles, sight seeing in the city, and love making. On the tenth day Douglas got a mysterious phone call, mysterious to Eilid in that Douglas refused to say who called save that he had to leave right away. Suddenly he was all action. They said goodbye briefly sharing what was an almost perfunctory kiss; Douglas's mind was clearly on other things. He promised to get back in touch with her as soon as he could. He waved wildly to her blowing kisses as he drove out of the terrace onto Great Western Road and then he was gone leaving Eilid the flat but with no means of transport.

Eilid had been keeping Sir Andrew updated on his grandson's progress until Charles was feeling much better and was allowed out of bed to take his first few faltering steps under the close supervision of the Staff Nurse. Sir Andrew got Fitz to drive him to Glasgow so that he could see the improvement in Charles with his own eyes. Sir Andrew, like anyone else, who had seen Charles before the operation, was astonished at the improvement. It was as though a different boy occupied the hospital bed. Gone was the gray pallor. His face was aglow; his green eyes bright and shining with the expectation of the new life that he could now see stretched out before him. He proudly showed off his scar to his Granddad.

"Wait 'til the boys at Strahearn see that," said Sir Andrew. "You'll be the talking point of the school." Charles grinned from ear to ear.

Sir Andrew talked to Eilid outside in the car park.

"Well what do you think? He looks amazingly well after such a severe operation."

"He's a different boy now altogether. He can see and feel that for himself. He's now desperate to get back to school and play rugby. I haven't had the heart to tell him yet that the surgeon has told me contact sports are out." Eilid looked at her Granddad.

"That's too bad," Sir Andrew looked crestfallen; "I thought he'd be allowed to play any sport now. I suppose the operation was harsher on him than I thought. He'll be very disappointed, but I suppose it can't be helped."

"Well it's the sawing the sternum that causes the problem. I'm going to tell him it's a temporary measure; I'll see how he deals with that. After all he's never played rugby before, so hopefully what he's never had he will never miss."

Eilid then mentioned Douglas in passing and where he might be, but Sir Andrew hadn't heard from him. Eilid began to think it very strange; it was as if he had disappeared off the face of the planet. Land Rover in Perth hadn't seen him, but they told her, that wasn't unusual as Douglas visited them only on about four occasions each year. Eilid felt so let down and depressed. There was no doubt in her mind now that she was in love with Douglas and she thought Douglas loved her, but all this time without even a 'phone call was making her very disappointed and a little bit concerned.

At the end of the fourth week in hospital Charles was up and walking about. George Eliot was delighted with his progress.

"He can go home now," he declared, "but before he goes back to school, and that will be after Christmas, I want to see him again. So there you are young lady, your son's going to be a healthy young man."

"Dr. Eliot, you've been wonderful, and so have all your staff. Why don't you take a break and come up to the Torridon Lodge as my guest for New Year. The weather is usually not too bad, the worst we get is usually in mid-January to mid-February, but you never know. I can promise you wonderful food and hospitality and it won't cost you a penny. Think it over and I'll call you later in the month to let you know how Charles is doing."

"I may just take you up on that, sounds really good. A traditional Hogmanay in the North of Scotland, I'll run that past my wife and I'll let you know when you phone. Now, there shouldn't be any complications, the wound has healed nicely, but if there is anything at all that gives you concern I want you to call me right away, all right?"

The taxi cab took off for Glasgow's Central Station with mother and son waving furiously at the nurses and staff who had assembled to see them go. Eilid and Charles were picked up in Perth by Ken Urquhart so that she could retrieve the Land Rover and continue their journey on to Torridon. Ken was delighted to see his visitors and he checked Charles out and pronounced him 'fit as a fiddle". Mother and son left early next morning as Eilid wanted to get home as soon as possible. She had asked Ken about Douglas but Ken had said he had not heard from him, nor could he give Eilid any clue as to where he might be. However as she prepared to leave the next morning Ken came up to her as she was packing the Land Rover.

"You really do miss him?"

He didn't have to say whom. Eilid nodded glumly.

"So it's that bad is it?" Ken wasn't pulling her leg either.

Eilid didn't protest her normal innocence. She looked at Ken with big sad eyes.

"I love him."

"You're sure about that?"

"Oh Uncle Ken, I can't get him out of my mind. Where the hell can he be?"

"Well, you know, I just think he's not altogether finished with the SAS. He's too old to do what he used to do but I think he still has connections and that he might still be useful in some way to the intelligence branch or some other military department. He has disappeared for long stretches before. He'll never tell you where he's been and certainly not what he's done, it's all pretty hush, hush."

"Well I hope he's got a good excuse if and when he gets in touch with me," Eilid tried to sound mad, but Ken could see she was in lower spirits than he had seen her for some time.

"Right, off you go, and I'll tell you what, I still stay in touch with some of his colleagues from his Commando days, I might just make the odd inquiry and if I find out anything I'll let you know."

"Oh would you? I'd be so grateful. Thanks Uncle Ken." And on came the soft kiss right on his lips.

Ken watched them as they drove off and wondered if anyone had ever told her that you kissed cheeks of relatives or other friends close to you, not give them a smacker on the lips. Maybe it's just because it's me he mused and went back into the house to a cup of coffee.

The welcome at the Lodge was effusive. Hamish spied the Land Rover coming down the glen and warned Mhairi. Lunch was a sumptuous affair and never had they seen Charles eat so much! They marveled at how well he looked.

"That's it," said Mhairi, "we'll get you to put some beef on that skinny frame of yours, that's my challenge, to have you put on a least a stone before you go back to Strahearn, then you can throw your weight around."

Charles just grinned with a look that said 'bring it all on'!

Hamish and Charles became even closer in the intervening months before he returned to Strahearn for the Spring Term. Now that Charles could walk the hills it made a tremendous difference. Charles loved the outdoors and his new found freedom. Any day that Hamish went on the hill, Charles went with him. At first Eilid and Hamish limited the length of his walks, Hamish letting him ride one of the hill ponies when he flagged a bit. Little by little Charles gained strength and, by his twelfth birthday, he could climb to the summit of Liathach. Beinn Eighe would have to wait a little longer. Stalking had finished for the season by the time Charles came home so the visits they made on the hill were unrestricted and more exploratory in nature. Hamish found Charles had an avid interest about the estate and Hamish had to constantly remind himself that this was altogether new for Charles. His learning curve was quick and, with the marked improvement in his health, his overall demeanor became jauntier. Hamish was to discover he had a quick wit and loved a joke. Eilid had postponed the cull on Hinds until December. As the weather got colder in the glen Eilid kept a close watch on Charles, any cold weather before his operation had simply floored her son. Now he could go out in the freezing wind and rain and keep up with Hamish together with the ghillie from Kinlochewe Hamish had started. The ghillie would just turn up now and again by way of keeping his face in front of Eilid, hoping that the job might become permanent.

Charles's twelfth birthday fell on a Monday. Both mother and son were pleased by two events. Because Charles's birthday was over the weekend Ken Urquhart visited the Lodge for the first time. Charles and Eilid greeted him with smiles and, in Eilid's case, multiple kisses. The Lodge immediately took to Kenny's fancy. The location was awesome and the weather, for the end of November, was fine. The skies remained clear with odd wisps of high cloud that made for spectacular sunsets. It was on the Saturday night that Ken took Charles in his car and drove towards Kinlochewe so that they could see the razor like outline of Beinn Eighe against the setting sun.

Uncle and nephew stood agape at the vivid reds and oranges transforming their Highland tapestry of hill and glen into a Technicolor wonderland. They returned in the dark with Charles telling Ken that he had never felt better and he was already putting on weight thanks to Mhairi's generous helpings and an appetite that never seemed to quit. There was no doubt about it Kenny told himself, it was as if he was sitting beside a different boy. Even Charles wispy hair seemed to have taken on a shine he hadn't seen before, his deathly pallor had gone to be replaced by rosy cheeks and his green eyes sparkled like never before.

They arrived back to discover that the postman had just delivered a birthday card for Charles. The envelope fascinated Charles. It had colorful stamps he had never seen but it was almost impossible to make out the postmark it was so badly smudged. Charles opened it up with Kenny and his mother looking over his shoulder their curiosity having got the better of them. Charles pulled the card out which was more like a post card with an imposing building flanked by statuesque pillars. Inside was blank except for Happy Birthday scrawled in big letters.

"Well who is it from?" Eilid strained to see the signature.

"Douglas," announced Charles.

"Douglas who?" Eilid asked astonished.

"Your Douglas of course," Kenny laughed.

Eilid grabbed the card from Charles. That was all that was written. She turned it over. On the back Douglas had written something. *'Charles, have a wonderful day and tell your mother she'll hear from me soon.'* That was it.

Eilid was speechless for a moment.

"How could he?" she exploded at her Uncle. "Charles gets a card with a wee note about you'll hear from me soon. He's got some bloody nerve has Mr. Hamilton."

"Where was the card from, though?" Kenny asked.

"I've no idea; Charles was the one who opened it."

Charles produced the envelope. Try as they might the reading of the postmark eluded them.

"Go get a magnifying glass, Eilid."

Kenny examined it closely. The postmark was blurred and faint and had bold, almost black cancel marks across it, but with a bit of effort Kenny made out the name Budapest on the franking.

"So where's Budapest Uncle?" Charles asked.

"Do they teach you children nothing at school? Bless my soul, where's Budapest. Eilid I suppose you know?"

"Hungary," Eilid said without hesitation.

"And where is Hungary?"

"Behind the Iron Curtain."

"Dead right, no wonder you haven't heard from Mr. Hamilton."

"So what you told me is true, he is still connected to the SAS?" Eilid sounded alarmed.

"Seems like it. I did ask around you know, I promised you I would but all his cohorts had long since severed their ties with the army. At least that's what they told me, it's a bit of a closed shop you know. I do think if my contacts knew anything they would have given me an idea without divulging anything classified, but you never know."

"Thank God," said Eilid, "at least we know he's alive. I'll sleep better tonight."

"Amen to that," added Kenny smiling broadly at his niece.

Kenny and Hamish made a pact to take Charles round to the corrie at Beinn Eighe on his birthday if the weather held. Kenny wanted to see the famous or infamous corrie for himself. It depended on your point of view and certain essential information, he told himself. Sunday morning was bright and clear as they left the Lodge at nine-thirty having just polished off one of Mhairi's full-Monty breakfasts.

Eilid saw them off with a few cautionary words.

"Remember it starts getting dark by half-past three you know, don't be lingering up there too long it's quite a trek for Charles so just keep and eye on him, he is only twelve and he's just had this major operation..." she tailed off as she saw her Uncle's withering look.

"Eilid, please," Kenny smiled.

"All right, all right, I'm sorry. I just get concerned, that's all."

Charles was excited about the hill walk. Hamish pointed to the gap between the Liathach and Beinn Eighe with his hill stick showing Charles and Kenny the path they would take to get to the corrie. Ken had a map which he spread out on a nearby rock.

"Right now, let's get our bearings. This is where we are now, and here's where we're going."

"Uncle Kenny, that's a great map, everything is so clear, even Hamish's cottage is marked on it."

"This is what is called an Ordnance Survey map on a scale of two and a half inches to one mile and all these lines you see are contour lines joining areas of similar height as you can see. Look how close they are here at the triple buttress which leads on up to the summit of the Beinn."

"And this is where we are going," Charles ran his little finger over the name. "Corrie Mick something."

"No it's not 'Mick' anything. Think of Mhairi's name and how it's spelled and how it's pronounced, it's a Gaelic name so you would pronounce an Mh together as a 'Vee' sound so it's Corrie Veechkerachar; got that now."

"Yes, oh Great Uncle," Charles said mockingly. "Did you used to speak Gaelic?"

"Of course. Anyone who comes from the Hebrides speaks Gaelic as their first language, and then they have to learn English."

"Does my mother speak Gaelic?"

"No more's the pity. Her mother, my sister Catriona does, but she never passed it on to Eilid. I think your mother knows a few words but I've never heard her converse in it. It's a great pity for it's a dying language. It's as if the English take over everything, land, language, the lot." For the first time Charles detected a bitter edge in his Great Uncle's voice.

"It all started with the Highland clearances, didn't it Uncle?"

"That it did lad, that it did. That young Pretender left behind a terrible legacy, a terrible legacy. Did you learn about him at school?"

"No, no Uncle. I've read all about him, Bonnie Prince Charlie. I've got the same name as him you know?"

"Aye well I know. Sure I was there at your christening. Charles Edward Stuart it is indeed. Maybe you can undo what the last one did and get us back our land." Ken Urquhart smiled ruefully at the twelve-year old.

What Ken Urquhart didn't realize that his words stuck with Charles for a long time to come.

"Are you two finished blethering?" Hamish was getting fed up with the conversation, which was going nowhere. "Let's get going or your mother will be sending out a search party for us."

In two hours they had reached the foot of the corrie. The Lochan gleamed like a shimmering jewel in the November sunshine. They all looked up at the huge scree slope leading to the soaring triple buttresses, which projected themselves out into the corrie. The air was still and the waterfall coming out of the lochan could easily be heard. It was truly a spectacular site. It was Hamish who spotted it first.

"Look at that, away up there, to the right of the right buttress, it must be a sheep, but how the hell did it get up there?"

They all instinctively reached for their binoculars and focused in on the white animal that was moving slowly across the dark brown face of the mountain.

"Well, I'll be damned!" Hamish cried out.

"What on earth is it?" asked Kenny.

"It's a deer, well a calf, an albino calf and it looks like it might be male. Fancy that, we'll maybe have a white stag if it survives the winter."

Charles stared intently through his binoculars. It looked like a white Bambi to him. He was fascinated as the little deer picked its way between the loose rocks on the steeper part of the face.

"Hamish, where's the mother?"

"Aye, that's just what's bothering me. I hope she hasn't abandoned the puir we soul. Let's climb up a few feet an' see if we can't get a better view. Do you all feel fit enough?"

"Let's go," Charles said enthusiastically. Kenny just nodded.

Up the scree slope they went following just the whisper of a path, which wended its way towards where Hamish had spotted the calf. As they climbed higher so the remains of the Stratocruiser's undercarriage came into view. Hamish had seen it many times before but it had a strange effect on Ken Urquhart once Hamish had explained to Charles and his Uncle what it was.

"My God, my God," was all that Kenny would mutter as he looked at the aluminum object glinting in the sun.

"It must have been a big plane," said Charles, "look at the size of the tires."

Kenny could not have imagined a more bizarre situation. Here he was with the boy who had been catapulted from the blazing plane into the snow to be rescued and illegally adopted by his niece. It was mind-bending stuff especially as Charles looked over the remains of the aircraft he had flown in completely unaware that he any connection with the tragic event of almost twelve years past.

"Was every one killed?" Charles asked.

Kenny had dreaded that question he knew was coming.

"As far as I know," Kenny said wishing Charles would get his mind back on the white deer calf.

Hamish was more affirmative. "Dead, aye dead, every last one, nae survivors."

Thankfully Charles moved on under Hamish's prompting his attention was now all on finding the white calf's mother. They stopped, turned and brought their binoculars back to where they had last seen the little deer. It was still there, standing very still. Then it gave a toss of its little head and started back in the direction it had come. Hamish followed its movements closely.

"Oh, there she is, just there, you can just see her head above that mound."

"Where?" Charles and Kenny chorused.

"See that gray mark just below where the calf is standing go left at about ten o'clock and you can just see her head."

Try as they might the hind remained invisible to uncle and nephew but they took Hamish's word for it and started back down the corrie and home. The extra climb up the corrie had extended their outing so they returned home in the gloaming with the sun disappearing behind Liathach.

Hamish said, "I'll just away to my cottage, to change for tonight's party. Mhairi's sure to be there waiting for me."

"By, but you're all the fly buggers, you are." Kenney rounded on Hamish in good humor.

"What do ye mean?" Hamish looked all innocence spreading his palms outward protesting his innocence.

"Well you know we'll get 'tongue pie' from Eilid for being away so long, you can just come to the Lodge with us and I'll run you home in my car."

"No seriously Kenny, Mhairi will be waiting for me."

"Aye, that *will* be right. Come on Charlie let's get him."

And with that Charles followed Ken's lead by putting his hand under Hamish's armpit and taking him with them as they walked to the Lodge. While Charles's strength was insignificant Kenny's was not. Hamish was propelled forward still protesting that he had to go home to change. Eilid was beginning to get slightly alarmed as she walked out to the front of the Lodge to see Hamish being frog marched towards her. She knew what was expected of her.

Arms akimbo she surveyed the hill party as Hamish was thrust up the front steps.

"Just where the Hell do you think you've all been?"

"Oh, God," Hamish groaned.

"Don't you 'Oh God' me Hamish Ferguson. What did I tell you before you left?"

"Not to be out too long."

"Right and what's this then. It's damn near dark..."

Charles cut her off. "Mother it was wonderful, we went up into the corrie to see a white stag, well he's not quite a stag yet but Hamish says he will be next year."

"Don't you dare change the subject Charles Stuart."

"But it's my birthday, mother!"

All Eilid's bluff and bluster disappeared. Her son was obviously in good health and in good spirits, he was right, it was his birthday.

"You're quite right. Come in all of you and tell me about this, this, white stag?"

Everyone was so busy getting into the Lodge that they didn't notice the headlights coming down the glen. It was an even bigger surprise therefore when the knocking on the door turned out to be Sir Andrew and Sir David Vickers.

"Granddad!" Charles yelled and launched himself at Sir Andrew.

"Well, well, goodness me, is this the wee boy I saw not two months ago?" Sir Andrew was not feigning surprise. To him the transformation in Charles was miraculous. Before him stood a fresh-faced youth, still skinny, but having gained some weight since his time in hospital. It was his color though that made Sir Andrew smile. Gone was the gray pallor, his great-grandson now looked like any normal child, it was wonderful.

"Eilid, how are you?" Sir David came round Sir Andrew to give her a hug and a kiss.

"Sir David, this is my Uncle, the famous doctor Urquhart from Pitlochry."

"Ah, quite, quite so, Doctor Urquhart, a pleasure," David Vickers shook Ken's hand warmly. "This is your first time here I believe?"

"It is, and by the way just call me Ken."

"Absolutely and I'm David I can't get Eilid to stop all this 'Sir' stuff, well not in public anyway and we're all like family here aren't we."

Ken smiled, nodding.

It was Eilid's turn to round on her visitors.

"All right you two conspirators, what's going on? Not a word, no warning, you just appear."

"Well, there's a wee bit more to it than that." David Vickers explained, "your Granddad and I went to Strahearn."

"Really, what for?"

"Little bit of damage control my lass, just a bit of damage control." Sir Andrew butted in.

"What do you mean?"

"Well your Granddad concluded that the school might not want to have Charles back after all the problems they had," Sir David went on. "I think he was right, right on the money. But the school was also looking for someone to be on the Board of Governors and, as Andrew is thinking of retiring, he brought me along as his nominee."

Eilid could see where this was all heading. "Don't tell me, the famous Ballantyne blackmail again!"

"I say, I say, I resent the use of that word. More like friendly persuasion wasn't it David?"

"Absolutely, absolutely. We had them eating out of our hand in no time. They can't wait to have Charles back, especially as we assured John Forsyth he was in the peak of health."

"Oh you two, you're two scallywags, that's what you are."

"Where did you find that word Eilid, I haven't heard it used in years?"

"Oh it was Miss Bain, my old school teacher's expression, but it fits you two perfectly."

"Bit dry around here David, isn't it?"

"Gobi Dessert old chap."

"All right, come and sit down. Macallans all round I suppose."

"You suppose correctly my dear, as always." Sir Andrew beamed at his Granddaughter and she beamed back.

Eilid went off to get their drinks.

"Did you drive up?" She called over her shoulder.

"We drove up all the way, we got Fitz to…" at that Sir Andrew tailed off. "My God David we are getting old, we left Fitz in the car, where can he be? He's not usually a man to hang back, is he? He was supposed to bring the luggage in, not that it's much, just an overnight bag and so forth, and a little present for the boy."

"I bet I know what's happened," Eilid was laughing now at the consternation the two knights of the realm were showing over their forgetfulness.

"What's that?"

"Hamish was heading to the cottage to change and then come on up with Mhairi, Fitz has given him a lift down and he'll be bringing him back"

"Oh, good for you, I thought we had offended the poor chap so much he must have taken umbrage." Sir Andrew grinned.

The threesome had just finished their drinks when true to Eilid's prediction Hamish, Mhairi and Fitz came through the door. Mhairi was dressed in her tartan hostess skirt, a white silk blouse complete with jabot and silver buckled shoes, quite the Highland lady as Sir David remarked. At twenty-five Mhairi was beginning to fill out a bit and had lost her pale anorexic look she had had in her teens.

While all the greetings had been going on Hamish had quietly disappeared to change out of his hill clothes to put on something more appropriate for the party. Fifteen minutes later he made a grand entrance wearing a kilt of Ferguson tartan. Mainly in green plaid interspersed with a blue check finally completed by a red stripe of two threads in the weave. He wore a white shirt with ruffs at the end of the sleeves and no jacket. His brogues were standard with crossover laces and his sporran was of sealskin with thistle interlink chains. A broad leather belt, silver buckle and sgian dubh completed the ensemble.

"Well, well, what have we here," said a quite astonished Sir Andrew. "By Jove but you Fergusons clean up well!" He stood back surveying brother and sister as they stood together.

"Hear, hear," Sir David joined in as the remainder of the party applauded.

Hamish and Mhairi both flushed bright scarlet embarrassed by the effusive compliments. Mhairi mumbled some excuse of having to be in the kitchen and rushed off to be closely followed by Hamish.

"I tell you what Eilid, you've worked wonders with those two, they're a credit to you and this Lodge, I've said this before, but they really are presenting themselves well," David Vickers gave one of his bear like hugs to Eilid who smiled happily at her Granddad.

"All right then birthday boy, what were you doing today?"

It was the moment for which Charles had been waiting.

"We saw a white stag high in the corrie. At first we thought it was a sheep, didn't we Uncle Ken?"

"Aye we did that, even with the binoculars my eyesight catch match Hamish's," Ken joined in. "Now don't exaggerate Charles it was a wee calf, but I have to say this, it was a white calf no doubt and Hamish declared it to be a male, so, as Hamish said, if it doesn't fall foul of other beasties and the weather, we'll have a white stag next year."

"That's fantastic, what a wonderful addition to the glen. Eilid we'll have to make it very clear that if this wee fellow survives he must be a protected species. A white stag will stand out like a sore thumb on these hills." Sir David deferred to Eilid

"I'll see that the warning goes out and I'll spread it around locally. I rather fancy the poachers won't come back to this glen for a while. I would think that might be the only danger. Like you I'm fair excited about the possibility of an albino stag. I haven't had a chance to talk to Hamish yet so where was it you actually saw the calf?"

"I can tell you mother. It was high up on one of the buttresses on corrie vee something"…Charles struggled to spit the word out. "What is it again Uncle?"

"Corrie 'Veechkerachar'."

"That's right, that's what it was. We also saw the wreckage of the big 'plane that crashed in the corrie didn't we Uncle?"

Ken Urquhart saw Eilid visibly pale at the words.

"Aye so we did. We didn't get close though, for it was about at that time Hamish picked up our wee white fellow." Ken looked closely at Eilid, but her face was a mask.

"That wreckage has been there for about as long as you have, Charles,"

Eilid smiled sweetly at her kilted son as she pushed him gently towards the dining room.

Ken Urquhart thought, by God that girl's got balls.

"By the way David, just when was that tragedy?"

"Damned if I can remember. All I know is some of the undercarriage still clutters up the corrie. RAF promised to remove it God knows when, but it never seemed to happen. Still who knows, some day...?" He tailed off. "You were here when that happened weren't you Eilid? In the glen I mean?"

"No. If you remember that was the year I went to my Uncle Kenny to have Charles."

"Ah yes, quite, quite so. So you're right it's coming up to be almost twelve years now, how time flies."

Kenny shot a sideways glance at Eilid but if she saw it she didn't flicker an acknowledgement.

"Right then, let's get into dinner," Eilid quickly changed the subject finally propelling Charles into the dining room.

The Birthday Cake gleamed with snow-white icing and twelve candles. Eilid was close to tears as she watched her son blow them out without as much as a hesitation. He wouldn't have been able to blow out one before his surgery she told herself. Her heart went out to him all over again. He never complained. After his operation he must have been in quite a lot of pain, but he had said nothing, and stoically accepted his lot, as he gradually got better. She could see by the way he acted he felt on equal terms with the people around him. She couldn't help but wonder on this night of nights what the future might hold for him. She had a new son, a new boy to love, to cherish and to lead into a new lifestyle. She wouldn't let him down.

Charles returned to Strahearn in mid-January as a bit of a hero for what was euphemistically called Spring Term. Rumor in the school had been rife. He had died on the operating table, he would never walk again, his father had abandoned him, he would never return to the school. All the scuttlebutt that a boarding school produces was meted out by one boy after another as they individually basked —albeit for a short time —in the glory of being the one who was 'in the know'. All of it was total fabrication, of course. Not one boy at Strahearn had a clue as to where Charles came from let alone any idea of how to contact him. But it made for good drama and chattering could be heard in the dormitories long after lights-out as the members of Charles's dorm conjectured on the fate of the pale anemic Charles Stuart.

The Headmaster, John Forsyth, had suggested that Charles return two days after the general return from the Christmas holidays. Forsyth was still apprehensive about the boy's condition. After all, he told himself, hadn't he just gone through major heart surgery? Let him come back after the rough and tumble of the start of Term and ease himself into school routine. The earlier impromptu visit by Sir Andrew Ballantyne, ostensibly to introduce Sir David Vickers to him and recommend Sir David to serve on the Board of Governors had done nothing to quell his apprehension that he had a major medical problem in his bailiwick.

He saw Sir Andrew's visit as a repetition of his first to the school with his stunning blond Granddaughter Eilid, when he had given him all kinds of assurances that Charles's breathing difficulties were of no consequence. He still reminisced about the kiss she had given him on parting. What wouldn't he give to see her again? I'm just a dirty old man he said to himself and then grinned hugely. I'd certainly give her more consideration he told himself as his thoughts strayed to the many fine women he had conquered in his youth. He broke away from his reverie of seduction and love-making to focus on the matter in hand. He would make sure that nothing happened to this boy. Breckinridge, that was the answer, he'd get Paul Breckinridge the most popular Prefect in the school, to watch over Charles Stuart. Already a sycophant, Breckinridge would readily take the Headmasters instructions to watch out for this weedy pupil and become his bodyguard, mentor and guide. He congratulated himself on his strategy; the school's potential liability would be in good hands.

Charles arrived at the local station with his trunk. Breckinridge and the Head were there to greet him. John Forsyth could not believe the transformation in the boy. From a ten-year-old weakling he had become a well developed twelve year old. It was indeed a miracle. Sir Andrew hadn't been lying after all. The effusive welcome back he gave Charles was all the more genuine. In fact he couldn't take his eyes off the lad. Charles's green eyes were now more prominent. Where before they had been dull and listless they now sparkled with life. There was a new vigor in the way he got off the train and shook hands. His thin emaciated body had filled out and he smiled at his welcoming party with a wide infectious grin. It occurred to John Forsyth, right then and there, that he could never remember Charles smiling, not once.

"So, young Charles, you are looking splendid. I thought your mother would have driven you down from, eh, where is it exactly now?"

"Torridon, sir, Glen Torridon."

"Ah yes. I should have remembered but as all the correspondence goes to your Great Grandfather Sir Andrew; your location just slipped my mind. Well anyhow, she couldn't make it?"

"She's behind in the cull, sir."

"What is she culling?"

"The hinds, sir. Normally she takes about sixty off the hill in a season, but she's only got about thirty, it's all my fault really with my health and everything, sir. I do want to apologize to you about collapsing like that."

"My dear boy, you could not have prevented that. I'm so pleased, aren't we Breckinridge to see Charles looking so well?"

It was rhetorical question but Breckinridge came in with a couple of "yes sirs" right on cue.

"Right then, let's get you to the Big House and you can tell me all about your mother. I take it she's in good health?"

"Yes sir, she is. In fact I've never known her to be ill. I never thought about that until you mentioned it now."

"It's all that fresh air and out on the hills and in all weathers that does it, I suppose."

"What does your mother actually do Charles?" Breckinridge couldn't even remember Charles but that was hardly surprising as he had only been in the school a couple of weeks before taking ill.

"She runs Torridon Lodge Estate and she's a stalker by profession, she's very good you know."

Breckinridge didn't know and didn't really care to know. Daddy was a stockbroker in the City of London and daddy made oodles of money without even breaking sweat. Breckinridge couldn't begin to imagine a life in the cold North of Scotland trying to eke a miserable existence out of a barren inhospitable land. He had seen pictures of the Highlands and Strahearn was quite as close as he wanted to be to that, thank you.

"Well bully for her. She shoots these poor animals then?"

"Of course; the Red Deer population in Scotland is increasing at an alarming rate. They eat the farmers' crops and destroy saplings planted by the Forestry Commission. They need to be culled."

"So your mum's a sort of Highland butcher then is she?" Paul grinned enjoying Charles's discomfort.

Charles began to feel that he and his mother were being made fools of by this Prefect who sounded very supercilious and superior as he talked down to what he considered a country bumpkin.

"She could outshoot anyone in this school, that's for sure." Charles leaped to his mother's defense. He had already taken a healthy dislike to Breckinridge.

"I doubt that," Breckinridge sneered. "I have my Marksman badge in the cadets and I'm pretty good, there aren't many better than me. I'm a crack shot." Breckinridge ended on a note of superiority.

Charles said nothing.

"Come on you two, I have Charles's trunk in the car. Stop waffling and come with me."

The Headmaster had heard some of the conversation and he hadn't liked what he heard. This was a side of Breckinridge he had never experienced and immediately he saw his mistake. Breckinridge was the wrong man for the job, if indeed there was a job. He was very impressed by the transformation in Charles.

The boys in Charles's dorm went wild when he returned.

"Come on then, show us your scar," they all demanded and when Charles lifted his pajama top to reveal the huge scar carved up the middle of his chest the silence could have been cut with a knife.

"Jesus, Charles that must have hurt?"

"Will it ever get better?"

"Can you really play rugger like that?"

"How long was the operation?"

The questions flew thick and fast. Charles basked in the attention. His first two weeks at the school had been miserable but he had never told his mother. The fact that he was so different from the other boys had singled him out for special attention. They had nicknamed him Casper after the cartoon character "Casper the Friendly Ghost" because of his pallor. Eventually that was what had lead to the pillow fight which had knocked him out for a time until he had come around in the school Sanatorium. The boys in his Dorm had reckoned on dire retribution from the Masters and Prefects but none came. That was why they gave Charles the tumultuous welcome. Most of the boys thought they had ended his life that Sunday in September.

For Charles the Spring Term was an awakening. He enjoyed himself like never before. John Forsyth soon ended Breckinridge's monitoring and Charles was left free to roam and to do anything he wanted save play contact sports. Rugger was out. Towards the end of the Spring Term the school switched from rugby to hockey and Charles, after a brief consultation between Eilid and George Eliot the surgeon, was allowed to play.

He was good. His hand eye co-ordination was, if anything, better than his father's. If Red Ericsson could have seen him wield a hockey stick in Scotland he would have got him on Canadian ice right away. He had all the aptitude to make a fine ice hockey player if contact sports could have been on his menu.

Charles seldom became involved in the school intrigue. He soon learned about homosexuality and how some masters took advantage of boys who wanted to learn more about themselves at an age that was on the threshold of puberty. He steered away from that, as his maturity took much longer. His puberty was still playing catch-up with his newfound physical development. His main activity in the evening was woodcarving during the hour of Activities, as it was called before Prep began. The skills he had developed as a wood carver from Hamish became more extensive as he learned to use power tools such as turning lathes, or drills with various characteristics. He already had a grand project in mind and that was to emulate the chess set his Great Grandfather had given him for Christmas in 1968. But this one would be even better and he had one idea in the back of his mind that would customize just for Sir Andrew, something he could cherish, something that would be unique and make him proud of his great grandson's achievement. But that was just a hobby. There was much more to Charles than that. Rather like a flower or plant whose growth has been stultified by lack of nourishment or light, he suddenly blossomed now the conditions were right.

Even John Forsyth took the time to 'phone Sir Andrew to tell him how happy he was at Charles's progress. The old man couldn't have been more pleased.

"You thought there would be problems John, didn't you?"

"No, no not really. Just apprehensive, I suppose."

"Come on John, you thought I was lying didn't you?"

"Let's just leave it at apprehensive. After Eilid blew away my misgivings on your first visit to the school, I was a bit concerned. Let's just leave it at that, shall we?"

The two men laughed.

"I know what you mean, John let's leave it at that. And by the way, thank you for the call. It's much appreciated."

"How is your Granddaughter then, Andrew?"

"Ah! I knew you'd want to ask about her. Haven't you seen her then? Does she not come down for leave-out weekends?"

"No I haven't more's the pity. Apparently she does come down from time to time at leave outs. If she can't make it there's a red haired lad with jug handles for ears comes for Charles. Both of them pick up Charles at the school gates and he gets dropped off there. Neither of them comes into the school. It's a bit strange, really."

"That does seem a bit strange. I'll have a quiet word with her. She has become quite sociable as she's got older, when she was in her twenties it was all you could do to get her to talk." Sir Andrew sounded puzzled.

"Well for God's sake don't tell her I said anything, I want to keep on her good side, especially after the problem we had with Charles."

"I'll be the soul of discretion, bye John" and with that Sir Andrew hung up.

By the time he came home for the summer vacation in July of 1971 Charles was the toast of the school debating team. He had a natural talent for getting to the heart of any matter. For his age, he possessed a flair for talking extemporaneously and holding the attention of others. He commanded rather than demanded attention. It had, so the masters thought, something to do with his green eyes. They could be almost mesmeric at times. He always entered debates of a political nature and his House Tutor saw him as a politician in the making, even at the early age of twelve.

In October of that year Charles was given special leave out privileges as the "Sirs" week in the glen had come round again. As the twentieth of October fell on a Wednesday that year it meant that Sir David's guests would be most probably be staying over two weekends. Eilid arranged for Hamish to pick Charles on Friday the fifteenth from Perth and take him back on the following Friday which seemed to suit the Headmaster. That meant Charles would have at least two or three days with Sir Andrew and, when everyone went home on the Wednesday, Hamish would take Charles back to school the next day.

The "Sir's Week" was still the highlight of the stalking season and many a would-be guest would try and kindle a friendship with Sir David to wrest an invitation for what had become the signature week of stalking in all of Scotland. But to no avail, Sir David had his regular six-some and nothing short of death or illness would change the list of invitees. Eilid had told Charles that it would most likely be Sir Andrew's last visit. He was now seventy-six and Eilid had heard from Fitz that his ability to get around had become quite impaired. In addition his eyesight had deteriorated to the point where he could no longer drive so Fitz had to drive him everywhere. While Fitz didn't mind, it was, he said, beginning to encroach on his fishing.

Charles had his present all ready. The chessboard was piano-hinged and the marquetry work was precise. He had spray coated the board with a new type of lacquer. Polyurethane it was called and the look of the Chess Board had a style and depth to it that was incredible, it was as if it had a deep glossy almost plastic coating. The chess pieces had all been carved by hand save for the pawns and the castles that Charles had turned on a lathe. Instead of knights that resembled horses Charles had substituted stags. That gave the set the uniqueness he had been planning. He was sure by next spring there would be a white stag in the glen and this, he thought, would add a certain poignancy to the gift. He was ready waiting at the school gates as usual when the Land Rover arrived right on cue driven by Hamish.

"What's that ye've got there, young Charles?"

"It's my Granddad's present."

"What is it?"

So Charles explained what he had produced at wood working class, which made Hamish really proud as he felt Charles was his true protégé in the art of woodcarving.

"Well we'll have to have a keek at that before Sir Andrew sees it."

"Why? I've wrapped it all up, you know."

"We can soon fix that. I'm just interested and proud of what you've done, and I'd like to take a wee look just to kill my own curiosity."

Charles was on to him right away. "You just want to check out the quality of the work, Hamish Ferguson, don't you?"

Dear God, thought Hamish, this child's too smart by half. "No, no, never not at all, I'm sure it's perfect." But his ability to be embarrassed gave him away as he reddened quickly.

Charles just sat back and laughed as the Land Rover crossed the river Earn and headed north to Torridon.

Saturday night at the Lodge was an outstanding success. Sir Andrew was in grand form and so were all the guests. Charles presented his chess set to his Great Grandfather who was truly amazed by the craftsmanship and the quality of the work. But most of all he marveled at the use of stags as knights. There was not one of Sir David Vickers's guests who did not appreciate the workmanship and thought that Sir Andrew's twelve-year-old grandson had put into the chessboard and the chessmen. The white stag, the one they hoped would be on the hill the following year, was the main topic of conversation. To a man they agreed that protection would be given if the calf survived, Sir David had heard of albino deer before, but to have one on his estate was an attraction he looked forward to.

"We'll have to play," Sir Andrew said having examined and set up the chess set carefully.

"I'm not very good Granddad."

"And I'm pretty rusty, so it'll be an even match."

Great Grandfather and Charles sat down to play and after a few moves with casualties on both sides the match slowed down until both players stared at the board not quite knowing what piece to move next. Charles was playing the white, Sir Andrew, black. Sir Percy, one of Sir David's more vociferous guests cast a casual glance at the game as he passed by smoking a large cigar heading for the sideboard that held an array of malts.

"White stag to take queen's pawn, young fella and it's check mate," he declared. "You've wiped out the next heir to the throne," he laughed.

Neither Sir Andrew nor Charles knew what he was talking about. They both raised their eyes with a puzzled look.

"Pretty simple stuff, you know. Queen's pawn is the Prince of Wales, Prince Charles who is now twenty-one, soon to be twenty-two, is as I'm sure you know heir to the Throne. Our young Charles is named Charles

Edward Stuart, after, one supposes, the Young Pretender. Memories of the '45 what? Take out the current Prince of Wales, eh?"

The elderly guest stomped off to get his whisky.

"Well his move is right," Sir Andrew exclaimed, "but what's all this other baloney?"

Charles laughed at the 'baloney' word; he hadn't heard it used for ages.

"Maybe he thinks with my name I'm a candidate to take over the country; Scotland I mean. My Uncle Ken is quite political, you know. He longs for some kind of reform to give Scotland its own Parliament back and to make Scotland truly independent. He wants the land seized by the English during the Highland clearances after Culloden returned to the rightful heirs or owners. Wouldn't it be thrilling if somehow that could come about, I dream about it, but that's all it is just a dream."

"Well my boy, it may be a dream, but some dreams can become reality if you want them badly enough. Now that you're truly well I can see a great future ahead of you. Come along then, enough of this, let's go and join the others."

Everyone was in the big living room where the log fire blazed away merrily. The scene was one of complete contentment. Mhairi's traditional Sunday dinner of Steak and Kidney Pudding had filled them all to capacity; the wine, a Chateau Palmer '61, had been superb.

"Bloody waste of great wine," Sir Percy Ponsonby-Smythe had declared as he drained another glass of the red velvet.

"I don't agree. Sir Andrew spoke out. "Anyway, it's my wine and when did you ever have such fine steak pudding."

"My dear chap, you're quite right, quite right." Sir Percy nodded his head sagely. "Tell me David, how do you keep that young lass here? I warrant she'd be a top chef in any fine London restaurant."

"She loves the glen. She's never been farther south than Inverness and she likes it that way. She's all found here at the Lodge and it's really Eilid who keeps the team together. There's a wee bit of an unfortunate story on her childhood, but I'm not going to go into that, not unless Eilid wants to pick up the story?" At the far end of the table Eilid shook her head vehemently.

"Aye, a wee touch of the domestic molestations I suppose?" Sir Percy clearly wanted to know more but David's look cut him off and the conversation died right there.

Eilid was exhausted. It had been a long week. Mercifully all the guests had decided they had enjoyed a surfeit of good stalking, great camaraderie, wonderful food and hospitality, so much so that they decided to a man to go home on Monday rather than go on the hill. Because of this Eilid decided to keep Charles in the glen for the remainder of the week and take him back to school to celebrate Halloween with his school friends.

Sir Andrew was the last to leave. Fitz had had the car ready for over an hour, but Sir Andrew was slowing down. He refused to have Fitz help him pack and it took him over an hour to put his few personal possessions and hill clothes, some of which had been at the Lodge for years into his duffle bag. Now he sat picking away at his breakfast in a disinterested fashion staring out of the dining room window as low gray clouds moved into the glen from the Black Cuillin on the nearby Isle of Skye. It was Mhairi who finally chased him off as she unceremoniously cleared away what was left on the table while he was still seated. Sir Andrew got the message.

"Right, right young lass, I'm going. Just give me time to finish my tea and I'll be on my way for the last time." The words were spoken with such a heavy heart that Mhairi, not realizing this might well be his last time in the glen, tried to disappear into the kitchen with tears welling up, but Sir Andrew was too quick.

"Come here, come here lassie, you've not to weep for me. I'm just a maudlin old fool. I'm just feeling a wee bit sad and sorry for myself, and why should I, my cup's more half full than half empty, I've got a beautiful Granddaughter and Great-grandson, and I count you and Hamish as amongst my dearest friends." All this did was to make Mhairi wail all the louder bringing Eilid down from upstairs to find out what all the commotion was about.

"Come on Granddad; put that young lass down, she's much too young for the likes of you!" She chided him gently, cutting through the murk of the moment. It did the trick. Sir Andrew broke into a broad smile,

"Just so, just so, but there was a day Eilid Stuart when I could handle young Mhairi plus a few others, mark my words."

"I know Granddad, I know. All you old men are the same. The chase is better than the conquest, isn't that a fact."

"Aye, indeed, indeed it is. The male ego aye needs to be fed. Right where's that bloody Fitz, we've got to be off," he suddenly snapped to, gave Mhairi a big kiss on the cheek and headed to the door to see Fitz standing, arms folded, with a look that said, thank God, at long last.

Eilid hugged her Granddad as Charles held onto his knurled hand.

"Bye my dear, don't be a stranger to the Neuk, come to me on leave-outs, Perth isn't so far from Peebles. You're welcome anytime. And Charles, thank you for the time and superb artistry you put into my chess set. You must send me photographs of the white stag if he makes it through to next year. I just thought, and I'm a bit late saying this but Fitz and I could drop Charles off at Strahearn, it's not that far out of our way, couldn't we Fitz?"

"That's very kind Granddad, but Charles and I are going to do a bit of exploring in the next few days and Hamish will run him back to the school on Friday."

"Oh," said Sir Andrew, "I thought you'd be taking him back. When did you visit Charles at the school last?"

"Why Granddad?"

"Just curious."

"Well when I go to pick Charles up I don't go in. It's such a waste of time. I've got to crawl up that long driveway and I'm sure the dirty old Land Rover doesn't go down too well. Now one of the new Range Rovers...that would be another thing altogether." Eilid referred to the new breed of four-wheel drive vehicles that the Rover Corporation had launched earlier that year and had caught the public's imagination as a luxury style vehicle suitable for either open road touring or driving on rough terrain.

"Well I'm sure David Vickers is not about to supply you with one of those, they're awfully expensive, so I'm told."

"Granddad, I'm only joking. I really don't like going into the school. But you want me to pay a visit, don't you?"

"Who me? No, no, my dear. What you do is your own business. I just thought it might be courteous to drop in once in a while. I'm sure John Forsyth would be pleased to see you."

I knew it, thought Eilid. John Forsyth's at the bottom of this.

"You don't have a problem with John, do you?'"

"No, not at all; in fact I like him. I think he's rather dishy. "Granddad," Sir Andrew heard the exasperation in her voice. "Granddad it is not just one thing, there's more than one, but all right, I'll make a point of saying hello to John when I take Charles back, satisfied?" There was even more exasperation in her voice now.

Sir Andrew backed off. "That would be most kind if you did that, I'm sure John will be pleased to see you."

"Granddad, goodbye," and she planted those disconcerting soft lips of hers on top of his and gave him a long kiss.

As usual Sir Andrew swooned quietly. I really do wonder if she knows what she's doing he asked himself for the umpteenth time. Then it was Charles turn to be given a hug and a kiss from his Granddad, as he called him, a firm hand shake from Fitz who couldn't believe the change in the boy since his first visit to Innerleithen, and off Fitz and Sir Andrew went leaving the Lodge empty of guests for the remainder of the year.

The next morning Eilid phoned John Forsyth.

"Mr. Forsyth, this is Eilid Stuart."

"Eilid, what a pleasant surprise," Forsyth sounded genuinely pleased. "And by the way John will be fine, when we're on the telephone at least."

"Thank you John. And thank you for giving Charles the extra time off to see Sir Andrew. He's getting on now and I think it may be his last year at Torridon."

"Quite, Charles explained that to me. It was never a problem. Charles is doing awfully well you know. The time off will have no impact on his studies I can assure you of that."

"That's fine. I thought I would bring him back on Friday, if that's all right with you and at the same time see a bit of the school. I really haven't spent any time there since my last visit more than two years ago."

"It will be my pleasure to show you around. Just arrive when it's convenient and I'll keep my day clear." John Forsyth sounded enthusiastic.

"That's very kind of you John," her soft Highland lilt did wonders for John's libido. He certainly didn't look sixty-one he told himself. Why, there was less than thirty years between he and Eilid. He dreamed on, wondering what she would be wearing, something low cut would be nice.

Friday the twenty-second of October 1971 turned out to be a bitterly cold day, a wind straight out of the north whipped around the Combined Cadet Force as they stood on Parade. Even the heavy Army Greatcoats couldn't keep the cadets from shivering. Eilid arrived as they marched smartly by. As she got out of the Land Rover the sergeant gave an "eyes left" to the platoons and they turned in unison towards the tall blond whose hair was being blown almost horizontally in the bitterly cold wind. Eilid smiled broadly and snapped a mock salute back to the boys. Some at the rear were so distracted they kept their eyes left too long and tripped over their comrades as they stared and wondered just who the attractive woman could be. Charles was fiddling about in the back of the Land Rover, so no one associated Eilid with Charles.

The whispering in the ranks started.

"Who is she?"

"Dunno."

"Is that the new Matron?"

"If it is I'm feeling sick already"

The whispering grew until the Sergeant yelled "squad" and they all shut up waiting for the follow-on command which never came.

John Forsyth was the picture of disappointment as he stared out of the entrance hall. Eilid was wearing a turtleneck sweater under her Barbour jacket, khaki corduroy trousers and a pair of well-polished boots.

She wore no makeup but she still looked glamorous. That's the test of real beauty, John told himself.

"Come in; come in out of that damned wind!" John opened one of the heavy oak double doors and beckoned to Eilid who had been now joined by Charles as they both watched the marching cadets disappear.

"Thank you, thank you John."

The Headmaster leaned forward to give her a peck on the cheek and he was rewarded by Eilid's soft warm lips alighting on his. My God the sap's rising already, his thought distracted him. He stood back to take a closer look.

"Well, that was a nice surprise. You look wonderful." John smiled disarmingly. "And you too young man. I do believe you've put on even more weight."

"Thank you very much. I'm not very well dressed but when I left this morning there were flurries of snow coming down the glen." Eilid explained.

Charles smiled at the Headmaster's remarks. It was true. Despite the hill walking and other activities in which Charles had taken part, Mhairi's cooking and the compulsory three-meals-a-day routine had certainly helped to fill Charles out.

"Eilid you look fine. You're dressed most appropriately. Both of you come to my study, we'll have a coffee and I'll get one of the porters to fetch Charles's bag and then he can report to Matron. As you saw it is CCF day today and Charles's House Tutor is taking some of the platoons on a route march. While I'm on the subject of the Combined Cadet Force I need to ask you if it will be permissible for Charles to join next year, which in the normal course of events he would anyway, but I thought that with, shall we say, his 'situation' you might want to consider the advisability of him becoming involved."

"Please mother?" Charles's green eyes became beseeching.

"I'm not sure John. It's kind of you to ask. Why don't I ask George Eliot, Charles's surgeon and I'll let you know what he says."

"Mother, please, the more I'm different from the other boys the more difficult it makes my life. If there's something we've got to do that

I think could be similar to playing rugger, I'll just back out. All the masters are aware of my condition, it won't be a problem, will it sir?"

Charles turned to look at the Headmaster eliciting support.

"Actually what he says is true Eilid, boarding schools are cruel places. Any perceived weakness is magnified and thrown back in the boy's face. I wish our schoolboys wouldn't be so cruel, but they are, especially the juniors." Forsyth smiled grimly.

"All right John, I understand what you're telling me. Charles, next year I don't want to hear any moans or groans about Cadet life, clear?"

"Yes mother, thank you, thank you." Charles kissed her, grinning like a Cheshire cat.

"While I'm on the subject of the CCF, I have a little task for you, if you don't mind."

"I'm intrigued."

"I understand from Charles that you're a bit of a crack shot. Now you saw the cadets marching down the drive."

"Yes I did. I was most impressed. They looked very smart."

"Thank you. Well, today's rifle practice down at the range. The range is located just on the right just as you swing through the gates. I wondered, as you're here, if you would give the boys some instruction."

"I'd be delighted. When do they start?" Eilid asked.

"You've got about an hour, spend say half an hour with the boys and then I'll be happy to show you around and let you see the improvements we've made since you visited last. Charles, if you go to the sewing room you can let Matron know you're back. I'll have your bag taken there and after that I'll take your mother to the range and introduce her. I'll come back here, I've got some calls to make and then we'll do the short tour, all right everyone?"

"Fine," said Eilid.

"You'd best be careful mother. These are .303 caliber and they weigh a ton."

"Sounds like remnants from the Second World War." Eilid commented.

"You are right, of course. Lee-Enfield No.4 Mark 1, standard Army issue, I'm sure you can handle them?" John Forsyth raised his eyebrows.

Charles just nodded and left the Head's study to find matron. Eilid turned to John.

"I haven't met a rifle I couldn't use but I've never used anything heavier than a 300 Magnum, and that was just to please some fool of a guest who thought he'd blow away half the stag."

She laughed at the memory and tossed her hair as John took advantage of her sweater filling out as she leaned back slightly. Then, in disconcerting move, she took John's arm, linked it through hers and exited towards the Headmaster's car.

John Forsyth introduced Eilid to the cadets assembled at the range. He said little about what Eilid did except for telling them that she was an expert with a rifle and that their undivided attention was required.

"Carry on then Lieutenant," he called out to the master acting as a First Lieutenant.

The afternoon was one of fascination for the cadets. The elder boys in the sixth form couldn't get enough.

"Miss, could you just show me again how I should hold this rifle?"

Eilid would get down beside the eager cadet placing the pupil's hands on the rifle for the second or third time, her blond hair spilling over the swooning teenager. While his friends hissed,

"Lucky bastard," or

"You shit Colvin, it's my turn now."

Finally having gone down the line of the first eight on the range ready to fire, she stood back to let the Lieutenant take over, as she gave them her final words

"Right. I've taught you all you need to know. Remember hold the weapon one hand on the stock just behind the trigger guard, one hand on the barrel as far up as is comfortable for you, twist both hands in opposite directions as if you were trying to unscrew the top off a bottle or wring out a cloth, take aim, breathe in, exhale slowly and when you're ready squeeze the trigger, don't pull, squeeze." Eilid looked them over. They were so young she thought to be handling those rifles.

"I know what I'd like to squeeze" one of the Cadet Sergeants said in a stage whisper.

Eilid heard the comment as the others all went into fits of laughter.

She normally would have ignored the remark but it so reminded her of the idiot who had flagrantly assaulted her and completely spoiled her nineteenth birthday party. She decided she would do something about it.

"What's your name Sergeant," she snapped.

"Breckinridge, ma'am."

"You have a first name?"

"Paul, miss."

The name was vaguely familiar to Eilid, and there was nothing that she remembered was complimentary.

"What would you like to squeeze then Paul?"

"Nothing miss. It was just a comment, I'm sorry."

"I see you have a marksman's badge," she pointed to the crossed rifles on the sleeve of his tunic, "let's just see how good you are, maybe you'll get to squeeze something other than a trigger."

There was complete silence in the ranks. Eilid's blue eyes blazed cutting through brain matter.

"Corporal."

"Yes ma'am."

"Put up two targets."

The Corporal did as he was bid. The Lieutenant, the master in charge looked on and said nothing. He was as fascinated as the boys, more so, in fact. He wanted to see if this blond could really perform.

The rifles were each loaded with five rounds. The Corporal gave the command, "Fire at will!"

Eilid spread-eagled herself on her Barbour jacket revealing her figure to the ogling cadets. Bam, bam, bam, bam, bam, she blasted off five shots so quickly it sounded as if there was a semi-automatic at the range.

Bam. Breckinridge's first shot went off. Then another and so on intermittently until the magazine was empty.

The cadets uncovered their ears, the noise had been deafening. The rifles were laid down breaches open. The Corporal went to get the targets. It was like the rifle club performance at Pitlochry all over again. Where the bull had been in Eilid's target there was a huge hole. Breckinridge's shots were all over the place; in fact one shot had missed the target completely.

"Thank you boys, now you've seen the importance of squeezing rather than pulling, any questions?"

"Mrs. Stuart." The Lieutenant spoke up. "Thank you for a wonderful display of marksmanship. Let's have three cheers for Mrs. Stuart…hip, hip hooray! The Cadet Force hoorayed to a man three times. Breckinridge hung his head wishing his quick wit had died on his tongue.

Standing in the background was Charles who had walked down to the butts and had seen the whole display. He couldn't remember when he had seen his mother quite so angry. He hadn't heard Paul Breckinridge's comment so he had no idea what had upset her so.

"All right Paul" Eilid confronted the cadet, "you can squeeze my hand just for that." Eilid proffered her hand and Paul took it, as a sign of let bygones be bygones and grasped it eagerly.

Eilid squeezed his hand putting all her strength into the 'handshake'.

"Oh, aah, oh," Breckinridge yelled as Eilid turned up the pressure.

"What was it you wanted to squeeze now Paul?" Eilid smiled grimly keeping up the pressure on his right hand.

"Please miss, please let go, I'm truly sorry." Breckinridge sank to his knees as tears welled up in his eyes.

"Aye, and I should think so too." Eilid released his hand, collected Charles and left an astonished Cadet Force with a wave and a smile.

The legend of Eilid Stuart lived on for many years long after Charles had left Strahearn and been accepted for Aberdeen University.

Red Ericsson was as proud as a father could be. He sat in the Hofheinz Pavilion in May of 1979 as his son received his degree in Chemical Engineering from the University of Houston. How he wished his mother could have seen him. Lance had grown tall, taller than Red and slightly heavier. His sandy hair and green eyes were Red's but from there down the nose, mouth and lips were Karen's. He turned to Agnes Anderson who was dabbing furiously at something she averred had got in her eye,

"Well, did you ever think you'd see this happen?" Red asked her.

"Oh no, never in a month of Sundays, but you've aye persevered with him and he's done you proud; Karen would have been so happy..." she tailed off dabbing furiously. "I'm so sorry Red; it's such an emotional moment."

"Hey, that's all right," he gave her a fierce hug; "steady now or I'll be joining you. Remember if it weren't for you, none of this would have happened. That school we sent him to, at your insistence, disciplined him in a way that neither you nor I could have done. I just hope it sticks."

"Red, promise me now that you'll see that it does. He can be a bad rascal that son of yours. Mind you, I haven't seen him for over five years, but I can't think much has changed.

"Well, I try to keep him on a short leash, but boys will be boys."

Red cast his mind back to when he was twenty-one; there wasn't a good looking woman he didn't try to bed when he was working on the drilling rigs. He smiled inwardly as he remembered the bar brawls and the drinking; those were the days, he thought to himself. I've changed, he thought, I've become introverted, I work my ass off and now there's not a woman I would look at, not for any time anyway. He knew he used women only as a physical necessity, and paid dearly for the privilege.

"Penny for 'em," said Agnes breaking into his self-analysis.

"Sorry Agnes, I was away again, thinking of what I was like at Lance's age. When's your flight?" Red decided he didn't want to go down that path for he knew from past experience that when Agnes got hold of a subject she couldn't let go.

"It's not until mid-morning. Not for me this stramashing to the airport at my age. I'll have a long lie in, collect myself, and then get your fellow, what's his name, to take me to Intercontinental."

"Fred, Fred Espinosa, my driver, that's his name. And what the hell is stramashing?"

"Well fine you know it's a Scot's word for getting yourself all in an uproar and getting out of sorts....see there you are, it takes four words or five words in English to describe it!" she said triumphantly.

"But I could have understood those, almost," and he shot her his infectious grin as he pulled her leg for the umpteenth time about her Scot's accent. "Agnes, seriously, it's great to have you here."

"Red it's great to be here. How's the new housekeeper working out?"

"This is her last week."

"How many is that you've gone through?"

"Too many. But there's hope on the horizon. We've got some English lady coming who just loves dogs. It's MacDuff whose been real strange and caused the problems. I just can't understand it. Ever since you left he's disliked anyone who's come into the house, to stay that is. He's such a gentle dog normally, it sure mystifies me."

"Well when I arrived this morning I got nearly bowled over, he was so frantic to greet me. He was up licking me all over like I was his long lost friend."

"That was because you used to feed him steak and all sorts of stuff, no wonder he misses you."

"You mean to tell me Red Ericsson that you don't give that dog the left-overs from Sunday dinner?"

"Don't know; it is Lance's dog you know."

"Well Lance will hear from me this very evening."

Red could bet with certainty that he would.

"Agnes, how are you?" Lance had come up on them as they bantered away while the graduates came up to the platform to receive their diplomas.

"Lance, my goodness, how you've grown. Congratulations, you've made me the proudest Godmother on the face of the planet. Now what's this I hear about MacDuff?"

Off they went arm in arm with Red bringing up the rear as Lance assured Agnes that MacDuff was the best fed dog in Houston.

Agnes had a wonderful evening. Even at seventy-two she could turn a head or two. Her iron gray hair had gone white, "all because of you two," she assured them. But she was still slim with a slight stoop in what had been a ramrod straight carriage. Red took her and Lance to Tony's, near the Galleria area, reputedly the best restaurant in Houston. No expense was spared and by the end of the evening Agnes confessed to being a little tipsy. Lance marveled at her constitution. Oysters Bienville to start, House salad, Steak au Poivre, and a to die for Grand Marnier Soufflé, washed down by two or was it three large glasses of Chateau Cheval Blanc and two large malt whiskies.

"Formidable" declared the French Maitre d', laughing as he helped Agnes from her chair.

"You know," she confided to Red and Lance in the back of the limo taking them home, "that's the best meal I've had since I was with your mother in Claridges, in London." With that she got all maudlin again and started sniveling.

"Agnes, let's not relive all this again, we've had a great night, Lance is on his way up in the world and your going home to your sister in Vancouver, all right."

"Red, I'm sorry. You've been too kind. I'm just a silly old woman haunted by my memories. You're right let's have a good time; where are we going to go?"

"I thought we were going home.........but......let's see if we can find some action somewhere." Red thought hard.

Then Red had a great idea. He looked at his watch, hell it was ten thirty, and he wondered why he hadn't thought of it earlier.

"Driver, take us to the Petroleum Club."

"Yes suh!"

Why hadn't he thought about this venue before? He asked himself but deep down he knew. In his innermost thoughts it was Karen's special place, the place they had gone to for their first date all those years ago with, what were their names? Michelle something and a Jim, slowly it came back to him it was Michelle Turner and her father was a doctor. He wondered what had happened to them, he wondered if they knew about Karen. He broke off his train of thought as the Limo reached Downtown and turned onto Louisiana.

Agnes was such a part of the family she deserved to go there, Red had no reservations about that at all. Lance would certainly like the attention he thought, and, after all it was Lance's special day. Agnes will just love the views from the club, he told himself. It was now located on the forty-third and forty-fourth floors of the Exxon building, right in the middle of Downtown Houston. The views from there were spectacular, the service impeccable, and the band, Red hoped, still as wonderful as he remembered it those long twenty-three years ago.

The high-speed elevator whipped them up to the forty-fourth floor. Red led his party into the restaurant.

"Mr. Ericsson, sir, so nice to see you. I guess this fine man is your son?"

"Yeah, Scratchy, this is Lance, and this is Agnes Anderson, a Scot's lady who is Lance's Godmother."

Scratchy was all over Lance and Agnes. "What a wonderful surprise, I guess we're havin' a celebration?"

"Yes we are," replied Lance. I've just graduated, Agnes has been in town for the celebration and my Dad has brought us here for a nightcap, although to tell you the truth, I don't think we need one."

"You speak for yourself, young Lance. Scratchy, take us to the bar. A place as prestigious as this has got to have some decent Champagne." Agnes was on a roll.

"Right away Madame," Scratchy proffered his arm and led the trio to a table by the floor to ceiling window.

"Red, this is wonderful, thank you so much for bringing me. I know this club has a special place in your heart. The views are wonderful."

Agnes looked out from the west elevation window to Memorial Park. She could see Buffalo Bayou meandering its way through the city like some dark brown serpent as it slithered its way out to the Houston Ship Channel and thence to the Gulf. The wine waiter brought a bottle of Cristal Champagne, unobtrusively popped the cork, and carefully filled each flute.

"Was this where you brought Karen all those years ago?"

"No. The club wasn't here then. It was on top of the Rice Hotel and it moved here in, I think, nineteen sixty-two or three. This venue is a wonderful improvement but I liked the nostalgia of the old place. That's emotion taking over now. Happy memories."

He looked hard into the bottom of his glass.

The limo dropped them off just before midnight. Red had told the driver to stop at the house entrance gates. The threesome walked arm in arm up the long driveway. Agnes was deep in thought. She had lived in this house with Lance and Red for almost twelve years. Those years had taken their toll. Not so much physically, she told herself, but the mental strain of constantly dealing with father and son had been enervating. Her visit had been one of joy and bitter memories. Seeing the portrait of Karen in the entrance hall reminded her of the Stahlman's.

"Red, what ever happened to the Stahlman's? Do you ever hear from them?"

"Jees, no, never. Rosemary died last year, you know. Just drank herself to death, so I'm told, she was seventy-three. I only heard about it through Ruth, my personal assistant. She's new, been with me for only about six months, but I kinda lean on her more every day. Anyway she saw something in the obituary column, I think, it was the Los Angeles Times and for some reason she knew of the connection. To tell you the truth I was real upset, and I would have thought Brett might just have called me. I got Ruth to make some enquiries but all she got was a staff member who said Mr. Stahlman was ill and hung up the phone. I didn't try after that."

'They were a strange pair really, weren't they?"

"Yup, they became strange. Loosing Karen just kicked away the bottom brick for them both, I suppose I didn't try hard enough, but hey, as I've said before, the phone works both ways, you know?"

"Well I think it's sad. Lance is all they had to remember Karen by, now if you had married someone else, I could see there might be a problem..." Agnes tailed off, fishing as usual.

"Christ Agnes, you never stop. If you've got the fishing rods I've got the jam jars."

"I didn't think it was all that obvious." She put on her famous Scottish pout.

'Oh come *on!*"

They both laughed at themselves. Red looked hard at Agnes.

"Happy?"

"Content."

"Well that's fine I guess. So let me turn the tables just a wee bit, as you would say, was there ever a man?" He held out his hands palms towards her in mock surrender. "Now I've known you for how long? And I've never asked the question."

"And I should think not too, a lady's affairs are private, and should remain so." Agnes became all haughty.

"Agnes," Red reached out from his armchair to the couch and held her hand in his. "This is Red, you know."

Agnes found herself wishing she wasn't so old and could be with the family. Life with her sister in Vancouver was fine, but the days dragged and she missed the excitement of 'Chateau Red' as everyone had nicknamed the huge house. She felt herself wilting slightly. Her mind went back, all those many, many years ago.

"Aye. Yes, I mean, there was someone. He was a captain in the Black Watch. We were going to get married and then the war came. He got shipped out right away. He was killed at Tobruk in the November of 1941. And that was that." She sniffled.

"I already was a nurse in Glasgow, so I joined up to help with the wounded. After the war my sister and her husband came out to the States to settle but Bob, her husband, got offered this great job in Canada and so they moved there. I liked Los Angeles, particularly the climate, so I stayed put. You know the rest."

Red didn't say anything. He stood up and by holding her hands he gently brought her up beside him. He leaned over and kissed her, first on one cheek, then the other. Agnes regained her composure.

"Away with ye' what's a handsome man like you at fifty cavorting wi' an old prune like me at seventy four.

"I happen to like prunes," said Red grinning, only missing a clout to the head as he was too tall for Agnes to reach him.

"Come on then, bed. I'm going to take you to the airport in the morning, I can get Ruth to reorganize my day, she's good at that."

"You seem to put a lot of store by this Ruth, you fancy her then, do you?"

That was Agnes. She never lost her Scottish directness. Subtle as a baseball bat behind the left ear, thought Red as he smiled inwardly. She still has my best interests at heart.

"Yes, Agnes, but not in that way. There'll never be another Karen, I'm certain of that, now *off to bed!*" He yelled at her, half joking, whole earnest. Putting her nose in the air, she went quietly in her own time; up the stairs to the room she had known so well for so many years.

MARISCHAL COLLEGE —
July 1979

Two months later in July of the same year, a similar graduation ceremony took place in the City of Aberdeen, Scotland. The July sun beat down on Eilid, Mhairi and Hamish as they made their way to Marischal Hall probably the most prestigious building in the Granite City, the other name by which Aberdeen is known. Marischal Hall was the second largest granite building in the world, only surpassed by the Escorial Palace outside Madrid, so Eilid had read as she swatted up on the graduation ceremony.

How quickly the last ten years had gone, she mulled as she packed her case for the trip to Aberdeen. Nothing much had changed at the Lodge, Hamish did more of the stalking during the season and Mhairi had matured, put on a bit more weight which suited her and was an attractive red-head of thirty-five. The romance that had blossomed between her and John Chisholm, her policemen, had fizzled out some five years earlier when John had been transferred to Kinlochbervie, virtually, as Mhairi had put it, to the end of the earth. In that she wasn't far wrong, go north but a few miles and there was the bleak wind hewn promontory of Cape Wrath. Regular visits became impossible and John soon found a new attachment and the letters and the occasional phone calls stopped.

While Mhairi was quite philosophical about the loss of her lover, Eilid had endured the pain and suffering of not knowing what had happened to Douglas Hamilton. The letter or card promised ten years earlier at Charles's twelfth birthday never materialized. It was as though Douglas had disappeared off the face of the earth. Sir Andrew tried in vain to find out what had become of Douglas, but each enquiry met with a dead end. He got enough out of one mutual friend who knew he had gone to Hungary, but after that, nothing. Sir Andrew tried in vain to console his Granddaughter. It was at that time he discovered how fond she had become of Douglas.

Eilid shook her head as she chased away the bitter memories. She had hoped against hope that some day a car would come down the glen, and there he would be, smiling broadly, craving forgiveness. But in those ten years it had never happened. She sighed out loud as she carefully folded a soft black full-length halter necked gown she had chosen for the graduation ball. The gown had a well fitting bodice and a full skirt and was virtually backless. She had tried to get various bras to go with the dress but anything she found could be seen from the back no matter how she tried to adjust either the bra or the dress. To hell with it she thought, I don't need a bra, and she would critically examine her nude self in the mirror moving this way and that to see if there was any untoward movement. Her breasts, she told herself, were just as firm as they had ever been, slightly larger than ten years ago, but that was all right, men liked that sort of thing. Then, ashamed at her thoughts, she would pull on a sweater to cover her self-generated embarrassment.

Her one great disappointment was that Sir Andrew was unable to attend Charles's graduation. He was now eighty-five and was desperately ill with cancer of the liver. Fitz had become his sole companion and acted like a male nurse as he tended the old man compassionately and watched his employer get weaker and thinner and more jaundiced every day. Just when he thought the end was near, Sir Andrew would rally, and try to overcome the hellish disease that gripped him. Fitz had spoken with Eilid two days before her journey and had told her that he doubted if her Granddad could last another two months and so it was tinged with that sadness she packed the Land Rover and set off with Mhairi and Hamish for three days in the Granite City to be at the graduation ceremony and the graduation ball. She told Fitz that she would make arrangements for Hamish and Mhairi to go back to Torridon and that she would travel south with Charles to Innerleithen to be with her Granddad.

The weather couldn't have been kinder as they made their way to Inverness in warm sunshine with fluffy white clouds occasionally playing hide and seek with the sun. As they had plenty of time, Eilid took the coast road going from Fochabers through the quaint and quaintly named villages of Buckie, Banff and Macduff. Then having got to Macduff she decided to avoid the longer way to her destination via Fraserburgh and Peterhead, so she backtracked a few miles and cut the corner of the Eastern bulge by going through Turriff and Old Meldrum finally arriving at Aberdeen late in the afternoon.

They drove down Union Street wide eyed as building after building gleamed and sparkled in the early July sunshine. Fitz, who had followed Sir Andrew's precise instructions to the letter, had made reservations for them at the Caledonian, one of the city's oldest and most prestigious hotels. Stinting nothing, Sir Andrew had Fitz reserve and pre-pay a suite for Eilid and separate rooms for Hamish and Mhairi. As they drove up to the four-star hotel they couldn't help notice some askance glances at the slightly battered and mud bespattered Land Rover as Eilid parked outside the hotel entrance. If the clients showed scant approval at their means of transport, there was none from the staff. The porters leaped to the attention of the tall blond and the attractive redhead paying little attention to Hamish. The young receptionist was pretty with a welcoming smile and soon had them all ensconced in their respective rooms. There were oohs and aahs from Hamish and Mhairi as they inspected the ensuite bathrooms equipped with huge fluffy white towels and complete with shampoo, conditioner and bath oil. Eilid was pretty much overawed with her accommodations as well. The sitting room off the bedroom was large by most standards and it overlooked the Union Terrace Gardens only minutes away from the train station. There was a large sofa which, the hotel porter informed her could convert into a double bed. Eilid thought that might become useful if Charles elected to stay the night, but she considered that highly unlikely, she was sure he would be celebrating with his friends most of the night.

She decided to luxuriate in a bath as she had two hours to kill before her son arrived, if indeed he was going to visit them at all, that evening. As she lay in the tub with her hair piled high on her head she again went over in her mind the events of the last ten years.

Charles had become one of the most popular boys at boarding school. In the intervening decade since his heart valve operation he had developed rapidly into a well built, handsome young man. His hair had lost some of the red and was now sandier in color. One of his greatest friends was Paul Breckinridge, the cadet sergeant that Eilid well remembered excoriating and embarrassing at Strahearn. His change of attitude, she had found out, had been prompted by the Strahearn Headmaster, John Forsyth, who had put great store in the boy's abilities and had been more than disappointed with Paul's demeanor and supercilious attitude as he came into his senior years. The incident at the rifle range had been well reported back to him and he had a talk with Breckinridge that didn't leave much else to be said. Forsyth then 'phoned Eilid to apologize in person only to be completely disarmed by her expressing her regrets at her show of temper. Forsyth had gone on to say that Breckinridge was truly sorry and that he had already made an approach to Charles on the subject.

A week after the rifle-range incident a letter of apology found its way to the Lodge at Torridon. Eilid was so impressed by the earnestness of the letter and the quality of the English she wrote back at once forgiving Paul and inviting him up to Torridon for one of the long leave-outs. Paul took to the Highlands like a duck takes to water. He loved the area, and, under Eilid's tutelage he did become a crack shot. Although Paul was four years Charles's senior they complimented each other perfectly. Paul was an extrovert, had a wicked sense of humor, and made everyone feel at ease. Charles on the other hand was the thinker, slow to react and with a much more composed approach to life than Paul. Charles was slightly taller than Paul, but Paul was the better built of the two. They became firm friends with Paul visiting Torridon on every possible occasion until at the age of eighteen, when he was made School Captain, Eilid invited Paul and his parents to the Lodge in the stalking season, took Paul on the hill and put him into his first stag. He didn't let Eilid down. He took out the beast with one shot at a difficult angle of just over 150 yards. He strutted back at the end of the day to the Lodge with his face bloodied with Hamish and Eilid grinning at his ebullience to show off to his parents the ten pointer he had just shot.

Mhairi, who had taken an instant crush on Paul, helped him wipe off the dry caked blood from his face and furtively poured him his first malt when his slightly shocked parents weren't looking. Reciprocity from Paul's parents was immediate. They invited Charles and Eilid down to their home in Haselmere, Surrey. While Eilid had always declined, Charles flew down to London many times staying in the Breckinridge's enormous home, which Charles swore to his mother was bigger than the Lodge. The other attraction for Charles was that Paul Breckinridge had a sister just one year older than Charles. While Emily Breckinridge could hardly be called pretty she was a lively and bright fifteen-year-old when Charles fist met her. She had her teeth in braces and her brown hair was pleated in pigtails. Her face was covered in pimples and her mouth seemed much too large for her face. She was also quite chubby and probably outweighed Charles by twenty pounds or more, he thought. Puppy fat, her mother called it.

By contrast Emily thought Charles was 'super' and vowed she would marry him when they were both a bit older. Charles, on the other hand, considered her a 'jolly hockey-sticks' type as well as a bit of a tomboy. He liked her directness, open honesty and her sense of humor. She could take the best barbs from Paul and dish it back with extra verve and bite. Over the years while Charles was at Strahearn they became firm friends. Emily loved to take Charles up to London, a place where he felt utterly at odds with society. He found out that it was almost impossible for him to cope with the speed and bustle of city life. It unsettled and upset him. He was not prepared for such a complete turnaround in life style as he experienced in London. One thing did come home to him very quickly though, London was the seat of power, power was control, and power was money.

Once at University he became more involved with the societies and the student's union. It was only once he was alone in Aberdeen did it dawn on him what a sheltered and protected life he had led up until he was almost eighteen. For eleven years he had enjoyed the solitude of Glen Torridon, then the protected and organized regimen of boarding school. So it wasn't until Charles attained the great age of nineteen years that he began to feel comfortable with city life.

It was when he was seventeen that his desire to find out more about the female form developed. When he had returned home from Strahearn the kiss and embrace that Mhairi gave him became quite a thrill as she pressed her breasts into his lanky frame. He didn't know quite what it was, but there was a stirring of something, somewhere, and he wanted more. In a way he was embarrassed with himself too. He, Hamish and Mhairi had always been the best of friends and it was thanks to Eilid's management style that they all dovetailed as friends. He wondered why, deep down, why he didn't experience those feelings for Emily Breckinridge. The boss, employee relationship had never existed in the Lodge yet everyone knew what was expected of them and they wanted to excel in everything they did just to please Eilid. Management style was something that Eilid had never studied. She seldom thought about it and it was probably the courteous way that Sir Andrew had always treated his employees that had influenced her most. People did things *for* Eilid, not *because* of her and Charles's people skills, everyone assumed, came straight from her.

If he had been popular with the boys at Strahearn he became a rave with the girls attending University so Paul had informed Eilid on one of his now rare visits. Charles was almost eighteen when he entered University and he immediately became *the* man of mystery. He never talked much about himself, his surroundings, or his parents. This gave him an aura that few students of his age group possessed and the ladies loved it. His charismatic style effortlessly charmed them. The tall, now over six feet, sandy haired, green-eyed softly spoken student became an instant heartthrob.

It became known to Charles via the grapevine that the ladies were plotting to capture his heart, if he had one, so one frustrated female student had been heard to mutter. Elaine Struthers, the blond bombshell now in her third year studying physics would unleash her formidable arsenal of charm and guile on Charles. Elaine was good looking and knew it. Tall, blond, hour glass figure perfectly proportioned, with baby blue eyes, a nose that fitted her to perfection and flawless white teeth, she could have probably made a fortune as a model but she had spurned the possibility of that for higher education. Even the professors had palpitations when she deigned to stop and talk to them in one of the quadrangles.

There was a general assertion by the male student body that Elaine was a PT merchant of the first order. No one knew of anyone who had deflowered her, although many had claimed to and many had tried. But there was not one shred of evidence to support the fact that Elaine had ever lost her virginity. The male community regarded prick teasers as the scourge of the dominant male student community. Charles had been warned in no uncertain terms by some of the seniors that not only could these teasers lead you on, you could get into serious trouble by association and inference and not even get your end away. It was with this warning that Charles acceded to the so-called trap that was being set. It was in one of the bars that the students frequented that the arranged meeting was scheduled to take place quite by happenstance.

It was a chilly December evening not long after Charles's eighteenth birthday when he and some of his closer friends were celebrating their win at rugger over St. Andrew's University in the St. Machar pub when the lady students sallied in to the pub. Elaine was flanked by two of her more attractive friends who knew their place and were quite happy to play second fiddle to the beauty queen. The lads were agog. The atmosphere electric.

The girls, all acting coy, ordered drinks, arranged themselves round a large table so that they all faced the bar. Charles's friends and some other students who were leaning on the bar turned to face the girls. One of the students who originated from Glasgow viewed the 'talent' appreciatively.

"Haw lassies, here's fellas…" he guffawed, considering his overture to be hilarious.

He was met with stony silence and even stonier looks.

Elaine broke the silence. "That's the problem right there, you are just 'fellas', there's not a gentleman among you. A bunch of louts, that's what you are." Her rebuke was made in a confident, well modulated voice.

The boys roared with laughter.

"Shit," cried one, "listen to Miss Prim. Just who do you think you are? Fuckin' Marilyn Monroe?"

"She's dead, and I'm not fuckin' anyone, you foul mouthed yob." Elaine hissed the words back. There was a long silence.

Charles, who was one of the students not facing the table of talent, turned slowly to look at the girls. No one seemed to notice except Elaine, who had only just heard of Charles Stuart let alone met him. She glanced up as he turned to see the tall good looking slim young man with haunting green eyes. The other girls were still preoccupied with the job of glaring at the males. Matters, thought Charles, were getting out of hand. What had started out to be a stupid bit of fun was about to turn into a rabble. Slowly he detached himself from the bar and sauntered over to the girls' table. One or two comments from the male supporters followed him.

"Get on yer Charlie, give her one!"

"Let's see if she *is* a blond, collars and cuffs Charlie, check her out!"

Without looking back Charles held up his right hand. The jeering stopped. Walking right up to Elaine he smiled, held out his hand and said,

"Elaine, I'm Charles Stuart, if you and I are supposed to meet I can't think of a worse place or worse timing." The green eyes glittered and his soft lilting voice was firm and calm.

Elaine reached over the table and gave him her hand. They shook hands, firmly but gently. Her fingers were long and slender, her hands soft and supple, and she smiled back and lighting up the gloomy bar. They held hands and looked into one another's eyes for a long time, too long as the protagonists on both sides started to whistle and yell. Charles leaned forward, for a moment Elaine thought he was going to kiss her, but all he did was whisper in her ear,

"Thank you for that. Let's meet tomorrow in the Bobbin, just off campus. Seven o'clock?"

Elaine just smiled and nodded.

"Can I buy you ladies a drink?" Charles took in the other six pairs of eyes as he swept round the table.

"Well you *are* a gentleman," one of Elaine's closer companions exclaimed.

"Thank you," said one or two others as Charles summoned the harassed waitress over to the take the order.

"See you later," Charles smiled his most captivating smile and sauntered back to the bar.

"Jesus Christ, what a bloody plaster!" one of his Inverness friends exploded, "here we were looking for some hot action and all we got was you playing bloody Valentino to Garbo over there."

"Yeah, Charlie, what was all that about, we set you to show her who's who and what's what by putting those little madams in their places and you welched out on us, you're a big shit!"

"Yep, that might be right, but I'm a happy one," he grinned from ear to ear.

"What's the deal then?"

"I can't say."

"Bollocks, of course you can. We'll find out anyway, come on Charlie what did she say to you?"

"Listen chaps; you were there the same as I. What did you hear Elaine say?"

"Hello or something earthmoving like that?'

"Precisely, that was it, buuut", he drew out the word letting everyone hang on his next word; "if you must know I'm seeing her again."

"Lucky bastard," said one.

"Poor bastard", cried another, "you know she's nothing but a PT merchant."

"I know," Charles was still grinning, "but so am I."

More incredulity from the mass of manhood erupted as they accused him of blatant lying about his sex life and his implied virginity. To all the jibes and taunts Charles remained staunchly phlegmatic, paid for the drinks and left the bar in turmoil. It was diplomatic action at its best.

Elaine and Charles became an item. For both of them the next two years were idyllic. They enjoyed one another's friendship as well as their love for one another. Charles became fascinated by Elaine's Physics' Degree and he found himself attracted by some of the subject matter, in fact if he hadn't been in love with politics, particularly those of his homeland, he at one time seriously considered switching. He discovered that if he wanted to do that he could not stay at Aberdeen but had to seek entry to another university.

The bath water was getting cold so Eilid ran the hot and topped the bath up. Her mind went back to 1977. She well remembered that it had taken nine months before Charles had considered introducing Elaine to her.

Not that Charles had qualms about his mother not liking or getting on with Elaine, he just wanted to be sure that he was right for her and she for him. It was in late summer of that year after he and Elaine had met when he took Elaine to Inverness by train from Aberdeen. Following Eilid's instructions the ever-faithful Hamish picked them up at the railway station and headed northward to Torridon. The weather had been appalling. Heavy purplish-bruised clouds hurtled in from the west. The rain was torrential; it took all of Hamish's skill to keep them on the road as the wind whipped up in dark squalls, one after another. Elaine had looked alarmed as she sat in the back with Charles's arm round her. The wonderful views that Charles had promised her of the Torridon hills evaporated as her did her good humor. This was a God forsaken place she had told herself, you would have to be mad to live here permanently. All conversation had stopped for some time now as Hamish, sensing the rising tension, informed them that they had only ten more miles to go as they turned due west onto the Torridon road and headed down the glen.

Eilid and Mhairi had been anxiously waiting for the Land Rover. They had been straining to see a blink of light through the sheeting rain but it wasn't until the Land Rover was about a couple of hundred yards from the Lodge that the rain abated slightly and they could see the headlights glare, so close was it to home.

"Come away in," shouted Mhairi as she held the Lodge door open and Elaine raced in from the vehicle with Charles's Barbour jacket held over her head in an attempt to stay dry.

Eilid remembered she was in the foyer of the Lodge to greet her.

"Elaine'" she held out her arms, "what a terrible way to meet."

"And this is summer," smiled Elaine ruefully. "You are of course Eilid, I've heard so much about you from Charles, and here he is," she turned from Eilid's welcoming embrace to wave Charles in to his mother's side.

"Hello mother," he planted a kiss on her cheek instinctively knowing full well that wasn't going to do. Eilid still kissed people on the lips, at least people with whom she was well acquainted. Charles had to succumb to a big hug and a long kiss.

"Please mother. That's enough."

Charles squirmed from his mother's grasp to go over to hold Elaine's hand as he properly introduced her to Mhairi and to Hamish.

Eilid and Elaine could have been mother and daughter, or even sisters Charles had to concede. They really weren't all that similar facially,

Eilid's chin was squarer than Elaine's but the fact that they were both blond, blue eyed and roughly the same height anyone could have reasonably thought they were related. The evening passed without a hitch and Elaine raved over Mhairi's dinner. The only thing Elaine would not do, Eilid remembered, was to join the Lodge party in a dram after dinner. She couldn't stand the smell of whisky she said and so she stuck to wine and chatted amiably to Eilid, Mhairi, and Hamish.

After dinner Charles, Eilid and Elaine were sitting in front of a blazing fire in the lounge relaxing, Mhairi and Hamish had gone of to bed about an hour earlier.

Elaine seemed enthralled as Eilid told her of how she got to Torridon, the tragedy of Auld John, the adventure with the poachers, the great White Stag who now roamed the surrounding hills and the future of the Lodge, all the time underscoring her story with the generosity of both Sir David Vickers and her Granddad. In the course of the conversation Elaine asked how Sir Andrew came to be her Granddad when Eilid's name was Stuart. Eilid had explained that she was Alasdair Ballantyne's daughter and that he, Alasdair, lost his life as a Battle of Britain hero. Her mother then married Angus Stuart of Glen Cannich some time later.

The torrential rain had given way to clear skies and a cold wind that whipped down the glen straight from the north-east. Despite the cold weather Elaine and Charles, with Hamish's help, had got into the little rowing boat at the Lochan and set of to fish for trout. After an hour they had given up without as much as a nibble. Dejected they headed back to the Lodge.

"Let's see if my mother can take us to find the White Stag. He's become famous now. Lot's of people stay at the Lodge after the season is over to try and see him." Charles had suggested to Elaine as they headed for the Lodge to see what Mhairi might have for lunch. When they got there Mhairi was nowhere to be found, nor Hamish. The Lodge was deserted.

"Well I know there's no one staying apart from you and me, but somebody is usually here. I notice the Land Rover is gone, maybe they've gone to the village to get something Mhairi needs." Charles had said, puzzled.

"Well it doesn't matter, does it darling, we've got you and me and we won't starve there's enough food in the 'fridge to feed an army. Let's just stay in and we'll be warm and comfy."

With that they got some left over quail which Mhairi had roasted some days before, a bottle of decent claret from the cellar and they sat down and had a marvelous sort of picnic lunch. Desert for Charles was Elaine, who decided after the intake of wine she needed to sleep it off, without any success. Charles was all over her. She was, he had discovered, quite sexually adventurous and they engaged in all sorts of games to arouse their mutual passion. Charles wondered where she had learned some of her little tricks, and there seemed to be no limit to her inventiveness; Charles relished it. Sated by food, wine and love making they fell asleep in each other's arms to be awakened late in the afternoon by tires crunching on the gravel outside the Lodge.

"Shit!" Charles sat bolt upright. "It's the Land Rover, Hamish, Mhairi and my mother must be back." He looked at his watch. "Christ it's five-thirty, we must have slept all afternoon." He turned to Elaine who was already sitting up in bed stark naked. God, thought Charles, she does have magnificent breasts, but this is not the time and place for an appreciation society, as he scrambled into his jeans and sweater.

"Slept all afternoon, did we?" Elaine laughed. "I suppose it was all a dream, all that erotic stuff you were performing, my God Charles I swear I had three orgasms!"

"It was wonderful darling, but I *must* get downstairs and find out just what the hell is going on." And before Elaine could say another word Charles had shot out of her bedroom. His long lanky legs took the stairs two-at-a-time and he was already in the kitchen when he heard the front door burst open and his mother's voice telling Mhairi to put the kettle on.

He sauntered through to see Hamish, his mother, Mhairi and Mhairi's clone come through into the lobby. The girl supported between Hamish and his mother was like the Mhairi as Charles remembered almost ten years earlier. Red hair, freckles, pale white anemic skin, listless blue, almost haunted eyes, red with weeping. Whatever hell she had been through was written in her physiognomy. She was painfully thin and she relied on her brother and his mother to help her to the large settee in the lounge. Mhairi rushed past Charles as if he wasn't there, filled a kettle and put it on the AGA. Charles who had so far said nothing raised a quizzical eyebrow at Mhairi.

"It's Allison, my sister," was all she had said as she went back into the lounge to join the others.

"We'll have a cup of tea in no time," she went down on her knees beside her sister and had looked up into her wan face.

"Allison, you're with us now, you'll be fine, you'll be fine." Eilid had said the words soothingly as she tried to stroke her hair but it was so matted and filthy she had to give up. Mhairi had got up and sat beside Allison to take Hamish's place. Hamish took the hint and went into the kitchen with Charles following.

"Hamish, what's up? I can see that's your sister and that she's not well, what happened?"

"Charles, now's no' the time or the place son, I'm that upset I could kill myself. I've no secrets from this family; I'll tell ye later or better still your mother will. Thank God there's naebody here this week, it'll give the wee soul time to recover."

Charles had seen that Hamish was wound up tighter than an eight-day clock as Catriona his Grandma used to say. He had never seen the ghillie so emotionally upset so he didn't push the conversation and walked away saying he would waken Elaine and ask if she would lend a hand with dinner. Charles told Elaine that something had happened to Mhairi and Hamish's sister but that he didn't know what.

"You want to come down and look at this poor wretch, it's as if she's been caged up like an animal," Charles had surmised. That statement was closer to the truth than either Charles or Elaine realized.

The next morning had dawned as one of the few glorious mornings that tend to be bestowed on the Scottish Highlands too infrequently. The skies were crystal blue, the wind had dropped to a mere zephyr, and the sounds of the hill carried for miles. A sheep bleating here and a stag roaring there, a grouse cackling as it rose from the heather in a beating flurry of wings. To the north the sharp peak of Beinn Eighe towered majestically, dominating the glen. Elaine's opinion of Torridon went through 180 degrees. Now she understood what Charles had raved about, the composition of hill, forest, loch and glen was probably as fine as anywhere in the world and the countryside had a mature serenity that she had never experienced elsewhere.

Elaine had sat on the front steps of the Lodge drinking it all in. There had been no sign of Mhairi, Hamish or Allison that morning which was unusual, normally breakfast began at eight and it was now half-past the hour. Eilid had suddenly appeared, walking towards the Lodge from the direction of Hamish's cottage looking grim.

"Morning Elaine, is Charles up?"

"Yes, I think so, I heard him messing around in the bathroom; can I help with breakfast?'

"Thank you, that would be grand. Tell Charles to get his lazy arse down here and you and I'll do the cooking, we're not going to see much of the Fergusons today, and I'll tell you about Allison."

The bacon was soon sizzling in the pan and the smell of coffee wafted up as Charles had busied himself with the less arduous tasks of making coffee and toast. In fifteen minutes their combined efforts had them sitting at the table wolfing down a fried breakfast. Finished eating Charles had pushed back his plate, refilled his mug with coffee and had asked,

"Okay mother, what's all this about Allison Ferguson?"

"Well it's a long story. Old Hughie Ferguson, the children's father was a boozer and a pedophile, with his own daughters anyway. Hamish left home when he was seventeen because he couldn't stand the abuse his father was dishing out to him and the different type of abuse he was meeting out to Mhairi."

"My God, how awful," Elaine had gasped.

"You haven't heard the half," Eilid had continued. "What happened yesterday when you and Charles went fishing was that Mhairi got a 'phone call from one of her father's neighbors to say that her father had died, very suddenly. It seemed to be a heart attack but at that stage they weren't sure. What followed was worse. They had found her father lying in the kitchen stone dead. They had been aroused early in the morning by the racket coming from somewhere inside the house. From finding old Hughie's body they followed the screams and shouts to a bedroom that was locked. They had to literally batter the door down to find a hysterical and weeping Allison in a terrible state. The room smelled like a.... like a...well for want of a better word, like a toilet. There was an old bed in the corner and, what were supposed to be blankets or sheets were rags, there was no carpet, no curtains. The window had been barred. In effect Allison had been a prisoner for God knows how long. Mhairi and Hamish have a tremendous sense of guilt over all of this. They both genuinely thought that at least one or two of the four remaining brothers had stayed at home. Clearly that wasn't the case."

"My God, how terrible. So you went off with Hamish and Mhairi this morning," Charles hadn't been able to believe what he was hearing.

"How old is Allison," Elaine had spoken up from her shocked silence.

"I know you're not going to believe this but she's twenty-six." Eilid had said.

"My God," Elaine had whispered through her teeth, "she looks eighteen."

"That she does, the poor lass has been so underfed and undernourished I'm sure it's stunted her growth."

"What else did you find out?" Charles wanted to hear the rest of the story.

"Not a lot. She's too shocked to say much, she's like a dog that's been whipped and starved into submission, not to mention what old Hughie got up to with her when he'd had a skinfull, which was just about every evening, from what I gather."

"My God," Elaine had said for the umpteenth time, "will she ever recover?"

"I don't know. Depends on the level of abuse. I haven't asked and I don't like to ask. I think Mhairi will get to the truth, but it's going to take time, a long time for Allison to get any where near normal."

Eilid had sat back steepled her fingers and sighed deeply.

"I should have known something like this could happen. All those years ago when Douglas Hamilton and I chased after the poachers Inspector Robertson quizzed Mhairi about her sister and what had happened to her. He knew all about her father and what he was like but Mhairi wouldn't discuss it, not to anyone. I suppose poor Allison became a replacement for Mhairi and old Hughie kept her locked up for fear she would run off just like all the other members of the family."

"Mother, you can't blame yourself for that. Who was to know what was going to happen?" Charles had told her.

"We all should have suspected, Hamish, Mhairi and me. Now it's too late, the damage is done." Eilid got up from the table and poured herself another cup of coffee.

"What's on the agenda for today then?" Charles had asked.

"First we're going to leave the Fergusons to themselves, next we're going to find the White Stag, how's that for an idea?"

"That would be wonderful," Elaine, had agreed "that would be a tale to take back to the University."

The threesome had soon cleared away the breakfast things and then took the Land Rover to the foot of Liathach. Eilid parked the vehicle and left the keys under the front bumper having told Hamish where they were going and to take the Land Rover if he needed it. The day remained warm and sunny and in two hours the party found themselves high above the corrie where Eilid had last seen the stag. The going was hot and they were all panting and perspiring. As they were about to breast one of the many ridges Eilid saw some movement off to her left. She held out her hand, stopping the others. Quickly she dropped to the ground and crawled to the skyline. Out came the faithful binoculars and she did a quick scan of the hill rising sharply in front of her. Sure enough, there he was, larger than life, like some white alabaster statue standing proud and erect looking down the glen. Eilid noticed that he was always quite alone. She had never seen him with hinds but then she had never stalked him in the rut, she kept well away from him as much as possible fearing that someone would betray her trust and try to kill the unique beast that roamed the corries between and at the back of Liathach and Beinn Eighe.

She motioned for the others to come forward and join her. Slowly Elaine and Charles moved upwards at a crouch to where Eilid was lying. She passed the binoculars to Elaine who in turn passed them to Charles.

"He's beautiful; he looks so big and so close."

"Aye, he's a big beast alright. Stay close to me and I'll get you nearer."

Eilid set off and right angles to where the stag was and in fifteen minutes Eilid had them looking down on the White Stag now only about eighty yards away. Elaine watched enthralled as the high-powered binoculars picked out every detail of the noble creature.

Suddenly, as if by some sixth sense, he looked around, raised his ten-point antlers and trotted off up over the next rise and out of view. The party slowly made their way back down the hill stopping occasionally to drink from the odd burn that frothed madly rushing downhill to join finally join other burns all clear and sparkling to decant into the loch. It was an idyllic day that Elaine would remember always. Back at the Lodge they discovered that Mhairi was in the kitchen and had been making venison stew. Could Allison join them for dinner? She had asked. Eilid had told her of course, how was she? Mhairi didn't know how to answer and tears sluiced down her face as she tried to cope with the enormity of what had happened to her sister.

Surprisingly it was Elaine who had calmed her. She went to Mhairi, as if related by some common bond, said not a word and hugged her gently at first and then more fiercely as the sobs racked Mhairi's body. As she reassured her Elaine quietly took a big handkerchief from the pocket of her jeans and wiped away the tears. Mhairi excused herself by saying she had to clean up, but Elaine would have none of it and had taken her to her bedroom and had used her makeup to transform Mhairi into a presentable state.

Hamish had brought Allison into the Lodge about ten minutes before dinner was about to be served. She looked almost worse than she had when Elaine first set eyes on her. The gaunt, saucer sized staring eyes, the thin pale face, the emaciated body, and the thin wispy red hair, almost the same color as Mhairi's but with a striking difference in quality. She glanced furtively around the people seated at the table; her haunted eyes bore witness of an abused life too dreadful to contemplate. Everyone smiled a weak smile of welcome hoping to comfort at her, but her downcast eyes didn't see any of them. Hamish helped her into her chair.

"Dinae fasch lass, you're with family, we're a' family." Hamish had done his best to reassure her. Elaine and Mhairi served the Scotch broth and Allison had it downed in no time. She was finished before others were half way through.

"By Jove Allison, you've got a boarding school appetite, racing colors on the cutlery and starting blocks on the elbows!" Charles had made an attempt at humor. But as soon as the words left his lips he could have cut his tongue out as he watched Allison hesitate, put down her soup-spoon and look to Hamish for help. Hamish just smiled,

"More soup?"

Allison had nodded frantically and before Mhairi could move Elaine had picked up Allison's bowl, gone into the kitchen and replenished it in one smooth movement. For the first time Allison looked up into Elaine's eyes and smiled a pathetic little smile.

"Tuck in, there's your sister's famous venison stew to follow." Elaine had smiled back.

Allison ate none of the stew, she picked away at what was on her plate but clearly the broth had satisfied her emptiness. She ate a little bit of potato with some of the gravy and that was it. Hamish and Mhairi were almost on a par with their sister. They picked at their food languidly while the hill party cleared their plates.

When the meal was over Elaine had insisted on doing the clearing away and the washing up, Charles helped grudgingly. The Fergusons and Eilid retired to the big lounge that was cooling down nicely after the heat of the day. Eilid poured the drinks but Allison refused, shaking her head violently saying she couldn't stand the smell of whisky. No one needed to ask or wonder why. Elaine and Charles joined the others later and while the conversation picked up a bit Allison sat silent until it was time to go to bed. Eilid had insisted everyone stay in the Lodge that night and the Fergusons had been clearly grateful of the offer. Hamish's cottage had two bedrooms but only two beds. Allison and Elaine for some reason seemed to be attracted to one another. In character there could not have been a greater contrast. The tall willowy figure of the blond compared to the thin emaciated wispy red head. Clearly Elaine had been shocked by the story of what had happened to Allison and she was making every effort to bring her into the wider circle of the Stuart family.

Eilid's opinion of Elaine had risen immeasurably as she watched how she spoke to Allison and how she got her, however falteringly, to join in the conversation. Elaine was talking about going to Inverness the following day to do some shopping. She had heard there were some fine knitwear shops in the city and she and Charles had planned the second last day of her visit to go there.

"I've never been to Inverness," Allison had whispered.

"Would you like to go?" Elaine had asked.

"I don't know."

"Away with ye," Hamish had said, "you'd love to go, wouldn't you?"

Allison had blushed and nodded.

"Would you like to come with me tomorrow?" asked Elaine.

Another nod, another blush.

"Well that's settled then, we'll go together. Charles can just stay here, he hates shopping anyway so it'll be just you and me.........how does that sound?"

"Marvelous miss," Allison had smiled weakly.

"Well I don't know I'm not that bad to go shopping, now am I?" Charles had appealed to his mother.

"Havers Charles you're the world's worse. I think it's a grand idea. It'll let Allison see the town and you girls will have a fine time, there you are, it's all arranged." And indeed it was. Elaine and Allison had left the Lodge before eight o'clock the next morning and did not return until eight o'clock that evening.

Eilid had clutched at the idea. She wanted to be able to speak to Charles on his own, for since Elaine had come to the Lodge the two had been virtually inseparable. Nor were her motives altogether self-serving, she could see that there had been an immediate bond between Elaine and Allison and after the trauma of the last two days she thought that a trip to Inverness with someone unrelated was the best thing for the distressed girl.

The transformation in Allison that evening had been amazing. Not just because of the change in her general demeanor but she almost looked attractive or so Charles had thought as she came through the door of the Lodge. Elaine had taken Allison shopping in a big way. Bag upon bag was carried out of the Land Rover. Allison had cast off the almost ragged skirt and sweater that she had been wearing when she came to the Lodge. A dark green shirt had replaced the sweater and a mid-length checked flared skirt in a soft warm browns and greens hid her emaciated legs. She wore shiny brown calf length boots, which Eilid had thought must have cost Elaine a small fortune, and her red hair had been styled and blow dried so that it flicked out at the end and gave her a sort of impish look, which was accentuated by the myriad of freckles covering her face.

Hamish, Mhairi and Eilid had given them both a warm welcome. Allison had actually smiled as she talked in a soft voice about the day's outing. Just the drive to Inverness had been an adventure for her.

"Come on," Mhairi had said eventually, "we're all starving, you can tell us all about it over dinner."

Allison sat next to Elaine with Hamish on her other side; Charles was relegated to sitting beside his mother. After the meal was over Hamish sidled up to Elaine and asked her what the family owed her. Elaine had been waiting for this. She was well aware of the independent streak that ran through all Scots, more particularly in the Highlands.

She had put both of her hands on Hamish's shoulders, looked him straight in the eye and said,

"Hamish, it is my pleasure, and I mean that. Allison has already offered to pay for the clothes so please don't either of you be too proud to accept a gift. We both know she's been through a lot and I repeat, it's a pleasure just to be able to see her smile a little bit. There are no strings, what's given is given, okay?"

Hamish had been moved to silence. Here was the third member of his family receiving generosity from the Stuarts or someone he reckoned who was soon to be related to the Stuarts. He had looked at the tall slim blond in front of him, smiled a tight-lipped smile and just nodded.

When Allison had heard that she could stay with her sister and brother she was overwhelmed and burst into tears, however this time they were tears of joy. Everyone, including Charles had thanked Eilid, who could not imagine doing anything else in the circumstances. She would have to write to Sir David and tell him of the extra staff she had taken on, she had explained to the assembly, but she told them that was simply a courtesy, which protocol demanded and that Sir David, in twenty years, had never challenged a decision she had made.

As they sat around having pre-dinner drinks Eilid had said dryly and without any humor,

"You know this damned Lodge has been a haven for molested women, let's hope we've seen the last of that"

It had been a toast they could all drink to and Mhairi hugged her little sister so hard Allison had to tell her to stop for fear of being, as she had said, "pit oot o' joint!"

Charles had driven Elaine to the station at Inverness the following day, as it was now time for her to go home to her parents who lived in Kilmarnock.

"When will we see one another again?" Elaine had asked him.

"Just as soon as I can get away from the Uni. What are you going to do, now you've graduated?" Charles had asked her.

"I thought I'd take a year off, travel abroad a bit, I've always wanted to go to America and Canada, I'm told there's some spectacular scenery in the Canadian west, but I don't know. I doubt if I'll ever see such beauty as I've seen here, it's truly idyllic."

"Aye, you're right, just as long as the weather stays fine," Charles had laughed remembering the day they arrived. He admitted they had been lucky, the spectacular weather had held for almost ten days, and they saw, as the drove south, high clouds drifting in from the west, a sign that high pressure was backing off and that they would soon be in a Southwesterly airflow again which would eventually bring rain.

They had hugged and kissed on the station platform and he had waved and waved until the train was out of sight so Charles had told Eilid. It was with a heavy heart he returned to the Land Rover and drove the lonely miles home. He had two weeks before University began again and he shared his thoughts with his mother that if and when Elaine went abroad she would remain true to him. It was, he had said, not an idle thought, many men would be attracted to her, that was a given, would she be attracted to them? That was the burning question that had preyed on his mind.

As if by some omen the next morning the weather had broken and dark clouds had scudded through the glen. Everyone felt depressed, except young Allison. The last few days had been of Cinderella-like quality and she had to pinch herself to make sure she wasn't dreaming.

THE GRADUATION BALL —
July 1979

Eilid came to with someone banging on the door of her suite. She had fallen fast asleep in the bath and had slid down sufficiently to wet some of her hair. Damn, she thought as she hauled herself out of the bath, I'll have to dry this before we go out.

"Coming," she yelled at the door. "Hang on a wee minute."

"It's only me mother," Charles bellowed through the door.

"Okay," she shouted back, slipping on the complimentary white toweling dressing gown the hotel supplied to its better guests.

She opened the door and Charles barged in.

"I've been knocking for ages, you know."

"I'm sorry I fell asleep in the bath, I was busy dreaming of the time Elaine came to Torridon. Have you spoken to Hamish or Mhairi?"

"Aye. It was Hamish who gave me your room number. They wouldn't tell me at reception. Security or something they said."

"Are we going out?

"Of course." Charles held his mother at arms length and gave her the once over. It never failed to amaze him how attractive she looked even when she was a mess. "You going to wear this tonight, Paul will love it." He smiled.

"Paul's here?" she asked incredulously.

"Yes, he is. He's looking forward to seeing you. Annnnd," he drew out the word, "guess who else is here?"

"Well, let me just think for a wee minute, you're like the cat's that got the cream Charles Stuart, don't tell me it's Elaine Struthers?"

"Damn, I don't have any surprises at all. She's back to see me graduate and she's looking more fabulous than ever, sporting a great tan you couldn't possibly get in Scotland."

"Well, well, fancy that, it'll be a wild night then. Are we all allowed to join in?"

"Mother for God's sake, you're only forty-one, well forty-two tomorrow, I may have to think about that, forty-two is really pushing it a bit."

Eilid gave him a cuff on the side of the head.

"I've been trying to forget about my bloody birthday, but Mhairi keeps telling me what a special party we're going to have, she's never been to Aberdeen before, so she's ready to paint the town." Eilid sighed deeply. She wasn't sure if she was up to this.

"You know I've never seen Mhairi having a fling. She's always been so reserved, always in control. I suppose when the guests are enjoying themselves she's still on duty. By the way, who's looking after the Lodge while you're away?" Charles asked.

"We left Allison in charge. There's no one there at the moment and she'll manage just fine. She's come on you know in the last two years. She's quite good looking in a gawky kind of way. She still doesn't say too much, I seriously doubt if she'll ever get over her years at the hands of that old bastard Hughie, her father. It's a damn good job he died when he did, or I might have assisted him to his final destination."

Eilid's eyes had taken on the hawk like look, with which Charles was familiar, as she thought about Allison's father and the harm he had wreaked on all his family. Charles, looking at his mother's jaw set didn't doubt that she would have done just that.

"Come on then mother, stir yer stumps and get dressed, I've invited them all to your suite for drinks before dinner."

"Well if a certain person would order some drinks to the room we might, just might, have a wee ceilidh before we eat."

"Consider it done." Charles made for the phone to call Room Service.

The evening turned out to be better than even Eilid could have expected. Paul met Elaine, and vowed that Charles was the luckiest man he had ever known, Mhairi reckoned that Paul had only come to Aberdeen to see her, and Paul being a gentleman to his fingertips didn't disappoint her. Not that it was a hard task. Mhairi wore a slim pencil like low cut dress and she looked breathtaking. Elaine and Charles were all over one another, to the point where Eilid had told Hamish, you might not like this, but you've got me for the evening.

Hamish didn't bat an eye. To be seen with Eilid in her long tartan hostess skirt complete with sheer white, almost see through blouse was an imposition he could well suffer. The maitre d'hotel in the Caledonian's restaurant gave them unsurpassed attention and the Stuart table acquired an aura that attracted all sorts of questions and comments from the surrounding diners.

Elaine was in grand form. She told Charles of her travels in Europe and then the United States. The American men, in particular, she had found difficult to deal with. She said that they lacked warmth, humor and subtlety, their main objective being getting her to bed in one way or another as quickly as possible. Her university training, she told Charles and Paul, had stood her in good stead.

"Oh so you were a prick-teaser then," Paul said laughing.

"Paul Breckinridge, if you weren't Charles's best friend I'd slap you down for saying such a thing, that's disgraceful."

And just when Paul got to thinking he had really overstepped the mark, she retorted, "and yes, as a matter of fact, I was!" She threw back her head and laughed gaily.

Most of the conversation was lost on Mhairi but she smiled and cuddled up to Paul as the evening went on. Eilid and Hamish were for the most part out of the conversation and they quietly talked about the things that interested them.

"Have you any regrets Hamish?" Eilid smiled her enigmatic smile at the man who was her right hand.

"About what?" Asked Hamish, always on the defensive.

"About what you've done with your life. We're not part of all this hustle and bustle, are we?"

"No, thank God for that, I couldnae stand it. I've no regrets. Thanks to you…and Sir David," he hurriedly added, "I've saved both my wee sisters and made something of them, I think I've made something of myself and I've you and you alone to thank for that. Sometimes I saw myself as Charles's father and now more often as an elder brother. I just wonder if he misses a father now and again?" He waited for the rebuke, which usually followed any mention of Charles's father. But this time there was none.

"Yes, you might well be right. I had a good father until things went haywire, he brought me up as best he could on his limited income and he taught me all I know about stalking. It was my birth father who was the crack shot....but that's a long story." She stopped and looked wistfully at Hamish.

Hamish glanced at the other end of the table where the youngsters, as he regarded them, were at full throttle laughing loudly.

"I've never asked you about Charles's father, not in all these years, and I'm not going to now. At least you got a topper of a wedding ring or engagement ring out of it." He looked at Eilid's ring finger where on occasions like this she wore her brilliant sapphire and diamond ring. "Come on let's slide up a wee bit and join the others. This is a night where we should all be happy."

Eilid smiled and said, "some day I'll tell you all about it, but you're right, let's join the children."

Eilid got to bed just before midnight leaving the others, including Hamish to head to the Beach Ballroom for some local activity.

Eilid's birthday dawned bright and clear. She had breakfast served in her room by a good-looking young waiter who pranced around in a hyper state trying to impress her with his efficiency. She had no sooner begun her breakfast when there was another knock on the suite door from room service delivering two great bouquets of flowers, one from Paul, and the other from Charles and Elaine, wishing her many Happy Returns. She was quite overwhelmed and the hotel staff assured her that they would arrange the flowers in vases just as soon as she had vacated the room. What wonderful service she thought!

The graduation ceremony started at eleven o'clock and all of her party had agreed to meet in her suite at nine-thirty prompt. Charles had to be present at least one hour before the ceremony began and he had told the others to be there not long after him as the seating of the guests took some time.

"At nine forty-five Eilid became concerned. Not one body had appeared, nor had the phone rang. She decided to call around. Hamish was the first to respond. He was, he assured her on his way. She called Mhairi…nothing. Then Elaine, it was Charles who answered the phone in a monosyllabic monotone.

"Was that the time? Dear God we've slept in." He and Elaine would be there directly.

At least Paul answered all bright and cheerful. He'd be there "toute suite". Had he seen Mhairi? Yes, she was somewhere around he conceded, trying hard to be vague. Eilid didn't pry. The 'children' had all had a good time one way and another. Suddenly she felt jealous. This was supposed to be *her* day. *Her* birthday, but with her son graduating, she felt she needed someone. Oh, if Sir Andrew could only have been there, anyone almost, to take away the loneliness and more than just a touch of bitterness that was building inside her. She had always considered herself self-sufficient but watching the young ones having their fling, as she described it to herself, made her resentful in a way she had never experienced before. Why could Douglas not be here? The only man she had ever loved, nae ever made love to, had deserted her. Her bitterness developed as she thought about the whole scenario. She had just turned forty-two, she felt old and alone and going to the ball with Hamish, her employee, as her sole companion.

In fifteen minutes they were all assembled in varying states of disarray save for Charles who had left immediately for Marischal College frantically trying to remember the instructions his professor had given all the graduands for the student procession into the ceremony.

At ten-thirty Hamish, Paul, Mhairi, Elaine and Eilid arrived at Marischal College. Elaine looked sophisticated and elegant in a dark blue pinstriped suit. Her blond hair had been cut to Paige-boy length and she looked stunning. Paul and Hamish had donned their kilts and wore tweed jackets and regular ties; the dress code did not permit bow ties. Mhairi looked very attractive in her long tartan hostess skirt and blouse but all eyes were focused on Eilid as they made their entrance. Years earlier, probably fifteen she thought, she had bought a mini-kilt. Minis were all the rage at the time and on a whim she had bought the skirt, if it could be called that, in a shop in Pitlochry on one of her visits to Ken Urquhart. The bitterness she had felt that morning drove her to do something that was quite foreign to her nature, and that was to make a spectacle of herself by wearing the mini-kilt to the graduation ceremony. Not that she didn't look spectacular, her long slim legs were displayed to their maximum, the blouse was tightly drawn accentuating her bust and her slim waist, and the whole ensemble was completed by a black velvet waistcoat and black patent leather shoes with silver buckles. Her long blond hair hung loosely over her shoulders, and she wore no make up save for a slash of vermilion lipstick, which matched the Royal Stuart tartan of the kilt.

To say she stopped the traffic was an understatement. Charles couldn't believe his eyes. Even Elaine was almost shocked to silence when Eilid had emerged from her bedroom dressed in the mini. She had told Eilid the whole effect was 'breathtaking' which was closer to the truth than she had thought she could dare go. Mhairi and Hamish talked in hushed terms convinced that their employer had finally lost her marbles. The effect on the guests assembled in the Mitchell Hall for the graduation ceremony was electrifying. To a person they all turned to stare and look at the tall blond in the mini kilt. One Professor was obliged to sit down and reach, so some said, for a glycerin pill to put under his tongue. Elaine figured all conversation stopped for about ten seconds, on recollection, and then started up louder than ever.

"Who the Hell is that?" one Professor spluttered.

"Don't have a clue," said another, "but I'm damn well going to find out."

Charles had drawn back from the platform so that his mother couldn't see the shocked look on his face. He turned to one of his Inverness pals graduating with him.

"Christ, Malcolm, what's my mother doing? People will think she's a bloody hooker."

"But a bloody good looking one, you have to admit," Malcolm grinned from ear to ear. He was well aware of Charles's sense of propriety and there was no doubt his friend was in shock. If the general consternation affected Eilid it certainly wasn't noticeable. She managed to remember to shorten her stride by watching Elaine closely, who glided to her seat.

Paul, Hamish and Mhairi, having already seen Eilid's outfit for the ceremony were more astounded by the grandeur of the building and the Great Window of Mitchell Hall. From what they could gather the window summarized pictorially, in the most magnificent stained glass, the history of Marischal College together with the Heraldic Shields of the first eight principals and twenty-two early benefactors and founders of the college.

Finally the ceremony began. The audience stood and sang Gaudeamus Igatur. Then came the opening address by the Chancellor of the University who was ensconced in a huge chair in the middle of the stage and there then followed the conferment of honorary degrees to a number of dignitaries. After a musical interlude the graduation ceremony began. The graduands were taken out row by row to stand at the side of the platform. Finally it was Charles's turn standing at the foot of the stairs waiting for his name to be called,

"Charles Edward Stuart," called the attendant. Charles had never felt quite so nervous. In full view of the assembly he slowly climbed the stairs making sure his hood was draped over his arm. The Sacrist took the hood from Charles's arm as he passed and Charles stood in front of the Chancellor, "Et te creo," said the Chancellor and Charles remembered to tilt his head slightly so that the Chancellor could touch it with the cap: that was Charles capped. He turned to his right and the Sacrist put the hood over his head. He had graduated. There was polite applause and yells of encouragement from his family and friends as well as from his colleagues who had already just graduated. Finally at the foot of the stairs he was handed his certificate from one of the Registry staff and he returned to the seat he had occupied when the ceremony started.

At last the ceremony ended and Charles could put on his trencher and join his assembled friends and their families in the quadrangle.

"Charles, who's the blond bird in the mini then?" Archie, one of Malcolm's friends, was just bursting to know.

"That's my mother, I hate to tell you." Charles sounded more than apologetic.

"Christ you have to be joking. We all thought it was Elaine's older sister."

"Some people make that mistake, but I assure you it's my mother."

"Can my father meet her, he's just bursting for an introduction?"

"Sure come on over." So Archie MacRae's father came forward and rounded on Eilid.

"Archie tells me you're Charles's mother? I'm Roger MacRae, from Beauly."

Eilid proffered her hand noting how Archie's father's beady eyes scanned her whole body mentally undressing her. Well, she thought, she had asked for that.

"Why I've heard so much about Archie from Charles, I'm pleased to meet you."

"The pleasure is all mine I assure you. And this young lady?" he turned to Mhairi.

"This is Mhairi Ferguson from Torridon."

"Well, I've never met such beautiful people all in one place at one time. I thought you were Elaine Struthers' sister but Archie put me right. Are you going to the ball tonight?"

"Yes, of course, we wouldn't miss it."

"That's grand, just grand, I'll see you there, put me down on your dance card," he said laughingly as he moved away.

Eilid sidled up to her son. "Congratulations darling, well done, Sir Andrew would be proud of you."

"Yes I reckon he would, I don't know what he'd say to you though?"

"What do you mean?"

"Oh come on mother, look at you. You look like one of the tarts you'd find down by the Docks.

"You mean you don't like my outfit?"

"Mother, I've *never* seen you dressed like that ever. I didn't even know you possessed something like that, and, while I'm on possession, what possessed you to wear the mini. I mean, for God's sake, it leaves nothing to the imagination. One of the Profs bloody nearly had heart failure, so I'm told."

"Charles, I'm sorry if I upset you. It's my Birthday. I felt just a wee bit neglected and sad this morning so I thought I'd brighten up your day. I mean I don't think it's offensive in any way, I'm wearing tights *and* knickers."

"Thank God!" Charles said without a trace of humor.

"I mean my legs aren't that bad are they?"

"No they're superb, it's just there's too much of them." Suddenly he caught what he had said and he burst out laughing. "I'm sorry mother I'm not laughing at you it's at what I just said. Anyway one thing's for sure the attendees at today's ceremony will never forget you and I would think you'll have to fight them off at the ball tonight."

Eilid smiled back. "I don't know about that, but I'm wearing a much more seemly dress tonight, you won't see my legs at all." She didn't mention it was bra-less, that would probably have set Charles off all over again.

The party started breaking up. Hamish and Mhairi decided to walk into town and were joined by Paul, who decided he'd better buy something typically Highland for his sister Emily who had wanted to come to Charles graduation so badly, but numbers were limited for both the Graduation Ceremony and the Ball. Charles and Elaine invited Eilid to have lunch with them on campus, but Eilid said she had things to do to a relieved Charles, and headed back to the hotel in a taxi. She was the center of attention again as she got out of the cab and headed for her room. Perhaps Charles was right, she thought, I'm probably mutton dressed as lamb. She hastened up to her suite and threw off the mini and put on her long tartan hostess skirt very much like Mhairi's.

She called Innerleithen and spoke to Fitz. The news was not good. Fitz was sure Sir Andrew was on his deathbed and urged Eilid to come just as quickly as she could. Next she called home and checked with Allison that everything was in order.

"Happy Birthday, Eilid, have you had a great time?"

"Well thank you, thank you Allison. I've had a great time. Hamish and Mhairi are enjoying themselves as well, thanks to you holding the fort. Everything's all right I take it."

"Oh aye everything is just fine, why would it not be?"

God, would Allison ever relax, Eilid thought, always on the defensive. She ignored the question.

"What would you like from Aberdeen then?"

"Oh I've no idea, I'll leave it to you. Maybe a book on Scottish traditional recipes that would be nice; I haven't Mhairi's talent for making food the way she does. She never goes by a recipe it's all up there in her head somewhere and she never tells me."

"Let me see what I can get you then. Look after yourself. Hamish and Mhairi will be home some time on Saturday. Charles and I are going to see Sir Andrew, we're going to take the train to Edinburgh and take a taxi from there, or maybe Fitz will send a car."

"Give Sir Andrew my love," Allison said although she had never met the Laird.

"I shall, never fear." Eilid hung up.

The six met again at seven-thirty in Eilid's suite for drinks before the Graduation Ball. Charles and Elaine had to agree that his mother had recovered from the dress code excesses of the mid-morning to a quiet elegance more befitting the mother of a graduate.

Breckinridge, of course, with typical Public School charm weighed in with,

"What happened to the mini Eilid? Not wearing it tonight are we?"

"Paul Breckinridge if I didn't know you better I would say you're setting me up, and I'd box your bloody ears, but as I know you're a gentleman and have an appreciation for the female figure, so I'll take that as a compliment."

"I wouldn't," retorted Charles.

"I know Paul so well don't I Paul, let's shake on it."

Paul had flashback to the Eilid 'killer grip' of years gone by.

"We don't need to shake on it Eilid, I want to be able to hold Mhairi at least through the first dance." He grinned knowingly.

"No, not at all. I insist. The first dance is mine." Eilid's blue eyes went electric.

Oh Christ, thought Paul I'll be maimed for life. He bowed gallantly.
"At your command Madame!" And finished off his whisky in a grand
flourish calculating that he needed to be well anaesthetized before that
first dance. Hopefully he would emerge unscathed but knowing Eilid's
penchant for payback he wasn't quite so sure.

By the time they got to the ball in a stretched limousine provided
by the hotel everyone was literally and metaphorically in good spirits. Mhairi and Paul had become inseparable, Hamish escorted Eilid,
Charles and Elaine held hands as if they would lose one another just by
letting go. Elaine looked fabulous. While Eilid had chosen black Elaine
wore a bright red flared ball gown. Charles and she waltzed around the
floor in a totally mesmeric fashion, eyes only for one another. Eilid and
Paul had a fun time as Eilid tried unsuccessfully to maim him once or
twice as they twirled one another on the floor. It was more a physical
challenge than a dance but Paul finally prevailed by holding Eilid so tight
to him she had no option but to follow his lead. Without question Paul
was a good, if not great, dancer. All eyes were on the Stuart party as they
took the floor for dance after dance.

Eilid's black halter-top dress was enhanced only by a double string
of magnificent pearls given to her by Sir Andrew. It was on one of his
many visits to the Torridon Lodge he had brought them to Eilid. They
had belonged to his wife, a gift he had given her when Alasdair was
born, and he felt they needed wearing. Eilid had not wanted to take the
gift but Sir Andrew had insisted. Eilid had put them away in a safe place
and forgot about them and wore them for the first time. It's ironic she
thought as she danced with her son, I've only got two pieces of jewelry
and neither have been bought for me nor belonged to me originally.

As she sat down at the table after the dance with Charles, Roger
MacRae rounded on the group.

"Ah, now then, there you are Eilid! My goodness but you look gorgeous if I may say so, and may I say the same to the other ladies present."

He oozed oily charm. His red face had become redder with exertion and his baldhead shone with reflected light. His dinner suit was far
too tight which only helped to make him appear fatter. Eilid hadn't realized from their first meeting that he was so short. He had to look up to
both Eilid and Elaine and even Mhairi seemed to be level with him.

"May I have the pleasure of this next dance?" He picked up Eilid's left hand as if to guide her to the dance floor when he saw the Eilid's other piece of jewelry, the sapphire and diamond ring. "Goodness me, what a magnificent ring, may I?" and he grabbed her hand and put the ring almost in his eye before Eilid could resist. "That's an absolute beauty, that must be all of a two and half carat stone, and the diamonds are good quality too."

"Do you know about jewelry then?" asked an astonished Eilid.

"Dear lady I *am* a jeweler. The best in Beauly and Inverness if you ask around," he beamed a sweaty beam at Eilid and then to the party.

"May I ask you where you got or rather who gave you this magnificent ring?"

"Charles's father," said Eilid bluntly and stopped right there.

"Well he must have been a man of means this is one of the most magnificent pieces I have seen for some time."

"So it's real is it," asked Charles who had never really believed any ring that large could be genuine.

"Real, real!" Roger MacRae almost shouted, "let me tell you, if you were to buy this ring today, and this probably came from a London jeweler, you would have no change out of ten thousand pounds."

There was a gasp from everyone in the group. They had all admired the ring but like Charles they thought it was just a piece of costume jewelry. Eilid had to sit down to get over the shock. Roger took her lead and sat down beside her.

"And let me look at these please." He looked up at the double strand of pearls. "Allow me if you will and he reached up to Eilid's neck and held the pearls softly between his fingers. "My word but you are a lucky lady, these are top quality pearls, very old, but quite exquisite. These have been plucked from the depth of some Pacific lagoon I've no doubt; these beauties never saw an oyster farm. Where, oh where did these come from pretty maid?"

Eilid was beginning to tire of this odious little man's condescending tone and his inquisitiveness. It had started out to be interesting but now she felt she was being appraised, as if she were up for auction. Still she didn't want to spoil what had been a wonderful day for her so far, so she indulged him.

"My Grandmother's"

"Ah, I should have guessed, I should have guessed. Come on then we missed the last dance with all my chatter let's try this waltz."

With that he took Eilid's hand and led her to the floor. Eilid had to concede that for a little barrel of a man he was a good dancer and very light on his feet. The floor filled up and as it did so Roger's hand moved down her bare back towards her hips. He had just realized that Eilid wasn't wearing a brassiere and he was immediately aroused. As they turned and turned so his right hand moved lower and lower on her buttocks. Oh God, thought Eilid, where do I find these people?

Quietly she took her left hand, grasped Roger's offending right, and planked it back in the middle of her back. Not to be outdone the wandering hand returned to her rear cleavage in less than a minute. Suddenly Roger froze as fingers tapped him on his right shoulder, he glanced right, no one, quickly left to see a tall gaunt figure hovering over him. Eilid had been so distracted by Roger's antics that she hadn't even noticed anyone approaching.

"Is it all right if I cut in Mr. MacRae?" the voice sounded quite menacing. Roger took one look at the haunted eyes and spluttered,

"Yes, yes of course, if it's all right with the lady."

Eilid looked at the thin gaunt shape in front of her and nearly collapsed.

"My God, Douglas, Douglas Hamilton, is it really you, and what's happened to you?"

"Eilid, it's a long story…thank you Mr. MacRae, we go back a long way." But Roger had already skedaddled and was nowhere in sight.

"Well, that took care of mister arse grabber, didn't it?"

Eilid was stunned, speechless. Then as the shock wore off she threw herself forward and hugged him with all her strength. It was then she discovered just how emaciated he was. Douglas was literally a shadow of his former self.

"Okay, steady, steady now, don't hug me too hard you'll break my bloody ribs of you're not careful."

"Oh, Douglas, Douglas, I can't dance, not now, not right now." Eilid was choked with emotion.

"Come darling, let's sit down."

She led him to her table and introduced him to Paul and Elaine. Charles was giving Mhairi a dance and Hamish had gone off somewhere, probably to the loo, Elaine explained. Quickly Eilid borrowed a chair from another table to make an extra place for Douglas. She wondered if Charles would remember him it had been so long ago and he had changed so much in the last, what was it now she asked herself, eleven years.

Charles and Mhairi returned to find Douglas with Eilid flanked by Paul and Elaine. Charles had to do a double take to make sure it was who he thought it was.

"Mr. Hamilton, my goodness, how *are* you? And by-the-way thank you for my birthday card all those years ago."

"Charles, first of all it's Douglas, I feel old enough without you calling me Mr. Hamilton, and I'm feeling a lot better now thanks to finding your mother and the 'Torridon gang' here. I wish I could have sent you a birthday card every year, but circumstances didn't allow. And this is Mhairi, of course," he turned to Mhairi on his left, held her out at arms length to take a better look at her.

"Well young lady, you've certainly changed, and for the better too, you look absolutely lovely. You all look lovely!" He spread his arms to encompass them all. Then Hamish finally appeared.

"Mercy me, it's Mr. Douglas, I hardly recognized you sir, whaur have you been?" Hamish grasped his hand and held Douglas's forearm in his left as they shook hands warmly.

"Well you might ask. It's along story. But I'm here, thank God, here at last. You can't imagine the times I've thought about you all, up there in that wonderful Highland glen where there's freedom all around. It's just so nice to be back. I knew it was my sweetheart's birthday and for a minute I didn't think I'd make it, but I pulled a few strings…" His voice cracked slightly as he fought off the surging feelings within him.

"Hamish. Get hold of our waitress and tell her to bring a bottle of whisky to the table, I doubt if they'll have malts, Johnnie Walker Black Label at least. See what you can do." Eilid took charge.

Everyone was seated all talking animatedly across one another. Elaine was asking Charles just who this Douglas Hamilton man was.

"As far as I know, it's the only man my mother has ever loved, but that was eleven years ago. After two years she never mentioned his name again. He is, I think, ex-SAS but right now he looks terrible. He used to be a good looking, well built man with a great sense of humor. Always in command of the situation is the way I'd best describe him. He first met my mother when Sir Andrew, my Granddad, well Great Granddad, actually, invited him for a week's stalking at the Lodge. It was quite a week. He and my mother chased off some poachers and helped in getting them arrested by the police, Mhairi met her boy friend, a young policeman, now long lost..."

"Aye and good riddance, is what I say..." Mhairi cut in on overhearing the conversation.

"Come on Mhairi, you had the hots for him, what was his name again?"

Mhairi colored. "John Chisholm, and I did not have the so called hots for him. You were just a wee boy then and you didn't know anything about it."

"You mean you didn't see me that time at the cottage when you and John were making out...." Charles laughed.

Mhairi went redder, Charles knew just how gullible she could be and he had touched her raw nerve of propriety. She was about to launch into a tirade of self defense when her brother arrived with a bottle of Glenlivet followed closely by their waitress with seven glasses and a jug of water.

"Here we go now," said Hamish as he pulled the cork on the bottle with a flourish and started pouring. Douglas and Eilid joined the group again as they had been in a huddle talking quietly to one another.

Charles took over. "To our long lost friend. Here's tae us, wha's like us, gey few, and they're a' deid!"

"By God I'll drink to that!" said Douglas with some of his old verve returning. Glasses were raised in salute towards Douglas,

"Slainte Douglas, welcome back!" they all roared, almost drowning out the band. Other dancers stopped in mid-step to see what all the commotion was about and seeing that it was all just good high-spirited fun they smiled and danced on.

It was one-thirty in the morning. From her bedroom Eilid lay awake listening to the odd revelers making their way home. Douglas lay beside her fast asleep. They had arrived at her suite just after midnight, leaving the rest of the party to dance the night away. Douglas looked and said he was exhausted. The Glenlivet had gone straight to his head and he needed something to eat fast. Room Service took their time but a plate of smoked salmon with thinly sliced lightly buttered brown bread did eventually find its way to Eilid's room, most of which Douglas devoured. Then he started to tell Eilid what had happened to him.

He had been in Budapest for about six months on a mission for MI 6 and he had been assured it was a short mission and the money offered had been good. It was shortly after he had sent the birthday card to Charles that he had been arrested, thrown in jail and tried as a spy. Despite all diplomatic attempts his captors refused his release and after six months in a Hungarian prison he was sent to one in East Germany. If things had been bad in Hungary they were much worse in East Germany he told Eilid. The food was inedible, dysentery and disease were rife, and it was only his superb physique that had kept him alive and the memories of Eilid, her son and the glen that, he was convinced, he would never see again.   Most of the inmates died after a couple of years in the dreadful conditions, and if they didn't die from malnutrition they died from beatings they received from the guards. The only thing on the credit side Douglas had said was that he was now fluent in German and knew quite a bit of Russian.

Finally he was released on a swap deal of spies between Britain and the USSR. His release had been just a week before Charles's graduation and he had been flown to England to be debriefed. He had then flown to Edinburgh and traveled down to see Sir Andrew completely unaware of the old man's terminal illness. He had been shocked by what he saw and he proposed to fly down to Edinburgh with Eilid and Charles the very next day.

Eilid had said she didn't know if there were flights from Aberdeen to Edinburgh. Douglas told her he wasn't sure about flights either but that it didn't matter he had a 'plane. Eilid had said she didn't understand. Douglas told her that he had, once again, 'pulled a few strings' and had a Piper Navaho at his disposal for a couple of weeks at least.

"But who is the pilot?" Eilid asked.

"Well me of course, you silly goose," he told her.

"I didn't know you could fly, you're such a man of mystery. You never told me you could fly."

"You never asked," said Douglass, "I'm not just a pretty face you know."

"Well while we're on that subject it has been prettier. Promise me one thing, please. I want you at Torridon and I want you for me. I want to feed you, well Mhairi will do that, the other bits for me."

"Can I guess what that is?"

"No need to silly," she closed her eyes and kissed him for the first time in eleven years. It was a kiss that went on and on and one that she would remember for a long time.

They had scrambled into bed and hugged and caressed one another as if it were the first time for both of them. But try as she might she couldn't arouse Douglas. She was in tears as she lay back on the bed frustrated and concerned.

"Shhhh. It's all right. It's going to take a little while that's all. I've even found it difficult sleeping in a proper bed," he told her looking down into her tear stained eyes. He kissed her gently, rolled onto his back and fell fast asleep.

The ever-efficient waiter who had looked after Eilid's every need since her arrival at the Caledonian delivered breakfast promptly at seven-thirty.

"Hungry this morning, Ma'am?" he said as he set up the table in the suite with two of just about everything.

"My son's joining me for breakfast," Eilid lied. The last thing she wanted was any suggestion she was sharing her room with anyone.

"Right you are Madame," the waiter smiled and backed out of the room.

Douglas came out of the bathroom as Eilid was pouring the tea.

"God, but I had a great sleep. I hope I didn't snore too much. I'm sorry about last night darling, but I've been all spooled up trying to get here in time for your birthday and Charles's graduation."

"There's nothing at all to apologize for. Now sit down and eat your breakfast before it gets cold. I'm going to call Charles and tell him we're flying down to see his Granddad. He'll be thrilled at that, I don't know where Elaine figures in his plans and we haven't talked about what he's going to do with his life. He can't become a stalker, he fancies doing something in politics, all to do with Scottish independence but that's a pipe dream."

"Well, I don't know. With all this North Sea oil around quite a number of folk are looking at Scottish independence in a new light, there may be more to it than meets the eye. One thing is for sure Scotland gets scant representation at Westminster and that's a wrong that has to be addressed. Take the M6 for example, the bloody motorway stops just north of Carlisle and then you're onto the old A74, a death trap. No north-south motorway for Scotland, at least not in the foreseeable future. It's a disgrace."

"Well you and Charles can put the world to rights on the way to Sir Andrew's. Let me call him if I can get him to wake up.

Elaine had elected to go to Torridon with Mhairi and Hamish, as she wanted to see Allison again. The Land Rover was left for Hamish and Mhairi to use, as they were anxious to get back to the Lodge.

By nine-thirty Douglas had the Piper refueled and sat waiting for Eilid and Charles. At just before ten o'clock Charles and Eilid arrived at Dyce Airport in the hotel car. Douglas sat Charles next to him in the co-pilot's seat with Eilid tucked in behind Charles The Navaho was fitted out to seat six so there was plenty room.

Charles put on the headphones handed to him and he peered out of the cockpit watching the engines splutter into life. There was an enormous array of instruments, which were much too complicated to understand. Douglas revved the engines taxied to the end of the runway, was cleared by the Dyce control tower for take-off, and sped down the runway for what seemed like only a couple of hundred yards before they were airborne.

Charles looked round at his mother. Eilid was sitting with her eyes tight shut, lips drawn tight and with white knuckles as she clutched the arms of the small seat. Charles nudged Douglas and pointed to his mother. Douglas burst out laughing and put the plane in a steep bank as they headed out of the Aberdeen area. Eilid opened her eyes in horror convinced the aircraft was about to fall from the sky. All she saw were two faces wreathed in smiles looking at her.

"It's all right for you two, I've never flown before. I have no idea how this thing stays up here."

"Well who's fault is that," yelled Charles above the noise of the twin engines, "the Breckinridges invited you down to London often enough, you'd have loved it."

"I prefer to stay closer to home thank you, and as for you Douglas Hamilton, take that daft smile of your face and pay attention to driving the plane."

"It's called flying the plane darling, and it's on automatic pilot."

"What does that mean?" Eilid was becoming alarmed again

"Forget it," Douglas laughed clearly enjoying Eilid's discomfort. He had never seen her like this, and indeed nor had Charles. It amused them both to see Eilid fuming at them both.

The flight to Edinburgh took less than an hour. Fitz had sent a car for them and soon they were heading out of Scotland's capital on the road south to Peebles. Eilid had spoken to Fitz had called earlier that morning and he told her that if she hurried she might just see her Granddad alive. Eilid had never heard Fitz quite so distraught. Clearly the driver had been told to use all possible speed and he drove the Volvo as if he was in some cross-country rally, squealing the tires on the corners of the fairly narrow roads as they headed rapidly towards the Scottish Borders. They arrived at the Neuk about fifteen minutes after noon. Fitz was at the door to greet them.

"Eilid, Mr. Hamilton, Charles, I'm so glad you're here. Believe it or not he's been asking for you."

"How long ago was that?" Eilid asked.

"Not half and hour ago, I told him you were coming. I never know whether he hears me or not, he's in an out of consciousness all the time. It's the morphine, you know, he's well sedated."

Fitz ushered them into the large bedroom. Eilid really wasn't ready for what she saw. Propped up in the bed was a wizened, yellowed little man. His eyes were shut and he seemed to be breathing with difficulty. Charles and Douglas held back. Eilid's eyes filled as she knelt by the bed, lifted his withered arm and kissed his hand. Gone was the fine, handsome aristocratic Grandfather she had known. Here was an old, old man who appeared to resemble a tiny child in a bed about four sizes too big for him.

"Granddad," Eilid whispered. If Sir Andrew heard there was no response. "Granddad, Charles is here and so is my darling Douglas. We've all come to see you." She continued speaking as she stroked his hand. Fitz coughed.

"I'm sure he can hear you. It takes a little while to get a response."

Charles came forward. He too was shocked and like Eilid his eyes were filled with tears.

"Granddad, it's Charles, Granddad!" This time Charles said it with more urgency.

The dying man's eyes opened. "Alasdair, Alasdair, is that you?"

"No Granddad it's Charles, it's Eilid and Charles."

Sir Andrew's eyes screwed up as if he was concentrating. "Charles, Charles, my goodness have you come all the way from Torridon to see me."

"Yes I have," responded Charles, "and my mother is here as well."

"Ah, right. Right you are. Does she still have her father's blond hair?"

"Yes she does," Eilid bent forward and kissed his forehead her blond hair spilling across her Granddad's face.

"Aye, I remember it well."

"Douglas is here too."

"Aye he's a fine lad, don't let him get away this time."

"My God," said Fitz, "this is the most lucid he's been in weeks."

"No I won't," Eilid said quite vehemently, looking at Douglas her blue eyes flashing.

"Aye, it's a bad time to be coming, the garden's a mess you know." The old man rambled on.

"Granddad it's fine, not as fine as when you looked after it, but Fitz has done a grand job." Eilid winked at Fitz, Fitz smiled benignly back.

"Promise me you'll look after Cannich for me," and suddenly his grip grew strong and he held Eilid tightly by the wrist. "Promise me now."

"I promise, I promise." Eilid didn't know what else to say. Clearly he was raving a bit but all she wanted to do was humor him.

"Ah, that's fine, that's fine, and Douglas you look after her now you hear."

"You know I will Sir Andrew, you have my word on it." Douglas had moved to the other side of the bed and held Sir Andrew's left hand in his right.

Suddenly Sir Andrew's eyes closed, his grip slackened as if the power had suddenly drained from him.

"I think he's had enough for today," said Fitz. "He tires very easily, but that was remarkable he's hardly said two words for days."

Quietly the foursome left the bedroom. Fitz had a cold lunch prepared of fresh poached salmon and salad. They ate silently, each in their own thoughts.

It was Charles who was the first to speak. "Fitz, what are you going to do after he dies?"

"Good question, I shall miss it here. I have enough saved to retire, not quite in the style to which I've become accustomed, but I'll be happy enough. Probably move to Edinburgh. There's a bit more to do there than fishing. I'm fifty-two now you know so I've got a few more years left in me yet."

That seemed to break the ice and they all laughed at Fitz who was sounding like an old woman. Finally it was time to go. The driver brought round the Volvo and they crunched over the gravel on the driveway and through the wrought iron gates. They were not a mile from the Neuk when Sir Andrew Ballantyne passed from this life to the next.

The funeral and Memorial Service, Fitz advised the Stuarts, was to be held a week later in St. Giles Cathedral, Edinburgh, a church of great antiquity in whose graveyard other members of the Ballantyne family were interred.

Douglas had flown the Navaho from Inverness to Stornoway to fetch Catriona, Eilid's mother, who had asked if she could pay her last respects to the man who for years had known her secret but had never divulged it to anyone, save to Eilid and then in a most proprietary way.

Now just turned sixty Catriona had few wrinkles and not one gray hair on her head. She was still slim but stooped slightly when she walked. Eilid was delighted she could come to Sir Andrew's funeral. She hadn't seen her mother for the past six years as her Grandmother, Granny Kathleen as Eilid called her, had been virtually housebound with senile dementia since the early seventies, finally expiring one week before her ninetieth birthday.

The funeral was a very formal affair. All of Sir Andrew's old stalking and fishing companions, many of them Knights of the Realm, attended as did the tenants from his estate in Scotland. All in all Eilid reckoned about three hundred and fifty people filed out of the church and paid their respects to Eilid standing, completely dressed in black, as the sole remaining member of the Ballantyne family. Finally the last man appeared at the door and moved slowly towards Eilid. He was small with a pronounced stoop so that the first thing that came into view was his shock of white hair. He proffered his hand and unbent himself to look at Eilid. He had hawk like eyes, which peered through a pair of pince-nez, balanced on a hooked nose that seemed too large for his almost elfin like face. He wore a black Crombie coat that must have been twenty years old.

He held Eilid's hand and looked at her directly, slowly and very deliberately.

"Ah, you are very beautiful, aren't you? Sir Andrew said you were quite attractive, but then he was always given over to understatement. I'm Clive Pritchard, Sir Andrew's old friend and solicitor."

Eilid shook his hand gently. He appeared quite frail although his eyes were bright and he had a keen grip on Eilid's hand.

"Thank you so much for coming Mr. Pritchard, it's very kind of you. I've met so many people today I don't know; everyone's been most kind. Are you going to come back to the Caledonian Hotel? We've got a Private room reserved."

"Yes, I might do just that. My flight back to London is not until later on this evening, let me just catch a taxi and I'll be along. I have some quite important matters to discuss with you."

"I won't hear of you taking a taxi, there's plenty room in our car and you can meet my Charles and Douglas Hamilton who has just come back from abroad."

"Ah so they let him out did they, Sir Andrew hoped they would."

Eilid couldn't believe her ears. All this time and Sir Andrew had known where Douglas was and never said a word. She couldn't contain herself.

"You mean my Granddad knew where Douglas was for all those years and didn't tell me?"

"Well it wasn't that he didn't want to tell you my dear, he couldn't tell you. Douglas's mission was top secret you know, but I'm sure you'll be glad to have him back."

"Indeed." Eilid was still stunned and shaken by Clive Pritchard's revelation. Taking Clive by the arm she steered him towards the waiting black limousine. Eilid did the introductions as Clive squeezed in between Charles and Douglas while Eilid sat beside Fitz facing Clive.

The Caledonian had laid on a wonderful array of hors d'oeuvres selected by Fitz. The wine and the whisky flowed and Eilid was engaged in earnest conversation wherever she turned. The stalkers and fishermen whom she knew all had a kind word and asked about Hamish and Mhairi and those who hadn't been to the Lodge in the past two years were told by Eilid that there was another Ferguson complementing the service and spectacular food that had become the hallmark of the Torridon venue. But there were many others she didn't know who were astonished that Sir Andrew had never talked about the tall attractive blond who claimed to be his Granddaughter. After two hours the gathering started thinning out and most left in high spirits. It was at that point that Clive Pritchard saw fit to pull Eilid away from the general company and sit her down in a far corner.

"Eilid," he started in a low confidential voice, "we have to meet sometime next week, preferably in London. I'm retired, of course, and I never expected Andrew would pre-decease me. We were great chums you know. He was at Oxford and I was at Cambridge and we met often on the rugger field, those were the days, I tell you, great times....grand times and his voice wavered and his eyes became reflective as he rolled back the years. We both survived the Great War, hoping that nothing like it would ever happen again, but it did and it claimed the life of your father."

He looked at her directly. "You have his fair hair and his eyes, those mesmeric electric blue eyes. Tell me do you shoot left handed?"

Eilid simply nodded.

"Are you good?"

"Fantastic," she smiled, almost flirting with the old man.

"Well down to business, I'm the executor of Sir Andrew's estate and you, Charles and Fitz need to come down to my offices in London. By all means bring Douglas if you wish. There are some important items to be discussed. Enough of business, I've had too much to drink, whose idea was it to have the malt whiskies available?"

"All of us really, Fitz did all the donkey work."

"Well, you tell him from me he's a fine donkey." He smiled a grim little smile at his attempt at humor. "Shall we say a week from today at my office?" He pressed a business card into Eilid's hand. It was neither question nor request and Eilid recognized it as such.

"We'll be there," was all she said as she ushered Clive to the door and into a waiting taxi to take the old solicitor to Edinburgh Airport.

The following week Eilid, Charles and Douglas found themselves in London. Paul Breckinridge had heard from Charles that he and his mother might be coming south to the capital and both he and his parents insisted they all come as their guests even if it was only for two or three nights. Charles and Douglas had promised to take Eilid sight seeing in the City if time permitted.

Eilid, for her part, couldn't believe so many changes to her life had happened in the space of less than two weeks. She had been reunited with Douglas, stayed in not one but two hotels both named the Caledonian, flown in a private plane and buried her Granddad. Life in Torridon she told herself just didn't take on this pace and she wasn't used to it. And now she was in London, a place she had vowed never to come. Being with Douglas and Charles helped. She would have been totally lost on her own and was almost paralyzed with fear by the voluminous traffic that sped round the narrow London streets. She did like Haselmere, however, and couldn't thank the Breckinridges enough for their hospitality.

On the second day in the City mother and son had an eleven o'clock appointment at the offices of Cobham, Barnett & Stroud just round the corner from Blackfriar's Bridge. They had decided to go into town by train rather than face the problems of fighting through the London traffic and then trying to park. Douglas came with them as far as the lawyer's offices and left them promising to be back within the hour saying he had someone to meet in the West End.

The solicitor's offices were dark and musty. Heavy Oak paneling and heavier Oak doors were in evidence throughout the building. They were ushered into a conference room by an officious female secretary wearing a dark green twin set, tweed skirt and flat brown brogues who peered through her glasses at them in supercilious manner which said, 'I really can't begin to imagine what you people are doing here.'

The conference room walls were lined with legal journals and books dating back to the beginning of the century. A solitary crystal light fitting fought hard with little success to dispel the gloom. After about ten minutes Clive Pritchard appeared clutching a large file of papers followed by a much younger man whom he introduced as Myles Newman. Once the introductions were complete Charles and Eilid sat at one side of the huge table and Clive and Myles at the other. Clive told his visitors that Myles would read Sir Andrew's Last Will and Testament as he, Clive, had failing eyesight. No wonder thought Eilid if he had worked in gloomy conditions like this all his life.

Myles Newman opened the file and with a sense of occasion took out what looked like an old parchment document and laid it before him. He cleared his throat,

"Mrs. Stuart, Mr. Charles Stuart, before I begin the reading of the will I have to inform you that according to our investigations you, Mrs. Stuart and your son Charles are the only known relatives of Sir Andrew Ballantyne, Baronet late of the Neuk, Innerleithen, Peeblesshire, Scotland. Sir Andrew did have a brother who went to Nova Scotia in the early twenties but all efforts have failed to locate Mr. Christopher Ballantyne. I take it you do have Charles's Birth Certificate with you?"

Eilid nodded.

"Good, then I'll continue." He opened the document in front of him and began to read.

This is the Last Will and Testament of me, Andrew Mackay Ballantyne of "The Neuk" Innerleithen, in the County of Peeblesshire, Scotland being of sound mind and body do hereby revoke all former testamentary dispositions made by me.

I appoint my Granddaughter Eilid Stuart Ballantyne of The Lodge, Glen Torridon, Ross-shire, Scotland and Sir David Vickers Bt. of Yew Tree Farm, Guildford, Surrey, England and Clive Pritchard QC of Cobham, Barnett & Stroud, Solicitors, of 54 Tudor Street, London EC 4 England (herein after called my Trustees which expression shall include the Trustees for the time being hereof) to be the Executors and trustees of this my Will. I bequeath all of my heritable goods and property to the Ballantyne Trust, which has been formed for the administration of my affairs after my death. The executor of this, my last will and testament and the management of the trust will remain in the capable hands of Clive Pritchard QC and my London Solicitors. In the event that Clive Pritchard pre-decease me then a nominee from said Cobham, Barnett & Stroud selected by Sir David Vickers will act in his stead in the formation of the Trust.

I give the sum of One million pounds sterling free of duty to the RAF Benevolent Fund and declare that the receipt of the treasurer or other proper officer shall be a sufficient discharge to my trustees.

I give a tenancy of my house, "The Neuk" at the aforementioned address to Liam Fitzgerald currently of the same address which shall continue until his death or until Fitzgerald decides to vacate the premises whereupon the first offer of purchase at fair market value shall be given to my Granddaughter Eilid Stuart Ballantyne. In the event that Eilid Stuart Ballantyne predeceases Liam Fitzgerald then the property shall be sold after the relinquishment of tenancy by public auction and the proceeds therefrom, less all taxes and charges for services rendered by the trustees, shall be distributed to the RAF Benevolent Fund.

I give a continuing tenancy of my land and estate at Glen Cannich, Invernessshire, Scotland to Angus Stuart, presently residing at the Old Farm, Glen Cannich for a period of ten years from the date of my death or the death of said Angus Stuart whichever comes first, the "Effective Date". Upon the Effective Date the Trust is empowered to assign, convey and make over all title and ownership of the Cannich Estate to Eilid Stuart Ballantyne. To ensure the proper maintenance of the estate the trustees shall make sufficient funds available from the Ballantyne Trust for the upkeep of the estate buildings and the grounds to a standard acceptable to a majority of my said trustees accepting and surviving that they shall at all times form a quorum for executing the purposes of this trust. The assessment of this standard shall be the responsibility of Eilid Stuart Ballantyne who shall submit an annual budget and report to the Trustees requesting funds as may be required before or on April 4th each year.

The Trustees are further charged with the management of my investments in such a way as to effect a payment to said Eilid Ballantyne of Forty-thousand pounds free of all duty or taxes as may at any time prevail. This stipend to be made on the 4th of July each year in perpetuity until her death.

In the event that Eilid Stuart Ballantyne predeceases Angus Stuart then at the Effective Date the Cannich estate shall be sold by public auction and the proceeds therefrom, less all taxes and charges for services rendered by the trustees, shall be distributed to the Special Forces Benevolent fund.

All of the foregoing with respect to Eilid Stuart Ballantyne, my illegitimate Granddaughter, is incumbent upon her changing her name by Deed Poll, or any other legal means available to her, from Eilid Stuart to Eilid Ballantyne within two calendar months from the reading of this Will. In the event that Eilid Stuart does not comply then all of the provisions of the Trust in respect to the first right of purchase of The Neuk, Innerleithen, the transfer of ownership to the Glen Can-

nich Estate and the annual stipend, shall be set aside and the properties disposed of by the Trustees in the manner specified after the original provisions and settlements on these properties has been made.

My final resting place shall be in the family vault at St. Giles Cathedral, Edinburgh that holds the remains of my wife Fiona Campbell Ballantyne and my son Alasdair Campbell Ballantyne.

In Witness whereof I have hereunto set my hand this the tenth day of August One thousand nine hundred and seventy-seven.

Newman stopped reading.

Clive Pritchard, steepled his fingers and looked down the table at Eilid and Charles.

"Any questions?"

"Well it's a bit complicated. I'm glad he left the house to Fitz, he'll be delighted at that, and that's appropriate. No one else could have done more for him in the last two years. I can't believe he let my father stay on at Cannich. Not long ago he was telling me I should go up there and move him out." Eilid's mind was buzzing as she tried to think about the provisions Sir Andrew had made.

"Really. Well I do know he talked to David Vickers about it and most other things you know. They were very close."

"Yes, I know. I'm surprised that Charles isn't mentioned at all in his Will."

"Ah, yes. I'm so sorry, quite forgot. There is a detailed schedule of things that Sir Andrew wanted individuals to have. It is attached to the Will but for the purpose of saving time I didn't get Myles to read it all out. After the first bequests there are others, which are relatively insignificant, and I'll gladly give you the list to read. There is, however, another letter, quite separate from the Will which he left to be given, unopened, to you."

Clive Pritchard reached into the file and produced a vellum envelope with the name Eilid scrolled on the front in perfect Copperplate. He handed it to Eilid.

"Thank you Mr. Pritchard. I have a lot to think about and I'll take this back with me and read it tonight at the Breckinridge's. I'm flattered that he wants me to change my name to Ballantyne, so I don't have a problem with that. Can you handle the details for me?"

"Certainly, we can do that for you. There are some forms to fill in but we'll do most of the work and just get you to sign them."

"Fine. If there's nothing else Charles and I will get on our way. We came in by train with Douglas Hamilton so we've got to find Douglas."

"I understand you won't have a problem with that Mrs. Stuart. I've been told that there is a gentleman waiting in reception for you." Myles Newman spoke for the first time since he had read the Will.

True to Myles Newman's word there was Douglas waiting for them.

"Well, how did it go?" Douglas looked at Charles, then at Eilid and back to Charles.

"I thought it went very well," Charles turned to look at his mother, "didn't you?"

"Oh, my word yes. We'll never have to want for anything. Sir Andrew's left me forty-thousand pounds a year to be paid every birthday, what do you think of that?"

"Extremely generous. Do you have to pay tax on that?"

"No, that's the good part. The Trust pays all of the taxes or gives me more money to pay the taxes due, it all sounds too good to be true. What made you think of the tax aspect?"

"Dunno, really. Just interested. The bloody tax man seems to take about half of what you earn and then piss it away on all sorts of Government projects which never seem to do any good for the public at large. I know I've seen it first hand."

"Do you mean some of the things you were involved in, in the SAS for example."

"Christ not a few of the things…almost all the things!" Douglas laughed a hollow laugh. Ironic isn't it, the thing they locked me up in jail for all those years, and I won't get into detail, but it's insignificant now."

"But you are looking better Douglas darling and feeling better."

"Granted, the external stuff will heal. It's the inside part of me that smolders away. Eight years of my life burned away for something that was totally needless. All those years I could have been with you, and Charles. Anyway let's not talk any more about me. What else did old Andrew do with his money?"

Eilid and Charles told Douglas all the provisions of the Will on the train journey back to Haselmere and browsed through the schedule of specific gifts attached to the Will. The painting of Alasdair hanging in the hallway of The Neuk was Eilid's for the taking. Sir Andrew's Gold Rolex Oyster was left to Charles; all of Sir Andrew's extensive gun collection also went to Charles, save for one item that was left to Douglas.

"Look at that Douglas, you're in the Will as well," Charles sang out as the commuter train rattled over the tracks on its way south-west to Haselmere.

Douglas didn't say anything, smiled and said, "Well the old buggar, he would do something like that wouldn't he?"

Late that night in the Breckinridge's home Eilid tossed and turned as she tried to get to sleep. Then, with a start, she remembered the letter addressed simply to Eilid. She reached into the large manila envelope into which Myles Newman had put all the paperwork associated with the Ballantyne Trust and pulled it out. The contents were neatly written in Sir Andrew's hand covering two sheets of stout vellum paper.

My Dearest Eilid, it began, *by now Clive Pritchard and you should be acquainted and you will know of the future I have mapped out for you. I trust you do not mind me reaching from beyond the grave, as it were, but I have a desire to preserve all things Ballantyne and to ensure, if possible, that Ballantyne money stays Ballantyne.*

There are times when we meet you remind me so much of Alasdair and, had he survived, I'm sure you two would have got on famously. I doubt if you will ever see your dear Douglas again. He is incarcerated somewhere behind the Iron Curtain and as I write this there seems little hope of him being released. So if you never get together again it is not his fault. He was sent on a mission by the British Government, a top-secret mission that there is no point in me revealing to you. I am actually in breach of the Officials Secret's Act divulging this much, but as I'm dead and gone it is quite academic. I know Douglas very well, better than you think, in fact, as I was his commanding officer in his early days in the

Commandos. That's something else you didn't know about me and I spent the early war years in British Intelligence, all very hush, hush. This much I can tell you. Douglas loves you very much, and you have confided in me that you love him too. I am so sad that circumstances could not have worked out better for you. You must be wondering why there is little mention of Charles in my Will. He is, after all, supposed to be your son.

Eilid stopped reading as the word 'supposed' leaped from the page at her and her hair stood on end and gave her that dreadful sensation that someone was walking over her grave!

Douglas and you are, or were lovers. I think the first time you showed one another your true affections was when Douglas came to Glasgow after Charles's heart operation. Without going into the details, Douglas told me that he made love to a virgin that night; there was no doubt in his mind. This prompts the question just who is Charles Edward Stuart? I asked Douglas to find out more, but before he could do that he was sent out of the country on the mission that now keeps him from you.

Eilid, I have always trusted you, and to my knowledge, you have never lied to me. That is probably because I never asked the direct question, which follows from the first, just who is Charles's father? It is because of this that I have a concern, not only for you, but also for his future. I have left you sufficient funds and property to take care of most eventualities and just in case there is some retribution in respect of Charles. The ownership of Cannich stays in the trust until he is in is his early thirties. There must have been an elaborate web of deception set up to avoid the discovery of the true identity of this young man and I hope and pray it (the discovery process) escapes you. Whatever you have done in the past must live with you, what's done is done. You have brought Charles up in the best possible way, I have helped with his education, his health is fine and he seems to be doing well at Aberdeen University. I know all the difficulties associated with being a single parent having been there myself, albeit for too short a time. Take care of him and what I have left to you, you must do with as you will. I am sure you will act wisely in a way that would elicit my approval. Goodbye, my darling Granddaughter,

Affectionately,

Andrew

Eilid stared at the letter in front of her until her eyes burned. She felt betrayed. How dare Douglas Hamilton reveal the most personal things to Sir Andrew! The obvious hurt. She had Douglas back but he knew, my God he knew, Charles was not hers. Not only did she feel betrayed, she felt dirty. All her guilt came flooding back as it had done the day on the hill when Colin Macalister, the assisting surgeon at Charles's original heart operation, had told her the child's father was not on the 'plane that crashed all those years ago. It was four in the morning when worry and exhaustion finally took over and she fell into a fitful and dreamless sleep.

DREW FINDLAY, HOUSTON, TEXAS — September 1993

The phone rang and rang. Houston sunlight filtered through aging Venetian blinds. Dust floated, suspended in shafts of bright morning sunlight. That was the only perceptible movement in the grubby apartment. The phone continued to ring, like an urgent messenger needing an answer. The apartment bedroom looked as if a bomb had hit it. No tidying hand had tried to clean the room or remove the litter that spread itself everywhere. Stale tobacco smoke poisoned any air that had managed to leak into the virtually stagnant atmosphere. Full ashtrays, empty beer, wine, Scotch bottles and scattered newspapers, some days, even months old, added to the disorder.

The figure in the bed stirred, wakened by the incessant ring of the phone. He stretched, coughed, stretched again and was about to make an effort to get up when it stopped ringing.

"Shit!" said the drunkard and fell back under the covers. Drew Findlay closed his eyes and tried to forget his splitting head. Then came the gut wrenching reality that hit him every morning; it was a sensation that never quit. As the booze and sleeping pills wore off the pit of his stomach contracted to give him that hollow empty feeling of despair as memory flooded back in to his now semi-conscious mind. It was as if each day he wakened he hoped some miracle had occurred and put the clock back six months and he was with his wife and three daughters. The miracle never came.

The phone rang again. It seemed even louder and more urgent this time. Findlay got out of bed, staggered a bit, tripped over his Docksiders, swore, and tried to find the phone. He could hear it okay, but where the hell was it? He moved some papers. There it was on the floor by the small side table near the only decent chair in the room. He screwed up his eyes just to make sure and lifted the receiver.

"Hullo," out came a croak. He cleared his throat. "Hello, Findlay here".

"Sorry Drew, did I waken you? It's Bobby, Bobby Rule"

"Yeah, well just a bit.... what's the time anyway?"

"Ten forty-five and it's Tuesday September 14th 1993…all day.

"Very funny".

"Listen, why don't you jump in the shower, take a lightly boiled Tylenol, get dressed and call me back in half an hour. I've got something that might just be of interest to you. Was it a rough night?" Bobby inquired.

"Same ol', same ol', Bobby. Another bloody bender. Thanks for thinking of me. You're one of the few left, seriously."

"Yup, I can imagine. Anyway, get yourself together. Half-an-hour, mind."

"Okay, okay, I hear you. 'Bye." Drew put down the phone. He looked at the disarray all around him. Christ, he thought, I really need to tidy this place up. He opened the door to the small living room and combined kitchen. It looked slightly better, but only slightly. He filled the coffee maker, switched it on and lit his first cigarette. The living room curtains came next. His eyes screwed up as the blast of bright light blinded him. He glared in the mirror on the living room wall. Jesus, what a sight. His eyes were blood shot to hell; his face stared back at him with a thick three day stubble.

He had started drinking on Saturday night; at least he thought it was Saturday night. He went down to one of the many bars on Richmond. In fact he started in a British bar, the Mucky Duck. He didn't have any time for American beer and they had some good English ale on draught. At least one good thing came out of England. He watched some of the soccer on the big screen TV which came in via satellite. He picked up a barfly called Mary Lou and it went down hill from there.

By ten o'clock he was on the Scotch, feeling no pain. He was just another faceless regular in a local bar. It didn't matter which pub he went into, everybody seemed to know his name so maybe he wasn't quite so faceless after all. Mary Lou seemed to know where all the action was and so he tagged along for want of nothing better to do picking up the tab as they drove from bar to bar until they both decided they needed to take a cab, abandoning Mary Lou's car in some car park on Westheimer. They had gone back to her place, which turned out to be an old, but in good order, two-bedroom apartment on Foutainview she shared with a girl friend

He remembered getting something to eat round the corner walking into Houston's close to Midnight. By that time Drew had about had it with too much booze and not enough food. Mary Lou could certainly hold her liquor; he had to give her that. She was tall, with quite a pretty face surrounded by masses of long dark hair. She was flat-chested or at least the sweatshirt she wore didn't reveal any bumps. Her waist was surprisingly slim and from there it all went to hell at least that was Drew's opinion. She had what Drew referred to as the horse bearing hips that seemed to be totally out of proportion to the rest of her body. It was as though a committee had designed her body. But beauty, as he kept reminding himself that night, can be from the inside. And, as the night went on, that certainly was true of Mary Lou.

She was good fun. Drew didn't want any more than that. At 52 he had seen and done most everything and having a quickie wouldn't take away the hurt that seemed to be like a cancer eating into him. It had only been six months with wounds still gaping and the scars still raw. He just wanted to forget, and the booze and the company did that, at least for a time.

By Sunday all the drink had been consumed. They had bought some beer but liquor can't be bought in Texas on a Sunday. So it was Monday morning before a half-gallon of Johnnie Walker Black Label was purchased and the topping up process began in earnest. He arrived back home at some time on Monday late afternoon. Mary Lou had retrieved her car and was sober enough, or so she had said, to drive him home. Armed with the remains of the Scotch and a six pack of St. Pauli Girl he left her at the security gate to the apartment promising to meet her at the Mucky Duck the following Friday. He certainly didn't invite her in…thank God.

Drew showered and shaved, put on a half sleeve shirt and slacks, smoked another cigarette and drank two cups of coffee. He was just beginning to think that Bobby Rule had forgotten him when the phone rang.

"You're late"

"Sorry," apologized Bobby. "I was on another call, in fact it's in relation to what I think might interest you."

"Go ahead"

"Drew, I've just had a conversation with an old friend of mine who's one of the original Texas wildcatters although he originally comes from Canada. You may have heard of Red Ericsson on your travels. This guy is the President and CEO of Petrotex. His corporate offices are here in Houston, just a couple of blocks from me. Well Red phoned me a couple of days ago and said he wanted an investigator to do some work for him in England; it's all pretty vague, but if you can come down to my office, I can fill you in on what I know."

"When do you want me?"

"How about some time this afternoon?"

"No problem, you know I'm not doing anything."

"Except drinking yourself to death."

"Don't lecture, Bobby. I know, I know. I'll see you at three.

Bobby's offices were typical of any successful attorney who could afford to occupy a downtown suite of offices. Known to his friends and adversaries alike as "Cool" Rule he commanded some of the best fees in Houston. Always a sharp dresser Bobby played the successful attorney up to the hilt. A member at River Oaks Country Club, Patron of the Arts, one time Mayor of West University; Bobby maintained a high profile.

Drew said hello to the blond, well-groomed receptionist. Various Persian rugs, doubtless of great value, lay on the hardwood floor with a variety of "objets d'art" to impress prospective clients into believing that the partners in the office knew something about art at its higher level.

Bobby came bouncing out to meet him. "Glad you could make it. Coffee?"

"No thanks."

"Have you played any golf?"

"Bobby you know the answer…"

"Right, okay, I shouldn't have asked, but I bet you could still play off scratch" Bobby carried on regardless.

Drew gave Bobby a withering look.

Bobby held up his hands in mock surrender, "Okay, come on in and let me tell you what I know and see if you're interested in taking on this assignment."

Drew sank into the leather wing back chair in Bobby's office, crossed his legs and said, "Okay, shoot."

"Drew, you look like shit. As a friend let me say you need to take this job, even if it's cleaning out the kennels. You've got to get your mind off things, get away, get out of that apartment, anything."

"Bobby, look, I know you're trying to help, but it's tough. Look at me I'm 52, on my own, out of work, pissed out of my mind half the time and that's because I like it. It's become an anesthetic; just don't judge me, not yet anyway."

"Drew, you know I'd do anything to help you. You and I go back a long way. Much of what you did helped me get where I am today. I'm only trying to help. I know you Scots won't accept charity, and it's not charity I'm offering. I'm trying to rehabilitate you, if that's the right word."

Drew stared at Bobby. He knew what his friend was saying to him made sense. He bowed his head as emotion overcame him. His eyes were tearing up and acid burned the back of his throat. He coughed. Bobby looked away.

"Okay Bobby, you've made your point. Now what the hell am I here for?" The old Drew was back for a minute, gruff, short and to the point.

"Right," Bobby began, "As I said to you on the phone, I've known Red Ericsson since he started out as a drilling specialist in the oil business at the age of twenty. He's become a legend and is a complete workaholic. He has international interests now, all over the world including some in the U.K. and, I think, why he wants you might be something to do with his U.K. investments. He asked me if I knew of an investigator who either was an expat or knew England real well. You, of course, sprang to mind. And don't take the red-ass at me saying you were English 'cause I know you're Scots, but as far as Red's concerned, it's all the same damn thing. So here's the deal, Drew. Red wants somebody to fly out to the U.K. and Red, and only Red, is going to give the instructions here. For a start let me tell you that this is real unusual. Red normally delegates all minor stuff to his Personal Assistant or some other person in his organization. So there's more to this than meets the eye. What the details are, I haven't a clue. All I know is that when Red wants something done, it gets done, fast. Money here won't be a problem, but he wants to meet you ASAP."

Drew thought for a moment. "Well, it might be of interest but I need to know more. Let's put it this way, I'll leave it to you to make the arrangements to meet this Ericsson guy. If I take on the job, whatever it turns out to be I'll also leave it to you to set up the deal for me. Just you draw up a contract that you think is fair and reasonable and, you know me Bobby, I don't want to rip anybody off, but I do want to fly in reasonable comfort and my expenses will be my expenses. I'll supply receipts and vouchers to back them up in the usual way. The fee will be what really motivates me. I know sod-all about the oil industry so before I meet this Red guy you'd better ask him if it's anything to do with his oil business for if it is, I'm not his man."

"Okay" said Bobby, "let me call Red sometime tomorrow, or today even, because he sounded real anxious and I'll get back to you."

Two days later Bobby came back to him to confirm he had an appointment with Mr. Ericsson at the Four Season's hotel in Downtown Houston. Drew thought it a bit strange that he was not to meet Ericsson in his office, but he figured there had to be a good reason. So he took a cab and arrived at the hotel just before the one o'clock appointment time. Drew, following instructions, called up on the house phone and spoke with Red's secretary who told him to take the elevator to the twelfth floor. Drew did as instructed. As the elevator doors opened, a well-groomed, attractive lady of about fifty, Drew supposed, greeted him. She had an ample figure with slim legs enhanced by the navy blue dress she wore. Her shoulder length auburn hair was tinged slightly with gray framing her face that had slight creases around sparkling brown eyes. The lady held out her hand and smiling said,

"You must be Drew Findlay? I'm Ruth Rivers, Mr. Ericsson's personal assistant."

"Nice to meet you" said Drew.

"Just follow me and I'll take you to Mr. Ericsson's suite. We're just about to order lunch so, if you tell me what you would like to eat, I'll organize it." Ruth said.

Drew said "Well, I'm not very hungry, but how about a little smoked salmon with some brown bread on the side. That would just be fine."

"Consider it done" said Ruth as she opened the door of suite 1256 and ushered Drew in.

Ericsson was on the phone when Drew entered, however, he quickly finished the call, got to his feet and strode over to greet Drew. "Drew, glad you're here. Sit down." Obviously, Ericsson was a man of few words. "Has Ruth taken care of lunch?"

"Yes, just fine" said Drew.

"Okay Ruth" said Ericsson "let's have that in fifteen minutes and that'll give me time to talk to Drew here and explain to him what I want." Ruth nodded and left the room.

Okay, thought Drew, this *is* going to be a short meeting.

"Drew" said Ericsson, "Bobby Rule filled me in on your background and you sound like you could just be the right kind of man I'm looking for. Before we go any further, there's a reason for me inviting you to meet me in this hotel. There are too many damned leaky barrels in my corporate offices and this is a private matter. So you can take it from what I'm saying that what we're going to talk about is an issue of the utmost confidence, secrecy, if you like. The only other person who knows anything about the project I'm about to discuss with you is Ruth. She's been with me for years and is totally loyal and trustworthy. If sometimes you can't get hold of me, just speak to Ruth and she'll pass on your information."

"I understand" said Drew. "All of my investigations are conducted with the utmost confidentiality and I leave it to you, Mr. Ericsson, to tell me how you wish me to communicate to you."

"Agreed" said Ericsson. "I'm gonna give you a private number where you can leave a message for me any time. Also, Ruth will let you have the number of a secure fax where the messages are stored in a private file. I am the only person who can access those messages. You'll be pleased to hear that what I'm gonna ask you to do has nothing to do with my business or the oil industry in general. Rule told me you might lose interest if it was anything to do with oil. What I'm gonna show you now might be somethin' and it might be nuthin'. And let me tell you now, Drew, that I'm not gonna even let you into my thoughts in this matter; I just want you to act on my instructions and report back to me when you have something. I can't make it any clearer than that."

Drew nodded. Red didn't mess about.

"Okay" said Ericsson, "and by the way, Drew, just call me Red, everybody does 'cept Ruth when she's bein' formal with other people. I want you to look at this."

With that, Red opened his briefcase that was on top of the desk he had been sitting at and produced a newspaper. Drew recognized the Glasgow Herald heading immediately. Red had circled a photograph on the front page. The caption below the photograph said 'Charles Edward Stuart newly elected leader of the Scottish Republican Party' and there followed two columns of narrative below the photograph. Drew looked at the date of the newspaper and noticed that it had been published about five months earlier in May of 1993. "Take this paper" said Red "and find out all you can about this man and, as I said, I want you to do it in the most discreet way. Bobby tells me you're good at what you do and I don't want people even raising an eyebrow at any of your questions. I don't particularly want it known that you live in the United States and I certainly don't want any of this to be traced back to me. When, and if, you find something out about this guy, then you can call me and leave me a number where you can be contacted. Is everything clear so far?"

"Well" said Drew "I hear what you say but can't you give me some motive or reason for you wanting to know more about this Charles Stuart? I mean, what do you want me to find out about him? Has he done something shady in the past that you want to know about or is it just general historical background? I'm sure you'll understand it makes it easier for me if I'm digging for dirt or for something to discredit the guy, I really need more detailed instructions if I'm going to achieve something without wasting your money."

Red turned his most piercing look on Drew. It was then that Drew noticed how green Ericsson's eyes were.

"Drew" said Red "I hear you, but I'm not about to explain. If you want this job, I just want you to find out everything, and I mean everything, about this guy, where he was born, who his parents are or were, where he was educated, everything! I can't make it clearer than that. Do you have a problem?"

"No, not at all" said Drew. "Just a lead-in would have been a bit more helpful but I hear you and I want the job."

"Okay" said Red, "I'm gonna go and leave you to have lunch with Ruth. I have some other things I have to do. Bobby will have the details of my deal with you and I expect to hear from you within a couple of months. Good luck."

Clearly, the meeting come interview was at an end. Ruth appeared from a connecting room and, at the same time, ushered in room service with Drew's lunch. Red shook hands with Drew, said something quickly to Ruth which Drew didn't catch, and left. "Okay" said Ruth, "I took the opportunity of ordering some white wine with your smoked salmon. They told me it was Scottish smoked salmon and it sounded so good I ordered enough for both of us; I hope you won't mind if I join you for lunch."

"Delighted".

The room service waiter busied himself setting out a table in the suite.

"I take it you live in Houston?" Ruth asked.

"Oh yes" said Drew. "I've lived here for just about thirty years now."

"You haven't lost your Scots accent, though."

"No, you're right; you never lose that unless you emigrate as a child."

Drew and Ruth sat at the table; the waiter poured the Chardonnay and left them to eat their lunch. Ruth turned out to be a very pleasant lunch companion. She chatted away amiably and asked Drew all about his background and what he did. Drew explained that he had been a detective in the Houston Police department, had taken early retirement had then been approached by a national insurance company to join them as an investigator into insurance fraud.

"That must be very interesting," said Ruth taking another swallow of what was an excellent Chardonnay. "Are you married?"

"I was" said Drew and diverted his eyes.

Ruth sensed his unease and guessed there might have been a messy divorce so she left it at that and didn't pursue the matter. But she liked what she saw. He was, she guessed, round about forty-eight, probably about six foot, maybe a tad shorter although his broad and massive shoulders perhaps made him look shorter. His graying hair badly needed cut and she liked his wide blue-gray honest eyes. You could trust a man with those; there was a quiet, resigned sadness in them she thought. His nose was a bit on the big side but it suited his square cut face. His pants hung loosely on him as if he had lost weight recently. It was the way his body tapered, she thought, that attracted her. She wished she could have had tight buns like that it made her envious. He's probably got plenty of attractive women, she mused.

As the lunch continued in a fairly lighthearted way she began to like Drew even more. Ruth had always been attracted to men. She liked men's company in or out of bed and while she was the very discreet with her affairs it was well known by Red that she was generous with herself.

Drew discovered that Ruth liked to play golf and had a number of lady friends with whom she traveled from time to time around some of the better golf courses in the Houston area. Clearly, she was a lady who was not only well paid, but used her money to live a pleasant and active life. She had never found the right man she confessed but she didn't really care. Her career was here with Mr. Ericsson and having Red to look after was a full time job she told Drew.

"I can believe that," he had said

As the lunch concluded, Drew said, "Can I ask you a couple of questions?"

Ruth said, "Well, I may not be able to answer, but go ahead."

"Sure" said Drew as he quickly reassured Ruth that he wasn't going to ask questions on anything he and Red Ericsson had discussed. "I just wanted to know something about Petrotex I know it's a huge organization, but I know absolutely nothing at all about the company."

"Well that's easy" smiled Ruth. "Let me give you our latest annual report and accounts. It'll make for some interesting reading this evening." She opened her briefcase and produced a very thick, glossy, well-produced document which had "Petrotex" in gold embossed lettering across the top of the cover sheet. Drew thanked her and put the document in his briefcase.

"Why don't you call me when you've met up with Bobby and agreed on terms? Here's my card, it's got my direct number on it and I've written my cell phone number on the back. You may need it from time to time if you take on this project".

"Thanks."

The wine at lunchtime had made Drew feel sleepy and he almost dosed off in the cab on his way home. That evening, having done a quick tidy up to the apartment, he opened the document Ruth had given him and started to browse through the report. He had just turned the second page when everything around him stopped dead. There, staring at him was a photograph of the guy from the Glasgow Herald, Charles Stuart or if it wasn't Charles Stuart it was bloody nearly his double. Drew sat stunned. What the hell, he thought, was Ericsson's game? What's this all about? He looked at the caption below the photograph and read the name of Lance Ericsson with the title of Chief Operations Officer of Petrotex.

SCOTLAND —
November 1993

The change in the note of the jet whine wakened Drew who had dozed off in the last hour of the flight as the pilot throttled back and put the nose of the Continental Airlines DC10 from Houston down for the gradual descent into London's Gatwick airport. Drew stretched and stirred as the surrounding noises and smells of breakfast being served added to the awakening process. He tentatively lifted his eye mask to be blasted by a shaft of bright light. He snapped the mask back just as quickly. God he thought, I feel bloody awful. His back hurt and his eyes were almost gummed shut. The offer of drinks at anytime and in any quantity in Business-First had been too much for Drew to turn down and he had just about drunk himself into oblivion on what was an eight and a half hour flight. He had been trying to cut back on the booze consumption out of respect for his attorney friend Bobby Rule who was responsible for putting him back to work. If Bobby saw me now, he thought to himself, he'd fire my ass and he'd be justified. He decided to try and straighten himself out before landing.

He eased off the eye mask again, stretched and looked around him. Most everyone was sitting up finishing a cooked breakfast, or sitting back browsing through a magazine or reading a book to kill the boredom of the last twenty minutes or so before landing.

The plane banked sharply as the aircraft was put into a holding pattern over the south coast of England. The co-pilot announced that local air traffic control had put them in the Gatwick stack for what he hoped would be a short fifteen minutes. Expected touch down would be in about half-an-hour.

About par for the course, Drew thought. London's Gatwick airport still only had one runway operating although a second runway was under construction. He darted quickly into a vacated toilet and did a quick wash and brush up before he got into trouble about leaving his seat while the fasten seat belt sign was illuminated.

He had just sat down when the No Smoking Sign lit up together with the announcement that they would be landing shortly. He looked at his watch. Three-thirty it read. He unscrewed the winder of his Rolex and moved the hands forward to nine-thirty. He still felt awful despite the coffee the pleasant dark-haired stewardess had forced on him.

The plane came through the low clouds at about four thousand feet. Drew looked out onto the drab November landscape and remembered why he was glad to have left Scotland all those years before. He glimpsed the M23 only a few hundred feet below them now as the Captain made his final approach.

The super smooth landing impressed Drew. He wondered just what kind of talent it took to land a wide-bodied jet liner without feeling even a bump. They were at the Jetway in minutes and there was the usual scramble to get off. Business/First class decanted first, so in next to no time, Drew found himself walking down the long finger of lounges and Jetways towards Immigration Control and Baggage.

Although he had become an American Citizen he still had his British passport. He waved it at a sour faced official who motioned him to come through without, it seemed, as much as a glance at the passport. He hung around in the lower area of the baggage hall waiting for the signage system to tell him on which carousel the bags would be delivered.

Finally carousel number 4 was selected, and he didn't wait for more than a couple of minutes before his brown leather suiter was in his hand and he had gone through the Green Light area of customs which was devoid of any personnel. Ten minutes later he was tucking into his British breakfast with tea that tasted like it should. Texas was the land of the iced tea, something Drew had never got used to.

He now had to get himself to London's Heathrow Airport and take a British Airways Shuttle flight to Edinburgh. He thought about the various options and he decided he'd take a taxi rather than the bus. He was, after all, traveling on Red Ericsson's money. He was off on the first leg of his investigation. Where was all this going he wondered as he dozed in the taxi on the way to Heathrow? He tried to remember when he had last been in Scotland but there were too many memories. For the first time in months, his mind concentrated on the job in hand, as he tried to plan his next move. Just who is this Charles Stuart, and his mother with the strange name of Eilid who had been mentioned in the Glasgow Herald article? And what was the Scottish Republican Party? He had never heard of it; Scottish Nationalists, sure, but Republicans, never.

The name, Charles Edward Stuart wasn't lost on Drew either. It was the same name as the young Pretender, or Bonnie Prince Charlie as he had been called whose 1745 uprising had nearly caused George 1st, German Geordie, as he was known, to flee the country as the Highlanders loyal to the Prince reached the city of Derby. The retreat and crushing defeat the following year at Culloden was well documented and marked the last civil war on British soil. The vanquished were then subjected to the vicious Highland clearances. Able bodied men were deported to the colonies, women and children put to the sword and their land seized by the English.

Was this new Charles Stuart also a pretender of sorts? And apart from looking similar to Red's son Lance, what possible interest could Red Ericsson have in him? It was a both a mystery and a challenge he was determined to resolve.

For the second time in twenty-four hours Drew Findlay wakened from a shallow sleep in an aircraft seat. His eyes opened as the British Airways 757 Shuttle flight out of London's Heathrow made its descent into Edinburgh airport.

Drew had decided that the first obvious place to look was the Registrar's Office in Edinburgh where all Birth, Death and Marriage records for Scotland are stored. He reckoned he would be there for about a day, would stay overnight and then, depending on what he found at the Registrar's office, he would go on to Inverness as he had an address for Charles Stuart at Glen Cannich.

He rented a Ford from the airport and drove to the Caledonian Hotel in Princes Street, the same hotel had he known it, where the mourners had assembled after Sir Andrew Ballantyne's interment more that thirteen years previously. From there he decided to go to the Register Office on Princes Street, just past the Sir Walter Scott monument. He needed to stretch his legs after all the flying, so he decided to walk. The lady at the Register Office was more than helpful. In no time he had a copy of Charles's Birth Certificate in his hands. Born

November 30th 1958 at 11:00 a.m. Father was stated as a Callum Stuart, profession Fisherman. Signature and qualification of the informant was a Doctor Kenneth Urquhart. Place of Birth was listed as "The Surgery, Pitlochry. There was nothing suspicious in that document but just to cross check he decided to pull the Marriage Certificate for Callum and Eilid Stuart. The assistant was away for ages and eventually came back and said she could find no marriage certificate for a Callum Stuart residing in Birnam. She could find plenty for Callum Stuarts, a common enough name in the Highlands, but none within a ten year spread of the birth date that she thought was a reasonable period on which to search. Drew concurred.

"You know," said the tiny assistant in a confidential-like voice, "they may not have been married."

"I'm beginning to think that," Drew frowned. "What do you think I should do now?"

"Well now that's a wee bit difficult sir, is this important like?"

"Sort of; I represent a rich relative of Callum Stuart's who immigrated years ago to the United States and he's left a sizeable amount of money in his will to him, or his next of kin. That's why I'm in a bit of a corner."

"You mean between a rock and a hard place, sir"

"Well if you put it that way, I didn't know you had that expression in this country."

"Och aye sir, I watch all the soaps on TV. Bloody wonderful they are, pardon sir. Wonderful they are." She covered her mouth with her hand in mock astonishment to mask her unprofessional language.

"So you, watch a lot of TV then?"

"I like the mysteries, Remington Steele and that."

"Really. Okay sleuth, what's our next step?"

"Well, we've got to find Callum Stuart's Birth Certificate. That could be hard. He might well have lived in Birnam, but born there? Now that's another matter. He could have been born in England just as easily, then we've no chance, no chance at all."

"Don't say that. Can you have a look?"

"Nae worries sir, if it's there I'll find it."

Drew sat down with his notebook trying to figure out his next move. So far nothing had struck him as suspicious. Two Stuarts getting married, coincidental maybe but there was nothing suspicious in that. Birth registered, perhaps born out of wedlock, whatever Red Ericsson was looking for it certainly wasn't here.

Elspeth, she had given Drew her name, was away for ages. He saw her coming as he put down his fifth copy of Scottish Field the magazine he had been poring over for the last thirty minutes or so. She reached the counter, caught his eye and held her arms up palms upwards.

"Not a sausage," she said.

Drew laughed, despite the disappointment. He hadn't heard that expression in years. "Well it was a long shot. Did you find *any* Callum Stuarts in Birnam?"

"There was one, but he's not our man. Born in 1873. Funnily enough he was a fisherman. But he would have been eighty-five when the baby was born, wouldn't he?"

"Yeah, you're right he's not our man. Thanks for your time and your help."

"Any time, my pleasure," Elspeth smiled.

"Have a pint on me," said Drew pressing a folded ten-pound note into her hand.

"Oh, sir; you can't do that, it's not allowed. I'll get the jail so I will."

"So who's to know?" Drew winked at her.

"Well thanks a lot sir, you're a real toff. If you ever need any help remember and ask for me. Elspeth's the name, searchin's ma game." She gave a high-pitched laugh, turned bright scarlet and disappeared behind the patterned glass screen.

Drew got back to the hotel late that afternoon. He had spent much of his time sitting in the Princes Street gardens marveling at the floral clock and the beautiful condition in which the grounds were kept. Even in late autumn the gardens looked attractive. After the Houston heat the cold weather made a pleasant change. He had been deep in thought wondering what to do next and he figured he had better get back and send a fax to Ruth at least advising her he had arrived in Scotland. The two-line fax sent from the hotel took less than a minute to dispatch to Houston.

He started to watch some TV in his room but the programs were all so bad he turned the set off and poured himself a Scotch from the mini bar in the room. He was proud of himself. This was the first drink he had had since getting off the 'plane at Gatwick. Something of a record, he thought. Maybe there was something in what Bobby Rule had said. Just get busy with something and get your mind off past events.

Elspeth had given him a copy of the Charles Stuart's Birth Certificate so he examined it more closely. It didn't give a lot of information. Name and Surname of the child. When and where born. Sex. Name, surname and rank or profession of father. Name and maiden surname of mother. Date and place of marriage. Signature and qualification of informant and residence, if out of the house in which the birth occurred. When and where registered and signature of registrar. That was it…except, there was one odd thing that caught his attention. The birth had been registered on January the twelfth 1959. That was about forty days after the date of birth on the certificate. He thought that was curious, but there could well have been genuine reasons for the delay. He filed that fact in the back of his mind.

Callum Stuart was named as the father, Eilid Stuart the mother and, as he had read previously, Kenneth Urquhart was the informant of the Surgery, Pitlochry. Date and place of Marriage column had been left blank.

Drew wakened at three in the morning sitting in the chair of his hotel room. He had fallen fast asleep with Charles Stuart's Birth Certificate still in his hand. He staggered to the bathroom, brushed his teeth, got undressed fell into bed and wakened up to the noise of a vacuum cleaner outside his door at ten thirty the next morning. He was instantly wide-awake. Gone was the gut wrenching feeling he experienced every morning. There was a pain, but it had mitigated. He supposed he was beginning to deal with reality. He shrugged those thoughts from his mind and picked up the phone.

"Room service," he croaked down the receiver.

"Mr. Findlay, what can we do for you?" the voice at the other end sounded friendly and helpful.

"Breakfast please; orange juice, dry wheat toast, bacon, sausage, eggs over easy, coffee."

There was a pregnant pause at the end of the line.

"Got that?" Drew growled.

"Beggin' your pardon Sir, but we stopped serving breakfast at nine thirty."

"You are joking."

"Afraid not sir."

"Jesus Christ, what kind of hotel is this?"

"Four star sir." The voice at the other end sounded less than confident.

"Get me the manager."

"Yes sir, right away sir."

Drew slammed the phone down. He should have known it. Bloody Scotland. They ran things to their timetable not to anyone else's.

The assistant manager was polite and unhelpful. Breakfast was served from seven in the morning to nine thirty. If sir required room service he could provide sandwiches and tea or coffee in twenty minutes. Drew told him to stuff it. He checked out of the hotel ten minutes later and took off for Perth proposing to head for Pitlochry as he needed to speak to locals who might have some idea of where he could find Ken Urquhart, the doctor who had been present at Charles Stuart's birth those thirty-four years ago. Just north of Perth he saw a sign for a hotel so he turned off the main A9 road and headed for the village of Stanley. He had to ask there where the hotel was and a friendly pensioner directed him towards Kinclaven, which was a few miles further down the road. There he found Balathie House Hotel and what a find it was too. It was built like some Baronial Keep or Castle complete with towers and turrets. The car park was virtually empty as he came down the long drive through well-kept grounds finally crunching on the gravel parking area.

His welcome was cheerful and friendly. Yes there was a room available, would he like to have dinner? "Absolutely", Drew said. The porter brought his bags from his car and took him up the wide staircase with a half landing to a wonderfully appointed room with views over a wide fast flowing river.

"What river is that?" he asked the porter.

"The Tay sir," he responded querulously as if Drew had taken complete leave of his senses.

"Of course, of course, I should have known. Haven't been in Scotland for many a year."

"Is this your first time with us sir?"

"Yes, yes it is. How far is it to Pitlochry?"

"It's just up the road a bit sir. Not far like, about twenty-five miles maybe."

"Right, sounds good then."

"The bar's on your left just past the entrance to reception, sir."

"Thank you, ahem…" Drew stalled.

"Peter, sir, I'm Peter."

"Well thanks then Peter," Drew said, pressing two one pound coins into his palm.

"Thank you very much sir," Peter backed out of the room.

Drew's stay at the hotel was an experience in fine dining and friendly local Scottish service. There were no airs and graces. The staff was efficient, friendly, and helpful. Dinner had been superb, breakfast marvelous. Drew resolved that if his Pitlochry visit took longer then he would gladly commute between Kinclaven and Pitlochry.

The trip to Pitlochry on vastly improved roads from those he remembered took just over thirty minutes. He stopped at one of the hotels in the center of the town and asked about Dr. Ken Urquhart. No one had heard of him. He went to one of the local pharmacies and asked again; nothing. But again the friendly staff directed him to go farther up the town and try at another chemist's there. He did without any success. Ken Urquhart had vanished. He was just about to leave when an elderly lady entering the shop heard the girl say they knew of no Doctor Urquhart.

"Who is it looking for Kenny Urquhart," she asked the assistant.

"It's the gentleman who's just left, just as you came in Mrs. Gilfillan."

With alacrity belying her years she quickly opened the door and chased after Drew.

"Hello, hello." Drew heard some voice behind him. He turned to see this elderly lady bearing down on him waving her umbrella.

"Can I help you?" Drew asked.

"I don't think so young man, but maybe I can help you. The lassie in the chemists tells me you're looking for Doctor Urquhart, Kenny Urquhart."

"Well, thank you, yes I was. A friend of mine in the United States asked me to look him up, just for auld lang syne, you know."

"Ah, of course; I should have known you weren't from here. You're too brown, much too brown to have lived in Scotland."

"Is Doctor Urquhart still here, then?"

"Oh no. He left years ago. He retired and went to live with his niece up north somewhere. That's a long time ago. He may not even be alive. Let me tell you that all us old yins still miss him. He was a wonderful man, and a great doctor. He used to live up the hill in Moulin. Why don't you go up to the hotel there? That was where he used to spend most of his time. Liked his whisky did Kenny, but it never affected his judgment, he was a marvelous doctor."

Drew did as Mrs. Gilfillan suggested and made his way up the hill to the Moulin Hotel and went into the bar. It was mid-morning and the bar was deserted. A gray haired barman approached him.

"Whit'll it be sir?"

"It's a bit too early to drink but I was looking for a Ken Urquhart, a doctor. I was told he used to live here. Have you ever heard of him?"

"Know him, know him; my God he was a regular for over twenty years."

"You mean you've been here that long?"

"Jesus, don't say it like that. I started here when I wis nineteen. Came from Glasgow. Ma faither kicked me oot the hoose. I lied aboot ma age an' got a job in the bar. I've bin here ever since. I'm fifty-three noo."

"Drew Findlay." Drew held out his hand.

The barman shook it warmly. "Johnnie Miller, at your service."

Drew sat down at the bar. "Okay let's have wee malt. Somewhere in the world it's six o'clock."

"Now we're talkin'; a man after ma ain heart!"

Johnnie didn't ask. He just reached for the bottle of Macallan and started pouring.

"I take it the Macallan's all right with you, it wis Kenny's favorite tipple, his niece's too."

"Fine," said Drew, "you mean you met his niece?"

"Jesus, don't remind me. A smasher, a bloody smasher she wis, legs up tae her armpits, tits oot tae here." Johnnie placed his cupped hands in front of him. "But class, Jesus Christ, she had class. Ask the boys who are old enough tae remember at the rifle club. They're still talkin' aboot it tae this day. Blew the arse right oot the bull she did. Five shots wan after the ither. So fast they thought it wis a bloody machine gun goin' aff. The Scottish Annie Oakley they christened her."

Drew held up his glass to stop the verbal diarrhea. Johnnie was on a roll.

"So tell me Johnnie, what was his niece doing here?"

"Oh the first time she came she had niver met her Uncle, then aboot a year later she came tae hiv the wean; a wee boy. Then she came back wan Christmas, Gawd, it wis years ago. Ah think the wee boy wis aboot ten by then. Her boy friend came too tae surprise her, we had a great time."

"Was he the baby's father?"

"Who, like?"

"The boy friend."

"Naw. Ah don't think so. He wis a real nice gent as well. His name wis........." Johnnie searched his memory, "Douglas something, that's whit it wis, Douglas. He liked Glenmorangie. Ah sometimes forget names but Ah niver forget whit they drink, funny that, isn't it?"

"That's the sign of a good barman," said Drew, "few and far between."

"Thank you, sir." Johnnie poured the second Macallan. "Good stuff, eh?"

"It is indeed. Anyway this Douglas man wasn't the father of the niece's boy, you don't know who was?"

"Naw, that's right. She niver did speak aboot him. Some o' the young blades tried their hand, so tae speak. But they had nae chance, nae chance at a'. The great thing wis that she wis niver nasty tae onybody. She aye smiled, made them feel that they were great guys, an' then wid bugger aff hame!"

"So what happened to Ken?" Drew was becoming a bit impatient with Johnnie's rambling and he needed to get on. On the basis that he would find Doctor Urquhart in Pitlochry he had decided to stay another night at Balathie. It was just too good a deal to turn down.

"Kenny? Aye, he retired at sixty-five, sold the hoose just up the road," Johnnie pointed his thumb over his shoulder to the rear of the hotel, "an' as far as Ah know went tae live wi' Eilid. But whaur he is noo, Ah hiv no idea."

"Do you know anybody who might?"

Johnnie thought about Drew's question hard and long. Eventually he said,

"Tell ye whit, go tae whit was Kenny's surgery, it's doon Scotland's Brae, Ah'll show ye the way an ask in there. Ah wid think that when Kenny left he wid leave an address whaur he could be contacted, mind you that's fifteen, maybe sixteen years ago. Maybe his replacement knows, but the wan that did replace him didnae stay long, naebody liked him. Mind you, Kenny wis a hard act tae follow."

"People liked him then?"

"Oh aye, he wis the best."

"Well thanks for the help. I'll do what you say. What do I owe you?"

"Ach call it a couple of quid, great tae talk tae you."

"Have one on me," Drew put a five-pound note on the bar.

"Man yer a real gent, come back an' see us, noo."

Drew followed the simple directions Johnnie had given him and was at the surgery in a couple of minutes. The young girl on reception was very pleasant. Yes, she had heard Doctor Urquhart's name mentioned but other than that she didn't know anything about him. She told Drew to wait for a minute. The doctor was just seeing his last patient and she thought Drew would be able to talk to him.

"Robert Findlay," the doctor shook hands and introduced himself.

Drew grinned back. "Drew Findlay."

"Well there's a coincidence," said the doctor. "Which part of Scotland do you hail from?"

"I live in the United Sates now," said Drew, "but originally Kirkintilloch, well Lenzie actually."

"Oh right, never been there but I've certainly heard of Lenzie, there's a mental institution there."

"You're right, Woodlea, I think it's called. I forgot all about its existence, actually."

"You've been away for some time then?"

"Uh, uh. About thirty years now, a lifetime."

"Indeed, how can I help you?"

"I was trying to get hold of Doctor Urquhart; I understand this used to be his practice."

"Yes it was. I was not Kenny's immediate successor but the doctor who took over didn't last long, a couple of years, then I came. But I do know about Ken Urquhart, he's dead I'm afraid, died three years ago."

Drew's heart sank. "Where was he when he died?"

"You know I don't know precisely. We had a phone number for him and when my nurse called to get some background information on a patient who had returned after some years, she was told that he had passed away. Let me see if I can find out just where it was."

"No, don't bother," said Drew, it's going to serve no purpose if he's gone, he's gone."

"Is there anything else I can help you with?"

"No, no there's not. Thanks for your time Doctor Findlay." Drew smiled, shook hands and left.

He got back in the car and sat silent. Another dead-end, literally. This wasn't getting him anywhere. He had to find someone who knew Charles and wasn't related to him. He drove back to the hotel dejected. He prepared a fax for Ruth Rivers, which virtually said nothing and got the hotel to send it off to her.

He was just turning to go into the bar when he saw some daily papers on the table in reception. He looked at one and the tabloid's headline screamed in bold print, 'Will ye no come back again?' And then below in smaller but just as bold it read, 'He's Back!' He flipped open the paper and there staring back at him was Charles Stuart!

He picked up the Scotsman, one of the more sophisticated local journals. Sure enough Charles was on the front page again. The headline read 'Bonnie Prince Charlie?' With a sub heading which read, 'Newly elected leader of the SRP claims to be a descendant of Bonnie Prince Charlie.' There then followed a short biography of Charles and his background. *Educated at Strahearn Public School and gained an Honors Degree in Political Science at Aberdeen University,* it went on to review his activities as a Scottish Nationalist and his popularity as the presenter of the current affairs program called Scotland Today on Grampian TV. Drew read on. *Despite attempts to contact Mr. Stuart calls had not been returned from his Cannich Estate. Neither was his mother, Eilid Ballantyne, available for comment.*

Eilid Stuart must have married again if she was now Mrs. Ballantyne. Charles Stuart was becoming more of a conundrum. Drew decided it was time for a call to his little girl Elspeth in Register House, Edinburgh. First thing after breakfast the following morning he put a call into Elspeth. She took down notes of what Drew's requirements and asked him to call back in an hour.

Drew spent the next hour walking round the grounds of Balathie House. He went down to the Tay, which was swirling angrily, a muddy brown after recent heavy rain. The debris of branches and even small trees floated by as the river raced on its way to Dundee where it disgorged into the sea at Carnoustie on the east coast. The hour went by slowly.

Elspeth had found only one answer to his questions. Yes, there was a record of Charles Stuart's marriage to an Elaine Struthers. It had taken place at King's Chapel at Aberdeen University in the spring of 1982. There was no record of an Eilid Stuart marrying anyone. There was no record of a Ballantyne marrying anyone not within the last ten years anyway. It was becoming clearer to Drew that he was really wasting his time and Red Ericsson's money.

He made his way back into reception to find Laurie, the manager's secretary who was on duty.

"Mr. Findlay, what can I do for you?"

"Laurie, have you ever heard of a school called Strahearn?"

"Sure. It's well known and *very* prestigious."

"Where is it?"

"Can't be more than twenty miles from here, if that."

"You're kidding."

"No I'm not. It's close to Bridge of Earn, that's on the Dundee road. Let me get you a map."

Laurie went into the office and produced an Ordnance Survey map of the area. She opened it up and Drew stood by her right shoulder.

"Here we are," she said pointing, "right here."

"My God it's on our doorstep. Okay can you book me in for another night please?"

"My pleasure, you're going to become quite a regular, I can see that. Is it your work that brings you here?"

"Well, yes and no. I haven't been in Scotland for years, I should have come in the spring though, it's pretty dull although today's been better. I thought it would have been colder."

"Don't say that," said Laurie, "that's tempting fate."

Drew drove through the gates of Strahearn at just before ten o'clock the next morning. He found the Bursar's office thanks to help from a polite schoolboy and sat down to wait for the Bursar finishing a phone call.

"You're not from the press are you?" the abrupt question was thrown at him by the florid faced man who came barging out of the office marked Bursar.

"No, my name's Drew Findlay," the bursar ignored the proffered hand, "and I'm not the press, nor anything to do with the press."

"I'm Norman Evans, the bursar, how may I help?"

"Why did you think I was from the press?"

"They've pestered the life out of me over this Bonnie Prince Charlie thing. The whole bloody world's gone mad. You must have seen the papers, and now TV has got hold of it, God knows where it will all end."

"I did see something in the papers. Let me explain before we go any farther. I'm a private investigator from the United States, I live in Houston, Texas, but I'm Scots by birth."

"Dear God," cried the harassed bursar, "private investigator, what next? I suppose you're looking for details on Charles Edward Stuart of that ilk."

"Right on the money," Drew smiled.

"Dear God, has it to do with his claim to the throne?"

"What do you mean what throne?"

'Well it's reported in some papers that he claims to be a direct descendant of Bonnie Prince Charlie, the Young Pretender of 1745 fame or infamy and as such he has more of a right to the British throne than the incumbent monarch. Nonsense of course, but try telling the press that."

"Wow!" Drew was taken aback. He hadn't read that in the paper, what a turn up he thought. He recalled Bobby's story on the fate of Red's wife and child thirty-six years earlier. What possible connection could there be between this man claiming to be a descendant of Prince Charles and Red Ericsson? The only common bond that Ericsson has is the uncanny likeness to his surviving son Lance, Drew thought. All of these thoughts coursed through his mind as the Bursar went on about the press, the media, and how harassed he was.

"Well it's not because of that," Drew continued, "I just want to find out more about this Charles Stuart for someone in the States who thinks he may be a relative. I'm looking for some background information, that's all."

"Why don't you just go to the mother, Mrs. Stuart? Her son's become an overnight celebrity, not that he wasn't before. His TV program Scotland Today was very popular. Most mothers would be delighted to rabbit on about their son. Mind you, he has great charisma and talent, I have to admit. He is an excellent communicator."

"I don't want to go near her and maybe alarm her. This has to be kept rather confidential."

"All right, I'll do what I can but that won't be much. He left the school in 1975 that's eighteen years ago."

"Are there not any masters who might remember him or anything about him?"

"Do you know I can't think of anyone who is left that would remember anything? We have over three hundred and fifty pupils and there's constant change. Most of the masters, who were here when the last Headmaster retired, are gone. Changed with the coming of the new Headmaster, it often happens that way you know, new broom sweeps clean and all that."

"Who was the Headmaster who retired?"

"Oh, that would be John Forsyth. Very competent Head; well liked too, so I gather."

"So you didn't know Forsyth?"

"Heavens no, he must be gone what, seventeen, eighteen years now."

"Indeed." This was getting nowhere Drew thought. He was about to wrap up the conversation as the Bursar was beginning to irritate him. But the Bursar was off deep in his own thoughts.

"Still pretty active though, still pretty active. Attends some of the FP dinners."

"Who? What?" Drew asked.

"Forsyth still goes to the Strahearn Club dinners every year. I think his wife goes too."

"What's the Strahearn Club?"

"Well it's the Club you join when you leave the school. Keeps you in touch with former pupils and you get the school magazine every year. The FPs have a dinner in Perth and one in London, at least I think it's Perth, maybe it's Glasgow…" He hesitated so Drew cut in.

"Do you know where Forsyth lives?"

"Not exactly; I think he's in Auchterarder. He bought a bungalow in one of the new developments. Let me ask Matron, she knows everything about everybody. She's been here twenty years and will remember John. Hang on and I'll call her."

Fifteen minutes later Drew was heading out the school gates with John Forsyth's address written in his diary. Auchterarder was only about twelve miles from the school and he found the house quite easily; it was located to the east of the town and was within walking distance of Auchterarder Golf Club, not far from Gleneagles. A trim, elderly lady answered the door and Drew introduced himself and gave her a rough outline of why he wanted to speak to her husband.

"Did you go to Strahearn, then?" She inquired.

"No ma'am. My father wasn't well off enough to send us to boarding school. But I did go to Lenzie Academy."

"As far as I know it still has a good reputation, but that's information from years ago we've sort of lost touch with all our friends in the scholastic field. John's gone out for a walk he'll be back shortly, I'm sure he'd like to speak to you. Do you live in the United States? You have a sort of American accent"

"Yes. Yes I do. If it's all right with you I'll wait in the car until John returns."

"You'll do no such thing. Come in and sit yourself down. I've just put on the kettle for a cup of tea; John will be back any moment."

They sat in the neat kitchen all light and bright while Mrs. Forsyth poured the tea.

"A chocolate digestive?" She offered Drew a plate of assorted biscuits.

"Wonderful," said Drew, "you can't get these in the States, well you can if you go looking but I've almost given up eating biscuits, or cookies as the Americans call them."

"Does your wife not buy them for you?"

"I'm not married, was, but not now."

"Oh dear I am sorry."

Drew shrugged not wishing to continue the line of conversation,

"That's the way it goes, I suppose." Mrs. Forsyth tried to sound sympathetic.

John Forsyth's timing could not have been better. The back door swung open and John came in clutching a brown paper bag.

"Ah, Alice, I knew we had guests. Saw the car outside." John was puffing a bit from his exertions coming up the hill, which led to the house.

He looked Drew up and down as he made a mental assessment. Not too tall, nice eyes, wavy hair going gray, broad, very broad shoulders, slim hips not carrying too much excess weight. Not bad for someone in their fifties. All of this took les than ten seconds; he hadn't been a schoolmaster and then a Headmaster all those years for nothing.

Drew waited still the scan finished.

He held out his hand, "Drew Findlay, pleased to meet you. I do hope you don't mind me coming along in this impromptu fashion without as much as a 'phone call but I was at your old school this morning and the Matron kindly gave me your address with no phone number, so here I am."

"John Forsyth." He shook Drew's hand not taking his eyes off Drew's. John looked in good shape for someone in his eighties. "Don't apologize, Alice and I could do with a little excitement from time to time, couldn't we Alice."

Alice smiled and nodded.

"So what brings you to this part of the world?"

Drew explained as succinctly as possible what his mission was all about. John listened in silence while Alice made a new pot of tea.

When he had finished John said, "Tell you what, young fella-me-lad lets go into my study, it's a bit more comfortable there and Alice can bring us our tea, won't you dear?"

"Yes, darling" she answered resignedly.

John led the way to the study. It had a familiar layout. A tooled leather inlaid burr walnut desk, a globe sitting by the side of the desk, a print of Monarch of the Glen, the famous painting by Sir Edwin Landseer prominent on one of the oak paneled walls. Other photographs and memorabilia hung all around with the odd golfing trophy exhibited. Then there were books. Books everywhere on shelves, tabletops, nooks and crannies, books filled every conceivable space.

John motioned to a tall winged back leather chair. Drew sat down.

"Right; Charles Stuart and his mother Eilid. You ask do I remember them? My God, I'll never forget them! Charles got into the school just before his twelfth birthday, actively sponsored by Sir Andrew Ballantyne. Sir Andrew and I were good friends. He was on the Board of Governors, a great benefactor to the school. I had reservations, not about the boy's intelligence, but about his health. He looked far from well. Sir Andrew really didn't come clean with me on that one. The lad had a heart problem. Bloody nearly lost him.

"How do you mean?" asked Drew.

"Damn nearly died on us. Took some fit or seizure; had us all up to hi-do. He was rushed to hospital in Glasgow and had a major, I mean major, heart operation to fix a faulty valve or something. Came out smelling like a rose. Couldn't believe the change. From white as a ghost, almost blue at times, to pink and healthy, that's the best I can do to describe it. After that he was fine. Passed his A levels with flying colors and then went straight to Aberdeen University, I think. Or did he take some time off? Can't remember. All I know is he graduated with honors either four or five years later."

"You met Mrs. Stuart or Eilid."

"My God yes." John dropped his voice to a confidential whisper. "Wish I had been a bit younger, eh. I was fifty-nine at the time. Gorgeous girl. Great figure, long blond hair, sharp blue eyes, she could easily have been a model she was so good looking. I had to fight off old Henry Blake the Bursar at the time. All over her he was, dirty old devil."

Drew smiled inwardly, there was nothing like a bit of hypocrisy to keep the ball rolling.

"So who in fact was she? How did she know, or what was her connection to Sir Andrew?"

"Well there's the thing. She was Sir Andrew's granddaughter, or so he said."

"How come her name was Stuart?"

"That's another thing. Her father was Alasdair Ballantyne and we assumed that Eilid's mother, a certain Catriona Urquhart had been married to Alasdair. But there's no record of any such marriage having taken place. Catriona only married once and that was to an Angus Stuart. I leave you to draw your own conclusions.

"This Catriona Stuart, did you ever meet her?"

"No. Eilid was hardly ever here. We certainly never met her mother."

"You said Catriona's maiden name was Urquhart. Any relation to Kenneth Urquhart, a doctor who had a practice in Pitlochry?"

"Yes. Her brother, Eilid's uncle. He came down lickety-split when Charles took his seizure. Very competent too, nice man. He cut through all the red tape that this National Health Service bombards you with. Got young Charles admitted to hospital in no time and with the best surgeon possible."

Alice came in with the tea and more biscuits. "Drew, may I call you Drew."

"Of course."

"It's getting near lunch. Would you like a sandwich or something, you must be famished?"

"No thanks Mrs. Forsyth. I'm fine really. But I tell you what, as you've been so nice and John's being so helpful why don't I take you to lunch, it would be my pleasure."

Alice's eyes gleamed. She looked over at John.

"Capital, that would be very nice. You don't have to do this, you know. There's not much in the village. There's Gleneagles just down the road but it's terribly expensive, so I hear, and not very good."

"I'm staying at Balathie House it can't be more than thirty minutes from here. Come on, let me give you an afternoon out and I'll bring you back. It's the least I can do. You're the first person I've met who knew both Eilid and Charles."

"What about Ken Urquhart, I don't know where he is now, but you should be able to find him, I think."

"I tried that and I do know where he is." Drew pointed up at the ceiling, heavenwards.

"Dear me; he's dead then is he?"

"He died three years ago."

"How sad. He was such a nice man, a man's man if you know what I mean."

"Yes I do," said Drew.

The drive to Balathie was quick and smooth. The Forsyth's enjoyed their lunch immensely and they were only too happy to adjourn to the bar where Alice had a gin and tonic and John had a large malt.

"So Eilid Stuart was a bit of a looker then?" Drew resurrected the conversation on the Stuarts.

It was Alice who butted in. "Yes she was very beautiful, John had trouble keeping his hands off her."

"Oh come on now darling, I'm just an admirer of the female form."

Drew could see John's eyes glazing over, going back all those years as he conjured up a picture of Eilid Stuart.

"She was quite the most attractive mother ever to come to the school." John said convincingly.

"Did she only come once?"

"No she came one more time that I can recall when she brought Charles back from an extended leave-out as I remember. It was towards the end of October. It was on Cadet Day, that's a Friday, we ran a Cadet Cadre course, bit of extra revenue, you know. She gave a display of shooting to the boys the like of which they had never seen, before or since. Quite remarkable apparently. I wasn't there but it became a legend at the school for many years."

Drew took a mental note.

"Really. She seems to make a habit of showing off with the rifle."

"How do you mean?"

"Oh nothing important. There was a similar incident reported at the Pitlochry Rifle club. But that was just after she had given birth to Charles. Did you ever meet Mr. Stuart?"

"No never, never a mention of him, neither by Charles nor his mother. It was rather strange that, usually a child will talk about his parents even if the father is no longer around. Didn't happen to my knowledge in this case."

"So she didn't wear wedding band or anything?"

"Oh God, how could I forget. Wedding ring or engagement ring more precisely. It was a huge sapphire surrounded by diamonds. She wore it on the fourth finger of her left hand. If it was real it must have cost a fortune."

"Can you remember the name of the hospital Charles was taken to in Glasgow?"

"Oh dear, it was such a long time ago. Let me think about that one. Alice can you remember?"

"What's that dear?"

"The hospital they took Charles Stuart to all those years ago. Can you remember the name?"

"Yorkhill, darling it was Yorkhill."

Drew made notes of everything that had been said without knowing the significance of the information. At least, he thought, he'd have something to give Ruth Rivers in his next fax.

He drove the grateful Forsyth's back to their home and had to waken John up to get him out of the car. They all shook hands and promised to stay in touch.

That evening Drew had a light dinner, a glass or two of wine, and sent the fax including all the detail he had amassed back to Ruth at Petrotex's headquarters.

Charlie Stuart chaired the emergency meeting of the Scottish Republican Party's headquarters in Inverness. Daily and evening papers littered the table. All bore headlines of some sort or another alluding to the coming of the 1993 rebellion, which considered the possible deposition of the Queen and the demise of her son Prince Charles by the new Bonnie Prince Charlie. The media was in full cry. All of the party council members had been sworn to silence. The words 'No Comment' were well used that day. Microphones had been stuck into members faces in an attempt to elicit some comment, any comment from members of the newly formed SRP.

"First of all, are we sure this room's not bugged?" Charles looked over to his security advisor an ex-Metropolitan detective who was into all the surveillance equipment available.

"It's clean, swept it again just fifteen minutes before we arrived."

"Okay," Charles addressed the assembled Party Members. "What in the name of Christ went on yesterday? I mean look at all this stuff. It's got us in the papers and potentially on television but this, as we all know is part of Lawrence's crap, which we told him to forget." Charles referred to Lawrence Ingles the would-be historian, philosopher in the party who had patched together the line of lineage to prove Charlie was indeed rightful monarch of the United Kingdom and Northern Ireland or, if he was not the rightful monarch, he at least could lay claim to the throne.

"Charlie," Bobbie Simpson, the party's press secretary spoke up. "None of our people, including Lawrence has spoken to the press or the media in any way, shape or form. We don't know where this came from but we'll find out who divulged this nonsense and we'll have him by the bollocks."

"Well I'm pleased to hear no one in the party is responsible and we'll have to find out who is. But why would we want to have whoever it was by the gonads? Think about this, we're an embryonic party, we've got no political muscle and we're on the front page of all the dailies, and we want to have this guy by the bollocks? Are you all bloody crazy? We are getting publicity, which, if we had to pay for, would wipe us out overnight!" Charles exploded.

"What do you want to do then?" Tom Caruthers, one of the more stable members of the party asked. "You work or worked in the media for ten years. You're well known, your wife's in the super model bracket and your mother, Charlie, is right behind. You have a star studded cast."

"We stall." Charles looked round the table. "There is nothing more endearing to the British public, the English in particular, than the Monarchy. Now according to the tabloid press it's being threatened. If we issue a retraction immediately we'll burst the bubble once and for all. We'll never get such inexpensive publicity again. Note, I said inexpensive, not cheap! Come on Bobbie how do we capitalize on this without going to jail?"

"We get Lawrence to do the talking. He's the man who drew up the chart. Let him explain the whole thing." Bobbie spread his hands palms upward.

"Do you not think that could be dangerous? Lawrence is such a flake, a couple of good questions and he's up shit creek without the proverbial paddle." Iain Fraser weighed in from the other side of the table.

"Iain's right. Lawrence would just get himself and the party in a mess. Let's keep the 'no comment' approach alive and if they try to contact any of us then we use the 'not available for comment' approach. The media will get all the more frantic and if they can't reach anyone in the party directly then they will try and get to us through our families, friends, and acquaintances at all who might be able to shed some light on the story they think they've got hold of."

Charles leaned back in his chair and looked round the table for any sign of disapproval. Everyone nodded quietly.

"I move for an adjournment," Tom Caruthers proposed the motion.

"Seconded," Bobbie Simpson said. And the meeting broke up.

In the crowded bar of the same hotel a bunch of journalists surrounded Fred Grundy. Fred was a hack journalist who had bounced from tabloid to tabloid in quest of a scoop that might bring him fame, recognition and some extra cash that he needed desperately to stay out of jail. Divorced, he owed his wife a small fortune in child support and had only evaded being brought to book by keeping one or two jumps ahead of the law. But now his goose was virtually cooked. His ex had managed to get hold of a private detective, whom Fred was sure she was screwing, she could never afford to pay a private eye, Fred knew that for a fact. This burly guy with huge feet, gray hair and even grayer deep-set eyes accosted him one evening in Inverness. He knew immediately he was, or had been, a cop. The private investigator pressed a business card into his hand and said he represented his divorced wife and he would be speaking to him again on the subject of money and not to leave town. Fred looked into the gray eyes and said he wouldn't even think about it. That was it. The private eye disappeared and the next morning a warrant was served on him by the local constabulary.

But now Fred was on a roll. His persistence and snooping had finally paid off. He was a celebrity. One of Fred's great sleuthing activities was to sift through the trash of various organizations. Seldom was paper shredded, not unless it was a government department and even that didn't happen all the time. It was amazing what he had uncovered in the past by doing that one simple task. Some of what he had found was enough to start an exposé on a person or a company, but there had been nothing really big until now. Drawn to the new Scottish Republican Party by the magnetic quality of TV personality Charlie Stuart he had been going through their rubbish late one evening and had come across a genealogical chart headed up "King Charles, the claim to the Throne". At first, he had only seen the King Charles bit as the papers had been torn into quarters but he soon pieced it together and searched through some more to find the preamble to the chart that Lawrence Ingles had written. This was dynamite! He could see his name in lights; money pouring in from interviews and TV appearances as he revealed what was being hidden from the public. The SRP thought they had someone who was entitled, *by birthright,* to sit on the throne of Great Britain and Northern Ireland.

He went back to his cheap motel, bought a bottle of equally cheap talking whisky and got quietly paralytic, drinking to his newfound good fortune.

He couldn't wait to get to the phone the next day in the place he had rented as an office in one of the new industrial estates east of the town. Then he started calling his 'friends,' as he liked to call them, in the newspaper world. He talked carefully about his find. He wasn't sure if it was a plot, he could get more information on that, but yes, he did have the authentic document, he was careful not to say authenticated document, which proved Charles Edward Stuart was indeed entitled to lay claim to the British Throne.

Could he fax it to them? No, he couldn't. This was a prime document of historical importance, in any case it was too big to fax. Could he get on the next plane to London, all expenses paid? Not a problem. He was only fifteen minutes from the airport. He would meet the representatives from the various interested parties at Heathrow, let them see the document and then go back to Inverness where great plans were being hatched by the SRP. This new party clearly meant business and it now looked as if they had the muscle to do it.

Once the press got their ducks in a row the idea of a possible new King Charles took root. The incumbent Price of Wales was having a bad time with the press, his personal life was a shambles, his marriage was failing, and his popularity had reached an all time low. Charles Stuart, by comparison, was a fine looking, and a believably regal replacement who had intelligence, charisma and possessed the common touch. Not only that; he was a Scotsman who spoke with a Scots accent, a rare commodity indeed.

While other more respectable papers held off sensationalizing Fred Grundy's scoop, the tabloids had a field day. It was those reporters who had attracted Drew Findlay's attention at his hotel earlier that week. Now Fred was holding court in the hotel bar and he loved every minute of it. The questions flowed thick and fast hardly giving him time to down the drinks that had piled up at his elbow.

How well did he know Charlie Stuart? Who in the SRP had given him the document? How long had he had it in his possession? Did the SRP know he had the document or had he come by it by some other means? Had he checked out the authenticity of the chart? Did he know Charles through his program on Grampian Television? And on and on.

Fred fielded all of these questions with vague responses. The last thing he wanted was to give definitive information that could burst his bubble but he did say that he had arranged an exclusive interview with said Charlie Stuart after which he would be more than happy to answer all questions more precisely. It was a lie, of course, he had only seen Charles host the Scotland Today program some months earlier but he wanted to impress on his fellow reporters that access to the SRP was exclusively his. Had he only known, Charles and his colleagues had just exited the hotel by the goods delivery entrance to avoid Fred and the likes of Fred. The paparazzi were everywhere.

Back in Perthshire Drew finally and reluctantly left the comforts of Balathie House and headed north towards Inverness. He had no idea of what he was going to do when he got there but he felt that to justify him staying any longer in the UK he should at least see his target. He had sent his last fax to Ruth Rivers telling Red that he had met Charles's old Headmaster and laid out all he had said about Charles and his mother. The next fax they would get would probably be from Inverness, he told them.

Red was out of town when Ruth received the fax from Drew that morning. She quickly scanned over what Drew had written. It made quite interesting reading. It didn't mean much to her but there might be something significant in it for Red.

It was the afternoon when Red called in from Morgan City, Louisiana where he was with Lance negotiating over some drilling rigs. Ruth told him she had at last got some information from Drew.

"About time too," Red growled. "What's he say?"

"You want me to read this out; it's like a mini-novel,"

"No kiddin'. Well can you kinda précis it"?

"How long have you got?"

"God Ruth just read me the highlights."

"Okay, keep your hair on, I'll do my best."

Ruth quickly went over the details of Drew's visit to the school explaining that Charles had gone to a private school and that his grandfather was, or had been a certain Sir Andrew Ballantyne. Then followed the meeting with John Forsyth. Charles's near death experience followed by major heart surgery.

"How long ago did all this happen?" Red was suddenly alert.

"Let's see, September 1969, I think it says."

"Go on."

The boy returned to the school the next year after successful heart surgery and then four or five years later went to university, in Aberdeen."

"Does he say anything about the mother?"

"Yep. Quite a lot. She certainly seems to have been a bit of a looker, so the headmaster thought, tall, long blond hair, lived in the far North-West of Scotland, was a stalker it says here, can that be right? You get arrested for that in Houston."

"It's probably something Scottish, sounds kinda weird, anything else?"

"Nope not much, just something about a ring, a big blue ring with diamonds, it caught his attention, at least that's what Drew's written."

There was a long silence at the other end of the phone. Then Ruth heard Red under his breath say,

"Jesus Christ. That's got to be Karen's ring."

"Red, Red, you okay."

"No, not really. Let me sit down." Lance, who had just come into the office Red was using to make the call, saw his father slump onto a chair near the desk on which the phone sat.

Red's face was ashen.

"Pop, are you okay?" Lance put his hand on his father's shoulder.

"Yeah, yeah, I'm okay. Just got a bit of a shock, that's all."

"What's up?"

"Just some old buddy of mine who passed away suddenly." Red covered up. He had to be sure, before he said anything to anybody.

He went back on the phone to a concerned Ruth.

"Red, Red are you sure you're okay?"

"I'm fine now. Here's what I want you to do. Phone Cedars-Sinai in Los Angeles; see if you can locate a Doctor Crawford, Jack Crawford. He used to be a cardiologist at that hospital. Don't be given the run around. He'll be retired, or he could be dead." He quickly considered that possibility, Jack Crawford would be eighty-something now.

"Anyway, whatever, see if you can get in touch with him, get a number I can call him at. Next get Bobby Rule to meet me first thing on Monday morning in his office."

"You have a meeting with Don Wylie at, eight sharp."

"Cancel it. Tell Bobby I'll be there at seven-thirty prompt."

"Suppose Bobby can't make that?"

"He'll make it. Just say Drew's onto something. Then get me a number where I can talk to Drew, quick as you can?"

"That's going to be difficult. He's traveling around in Scotland, God knows where he is."

"He said he'd be faxing back shortly didn't he?"

"That could be a couple of days, maybe more."

"Jesus Christ Ruth, do I have to do your job for you?"

"No sir you don't." This was Red on the rampage. She hadn't heard him like this for a long time. "I was just pointing out..."

"I know what you were pointing out. Phone the last fuckin' hotel he stayed in and find out if they know where he went." Red's strident voice cut right across hers.

"Yes sir!" Came Ruth's terse response.

"And call me at home tonight. We're flying back tonight from New Orleans and I'll be home by about eight."

"Yes sir."

"Goodbye." Red slammed the phone down before Ruth could say anything else. "Goddamn women!" He said to himself out loud.

"Who's the Drew guy?" Lance looked over towards his father.

"Who?"

"You asked Ruth to find out where Drew was. I'm only asking who is Drew?"

"Nobody you know," Red snapped back. He was not in the mood right then to go into explanations. All of that would come in good time.

Lance and Red hardly exchanged two words on the flight back home. Red's mind was racing. Findlay would not have any idea of the significance of the things he had found out from John Forsyth. Thank God, Red thought, he had found the ex-Headmaster. Without his recollection, the trail would have gone cold. He was now sure Charles Stuart was Jens. How this had come about and how or what had happened was a mystery, but it wouldn't be a mystery for long. Findlay would find out one way or the other. The Petrotex Learjet touched down at Ellington field just after seven o'clock that Friday and Red was home in forty-five minutes contra-flowing the mass of traffic that headed south on Interstate 45 for the weekend.

He had just poured himself a Scotch when the doorbell rang. It had to be Ruth. She had a pass for the electronic gate. He was right; she was standing in the front vestibule looking very attractive in a light beige colored suit. He smiled at her.

"Come in."

"I'd rather not thanks. I've tried my best to locate Drew Findlay but it's now two in the morning in the UK. I tried the hotel near Perth where he's been staying but they have no idea of where he might be. I got the evening staff. They said I should try in the morning. I'll call at nine their time."

"That's in about seven hours from now. Look come in; let me get you a drink."

"No. Red it's very kind of you but I'd rather not." Red could recognize a pout when he saw one. He remembered Karen, Queen of the super pout.

"I insist."

"Red. I'd rather not."

"I want to apologize for today."

Ruth was past him over the threshold before he could say another word. She headed straight to the bar in the family room.

"Do you know, I've been with you all these years, rain or shine, and until today there are two words I've never heard addressed at me? One is the 'F" word. I can live without that, thank you, and the other is 'apologize' I cannot wait. Oh yes, and I'll have a Crown and seven."

Red poured them both drinks and sat on the large settee opposite.

"Let me tell you what all this is about."

Ruth sat mesmerized as he told her all about Karen and Jens, and what had happened. How the chance letter from an old friend visiting the UK with the newspaper photograph of Charles Stuart came to him and started him playing mind games. He told Ruth how Jens body had never been found. Not a trace. Suppose, just suppose, he hadn't died. Someone had found him alive by some miracle and hadn't gone to the authorities and adopted him as their own. This was the straw he was clutching. Now it wasn't so much of a straw, there was more to Eilid and Charles Stuart than met the eye. He was now sixty-five. Just think, he said, I've been deprived of my son for the best part of thirty-four years.

At the end of his dissertation he almost had Ruth in tears. It was the first time she had seen Red's true emotions and it was the same for Red. Ruth and he had always had the most professional and efficient of personal assistants. Despite the fact that Ruth was better than just attractive Red had never once shared his personal life with her unless it was connected to his business in some way. They had a mutual admiration for one another but the feelings stopped there.

"I'm sorry Red. I had no idea what you went through, that must have been real tough."

"It was. But it's over thirty years ago and the mind becomes numb to issues that were so painful then. Now they're all back in front of me again."

"What happens now? And by the way I've got Dr. Crawford's number for you. He's retired, of course, so this is his home number. I had to use all my wiles to get this from the hospital. He lives in Orange County; it's only about six-thirty there."

"What about Bobby?"

"Oh, right. I forgot about that. He's on. Seven-thirty in his office."

"Good, well done. What we've got to do now is to find out whether this Charles Stuart is really Jens and it depends on how good this Findlay guy is. That's one of the questions I have for Bobby. At this stage in the game I would think the prime source for information is his mother, the Eilid Stuart dame. She may or may not be the person responsible for taking him in the first place. It's all a mystery right now but to me the ring is the key. That's the ring I gave to Karen for Christmas 1958, I never did see that ring but I ordered it from a jeweler in Bond Street, London. They couriered over a brochure to let me see what they could offer and I chose a three carat sapphire surrounded by diamonds. Now it sounds like this Eilid woman is wearing Karen's ring or it could just be coincidence. That's what Findlay's gotta find out for me."

"Red you know I'll do whatever it takes to help."

"Ruth you're a good lady. Just keep it all to yourself right now, that's all I ask. I sure don't want things goin' off at half-cock. So keep me updated on where Findlay is 'cause I need to talk to him real quick."

Ruth had finished her drink by this time. She rose to leave.

"Will I see you tomorrow?"

"You bet. And Ruth, thanks for coming in and listening to me, I sure appreciate that." Red grasped her by the upper arms held her firm and planted a big kiss on her forehead.

Ruth hugged Red back and made for the door before her emotions played tricks on her again. It was a side of Red Ericsson she had never seen in all of the sixteen years she had worked for him. She drove down the wide drive with more than just a touch of euphoria.

Bobby Rule was waiting for Red when he came swinging through the door at seven-twenty the following morning.

"You're early," said Bobby as he and Red shook hands.

"Yup, I think we may have something."

Bobby took Red into his office. "Okay shoot"

Red told him about Drew Findlay's latest fax, and the conclusions he'd drawn from it. He then asked Bobby just how good Findlay was. Bobby said all the right things; reliable, honest, hard working, maybe drank a little too much now and again, but didn't elaborate on Drew's family situation.

"What do you want him to do now?" Bobby asked when Red had finished.

"Get to the truth. If this is Jens…"

"Red don't get your hopes so high, it's been thirty something years…"

"Thirty-four," Red cut in.

"All right thirty-four years, the ring could just be a coincidence. What else is there?"

"I got hold of Jack Crawford the doctor who was Chief Cardiologist when Jens was ill. It was he who told me to get Jens to London. Well I phoned Jack, he's retired now, but of course he remembered the tragedy. Now what they did on Jens is called a shunt, it's not a permanent solution, and he would have needed more heart surgery in eight to ten years. Well guess what, this kid collapsed at school, a boarding school by the way, and according to the Headmaster Findlay talked to, they just got him to the hospital in time. Whatever they did fixed him up real good, 'cause he went back to school and finished his four years of education there and went on to university."

Bobby sat silent for a moment, then he said, "I think it was Ian Fleming in one of his James Bond books who said, 'the first time is happenstance, the second is coincidence and the third time it's enemy action.' So far we have two. The ring and then the heart operation, we need a third. Where does this lady with the strange name live?"

"I've no idea. Scotland somewhere. I suppose Findlay might know."

"Okay, here's what we do, you said he had found a Birth Certificate and it all looked in order?"

"Yes."

"Get him to re-check that. If there's a father in the record we want to know who it is and where he came from. Then let's find out where Mrs. Stuart is living now and where she was living when the aircraft went down. If Findlay can get the answer to some of these questions we might have the third item. Then we need to take this whole thing more seriously."

"It might be a couple of days. We don't have a clue where Findlay is."

"Why not?" Bobby frowned.

"Well he faxes us from time to time. His only real contact is Ruth for I'm out of town most of the time."

"Red, buy him, or tell him to buy a frickin' phone."

"Do they have those in the wilds of Scotland?" Red frowned.

"Jesus Red, how would I know? You're the guy who's working in the North Sea."

"Do you know I never considered that? I must be getting old. I'll get Ruth to set it up."

Red left and went straight to the Corporate Headquarters and breezed in on Ruth.

"Can you get Findlay one of those cell phones?" The ones that work off a satellite. They have them in the England don't they?"

"Sure can, and sure have. I just need to know where he is."

"Still no news."

"Nope. Drew's gone cold on us"

"Well let me know the minute you make contact."

"Fine. You'll be the first to know."

"Yeah and the only one to know, apart from you. You know to say nothing of this, not even to Lance."

"My lips are sealed," Ruth drew an invisible zipper across her lips and smiled her sweetest smile. "Thanks for last night. There's just one thing."

"What's that? You never did say 'sorry'."

"I did."

"No you didn't."

"Okay. I apologize. I was upset. I am truly sorry."

"Accepted. By the way Don Wylie, you know you canceled this morning on him."

"Yup."

"Well he wants to know if you can do lunch, at the Petroleum Club. He says he's got some hot information he wants to pass along."

"Okay. Tell him okay. It'll be a liquid lunch, for Don anyway. He's a minimum three Martini man.

Don Wylie was one of the 'good ole boys' in the Petroleum industry. He always seemed to be on the inside track of something in the business. Maybe it was because his wife wrote the gossip column in the Houston Post.

Back in Inverness Drew was getting nowhere fast. The general furor
that had erupted with the revelation from Fred Grundy that Charles
was a descendant of Bonnie Prince Charlie had the media all over the
place. Drew was fortunate that the manager at his previous hotel had
offered to phone ahead to reserve a room at the Station Hotel hard by
the railway station as the name suggested. It was a charming hotel with
friendly staff. Not quite so well appointed as Balathie House but it was
packed. Not one room was available. Getting information about Charlie
Stuart was easy. Getting *to* him was impossible. Drew now figured that
he had to get to see Eilid Stuart by some other means. He had originally
thought to do this through having a conversation with Charles, but he
had already discounted that approach as the media kept trying to ensnare
the evasive Charles to get some comment from 'the horse's mouth.'

He plied the concierge in the hotel about the possibilities of stalking in the area. The concierge was more than helpful. He had missed the
boat this year. Stalking and culling the stags finished on the twentieth of
October. But for next year, why, there were estates all over the place.
What did the gentleman have in mind? Drew told him it would be his
first time on the hill. What could he recommend? The concierge said
just about anywhere was as good as the other. It would depend on the
time of year, the weather and then the stalker. Drew asked if he wanted
the best, the very best where could he recommend. The concierge told
him Torridon Lodge but the possibility of getting in there was like trying
to interview Charlie Stuart. Not a chance. Drew asked, "why?"

"Sir, Torridon Lodge is a class act. It's a legend. Not only is the
stalking good but the food prepared by Mhairi Ferguson is world class.
So I'm told. I wouldnae know. Unless you know someone close to the
Estate owner or the stalker, Mhairi's brother Hamish, you'll have nae
chance of getting to stalk there. It was Charles's mother who made the
place famous, you know."

"I didn't. You mean the Charlie Stuart who everyone is talking
about?"

"The very man. Eilid Stuart, his mother, that's who taught Hamish all he knows."

"You don't say. Can I visit there?"

"Sure, sure; it's a wee bit far, mind you."

"How far is far?"

"About sixty miles, it's a fair run."

Drew permitted himself a smile. It was amazing how the locals thought sixty miles was a long way. If only they knew, he thought, you could drive sixty miles just about and never leave the Houston Metroplex.

"Great thanks for your help." Drew was now set in his mind he'd go to Torridon. He must be able to get information about Eilid there.

The day dragged on. He had nothing to do. Shopping was something Drew never did, but he wandered through the streets of Inverness browsing. Charlie Stuart's photograph was everywhere. The locals had caught the "Bonnie Prince Charlie" fever and Scottish flags, the St. Andrew Saltire and the Royal Flag of Scotland, the Lion Rampant were fluttering from just about every building. It was about four in the afternoon and already starting to get dark. Drew made his way back to the hotel, went to the bar, and after a couple of malts, had a conversation about freedom for Scotland with a bunch of reporters from the south. He broke away and had dinner on his own.

The morning dawned bleak and cold. There was a wind coming off the Moray Firth that would have cut you in two. Drew ate a hearty breakfast, as he had no idea when he would eat again that day, and pulled out of Academy Street just after nine o'clock. The high whitish-bellied clouds began to look more ominous as he sped northwest on virtually empty roads. As long as it didn't snow, he'd been fine he told himself. He checked the fuel gauge the tank was almost full. The concierge had warned him about getting petrol before he left Inverness.

His thoughts turned back to Houston. The weather would be just about perfect he thought. Seventy-five degrees, clear blue skies, light winds, perfect golfing weather or nipping down to the beach at Galveston. That did it. The horrors came back again with a vengeance. He could see his three girls laughing and splashing about in the brown uninviting surf that came in from the Mexican Gulf. It was so bad he had to stop the car in a lay-bye. Fifteen minutes passed before he could take control of himself. He put his hands back on the wheel but he was shaking uncontrollably. He couldn't possibly drive in this state. He sat staring into space for another ten minutes. Finally he conquered his monsters from the Id. He drove on with no enthusiasm. The surrounding countryside was bleak, foreboding even. The skies became darker, grayer and the wind had picked up noticeably. He arrived at Kinlochewe about an hour after he left Inverness. The simple finger signpost read ''Torridon 10'. He turned left into the glen and headed due west.

Slowly he went down the single-track road as flurries of snow began to dance around his car like eddies in a stream. One minute all encompassing, as if he and the car were in some kind of whirling vortex with no end and no beginning, then the snow would let up and he could see the road more clearly and the tiny flakes caressed the car as if they had no shape or form, deceiving in their apparent softness as they fluttered down from an unseen sky.

It seemed to Drew as if he had been driving for at least an hour, in fact, it was only fifteen minutes. He caught the sign Torridon Lodge on his left and turned up the well-metalled road. The snow had almost stopped and he was thankful. The last thing he wanted to do was to miss the Lodge and go on driving for God knows how long.

There were no cars or trucks at the entrance; in fact the Lodge looked deserted. He parked outside the main entrance and got out of the car. A blast of dry icy air took his breath away. By God but it's cold, he thought, why would anyone want to live in this part of the country. He knocked politely on the double entrance door. Nothing. Just the eerie whistling of the wind as it came down the glen and rattled the odd window of the Lodge. Drew tried the door. It swung open on well-oiled hinges. Inside was nice and warm. He called out,

"Anybody there?" Dead silence. He walked forward into the main hallway. On his left he could see a well-appointed lounge or sitting room, to his right the dining area with what looked like a large refectory table and twelve chairs.

"Hello, anybody at home?" He tried again.

My God, he thought, this is like the Marie Celeste. To the left in the living room there was a bar. On the bar was a large silver tray with about six good malts in various stages of depletion. He walked forward to examine the tray. It was a beautiful example of scrolled engraving. There was a plain oval in the center of the tray. He moved one of the bottles to read the inscription.

'To the Clan Ferguson, without whose help none of this would have been possible. With love and affection, Eilid Stuart Ballantyne, January 1st 1980.'

Eilid Stuart Ballantyne, he said to himself. How odd. She couldn't have married, well not the Ballantyne he had heard of anyway. He picked up a bottle of the Macallan 18 year old malt.

"I can see you're a man of good taste."

A voice boomed behind him. Drew didn't flinch, he was used to surprises. He turned round slowly. Hamish was standing in the middle of the room dressed in his breeches, long woolen stockings, a green plaid shirt and a brown half-sleeved sweater.

"What can I be doing for you?"

Drew stepped forward, putting the bottle back on the tray. "You must be one of the Ferguson Clan, eh?"

"Hamish Ferguson," Hamish stuck out his hand. Drew shook it warmly.

"Drew Findlay, pleased to meet you."

"And what brings you to Torridon Lodge in such terrible weather?"

"I had asked about stalking in Inverness and the concierge at the hotel told me that Torridon was the place to come, so I thought I'd pay you a visit."

Hamish's wide grin accentuated his wing nut ears. "Aye, we have that reputation, built up over many years of course. But you'd have to be knowing Sir David and have a wee bit experience with a rifle before you got on the hill."

"Well I've used a rifle before, but who is Sir David?"

"Sir David Vickers, the Estate owner. He lives just outside of London but he hasn't been here for years. He must be in his nineties now;

aye he'll be ninety-three. He was born in 1900 so his age is with the century. Only his friends and friends of friends come now. But you can apply, you'll have to fill in this wee form," Hamish reached over to a desk in the lounge and pulled out a piece of paper, "fill this in and if there's a cancellation and you get drawn in the ballot, we'll let you know."

"Jesus, I didn't know it would be so complicated. I live in the United States, but I am Scots."

"By God you could have fooled me. You must have lived over there a long time."

"About thirty years."

"So you moved to the States when you were twenty-something."

"Quite right, I was exactly twenty when the family moved there."

"Fancy that then, you'll be the same age as me, the big five-oh?"

"Fifty-two actually. How long have you been here?" Drew was warming to the conversation.

"Since I was seventeen. Mistress Stuart took me in as a ghillie, God bless her, she had just been made Stalker then and she took a chance on me."

"And you never let her down?"

"Not in any big way, ever." Hamish wondered what all the questions were about. He sniffed police. The man looked like a policeman. Hamish watched his soft gray eyes harden suddenly.

"That's why you got the salver?"

"Aye, I suppose you could say that. Anyway, fill in the form, let me have it and if you're lucky we'll maybe see you next year." Clearly the conversation was over. Hamish wanted him out the door.

"So Eilid Stuart is no longer here?" Drew had to ask the question.

"No."

"Where did she go then? And why does she have Ballantyne as her surname?"

"Why would you be wanting to know? Are you from the press?"

"No I'm not from the press, I was just curious."

"Aye, well your curiosity will just have to remain dissatisfied. She moved away years ago after her grandfather died."

"You mean Sir Andrew?"

That was Drew's big mistake, he had pushed too hard.

Suddenly Hamish was staring at him twelve inches from his face.

"Right mister, just who the hell are you? You know too much and you've got too many questions, awa' back to where ye came from before ye get hurt." Hamish had his fists clenched by his side and his accent had become more pronounced.

Drew realized he had over stayed his welcome.

"Hamish, I'm sorry. I represent a Ballantyne relative living in the United States who has no family or relatives. He asked me to find out about the Ballantynes in this country. He's a very wealthy man."

Some of the distrust left Hamish's eyes. The inheritance trick seemed to have worked again.

"So why would you come to Torridon?"

"I was told, wrongly now as it turns out, that this was Sir Andrew's Estate."

"That's the trouble wi' townies, they get it all mixed up. Sir Andrew used to come here every year but that's a long time ago now. He was Eilid's grandfather, that was why he came 'til he got too old to go on the hill. He left her everything, well not everything, but his estate at Cannich is hers. She's a wealthy lady, she'll no' be needing your American Ballantyne's money."

"That's why she changed her name then?"

"Aye, it was a condition in the will; after all she was really a Ballantyne." Hamish explained.

"And she lives at the Cannich Estate?"

"Aye she does, with my wee sister Allison, who cooks near as fine as Mhairi and she helps her run the Lodge there."

Drew could go now. Hamish had given him all he needed to know. Eilid Stuart was now Eilid Ballantyne and she lived on Cannich Estate. He headed for the door,

"I'll mail this to you," he waved the piece of paper in Hamish's direction, "and thanks for your hospitality."

As drew drove off, Hamish looked at the disappearing car in concern. Maybe he shouldn't have told that man all about Eilid, but he was so willing to help it had all just spilled out. Ach, he thought, what can be the harm? The man could find out about Eilid in a hundred places, she was so well known.

Drew returned to the hotel just after lunch. He looked at his watch ten past two it read. He thought he'd better fax Ruth in Houston; it was just after eight in the morning there so she'd get it just before nine.

The hotel was nice and warm so he sat in the lobby by a roaring fire and printed out what he had found out about Eilid. He still hadn't been able to get to speak to Charles and he didn't want to get embroiled in the local political ramifications. They wouldn't understand a word of what he wrote anyway. He gave the fax to the young attractive dark haired girl at reception and she promised to send it off right away. Drew sat back down in the comfortable chair again and he was dozing off when the young receptionist came over to him.

"Mr. Findlay, are you Mr. Drew Findlay sir?"

"I am, young lady."

"Well there's a lady on the phone from America and says she wants to talk to you, it's urgent like, she says."

Drew raised his eyebrows. "Really, where do I take it?"

"Go over to that booth there, sir" the receptionist pointed, "I'll put you through."

"Drew, this is Ruth Rivers, how are you?"

"Fine, I guess you got my fax?"

"You bet. That's why I'm calling. Red wants to talk to you right away. He needs to tell you something."

"Okay, does he want to speak to me now?"

"Yes, he's pacing around in his office like a caged tiger. We've been trying to find you for over three days, I think he wants you to buy a mobile phone so that he can contact you more easily, anyway I'll put you through."

The line went silent.

Then Drew heard Red's booming voice.

"Where the hell have you been, man?"

"Traveling."

"Where are you now?"

"Inverness. I just sent you a fax on hotel letterhead."

"I know, Ruth just gave me it. Are you staying there?"

"Yes. I'll be here for at least another day. I've discovered where Mrs. Stuart lives."

"Son-of-a-bitch. Well done. Have you got time to listen right now?"

"Shoot, I'm all ears."

So Red started to tell Drew all about Karen and Jens and what had happened. Drew listened sympathetically. He had first hand knowledge of just how the man must have felt all those years ago. In the midst of the one way conversation he began to see where all this was going; especially when he told Drew about Jens's operation and the necessity for a more permanent solution to right his health, requiring another operation eight or ten years farther on. Then he told Drew about the ring. It was all too much of a coincidence, he said finishing up.

"Drew, I think Charles Stuart is my son Jens. My wife gave birth to identical twins; one was just smaller than the other due to his heart defect. He looks like Lance, he's just a bit thinner, that's all. I have no idea of how this woman came by him, but by Jesus Christ Drew, you're going to find out, and if it is Jens, watch this space."

Drew was silent. His mind was racing. "Red, where did the plane crash?"

"Jeez, I can tell you that. In Torridon or Glen Torridon; it hit the top of Ben Eh or a hill with that name. I've been up it, to scatter Karen's ashes," his voice shook slightly. "The plane crashed and ended up in what the Scots call a corrie or something."

"That's right, a corrie's right. Listen I've just come from Torridon, from what you'd call the hunting lodge, Eilid Stuart was the stalker there all those years ago. We're talking 1959 aren't we?"

"Yup."

"Well she and Charles lived there for years. I've just spoken to the stalker, Hamish Ferguson, he's almost the same age as me, been there all his working life. Not very talkative at first, but he came round and gave me enough of what I wanted to know. I think I'll pay a visit on Madame Stuart, who, by the way, has changed her name to Ballantyne."

"Why did she do that?"

"Something to do with her grandfather, who was a Sir Andrew Ballantyne. Her mother was married to Sir Andrew's son, although according to John Forsyth the ex-Headmaster from Strahearn, no one could find any record of a marriage to the son. I think Eilid is, as we would say, the Laird's or the Laird's son's bastard. What happened to him I don't know yet, but I'll find out. There are more questions than answers at the moment, but leave it to me, I promise you, I'll get to the bottom of this."

"Thanks Drew, Bobby said you'd come through."

"Well, now that I've got information can we say that I'm more motivated, if that's the word? I've been trying to play cards with half-a-deck up until now. Why did you not tell me all this up front? I felt I was spending your money to no purpose"

"Drew, let's just say I dared to hope. I felt like a stupid old fool sending you on a wild goose chase. Now I don't feel so stupid or so old."

"Hey, amen to that."

"Drew, go and get yourself a cell phone. One of the best. Get one of these deals that communicate by satellite, so it doesn't matter where you are in the world, I can get hold of you."

"Red, those things cost a fortune." The minute Drew uttered the words he knew he had made a mistake.

"Drew, buy the damn phone, okay?"

"Consider it done."

"Okay. Give the number to Ruth when it's set up."

"I will."

"Bye." And Red was gone.

Drew went back to the comfortable chair near the fire. He closed his eyes. His head was reeling from his conversation with Red. What a story, and what if it was true? It would change everything that was happening in the newly founded Scottish Republican Party. Charlie Stuart would be an American citizen. What irony. The Pretender to the British throne and leader of the breakaway Scottish Republican Party was an American, Jesus the spin-doctors and the media would have a field day. It was mind-boggling. The next steps he took would be critical. He was dealing with an unknown quantity. He went over in his mind what he knew about Eilid Stuart so far. Most of it had come from Johnnie the barman at the Moulin Hotel and John Forsyth, Charles's ex-Headmaster. Blond, attractive, well that was then, a crack shot, both of his contacts had told him that. This lady would be no push over. He could imagine her being intensely private, a person of few words, not aware of her stunning good looks and shunning men when she was younger for some good reason. There were hidden depths there; how to plumb them was another matter.

Then there was the ring. If he could prove that the ring Eilid was wearing or had worn was the original purchased by Red way back in 1958, that would be enough indeed to implicate Eilid Stuart in Red's theory that his son Jens was alive and was indeed Charles Stuart. Drew suddenly had an idea. After some trouble he got through to Ruth Rivers again some thirty minutes later.

"Drew," she laughed a deep throaty laugh, "we'll have to stop meeting this way. What can I do for you?"

"I need to speak to Red."

"He's in a meeting hon. Give me the message and I'll get back to you."

"I really need to talk to him now, it's a question only he can answer and it's kind of critical that I have a word."

"Okay, you're the man. Hold on."

Drew hung on for what seemed like an eternity then suddenly,

"Drew, this is Red, whatcha got?"

"It's what you've got I'm after. Listen, when you bought the ring and other gifts you told me about, did you buy them sight unseen?"

What d'you mean sight unseen?"

Drew took a deep breath,

"Did you see the goods or a picture of the jewelry before you made the purchase?"

"Oh, oh, I see what you mean. Yeah I did, I think I did. It's a long time ago. The jewelers sent me some kind of fancy brochure, I remember now. They got it to me before Christmas, by courier as I recall."

"Do you have that brochure now?"

"Are you kiddin'?"

"Just asking."

"Jesus Drew that was thirty-odd years ago."

"I'm well aware of that; do you think you can find that brochure?'

"Not an idea. We lived in Los Angeles then. Correction, I lived in L.A. then. The only one who might have known its whereabouts would have been Agnes Anderson, she was Karen's nurse you know, who went over to London with her, but she died four or five years ago. It was a helluva long time ago; I have no idea where it might be."

"Now you know the sort of problems I'm running into," Drew countered not without a touch of sarcasm. "Why don't you try and find it, I need something that will shake this lady to her very foundations and if you have that brochure, and if she still wears the ring a confrontation with that kind of evidence would be hard to shrug off, don't you think?"

"What if it's not my ring?"

"That's what I want the bloody brochure for." Really, thought Drew, there are times…

"Well, I'll do my best. I didn't keep much of Karen's, you can understand that." Red didn't sound very enthusiastic.

"Better than you can ever know. But listen, you wouldn't keep that with any of her stuff, would you. That's more like something you'd put in your desk drawer, isn't it?"

"Okay smart ass; I'll give it some thought. And if I find it?"

"Get it to me ASAP."

"You mean mail it or FedEx it?"

"No I don't. Send it over by courier. Reverse the process the jeweler used if that's how it came to you all those years ago."

"I can always send it over in the Lear."

Christ, thought Drew from the sublime to the cor-blimey.

"Whatever. But I'm not going to confront Madame Stuart now Ballantyne without something that will get her to sit up and take notice. So before I put my big foot in it I'd just like to have some proof, not conjecture, proof that that ring is Karen's. Does that make sense?"

"I'll look through the house tonight, I promise." Red sounded more positive.

"Okay, that's a deal. I have to go back to London to get that satellite phone, there's nothing like that up here so that'll be tomorrow. I'll ring Ruth once it's enabled and you can then speak to me direct. If you find what we're looking for I'll stay on in London and meet the courier or the 'plane or whatever."

"Call me tomorrow. I might just sneak away to the house earlier."

Getting better all the time, thought Drew as he hung up.

By noon the following day Drew was in Tottenham Court Road, London browsing through a store that specialized in security and spy equipment looking for a mobile phone that worked via satellite. The monthly cost of running the thing was enormous, and that was before you made a call. However, his American Express card worked, by two o'clock the phone was enabled, and he was ready to go. Anxious to see if the reception would be good he called Ruth in Houston. She came through loud and clear.

"My God," said Drew, "it's better than a land line." He gave Ruth the number and told her to get Red to call him as soon as he appeared at the office. Ruth promised to do that and told him that Red had left early the previous day to "rummage," was the word she used, for some old document or other in his massive house.

Drew made his way back to the West End and checked into the Lowndes Hotel just off Lowndes Square in London's Belgravia. It was a fairly modest hotel by London standards, but it suited Drew for what he hoped would be a short stay in London. He was contemplating going to have a drink at the bar before going out to find a restaurant when his cell phone rang. It was Red.

"I tell ya boy, we got lucky."

"You found it?"

"Yup. I was about to give up, I had bin through everything when I remembered I had given my old desk to Lance when he was studying at college. So I went up to what was his room and started goin' through all his things and there was one drawer at the bottom missing its handle, it was just a knob, like you would pull, well I levered that sucker open and bingo! There was all my old stuff from way back. I figure the drawer had never been opened for all those years. At the back was the brochure sent to me by Aspreys, I remember now that was the name of the jeweler. The ring I bought Karen is right on the outside with about two others. It's the only one with an oval sapphire so you can't be wrong footed. Now Lance has some guys goin' over to the UK not tomorrow but the next day and they fly into Gatwick on Saturday morning. Is that goin' to be okay?"

"Yes, that'll be fine. I really want to mull over the best way of doing this and the couple of extra days I have in London will help me do that. I'll have to send Ruth my expenses to date; I'm running a bit low on cash." Drew thought he had a better chance to talk money now that his visit didn't seem to be a wild goose chase any longer.

"Drew buddy, just you tell me how much; I'll send it over with Lance's guys."

"Let's say a couple of thousand just to be going on with. The exchange rate is pretty bad right now, so you don't get much for your dollar."

"Consider it done. I'll get Ruth to call you and give you the name of the guy who will have the money and the jeweler's brochure." Red was all action now. It was as if he could smell blood.

Drew went down to the bar feeling better as well. *He* could certainly smell blood and he hadn't even started getting down to business. He just had to find out more about Eilid Stuart or Ballantyne as she now styled herself. Where to start was the problem. He ate a fairly disinteresting dinner. He wasn't sure whether it was the food that wasn't to his liking or the impatient mood he was in.

Suddenly it came to him. He had been thinking about John Forsyth the very helpful retired Strahearn headmaster when it occurred to him that Charles had to have school friends, none better than to give him an insight into Charles and, hopefully, his mother. From his dinner table he pulled out his new high-tech toy and dialed John Forsyth's number hoping it wouldn't be too late in the evening.

It was Alice Forsyth who answered. No, no they were not in bed and John would come to the phone right away.

"What can I do for you?" John's cheerful voice came over the phone. "You know we're still talking about that wonderful lunch you gave us, quite made our week, that did."

"John, nice to hear you are both doing well. I've got some more questions for you on our mutual friend Charles Stuart."

"Oh right, he's making quite a name for himself in the papers eh? Pretender to the British throne? Bloody poppycock."

"Why do you say that?"

"They, whoever wrote this article, doesn't know their history. Someone has already claimed to be the rightful heir to the Stuart dynasty."

"Really?"

"Yes really. Not terribly well known but the most direct, or indirect, descendant of Bonnie Prince Charlie, depending on which side you stand, is the Seventh Count of Albany. He styles himself His Royal Highness Prince Michael of Albany. Belgian chappie but came to live in Scotland in the mid-seventies I think, but the most significant item of note is that he was elected as President of the European Council of Princes just this year."

"Where do you get all this from?" Drew was fascinated.

"Read all the papers from home and abroad. Nothing much else to do, my golf has gone to hell. So there we are. Charlie boy will have to overcome that one before he starts another bloody fiasco." Forsyth ended on a triumphant note.

"Do you have any of these articles? I'd love to read them."

"Well, now I'm not sure. Alice chucks stuff out, you know, she's such a busybody, but I'll have a look. If I find something how do I get in touch?"

Drew gave him his mobile number assuring him that no matter where he might be he would get either John's call or any message he left him.

Drew was at Gatwick to meet Red's crew as they deplaned. Continental's flight 4 was right on schedule and he held up a sign with the name of the foreman who was to have a large envelope for him. The foreman soon spotted him and the exchange was made after he asked for some ID. Drew, quite impressed, flashed him his Texas driver's license and asked if he could run the five crewmen anywhere. They politely declined saying that they were being taken care of by the London Office and Drew left them to head back to the hotel.

Inside the bulky envelope was the old Aspreys brochure all wrapped in bubble wrap and another thick bulky envelope that held ten thousand dollars and a letter from Red! Drew had never seen that much money, not in cash anyway. He counted out the crisp one hundred dollar bills. Ten thousand, he had asked for two. He read the short note.

Drew, you are doing a hell of a job. Just so you do not go Scots' mean on me, use this to advantage. Talk to you soon.

Red.

A man of few words, he should get on well with Eilid, he surmised. Then he focused on that fleeting notion. If they ever were to meet, boy that would be some meeting. Oh to be a fly on the wall!. Would they ever meet that was the question? Assuming all that Red conjectured about had happened and by some miracle Jens was alive and Eilid Stuart had knowingly kept his son from him, brother, skin and hair would fly. The legal implications were just too much to consider. He had already considered the irony of a US citizen leading the Scottish Republican Party and the media's reaction.

There was nothing else for it. He had to go back to Inverness and get hold of Eilid Stuart and confront her. He checked out of the Lowndes Hotel and made his way to Heathrow. There was only one flight to Inverness on a Saturday and he wanted to set up a bank account and get some of the dollars changed into Sterling. As far as he knew the only banks open on a Saturday were located at airports. By one-thirty he was in the air with five hundred pounds in his wallet, a new checkbook and a

Switch card which was as good as a credit card, he was told, because the money would get debited out of the bank account he had just set up.

By four o'clock that afternoon he was ensconced once again in the Station Hotel in Inverness with an almost brand new Range Rover that he had rented from Hertz. Before setting out for his impromptu visit to Eilid he thought he would have one last shot at getting hold of Charles Stuart. The hotel concierge directed him to the SRP offices, which were within walking distance of the hotel. Drew fully expected the offices would be empty on a Saturday especially this late in the afternoon. It was almost dark as he made he reached the door emblazoned with a Lion Rampant etched on the glass and the motto in Latin 'Neo Me Impune Lacessit', translated by the Black Watch Regiment as 'Whau Dare Meddle Wi' Me" or more correctly 'No One Treats Me with Impunity' scrolled underneath the lion. He was just about to try the door when it opened and Charles Stuart came out and nearly walked into him.

"Sorry. I'm very sorry; it's so gloomy I didn't see you. Can I help you?"

"I was hoping to speak to Charles Stuart, and I'm not from the press," Drew hastily added.

"Well if you're not from the press, you've found him." Charles smiled.

Drew could see from his slightly lopsided grin why people liked him. Tall, slim and attractive he had eyes that locked onto yours and engaged you right from the start. He had no doubt that Charles would be an effective politician.

"Drew Findlay," Drew stuck out his hand. Charles grasped it in a firm handshake. "I'm from the United States, I live there now but I'm originally from Scotland. I represent a certain Mr. Ballantyne who has left a considerable estate to his closest living relative, that's what brings me to Scotland and Inverness."

"Why would you want to talk to me then, Mr. Findlay, my name's Stuart?"

"Your great-grandfather was Sir Andrew Ballantyne, was he not?"

"You've been doing your homework." Charles frowned. "Look we can't stand here talking, let's go back into the office, it's more comfortable there."

"What about going to the Station Hotel where I'm staying, we could get a drink and they have a nice log fire in the lobby area."

"That would be great, but you forget who I am or rather what I've become, we wouldn't get a minutes peace. Come on back in, I'm sure we can find a bottle of something acceptable, the SRP could hardly have a dry office, could it now?" Charles opened the door and gestured for Drew to go through.

"You're quite right, I forgot about you making claim to the throne."

"Well we're just about to undo that one. It was a bit of fun at the time, not perpetrated by anyone in the party. I'll tell you about it or you'll read about it shortly. The publicity has been wonderful, though. It's put the SRP on the map. We just have to maintain the momentum, that's the difficult thing." Charles talked as they went up a short flight of stairs and he threw open what was the door to his office and beckoned Drew to sit in one of the massive leather swivel chairs in front of his desk.

"Go ahead." Charles leaned back in his chair.

Drew licked his lips. He needed that drink. Charles seemed to have forgotten all about finding the 'acceptable bottle'.

"It's just what I said earlier, I was trying to locate your mother and I did go to Torridon last week. Someone thought she might be there."

"Oh, I remember now. You met Hamish didn't you?"

"That's right."

"Aye, he phoned me in a great state of agitation not knowing whether he had done the right thing by telling you where my mother lives. I told him not to worry. My mother's whereabouts are local knowledge. So you've seen my mother?"

"No I haven't. Hamish told me Glen Cannich but I'm sure it's a big Glen."

"Aye, of course, Hamish wouldn't think, he just assumes everyone knows what and where he's talking about. So do you want to see my mother or me?"

"Your mother actually. But I just got back into town, I had to go to London and I thought I'd try and see you. Tell me about your father?"

"I never knew him and my mother doesn't talk about him, ever."

"You mean you don't know his name?"

"Of course, as far as I know everyone has a Birth Certificate and mine lists Callum Stuart as my father and that's it."

"What age was Callum Stuart?"

"I've no idea."

"Did you ever try to find out?"

"Well I got curious when I was at school and we were doing this genealogy thing, I have to confess I did try to find a Callum Stuart. I found plenty but only one in Birnam or thereabouts. That Callum Stuart was eighty-five when I was born so it couldn't have been him. I stopped then. There are Callum Stuarts all over the place but I let it go."

Drew was convinced that Charles was telling the truth. He had only turned up what Drew had found for himself in Edinburgh.

"Well thanks for your time," said Drew, there was nothing more to be gained by questioning Charles. The father was never mentioned because *there never was a father*. Drew was now convinced more than ever that Red Ericsson was right, Charles Stuart *was* Jens Ericsson. He sat back for a second mulling over whether he should drop the bombshell on Charles, but he rapidly thought the better of it. If this person opposite him was really Jens Ericsson it had to come from Eilid his mother or surrogate mother as it might turn out.

Drew went to get up.

"Hold on a minute, what dreadful hospitality. I did say we had a bottle somewhere. I quite forgot. Come on, let's have a dram, I've had a hell of a last two weeks, do you mind?" Charles grinned.

"You've twisted my arm," Drew grinned back.

Charles produced a bottle of Talisker from a drawer in the office and went off holding a crystal jug to find some water and some glasses. He was back in seconds pouring as he came back in through the door.

"Where do you live in the States?" Charles asked, sitting behind his desk again.

"Houston, Texas. Cheers," Drew lifted his glass.

"Slainte," said Charles, "here's to you and yours. Do you have a family?"

"I had, but not any more, it's a long story." Drew was amazed that he could actually get those words out without the customary choke. Fortunately Charles didn't pry.

"How about you?" Drew asked.

"We've been very lucky. I have two boys one eight and one six. We were going to try for a third, Elaine wants a girl but then the SRP came along."

"What did you do before you entered politics?"

"I was with Grampian Television. I became anchorman for a program called Scotland Today. It's a sort of Panorama type program but with the emphasis on Scotland. I've been doing that for eight years, well I mean I've stopped now, can't get used to that, it became part of my life."

"Do you think the SRP will become a major player in Scottish politics?"

"Only if we can be a credible alternative to the Scottish Nationalists, the SNP. This sounds like you doing my program," Charles laughed.

Drew was finding all this quite interesting.

"So how did you get into television?"

"By accident I suppose. One weekend at Torridon I met a film crew and a producer from Grampian Television, the Independent Television service for the Highlands and Islands in Scotland. The producer was doing an article on Torridon Lodge extolling the virtues of Hamish and Mhairi Ferguson the brother and sister team who run the place as if it were a five star hotel. I got on with the producer, a David Henderson, like a house on fire. He not only liked what he saw and heard from me but he shared the same political views as I do on Scotland becoming an independent country. I went for a screen test and the rest is history. I helped produce the program at first. Those were stirring times; we did more to fire the public's imagination on Scottish Independence than anyone. The media's very powerful as you probably know living in the US."

"Sure. To my mind it's over the top. So, tell me where do you live, in Inverness?"

"No, I just live up the road from my mother. She lives in the farmhouse, totally remodeled of course, and I built a house for Elaine and me with our back to the mountains looking south over a lochan it's a pretty spot."

"What about your mother's father? Wasn't he a Stuart as well?"

"Angus Stuart, he died a long time ago, 1977 I think it was. I was only nineteen at the time, still at university. I never met him. He didn't want anything to do with Eilid. She said he had been a really good father to her until he discovered that she was Alasdair Ballantyne's child, that's when the shit literally hit the fan. After he died the house lay vacant for years, then my mother decided to leave Torridon and go back to Cannich."

Drew listened to all of this free information. So Eilid Stuart or Ballantyne was Sir Andrew's *bastard* granddaughter. Eilid's history became more and more curious.

"So how do I get there?"

Charles drew a map and told Drew how to get there. He suggested that he should phone his mother and tell her about Drew's impending visit. Drew thought that would be a good idea, at least to Charles he seemed harmless and the fact that Charles had vetted him before meeting Eilid would be in his favor.

Charles and Drew said their goodbyes about ten minutes later. Charles had suggested that Drew should call on Monday rather than a Sunday, not that his mother would mind, she seldom attended church, but that it was the day for the family to get together. Allison Ferguson who moved with Eilid from Torridon now lived in the Cannich Lodge.

It was she who cooked Sunday dinner and that was not to be missed, Charles assured him.

Sunday dawned clear and cold. Drew had nothing to do and the city virtually closed down on a Sunday. The hotel was now almost empty. The reporters had all gone back to their respective homes or to chase more newsworthy items elsewhere. The 'no comment' strategy had played itself out. No news was bad news as far as reporters were concerned. Fred Grundy, the man behind it all stayed on in the hope that there would be more startling and exclusive revelations from the SRP.

Drew decided to go for a drive. He went back up the road to towards Torridon but instead of turning down the glen he headed north a few miles until he reached Loch Maree. The scenery was fantastic. There was a dusting of snow on Slioch the solitary mountain that guards the south-east end of the Loch. The waters looked gray and uninviting but the combination of hills, forest and water made Drew appreciate why some people would want to live there.

The weather remained the same on Monday. Drew drove down the side of the dark and foreboding Loch Ness glancing to the left now and then just in case the famous monster Nessie decided to reveal itself. When he reached Drumnadrochit he left the loch side and headed due west through Glen Urquhart and on to his destination. He found Cannich without any difficulty and turned up the dead end single-track road leading eventually to a loch created by the Scottish Hydroelectric Board just after the Second World War.

For some reason he felt slightly nervous. This was the moment of truth for him, so to speak. If he screwed up now all his efforts would be to no avail and the hope that sprang in the heart of Red Ericsson could be dashed forever. He had gone about five miles. There on his right was a bold sign carved on a slice of tree trunk hard by the entrance gate. 'Stalker's Cottage' it read. He stopped the Range Rover by the gate and unlatched it. It swung open easily on well-oiled hinges. Drew drove through, got out again and closed the gate behind him. The cottage had clearly gone through substantial improvements and alterations. All the windows were of hardwood, teak, he guessed and double-glazed. Attached to the front elevation was a large semi circular double-glazed porch with a variety of plants, some still flowering despite the chill

November weather. By the entrance door, again hardwood with a fan-light, sidelights and glazed panel all in obscure Georgian wired glass there was a long brass molded handle connected to a chain which ran up the wall some way and then disappeared through the rough hewn stone wall. Drew pulled gingerly pulled on the handle. He could hear a bell tinkling inside. Silence.

He looked around. A Range Rover was parked by a wooden building, probably an old stable he told himself. He began to have doubts. Maybe the seemingly friendly and co-operative Charles hadn't called her. He stepped back from the entrance and looked to the north up the hill behind him. The track leading from the farmhouse soon disappeared into thick woodland probably to emerge at the end of the tree line. There was no one there. Well, he thought, that was a wasted journey he took his hands out of his pockets with the key for his Range Rover and turned round right into Eilid Stuart. Drew got the fright of his life. He hadn't heard her coming and he jumped about six inches.

She stood eying him up and he she. A 30-06 Mannlicher Alpine rifle was slung over her right shoulder. She was dressed for the hill, long brown woolen stockings led to green corduroy breeches, a brownish checked shirt, the collar of which could just be seen poking out from a well worn dark green sweater in turn covered up by a dark green Barbour jacket. Her blond hair was pulled back in a ponytail and her face was devoid of any make up. She was beautiful, though. It was the only word that sprang to Drew's mind as they weighed one another up for what must have been all of ten seconds.

Eilid flashed him a perfect smile.

"I'm sorry I didn't mean to startle you. You must be Drew?"

"Yes, Drew Findlay."

They shook hands. Eilid's grip was as strong and firm as Drew's.

"Aye Charles phoned me. He was a bit vague about your visit and he wasn't sure of the time."

"I'm sorry about that. I don't think we did discuss a time, we got wrapped up in Scottish politics."

"Uh, uh, that's my boy all right."

Drew permitted himself a sarcastic thought. 'That's not your boy all right,' but he smiled back at her.

"Yes he was very generous with his time, quite a gentleman. I understand he lives near you?"

"Yes, just up the road a couple of miles. Look, I'm sorry I'm not being very hospitable but I've just shot this hind. I haven't started culling the hinds just yet but this one was wounded, someone had shot at her and broken both her legs. God knows where, not on my march I hope, she was almost completely crippled. I saw her last night so this morning I thought I'd catch her early. It took me longer than I thought she had hidden herself very well in the forest over there," Eilid pointed to a spot behind her, "so I'm later than I thought I'd be."

"That's not a problem. I'm not in a rush to go anywhere."

"You're sure."

"Not a problem."

"Would you mind coming with me 'til I bring her back. A wee help with a lift into the ArgoCat wouldn't go wrong. I'm not as young as I used to be."

"You look pretty good to me."

"Thank you. If you just wait here I'll get the Argo."

Drew watched as she climbed into the Range Rover and backed up to the old stable building. Then she hitched a trailer complete with ArgoCat to the vehicle and pulled forward beckoning on Drew to get in. Drew wondered just how old she was. She looked mid forties, maybe a little older. He surreptitiously glanced at her neck as they drove towards their destination but it was hard to see clearly with all the clothing she was wearing.

Eilid didn't miss a trick.

"What are you looking at?"

"Oh nothing, I was just looking at the scenery."

"Mmm."

Drew felt embarrassed.

"How far is it?"

"We're here. Well at least this is where I unload the Argo. On you come."

Drew was fascinated. He had never done anything like this ever. He sat in the front seat of the ArgoCat as Eilid started it up and steered forward by means of two levers, one with a throttle attached. The Briggs and Stratton 656cc engine fired away sounding just like an overstressed lawnmower as the ArgoCat moved forward on what seemed to be small plump under-inflated tires over the river, up the bank on the other side taking the rough terrain in its stride and on into the woodland. They hadn't gone more than a mile when Eilid turned the Argo through one-eighty degrees and stopped by the body of the hind. Drew marveled at her eyesight. He hadn't even seen the body even when they were right on top of it.

"Okay. Just wait a minute I've got to gralloch it, that's field dress it to you Americans, Charles tells me you're from the United States."

"I'm Scots actually," Drew said with some feeling.

"'Uh, uh. Where from?"

"Near Glasgow, but I've been away since I was twenty-two."

"So that's almost thirty years then, for you look about fifty."

"You're quite right, have you been speaking to Hamish?"

Eilid looked up as she zipped open the belly of the hind. The sweet smell of deer innards wafted up towards Drew. He backed off slightly.

Eilid had taken off the Barbour and rolled her shirtsleeve way up on her left arm to scoop out the intestines of the beast. She neatly side-stepped as she rolled the hind over and the innards slipped out. She picked up the stomach and intestines and threw them into a convenient hole in the ground a short way from the body. She wiped the blood off her arm with some grass she plucked from the forest floor.

"Right, this is where you come in, Drew isn't it?"

"Yes, Drew it is."

Pick her up by her hind legs, I'll grab the front and we'll just swing her into the back of the Cat."

Drew followed Eilid's instructions and applied all his strength to the lifting process. The deer suddenly shot up in the air and into the Argo as if propelled by some magical force.

"My word, I'm impressed. I hardly got my hand on it." Eilid stood back and looked at Drew again.

"I'm sorry I thought it would be a lot heavier, it can't weigh much more than a hundred pounds."

"Aye you're right, about eight stone I'd say just looking at her. Where did you get all those muscles?" Eilid looked at him with what seemed to be renewed interest.

"It's a long story."

"Maybe we'll find out. Come on then, let's get back." The process was repeated in reverse and by mid-morning they were at Cannich Lodge with Drew lending a hand as he and Eilid hung the hind in the Estate's larder.

"Come on we've done enough, I'll butcher her later today. Let's go back to the farm and you can tell me what's on your mind."

Eilid drove the short distance back to the farm in virtual silence. She quite liked the cut of Drew Findlay. There was something about him though that she couldn't put her finger on. She was a good judge of character having dealt with an enormous variety of people who had come to Torridon or Cannich for the stalking season.

Drew likewise tried to weigh Eilid up. She fitted the description given by the few people he had talked to about her. Words were used sparingly; she was extremely attractive and seemed to be in complete control of herself. She certainly knew what she was doing. Drew had already noticed the ring wasn't in evidence. To his mind that was the first set back. He had enjoyed the morning so far and it had helped to break down whatever barriers existed in each other's minds. He decided to throw away the rich dead relative approach. Eventually he would have to move from that story to get what he had really come for; he decided to as blunt and direct as possible.

"Sugar?" Eilid asked. They were now in the sun porch as Eilid called it and it was, Drew had to concede, very pleasant. Eilid had made a pot of tea and Drew was sitting in a comfortable chair at a modern round glass table. There were plants and small ferns all over what effectively was a conservatory and, even although it was late into November, the waning sun still manage to throw a pleasant warmth through the double-glazed roof. The views to the south, east and west were all spectacular. He wondered why he hadn't spent any time in the Highlands during his youth; it was just that working in the family business time never seemed to permit.

"Thanks, two please, no milk."

"Well now, there we are. Charles spoke warmly of you. You and he seemed to hit it off." She smiled at her visitor.

"Well there's not a lot to dislike. He's very personable indeed. As I think I said he and I share the same views on self-determination for Scotland."

"Ah then, you two would get on famously. Now who is it you're looking for?"

Eilid smiled again, but her eyes were icy cool as she looked over at Drew.

"I'm not really looking for anyone. I'm trying to find out information *about* someone"

"Who might that be?"

Drew took a deep breath.

"Your son, Charles Edward Stuart."

"Why did you not ask Charles when you saw him?"

"Because I don't think he has the answers to my questions."

There was a long silence.

"Just where are you from in the United States?"

"Houston, Texas."

"So you flew all the way from Texas to ask *me* questions about my son?"

"That's right. I want you to have a look at this please." Drew reached into his inside jacket pocket and pulled out the photograph of Lance

Ericsson he had cut out from the Petrotex Annual Report and Accounts. He passed it over to Eilid.

Eilid looked at the photograph for some time.

"Just who is this person?"

"His name is Lance Ericsson, and I have reason to believe he's Charles's twin brother."

Drew looked closely for any reaction. There was none. Just stony silence, Drew was sure he could hear his heart pounding as he held his breath still waiting for a reaction.

"I'm afraid you have come to the wrong house and I resent your implication. Please go."

Eilid slowly rose from her chair pushing away the teacup.

"Is that all you've got to say to me?"

"Indeed it is. You're lucky to be getting that." Eilid's lips were pursed tight and Drew could see she had paled visibly despite her tanned face.

Drew had shocked her to her very foundation he could see that, now her aggressiveness ebbed away in the sadness of her eyes.

"Eilid, let's not go down this path, please. I know too much. Charles's father has so much money he'll take legal action to prove what I have just told you. I beg you do not do this."

"Are you a policeman, then?"

"No I'm not. I used to be a long time ago. I am a sort of retired insurance investigator, brought out of retirement to do this job. There's one other thing I need to show you," he dived into his inside pocket again before Eilid could remonstrate further and produced the brochure with the ring. Drew thrust it under her eyes.

"You have a ring just like this, don't you?"

Eilid sat back down in her chair. Drew did the same. They stared at one another across the table.

Eilid's mind was racing. This was the moment she had dreaded all of her life. The one stupid, selfish act she committed thirty-four years ago had come back to haunt her like some Shakespearean ghost. She knew now it was over. She could see by Drew Findlay's mettle there would be no stopping him and her life would become a misery, as if it couldn't be miserable enough. She sat looking at Drew who had never taken his eyes from hers. Silently a tear rolled down her cheek and Drew knew he had won.

"Why don't you tell me all about it?" he had begun to feel sorry for her already. He reached out with his hand across the table to hold hers.

"How did you find out?" she wiped away another tear with her sleeve and gave Drew her right hand clutching his nervously.

"It was a simple thing really. Just a photograph of Charles in a newspaper and one of Mr. Ericsson's friends saw the amazing likeness and sent the newspaper clipping to him. I've been here, in the UK, for nearly three weeks trying to fit the pieces together. It's not been easy. You or your Uncle covered your tracks well. If it hadn't been for John Forsyth, Charles's old headmaster, I don't think I would ever have got a lead."

Eilid hardly heard a word. Her tear filled eyes stared back at him.

"I'm going to lose him, aren't I?"

"That's not for me to say. But I have to tell Mr. Ericsson what I've found. He may take into account some mitigating factors. Just how did you get hold of the baby? Would you please tell me?"

Eilid dried her eyes, poured another cup of tea for them both and related to Drew the events of January eighth almost thirty-five years ago. The horror of the crash, the miracle of finding the baby alive, the Herculean task of bringing the child off the hill. Then her assumption that both parents had been killed in the crash followed by the hair-raising drive to Pitlochry and finally getting her Uncle to attend to the child and registering the birth as her own.

"But your Uncle was a doctor, a man of high integrity, how did you persuade him to register the birth?"

Eilid told Drew of Ken's heavy drinking bouts and how, because of a badly written prescription, he had hastened the death of one of his patients. How he had confessed to Eilid when he was in his cups of his having practiced euthanasia on that patient and how she had used this as leverage to get him to do her bidding. Despite the fact that her coercion of her Uncle didn't happen quite as she described, Eilid wanted to clear her dead Uncle's reputation from any blame.

Drew listened fascinated as Eilid recanted the years of difficulty with Charles's health never really knowing what was wrong. Then she told him the story of Colin Macalister coming to Torridon and finding out first hand from one of the attending physicians at the baby's operation what had transpired. Armed with that information her Uncle had been able to diagnose Charles's condition, which led to another operation miraculously giving him a normal life.

"And Charles knows *nothing* of this?"

"No, no. That's what's bothering me. I can't imagine what he'll think of me."

"Did he never ask you about his father?"

"He did when he was younger and I just told him his father died in a tragic accident and he never asked again. I think Sir Andrew Ballantyne made up for not having a father. He doted on Charles."

"And Sir Andrew thought he was your child?"

"Well, yes and no."

"You revealed your secret to him?"

"Heavens no. I think just before he died he found out something from the man who was my only lover that I never had a child. He left me a personal letter in his will. Now that you have all this information what are you going to do? You'll never have been deprived of children I suppose, you have a family?"

"I can't begin to tell you how far that statement is removed from the truth. Yes I was married, I had three daughters and a wonderful wife and they were taken from me in a fiery crash on one of the freeways in Houston. Do you know you're the first person in almost a year that I've been able to talk to about it without tearing up?" Drew put down the teacup as his hand began to shake. Steady now, he told himself. Taking a deep breath he continued.

"I lost my mind, literally. I sold my home with all the memories in it intact. I wanted no part of it. I moved into an apartment and started drinking myself to death. If it wasn't for this case and my friend Bobby Rule, a Houston attorney, I'd probably be gone by now.

All of this has given me a new perspective on life, it won't and can't change what happened but I'll tell you this, I will do what I can on your behalf. It won't be easy, Red's a tough man and I don't know him personally, but Bobby does."

Eilid looked at Drew in a different light. She could see he was a kind person at heart and he had just confided his dreadful experience to her. It was as if a touch of bonding had taken place between them by way of their respective adversities. Drew's offer of help was akin to a beacon in the gloom of what could turn out to be her Armageddon.

"Drew, that's terrible, awful. I can't imagine how you must have felt or feel, even now. I am so sorry for you; I should not have said what I said. It's my selfish streak coming out again."

Eilid stretched out again and grasped Drew's right hand.

"I just want to know what's going to happen to me. Charles is all I've got in life, plus Elaine and the two boys. What's going to happen do you think?"

"I wish I knew. It's a conundrum. Charles is thirty-four, soon to be thirty-five. Technically, he's an American citizen. Also technically you abducted him or kidnapped him, I can't imagine any court not seeing it like that. You have deprived a father from raising his son. Had you gone to the authorities and reported the baby's survival that would be another matter. But you connived, and indeed colluded, with your uncle to keep him to yourself. Charles is now leading the Scottish Republican Party and he's *American*...there's one for the press after all the hoo-ha about his claim to be in line for the throne. Can Charles decide his future? After all, he's well past the age of majority. He's a popular, intelligent and charismatic man, just the man to lead Scotland or Petrotex into the future. Do you see the problem?"

Eilid sat stone-faced and just nodded.

"Look, I've got to report back to Red. He may not be around; he travels all over the place. I go through his personal assistant Ruth Rivers and I'll fax her what I've found out. Meanwhile I suggest you meet with Charles and fill him in on what's happened. How much or how little you tell him I'll leave to you." He reached forward and held her hands in his. "But Eilid, you need to tell him, he can't hear this from a third party."

Eilid nodded again. "What is his actual name? Colin Macalister told me but I've forgotten, it's such a long time ago."

"Jens, it's Jens Ericsson."

"That's not nearly as nice as Charles Edward Stuart now is it?" And for a brief moment the old Eilid was back with a ring in her voice and some of the fire back in her eyes.

"No it's not, but that was the name he was given. I've one more question, and it's important for I'll be asked. The ring, how did you come by the ring?"

"It was round the baby's neck, on a piece of yellow ribbon. I even kept the ribbon."

"Thank God," said Drew fervently, "you know that Red's wife lost her arm in the crash, I'm not sure which one, but I'm willing to bet Red will think you took that ring from his wife's finger."

"He's not alone. My Uncle Kenny and I almost had a fall out over that. He accused me of being a grave robber."

"Jeez, a man of mixed principle's eh? Pinch the kid, but where did the ring come from? Amazing, truly amazing."

"Well whatever. He was instrumental in saving Charles's life twice. He was a good man. If his wife hadn't left him for some Irish navvy he'd have been all right. I don't think he ever got over the humiliation of that happening."

"Sorry, I shouldn't have said that. I'm beginning to be judgmental now and I vowed I wouldn't do that. I'm sure your uncle was a fine doctor, everyone in Pitlochry spoke very highly of him."

"My God, you've been to Pitlochry?"

"Well that was the place of birth on the Birth Certificate that was issued. I met some guy in the Moulin Hotel bar who will never forget you."

"Don't tell me.........Johnnie."

"The very man. Johnnie Miller, still there after all these years. He was madly in love with you, still is, I think. He couldn't wait to tell me about your evening at the rifle club, the Scottish Annie Oakley they christened you."

Eilid smiled a wry smile. "Aye, it was a long time ago. I was just showing off, but the men were quite impressed and my Uncle Ken thought it was a great display. I was pretty good you know."

"You also had a boy friend, Johnnie couldn't quite remember his last name but he remembered what he drank."

"Yes, that's Johnnie all right. It was Douglas, Douglas Hamilton. The only man I ever loved and I think who truly loved me."

"Where is he now?"

"Gone. Like your family gone to what we think is a better place. He died of AIDS. He was incarcerated in some Soviet prison. Who knows what happened but he was given injections for a virulent strain of tuberculosis and it was a dirty needle. He certainly wasn't a queer."

"When did he die?"

"About six months after Charles graduated. January 1980. He attended the Graduation Ball. I hadn't seen him for more than twelve or thirteen years. It was a complete surprise and a shock let me tell you. He came up and did an "excuse me, can I dance with this lady?" routine. I hardly recognized him. He was so emaciated. I just thought it was his being starved in prison, but it was more sinister than that. He kept catching anything that was going round; flu would become pneumonia and so on. Then he was diagnosed HIV positive and it went rapidly downhill from there into full-blown AIDS. It was awful. Latterly he didn't know me and it wasn't the Douglas Hamilton I knew when he died."

"Christ, you've been through it too. I can see now why you want to have Charles around, he and Elaine *are* all you've got." Drew bit his lip; he too was getting emotional about the whole thing.

Eilid just managed to stay dry-eyed and just nodded. She got up without saying anything and wandered into the large living room. Drew sat lost in his own thoughts. He couldn't believe he had talked about his wife and family the way he did. Was this all part of some healing process as in 'life must go on'? He didn't know and he didn't much care. He had taken an instinctive liking to Eilid and he thought she to him.

He felt he had outstayed his visit and got up to make his way to the door when Eilid walked back in with a bottle of Macallan and two glasses. She nodded her head at him to sit down as she put the bottle and the glasses on the table.

"We both could do with this, not unless you've gone tee-total?"

"Chance would be a fine thing. At least I've cut back, I've been pretty stupid and doing this job for Bobby Rule has helped me put my life in a different perspective. Go ahead and pour."

Eilid filled the two crystal glasses up with about three fingers of malt.

"Water?" she asked.

"Just a tad. I've never been able to enjoy Scotch neat unless it's the Macallan 25 year old when adding water would be sacrilege."

Eilid add a couple of splashes.

"Drew, please tell me what you think will happen. I've lived with this dreadful fear of discovery all these years; I've been a selfish, silly old woman. Slainte," she lifted the glass in a mock toast.

"Slainte mhath" 'Good Health to you', Drew responded in Gaelic. "What do you mean

'old woman' you aren't close yet."

"I'll be fifty-six next birthday,"

"When is your birthday?"

"Fourth of July."

"Your kidding, American Independence Day. There's got to be some kind of irony there," Drew smiled for the first time. "Let me tell you, you look closer to forty-six than fifty-six."

"That's very kind of you, if you really mean it."

"Look at you. Your slender, *very* attractive, very fit, I think you're just…" Drew hesitated,

"Well?"

"You're very attractive… no, it's more than that, serene I think that's the word I would use, you have this sort of serenity about you."

"You're being very kind. But then my body hasn't been ruined with the child bearing, has it now?" Eilid smiled a grim little smile.

Drew smiled back. "To answer your question, which I think I've already answered in a round about way, I truly do not know. I'm not a lawyer or attorney, as they call it in the States, but my first thought is that Red will overreact. Apparently the loss of his wife was, and I know now how he feels, a deep and lasting loss. He never remarried. He'll go bananas when he finds out that Jens is alive. He'll probably want to 'sue yor ass' as the Americans love to say. But why would he do that? To punish you that would be his only reason. To my mind that's silly. He already has more money than God. It would be to no purpose. But then he'd say, and I'm playing Devil's Advocate now, why should she get off scot-free? That's the difficulty as I see it. Try to empathize. He's been denied his son for thirty-four years he'll want to lash out. Maybe between Bobby and me we can make common sense prevail but emotion is sure to take over, at least initially, he may even want to destroy you, just for the hell of it, he's a very powerful man." Drew finished his drink at a loss to say more, all this was just a guessing game.

"Do you think he'd want to take Charles back to the United States?"

"Would Charles want to go to the United States? That's the question I'd be asking myself. His life is here with his wife and children there's no kind of magic eraser that can wipe out the past and allow someone to relive it to a different set of circumstances and rules. Red might jump up and down, but at the end of the day his son's life is a fait accompli. And that's what's going to piss him off."

"What's the other twin like, is it Lance?"

"Don't know I've never met him. Bobby doesn't speak very highly of him. He said to me that he models himself on J.R. Ewing from the old TV show Dallas. He's just turned thirty-four and is not to be fooled with. Just a case of too much money too soon. Bobby calls him the Playboy of the Western world."

"He looks fatter than Charles, but that's to be expected, up until the age of ten or nearly eleven Charles was a thin wan wee chap."

"Eilid, I've got to go. I have to send my report to Ruth or Red. Let me do that and I'll come back when I get a reaction. What's your phone number?"

They parted with a hug in the neat garden and Drew climbed into his Range Rover to make his way back to Inverness. It was already mid-afternoon and the long Scottish twilight was setting in. The dipping sun was directly over his shoulder, with crimson and gold tinting the peaks as he made his way down the single-track road to Cannich village. His mind was in disarray. Thoughts flashed in and out, would Eilid tell Charles? And when? What would Red's reaction be? That was the one he dreaded.

However his mind twisted and turned so much so he couldn't divorce himself from the actions and reactions that would take place over the next twenty-four to forty-eight hours. He was a hired hand. He had no place in the determination of this mammoth problem. He arrived at the Station Hotel without any recollection of the journey back.

The receptionist in the hotel was only too pleased to give Drew, now a regular resident, the use one of the hotel's computers. It was seven in the evening when he finished with the word processor, printing out the wordy four-page document and faxing it to Houston for Ruth River's attention.

He celebrated dinner with a fine bottle of claret, which perfectly complemented the venison steak he ordered. He was done; it was all over. He sat in the now almost empty dining room staring blankly at the wall. Instead of elation for a job well done, he felt drained and depressed. The thought of going back to the US had no appeal; there was nothing to go back to. He left the table and had just got to his bedroom when his mobile phone rang. It was Ruth.

"Jeez dude, you must feel like the cat that got the cream!" She sounded elated.

"Sad really."

"What, for the bitch that took Red's son?"

"No. For both of them. What did Red say?"

"He hasn't seen it yet. He's out on a platform somewhere in the Gulf and I don't expect him in 'til late tomorrow. I'm sure not going to go over all this on the phone, but he'll be excited and mad all at the same time. Are you going to be around?"

"That's a good question. There's no reason for me to be here now, my works over. I'll probably start making tracks for home tomorrow."

"Whoa there, Drew. Not so fast. I'm sure you're keen to get out of that crap weather and get home to some sun, but I'd wait for Red to call the shots. My best guess is his first step will be to see Bobby Rule."

Yep, thought Drew. He didn't comment on Ruth's intuitive guess, but he said, "Fine, that's okay by me I'll wait a day or two. The weather's not been too bad. Pretty cold in the mornings but it is sunny and bright with just beautiful scenery."

"Well, you take care, y'hear; hey, and Drew, well done."

"Thank you. I just hope it works out okay."

"Me too." And Ruth was gone.

Drew was feeling really tired. It had been a day of emotional upheaval for the parties concerned. He wondered what Eilid had done with Charles. He was sitting at the end of the bed talking off his shoes when the phone rang.

"Drew Findlay," he answered.

"Drew, this is Charles Stuart. I have to talk to you."

"Where are you?"

"Downstairs in the lobby."

"Give me five minutes and I'll be down."

"I'll be at the bar," said Charles tersely.

Drew put his shoes back on, ran a comb through his gray wavy hair, and made for the elevator. He glanced at his watch. It was almost ten-thirty. When he arrived down stairs Charles was the only person in the bar, a glass of lager in his hand. As Drew entered he moved off the bar stool and sat at a table in a far away corner.

"What'll it be?' Charles asked.

"I'm fine right now...I take it your mother has spoken to you?"

"My God did she ever. Elaine and I are stunned, that's the only word for it. I had to come here for corroboration, I think she's gone stark raving mad, and at times she was almost incoherent."

"I can imagine." Drew averted his eyes to a beer mat on the tabletop. "I think I've just turned a number of lives through 180 degrees today, and I'm truly sorry. I'm only the messenger, but it's a hell of a message."

"So it's all true, is it?"

"Well I don't know exactly what your mother had to say but you were certainly not born Charles Stuart and you're not Scots."

"Jesus Christ, I can't take all of this in. What possessed her to do this?"

"I wish I could answer that one, not that it would make you feel any better. She was young, she jumped to the conclusion that you had just been orphaned and she used her strong will to get her uncle accept and carry out her wishes. As I often tell people the only thing you do in a hurry is make a mistake, and Eilid's was a cracker. I take it you had no inkling of this?" Drew looked at Charles closely.

"Absolutely not. I did often wonder why any mention of my father was a sore subject, that when I was young, and in truth I gave up probing because she got so upset and there was never any answer. She didn't lie; she just said it was not for discussion. When you're a kid that's the end of it."

"What are you going to do?"

"That's easy. Nothing right now except look after the only parent I've ever known. The legalities of this are too involved to even ponder. What do you think this Mr. Ericsson is going to do?"

Drew breathed a great sigh ands softly said, "I only wish I knew. He's out of the country and doesn't know yet, but he'll probably know tomorrow."

"I hear he's very wealthy?"

"Yep, more money than he knows what to do with, so I'm told."

"And I have a twin brother?"

"You do."

Charles sat shaking his head in disbelief.

Drew said, "I'll have that drink now, what's yours Charles it's on me?"

"I'll have a large whisky, thanks."

Drew called up two and their conversation started up again.

"You know Charles what Red, that's Ericsson's first name, a nickname really, needs to understand is that without your mother being at the right place at the right time you wouldn't be alive, that's a strong mitigating factor, I think. Did she tell you how she rescued you?"

"No we didn't get into detail. She was weeping so much; it was hard to make out what she was saying. In all my years I've never seen her cry like that. The first tear I ever saw her shed was at Sir Andrew's funeral."

"Well it was quite an affair, let me tell you." So Drew went on to relate how amazingly innovative Eilid had been in getting Charles off the hill alive. Drew had just finished relating this to him when Charles stopped him in mid-sentence.

"In the belly of the beast eh? You know when my mother grallochs a deer that smell, that sweet pungent odor, is somehow familiar and I hate it, I don't like it. You don't think it's stored in my subconscious somewhere do you?"

"Nothing would surprise me. The human mind is a wonderful thing."

Lance Ericsson swung out of the bed pulled back the covers and gave a playful slap to the generous buttocks that came into view.

"Yah know baby you're not a bad piece of ass for a lady of your age."

"Gee Lance you say the sweetest things, you're a real charmer." Ruth's acidic sarcasm didn't dent Lance one bit.

"Come on Ruth, let's be honest, you can't get enough, and we go at it real well. You're the best. I'd love to know where you learned some of your tricks, though."

"That's a ladies secret."

"When's my Daddy due home?"

Ruth looked at her ladies Rolex on the bedside table.

"You know, he should be home by now, why?"

"Jest wondered. I ain't doin' anything great tonight, he's not likely to call you, is he?"

"Well you never know, why?"

"Well I had jest such a fine time I figured a tad more of that there Champagne and you an' me could hump a bit more, but if the phone's gonna ring..."

"Taken care of," Ruth pulled the jack connection out of the wall. We're all private honey. Champagne's in the 'fridge." Ruth pointed to the small refrigerator in her bedroom, her latest acquisition.

"Hey that's new, ain't it?" Lance peered at the all white appliance.

"All thanks to you hon. I just got tired of running out into the kitchen buck naked to fetch drinks, so I thought I'd get the vitals a little bit closer to home, so to speak."

"Well that's jest swell. Allow me."

At that, Lance pulled the spring-loaded sealer cork out of the bottle and started to fill two glasses. He glanced up at Ruth and raised his eyebrows,

"I take it this is okay with you Ruthie?"

"Sure thing. If you can go, I sure can."

Two hours later the bottle was empty and neither Ruth nor Lance were totally in control of their mental processes.

"Tell yuh what Ruthie," Lance slushed, "we need somethin' to eat."

"Sounds like a good idea lover. You gonna get a to-go?"

"Yeah, why not. There's the Chinese a couple of blocks away. You phone."

"Jeez okay, I'll have to plug the phone back in."

No sooner had she done that, and before she could dial the Chinese, the phone rang. It was Red.

"Ruth where the hell have you been?"

"I've been home all night, honest."

"Well your phone's been ringing off the wall, no reply and no answering machine."

"Oh I'm sorry Red. The line had been disconnected from the jack."

"Jesus, how did that happen?"

"The maid, probably the maid."

"Did yuh hear from Drew?"

"I did indeed. It's Jens, he's proved it's Jens."

The words weren't out of her mouth when she could have cut her tongue out. She looked over at Lance lying on the bed. He had heard her all right and he was looking over at her with that strange look as if he had just eaten something that disagreed with him.

'Jesus Christ," Red hissed, "I knew that guy could do it. My son's alive, I, I… I can't believe it." Red's voice faltered as the enormity of what Ruth had said sank in. Can I phone him?"

"Well not now. It's seven-thirty here; it'll be one-thirty in the morning over there. He's probably in bed."

"Well he can get out of bed. I have to congratulate this guy. Did he say much to you?"

"He didn't call. He sent a long fax. It's locked in my desk drawer. Do you want it this evening?"

"Only if I can't get Drew on the phone. I have his cell number but there's no answer, I don't have the hotel number."

"I'll get you that."

Ruth went over to the dressing table and bent over to retrieve her handbag when Lance grabbed her from behind and started to play with her breasts.

"Lance," she hissed, "it's your father on the line, for Christ's sake."

"What's goin' on?"

"I'll tell you in a minute."

Back she went to the phone and gave the Inverness Station Hotel's number to a grateful Red and hung up.

Ruth turned to Lance.

"I've got to get dressed. Five gets you ten your father's going to be around any minute; he's ecstatic and alone, a bad combination. He can't find you here, that's for sure."

"What's all this Jens shit? What were you and he talking about?"

"Lance, this is your father's project, I'm not at liberty to say."

"Bull shit, li'l lady, you and I are goin' to have a conversation, right reason or none. So c'mon, I know my brother who died was called Jens, so what's the scoop?"

"Lance I can't tell you. I've said too much already, please, your father will kill me."

"If I don't kill you first!" Lance exploded and grabbed Ruth by her hair and pulled her face to within an inch of his.

"Lance, please you're hurting me…"

"I haven't even started yet," he spoke through clenched teeth with a breath soured by the Champagne. Ruth tried to back away. "C'mon, what's goin' on? I ain't leavin' 'til I find out."

Ruth said nothing. Lance let her go, staggered back slightly and threw a wild punch that connected to the side of Ruth's head. Still stark naked she fell back and hit her head on the bedside table as she fell. She began to cry.

"You big shit," she sobbed. No man's ever hit me, not one. I hope it *is* your brother Drew's found, for if it is he has to be a better man than you. I can't wait to meet him. Now go before I call the cops or your father or both."

Lance looked at the cringing female in front of him and drew back his foot to give her a kick. But he staggered a little, again due to the Champagne, and as he went to move forward and deliver the kick Ruth had grabbed her handbag and Lance was looking into the wrong end of a .38 snub nosed revolver.

Ruth glared at him. Lance glared back. Nothing was said for what seemed like ages.

"Okay, you win, let me get dressed." Lance backed off to go into the bathroom.

"Not a chance. Your clothes are on that chair over there. Dress in here and then go."

"You ain't heard the last of this Ruthie, I'll find out what's been goin' on and when I do watch this space, 'cause you won't be in it."

"Just fuck off!"

"My, my, dirty words, whatever next…" Lance scrambled into his pants, threw on his shirt, pulled on his boots grabbed his leather jacket and made for the door with Ruth not far behind. He slammed the door behind him and Ruth sank to the floor exhausted and broke into tears again. She was shaking like a leaf and her sobs were uncontrollable. Suddenly she realized she still had no clothes on and she staggered back to the bedroom pulled on a white toweling bathrobe and sat on the edge of the bed her mind reeling. After fifteen minutes she had calmed down sufficiently to go look at her face in the Vanitory mirror. There was a bright red weal under her left eye and already her cheek was going dark purplish blue.

She rushed to the kitchen to get an ice pack to hold to her face to try and reduce the swelling and the bruising. I should have known, she told herself; Lance was a shallow egotistical shithead. Others had told her what he was like as they left Petrotex fired by Lance on some spurious pretext or another but she had never thought she would become involved with him. It was her own fault. Red had never shown the slightest inclination to be associated with her sexually and underneath she resented that. She had done her best to attract him, she dressed well, was efficient to the point of being anal when it came to his likes and dislikes, but never, never once had he given her any sign that he was interested in her. It was only recently when she had been to his house that he had showed some emotion and ended up giving her a hug and a perfunctory kiss. The fact that his son had made a play at her had boosted her ego. Hell, here she was pushing fifty and she had a toy boy almost twenty years her junior. Now her affair had backfired. She prayed Red wouldn't come round to her apartment that night.

She wakened at six-thirty. It was still dark. A Blue-Norther had swept through some time in the night and when she looked outside the weather looked blustery and cool. She ran the shower and looked at her face in the mirror. There was no way she could hide the bruising, not without a heavy pancake makeup. Ruth prided herself in her complexion. She had never used heavy makeup and what makeup she did use she used sparingly only to accent what she thought were her better points. This morning it would have to be a plaster job to avoid Red's critical eye. She was glad he hadn't phoned again or come to visit her as she thought he might. Enough was enough for one evening.

She was ready to go at seven fifteen, but she couldn't find her keys. Where the hell were her keys for the office? She always had them in her handbag. She was sure they had been there the previous evening when she pulled her gun on Lance. That was a scary moment. Her car keys were in the pocket of her coat, but her office keys were more important. These were the keys to Red's personal filing cabinets, the key to the fax locked box and various other highly confidential files around the executive suite of offices. There was nothing she could do she had searched everywhere. Then she had an awful thought. Lance, could Lance have taken her keys? How could he when she had always been near her handbag? Then she pieced together what had happened when she went back to the phone with the phone number of the hotel in Scotland Lance would have had the opportunity to take them out of her bag. They were on a Dooney and Burke leather key chain and wouldn't be hard to find. That's why he backed off so quickly when she pulled her gun. He already had means to gain access. She had to get to the office right away.

She pulled out of her apartment driveway at about fifty miles an hour. She gunned the Lexus 300 down Chimney Rock towards the Southwest freeway and joined the already crawling traffic past the 610 Loop on towards Downtown. Her heart was pounding. How could she explain all this to Red? She had never lied to him she never had the need. This was different. The malevolence that showed on Lance's face came back to haunt her as she maneuvered her car through the rush hour traffic.

She got to the office on Louisiana and parked in her executive space. She took the elevator straight to the twenty-second floor and had to get security to let her into her office. That had taken another precious ten minutes. Her keys were lying right in the middle of her desk. She would never have left them there, of that she was certain. She opened the locked box on Red's personal fax machine. Nothing. My God, she thought what am I going to do? Then she remembered. With all this panic she was losing her mind. She had put them or more importantly locked them in her desk drawer. Breathlessly she opened the drawer. Nothing had been touched they were still there. She collapsed in the chair at her desk just as the door swung open to reveal Red standing in the threshold.

"How are you?" Red asked.

"I've been better."

Ruth cast her eyes downward.

"Did you get hold of Drew?" She asked.

"Did I ever. Wakened the poor bastard up, he was a tad upset. We talked for over an hour."

"Well if you waken someone in the middle of the night, what would you expect?"

"Nothing to do with that. What's wrong with your face?"

"Walked into the fridge door."

"Yeah, right. What was the fridge's name?"

"What did Drew say then?" Ruth had to change the subject.

"Well he told me everything verbatim from the Stuart woman. Don't get me wrong he did a fine job. It could all have gone the wrong way. The most interesting news by far was not what he put on the fax."

"What was that?"

"Well, after he had sent you the fax, he's in the hotel about to jump into bed and Jens or Charles, if you like, calls him from the hotel lobby and they have a head to head discussion in the bar for about two hours. What do you make of that?"

"What did Charles say?"

"His mother had gone to see him that afternoon just after Drew left her and gave him the whole enchilada."

"God, straight from the horses mouth, no holds barred, he must have been shattered." Ruth couldn't imagine what that revelation had done to Charles and his family.

"Yeah, that would be a fair comment. Drew asked him what he was going to do and he said nothing. His mother was the only parent he had ever known and he wasn't about to change anything. It's a typical reaction."

"More important Red, what's going to be your reaction?"

"Good question. I've gotta see Bobby. I've told Drew to stay on if he doesn't mind until I have a game plan. There are so many knock-on effects with this I can't think straight. Emotionally, I've about had it. It's like the second resurrection, and I don't mean that in any kinda blasphemous way, the son I thought was dead has risen. He's alive and well and he doesn't know me." Red had to grab his handkerchief, as his feelings got the better of him.

Ruth stepped forward and gave him a hug. She met with no resistance as she held Red tight to her.

"Red," they were still standing holding one another, "when are you going to tell Lance?"

"I don't know yet, but it's gotta be soon. He cannot find out 'cept from me. Do you think he'll like having a brother?"

Red could feel Ruth tense, as she said, "No, he won't like that at all."

"You mean that for real, don't yuh?"

"I'm sorry to say I do. Lance has had everything his own way for too long, I think so anyway, but I could be wrong."

Red held her at arm's length and looked her straight in the eye.

"And I had this gut feeling that you and Lance were maybe an item. That can't be so, eh?" Red grinned as Ruth made a face.

"I used to get along with him just fine, but lately…" she tailed off for fear of saying too much.

Red looked at her more closely. "Boy that sure is some shiner you have there, fridge door my ass. You should choose your men more carefully."

"Amen to that."

"He's not giving you trouble is he? 'Cause I can have that taken care of in a New York minute."

"No, no, everything's cool."

"You sure now Ruth?"

"Sure."

"Let me get back to Lance then. Are you sure Lance is going to be unhappy about having a brother?"

"Red, it's hard to say. I think I know him well enough to tell you he'll see the brother as competition. You can tell him he doesn't have to worry, but look at it from his perspective. You have choices now that didn't exist until you found Jens was alive. Your attention will be diverted from Lance, that's to be expected. You have to play catch-up with the twin you thought was dead. I'd be willing to bet he's gonna be one big unhappy guy, and that's bad. When Lance is unhappy watch out, nothing nice is about to happen. Right now he's the big cheese in Petrotex right after you, when you retire he's it, whether your people like it or not."

"Level with me Ruth, Lance ain't popular is that what you're telling me?"

"No comment."

"Ruth come on I have to know. I've given Lance pretty free reign since he came on board, but I have to admit I don't get too close." Red looked hard at Ruth her arms akimbo.

"You sure you want to hear this?"

"Yep. Give it to me straight, get to the bottom line."

"Red, Lance isn't just disliked, he's hated. This is not a very ladylike expression but basically he's a big shit. He abuses his position, he can be real evil. He runs rampage at times and we've lost some valuable people over the last two or three years since he became COO. You want me to go on?"

"No, I value your opinion. Thanks for your candor. I kinda thought as much, I just didn't have the guts to admit it to myself. What a goddam mess. Maybe meeting Jens will get him to straighten his act out."

"Red, you might be right, but, as I said, I wouldn't bet on it." Ruth looked straight into Red's downcast eyes.

"Okay. I hear you. Listen thanks for your help in all of this. Sooner or later I'm going to have to go over to Scotland, but the timing's not right I guess. Call Bobby for me and see if we can set up lunch. I want you to come and take notes."

"The Club?"

"Yeah, let's do the Club. I'm off to read all this," he waved Drew's fax in her face.

Lance sat in his palatial office with the door closed. He had read Drew Findlay's fax after he picked her keys out of Ruth's handbag. Stupid bitch, he thought, fancy pulling a gun on me, me Lance Ericsson. He wondered why his father had been so secretive. He had heard the name Drew mentioned a couple of times in the last couple of months but it had meant nothing to him. Now his twin brother was alive and well in Scotland, Jesus what a hell of a deal.

He knew nothing about Scotland but he was willing to bet that Jens wasn't living in the lap of luxury. He had better act quick, he thought, before too much damage could be done. All of that which he surveyed was his by right and birthright. He was not about to split anything with anybody, especially with a brother whom he had never known. He sat deep in thought for about thirty minutes. A plan started to form in his convoluted mind.

That afternoon, somewhere in South Beach Miami, a phone rang.

"Ola, thees ees Felix."

"Hey Felix ole' buddy, how you been? This is Lance here."

"Ah. Meester Lance. I think about you many times, always when I see the good-looking weeman, I theenk of our times togeether. What you need Felix to do for you?"

"I need somebody whacked."

"He ees here in Miami?"

"No. Not even in the US."

"Wheech country?"

"Scotland."

There was a long pause.

"Where ees thees Scotland?"

"In the United Kingdom"

"Eh?"

"Britain, fucking England, if you like." Lance was getting exasperated

"Why you no say Eengland? This place I know."

"You bin there?"

"No neever, but I hear of Eengland, it is full of Eenglish, no?"

"Yeah, it is. Scotland's to the North of England."

There was another long pause. Lance was beginning to have second doubts about Felix's ability to do this job.

"Thees weel be deeficult, maybe. How many men you want?"

"As many as it takes, I'll pay top dollar."

"Leave thees weeth me, Mr. Lance. I get back to you manyana. I call you on thees number."

Lance hung up.

Lance knew he could trust Felix not to rat on him; He was the only person he thought he could trust to handle a deal like this.

Felix had come to him by way of one of the Petrotex production platforms anchored out in the Mexican Gulf. Felix and his family of two girls and a boy plus his wife had escaped from Cuba in what was quite a sturdy boat. Heading for Miami, where they had friends, they were blown completely off course and ended up in the vast expanse of the Mexican Gulf. Fortunately for the Savio family Felix had fitted an outboard motor to the boat. It refused to work after a storm pounded their small vessel and soaked everything. Felix, as Lance soon found out, was a skilled mechanic. He stripped the outboard down to its components, fixed the problem and in a short time powered the boat, albeit slowly towards the north. He used the sails when the wind was favorable and the outboard at night. Their provisions had run out and after four days at sea he was about to give up all hope when he saw the lights of the Petrotex platform on the horizon. Three hours later the family was hauled on board, given food, water, and a place to stay.

Lance's helicopter had landed at dawn on one of his routine inspections. The crew foreman was about to call up the Coast Guard when Lance stopped him. Lance was fluent in Spanish and soon realized that if he reported the boat to the authorities the chances were that they might be returned to Cuba. Felix, for his part, pleaded with all his might not to be turned in to the authorities. For the Savios Lance became the knight in shining armor. He simply bundled them aboard the Petrotex chopper and landed them on the roof of the Downtown Houston office. There was an evil method in Lance's apparent generosity. The Savios were now illegal immigrants and as such would be subject to arrest and deportation. However Lance gave them quarters in his home and Felix acted as his chauffeur when required. Felix was cheap labor for Lance paid them a pittance but to the Savios this was paradise. While the money wasn't good, basically they lived all-found in Houston.

After a year in Houston, however, Felix soon found out that he and his family, while beholden to Lance, were virtual slaves. Eventually he contacted relatives who like Felix had escaped from Cuba and who lived in Miami. Felix then concocted a story of illness and hardship begging

Lance to be allowed to go to Miami and take care of his relatives. Reluctantly Lance agreed on the condition that Felix would help him with any future wishes Lance might have. Felix readily agreed and to date Lance's requests had been undemanding. Montecristo or Bolivar cigars smuggled in from Cuba were his greatest vice so far. Lance had known that Felix was connected to some of the Cuban mafia so it was Felix he called to organize the removal of his twin.

Two days had gone by without a word from Felix. Lance was becoming concerned. His father had now told him that his twin brother Jens was alive and well in Scotland. He said he was going to talk to Bobby Rule and that he would consider his options. Lance faked surprise, astonishment and then delight at his father's revelation. Lance had asked his father what might happen. It was during this discussion that Red revealed roughly where Charles and his family lived telling Lance not only was Charles a TV personality but that he was also the leader of the breakaway Scottish Republican Party committed to self rule for Scotland and devolving from the United Kingdom.

For the first time Lance thought about aborting his plan to have Charles removed. But then when he asked his father if he thought Jens or Charles would want to live in the United States he was shocked to hear his father say he would make every effort to bring him back to Houston. Red knew that Charles's initial reaction had been to do nothing and stay put, so Drew Findlay had indicated in his detailed fax. However, Red told Lance the day might come when the US would appeal to Charles and his family. He was, after all, an American Citizen. Red told Lance that once the news of Charles's, née Jens', nationality was revealed, his political life would be over. Red couldn't think of any greater irony in the fact that an American citizen was trying to bring independence to Scotland. He didn't know it then but Drew Findlay shared the same thought.

Red and Ruth were back in the corporate office by three o'clock. The lunch meeting had been very animated and Red had done most of the talking. However, the discussions with Bobby posed more questions than answers. Bobby had kept his discussion focused on what Red could and couldn't do under US law. Bobby explained that as no crime had been committed on US soil and as there was, as he put it, no connectivity between Eilid Stuart and Jens in the US; a kidnapping charge would not hold up in court. He had no idea how Scots Law would apply but he did point out to Red that there was a distinct difference between English and Scots law in relation to family law and other matters and that he should elicit the help of a Scottish law firm when he traveled to Scotland.

None of this was of any help to Red who had fumed impatiently as he and Ruth drove back from the Petroleum Club.

"That was a waste of time, goddamn attorneys," he complained to Ruth.

"Well what did you expect Bobby to say? It's a tough call. You're asking him to predict not only what Eilid might do if you take legal action, but what Charles *and* his family might do."

"I hear yuh. But he could be a bit more positive, he shilly-shallied all the time."

"That was when you told him, if I remember right, to 'sue her ass'. As he said, 'what do you think that'll achieve?'"

"So you think I should let her off scot-free? Shit, there's a pun there somewhere. But seriously, I want her to know that she's deprived me of my son for thirty-four damn years."

"I sure can see your point, but don't you think it's gone past that stage. If you had discovered Jens alive when he was a child that would be another matter. But he's a man, a father, probably being a fantastic father to his kids as he never had one."

"My point exactly." Red glared back at her. "All right, tell me what you would do?"

"Well I'm not you, and I've never had kids, but that's the way I wanted it. I would get myself over to Scotland, and I would go and see this Eilid Stuart dame, or Ballantyne or whatever the hell her name is now, and I would introduce myself to her. Then I would get her to introduce you to Charles or Jens and his family and go from there. Reading between the lines of Drew's report, she has real upset about what she did all those years ago. She made a stupid decision or mistake and she has lived with that guilt all her life. If you start throwing legal papers around, not only will you piss her off you're sure to alienate Jens, that's a given." Ruth looked her boss straight in the eye.

Red took a deep breath. "She'll probably blow my ass off with that rifle of hers, that's what might happen. I do not know, I really don't. All these years I wondered what happened to my son's body. I accept that without her being there he would have died; there's no question. But to kidnap him, that's what she's done, an' no mistake, that's a crime, and a crime that requires punishment. I'll see Bobby again in a couple of days. He's off to research Scots Law or something. Maybe they hang you for kidnap over there, who knows."

"Well, I understand you're pissed, but I don't agree with the route your going to take."

"I haven't made my mind up yet."

"Sounds like you have," Ruth walked away slowly. She had work to do.

"Goddamn women," she heard Red say as he turned on his heel and went to his office.

Felix came through on Lance's mobile phone on day four after the initiating call. The gist of the conversation was that no one in Miami would touch the proposition. His fellow Cuban contacts had heard that Scotland was a cold and inhospitable place, especially in the winter. But Felix's patron had another idea; he had close ties to some of the Mafioso in New York. Felix said he would handle the deal for Lance. He needed $250,000 up front with the same amount paid at completion. Even Lance balked at the cost, this was just too steep, and he told Felix. $150,000 up front, $150,000 at successful completion that was the best he could do.

Felix went away with his tail between his legs to try to negotiate on Lance's behalf.

Two days went past and Lance had heard nothing. He would have to think of something else. Getting the torpedoes in from New York didn't appeal to him at all, there was, he felt, too much exposure. His quiet little arrangement with Felix was unraveling fast.

At the weekend, however, Felix came back. $400 large was the best he could get. $200,000 up front, $200,000 when the job was done. That was the best he could get from the boys in New York. The police were tough in England on guns. Handguns especially. The New York mob would have to rely on their London cousins to supply the necessary weapons and a driver. Did Lance know they drove on the wrong side of the road?

"Yeah, Felix I know they drive on the wrong side of the road but that's no big deal I've driven there. Anyway tell your guys thanks, but no thanks. The price is just too steep. Lance hung up in anger.

Lance thought hard about the offer, he had forgotten about Britain's tough stance on firearms. When he remembered that it was becoming increasingly difficult to get handguns of any kind, Lance started to form his own plan.

His next ploy was to get all sugary with Ruth, as he needed as much information as he could get. Damn it, he thought, if he had only copied her keys when he had them, he could have had access to anything in her office. He figured he had most of the important details that had been passed on in the fax transmission from Findlay but he needed this operation to go well and more information on Charles Stuart and his family was essential.

His task of making up with Ruth evaporated when he saw neatly typed details of Charles Stuart lying on Ruth's desk. It had everything, address, phone number, but that was listed as an office number, his mother's address and a short bio of him, which Ruth had copied from one of the many newspapers reporting his leadership of the SRP. All he needed now was a photograph. Quickly he photocopied the papers on Ruth's machine and had just stuffed them into his pocket when Ruth came through the door.

"Hi Ruthie, how are you?"

Ruth turned her head to show off the weal that could still be seen, even with the most judicious use of makeup.

"Just peachy, can't you see. Now piss off before I get mad again."

"Hey, Ruthie, I'm real sorry. It was the drink, all that Champagne, it was my fault, I'm sorry. Let's you an' me make up?"

Ruth stared at him her nostrils flaring and her big brown eyes hardening.

"You don't get it, do you? You asshole, you're the first creep who's ever, ever, hit me and I've been round the block a few times. We sonny, are through, if we ever were more than just fucking around. I made a big mistake. Your father is the perfect gentleman; you wouldn't know the meaning of the word. Now go!" Ruth pointed to her door just as Red came into view.

"Hey Ruth what's up?" Red came into Ruth's office.

"Nothing, Lance is just leaving."

"I was just trying to get a picture of my resurrected brother, there's no harm in that is there?"

"Ruth will know where that is son, don't you Ruth?"

"All we have are the newspaper photographs and they're not very clear, but sure if Lance wants one I'll give him one." Ruth bit her lip, I would love to give him one, she thought, right in the frickin' eye. However, she smiled, unlocked her filing cabinet and handed out one of the many newspaper clippings she had amassed since she knew Findlay was onto something.

"Jesus," said Lance, "he is kinda like me. Just a bit thinner, that's all."

"He probably does some kind of physical work," Ruth's acid boiled over.

"Gee, thanks Ruth. Thanks Pop. See y'all, I've got work to do." Off went Lance and if either Red or Ruth had suspected for one second what Lance was up to they would have had a fit on the spot.

For Charles it had been an exhausting twenty-four hours. He hadn't got back home until almost two-thirty in the morning. Drew Findlay had confirmed all his mother had told him the previous afternoon and more. He still found it all hard to believe. Yesterday he was Charles Stuart, British Citizen leader of the Scottish Republican Party; today he was Jens Ericsson, Citizen of the United States of America. Elaine had been wonderful. She had looked after his distraught mother who had confessed to "acquiring" him by way of saving his life in January 1959. She had not elaborated. She begged his forgiveness and confessed to her obsession about wanting a child without a man touching her. She had deprived him of a father, a father who was alive, well and wealthy, living in the USA.

Charles had never seen his mother so upset. He thought he had seen her at her worst at Sir Andrew Ballantyne's funeral, but her grief was to the power of ten compared to that sad day. He did all he could for her but she would not be consoled. Finally Charles lost patience her, grabbed her from the chair in which she was sitting, held her by her shoulders, looked into her tear streaked face and said,

"Mother, I love you, I've always loved you. If you had told me what you're telling me now at the age of ten or eleven who I really was it would not have altered anything in my life. My love for you, for this country, stems from you and all of the things you have taught me. I live this wonderful life. I have Elaine as my wife and that will not and cannot change. Bring on Mr. Ericsson from the States, from what I understand I may have been deprived of a father but I would have been certainly shortchanged for a mother. So dwell on that. What I've learned today has shocked me, but it hasn't changed things for this family, and me in particular. We're still with you and we aren't going anywhere soon. Dry your eyes, stay for dinner and let us celebrate about what we have, a respected and loving Scots family. It cannot get much better than that."

Charles's emotional speech affected both Eilid and Elaine so much that Elaine found herself almost in tears clutching her mother-in-law who was now sobbing with such intensity that Elaine thought she was about to have a seizure.

While Charles's intentions of having his mother stay for dinner were meant to be in the best interests of them all, the meal itself turned out to be a somber affair. Elaine dished the food with little relish and it was eaten with less. Conversation was stultified, only the wine flowed freely. By just after nine o'clock Eilid was dropping from worry and lack of sleep. Elaine gently guided her upstairs to one of the spare bedrooms, helped her to undress, kissed her gently and tucked her in. She reckoned that her mother-in-law was asleep before she gently closed the door. She peeped in to see how the boys were doing and they too were in dreamland. She tiptoed downstairs to Charles.

"Charles, I don't want to be married to a yank," she smiled and looked into his eyes.

Charles laughed. "Thank God for a little levity, what a bloody day. Look I have got to go and see this Findlay chap. I want more detail, more information. I don't think my mother is acting rationally and I've got to see if all of this is true. It's like something from a play."

"On you go, but be careful round the Loch, there's some daft buggers driving at this time of night. And you've had just a bit too much wine."

"I'll be careful darling. I'll be back in the wee small hours. Look after my mother, she's not very stable."

"She'll get over it Charles, she's the most stable thing in our lives, she'll get over it, trust me." Elaine kissed her husband gently as he left for Inverness.

Charles's mind was swimming as he drove the twenty odd miles to Inverness. He already had met Findlay and he seemed a reasonable person. Charles guessed that he couldn't have told him the truth about his reason to meet his mother. That would certainly have let the cat out of the bag. Therefore, he had forgiven Findlay the white lies by the time he arrived at the Station Hotel.

He would never forget what followed that evening. Findlay was a brilliant raconteur. Charles sat spellbound as Drew told the story he had pieced together from his investigations and from the people he had met in his quest to find Charles. His rescue from the corrie at Ben Eighe was almost unbelievable and he had confessed to Drew that the smell emanating from a gralloched deer nauseated him like no other.

He asked Drew what his father was like. Drew gave him a copy of the Petrotex Report and Accounts with his father and brother's photographs. Charles stared at them avidly.

"Lance is like me isn't he?" He looked at Drew.

"Looks like it. A bit heavier, I would say, but that's a photograph. I've never met the man."

"You met my father though."

"Oh yes I met your father. Doesn't waste words your old man, very much to the point."

"Do you know him well?"

"No. Bobby Rule does though. He's the attorney who was the person responsible for me being here. I would imagine you'll be meeting them both pretty soon."

"I must say I'm not looking forward to that. From what my mother told me Ericsson lives in Houston, that's in Texas isn't it?"

"Yup, the Lone Star State."

"You live there as well?"

"Yes I do."

"What's it like, I've never been to the United States?"

"Totally different to anything you have in the Highlands. It's flat, very flat. Most of Houston isn't even one hundred feet above sea level. You can drive fifty miles and still be in the city. Without a car you're not going anywhere. It's a huge metropolitan conurbation with a population of over four million."

"My God, I'd feel lost. So would my family," Charles added almost as an afterthought. "How come you ended up in Houston?"

"It's a long story and it's getting late. Some other time." Drew was not about to go down his personal memory lane despite having been invited twice in the same day.

"I'm sorry; I just forgot how late it is. One last question, what do you think is going to happen to my mother? Today's events have just shattered her."

"I wish I knew. From what I saw of her today and her forthrightness and honesty about what happened with you gives me a great deal of respect for her. I've tried hard to empathize, in other words what I would I do in Red Ericsson's position? He could go all legal, Americans resort to litigation at the drop of a hat. The first thing he'll think of is suing your mother."

"My mother's not got any money; we'll not of any significance. She continued my great grandfather's trust, well the person I thought was my great grandfather anyway, and the Ballantyne Estate is in a new trust she had drawn up with me as benefactor. What would he gain by suing her anyway?"

"Satisfaction. Moral satisfaction. Ericsson doesn't need the money; he's wealthy, very wealthy. Charles, do you think I could meet up with your mother again? I like her, and as I said, maybe she could talk to me. As a detached third party she might give me some grounds to argue her case, not from any legal standpoint for what she did, aided and abetted by Kenneth Urquhart, is wrong. For my part I'm whiling away the days in Inverness waiting for instructions, on what I haven't a clue. My job here is done, complete, I came to find Jens Ericsson and I have." Drew got up from the table in the bar as if to leave.

"Let me speak to my mother. I'll call you in the morning. I still can't believe all you've told me, what a mess, what a bloody mess." Charles shook Drew's hand and left. Drew signed the bill and headed to bed.

TORRIDON LODGE —
Christmas 1993

True to his word Charles phoned Drew the next morning. Yes, he had got home safely and yes, his mother had slept well, and while she did not appear to be quite back to normal she was better. He thanked Drew for his concern. Drew asked if he might visit Eilid again and Charles confessed to having forgotten all about Drew's request, would he hang on and he would ask her.

Drew waited all of five minutes before Charles came back to him.

"Drew, have you got to stay at the Station Hotel for any reason?"

"No, not really, why?"

"Well Elaine and I got to thinking. Our closest friends are, of course, Hamish and Mhairi Ferguson up north in Torridon. Christmas is only a few days away and because of all this upset we've decided to go to Torridon and be with Hamish and Mhairi for Christmas and come back here in time for Hogmanay."

"Oh right. That's not a problem for me. I can see your mother any time it's convenient for her. The only thing I'm not sure about is Red Ericsson. He may want me back in the States…"

"Drew," Charles cut in, "Drew, we want you to come with us. Come to Torridon. You met Hamish briefly and so far, of course, no one knows about your revelation except family. But they've got to be told and I just think you'd enjoy yourself as well as being able to explain, and help my mother explain a few things."

Drew was overwhelmed.

"I can't think of a nicer invitation. I'd be delighted to come, if you're sure."

"Not only am I sure, my mother wished it as well. She told me a bit about your background, so I know you'll be feeling lonely at this time of the year. So come on, join my family and we'll all enjoy Christmas together."

The next day Charles and family, including Eilid and Allison Ferguson, arrived at the Station Hotel in time for breakfast. Drew thought there was a certain irony in buying breakfast for Red's son and his family and he smiled enigmatically to himself as he squared his account with the hotel using Red's money.

Charles's two boys, Roderick and Duncan, wanted to sit in Drew's Range Rover so it was decided that they would buckle up in the back. Allison was to sit in the front beside Drew and give the adults a little more room in Eilid's Range Rover for the 60-mile trip to Torridon. The weather had turned ugly. Purple bruised clouds raced across the sky and just as they left the hotel snow started to fall heavily. The parties left quickly for fear that the roads may just present them with difficult driving conditions. However as they moved farther to the west through Garve and on to Kinlochewe the snow became softer and wetter, finally turning to rain as they headed down Glen Torridon to the Lodge the wind having backed to the south-west. Drew noticed that Allison became more animated the closer they got to the Lodge. The boys too were getting restless but overall they were well behaved. The sudden re-involvement with children had made Drew pensive and withdrawn. Allison, still shy with strangers joined Drew in the prolonged silence in the front of the vehicle while the boys chattered away amongst themselves occasionally asking how long would it be until they got to see Uncle Hamish and Aunt Mhairi.

The welcome at the Lodge could not have been more effusive. Everyone hugged and kissed each other while Hamish and Mhairi politely shook Drew's hand. The party traipsed indoors to find a huge welcoming fire and a tall, Christmas tree waiting to be decorated. The silver salver Drew had seen on his first visit had an even greater selection of malts than before. Mhairi and Allison showed everyone to their respective rooms while Hamish fetched the luggage from the two Range Rovers.

Drew looked down the glen. The cloud was just beginning to lift from the top of Liathach with Beinn Eighe's sharp peak still hidden from view. So this is where it all took place, he ruminated. He tried to imagine what the conditions must have been like those thirty-four years earlier when Eilid had rescued Jens Ericsson from certain death. He had immediately taken a liking to the whole family, not just Eilid. The resemblance between Eilid and Elaine was remarkable. They could have been sisters from all outward appearances. However, there any similarity stopped. Eilid was calm, serene and deliberate, Elaine quick and cheerful. She had the boys well disciplined. They could go so far but when they pushed the envelope, she was quick to step in with a quiet word of chastisement. He stood, still deep in his thoughts, comparing Charles to Eilid, and from his immediate character read they certainly could have been mother and son. So lost was he in his reverie that he didn't hear Eilid approach.

"A penny for them Drew."

"Aye that's about all they're worth, believe me."

"Thank you for coming."

"No. Rather it's thank you for having me. I had forgotten all about Christmas, you know. The seasons have just come and gone." He smiled grimly at Eilid.

"Drew I want you and Charles and Hamish to join me tonight after dinner. It's going to be hard, but I have to tell Hamish, God bless him. All those years together and I never told him about Charles and he never asked. He got close once. That was when we went to Aberdeen for Charles's graduation. Hamish tried to talk about Charles's father then and I stopped him dead. It was on my forty-second birthday you know. I upset him so much."

"Who, Hamish?"

"Oh no, sorry, my mind wandered off again. Charles of course."

"What did you do?"

"I wore a mini-kilt to the graduation ceremony."

"You're joking?"

"I wish I was. A Royal Stuart tartan mini-kilt complete with a Prince Charlie vest and silver buckled shoes."

"You must have stopped the show?"

"Something like that. Just a silly old fool really."

"Silly perhaps, fool maybe, old never." The words were out of Drew's mouth before he realized it

"Thank you Drew. That's the nicest thing anyone has said to me in a long time. After dinner then?"

"No problem." Drew smiled and at that Eilid's face lit up. Once again Drew realized just how attractive she was.

When Sunday dinner was over Allison, Elaine and the boys all helped with clearing the table and the washing up. One of the latest acquisitions to the kitchen equipment was a dishwasher. How Mhairi loved her dishwasher. Everything went in the dishwasher save for the crystal glasses. Those were still washed by hand.

The others, Eilid, Hamish, Mhairi, Charles and Drew sat in a circle at the far end of the large living room. Hamish dispensed drinks all round.

"Where to begin?" Eilid put her hands together as if in prayer and rested her chin on them. Her blue eyes swept the group, their sharpness and clarity slightly misted.

"Hamish and Mhairi, you have been like second children to me. I owe you a debt of gratitude as well as begging your forgiveness. Charles is not my son. I have never given birth to anyone in my lifetime and I deeply regret something I did more than thirty years ago. Drew Findlay, who has been kind enough to come along and spend Christmas with us is Scots, like us. He lives in Houston in America, or the United States to be more correct. He is acting as a private investigator for Charles's father.

She looked over to Hamish and Mhairi. Both sat staring, seemingly stunned by the revelation.

"I'm going to ask Drew to relate all of the facts to you that includes the details of how Jens Ericsson became Charles Stuart."

Eilid leaned back in her chair, nodded to Drew who took a deep draught of his whisky and started to speak.

"I'm here as Red Ericsson's representative for the time being. Nothing that is said between these four walls will ever go back to Mr. Ericsson or his employees or attorneys. I am deeply grateful for Eilid and Charles's invitation to spend Christmas with you. I recently suffered a deep loss and for you to open your doors to me in this way has done more to put my life in perspective than I can say. So thank you all for that." Drew took a deep breath.

"It was in September this year that an attorney friend of mine…"

Drew talked for almost forty-five minutes. As a raconteur he was once again superb. When he finished speaking there was a long silence. He had held his audience spellbound by the stories of Charles's rescue from Bein Eighe and the search for the truth. He did not forget to tell the Fergusons of Eilid's immediate co-operation in coming forward with the truth.

It was Hamish who broke the silence. Getting up from his chair he went over to Eilid and knelt by her side. He took her hand in his, and looking up into her eyes, he said,

"Eilid, I knew there was something hidden in Charles's past and I'm glad the truth is out. Whatever happens we are with you. You say you have never given birth to anyone, well let me tell you Mhairi, Allison and I were re-born because of you. We are all the better for knowing and loving you."

Eilid looked at Hamish and rose as he did. They embraced. No words were necessary.

Charles also rose to be by his mother's side.

"That makes three people in the world you've saved. If you hadn't been on that mountain on that day at that precise moment I would never have lived. All of those wonderful things that have happened to me never would have been. I know that after the rescue you should have acted differently but you didn't, and, as I said before on the day you came to tell me the truth of who I am, you are, and will always be my mother and I will always be your son."

Charles leaned forward, kissed her gently and went back to his chair.

As Charles sat down Mhairi stood and said,

"Eilid, I agree with everything Hamish has said, God knows where we would be now without you. We are behind you no matter what."

Hamish turned to Drew,

"I knew you were the police whenever I met you, don't you remember?"

"Indeed I do"

"So tell me what happens now?" Hamish continued.

"That's the hard part. I've no way of knowing which way Mr. Ericsson might jump. He's going to do, or rather must do something. He's probably hurting right now thinking of the years he's been deprived of a son, a son he thought was dead."

Just at that point Elaine and Allison joined the party. The circle widened to accommodate the two ladies.

"Well, did we miss anything?" Elaine asked.

"Not much more than you know already. I suppose you told Allison all about Charles?"

Eilid looked at her daughter-in-law and then to Allison.

"Yes, you're fine, aren't you Allison?" Elaine asked.

"A wee bit shocked, but Charles isn't going away is he?"

"No, he's not going anywhere Ali," Hamish got up and hugged his little sister.

Hamish replenished the drinks and the party spread out encircling the glowing embers of log fire.

"Tell me Drew, how did you end up in a place like Houston? You promised to tell me you know." Eilid walked over to the tray and put a little more water in her Macallan.

"It's a long story."

"So you keep telling me. Come on now you've got an audience and we've nothing much else to do." Eilid sat down.

"Aye come on Drew, tell us all about yourself," Hamish chimed in. He already enjoyed listening to Drew and there was nothing like a good story to while away the long winter nights.

"Well all right then. Let me see where to start."

"Did you get those broad shoulders by working out?" It was Elaine who asked the question.

"Sort of yes and no. Not quite working out in the way that you mean. I was about sixteen or so and my father had a small transport business in Kirkintilloch, we lived in Lenzie. We owned about nine trucks of different sizes and tonnage. Well one of the trucks delivered sand to a pig iron foundry in Kirkintilloch, ten tons at a time. Well, to get the sand into the foundry it had to be shoveled from the flat bed of the truck through a bolt hole in the foundry wall that was about five feet above the level of the truck."

"Why could they not have the bolt hole level with the truck?" Charles spoke for almost the first time that night.

"Good question. Well the bolt hole had been made for unloading from a railway wagon but with the nationalization of the railways, and I'm talking the late forties early fifties, many spur railway lines were closed down. So we had to shovel the sand from the truck into the foundry. My grandfather, a mean old bugger, used to supervise me shoveling. The first thing he taught me was how to hold the shovel to get maximum leverage out of the shovel, then he taught me to switch hands, that is shoveling right handed and then switching left handed. That way you could pace yourself and shovel for much longer without tiring. If I forgot to switch my grandfather had this piece of knotted rope and he'd beat me over the back with it 'til I changed over."

"Jesus, he was a mean old bugger, wasn't he?" Hamish butted in.

"Aye he was mean all right but it taught me a good lesson and should have made me a bit of money. One day the word got out, probably spread by my grandfather or my two uncles who worked in the foundry, that I could shift the whole ten ton in under an hour. When the foundry boys heard this they backed a massively built worker to take me on in a competition. Well my grandfather was like a man possessed, rushing round and collecting bets from all the men. We tossed for who was to go first and the muscle man won and he went to work at a hell of a pace, but he didn't know about changing hands, and eventually his shoveling got slower and slower, until an hour went by before he shoveled the last of the load into the foundry."

"Ah so you won!" Charles exclaimed.

"Sure by more than ten minutes. My uncles and my grandfather made more than fifty quid that was a fortune in those days. When I think back on it now we were lucky to get out of the bloody foundry alive; and do you know I never saw a penny of it!"

"I don't believe it; after all you did the work. Your Grandfather was a mean old man, wasn't he? So did you make more bets after that?" It was Elaine this time who, like the others had become fascinated with Drew's story.

"Not much. I had one or two takers but the money was never the same. After they saw what I could do they all backed off. But that's the story of how I got the Popeye forearms and the strong shoulders."

"So you were a truck driver really?" It was Hamish again who asked the question.

"Well on and off. I was a pretty good golfer, nearly turned pro; I suppose I would have if we had stayed on in Scotland. What made us leave was the Labour Government. They were busy nationalizing the transport system. At first, we thought we might be too small for nation-alization but then my father became not so sure. We had relatives in New Zealand and the US, so we literally tossed a coin and we came to Houston, simply because relatives we knew lived there. It was funny really, looking back on it. We arrived in Houston in July; we had come from New York by train. Well, I was first off the train dressed in my tweed suit and nearly died. It must have been about ninety-five degrees with about ninety percent humidity. I rushed back on the train and told my parents they couldn't go out there. We had never experienced heat like it. I still find the heat and humidity too much in the summer."

"How long does it stay that hot?" Mhairi asked. She couldn't imagine temperatures in the nineties. On the odd occasion when they had good weather the temperature would get up to almost seventy-five, Mhairi felt like she was going to die from heat stroke.

"Depends really. But you can count on it getting into the nineties late May, early June and lasting through to the end of September. The saving grace is that all homes and commercial buildings are air-condi-tioned. Without that you couldn't live a reasonable life."

Drew wondered why indeed he did stay there after he spoke. He had nothing or rather no one to hold him in Houston now. It was strange how long it had taken for that thought to filter through, but then he hadn't been this rational for nine months, he told himself.

"So what did you work at?" Charles asked.

Well at first I became a Security Guard, and then when I became an American citizen I joined the Houston Police Department, and became a detective in the drug enforcement division. I did not like that much. All those kids poisoning themselves while the pushers and the dealers get rich. So I got head hunted by this insurance company who wanted me to look into insurance fraud and you know the rest."

"Did you never marry?" Mhairi asked unaware of the tragedy that had overtaken him.

"I think it's my turn to help you now as you've helped me." Eilid took the initiative.

Drew smiled a wan smile at her and simply nodded.

"Drew's family, his wife and three little girls were killed in a car crash about a year ago. Drew told me about it when I accused him of not knowing what it was like to lose a child. It was when I thought Charles could be taken from me."

"Oh Drew, I'm awful sorry, I should never have asked." Mhairi's embarrassment was for all to see. She bit her lip lest her emotions got the better of her.

Drew got up and kneeled down beside her and put an awkward arm around her shoulders.

"You weren't to know. Eilid was the first person I have talked to about it. You might almost say that this job or investigation I've got into has been therapeutic. They say time heals, and I thought it never would, but since coming back to Scotland, some things in my life have taken on a new perspective. So you're not to worry, I'm doing fine."

Drew gave Mhairi a fierce hug and went back to his chair.

"So Drew will you come back and live in Scotland?" Charles asked.

"If you get Scotland its independence that would certainly be a strong pull." Drew smiled at Charles and went on.

"You know it was only when I was describing Houston to Mhairi that the thought occurred to me that there's nothing to keep me in Houston now, never mind the United States. I'm too old to start over again, I mean having children, and even if I wasn't I don't think I would want to go through that deal again."

"Havers man, you're not too old. You're about the same age as me. But then I've never been married and I don't have children, well not any that anyone here knows about." Hamish laughed and winked furiously at Drew. Drew just smiled back. He could imagine the folks in the Highlands had their own little ploys that they thought no one knew about.

"Thanks for the vote of confidence Hamish. I have to tell you all that Mr. Ericsson is going to come over to try to meet you, Charles, some time soon. I don't know when that will be, not this year anyway but I've been told to stay on in Inverness as he wants me to be here and wait his arrival."

"Suppose I don't want to meet him?" Charles asked.

"Well I don't think that would be very helpful, do you?" Elaine chimed in.

"It's not very polite, if that's what you mean, but what would be the purpose of his visit?" Charles leaned back looking at Drew.

"That's a pretty daft question to ask now, isn't it? Put yourself in the man's place. He thought his son died with his wife thirty-four years ago and now he's found him alive, well and prospering. Why would he *not* want to meet him is more the question?"

"Drew you're quite right of course." Charles conceded. We are just all at sixes and sevens over this revelation. Mr. Ericsson can't put the clock back, that would be insane, but he can meet and maybe associate with me. What the legal implications are we have no idea. We're going to try and find out after the holidays, and that will be from a Scot's lawyer's perspective. Having only heard about US jurisprudence and how it can be manipulated I say God help us if the US lawyers are persuasive with their rich client. They'll probably want a life sentence for Eilid for kidnap; anything's possible." Charles finished, sighing deeply.

"Yup I think you've summed it all up pretty well. And you're right. Red Ericsson has a deep wallet and there's nothing an attorney likes more that that; a dripping roast for a client."

The debate on the Stuart family's fate went on for another hour until, as the embers began to lose their glow, the guests and the keepers of the Lodge went off to bed. Only Drew and Eilid were left deep in their own thoughts.

It was Drew who finally broke the silence.

"Well I'd better be getting to bed. Hamish told me that if the weather improves he's going to take me up around Ben Eighe."

"Well you'd better wrap up. It's going to be cold and it's a long way, especially if you've to plow your way through snow. But if the skies clear it's worth the effort just for the view."

Drew stood up to go. "You know Eilid, you've got a fine family, all of the people I've met here today are like family to you. You should be very proud."

"I was until you came along." She gave him a wry smile. "You're a kind person; I can see that now, thank you for doing your job in a friendly way. Elaine and Charles are concerned about you, you know. Elaine is a very perspicacious person she says she can see the hurt in your eyes."

"I'm impressed. Where did you find the word perspicacious come from?"

Eilid's face lit up as she laughed.

"I'm sorry, I couldn't think of anything more suitable. I did go to school you know, I'm not just a pretty face." Her mind reached back as she used one of Douglas Hamilton's many expressions.

"Hah, there's no answer to that," said Drew, "without getting myself into trouble. I'll see you in the morning."

Eilid rose pushing her hair back from her face.

"Drew, thank you." She stood before him and taking his face in both her hands she planted a kiss full on his lips.

Drew didn't know what to think. An emotional ember rekindled somewhere within him. When their lips parted all he could think of saying somewhat breathlessly was,

"Thank you for that."

He went to bed and lay awake for two hours going over in his mind what had happened that evening. Was Eilid up to something? Or was she just naïve? Why did she kiss him like that? He had warmed to her from the moment they first met, and he thought she reciprocated his feelings. Was their truly any depth to that kiss? He hadn't responded. Should he have, he wondered? And finally the plethora of second-guessing numbed his mind and he fell into a deep sleep.

Drew wakened just after eight o'clock. He had slept better than he had in months, neither drug nor alcohol induced. The smell of bacon frying and coffee brewing wafted through his bedroom door. Quickly he bathed and dressed and was downstairs in about fifteen minutes to join the family for breakfast.

Later that afternoon Drew took a call from Ruth on his cell phone.

Drew answered. "What's going on?"

"I thought you'd like to know. Red's decided to make the trip"

"Really, so you've got him organized for the big visit?"

"Yes I have. He's flying commercial, First Class of course."

"I thought he'd take the Lear."

"So did I. But the Lear's only got a range of fifteen hundred miles tops and at this time of the year re-fuelling stops can be a bear if the weather's bad." Ruth explained.

"Right, I see what you mean. So what's the date?"

"Let me check my diary. Okay, here we are. He flies out of Inter-continental on January 15th, that's a Saturday so he gets into London Gatwick early on the Sunday morning about six-thirty."

"And he wants me to meet him?" Drew asked just the same but he could have bet on the answer.

"Got it in one."

"That's not a Continental flight is it? Because it usually gets in around nine-thirty in the morning."

"No he's flying British Airways, Continental don't have full first-class, they have this Business-First deal."

"Okay. I'll get the flights booked to Inverness from Heathrow on the Sunday. Where will he want to stay?"

"With you of course."

"Great. Consider it done. Oh, and another thing, before I forget, is he coming over with a army of lawyers or is he going to be alone?" Ruth caught the sarcasm and the inflection in Drew's voice as he asked the question.

"As far as I know, all on his lonesome; Bobby did a fine job. He told him to figure out the lay of the land before he went into battle, and guess what? For once Red listened. Maybe he's mellowing in his old age, it's not before time. How are you getting on with the Stuarts and the Eilid lady?" Ruth asked.

"Real well, as you would say, almost too well. The Stuart family is very nice, they have two boys, wild at times but good fun to be around. Eilid is just…well just great." Drew closed his eyes thinking about the two day old kiss.

"You falling in love with her?"

There was a long pause.

"You know, I don't know," Drew answered honestly.

"Well, let's flip the question; is she in love with you?"

"Jesus, Ruth, mind your own business. If I knew the answer to that I'd be able to answer your first question."

"Just asking, a girl's got to ask you know?"

"Yeah, I know. Talk to you in a couple of days unless something happens your end, I know you'll call me, bye." Drew hung up.

Drew returned to the big living room in the Torridon Lodge. It was hard to believe Christmas was just two days away. Charles's kids had been having a great time. Allison, Mhairi and Hamish had all pitched in to decorate the Christmas tree that stood tall in one corner. Elaine and Eilid had gone off shopping to Inverness and it suddenly occurred to Drew that he didn't have anything to give anyone for Christmas. You're useless, he told himself. Here he was sharing this family's hospitality and he didn't have a thing to give them. He hated shopping and by now it was almost too late. He was in the boonies as far as he was concerned and the only real shops were in Inverness. He vowed to take off the next day for a shopping spree until he remembered it was Christmas Eve. All the memories came flooding back. This was the one day in the year he went shopping with his girls when he bought all sorts of stocking fillers and a special gift for his wife. He sat down heavily in one of the armchairs and stared into the log fire.

"Aye, there you are now, what's on your mind?" It was Hamish bringing some more wood to the fire.

"Oh nothing. Just thinking of old times at Christmas."

Hamish dropped the logs in the basket.

"Aye, it must be tough. I have no idea of what ye've gone through. I hope I never will. I wish I could share your sorrow Drew, you're a fine man."

"Ah, so now I'm a tragic figure?"

"Only if you want to be; we're all just sorry you lost your family, and in a way we're trying to put a wee bit of it back, can ye accept that?"

"Yes I can. You have all been so nice, and I know not for all the wrong reasons, I like you all, believe me."

"As one of they Jewish people we had as a visitor once said, "What's not tae like? Eh.""

Drew laughed. He had left that expression well behind him since his return to Scotland.

"You'll have a dram?" Hamish was already at the silver salver.

"Why not? Just a wee splash of water."

"So what's going to happen now?"

"Well we're going to get Mr. Ericsson flying across to meet Eilid and of course Charles, that's not going to be until the middle of January. I've just heard from Mr. Ericsson's personal assistant and she has him coming in to London on the 16th I think it is, I've to be there to meet him."

"Does Eilid know about this?" Hamish raised an eyebrow.

"No you're the first. I've just been talking to the States. I'll discuss it with Charles and Eilid over dinner. Now that we all know about Charles there's no reason not to have you and your sisters join in the conversation."

"You might just want to run that by Eilid for a minute, I know we're a' like family but I would jist ask."

"Not a problem, I will, thanks Hamish." Interesting, thought Drew. So there is a line somewhere that separates employer and employee.

Although he was short on detail Drew ran the proposal of a visit by Red past the Stuarts. There was a great deal of diffidence displayed by Charles, but in the end, Eilid prevailed. She argued that she could hardly prevent Mr. Ericsson from meeting his son and she concurred with Drew who suggested that if there were any obstacles put in Red's way he would immediately become belligerent and litigious. Eilid had no objections to the Fergusons hearing the discussion but there was not a comment from any of them. Only Elaine made the comment that the first meeting should be with Charles. She quite properly did not want her sons confused by all that was going on. Right now, she felt that they only required being on a 'need to know basis' and Charles readily agreed with her.

Again that evening it was Eilid and Drew who were last to go to bed. This time it was Drew who kissed Eilid goodnight, but there was something withdrawn about her and while she kissed him tenderly Drew felt it was without the same enthusiasm she had shown earlier. Once again he lay awake wondering about the upcoming meeting. He was now as apprehensive about Red and Eilid meeting as he had been when he drove to Cannich for the confrontation.

Christmas Eve dawned clear and cold. Eilid and Elaine decided to take the boys for a walk on the hills to see if there were any signs a white stag. The great white stag from Charles's childhood was but a memory but Eilid had always hoped there would be a genetic throwback and that another might yet appear inn the glen. Whatever her wish it was enough of a good story to get the boys out in the clear fresh air.

Drew decided he would go shopping and was surprised when shy Allison asked if she could come with him. Drew said he would be delighted and so they left Torridon at about nine-thirty and headed towards Inverness.

Allison at forty-three had filled out and, like her sister before her, had long stopped looking anorexic. Her red hair, cut to pageboy length, glistened and her figure, while not as full as Mhairi's was slim and neat.

She was dressed in blue jeans and a dark green tight turtle neck sweater, which accentuated her tall slender neck and made the most of her small bust. She never smiled a lot but when she did it was an infectious impish sort of grin that made people return the smile spontaneously.

As they drove through Achnasheen Drew asked her what she had in mind to buy for her brother and sister.

"I've already bought their presents but all my wrapping paper and bows and things are back at Cannich Lodge and I've got to get something extra for someone as well."

"I'm sure Mhairi would have let you have some paper and stuff if you had asked her, Drew said.

"Well to be truthful I just wanted to go out for a minute and when I heard you were going to Inverness I thought I'd invite myself along," she smiled shyly, "I hope you don't mind."

"No, of course not, having someone with a bit of local knowledge is very handy when it comes to Christmas shopping, and besides it's not often that I get to go out with a pretty girl."

Allison threw back her head and laughed. "Goodness, I'm hardly a girl; I'm forty-three you know?"

"No I didn't, you don't look a day over thirty." It was no lie Drew told himself. "So tell me if you're forty-three, how old is Mhairi?"

"She's two years younger than Hamish she'll be forty-eight now, sounds ancient doesn't it?"

"And not one of you has ever married?"

"No. Mhairi had a boy friend or two, but it never came to anything. I've never had a boy friend. I don't like men much, I mean in that kind of way."

She blushed deep crimson thinking she had offended Drew.

"Well I'm surprised. I thought a good looking girl like you would have all sorts of boys chasing you, what happened to put you off men?"

Allison hung her head and looked hard at her boots.

"I'm sorry," said Drew, "did I touch a raw nerve?"

Allison merely nodded and the silence continued for the next two miles. Suddenly she sat upright and stared through the windshield.

"My father wasn't a very nice man. I think that's why Mhairi and I never married."

"So Mhairi left home as well because of your father?"

Allison just nodded vigorously. He was sure 'wasn't very nice' was a massive understatement. My God thought Drew, what kind of society had he found? It was one of abused and bruised women. No wonder they had stuck so closely together for all those years. It was more than loyalty, they shared a kindred spirit. He drove on thinking of Eilid and the kiss they had shared two evenings ago. They too could be kindred spirits with all the scars they had both accumulated.

"Drew, is it all right if I call you Drew?"

"Of course."

"Drew, instead of going to Inverness why don't we stop in Beauly. It's got a grand wee gift shop and there's a very good woolen shop there with all sorts of sweaters in lamb's wool or cashmere even. I've always dreamed about having a cashmere sweater, it's so soft. They even have many bolts of tartan plaid; you could get yourself a kilt made."

"You know I had a kilt once, I have no idea where it went. Anyway let's go with your suggestion and visit Beauly."

Allison's change of venue turned out to be a fine one. There were plenty places to park in the village and the Gift Shop was a real find. They had the usual tourist tack but some of the jewelry in silver was very attractive and well made. Drew chose simple brooches for all the ladies with different colored Cairngorm stones and a fine stout antler topped thumb-stick for Hamish. Presents for Charles and the boys proved more difficult so he and Allison crossed the road to the woolen shop. There he bought three fine sweaters, Allison helping him pick the correct sizes. Then he had a mad moment.

"Allison, do me a favor. I left my phone in the Range Rover, could you nip over and get it for me, it's about the time I get called from the States, and I'll settle up here."

"Sure," said Allison taking the keys from Drew.

She had just gone out the door when he got hold of the sales lady by the arm and said,

"Quick, let me have four cashmere ladies' sweaters in that Lovat green color, one to fit the lady who was with me, two a size larger and the fourth a size larger again."

"I'll not have time to wrap them sir," the sales assistant said, "assuming you don't want the lady to see your purchases."

"Just put them in the same bag as the sweaters, I'll wrap them myself."

"That's six hundred and eighty pounds altogether sir."

"Dear God, how did it get up to that price?"

"Cashmere's expensive sir. Each of the lady's sweaters is more than a hundred each. Is that all right sir?"

"Yes sure. It's just I don't shop very often."

Allison came back into the shop just as Drew finished paying for the goods by credit card.

"Here's your phone Drew, you'll never guess, I met an old school friend across the road, he and I went to the same school in Garve. He now lives in the town, and guess what again, he wants to come to the Cannich Lodge and see me after the New Year."

"Is he married?"

"No, that's just it he lost his wife to cancer about four years ago. Imagine that, dead at thirty-six, hellish isn't it?"

"It is indeed. That was my wife's age when she died. She was a lot younger than me," he said by way of explanation. "I thought you didn't like men?"

"I don't normally, but I know Robert, and he knows a bit about me and he's very nice."

"So the trip was worth while then?"

Allison for the first time grinned from ear to ear like a love struck teenager.

"Oh yes, thanks for letting me come with you."

"Jesus," said Drew quietly, "we'll get you women married off yet."

"What was that?"

"Nothing. Nothing Allison, just talking to myself. Okay, now where's the Liquor Store around here?"

"I don't think we have one of those. What would you be looking for?"

"Some Scotch, Macallan if I can get it. I've been drinking Eilid and Hamish out of house and home and I've not made one contribution to the Lodge bar."

"Oh you'll get that in the licensed grocers. That's across on the other side of the street, but don't worry about the whisky, Hamish gets plenty from the visitors who come up to stalk. I've seen him get over fifty bottles in a good stalking year, that's more than one-a-day!"

"You're right it is. But I'm still going to buy some and after that we'll have lunch, how about that?"

"That would be lovely Drew."

Two bottles of 18 year-old Macallan and a pub lunch later they set out for Torridon. By three-thirty it was already getting dark despite the cloudless sky. Drew drove carefully just in case there was any ice on the road.

On the drive back Allison bubbled all the way. She told Drew how excited she was about being with her brother and sister over Christmas. She voluntarily told Drew about how her father had died and how Mhairi, Hamish had come to rescue her and how wonderful Eilid had been to give her board and lodging. She loved every day at Torridon Lodge, she felt like the Stuarts and the Fergusons were one big happy family.

"So how long is it since you've been here for Christmas?"

"It must be about thirteen, no, twelve years. I left Torridon about a year after Eilid moved back to Cannich when she offered me the cook's job at her Lodge. That was in 1981.

"So this will be quite a treat for you, I suppose?"

"It's just marvelous. I miss Hamish. He's so nice to me; I'm the baby of the family, you know. He blames himself for leaving me alone with my father, but he wasn't to know. He thought at least one of my brothers was with me."

The Lodge was bright with welcoming lights as they made their way down the glen. Hamish had the fire blazing and Charles's boys were sitting quietly both reading books.

"Do you see those two?" Elaine said as Drew and Allison came in, "they climbed all the way to the top of Beinn Eighe, no wonder they're quiet. I've been giving Mhairi a hand making stuffing for tomorrow's turkey. We are actually going to have a good old-fashioned turkey for Christmas dinner, does that sound good?"

"Super," chorused the boys, to which Drew added, "I don't know when I had turkey last, it all sounds marvelous to me."

Christmas Day was sensational. Charles's two boys had been up at the crack of dawn, which wasn't too early as it was almost eight in the morning before it started to get light. Breakfast was served first and then everyone assembled round the Christmas tree to open his or her presents. It brought memories flooding back for Eilid as she remembered all the wonderful Christmases she and Charles had shared with Hamish, Mhairi and latterly Allison. Then she remembered her first Christmas with her Uncle Ken in Pitlochry and Douglas Hamilton, both now only memories.

Drew sat quietly drinking his coffee with his own memories of what turned out to be the last Christmas for he and his family. If only he had known what was going to happen he would have made it the best Christmas of all time. But, as he told himself, fate doesn't allow you those little luxuries. His new found philosophy was smell the roses while you can.

When the excitement had died down a bit and the boys had gone off to examine all their presents he distributed his offerings to the ladies first and then the men. The boy's sweaters he gave to Elaine, as he didn't want to dull their enthusiasm with such plain gifts.

Allison shrieked when she opened up gift of the cashmere sweater.

"Oh my God, you dear man, I didn't see you buy these, did I?"

"No you didn't. You were too busy fetching my phone and talking to your friend Robert"

"By Jove you were fly. You know I didn't say anything but I thought to myself it's about six o'clock in the morning where you come from and I'm sure no one works on a Saturday."

"Well done. You'd make a good detective." Well, thought Drew, Allison is a lot sharper than I gave her credit for.

Eilid, Mhairi and Elaine tore at their parcels when they heard the word cashmere mentioned. Out fell the identically colored green sweaters. They all looked at one another and descended on Drew each giving him a hug and a kiss.

"Drew, you are much too generous. I've always promised myself cashmere but the price is so prohibitive I just never bought myself anything. Thank you again." Eilid smiled her warmest smile and rewarded him with another kiss.

"Thank you as well from me, come on then girls we've got to try them on," said Elaine

"Aye, right away," cried Allison and Mhairi in unison.

Three minutes later the Ferguson sisters, Eilid and Elaine paraded into the lounge wearing Drew's sweaters.

"Wow!" cried Charles, "look at the sweater girl parade." All the men did a second take and even the boys showed interest. The sheerness of the cashmere accentuated all their vital statistics to the full.

"I think you've done us all a favor Drew," said Charles. "The ladies look fabulous don't they?"

And to a man they all agreed.

The Houston flight was late by just over two hours. Drew had called earlier in the morning to check on the ETA of the British Airways flight and had been told with typical British efficiency that it was due to land at zero six-thirty hours on schedule. He had stayed at a local hotel and checked out just on six o'clock and made his way to Gatwick's North Terminal to be told that the flight was due to land at eight forty-five. Damn, he told himself, he could have had another hour or so in bed.

A blizzard had swept the country from north to south earlier in the week. All movement by road, rail and air was disrupted and only now was getting back to normal. Snow still lay on the ground and the temperature hadn't got to above freezing for five consecutive days. Red would be pissed thought Drew, and he was right.

He came out of Customs & Immigration like a bullet from a gun, looked round for Drew, gave him a curt nod of recognition and kept on walking. Drew caught up.

"What a damn flight. It was one thing after another. First some prick decided they weren't going to fly and they had checked their bags so that took about an hour to get them out of the hold, so we lost our slot. Air Traffic put us on hold for another hour so we were just over two hours late when we took off." Red fumed.

"Did you sleep much?"

"Na. About a couple of hours, the service was good though. Shit, there was only one other person in first class."

"Have you spoken to Mrs. Stuart or Ballantyne or whatever?" Red was all business.

"Yes, I have. She's quite prepared to meet with you. She thought that you and she should meet first and after that you could meet Charles. The family would come later. It's up to you."

"How d'yah mean it's up to me! Christ man, she's already dictating terms and conditions. You would think I was the person outta line here...." Red tailed off in anger.

Drew kept quiet. There was nothing he could say at that moment to try and cool Red down. He did not want to appear to be supporting the Stuarts, after all the man he was now with was paying him to do this job. The best he could try and do was to stay neutral, become an arbiter, if that was the right word.

"What do you think? You must have some opinion, eh?"

"I can see both sides. Right now the only good news is that you're here without an army of attorneys." Drew chose his words carefully.

"That can change real soon, believe me."

Drew believed him. Just about everyone was on a tightrope. A little too much one way or the other and they would all fall off.

"I'm sure you're right, can I take your bag?"

"Thanks," said Red handing it over. It felt light but he noticed it had been checked instead of just being hand baggage.

"I'm surprised you checked this."

"Another mistake. I travel so little commercially when the broad at check-in said, 'check the bag, sir?' I said go ahead. Dumb, real dumb."

"You've got a lot on your mind."

"You're right I have. It's a mess; a real mess." Red sounded quite dejected.

For the first time Drew felt sorry for Red. Ericsson was a tycoon used to getting his own way, *making* things go his way if necessary, now, instead he was walking on walnuts maneuvering as best he could to approach the problem reasonably. Drew figured it wouldn't take much to make the situation explosive.

"Right now we've got to get to Heathrow," Drew explained, "there's only one flight to Inverness on a Sunday. We're in good shape at the moment but with the weather the way it is you never know, the M25 can become a parking lot in minutes."

The thin cloud covering gave way to brilliant sunshine by mid morning. The flight to Inverness was on time and the view from the Boeing 737 was spectacular particularly when they reached the Scottish Highlands.

Red was clearly impressed with the scenery, or so Drew thought, as he peered out of his window when the Captain banked the aircraft to provide a spectacular view of Ben Nevis and the surrounding Mamores.

Suddenly Red gripped Drew's arm.

"Can you get a drink on this 'plane?" His eyes had a haunted look.

"Sure, in fact the flight attendant's are coming up the isle with the cart. You can get anything you want. Are you okay? You look as if you've seen a ghost."

"Pretty much. Drew get me a large Scotch, please."

Drew rang the flight attendant call button and a small attractive flight attendant approached full of efficiency.

"Is there anything I can get you sir?" The young girl smiled.

"Large Scotch for the gentleman over here please."

"Have I got to drink alone?" Red looked hard at Drew.

"Make that two miss."

"The drink cart is on its way sir, it'll be here any moment."

"I can see that Miss but we need them now, more for medicinal purposes if you like," Drew looked into her eyes and motioned with his towards Red.

"Are you all right sir?" The attendant could see how pale Red had gone.

"I will be when I get that Scotch," Red barked.

The attendant said nothing turned on her heel and in less that sixty seconds Drew and Red had their whiskies.

"Is it the jet lag?"

Red ignored the question.

"I've been here before. I've seen all this just as it is before."

"Is this you're imagination or have you been to Inverness before?"

"I've been before. I made this same trip, saw the same scenery, and saw the same mountains and it was on the same date I think. What's today?"

"January 16th."

"You know I think it was the same date."

"Recently or a while ago?"

Red took a big sip of his Scotch.

"A lifetime ago. Thirty-four years to be precise. I came to identify and recover Karen and Jens."

"Jesus, you would, wouldn't you?"

"It all came back in a rush, real strong. It was like something I had erased from my mind, I guess like lookin' in on yourself from the outside, if you know what I mean?"

"Yes, I do know what you mean." Drew had experienced one or two of those extramundane experiences since the loss of his family.

"You want to talk about it?"

"Yes, sure I can. You don't know a helluva lot about me. I can talk about it now. They say time heals the pain, well let me tell yuh, it doesn't heal, just deadens, that's all just deadens."

Drew hoped Red was right. It couldn't happen fast enough for him. Red leaned back, stared at the underside of the overhead bin and recounted to Drew all that had happened thirty-four years earlier when he had come to Inverness with Beverly Schwartz and Hank Kelly's mother.

Drew listened in fascination as Red rolled back the years and described the morgue scenes and his decision to cremate Karen and cast her ashes to be with where he thought lay the remains of his son.

"You mean you climbed to the summit of Beinn Eighe?"

"Pretty much. I had help from the RAF, they kinda jump-started me with a lift into the corrie, I think it's called, and the chaplain and I had to walk the rest of the way to the top. There were bits of aircraft all over the place. It struck the very summit you know, I figure another fifty feet higher or so and they could have been home free."

"What was the cause of the crash?" Drew asked.

"Engine failure pure and simple. Bad weather, the plane started icing up as it got lower trying to head for Dalcross and that was it. No survivors. Well we thought there were no survivors, but thanks to you that ain't so."

"I truly do not know if I've helped you or not. Charles Stuart *is* Jens Ericsson but you and I are the only ones who believe that. Well, that's a bad way of putting it. Nobody doubts the veracity of what I've found out and been told, it's just that they can't change a lifetime built by love, care, and good education. You are a grandfather, you know, that's an interesting thought."

"You are kiddin' me." Red's eyes took on a bit of their original shine.

"No, I'm not. Charles and Elaine have got two fine boys, Roderick, they call him Roddy, who's eight and Duncan who is six."

The plane was on final approach now and snow still covered the surrounding countryside.

"Just one thing I need to know before we land, Karen's ring, the ring that finalized your suspicions, just how did this Eilid dame get hold of that?"

"I thought you would want to know that. It was round the baby's neck on a piece of yellow ribbon."

"Eilid tell you that?"

"Yes she did and I believe her. Her Uncle, the doctor who helped her, shall we say acquire Jens, for want of a better word at the moment, asked the same question and apparently was not immediately convinced she was telling the truth. I found that amusing in a strange way."

Red said nothing as the aircraft taxied to the Jetway. They had checked nothing so they went straight to the car park where Drew had parked the Range Rover. As they drove off to the Station Hotel Red suddenly said,

"I believe her."

"What?"

"I believe her about the ring."

"Sorry my mind was away on something else, why would you believe her?"

"Because Agnes told me the ring didn't fit and she supposed Karen had put it back in its box, so now we know. Okay, when do I meet this lady?"

"I'm going to phone her when we get checked in at the hotel and we'll go from there. What's your time frame Red?"

"Hey, let me tell yuh, wide open. I've waited an eternity for this and no other agenda is gonna screw it up. I'm here for as long as it takes."

"As long as what takes?" To Drew the words sounded ominous.

"I don't know…I wish I did. Bobby Rule's been no help either. He can tell me what he thinks my legal rights are, but that's in the US, we're in Scotland. I have a son who doesn't know me and I don't know him and he's got a wife and kids…jeez what a situation.

"Red, you know, I think you'll like Eilid. She's not like any person you've ever met."

Drew pulled up outside the Hotel.

"We'll see. Describe her to me over dinner, will yuh, I'm gonna have a hot bath and I'll call you. Will you be in you're room?"

"Yes. I'll be there. If the lines busy call my mobile, okay? And by the way I got you a room with a sitting room, it would be called a suite in the States, I think it might be the same here but the bird on reception said did I want a sitting room and I said that would be fine. Oh, and another thing, it comes with a bar."

"Great, hey and Drew, thanks, thanks a lot."

"You're welcome."

The two men got out of the Range Rover as the porter bustled up to take their bags. Five minutes later Drew had Red checked in and on his way upstairs to his suite.

Drew phoned Eilid but there was no reply. It was only 4:30 but being dark he thought she would be home. Then he remembered; it was Sunday and she and Allison traditionally went to Charles for Sunday dinner. As it was the off-season for stalking Allison cooked dinner, an arrangement that Elaine loved. It gave her a least one day off from the daily grind. He was about to call Charles then changed his mind. He would call later that evening when Eilid was home, he was getting quite used to their conversations about all manner of things.

Had he known it Eilid too was becoming used to spending more time on a telephone than was normal for her. She felt that some male contact after the years of loneliness from Douglas Hamilton's death was quite nice. She liked Drew, she had decided. He was like her in many ways. Honest, utterly reliable, not given to talking too much he could be an asset to the family if he were used in the right way. He certainly didn't push himself on her despite the fact that she knew instinctively he liked her. That was always a big attraction to her. Douglas had been the same way, seemingly indifferent and then became the only lover she had ever known.

Drew and Red had dinner and then retired to Red's suite where over a couple of drinks they discussed how to approach the first crucial meeting with Eilid. Drew had used the word crucial because he had said this would determine how future meetings with Eilid and then Charles might go. Drew described Eilid as best he could. Outwardly he told Red she was pleasant, very attractive, kept her thoughts very much to herself and didn't engage in pointless conversation. She could be abrupt and to the point but never aggressively so. She was very apprehensive about her first meeting with Red so she had told Drew and Drew felt Red ought to know that. There was sensitivity there, he told Red. She knows she's done wrong; it's up to you how you handle it.

Red appreciated Drew's honest assessment of the situation and told him to call Eilid and set a time that would be convenient to her. Just don't make it too early in the morning, he asked. Drew understood completely, He had already been through the jet lag experience where eight in the morning in the UK was two in the morning in Houston. It took a few days to adjust.

Drew called Eilid at nine that night. She sounded pleased to hear from him.

"Mr. Ericsson get here all right then?'

"No problems. His flight was a couple of hours late I could have had another two hours in bed," Drew told her.

"My you poor soul," she mocked, "not used to getting up early then are we?"

"Not when there's not a point to it," said Drew. "Red's keen to meet you. How do you want to play this?"

"I've thought about this very carefully and you know I value your opinion; how about this? The Lodge is empty, we can have a fire lit in the big room and Allison can cook us lunch. I thought Mr. Ericsson might like a taste of Scotland. He probably hasn't been here before."

"Well yes he has in fact, thirty-four years ago when he came to Inverness to identify his wife."

There was silence at the other end of the line.

"Eilid, Eilid, you there?" Drew thought he had lost the connection.

"Yes, I'm here. My God, I never thought about that."

"There was quite a bit you didn't think about in those days, wasn't there?" Shit, that wasn't very clever Drew told himself, it just sort of came out.

"Thank you very much."

Drew could feel the instant chill from the other end of the phone.

"I'm sorry, that was unnecessary. I think your suggestion is a good one, it sounds quite attractive, let me see what Red thinks and I'll get back to you." Drew was about to hang up and he heard Eilid again,

"Drew, Drew, I take it you'll be there?"

"I wasn't planning to be. I was going to make the introductions and buzz-off. I think this is your and Red's party. I don't think I need to hang around to be referee; he's been quite reasonable so far, so don't count me in for lunch." Drew thought that the last thing Red would want was someone who was not 'family' present.

Drew ran Eilid's proposal to Red over a late breakfast. Red was quite amenable to Eilid's suggestion. So Drew went back to Eilid and asked what time she wanted Red there and between them they thought twelve-thirty would do.

"This is beautiful country isn't it?" Red looked all around as they sped south down the Loch Ness shoreline towards Drumnadrochit.

"Yes it can be very beautiful at times and very dreich as well."

"I know dreich, thanks to Agnes Anderson. She was always using Scottish expressions and I used to pull her leg about it. She was a fine lady."

"Who was Agnes Anderson?"

"Why she was my savior. It was Agnes we seconded to go to London with Karen; she was a nurse in Cedars-Sinai in Los Angeles. She came home a week before Karen to be at her sister's at New Year. She blamed herself for not being with Karen, which is nonsense of course. Then became like a surrogate mother to Lance. She moved with me to Houston then in 1974 she went to live with her sister permanently in Vancouver. She was sixty-seven then and I saw to it that the lady had enough money to keep her in a comfortable retirement."

"Is she still alive?"

"No, more's the pity. She'd have given anything to be here and to see Jens alive and well. She was seventy-eight when she died that's over eight years ago."

The Range Rover pulled up outside the Cannich Lodge dead on twelve-thirty.

Drew and Red got out and looked around. The drive up the glen had been spectacular there must have been more than a hundred and fifty deer mulling around the roadside looking for Eilid's generosity with the hay that she distributed every year.

Drew looked at Red. "Nervous?"

"Yes, I am, and I don't know why. It's as if I'm about to meet a legend and this is my son's kidnapper, Jesus my mind's like jello."

"That's funny, but I had the sweaty palms driving up to meet her for the first time as well. Strange that isn't it? Oh, here she comes."

Eilid came down the front steps of the Lodge looking radiant. She was wearing Drew's cashmere sweater and a long hostess skirt in Royal Stuart plaid.

She looked straight at Red without flinching and proffered her hand.

Red grasped it and looked straight back at her.

"Eilid Ballantyne," said Eilid.

"Charles's father," said Red.

Drew put his hand to his head. Dear God he thought, what an opener. He was glad to be an onlooker. Eilid's eyes were at their icy bluest and Red's were just as focused with the fire of Emeralds. The atmosphere crackled with static.

"Please come in," Eilid sounded rather breathless as she ushered Red into the Lodge.

Drew followed a few polite steps behind.

"This is Allison Ferguson; she'll be serving us lunch today. Allison came forward and almost did a curtsy in front of Red.

"How-do-you-do," whispered Allison.

"Red Ericsson, and I'm jest fine thank you."

"Allison, this is Charles's father," said Eilid

"Ooo", went Allison, "I can see now where Charles gets his green eyes from. It's a pleasure to have you at Cannich Lodge."

"Well thank you li'l lady." Red smiled grimly.

Eilid went into the great room and Red followed.

"Can I offer you some of Scotland's finest malt?" Eilid began.

"Sure, I drink Bourbon as a rule, but a Scotch will be jest fine."

"Okay, you two seemed to be settling in so I'll push off. Red, call me when you're through and I'll be here. I'm not going to be very far away." Drew was going to visit Charles and Elaine but he didn't want Red to know that.

"Are you sure you won't stay for a drink?"

"That's very kind Eilid but I have to go. Red, okay?"

"Sure go right ahead. Eilid and I will be jest fine." Red settled down on a sofa and Eilid placed his drink on a small side table.

Drew said goodbye to Allison and stepped out into the raw weather.

"Have you had Scotch Malt before?" Eilid asked.

"Yup. Agnes Anderson was a Scots nurse at the hospital where Karen had the twins, and who we persuaded to come over to England to be with Karen and Jens at his operation, she drank malt. I think it was called Glenmorangie, would that be right?"

"Yes, Glenmorangie is one of the more famous malts." Eilid confirmed the name.

"Well, I didn't dislike it but for me it was kinda bland, now this here is different entirely, this I could get to like."

"Well it's 18-year old Macallan, probably the best malt to come out of Scotland, at least I think so."

The silence that followed was prolonged and deep as each side weighed up the other recognizing that the pleasantries were over.

It was Eilid who spoke first.

"Mr. Ericsson I owe you the deepest of apologies. What I did or have done was wrong. I was just twenty-one and for reasons that I don't want to go into I wanted a child without any male attachment or commitment. Believing that the parents both perished in the crash, and for my own selfish reasons, I took Jens and made him my own. I'm sorry, truly sorry."

"Well I suppose I have to thank you for that, at least it's a start. Eilid, can I call you Eilid?"

Eilid nodded.

"And you call me Red. We may fall out eventually and I know y'all are more formal in England but I believe in using first names, okay."

Again Eilid nodded.

"Eilid, I need you to tell all about this right from the git-go. Sure, Drew's sent me the story in writing but I want to hear it from you, all about my son from your first meeting right up to today. And I'm gonna listen, I won't interrupt because this is my chance to play catch-up in my son's life. Can you understand that?"

"Yes, yes I can. Let's eat and I'll tell you all about your Jens, my Charles."

Allison served a light lunch of Scotch broth followed by poached salmon and fresh asparagus. Eilid had some Mersault on hand which Red drank mightily.

"I tell you what, you may not know about oil wells but you sure know how to pick good liquor, this wine is wonderful."

Back to the big room they went quite replete and Eilid started to talk in her soft unaccented lilt.

Red sat back and listened, from time to time closing his eyes as Eilid took him through all the ups and downs of Charles's life. Finally, about an hour and a half later she finished.

Red sat back, his fingers steepled, deep in thought.

"Can I jest ask you one thing?"

"Of course."

"At any time during Jens's life did you find out that he had a surviving parent?"

"I could lie to you, but I won't. The answer is yes, I did. But by that time Charles was eleven and not well. It was a complete coincidence but the surgeon who assisted at, shall we say, Jens's operation came up to Torridon to stalk. When we went into the corrie where the plane crashed, there are bits of the aircraft still there to this day, he recalled the operation and told me that only the mother and a nurse had been with your son at that time. But it was too late. I thought I was going to lose him. I thought he might die and I wanted to be with him if that happened....but he didn't and I did nothing."

"You sure are some lady, you wanted that boy at all costs, and you weren't goin 'to give up nuthin' were you? Here's the bit that bothers me lady, if some friend hadn't sent me that photograph from that Scottish newspaper and I hadn't taken a flyer at it I would have gone to my grave never knowing what happened to my boy. I jest thought the likeness was too good to be true. But it was a chance, a slim chance at best and I threw a few thousand dollars at it. I jest need you to chew on that one for a minute."

"I've already chewed on that, as you say, many times. I have no excuses and no answer except to say once again that I'm sorry."

"Have you ever had a husband? What I mean is how come you're a Ballantyne and not a Stuart?"

"No. I've never been married. It was a provision of my grandfather's will that I changed my name to his, that wasn't hard to do. Sir Andrew was a fine man."

"It's kinda ironic don't you think, here's my boy Lance with only a father, who never remarries and here's Jens with a surrogate mother who never gets a man. Jesus, maybe, jest maybe, we have something in common."

"I had a boy friend, but he died. I think had he lived we would have got married."

"He know about Jens, or Charles?"

"No, not even he."

"How many people did know then?"

"My Uncle Ken you heard me talk about, he was the doctor and my mother, that's it."

She was going to add that Sir Andrew had suspicions but there was no point in that.

"Boy you sure kept it under wraps, did no one ask who the father was?"

"Many times. I just lied and said he was dead and that I didn't want to discuss it."

"Well yours is a helluva story. I can't believe that a fine lookin' woman like you hasn't been snapped up by some wealthy man."

"It takes two," was all Eilid said.

"There's no doubt you saved Jens's life. If you hadn't been there at that time and in that place he would be gone. I have to thank you for that and curse you for everything else. You tell me, what are we going to do? For I don't have an answer. You're guilty of kidnapping, of keeping a son from his father and family and I'm sure the law in *any* country has something to say about that. I can prosecute you to the full extent of the law but where does that put me? Does that make Charles or Jens love me? I doubt it. But I think you have to be punished, for a crime like this you should not get off scot-free." Red sat back and looked hard at Eilid

"I think I have had about as much mental punishment as I can take. It has preyed on my mind, not just recently, but over the years just what would happen if my secret got out. If you want vengeance, then I'm sure the law has all the tools to equip you to make my life even more miserable. But you didn't come all this way to do that. You're here I hope to gain something. Right now, you've nothing to lose. Take me to court you'll alienate Charles and his family, but Red you've got everything to gain. Let's call a truce. Let's work together instead of against one another. If we fail then you have lost none of your options. Look it's getting dark already and I do have somewhere to go tonight. Let's look at the sunset, it promises to be very fine." Eilid stopped talking she felt the visit had lasted long enough.

Without another word Red got up and headed for the door pulling on his overcoat that he had fetched from the closet where Allison had hung it.

Eilid put on her Barbour and followed. They looked up the glen towards the Loch and the west. Fine mares' tails lit up the sky in colors of pink to deeper fiery red and then to crimson as the sun was slowly swallowed by the horizon. The stark whiteness of the snow-covered mountains accentuated the Highland tapestry and both Eilid and Red gazed in awe at the wonderful spectacle of color enhanced by the utter stillness in the glen.

"It's fantastic, it sure is. You know I was born in Canada on a farm. I lived there until I graduated from university. This brings it all back to me. I can't remember when I was in the countryside last. I drive through the hill country in Texas but I don't stay in it, not for more than a night anyways. Eilid, I agree to your truce. Recriminations at this stage ain't goin' to get us movin' forward, and you're right I don't have anything to lose and everything to gain. Let me call you and we can set up another meeting. The way I feel right now is I don't want to meet with Charles real soon and that's just because I want to know what to say to him and his family. Let me take my time with this one, okay?"

"Thank you. I'll wait for your call. You want me to call Drew and tell him to pick you up?"

"Would you do that? I forgot I didn't have my veehicle here. Tell him I'll be walking towards him. It's cold but it's dry. The walk will do me good. Eilid goodnight,"

They shook hands and Red strode off down the Lodge Road to meet up with Drew.

Eilid went back into the Lodge a half smile on her lips at the way Red had pronounced vehicle in two distinct syllables; vee-hicle, she said to herself over and over.

"Allison, I'm going home. Thank you for lunch," Eilid called into the kitchen.

Allison came scooting out of the large walk-in larder.

"How did you get on? He looks really nice, old but nice."

"I think I agree. Not the old part. We got on not too badly." Eilid weighed her words carefully. "I'm going home and then I'm off to report to Charles, I'll see you tomorrow."

Charles, Elaine and the two boys were just sitting down to dinner when Eilid arrived.

"Do you want some dinner, mother?" Charles asked.

"No thanks, I'm fine. Allison treated us to a grand lunch today."

"Well how did it go?" Elaine asked.

"He's quite pleasant, given the circumstances. He doesn't beat around the bush. Just told me straight out what he thought. He's going to call me and we'll talk again. While he's keen to see you all he's thinking hard and long on what he's going to say and how you're going to react."

"So he's not threatening litigation?" Charles said.

"Not right now. He doesn't want to anything that might jeopardize any future relationship with you, and I mean the family when I say you. How did you get along with Drew?"

"Fine. He's a good man that. He played with the boys a bit, they had good fun."

"Yes they did, didn't you boys?" Elaine turned to the boys.

"He's super fun Gran; he taught us how to play cops and robbers."

"But you can see the sadness in his eyes," Elaine said, "he's missing his family so badly you can almost feel it. You really like him, don't you Eilid?"

"Yes, I do. He's not Douglas Hamilton, but there's something about him I could get to like," Eilid smiled one of her enigmatic smiles.

Back at the Station hotel in Inverness Drew and Red went over the meeting. Drew was pleased to hear that Red had acted more than fairly. Red suggested that the next day they spoke with a local lawyer just to find out what the law said about Charles's case on citizenship. Was he Scots by absorption or was he still an American citizen? Drew imagined the latter and said so to Red, but Red wanted to be sure.

The weather had suddenly changed, heavy squalls thundered in from the west in the morning turning to torrential rain that afternoon. The rain continued the next day as Red and Drew made their way to a local solicitors office in Inverness who cam highly recommended in local circles.

Bill Whyte had practiced law for well over forty years. His hair was now silver, his eyesight failing and he suffered from heartburn that he treated with curiously strong peppermints, which he sucked on all day. He considered that he conveyed the epitome of professionalism, his height and weight were in balance and he was considered, by his female clients anyway, to be an attractive gentleman.

He sat back with his glasses perched on the end of his nose and listened to Mr. Ericsson, his new client from Texas, who was spinning some hypothetical tale about an American child who had been acquired by a person or persons unknown say, thirty years ago in Scotland, and had brought this child up as their own. Now their dark deed had been discovered and the child, now a man, was not sure of his citizenship status.

"What, Mr. Ericsson, does this man currently think about his status?" The lawyer sat back and clasped his hands.

"He thinks he's British for sure."

"What would make him think that?"

"He's got a British birth certificate that ain't correct."

"You mean it's a forgery?"

"No. I mean he was registered as being born in this country which is or was not true."

"And how did this entire hypothesis come about?"

Red was becoming impatient with what he considered the lawyer's pedantic attitude; Bobby Rule would have given him an answer in a heartbeat.

"I don't want to go into all that," Red sounded impatient.

"But you have the original Birth Certificate?"

"Why sure I have," blurted out Red.

"Ah, there we have it, have we not? This is not hypothetical then, is it?"

"Yeah, I suppose." Red looked over at Drew who had been sitting quietly listening to the conversation between Red and Bill Whyte. Red just raised his eyebrows to say, I blew it.

"Well, now that we can move out of the realm of fantasy, I have never heard of such a thing, nor do I suppose has any other solicitor in this country. But if what you tell me is true then upon production of the American Certificate of Birth and an examination of the British Birth Certificate the problem would be immediately resolved. I take it the name is the same on both certificates?"

"Absolutely not," Drew chimed in. He could see Red was becoming frazzled. "The child's name was changed and he was registered in the name chosen by the new parents." Drew used the plural as it divulged less.

"Mercy me, but can you challenge the identity of the person on the British Certificate?"

"Yes we can and we have, but we cannot at this stage divulge any more without revealing the identity of the perpetrator." Drew decided that he and Red had given the lawyer more than sufficient information to be able to at least guide him in an assessment of the situation.

"Well I have to tell you that this whole thing is most bizarre, most bizarre. It's quite fascinating really. This man could apply quite properly for a British passport by supplying all the necessary documentation in his British name, for want of a better expression, then turn round and apply for a US Passport using quite different criteria. In effect he has dual nationality and a different legal name in each country. Fascinating really."

Drew had to hand it to Bill Whyte. He had quite effectively thought outside the box. To Drew and Red, Charles or Jens could be one thing or the other, but not both.

Drew looked at Red. Red looked at Drew.

"Shit we never thought about that approach, who is to know?"

"Gentlemen, gentlemen I'm certainly not recommending you take that path. Clearly there has been a highly irregular transaction made by the person who falsely recorded the birth. Do we know if this was the father?"

"The attending physician," said Drew.

"Is he still alive?"

"No, long gone, dead," said Drew again.

Bill Whyte smiled. "Then it is entirely up to you Mr. Ericsson. If you go the proper route then you would have to expose the person or persons who were responsible for committing perjury and this could have very serious consequences indeed for that person or persons. But if you wish your son to have dual nationality but under a different name it's highly irregular but not impossible. I mean there is nothing to stop someone immigrating to Britain with a genuine American passport, changing their name by deed poll and then applying for a British passport in their new name once they had achieved citizenship. I've never heard of it being done but that doesn't mean to say it can't be done. I take it Mr. Ericsson this *is* your son we're talking about."

Red nodded.

"So you've discovered this after how many years?"

"Thirty-four," said Red.

"Have you met him?"

"No, not yet. I'm feeling my way. I'm not sure how I should react."

"Quite, quite, I understand. I take it he knows you're here?"

"Yes he does," answered Drew, "but he hasn't even spoken to his father yet."

"But that will come. Is he your only child?"

"No he has a twin brother back in the States." Drew saw where all this could be going.

"Goodness, curiouser and curiouser, my word I sound just like Alice in Wonderland," said the solicitor drawing blank looks from Red and Drew alike. "So there's a question of estate is there?"

"Yes, there could well be," Drew answered.

"Would the British named gentleman have an interest in the US estate?"

Drew chose to answer again as he gripped Red's upper arm to restrain him.

"We haven't discussed anything like that yet, but if push came to shove, I would think so."

"Hey, don't be so quick, this is my estate you're shovin' around." Red could contain himself no longer.

"I'm only saying we haven't discussed it, have we Red? So don't take the heavy red-ass."

"What pray tell me is the 'heavy red-ass'?" Bill Whyte arched his eyebrows.

"A high level of irritation or exasperation." Drew thought he summed it up pretty well.

"Well I never, what a quaint expression, it is Texan I take it?"

"You bet," said Red flaring his nostrils.

Bill Whyte was nothing if not a diplomat.

"Well if there's nothing else that I can help you with at the moment feel free to come back to me, our firm does handle estate planning so if you feel you wish to avail yourself of those services, we shall be happy to help." He rose from behind his desk.

"What do we owe you?" Asked Drew.

"Nothing, nothing at all. I hardly gave you a definitive answer; let's just call this an introductory consultation."

"Well that's sure kind of you, the attorneys I know would have taken at least two hundred bucks from me for that conversation."

"Well you'll be pleased to hear that we're not quite so mercenary in this country; thank you both for coming and I hope your problem resolves itself to the satisfaction of all." Bill Whyte shook hands and ushered them to the door.

Drew and Red left the law offices and headed back to the hotel. It was already getting dark and the earlier rain had now turned to snow.

"Jeez," said Red, "this sure is some weather they have here, it's like the four seasons in one day. And the days are short in these parts at this time of the year. It was the same when I was a kid in Canada, but the pay-off is in the summer when the nights are short and the days are long. So whadya think, Drew?"

"It's a bloody interesting concept. Two passports, two names, two completely different identities. That can't be legal. Christ it smacks of James Bond. Preposterous really, but possible. If you go down that route no one even gets bruised. Again you have your options you can get as difficult as you want or as benign as you want, I'm sure Eilid would never have thought of Bill Whyte's approach. I think it's quite clever."

"I'm meeting her tomorrow, remember and we're going on a walk to see some of the estate. How big is it anyway Drew, do ya know?"

"About sixteen thousand acres, in all."

"Hey that's not half bad, even by Texas standards. I sure hope she's only letting me see a corner of it, I ain't walking far in this weather."

"Red, you'll enjoy it. The weather is supposed to improve. Do you have something to put on your feet?"

"For some reason I brought the boots I purchased all those years ago, so they'll be fine,; changin' the subject for a minute I can see what you mean about her bein' different."

"I told you," said Drew, "she is very nice you know."

"Nice ain't the word I'd use. She's sensational, she's sensible and you told me she was good lookin', well she's better than that. How old is she, she must be in her mid-forties."

"Fifty-six," said Drew.

"Jesus, just nine years younger than me, hell there's hope for me yet!" Red laughed.

"You certainly don't look sixty-five,"

"Why thank you Drew, I keep telling myself I don't feel sixty-five but then there are days when I feel ninety-five. I'm lookin' forward to my day; maybe I can meet Charles and his family after that."

"You can drive yourself if you like; I'll give you the Range Rover."

"Gee, thanks but no thanks. I've driven on the right side of the road all my life and that single-track deal frightens the shit out of me. Jest you drop me off and I'll be fine. If I get on well with Charles maybe, jest maybe, he can drive me back."

"Red look on the bright side you might be invited to stay."

"Yeah, who knows, stranger things have happened. I think if I'm gonna be invited to stay anywhere it would be at Miss Eilid's."

Drew didn't reply. Red was smitten. This was the second time he had talked about Eilid in friendly terms; bugger me, thought Drew, and I thought I had a chance. He had considered all the possibilities and staying in Scotland and wooing Eilid was one of them. Now his plans started turning to mush, well maybe. He was jumping the gun a bit. At least Eilid had kissed him a couple of times; he was one or two up on Red.

The two men dined together and then sat in Red's sitting room quietly depleting a bottle of Macallan. Since Red's introduction by Eilid to the smooth malt he had talked of little else when it came to drinking. It was about eleven-thirty and Red and Drew's discussion had forked over every possible tactic on the best way to get close to his lost son and newfound grand children.

Drew had never heard Red talk so much. The whisky helped, he was sure of that, and the thought of getting close not only to Charles but to Eilid seemed to attract him like a moth to a flame and so he would ramble on going this way and that until Drew was exhausted listening to him.

Drew waited until Red had stopped for breath and he politely excused himself and headed for the door, he was just saying goodnight for the third time when his mobile phone rang. He snapped the phone open to hear Ruth River's agitated voice on the other end.

"Ruth, Ruth, slow down. I can't hear you too well."

"Drew, is Red there?"

"Yes he is, we were all just going off to bed."

"I'm real sorry Drew but I think this is something you and Red need to know about."

"Okay shoot, or do you want to speak to Red?"

No I'd rather you hear this first; listen we've lost Lance." Ruth sounded agitated.

"How do you mean?"

"I mean he's taken off somewhere and no one here in Corporate has a clue where."

"Did he go out of town?"

"Yeah, you bet your ass. He's taken the Lear."

"Shit, haven't the pilots got to file a flight plan?" Drew asked.

"Yeah but not to their final destination. This deal's got a range of fifteen hundred nautical miles so if they are going beyond that they can re-file from their next destination."

"So you're going to tell me their first stop?"

"Baltimore, and we have no interests in Baltimore."

"What the hell's goin' on?" Red was getting impatient as he was getting only one side of the conversation between Drew and Ruth."

"Ruth, do me a favor, call back on the hotel number, we've a speaker phone in Red's sitting room and we can both listen to you there."

Less than a minute went past and Ruth was back on the line.

"Red, Drew, can you hear me?"

"Yep, honey, go ahead, what's this about Lance?"

"Well most likely it's nuthin' to be alarmed about but he's taken off in the Lear and we don't know where he's goin'"

"Hell Ruth, he is the COO, he's got every right to take the 'plane, which way was he headed?"

"Out east, Baltimore, Maryland."

"Well hang loose. He'll be fine. If there are any other problems get hold of Drew on this fancy phone of his and he'll get hold of me. Okay Hon, everything else okay?" Red asked.

"Yes boss, we're doin' good. Drew can you call me back, I have a question about some of these expenses."

"Sure, not a problem. Get back to you in ten minutes."

"What's she goin' on about goddamn expenses, we're talkin' chicken shit."

"Calm down Red, she's only doing her job, I probably sent in duplicates or something. Sometimes I fax them and then I follow up with a hard copy by mail."

"Well okay, but I'm goin' to bed. I have to be spry for my little lady tomorrow."

Drew exited quickly and went to his room. He called Ruth back on the mobile.

"Red hasn't a clue, on what Lance might be planning, has he?" Ruth's voice was brittle, on edge.

"Well I'm sure he can't. Believe me Red's doing a great job. He's stated his case and his blunt opinion on Eilid's actions but he's backed off and is trying to build a bridge between Eilid and Charles and his family. You don't think Lance is heading our way, do you?"

"Listen Red, this is between you and me, Lance and I had a thing goin', huh, more fool me. The night that he found out that his brother had been discovered he was not a happy guy. Beat me up the bastard did or tried to, damn good job I got to my .38 before he really worked me over. Knowing Lance as I do, he could do anything. I'll try and get more info on the flight but it's late here and I know it's near midnight for you guys so just be careful and be on the look out."

"Thanks Ruth I will and thanks too for your candor, it's appreciated. You know anything you tell me stays with me. Goodnight."

Once again Drew lay in bed thinking. This time it had nothing to do with Eilid Ballantyne. His mind was racing. Suppose Lance had taken off early that morning it had been almost five o'clock Houston time before Ruth found out he was gone. Lance could be half way to them by now. He fell asleep not realizing just how right he was.

DALCROSS, INVERNESS —
January 19th 1994

Lance too was asleep as the Learjet approached Keflavik in Iceland for a refueling stop. This would be the last; the next stop would be Dalcross Airport at Inverness.

The Learjet Captain was a new junior addition to the aircraft personnel. His senior was on vacation and when Lance wanted to go "yesterday" as he had put it the junior jumped at the chance. What an honor Joel Childress thought to be flying the second in command in Petrotex. He planned the route meticulously, Houston to Baltimore, that kept him out of the New York/Boston Air traffic control system. Baltimore to either Goose Bay or Gander, depending on weather he could choose one or the other, on to Keflavik in Iceland to finally arriving at Inverness in the dawn hours. The whole flight would take just over eleven hours he calculated including refueling stops. Joel had actually shaved half an hour of his ETA, as there was a strong tail wind.

Lance wakened as the plane banked steeply to come in for a final approach at Dalcross. He looked outside and was appalled to see a bleak snow covered landscape. His next task was to get past Immigration and more importantly through Customs and Excise without them discovering his rifle. He had thought carefully about this. The aircraft was loaded with seismic equipment all of which belonged to Petrotex and he had placed the rifle in a large container with some of the seismic gear. He doubted if H M Customs crew would give it more than a cursory glance but if the rifle was discovered he could claim no knowledge of it. It was after all his father's old Browning .270 and Lance had made sure that none of his prints were anywhere on the rifle.

As it turned out he was right. There were no problems with Immigration and the Customs Officer looked cold and pale and sported a ten o'clock shadow. He looked as if he had just got out of bed. When he heard it was a Petrotex aircraft that he considered was most certainly on North Sea oil business he virtually waived Lance and his pilot and co-pilot through customs. Lance had also told him that they would be leaving later that day. By the time Lance had a rental car organized and the equipment stored in the hotel luggage room it was just past nine-thirty in the morning. He had to get some more sleep. The previous day had been hectic arranging to get over to Scotland and to do the job for which the idiots from New York had wanted four hundred large.

Lance took a hot shower, shaved and fell into bed setting the alarm for a one o'clock afternoon wake up. He was in a deep sleep when the alarm went off and it took him all of fifteen seconds to reorient himself and to remember where he was.

He opened up the road map he had bought at one of the local gas stations and he now pored over the two and a half inches to one-mile Ordnance Survey scale. Everything, including dwellings, barns, both-ies and dykes were all detailed. He saw Cannich cottage, that's where Charles lives he told himself erroneously. All he had to do was lie in wait. It would be cold but he had brought his insulated camouflaged coveralls that he could put on over his duvet jacket he wore when he went out on offshore rigs. He would be warm enough providing he hadn't to stay put for what was left of the day. His plan was simplicity itself. Charles would come home, he would lie in wait, one shot and that would be it. However the simple plan was unraveling slightly. He had miscalculated the daylight hours in this part of the world, what if Charles came home in the dark? He asked himself. He hadn't quite covered that point but now that he had recognized the potential problem he could deal with it.

Off he went to a local hardware store and bought a thin but powerful flashlight and a roll of what was, he supposed, the equivalent of duct tape. If it came down to it he could tape the flashlight to the underside of the rifle and work with that. He figured on being within close range, the chance of missing would be almost impossible.

When he left the hardware store he checked he had everything and left Inverness at about fifteen minutes after two o'clock. He arrived at Cannich in about forty minutes. It was almost three in the afternoon. The sky was still clear as the snow had stopped and the sky was now a clear icy blue. Snow still lay at lower levels and the surrounding mountains glittered like Alpine peaks. He drove up the hill out of the village and wended his way up the glen. He set the trip on the odometer to zero. According to the map Cannich cottage was almost exactly six miles from the village so he drove at a moderate speed until the trip read five miles, then he slowed the car down as he drove the last mile. He didn't have to look very hard; there was the sign on a shingle which was taken from one of the dead Douglas Spruces that Eilid had cut down. "Cannich Cottage" it read. Lance had arrived. He felt immediately exhilarated. His plan was on schedule, he would make no mistake. He took a quick glance at the cottage, there were no lights on but he could see a thin wisp of smoke coming from the one chimney. Other than that there was no sign of life.

Turning the car around he headed back down the road about half a mile and parked it in one of the many lay-bys, the front of the car facing east down the glen. He looked around as he put on his duvet jacket and then pulled on his camouflaged all-in-one coveralls. That was the other slight flaw in his plan. As camouflage for the surrounding terrain they would have been superb. The greens and browns would have made him almost invisible in the bracken and heather that proliferated the hill. But now there was snow, and lots of it, the usefulness of the camouflage was totally negated by the winter conditions. If he didn't take care to conceal himself properly he would stand out like a sore thumb. Slowly he walked back up the road the farm. Just before he got to the short driveway into the farm he left the road and went up the hill to the northeast of the house. He came to a gully with a burn at the foot of it. The water in the burn gurgled and frothed as it bounded over small rocks and bigger boulders making its way to the Cannich River. He stopped and looked around. This was an ideal spot. The side entrance door was in clear view; anyone coming to the door was in Lance's direct line of fire. He nestled down in the hoar covered bracken and removed the Browning from its canvas holder. He made a roll out of the holder and placed it at the front of the rifle, spread himself out and looked through the telescopic sight. Fantastic! He thought, if Charles gets home when it's light then it will be his last homecoming. Lance, driven solely by greed and avarice was about to murder his twin whom he had never met. He settled down to wait as the sun started to settle over the frozen horizon.

Eilid and Red had spent a wonderful day on the hill. She had got him to climb the highest peak on the estate and the views from there were breathtaking. To the south they could see the Grampian peaks, to the east lay the Moray Firth and the city of Inverness. To the west they could see the peaks of Kintail and due north lay the Torridon range. They stalked some deer just for the hell of it and laughed when Eilid clapped her hands and the hinds galloped off in a frenzy while the older stags hardly moved.

"Gee, those big guys don't frighten easily do they?" Said Red.

"No. Not now, they know the rut's over and they're no longer in danger, they're smarter than you think."

"Ain't that something?" Red was amazed.

"To night you'll see them come right down to the road and you can feed them a Mars Bar. They love that," said Eilid.

"You're kiddin' me."

"No I'm not. Do you have Mars Bars in the States?" Eilid asked.

"Yeah we do. But our Mars Bar is different. The equivalent of our Mars Bar is called a Milky Way. Don't ask me how I know that, 'cause I'm not big on candy. Karen now, she was different. She had a sweet tooth that wouldn't quit." He smiled at the memory.

"You must have loved Karen completely, has there never been anyone else?"

"What made you ask that?"

"It's the way you say her name, the way you look, just at the thought of her."

"Yep. I suppose you're right. Karen was so special. We fell in love the first time we met, well, I fell in love with her, she took a little bit of persuading. I was kinda brash, and I was a womanizer, I admit that. But she sure changed all that in me. Hell we only had about two years together. It's been tough."

"I think I know how you feel. With me it was Douglas Hamilton. He was the only man I ever loved and ever wanted to love. When he died I was heartbroken. It took me a long time to recover, and since then there's been no one. But I'm an old granny now, who would want me?"

"Hey, let me tell you, I'd park my boots under your bed any day!" Eilid didn't think Red was joking for he looked her straight in the eye as he said it.

Eilid didn't know what to say. There was a rush of emotion that welled up inside her only to be quelled by her common sense cutting in telling her not to be so stupid.

"Well I don't know whether I should take that as a compliment or not, it's not often older men hit on me." She thought that was a rather trite but smart answer.

"Hell don't be so picky. There's only nine years between us."

"Right," said Eilid getting back to business. "It's getting late and we'd better start down we don't want to be benighted do we?"

"Benighted, ain't that something the Queen does?"

"No silly. God you Americans. It means caught out on the hill in the dark."

"Oh sure, I see what you mean, yep let's go. Let me tell you something before we start down and I mean this. First of all this has been a hell of an experience for me, when I found out that Jens, your Charles, was still alive I could have cut your throat, that's how bad I felt about this whole deal. Now I haven't met Jens yet but from what I hear he's a fine man and he has a nice wife and kids. Meeting you though has been kinda exceptional; you're nothing like I thought you'd be. Today's been very special for me. I never realized how much I love the countryside and how much I enjoy spending time in it. I've been wrapped up in my business since Karen died and I haven't been able to see the wood for the trees. I know that's a real old well-worn cliché but that's the way it has been. I want to change all that if I can. So thank you for all you've done so far."

To Eilid, who was not used to emotional outbursts, it was quite a speech. It seemed that Red was absolving her of all blame in the denial of his twin son for all those years. She could hardly believe her ears.

"Red, that's very nice of you. I believe we still have some issues to talk about but I think we're making progress. Incidentally I did tell Charles to come to the house round about four o'clock, he wants to meet you and I think the timing's right."

"That would be the perfect end to a perfect day, lead on lady, lead on."

Charles mind was all over the place as he drove towards his mother's house. What do you say when you meet the father you never knew you had? He hadn't a clue where to begin. He was sure it was going to be an emotional moment for them both. He was so used to public speaking he was quite nerveless in front of the lights and the camera but this was different. He positively had butterflies in his tummy as he tried to scope out which way the conversation might go. Would his father be aggressive? Or would he give him a hug? There was no way of knowing. Still thirty minutes from now the initial introductions would be over and he would know better then which path to take. It was almost four o'clock now but there were no lights on in the house as he pulled into the driveway. Never mind, he thought, I have my key and I'll get the kettle on in time for my mother and father's return, they'll be cold being out there half the day. He mused at his use of the word 'father' for the first time when he thought of Red.

From his concealed position Lance watched Charles's car pull up. He looked at his watch. It was just beginning to get dark but he would have a clear shot despite the gloaming. What happened next engraved the events in the minds of three people for the rest of their lives.

Eilid and Red were about two hundred yards away and they saw Charles arrive, get out of the car and make his way to the side door. As he opened the porch door, which was never locked, there was a loud crack as Lance's Browning went off. Charles spun round and fell heavily. Eilid couldn't believe what she had heard or seen. Instinctively she fell to the ground and pulled Red down beside her.

"What the hell's goin' on?" Red cried out.

"Charles has been shot…stay still and be quiet."

"Merciful Christ, that's easier said than done."

"I know," hissed Eilid as she scanned the land surrounding the house with her telescopic sight. "I want to see who did this."

Lance could see Charles moving slowly forward trying to reach the shelter of the porch. Damn, thought Lance I haven't killed him. He took a quick look around. There was no one. He stood up from his position, moving forward, rifle at the ready. That one movement was all that Eilid needed as she brought the rifle past Lance's face for a heart shot, she virtually froze, it was as if she had Charles in the scope, thoughts rushed through her head in a nanosecond as she pulled the shot. The Mannlicher Alpine boomed. Lance was thrown off his feet as the bullet struck; his rifle went sailing and landed some twenty feet away from him.

"Christ," he said to no one in particular, "where did that come from?" His shoulder stung like hell but he wasn't dead, that much he knew. He struggled to his feet and went after the rifle. By this time Eilid and Red had both rushed forward with no regard for their own safety but Eilid saw the camouflaged figure stand and stretch for his weapon. This time she fired into the air as she was on the run. The noise was deafening and it was enough to make Lance take to his heels with Eilid in close pursuit. Lance got to the road as Eilid stopped briefly to see if Charles was alive. Right away she could tell it was a shoulder wound very similar to the one she had inflicted on Lance except it was Charles right shoulder.

"Look after him Red!" Eilid yelled as she continued the pursuit. She had the man in clear view and she wasn't going to let him get away, not under any circumstances.

Lance ran as if the very hounds of hell were after him. He could feel the left side of his body becoming warm and sticky as his blood pumped out of his wound at an ever-increasing speed because of his exertions. He just *had* to get to his car and take off. He glanced over his shoulder his pursuer was right behind and seemed to be gaining slightly. He redoubled his efforts but his legs seemed to have gone to jelly. He wondered just how badly he was shot.

Red meantime was kneeling beside Charles. He had ripped off his anorak and his sweater and made a makeshift pillow to put under Charles's head. Quickly he took the key that was still in Charles's hand and opened up Eilid's house. He rushed into a bedroom and grabbed the sheets and blankets from the bed and made out to the porch again. There was a great pool of dark blood on the slate slab and it was getting bigger. This was when he wished he had some first aid experience. Red's face was ashen as he watched his son lying before him unconscious. His mind was in turmoil. What should he do next? The phone, his mobile phone he had never used it since he came into Britain but like Drew's it was supposed to work anywhere in the world. He stabbed out Drew's number and heard the phone ring.

"Drew Findlay here," said the voice.

"Drew, Drew thank Christ I've got you. Where are you?"

"I'm with Elaine and the boys at Charles's house. We knew you were going to meet him today…

"Drew, Drew," Red frantically cut him off, "there's been an accident, Charles has been shot."

"How bad?" Drew asked tersely.

"It's his shoulder, it's bleeding badly but I think he'll live if we can get help to him."

"I'm leaving now, I won't say anything to Elaine otherwise we'll have the boys all upset not to mention the state she'll be in. Where's Eilid?"

"She's off running after the guy who shot Charles."

"Okay, save your breath I'm on my way you can tell me later."

Red looked down at Charles, he was opening his eyes; they were green, deep green just like Red's.

Charles struggled to speak.

"What happened?" he rasped. "Who are you?"

"I'm your dad, that's who I am," choked Red. "And I'm here to look after you."

Red didn't know it but for the first time since he knew that Karen wasn't coming back tears streamed down his face.

"Hi, dad," croaked Charles and tried to lift his right hand. Red grasped it with all his might.

"Welcome home son, it's been a long time coming."

Drew gunned the Range Rover through the twists and turns in the narrow road and he was at Eilid's in two minutes. Quickly he took charge. He had never seen Red as emotional as he was now.

"Red, you take care of yourself, I've done first aid, let me get an ambulance to us right away." He dialed 999 as he looked at the recumbent Charles.

"Emergency which service do you require please," the soft unhurried lilt of the emergency operator came through..

"Ambulance and police. Ambulance as soon as possible please, someone's been shot."

He gave the operator all the details and left her his phone number. He was still slowly pulling off the bedding Red had placed over Charles to get to the wound. There was a gaping hole in Charles's right front shoulder. What a shit thought Drew, shooting your brother from behind. There was no doubt in Drew's mind that Lance was responsible. The entrance wound was small, just below the shoulder blade and the exit wound ballooned into something that was just a bloody mess. He went into the house and looked in the bathroom cabinet. It was all pretty small stuff. Then he remembered that Eilid kept a full-blown First Aid kit with field dressings and everything at the Lodge. She had done this ever since Auld John had been shot on the hill. Quickly he dialed the Lodge. As he expected Allison answered. He told her the circumstances and asked if she could bring the First Aid kit as quickly as possible. Allison just gave him a quick 'yes' and hung up the phone.

Eilid could see the car in the lay-by. She knew instinctively that was where the gunman was headed. She had gained on him slightly but there would still be sufficient time for him to get in the car and he'd be gone. He was there now fumbling with the door lock. She had to do something drastic. She threw herself down on the opposite side of the road on a grassy bank and took aim at the tires on the car. Blam! Blam! Blam! Three shots, three flat tires. She squeezed the trigger to take out the fourth. There was a click, her magazine was empty. Quickly she reached into the pocket of her Barbour, put a bullet in the chamber and took out the fourth wheel. The noise of the gunfire had made Lance dive into a ditch near his side of the road. Gingerly he peeped out once the shooting had stopped to see Eilid up and running again. He cranked the car up and took off. The flat tires flapped wildly and he couldn't get any speed up. He was going downhill now and gathering a bit of speed heading to where a wooden bridge crossed the river. He tried to turn the car to take the bridge but the ripped tires had no traction on the icy road and the car slid sideways and tilted over almost toppling as he hit the bank on the left. He had only put another hundred and fifty yards between him and Eilid but it least it gave him a start. Off he took again but his feet felt like lead and he had a salty taste in his mouth. The pain in his shoulder was now excruciating and he knew he couldn't go on much farther. Rather than stick to the road he plunged into the trees along the river bank and disappeared. Eilid was still running but she was tiring. While she ran on grimly after the gunman her mind was with Charles, all the time hoping and praying her son would be all right.

She entered the woods at the same place where she had seen Lance enter. His trail was easy to follow; every so often there would be a splash of blood as he wove in and out of the small silver birch that grew close to the riverbank. Suddenly Lance came to the part of the Cannich River that cascaded down in a steep waterfall towards the village and decanted into the River Glass. He could see the road on the other side but he didn't know whether he should go across or not. He stopped for a second to consider his options. It was then when a young stag, having been startled by Eilid, came crashing through the trees close to him. Lance didn't see the beast but the noise indicated to him that Eilid was now right on his tail. He started to cross where there seemed to be plenty of rocks sticking above the fast flowing current. He was almost across when he made the fatal mistake of turning round to look for his pursuer, the rock he was on coggled and he lost his balance. Had he not been weakened by his loss of blood he might have staged a recovery, but as he fell his head hit another rock and he rolled into the deep flowing race of the waterfall. Eilid heard him cry out as he was swept downwards and out of sight.

It was morning when the police found his body washed up on the side of the Glass that flows hard by Cannich village. The police called Drew first as he had left his mobile phone number with them. Red, Eilid and Charles were in Inverness where Charles had been taken to hospital. The surgeon had said he was a very lucky man the bullet had made a clean entry and exit; no bones had been hit. The hospital would keep him in overnight for observation, pack him full of antibiotics and send him home sometime the next day.

It was Drew who was left to tell Red about Lance. He paced up and down in his hotel room wondering how on earth he was going to break the news to him. Ruth Rivers had already been on the phone telling Drew that she suspected Lance was indeed heading their way. Drew told her he knew but didn't elaborate.

Red and Eilid made it back to the hotel at 10 o'clock the next morning. They had stayed at Cannich overnight and hurried to the hospital early that morning to find out how Charles was. Drew went to Red's sitting room looking as grim as he did the day the police told him he would never see his family again.

"Red sit down, I'm glad Eilid is with you, I think you'll need her support."

"It's Lance isn't it?"

"How do you know?"

"Well this morning the company I use to fly my planes phoned me from the States, it must have been about one in the morning over there, and they asked me if I was using the Lear to come home. Their pilot had called and said he was in Inverness, that he had flown Mr. Lance in and was his father coming back with him? Lance had told him and the authorities at Inverness airport he'd be flying out the same evening and when that didn't happen and Lance didn't show up he thought he'd better call his management. So he did. So where is Lance?"

Drew gripped him by the shoulders, looked straight into his green eyes and said,

"Red there's no easy way to tell you this, he's dead."

"Jesus Christ, you can't be serious."

"I wish I wasn't. It was Lance that Eilid chased last night; it was Lance who tried to kill Charles yesterday afternoon. He slipped just at the waterfall and was swept into the river and drowned, that's what the police think anyway. But he was also wounded, that was Eilid's shot that stopped him finishing off Charles."

Red sat and buried his face in his hands. Eilid looked on ashen. Drew poured a Scotch for them all. He proffered it to Eilid.

"No, no thanks Drew, not just now."

"I thought when I heard about the Lear being used he had just gotten jealous about me meeting Jens and he came over to spoil my party, but I didn't think he was capable of this. How did he get the rifle he used?"

"We don't know," said Drew. We picked it up after we got Charles off in the ambulance it was a Browning .270 caliber."

"Jesus, I have a Browning .270. Used to use it for hunting. It hasn't been fired for years. You know it's not meant to be that I ever have two sons. No sooner do I find the one I lost than I lose the other. It just hasn't sunk in yet that Lance was that mean and that *bad,* that's the word, jest plain bad. Ruth tried to tell me what a bastard he was, but I didn't want to listen."

"Red, oh Red I'm so, so sorry." Eilid was on her knees holding Red's left hand which hung limply from his body.

"Hey, Eilid, it's not your fault. This is not your fault. Drew where is Lance?"

"He's at the hospital, I think the same one Charles is in. They're doing an autopsy, that's standard procedure in sudden death."

"Jesus Christ what a mess, I never even thought for a minute, not a damn minute that Lance would do a thing like this, did you Drew?"

"Well to tell you the truth I didn't think Lance would do anything until Ruth's call last night. But who would have thought that events would have moved so quickly?"

"Yeah okay, you're probably right. I'm just a crazy old fool."

"No your not," said Eilid vehemently. "Drew, Charles is getting out sometime this afternoon. I've told Elaine what happened and of course she's just thankful that he's going to be fine. The boys took it in their stride but they're young and they see this thing on television and think nothing of it. There will be an inquest of course and I'll be hauled over the coals at that. You're not allowed to shoot at people in this country whether or not in self-defense."

"Jesus, try telling that to the people in Texas or anywhere in the States for that matter, there would be a riot." Red looked at Eilid but she avoided his eyes.

"What amazes me is how Lance managed to bring a rifle into the country, either Customs and Excise were lax or he had some clever method of concealing the weapon." Drew said.

"You said the rifle was a Browning .270 didn't you?" Red asked.

"Yes it was. A fine rifle but a pretty old model." Drew replied.

"Well we might not know how he got it into the country but I can tell y'all that it's most likely my rifle."

The phone rang in the sitting room of Red's suite. It was the Inverness police asking if Red could go to the hospital and identify Lance. Red told them he'd be there in twenty minutes.

He turned to Drew and Eilid. "I get the real impression that history is repeating itself. Last time I went to the morgue it was to identify Karen thirty-four years ago, now it's her son. It's a real bitter pill to swallow." Red shook his head is disbelief. The others stayed silent lost in their own thoughts.

Finally Drew said, "Red, if you want me to tell Ruth what's happened I'm sure she'll take care of arrangements. The Lear is still at Dalcross, you go home with Lance."

"Yeah, thanks for that Drew, yeah you'll have to let Ruth know about Lance, but as for goin' home, not right now. Lance is going to be with his mother. I'll see y'all later, make yourself at home." Red waved his hand round the room and left to go to the horrors of the hospital morgue once more.

Elaine phoned Drew on his mobile and told him to tell Eilid that Charles was fine and they were just leaving the hospital and heading straight home to the boys. Drew passed on the message but if Eilid heard him she gave no sign. Drew could see she was in some sort of traumatic shock. She just couldn't come to terms with what had happened.

"Drew, you need to be here for Red. I need to go back to Charles and Elaine. I'll see you all in the morning. Tell Red to come over whenever. None of us will be going anywhere." Eilid left in a somber mood.

That evening Drew and Red sat in Red's sitting room armed with two bottles of Macallan, got completely rat-faced and finally staggered off to their respective rooms to the deep oblivion of an alcohol induced sleep.

The next morning two very hung-over gentlemen made their way to Glen Cannich drove past Eilid's cottage and headed straight for Charles's home. The events of the last forty-eight hours were like a bad dream. Charles was all bandaged up with his right arm in a sling, but, apart from looking very gray, he seemed to be in reasonable spirits. Drew went off to the kitchen to talk to Elaine while she made some coffee diplomatically leaving Charles and Red to renew their relationship in a less dramatic way than their first encounter.

"How is Charles?" Drew asked. "He's been through a hell of a lot."

"Hmm, your right, we all have. He just can't get used to Lance and his motives. I mean even if they had only met and talked. Charles was never going to be a threat to Lance. It's so tragic. They live for thirty-four years unaware of each other's existence, and they never get to talk, or meet or . . . . . ." Elaine tailed off at a loss for words.

Drew picked up the conversation again,

"You know we should have done more about this, by we I mean Ruth Rivers and me. She knows more about Lance than she's letting on, I think they were having an affair and for some reason it went sour. Ruth knew how upset Lance was when he finally heard that his twin was alive. I should have realized when Ruth told me about Lance going missing there might be an attempt to take Charles's life."

"All I know is that since the people in the United States became involved it's been a nightmare." Elaine pursed her lips looking grim. "I don't know how Charles is going to get over this, meeting his father and losing his brother all in the space of an hour. I know Eilid is in a dreadful state. Charles went to visit her this morning and she was still in bed and wouldn't come out to see him. Charles thinks she blaming herself for everything that's happened to Red and she doesn't even know how to begin to make amends. So we have another disaster. I have never known Eilid to be like this. I have to confess she's got both Charles and me worried." Elaine sounded bitter.

"I can imagine she's taking it very hard. What was coming round to being a reasonable event with Red and Eilid obviously hitting it off just turned to dust. Red is now left with only one son and not the one with which he's familiar, it's got a big time 'mea culpa' written all over it. There's nothing you or I can say or do. What a triumvirate, Charles, Eilid and Red." Drew finished by just shaking his head.

"Where's that coffee then?" Red shouted as he came from the living room into the kitchen.

"Right here," said Elaine pointing to the percolator. "Have you two finished then?"

"Yes, to answer your question we've had as good a conversation as you could expect in the circumstances. I just can't get to grips with losing

Lance. I don't think it has sunk in yet, my brains gone kinda numb, but we have to go forward. I'm going to go down to Eilid's to talk to her. Lance's cremation is going to be in Inverness on Monday, I'd like y'all to come to that and then I have to scatter those ashes, that'll be the next day, and I'd like you to be all there for that as well."

"Where are you going to scatter Lance's ashes, you clearly have a place in mind." Elaine held Red's hand as she looked into his dull sad eyes.

"From the summit of Beinn Eighe. I did the same thing with his mother's ashes in the January of nineteen fifty-nine. I said to myself then I'd never be back there ever, but you should never say never, it's like tempting the fates. Can I count on you being there?"

"Of course," they chorused.

"Well thank you for that; come on Charles let's go and see if we can't talk some sense into your mother." Red put his hand on Charles's good shoulder as they headed out the door.

Charles had to use his key to get into his mother's house. The place was in darkness so he went around putting on lights as Red stood watching him. Red knew that Charles had turned into a fine man. There were marked differences between Charles and Lance in attitude and style. Charles was quiet, thoughtful but very assertive in a friendly way. There was none of Lance's brashness or impetuosity. In short, Red thought Eilid had done a fine job raising him.

"Mother, it's Red and me. We're here to see you."

"Charles, that may be, but I do not want to see anybody, I'm not very well so I'm keeping to my bed." Eilid's muffled voice came through the bedroom door. "Please tell Red to go away, I don't want to see him, not just yet."

"Well you're going to have to see him," Red said as he slowly opened the bedroom door. He could see Eilid's long blond hair on the pillow and she propped herself up on an elbow to look at him as he came through the door.

"My God, can a body not have any privacy. Please leave me."

Red continued to advance with out a word.

"Please Red, I've done enough damage to you as a person, I've destroyed virtually all you had left in life. You must persuade Charles and Elaine and the boys to go with you, it's the only way."

"Eilid be quiet. I knew you'd be thinking this way. If you hadn't shot at Lance there's no doubt in my mind we'd be having a funeral for Charles, no doubt at all. Please listen to me."

Red sat on the bed and caressed her forehead. It felt fevered. "I need a favor. I want you to come to Lance's funeral and to the scattering of his ashes; he's going to be beside his mother. Now I want you get up and we'll talk this whole thing through, do you hear me? Elaine's told me she's never seen you like this, so if you really want to help, please be with me and get me over this whole mess."

There was a long silence. Red got up from the bed and headed towards the door as he went to leave he heard sounds of Eilid moving back the bedclothes.

"You can look, I'm perfectly decent."

Red turned to see from the puffy eyes and the swollen lips that told him she had been weeping for what must have been half the night.

"I don't know what to say to you except that I'm so sorry things turned out this way, not in my wildest dreams could I have imagined all that has taken place in the last two days."

Red took her by the waist and hugged her gently. He met with no resistance. Then Eilid pulled him closer to her and he could feel the soft warmth of her femininity. They stayed in that tender embrace until Charles yelled through the door,

"Are you two all right in there?"

"Yes, we're fine," said Eilid. "I'm up and I'm coming out, just give me a minute."

Red came out of the bedroom first and gave Charles the thumbs-up sign. Charles smiled; he was beginning to like Red. In fact, the more he thought about having a father it didn't seem to be such a bad thing after all.

The two packed Range Rovers made their way slowly down Glen Torridon the following Tuesday. Eilid drove hers with Red in the front, Elaine and Charles in the back. Drew drove his rental with Allison and Charles's two boys in the back. There was little conversation in either vehicle; the events of the past few days had just about numbed the minds of everyone.

Lance's funeral, held the day previously in Inverness, was a somber affair. If Eilid was there in body she was absent in spirit. Red held her hand through the whole ceremony but her eyes stared vacantly ahead as the minister went through the service. Charles, Elaine and Drew sat quietly at the back of the Chapel all deep in their own thoughts as the Crematorium curtains slid silently across the coffin indicating its descent to the fiery furnace.

Hamish and Mhairi were standing outside the Lodge in the sunny but bitterly cold weather to welcome everyone and be introduced to Red Ericsson. Drew had called well ahead and told Hamish about the terrible events and why they were on their way to Torridon. Hamish took it all in his stride but Mhairi seemed terribly upset by what had happened, knowing that Eilid would be on a guilt trip of major proportions, and in that she was right.

But there was also some other bad news that they had to pass on. If incidents come in threes then this was the final one. The introductions were all made and the party quickly made their way into the Big Room and the roaring fire. Hamish held Eilid's hand.

"We just had a phone call from London, and I hate to have to tell you this but Sir David died this morning."

"My God," wailed Eilid, "will this ever, ever end. It's like a never ending Nightmare."

Hamish hugged her.

"I know it's too bad, but he had a good innings, I mean ninety-three is a fair age and from what I understand his health had been failing for some time."

"Oh I suppose that's true. Normally I wouldn't be so upset but it's like nothing good is ever going to happen to me again, I'm sorry Hamish it's just the way I feel right now."

"Who was Sir David?" Red asked.

"The Estate owner, Sir David Vickers. He was a fine man, a great friend of Sir Andrew and Eilid's employer and friend for well nigh over twenty years. And he was as kind to us as he was to Eilid." Hamish finished.

"So who owns the Estate now?"

"That's a good question; Sir David's lawyer said he had instructions to sell it upon Sir David's death."

"Is that so Hamish?" Eilid butted in.

"Aye it is that. That's why Mhairi and I are no' looking so pleased either, I think we'll be okay, but with a new owner you can never be sure."

"What would an Estate like this sell for?" It was Drew who asked the question.

"I can give you an idea," said Charles who had been listening to the conversation. "An Estate this size almost next door to us went for six million last year. Now it had a good beat on the Glass and that would add a bit to the price, but with forty-five stags to take off the hill each year, and the grouse shooting it won't be far away from five to five and a half million."

"Jesus, who would have that kind of money?" Hamish whistled.

"Me for example," said Red. "Jest tell what that is in real money, I mean dollars."

"About eight and a half million bucks." Charles did a quick calculation guessing at the exchange rate.

"I might be interested, real interested. Half the damned Ericsson family is scattered or is about to be scattered hereabouts," Red said with no attempt at humor. "Eilid let's you and me talk about it, I could get to like this place, even retire here, well in the summer anyway. Hamish," Red turned to face Hamish, "has the minister arrived yet?"

"Aye, aye of course, I should have said. With all the commotion I jist forgot. He's up in one of the bedrooms changing into his climbing gear, and while I'm on the subject we'd best be going, it's a gey long way and the days are short. As for you Charles, I don't think you should be going wi' that arm of yours in a sling, eh?"

"I'm going, and that's final. Have you been talking to Eilid because we've just had that conversation."

Hamish held up his hands in surrender. "By God but yer as pig headed as that mother of yours." Then he clapped his hand over his mouth suddenly realizing what he had just said. He looked at Red. "Sorry, I'm awfy sorry."

"Well don't be." Said Red. "If I've got used to it so can you. Come on let's get this show on the road. And for the record I can be real pig headed or mulish about things as well, so you've covered all the bases."

The white arête of Bein Eighe stood out starkly against the icy cobalt sky as the funeral party made its way to the summit. An observer with good eyesight would have been able to see the slow moving column of people occasionally breaking the skyline as it inched its way through ice covered rocks towards the razor edged peak.

The climb had been harder than expected, in fact without the aid of Hamish Ferguson, Red, Elaine and Charles would not have made it. Hamish went back and forth continually to help them over difficult passages where they had to climb over rocks partially covered in ice. The minister who had been seconded to officiate was a young lithesome fellow who was clearly an experienced climber and he too helped both Elaine and Charles when parts of the climb got fairly difficult.

Finally they were at the summit. The views were breathtaking. Loch Maree with the great white hump of Slioch to the East and North, the snow covered Cuillin of Skye to the South and West and closer at hand the great white mass that was Liathach and just beyond that the peak of Beinn Alligin.

For Red it was just as emotional a moment as it had been thirty-four years previously. The minister gave the final valediction and Red cast his son's ashes into the stiff breeze carrying Lance's remains to mingle with those of Karen the mother he never knew.

Red shook hands with the men, and hugged and kissed the girls. Hamish led the way to commence the long descent. Charles, Red and Eilid went arm in arm on the lower slopes when the terrain permitted, Drew, Hamish, and Elaine also joined hands, only the minister was companionless as he walked alone in front of them.

No one knew for certain what the future would bring. Hamish and Mhairi had perhaps found a new owner, Charles a father, Elaine's boys a grandfather and Eilid two suitors. For the Stuarts and the Ericssons the circle was complete.

GLOSSARY

For Scots reading this book the vernacular I've used in certain passages will be familiar to them. However, for those not acquainted with, shall I say Doric Scots, they will find some of the words I've used together with certain expressions incomprehensible. This glossary is intended to help Sassenachs through this cultural minefield.

A':	All
Aboot:	About
Aff	Off
Ah	I
Ah'll	I'll
Ah've	I have
Auld	Old
Aw	All
Awa	Away
Awfy	Awful
Aye	Yes
Bairn	Child
Bairned	Getting pregnant
Bothy	A hut or small cottage
Bollocks	The word is often used figuratively, most commonly as a noun to mean "nonsense" or as an expletive following a minor accident or misfortune, but also in a number of other ways: as an adjective to mean "poor quality" or "useless" e.g. "a load of old bollocks!"
Cairngorm Stone	A semi-precious quartz stone
Cannae	Cannot or can't
Ceilidh	Gaelic for a social event or party with Celtic music and dancing.
Corrie	A steep-walled semicircular basin in a mountain.
D'ye	Do you
Dae	Do

Daein'	Doing
Didnae	Did not
Disnae	Does not
Doon	Down
Dreich	Dismal, gloomy viz. a gey dreich day – a very dull dismal day.
Frae	From
Faither	Father
Gey	Very
Ghillie	Hill laborer
Gie	Give
Gralloch	Gaelic for field-dress, to remove the offal from a deer. Disembowel.
Guid	Good
Hame	Home
Havers	To talk nonsense
Haud	Hold
Hebrides	Islands off the Scottish west coast
Hen	Affectionate slang term (female only)
Hiv	Have
Hivin'	Having
Hogmanay	New year's Eve
Hoose	House
Intae	Into
Jist	Just
Jalouse	To guess or suspect
Ken	Know "ye ken" = you know
Laird	Scottish Lord. Owner of a landed estate
Lass, Lassie	Woman; young girl
Mannie	Man (diminutive)

March	The Estate Territory in the context of "stay on our March".
Mhairi	Pronounced "Vari"
Nae	No or Not
Niver	Never
No'	Not
Nobber	Young Stag
Noo	Now
Och Aye	Oh Yes
Oor	Our
Oot	Out
RAF	Royal Air force
Sassenach	From the Gaelic *Sasunnach* originally meaning Saxon.
Shieling	A Shepherd's Hut or a temporary shelter usually on high ground.
Slainte!	Gaelic for good health pronounced Slawncha
Slainte Mhath	Good Health to you (response). Slawncha-va.
Stupit	Stupid
Tae	To
The noo	Just now
Wan	One
Whaur	Where
Wi'	With
Wid	Would
Wis	Was
Wouldnae	Would not
Ye	You
Ye'll	You'll
Ye've	You've or you have
Yer	Your

SCOTTISH MOUNTAINS AND OTHER FEATURES NAMED IN THIS BOOK

(Names in parentheses are other names by which these peaks are chronicled)

Beinn Eighe	(Ruadh Stac Mor - Big Red Stack) File Hill
Corrie Mhic Fhearchair	(say Corry Veechker*a*char)Corrie of the son of Farquar
Liathach	(Mullach an Rathain – Summit of the Pinnacles) The Grey One
Slioch	The Spear
Beinn Alligin	(Sgurr Mhor-Big Peak) Jewel Hill
Loch Maree	After St. Maelrubha (pronounced 'Malru*a*') who was the second Scottish early saint after Columba.
Beinn Vrackie	Speckled Hill

ACKNOWLEDGMENTS

Without the help, advice and encouragement from my friends listed below this book would never have been written.

Donald Fraser	Master Stalker
Patrick Roughneen MD FRCS	Cardiovascular Surgeon
Bill Myers	Chemical Engineer (Retd.)
Rebecca Davis	International Attorney
Iain McLeod	Professor of Structural Engineering (Retd.)
Patrick Childress	Artist and Erstwhile Golfing Buddy
Bill Whyte	Solicitor (Retd.)
Dave Findlay	Golf Professional
Nick Baker	Naturalist
Murie Ronald	Landscape Architect
Deborah Rodrigue	Personal Assistant
Nicholas A. Veronico	Author of Boeing 377 Stratocruiser

And last but not least my wife Nancy, who must have been sick and tired of reading and editing and my daughter Gill who gave me encouragement.

My deepest thanks to you all.

Martin MacDowall

June 2007

All of the locations and venues in this book exist. Some of the accommodations are a part of my imagination particularly The Lodge at Glen Torridon. There does exist the Torridon Hotel, (now called just The Torridon) once a home of the Earls of Lovelace, so with a stretch of imagination this could well be The Lodge. There is no Torridon Estate as such.

I was nineteen and a member of the Junior Mountaineering Club of Scotland (JMCS) when I first went to climb the Triple Buttresses in Corrie Mhic Fhearchair and saw the aircraft wreckage in the Corrie.

This wreckage belongs to a WW II Lancaster Bomber which tragically crashed on March 14th 1951 (March 14th coincidentally being my birthday.)

This discovery fired my imagination in such a way that I began to wonder what would happen if a commercial airliner crashed in this locale. The remoteness of the site and the difficulty of access made me consider the difficulty of any rescue attempts that might be required, so White Stag to Queen's Pawn was born.

As a mark of respect to the crew members who died in this tragic accident I list them here in remembrance. If you visit this site please treat it with respect and deference.

A memorial plaque is fixed to the blade of one of the propellers still in the Corrie, and reads:

In memory of the eight crew members of Lancaster TX264. Which crashed on this site in the early hours of March 14th 1951

F/Lt Harry Smith DFC (29) Pilot RAF

Sgt Ralph Clucas (23) Co-Pilot RAF

Sgt. Robert Strong (27) Navigator RAF

Sgt. Peter Tennison (26) Air Signals RAF

Sgt. James Naismith (28) Air Signals RAF

Sgt. Wilfred D. Beck (19) Air Signals RAF

Sgt. James W. Bell (25) Air Signals RAF

Sgt. George Farquhar (29) Flight Engineer RAF

Beinn Eighe is Britain's oldest National Nature Reserve. It was set up in 1951 primarily to protect the ancient pinewood west of Kinlochewe, but the reserve embraces a vast area of 48 square kilometers (18.5 square miles) stretching from loch-side to mountain top. A huge cluster of rugged peaks, ridges and scree-covered slopes between Loch Maree and Glen Torridon forms part of this national jewel, most of which is owned by Scottish Natural Heritage. The importance of the whole of Beinn Eighe — for wildlife, geology and enjoyment of the natural Highland scene — is now recognized worldwide.

9112306R0

Made in the USA
Charleston, SC
11 August 2011